W9-ACH-826

TO LIVE AND DIE

To Live and Die

COLLECTED STORIES

OF THE CIVIL WAR,

1861–1876

Kathleen Diffley, editor

Duke University Press

Durham & London

2002

PS
648
.C54
T6
2002

© 2002 Duke University Press

All rights reserved

Printed in the United States of America

on acid-free paper ∞

Designed by C. H. Westmoreland

Typeset in Monotype Fournier

by Tseng Information Systems, Inc.

Library of Congress Cataloging-

in-Publication Data

To live and die : collected stories of

the Civil War, 1861–1876 /

edited by Kathleen Diffley.

p. cm.   Includes bibliographical

references and index.

ISBN 0-8223-2887-9 (cloth : alk. paper)

1. United States — History — Civil War,

1861–1865 — Fiction.   2. American fiction

— 19th century.   3. War stories, American.

I. Diffley, Kathleen Elizabeth.

PS648.C54 T6   2002

813'.4080358 — dc21   2001054485

481708o7

for my folks

CONTENTS

AFTERMATH

ACKNOWLEDGMENTS

This volume first began to emerge in the shadow of a larger project some years ago. Because that examination of Civil War print culture continues, I am particularly grateful to Ezra Greenspan, Timothy Sweet, and the anonymous referees at Duke University Press for reading this collection's whole manuscript and talking back. Their care and encouragement have been as welcome as the advice meant to save me from any errors that may remain. Colleagues at the University of Iowa have been similarly generous, especially Margaret Bass, Corey Creekmur, Joni Kinsey, Rob Latham, Tom Lutz, Leslie Schwalm, Harry Stecopoulos, and, most important, Laura Rigal across the alley between our homes. I am intellectually beholden to them all and personally touched. For the time to listen as well as to write, I am also grateful to the National Endowment for the Humanities for the fellowship that saw this book through, to the University of Iowa for a Faculty Scholarship at a crucial editorial juncture, and to the Howard Foundation for a semester's leave when this volume of neglected stories began to coalesce.

As a student of American periodicals accustomed to deserted stacks and basement storage, I have been further buoyed by how willingly local libraries, regional museums, state archives, and historical societies as well as colleagues elsewhere have offered their assistance. Tracing obscure stories and fugitive authors has been an engaging task thanks in part to Sharon Y. Steinberg at the Connecticut Historical Society, Carolyn M. Picciano at the Connecticut State Library, Cindy Murphy at the Connecticut Valley Historical Museum, Nicholas Graham at the Massachusetts Historical Society, Elizabeth Marzuoli at the Massachusetts State Archives, Colleen Couture at the Old Sturbridge Village Research Library, Lorraine Murawski at the Sturbridge Town Hall, Victoria Brehm at Grand Valley State University, Celia Snyder at the Illinois Civil War Project under ILGenWeb auspices, Nicolette Doerfler at Illinois College, Linda Garvert at the Sangamon Valley Collection in Springfield's Lincoln Library, Shirley Aleguas at Illinois's Morgan Area Genealogical Association, Todd Gernes at Providence College, Jerry Mounts on the 52nd Indiana, Glenn McMullen at the Indiana Historical Society, Dennis Northcott at the Missouri Historical Society, Gary L. Burns at Maryland's Historical Society of Cecil County, Ervin Jordan at the University of Virginia, Margaret Greene Rogers at the North East Mississippi Museum, Laurie Verge at the Suratt House Museum, Andy Butler at Virginia's Meadow Farm Museum, John Coski at the Museum of the Confederacy, Jeffery Hartley at the National Archives Library Information Center, Louise Arnold-Friend at the U.S. Army Military History Institute in Pennsylvania's Carlisle Barracks, Kathleen Fernandez at the Ohio Historical Society, Andy Waskie at the Grand Army of the Republic Civil War Museum and Temple University, Cheryl Torsney at West Virginia University, Christa Lembeck LaPrade and Gregory Stoner at the Virginia Historical Society, Catherine Pollari at Hampden-Sydney College, Kathleen Chappell at Virginia's Alexandria Library, Vicky Jones at Virginia's Fauquier County Public Library, Kathryn Depret-Guillaume at Virginia's Fairfax County Public Library, Leon Jackson at the University of South Carolina, Henry and Patricia B. Mitchell of Foodways Publications, and the Free Library of Philadelphia. For his abiding generosity and goodwill, I am especially grateful to Trevor Plante at the Old Military and Civil Records of the National Archives. Naturally, my debt to ongoing digital projects that make nineteenth-century records a double-click away is immense, like that of other students of the Civil War who also lean heavily on the Making of America's Web site access to the *Official Records,* or more properly *The War of the Rebellion: A Compilation of the Official Records of the Union and Confederate Armies (1880–1901).* If these historical custodians had been less forthcoming, this volume might have remained opaque.

In the years it has taken to make stories, authors, and glossary entries less mysterious, I have also relied on the research and judgment of graduate students, some of whom have already begun careers of their own. My thanks to Ritch Adams, Greg Bales, Sharon Kennedy-Nolle, Heidi LaVine, Luke Mancuso, Jen McGovern, Pat Murphy, Derek Oja, Cindy Stretch, Mary Sylwester, and, above all, Marty Gould. Iowa's Department of English has generously underwritten the cost of bringing magazine illustrations to these pages. On that score and many others, I have further counted on the willing assistance of Iowa's University Libraries, particularly Sid Huttner and Kathy Hodson in Special Collections, Ann Ford in Reference, and pretty much everyone in Interlibrary Loan. I have also leaned on retired reference librarian Helen Ryan, who has done more work on elusive glossary entries than she probably cares to remember. More recently, I have benefited from the patience and good grace of Ken Wissoker at Duke University Press. His interest in this project began with a Sunday morning call years back and has since kept a burdened agenda manageable, while his sheer cordiality has lifted my spirits.

My son Sam tells me that this book should be dedicated to him and his brother Coleman, as well as my husband Jude, for all of the things they didn't say and could've. Since they are family, I guess they are my "folks" in a sprawling nineteenth-century sense that reminds me how much upheaval customarily roils domestic routines and throws most people back on the saving kindnesses of home. And yet, older debts and unwavering faith make this book more rightly for my parents, John and Betty Diffley, who have eased my professional and household snarls for years and who made other, earlier households warm. Old times there are not forgotten.

DAILY EMERGENCY: CIVIL WAR STORIES

OF THE WAR GENERATION

Dawn comes slowly to Charleston in April. When a storm threatens, as it did on the morning of April 12, 1861, freighted clouds make the darkness linger, though on that morning few people kept to their beds. At 3:20 A.M., Major John Anderson had received an official warning that Fort Sumter would be fired on within the hour. It was thus no surprise when a 10-inch shell flashed red against the night sky and cannon across the fortressed harbor began to boom. As dawn spread, the sky began filling with smoke, and from the shore it grew difficult to see how the fight was progressing. But on roofs and church steeples, in city streets and along the Battery, people crowded to watch the exploding shells, the embattled harbor, and the sudden spectacle of war. As "The House-Tops in Charleston during the Bombardment of Sumter" (frontispiece) reveals, they were themselves becoming part of a riveting scene, part of a national drama that was already underway.

For the next four years, it was a drama that newborn magazines were poised to share. With the resources to send artists to the field and the readership to ensure that many would see the smoke of battle secondhand, illustrated journals like *Harper's Weekly* quickly became mainstays on which anxious Americans came to rely. Before, during, and after the war's tumultuous events, magazines of various sorts continued to crop up and to find as willing an audience as Charleston's bombarded fort. When the special artists who later sketched battlefields and camp scenes, glory and longing, finally came home in 1865, *Harper's Weekly* would declare: "All over the country thousands and thousands of the faces and events which the war has made illustrious are tacked and pinned and posted upon the humblest walls."[1] So fetching was magazine artistry, in fact, that the dismay of Charleston's spectators is still palpable, even though the engraving testifies more to art department imagination than to the documented euphoria of the city's crowds. What magazines made sense of was the anxiety of their readers, who were often far from reported events. More than newspaper bulletins and broadside appeals, new weeklies and monthlies offered ways of seeing the war, in pictures and in prose, for growing numbers of subscribers who passed their pages along.

So when Daniel Aaron complained years ago that the Civil War was "unwritten," he was only partly right. True, there were plenty of personal accounts and memoirs, even a fair enough range of poetry, commentary, and latter-day fiction from William Faulkner and the Southern Agrarians to give Aaron's *The Unwritten War: American Writers and the Civil War* (1973) both reasonable heft and remarkable shelf life. What he lamented, however, was the absence of a transcendent American masterpiece, an epic with sufficient distance on Appomattox to enable scope, with sufficient ambition to ferret out the causes of the war, and with sufficient honesty to tackle race. The problem, countered Leslie Fiedler, was that Aaron was looking for the real war in all the wrong places and, arguably, all the wrong genres.

In his turn, Fiedler proposed an "inadvertent epic" running from Harriet Beecher Stowe through Thomas Dixon and D. W. Griffith and Margaret Mitchell to Alex Haley. His effort to recognize history's rumble in the groundswell of popular texts missed wartime responses, to be sure, but the resulting genre was boldly domestic, polyvocal, and engaged in tackling race head-on.[2] Fiedler's *The Inadvertent Epic: From "Uncle Tom's Cabin" to "Roots"* (1979) was intent on achieving scope across haunted time and "many hands," one sure way of tracking the Civil War's racial legacy beyond the constitutional abolition of slavery in 1865. And yet even his synthetic approach neglected the one right place for discovering what many Americans imagined while cannon were still hot and losses were piling up, the one right place for unearthing the alarms, misgivings, and settling purposes of wartime life, the one right place that Stowe herself sought once *Uncle Tom's Cabin* was underway: namely, midcentury magazines.

Delving into these at last, *To Live and Die* retrieves thirty-one stories of secession and its aftermath, stories culled from the hundreds that circulated in popular magazines between the fall of Fort Sumter in 1861 and the celebration of the American Centennial in 1876. These were among the earliest efforts to make creative sense of domestic crisis, when first the war and then Reconstruction were still in progress. Assembled here, out of their original welter, they constitute what might be called an "inadvertent novel" of the times, a collective narrative that provides a first seismic reading of the war's upheaval. When stories published even after the war are arranged to plot the country's unfolding drama, as they are in the pages to come, the war they register is still close, still one of sudden confrontations, backwater misfortunes, and the peculiarities of ordinary dislocation that could be shared for the first time in print. As imaginative ventures, these stories favor exactly those "pedestrian details" that Aaron saw choking epic sublimity, but that readers may once again find catching them up in the wartime clash first seen from the housetops of Charleston.

FIGURE I.
"The Nation's Birthday," *Harper's Weekly*, 15 July 1876, 576–77

In 1861, those housetops were alive with memories of the country's first war. Even New York's *Harper's Weekly* acknowledged the near revolutionary grounds on which Southern states would fight. "They are thoroughly persuaded that they are right, and that their cause is the cause of God and independence," the magazine editorialized just one page after Charleston's harbor view.[3] Across the years of war and rebuilding, the revolution's legacy remained a public preoccupation, so much so that Thomas Nast's double-page illustration for "The Nation's Birthday" in 1876 pictured Columbia as the "Teacher of Liberty" coupling the Declaration of Independence with the Emancipation Proclamation to spread the country's example throughout the world (Figure 1). Between the fall of Fort Sumter and the Centennial celebrations, between the Charleston housetops in 1861 and the country's lesson some fifteen years later, the revolution's legacy was strikingly reconceived in ways that the stories of *To Live and Die* illuminate.

3

FIGURE 2.

"The Gettysburg
Monument," *Harper's
Weekly*, 17 July 1869,
456

At Gettysburg especially, both the lessons of war and the readiness to in-
scribe them were insistent. Not only were more magazine stories written about
the three-day battle than any other, but the urge to commemorate the Confederacy's sharpest inroad and the Union's bravest rebuff led to a sculptural
commission that helps to define a period of transformation. On July 1, 1869,
exactly six years after the battle began, the Gettysburg Monument to the Union
soldiers who fell was dedicated on the spot where Abraham Lincoln delivered
his eloquent address. As *Harper's Weekly* noted when engraving a photograph
of the occasion (Figure 2), the massive tribute to the "unknown dead" was
large enough to include several allegorical figures.[4] At the monument's base
were four statues representing War, History, Peace, and Plenty, as well as their
gendered relations: the soldier appeared to tell the story of war to the muse of
history, listening with "stylus" in hand, while the mechanic of peace seemed
to join the goddess of plenty carrying the "fruits of the earth" (458). Above

them rose a fifth statue representing the "Genius of Liberty," which was most immediately defined by the laurels of victory held in one hand and the sheathed sword of power held in the other, and yet that "colossal" figure significantly rested on its allegorical base. The commemorative message in 1869 was that liberty had been won through the force of arms but would be grounded on the force of words amid the peace and plenty that the occasion's spectators already enjoyed, a message that Lincoln's moving sense of "unfinished work" anticipated and this collection amplifies.

In *Harper's Weekly,* the dedicated monument retained some of its scaffolding, a useful reminder that the meaning of "liberty" was still under construction between 1861 and 1876, when stories of the war were first told. The figure of War also predominated in the magazine's engraving, where History was caught in shadow to the side and Peace with its Plenty was effectively hidden. That, too, can be significant for any effort to recollect how the war was initially seen, since its events were as insistent as the monument's soldier. For that reason, chronology and thus narrative setting in this collection are uppermost, rather than the dates of story publication and the peacetime negotiations that always seem out of sight just around the corner. Still, Pennsylvania's parochialism in recognizing only the Union dead has been set aside in these pages for a wider acknowledgment of the war's expense and its manifold opportunities. Because the stories in this volume come from literary magazines across the South and West as well as the culturally dominant Northeast, they trace a "real" war that ultimately joins Northern and Southern allegiances with a Western slant, that integrates battlefield and home front, that reckons fitfully but insistently with race, that points to the ascendancy of paramount national citizenship, and that marks a new colloquial vitality in prose. At Gettysburg, a muse with a stylus shadowed a soldier with a rifle to guarantee the foundations of American liberty, a vision that Daniel Aaron missed and that this inadvertent novel restores. Yet it is wise to remember that the story of an abolitionist parson in prewar Kansas that opens this volume was published in 1874, within weeks of the "true story" that closes the collection in the remembered words of an outspoken black cook. If the war's events are justifiably insistent, the social "progress" they suggested in the stories writers told was at best uncertain and tantalizing.

For many, the details of these recovered stories may be most striking in their idiosyncrasy, like the magazines from which the stories have come. The voices of the Civil War were diverse and clamorous, it turns out, especially when more regional publications came to jostle the general interest monthlies that were established just before the war began. Some of the periodicals that were filling with war stories are as familiar today as the *Atlantic Monthly* in Boston and *Harper's New Monthly Magazine* in New York, both founded during the

1850s. Others emerged in just such publishing centers but earned more fleeting reputations, like Boston's *Continental Monthly* (1862–1864), New York's *Galaxy* (1866–1878) and the revitalized *Putnam's* (1868–1870), and Philadelphia's *Lippincott's* (1868–1916). Still others spread across the country to challenge the commemorative sway of the Northeast: periodicals like the *New Eclectic* (1866–1868) in Richmond and then the *Southern Magazine* (1868–1875) in Baltimore, the *Southern Monthly* (1861–1862) in Memphis, the *Land We Love* (1866–1869) in Charlotte, the *Overland Monthly* (1868–1875) in San Francisco, the *Lakeside Monthly* (1869–1874) in Chicago, and Frederick Douglass's *New National Era* (1870–1874) in Washington, D.C. Less cosmopolitan writers in their pages noticed stranger people in messier places at odder moments: a pawnshop owner whose bombazine morning gown and grizzly beard in Chauncey Hickox's "Job and the Bug" only partly disguise his secret agenda, a Southern scout who hides with his buckhorn knife among the bullfrogs off an island in the Potomac in William H. Kemper's "The Sergeant's Little Story," a frontier regiment along the Gulf coast in Richard M. Sheppard's "Sentenced and Shot" that inches toward mutiny during the war's final months. Away from the time-honored battlefields of Virginia and the sheltered cottages of Massachusetts, theirs is a surreptitious war that the urban *Harper's Weekly* (1857–1916) just began to suggest, despite circulating far more stories to far more readers than any other magazine could claim.

It is fair to say that other collections might have been assembled to illustrate how the war generation responded to widespread disruption. If coverage and circulation ought to count for more than regional disparity in the statistical scale for example, then the sheer number of contributions to *Harper's Weekly* might have weighed more heavily when choices were made. In addition to on-the-scene reports, the magazine published more than a hundred Civil War stories, largely unsigned, before turning its attention and huge readership to other events after 1866. Many of these narratives concern matters that claim only a small part of *To Live and Die*, where guerrilla demands, mistaken casualty reports, family sacrifice, and substitute soldiers appear less often. Because *Harper's Weekly* on the eve of civil war had a subscriber list of well over one hundred thousand, and an audience of several times that number once issues read aloud were passed around, it is worth noting these recurring emphases. They reveal whose war more Americans were first invited to see. There is also the matter of brevity; in the shorter narratives that *Harper's Weekly* preferred, there was more outspoken opinion from a disproportionate number of Southern Unionists, lady teachers, soldier letters, and newspaper reports, which may simply underline the ready politics and brisk composition of a weekly newsmagazine. By contrast, literary monthlies were distinctly less partisan, and they published better-crafted fiction whose greater length suggested a more complicated war and a better-heeled if less numerous reading public.

A different collection might also have arisen from the cultural life that was evidently shared across the Mason-Dixon line. No matter where magazines were published, there were plenty of unusual references that went unexplained in one story or another to suggest a ready knowledge that has since melted away, references to such things as Bob Ridleys, Shaker bonnets, Julien soup, the rebel cheat counties of West Virginia, jade-hoppers, and "sure enough" coffee. During a time when the Union and the Confederacy faced off at gunpoint, when the peace made at Appomattox was subsequently enforced through military districting and the reoccupation of the South, so common a culture raises intriguing questions. Who once sang "Ever of Thee" or "Her Bright Smile" or "Safe in the Kingdom" so regularly that a hymn title or a snatch of lyrics could jog the memories of readers without fuss? What cultural trafficking made Belshazzer, Mrs. Jarley's wax-work show, Alonzo and Imogen, Chang the giant, Bill Sling, Japan lilies, corn-dodgers, the waters of Marah, and the Ellsler twirl (for instance) a relatively simple and undeciphered stock-in-trade for mid-century writers on their way to national memory of the war? Another collection might be made from such things held in common, from secret society pins and shared watering holes, and from the cultural custodians whose bricks and straw came so readily and now so mysteriously to hand.

But the story of civil war as daily emergency and liberty's crucible showed up in literary magazines consistently, more than enough to upset easy distinctions between North and South, male and female, free and enslaved, even Standard English and unlettered dialect. When neglected regional journals are examined beside familiar sources, recollections of the war take on an intensity that prompts more significant questions. Until recently, for example, the distance between battlefields and cottages has tended to grow when historians have looked back to the Civil War. At the time, however, violence and sanctuary seemed much more entangled. In magazine stories, bushwhackers carry the war to the most out-of-the-way homesteads, spies work households from the inside, journeying paymasters rely on the kindness of border women, and soldiers turn out to be girls. Ellen D. Larned's "Three Days of Terror" brings the New York draft riots and class-bound threat to the doors of Twenty-Second Street; Rebecca Harding Davis's "Ellen" shows what the open road of wartime removals means to an abandoned girl in search of her enlisted brother. The widespread dismay these stories reveal makes it harder to isolate the home front from blundering disaster and harder to detach captains, lieutenants, and civil servants from the amenities of home.

Further complicating the routine separation of gendered spheres is the narrative fate of slaves and their sporadic but undeniable claim on magazine readers after 1861, especially as the cries for liberty and justice gathered strength. *To Live and Die* opens with a prewar vigilante attack on the underground railroad and a Kansas parson in Henry King's "The Cabin at Pharaoh's Ford"; the collection ends with a black cook's loss of her remaining son in Mark Twain's "A True Story," a narrative sustained by dialect as a freedwoman speaks out where King's fugitives mutely slip away. Between silent exodus and personal joy in this patchwork novel, a poor white woman defends emancipation in "A Letter from the Country," a slave family abandons a Virginia plantation to follow the Union army in M. Shele De Vere's "The Freedman's Story," and a black private in "Buried Alive" climbs out of Fort Pillow's massacre of colored artillery troops and a living grave. That desperate soldier struggling to free himself anticipates Twain's resilient cook serving Union officers in a confiscated plantation kitchen, an image of Southern sanctuary blasted on behalf of newly paramount national liberties and the fresh promise of rights unhampered by race.

Ultimately, since most of these narratives are taken from literary magazines, they are about the evocative power of language as well as the particular ways in which the nineteenth century's colloquial verve took hold, even in the dialogue given once silent slaves. Some stories are comparatively bleak: in Ross Guffin's description of the Western war on smugglers in "A Night on the Mississippi," the escalating danger of a Union detail's trip to a snowbound island derives from a closely watched material world, where wisps of breath freeze instantly. Other stories turn suddenly comic: in Confederate Gray's "T. J.'s Cavalry Charge," a horse rolls over and a disheveled volunteer complains, "There now, won't Betsy give me particular fits!" Still others seem to run on sheer talk, like that of Twain's Aunt Rachel declaring, "Den I was just a-*bilin'!* Mad? I was jist a-*boomin'!*" As early as the 1860s, narratives like these chronicled a war whose hard surfaces and verbal rhythms would prevail in American fiction for years to come.

This is the world the storytellers made, and theirs was a mediated war that helped patch together a nation reconceived in liberty. It was a nation that readers could literally envision. At a time when special artists traveled with the armies and photographic operatives hauled costly equipment to nearby battlefields, representative patches were often pictures, at least on other magazine pages. Although short American fiction was not generally illustrated midcentury, a collective narrative like this one that recalls how the war was first seen deserves to be read as *Harper's Weekly* once was, for the pictures as well as the prose. Not surprisingly, those period pieces varied. Most were drawn for magazine publication by artists like Alfred Waud, Winslow Homer, Thomas Nast, and Frank Vizetelly, whose work reappears on the following pages. Some were alternately redrawn for the wood block from photographs, like "The Harvest of Death—Gettysburg" that here accompanies General John D. Imboden's account of the defeated Lee. But the wood engraving of the photograph's littered field misses the shock of Gettysburg's rotting corpses, because the art department combined three separate photographs, whose empty skies, lonely corpses, and abandoned detritus were not nearly as stark when recomposed as a single engraved view. Such mistranslation recurred when photographic landscapes, rather than simpler portraits, were engraved, and for that reason new wet collodion images competed at a disadvantage in wartime magazines. Because *To Live and Die* is attentive to magazine culture rather than to the new visual technologies that had not yet overturned art department habits, the war's startling photographs make as fitful an appearance in the following pages as they once did in the newsmagazines that favored cheap reproduction over silvered detail.

The more telling contrast in these selected illustrations should lie between the wartime images of *Harper's Weekly* and those of the *Illustrated London News*, which began its transatlantic coverage in the North. When artist-correspondent Frank Vizetelly sketched the Union rout at Bull Run in disturbing detail, however, he lost permission to travel with the Army of the Potomac; after waiting fruitlessly for a reprieve, he joined Confederate forces and covered the war for British readers from a Southern perspective. The engravings made from his sporadic drawings accompany some of the stories appearing here from Southern magazines or those set along the Potomac, generally stories first published without the pictures that most magazines could ill afford. More than once, as it happens, Vizetelly's view of the Confederacy actually graced the pages of *Harper's Weekly*, which printed his intercepted drawings while adding substitute prose. His eyewitness work for "Bursting of a Shell in the Streets of Charleston, South Carolina" (Figure 3) appeared intact during January 1864, for example, but the Harpers merely credited "an English artist" after passing the drawing along to London, and they trimmed his inconvenient caption: "The Federals Shelling the City of Charleston—Shell Bursting in the Streets." [5] For Vizetelly, it was the independence of the Confederacy and the liberty of Southerners that were under attack, as his later account of the siege for the *Cornhill Magazine* demonstrated. Neither of those concerns was glossed by the pirating *Harper's Weekly* when the "same" illustration appeared, a sign of how much prose can count in the war readers think they see.

How widely conflicting messages were once disseminated thus depends on the particular journals in which contributions were published and the particular agendas of journal editors, which had long intersected with public debates

FIGURE 3. "Bursting of a Shell in the Streets of Charleston, South Carolina," *Harper's Weekly*, 9 January 1864, 28

and market concerns in strikingly different ways. As far back as 1835, when President Jackson asked Congress to forbid the postal circulation of volatile abolitionist papers, William Lloyd Garrison had been outraged and Louis A. Godey must have shrugged. As editor of the weekly *Liberator* (1831–1865), Garrison had declared that he would be "as harsh as truth, and as uncompromising as justice" on the subject of slavery. He wanted his voice to be heard beyond the narrow streets of Boston, and he welcomed the slave insurrections and mob violence that white Southerners increasingly feared. Godey, by contrast, wanted the widest possible circulation for his *Lady's Book* (1830–1898), which was launched in Philadelphia and already on its way to reaching the 150,000 readers in the North, South, and West who would subscribe by the eve of the Civil War. For the "fair Ladies" to whom he appealed, Godey designed "a magazine of elegant literature," steadfastly sidestepping the kind of censorship that Garrison protested and that even Andrew Jackson could not finally turn into law.[6] As more literary journals began to appear around the country by midcentury, they ranged self-consciously along a political spectrum from zeal to serenity that Garrison and Godey had long since laid out.

Closest to Garrisonian agitation were the *Atlantic Monthly* and the *Continental Monthly*, both Boston journals that were founded on antislavery principles, though they were as different in literary circles as giant and dwarf. More agile and less stern were several magazines in New York: *Harper's Monthly* favored literary neutrality over the *Weekly*'s outspoken opinion, but both magazines were temperate "family" forums by Boston standards. *Putnam's* was more thoroughly committed to encouraging original literature and Republican policy in its postwar years, while the *Galaxy* sought greater vitality if less rectitude in promoting writers from across the emerging nation. Still, reconstructing Southerners found their warmest Northern reception in *Lippincott's*, a Philadelphia journal that willingly stepped in for the reticent *Godey's* to welcome ex-Confederates hoping to be paid for their work.[7]

That was scarcely an option in the South, during or after the war's devastation. The *Southern Monthly* flared early and boisterously in Memphis before disappearing when Union gunboats arrived, a fate that the *New Eclectic* avoided by assembling its often pirated pages in postwar Richmond and then moving to Baltimore. Greater originality, absorbing Charlotte's the *Land We Love,* and an upcoming affiliation with the new Southern Historical Society prompted a change of name to the *Southern Magazine,* but the journal's coffers were still not robust enough in the 1870s to compete with Northern pay. The lure of greater compensation in Boston also enticed editor Bret Harte away from San Francisco and the *Overland Monthly,* but he left behind a brash Western magazine that remained as alert to the peculiar echoes of upheaval as Chicago's *Lakeside Monthly* was to the war's odd ambivalences. By comparison, as the following pages reveal, the *New National Era* in the nation's capital was more attuned to shorter, anecdotal fare that gained dimension when published in Frederick Douglass's postwar journal for mainly freeborn blacks. Although the magazine's literary material was often copied from larger journals with greater resources and presumably white contributors, the snatches of narrative on Douglass's pages then appeared cheek by jowl with sharp political essays by black commentators whose editorial aims could also transform the way stories were read.[8] In the literary marketplace of the 1860s and 1870s, the lesson of Vizetelly's intercepted drawings is worth remembering since no reprinted and thus migrating story was ever quite the same.

Of course, stories migrated from magazine to magazine less often when established authors were paid for their contributions and competing editors respected such arrangements. Yet, between the attack on Fort Sumter and the end of Reconstruction, few better-paid American authors wrote Civil War stories. At $200 and more per contribution, Harriet Beecher Stowe was earning premium rates for submissions to the *Atlantic Monthly,* considerably more than the $300 she had received for serializing *Uncle Tom's Cabin* in the *National Era* (1851–1852). During the 1860s, however, Stowe was more drawn to spiritual grace and serialized *Agnes of Sorrento* in the *Atlantic* (1861–1862); thereafter, she wrote about ministers and oldtown folks, chimney corners and home papers, Sojourner Truth and Lady Byron, but infrequently about the war. Similarly, *Putnam's* paid Herman Melville the magazine's highest rate in the 1850s, $5 per printed page for stories like "Benito Cereno," up from the $3 that other writers received. But in the 1860s, Melville turned from fiction to the poetry that appeared occasionally in *Harper's Monthly* before being published as *Battle-Pieces and Aspects of the War* in 1866.

At about that time, the *Galaxy* commissioned Walt Whitman's "Carol of Harvest for 1867," a poem about the war's passing blue-clad armies that the magazine paid $60 to publish in September of that year; with similar largesse, the *Galaxy* also brought out Whitman's essays "Democracy" (December 1867) and "Personalism" (May 1868), which would become the better part of *Democratic Vistas* by 1871. In these several genres and throughout the postwar years, Whitman called upon his experiences as a wartime nurse, but he had left short fiction behind with the temperance tales of "Walter Whitman" in the 1840s. Nathaniel Hawthorne, who died in 1864, contributed an essay entitled "Chiefly about War Matters" (July 1862), for which the *Atlantic Monthly* was pleased to pay top dollar and then double that figure for the essays on contemporary English life that Hawthorne submitted after wartime inflation pushed rates up in 1863.[9] Hawthorne, Whitman, Melville, and Stowe had all written earlier stories as the antebellum genre evolved, but none of them contributed Civil War stories to the magazines of the 1860s and 1870s. By then, reputations were more often in the making as short war fiction first began to appear, and lower "tyro" rates for newcomers plus the pressure of hasty promises and subsequent book publication meant that Civil War stories could still be read more than once and in substantially different contexts.

A handful of authors on the cusp of national reputation may reveal how protean midcentury tyros could be, how elusive name recognition was for many, and how much more context could count when their stories were read. Rebecca Harding Davis, for example, had only begun her magazine career when "Ellen" (*Atlantic Monthly*, July 1865) was published, after the lively success of her now classic "Life in the Iron Mills" revealed Wheeling's factory conditions to the *Atlantic*'s readers in 1861. During the magazine's war years, Davis contributed several remarkable home front stories while also writing headlong and near anonymously for *Peterson's*, a Philadelphia women's magazine that had topped the circulation of rival *Godey's* by the time war was declared. In July 1863, an earlier version of "Ellen" appeared in *Peterson's* as part of an issue that opened with plenty of engravings (of a lace cape, a "senorita dress," hair styles, and children's fashions), as well as sheet music for Alice Hawthorne's "Yes, I Would the War Were Over" and patterns for a handkerchief border. Davis would later insist that this first submission was a fictionalized version of the incidents she then retooled for Boston publication, but the story of a trusting sister who seeks an Ohio regiment in the fractious border country south of Wheeling was close enough to look like plagiarism to the editors of the *Atlantic Monthly* before matters were resolved. When the revised "Ellen" was linked in their prestigious pages to "the author of 'Life in the Iron-Mills' " and surrounded in 1865 by contributions written with greater care, such as John G. Whittier's poem "The Changeling" and Bayard Taylor's "Winter Life in St. Petersburg," the refashioned narrative seemed purposely fragmentary, its addled heroine disturbing, and Davis's story of the war's first months entirely different in its import.[10] Like wandering women on subsequent magazine roads, this later Ellen is led into a world of bewildering uncertainty and a twice-told story of unraveling narrative guarantees far from the *Peterson's* reassurance of ready-made patterns.

By comparison, Louisa May Alcott's hospital ward in "The Brothers" (*Atlantic Monthly,* November 1863) is orderly, feminized, and recuperative, though her wartime scene offers less of the familial reassurances to come in *Little Women* (1868–1869) and more of the unsettling logic that Alcott gave her early, pseudonymous stories for less distinguished magazines. The reason became clearer after the author's postwar rise to fame, when "The Brothers" was reprinted with her *Hospital Sketches* in 1869 and retitled "My Contraband." In both versions of the story, Alcott pits Northern principle against Southern transgression by pitting a slave soldier against his master and half-brother. But where her earlier title emphasizes familial and then sectional clash, which is narratively resolved when the colored 54th Massachusetts assaults Fort Wagner, "My Contraband" as a title foregrounds the story's unexpected triptych, the "mistress" inserted between the two brothers, and therefore what Elizabeth Young terms a shift "from male injury to female healing."[11] Where Davis points to the shared blood that holds families together in precarious times, Alcott takes the violated safety of slave cabins as fundamental, with almost as much national consequence in the *Atlantic Monthly* as a white nurse's gentle hand. The bad blood of reckless plantations suited the abolitionist cause that put a liberty cap on the magazine's rippling banner in 1865 (Figure 4), but the migrating story's later title and the postwar volume's recurring hospital nurses indicate who was gently angling to assume the Southern master's authority.

Outside the *Atlantic Monthly*, it was certainly possible to achieve professional success without the hurried writing for which both Davis and Alcott got paid, but it was that much harder to make a living and particularly so for Southerners, no matter how often their work appeared in print. Richard Malcolm Johnston published his first tale of rural Georgia life in a New York sporting journal

FIGURE 4. Title Page, *Atlantic Monthly*, January–June 1865

called *Porter's Spirit of the Times* (December 1857). He then collected the tale with three more for Augusta publication as *Georgia Sketches* (1864), reworked these and wrote others for Baltimore's *New Eclectic* (1869–1870) and the *Southern Magazine* (1871–1872), and collected these again in several arrangements as the *Dukesborough Tales* (1871, 1874), published likewise in Baltimore. But only after New York's *Scribner's Monthly* began accepting his stories in 1879 did he sign his own name and receive any recompense, and only after sixteen migrating stories were collected yet again by Harper Brothers in 1883 did he become a national sensation. In this wayward saga, "Mr. Williamson Slippey and His Salt" (*New Eclectic*, October 1870) was sometimes quietly ignored; it was the only story set as late as the Civil War and as far from central Georgia eccentricity as commercial Atlanta, peculiarities skewing the otherwise affable sketches that were picked up in the North more readily.[12]

Not that earlier fame would necessarily have helped. While Johnston was scraping together a living, Mark Twain was already much better known. At $20 per printed page, he was also much better rewarded when "A True Story" first appeared in the *Atlantic Monthly* (November 1874). That was actually the problem. Twain's reputation for humor so influenced reviews of his subsequent *Sketches, New and Old* (1875) that *Atlantic* editor and reviewer William Dean Howells felt he had to rescue the story of Aunt Rachel from misreading. Well before *Huckleberry Finn* was excerpted in the *Century* (1884–1885) and *Pudd'nhead Wilson* was serialized in the same magazine (1893–1894), Twain signaled his unanticipated moral reckoning by republishing "A True Story" with "Facts Concerning the Recent Carnival of Crime in Connecticut" (1877), a more serious companion in a volume advertising the stately Little Classics series and the smaller Vest-Pocket Series that circulated such writers as Emerson, Whittier, and Hawthorne.[13] As both Johnston and Twain discovered, the impact of any migrating story had a great deal to do with the company it kept, the same lesson that Davis and Alcott had learned by heart.

These four tyros were not the only members of a new literary generation to write about wartime crisis, and even their later celebrity is not reason enough by itself to include their stories in a volume of the war's first literary traces. After all, Henry James published several Civil War stories in the *Atlantic Monthly*, as did John W. De Forest and Rose Terry. But James's interest in detailed psychological study makes his war narratives as inert as his war heroes and as coolly removed from events. Instead, it was magazine unknowns such as William H. Kemper and Richmond Wolcott who acknowledged the desperate times that more willing volunteers could not escape. De Forest's short fiction, which also appeared in *Harper's Monthly* and the *Galaxy*, has the snap of Fred B. Perkins's story about Wall Street speculators or the otherworldly appeal of the *New National Era*'s "Believe in Ghosts!" But his attention often focuses on Reconstruction's complexities rather than the war's intrusions. Rose Terry reveals how distant the war could seem when its events figure so peripherally in the domestic life of her New England characters, a useful reminder but one that does not touch the challenge Daniel Aaron raised or mitigate the tumbling immediacy of war in narratives from less touted authors or in less predictable magazines. Although some of the war's first stories migrate once again anonymously in the following pages, where forgotten writers like Chauncey Hickox and Ellen D. Larned are about as opaque as "Izilda" and "Confederate Gray," it is worth remembering that Twain himself was so unfamiliar to the Eastern audiences devouring magazines in the 1860s that *Harper's Monthly* attributed his first published submission to "Mark Swain."

For magazine subscribers, Civil War stories were usually less about their authors than about their settings, especially when editorial policy could make periodical fare less attributable to individuals than to magazines. *Harper's Weekly*, the *New National Era*, and many of the Southern journals specifically resisted crediting authors; even magazines that did help build reputations would not often describe the little-known American contributors of short fiction and would sometimes delay revealing their names until issues were bound with a table of contents. Consequently, regimental veterans who had never written much magazine fiction could revise firsthand accounts with some marketplace success, but they could not always be distinguished from the publishing authors who relied on news bulletins or the occasional contributors who remain unfamiliar to this day. In magazine prose shaped by both inherited conventions and unanticipated events, by readerly expectations and wartime loss, it was less particular tellers than particular tales that helped make the war make sense. Above all, it was the narrative practice of entangling invention and evidence that counted when events were raw and that counts again as *To Live and Die* recalls the war's rough chronology.

Traditionally, because most readers and editors lived in the East, the war's story begins with the election of Abraham Lincoln, the secession of Southern states, and the firing on Fort Sumter, when the war's big guns first rolled into play. The clash of arms in the battles that followed is for many synonymous with the Civil War, and the distant smoke of military engagement is still as riveting as it once was for the citizens of Charleston on their housetops. As Gary Gallagher has observed, battlefield news was eagerly consumed throughout the war, a good reason now to privilege what Gallagher sees as "the vital ways in which military events influenced the homefront."[14] So the trajectory of the war in *To Live and Die* is also defined by its unfolding battles: the sudden rout at Bull Run in 1861, the unexpected expense of Antietam in 1862, Pickett's frontal assault at Gettysburg in 1863, and Spotsylvania's nighttime offensive in 1864.

But where war correspondents hammered out newspaper copy with summary leads and thus breaking information, contemporary magazines told battle stories with a more protracted difference: Chauncey Hickox's "Job and the Bug" arrives at the road to Bull Run through the Washington miasma of doubtful allegiances and the pawnshop suspicions of a ragtag boatman's son; "On the Antietam" follows part of a Union regiment to a neglected corner of the Maryland field. Stories with a further difference arise from the Southern perspective on such engagements, the martial euphoria that sends Confederate regiments to Virginia in Izilda's "A True and Simple Tale of '61" and the hasty ride that sends a rebel courier out of Maryland in Kemper's "The Sergeant's Little Story." The later Confederate drive into Pennsylvania can also be recalled contrapuntally: the panoply of Pickett's charge when seen by Union soldiers along Cemetery Ridge in "The Fourteenth at Gettysburg" gives way to the logistical nightmare of spiriting Lee's army trains south in General Imboden's "Lee at Gettysburg." If Davis's "Ellen" is twice-told in midcentury literary magazines, the war's military trajectory is double-voiced there and in the pages to come.

Such a pairing of stories is most revealing when the damaged, rain-swept Spotsylvania of "A Night in the Wilderness" is read against the light-hearted Western skirmishing of Richmond Wolcott's Shiloh in "Hopeful Tackett — His Mark," both exceptions that prove a curious narrative rule. No matter what slaughter took place on Eastern battlefields, the stories told about them tend to follow heroic soldiers; no matter how essential the war in the West was to eventual Union victory, its stories tend to be ruthless, lowdown, and closer to damaged homes, even in this collection. And yet, exactly the opposite happens in these paired stories. What makes "A Night in the Wilderness" unforgettable are the "bodies chopped and hacked by balls" that litter the grim Virginia woods, as they did the Gettysburg plain in photographer Timothy O'Sullivan's "Harvest of Death" and the Antietam cornfields that witnessed the single bloodiest day in American military history. Yet magazine stories about Gettysburg and Antietam regularly substituted tidier landscapes and just as regularly transferred the war's unnerving brutality to Kansas cabins, Missouri bushwhackers, Mississippi smuggling, Tennessee massacre, or Louisiana mutiny. The practice persisted even when magazines in Chicago and San Francisco began publishing war stories after Confederate forces admitted defeat. Although all of these portraits of a Western war are authentic, it is also true that the Tennessee battle at Shiloh church ended the war's first year with staggering casualties, and yet Hopeful Tackett volunteers to fight for the star-spangled "banger" like many other Northerners without shoulder straps. One explanation may be that Wolcott's story appeared in Boston's *Continental Monthly* just a few months after the battle while the war was still in progress; it is also worth noting that Massachusetts regiments and the magazine's abolitionist readers paid far less of the cost for Western victory than Wolcott's own 10th Illinois. By contrast, "A Night in the Wilderness" was published after the war in the less ideological *Galaxy*, where Spotsylvania's grueling attack could become part of Grant's Western "butchery" as he approached Richmond.

At the very least, magazine storytelling consistently suggests that it matters who was telling which story when and to whom, matters enough in this collection to augment the paired stories of battlefield clash with the troubling stories of home gone wrong that befuddle traditional tallies of victory and defeat. Shifting perspective makes the fall of New Orleans in April 1862 both the whopping opportunity of New York merchants in Perkins's "Thomas Elliott's Speculations" (*Harper's Monthly*, February 1863) and the disquieting hint in Nora Perry's "Mrs. F.'s Waiting Maid" (*Harper's Monthly*, June 1867) of an occupied people's resistance well into Reconstruction. Female soldiers, prison despair, draft riots, and slave family migrations all once prompted stories that further defamiliarize a conventional military narrative by insisting on the war's relentless intrusions. Instead of Lincoln's house divided, what emerged in the ongoing magazine war was a house invaded, sometimes comically. In Richmond, a confidential secretary in Edward Everett Hale's "The Skeleton in the Closet" learns that the discarded hoopskirts of his womenfolk have tripped couriers, clogged gunboats, and worse, much worse. More often, however, such stories suggest the war's permanent wounds, like the amputations in Silas

Weir Mitchell's "The Case of George Dedlow" or the lingering malice of the Old Dominion in "Believe in Ghosts!" Gathering urgency in postwar magazines, the figure of the house invaded reveals both an abiding Victorian conservatism and a sharp Reconstructive break with the founding premises of the country's Constitution.

The fundamental and yet half-hidden significance of race in the magazine world of *To Live and Die* is finally worth confirming and is actually part of the book's title, which inaugurates this collection's inadvertent plot in much the same way that Lincoln's inauguration in 1861 hurried the events of the war. The line comes from the minstrel song "Dixie," which was written in the antebellum North and appropriated by the wartime South after its popularity spread across the country. "Dixie" was so widely sung, in fact, that Lincoln requested the band to play it when he heard that Lee had surrendered at Appomattox. More recently, thanks to the research of Howard L. Sacks and Judith Rose Sacks for *Way Up North in Dixie*, it has become clearer that the song emerged in rural Ohio, where the black Snowden family made music and where minstrel Dan Emmett first heard the jingle of notes and colloquial longing that would forever be part of his legend.[15]

All three claims to "Dixie," from the minstrel North and the wartime South as well as a black oral tradition long ignored, suggest the braiding preoccupations of this volume, whose stories stretch from abolition to assassination, from Boston to San Francisco, from wedding parties to mangled corpses, and from state glory to national citizenship. Their unfolding plot rightly ends after the armies disbanded and rightly begins during the 1850s in the Western territories, as the *Overland Monthly* once persuasively demonstrated. Taking its cue from regional challenge, then, this patchwork novel opens in Kansas, where relocating Northerners, Southerners, and slaves first stake their claims on national destiny and first discover at Parson Brewster's "ark" who would live and who would die.

NOTES

1 *Harper's Weekly* (3 June 1865): 339.
2 Fiedler began *The Inadvertent Epic: From "Uncle Tom's Cabin" to "Roots"* (New York: Simon and Schuster, 1979) with a determination to rescue Stowe's best-selling novel from the literary critics and aesthetic judgments that Aaron valued, particularly when measuring "artistic creativeness" in *The Unwritten War: American Writers and the Civil War* (1973; rpt. Madison: University of Wisconsin Press, 1987). Edmund Wilson ranged more widely in *Patriotic Gore: Studies in the Literature of the American Civil War* (1962; rpt. New York: Nor-

ton, 1994), a substantial volume that considers diaries and journals as well as more public texts; but Wilson's attention to prose style and literary endeavor tends to favor a thoughtful few, much like George M. Fredrickson's *The Inner Civil War: Northern Intellectuals and the Crisis of the Union* (1965; rpt. Urbana: University of Illinois Press, 1993). More recently, Fiedler's challenge to reconsider popular reading habits has been taken up in my own *Where My Heart Is Turning Ever: Civil War Stories and Constitutional Reform, 1861–1876* (Athens: University of Georgia Press, 1992), as well as by scholars like Jim Cullen in *The Civil War in Popular Culture: A Reusable Past* (Washington, DC: Smithsonian Institution Press, 1995), Elizabeth Young in *Disarming the Nation: Women's Writing and the American Civil War* (Chicago: University of Chicago Press, 1999), and Alice Fahs in "The Feminized Civil War: Gender, Northern Popular Literature, and the Memory of the War, 1861–1900," *Journal of American History* 85 (March 1999): 1461–94, and *The Imagined Civil War: Popular Literature of the North and South, 1861–1865* (Chapel Hill: University of North Carolina Press, 2001). All of these studies are more cordial to what Robert A. Lively once called "the mass product" in *Fiction Fights the Civil War: An Unfinished Chapter in the Literary History of the American People* (Chapel Hill: University of North Carolina Press, 1957), his survey of 512 Civil War novels.

3 "The War," *Harper's Weekly* (4 May 1861): 274. The vista from "The House-Tops in Charleston during the Bombardment of Sumter" appeared on the issue's cover and was the magazine's first view of the outbreak of hostilities.

4 "The Gettysburg Monument," *Harper's Weekly* (17 July 1869): 458. The several pages devoted to the festivities that Theodore R. Davis sketched for the magazine include engravings of "relic-seekers" and the "Gettysburg Spring Hotel" that suggest how quickly the battlefield became a Civil War mecca.

5 See *Harper's Weekly* (9 January 1864): 15, as well as the *Illustrated London News* (5 December 1863): 561, and Vizetelly's later account of the Union siege in "Charleston under Fire," *Cornhill Magazine* 10 (July 1864): 99–110. The best discussion of Vizetelly's venture into the Confederacy remains W. Stanley Hoole, *Vizetelly Covers the Confederacy* (Tuscaloosa, AL: Confederate Publishing, 1957), 19–48. See, too, William P. Campbell, *The Civil War: A Centennial Exhibition of Eyewitness Drawings* (Washington, DC: National Gallery of Art, 1961), especially 11–13, 29, 36–39, 43, 51, 53, 61, 80, 107, 134–38; and my " 'Musquitos,' Rattlesnakes, and Perspiration: The Civil War's Special Artist for the *Illustrated London News*," *Books at Iowa* 63 (November 1995): 3–13.

6 The contested use of the mails during 1835 is thoughtfully considered in Richard R. John, *Spreading the News: The American Postal System from Franklin to Morse* (Cambridge, MA: Harvard University Press, 1995), 257–83; Donna Lee Dickerson, *The Course of Tolerance: Freedom of the Press in Nineteenth-Century America* (New York: Greenwood, 1990), 81–113; and W. Sherman Savage, *The Controversy over the Distribution of Abolition Literature, 1830–1860* (Washington, DC: Association for the Study of Negro Life and History, 1938), 9–81. For Garrison's editorial policies and the *Liberator*'s strategic function in the fight against slavery, see Robert A. Fanuzzi, " 'The

Organ of an Individual': William Lloyd Garrison and the *Liberator,*" *Prospects* 23 (1998): 107–27; David Paul Nord, "Tocqueville, Garrison, and the Perfection of Journalism," *Journalism History* 13 (summer 1986): 56–63, and his sketch in the *Dictionary of Literary Biography* 43 (1985): 232–47; Donald M. Jacobs, "William Lloyd Garrison's *Liberator* and Boston's Blacks, 1830–1865," *New England Quarterly* 44 (1971): 259–77; and Frank Luther Mott, *A History of American Magazines* (Cambridge, MA: Harvard University Press, 1938–1968), 2: 275–96. Garrison's own declaration appears in "To the Public," *Liberator* (1 January 1831): 1, and the remarks on Godey's *Lady's Book* were made by Sarah Josepha Hale in "Louis A. Godey," *Godey's* (February 1850): 87. For an overview of that magazine during its early years, see Isabelle Lehuu, "Sentimental Figures: Reading *Godey's Lady's Book* in Antebellum America," in Shirley Samuels, ed., *The Culture of Sentiment: Race, Gender, and Sentimentality in Nineteenth-Century America* (New York: Oxford University Press, 1992), 73–91, as well as her *Carnival on the Page: Popular Print Media in Antebellum America* (Chapel Hill: University of North Carolina Press, 2000), 102–25; Edward H. Sewell Jr., "Louis A. Godey," *DLB* 73 (1988): 139–45; Allison Bulsterbaum's sketch in Edward E. Chielens, ed., *American Literary Magazines: The Eighteenth and Nineteenth Centuries* (Westport, CT: Greenwood, 1986), 144–50; Mott, *A History of American Magazines*, 1: 580–94; and Lawrence Martin, "The Genesis of *Godey's Lady's Book*," *New England Quarterly* 1 (1928): 41–70. For persuasive arguments that "a magazine of elegant literature" was nonetheless politically charged, see Amy Kaplan, "Manifest Domesticity," *American Literature* 70 (1998): 581–606; and Patricia Okker, *Our Sister Editors: Sarah J. Hale and the Tradition of Nineteenth-Century American Women Editors* (Athens: University of Georgia Press, 1995), 38–58.

7 For detailed coverage of all these magazines, see Diffley, *Where My Heart Is Turning Ever*, xxi–xlii. More specifically, for discussions of Boston's *Atlantic Monthly*, whose circulation high in 1866 surpassed fifty thousand, see Ellery Sedgwick, *The Atlantic Monthly: Yankee Humanism at High Tide and Ebb* (Amherst: University of Massachusetts Press, 1994), especially 68–159, and "The Atlantic Monthly," in Chielens, *American Literary Magazines*, 50–57; Louis J. Budd, "Howells, the *Atlantic Monthly*, and Republicanism," *American Literature* 24 (1952): 139–56; and Mott, *A History of American Magazines*, 2: 493–515. For the *Continental Monthly*, whose unspecified circulation was comparatively small, see Mott, *A History of American Magazines*, 2: 540–43.

Useful treatments of New York's *Harper's Monthly* appear in Sheila Post-Lauria, "Magazine Practices and Melville's *Israel Potter*," in Kenneth M. Price and Susan Belasco Smith, eds., *Periodical Literature in Nineteenth-Century America* (Charlottesville: University Press of Virginia, 1995), 115–32; my "Home on the Range: Turner, Slavery, and the Landscape Illustrations in *Harper's New Monthly Magazine*, 1861–1876," *Prospects* 14 (1989): 175–202; Barbara M. Perkins's sketch in Chielens, *American Literary Magazines*, 166–71; Eugene Exman, *The House of Harper: One Hundred and Fifty Years of Publishing* (New York: Harper and Row, 1967), 69–79; and Mott, *A History of*

American Magazines, 2:383–405, which notes that by 1864 the magazine's circulation had returned to its prewar high of about two hundred thousand. For *Harper's Weekly*, see Andrea G. Pearson, "*Frank Leslie's Illustrated Newspaper* and *Harper's Weekly:* Innovation and Imitation in Nineteenth-Century American Periodical Reporting," *Journal of Popular Culture* 23 (1990): 81–111; Exman, *The House of Harper*, 80–93; and Mott, *A History of American Magazines*, 2: 469–87, where the magazine's circulation is said to have reached 160,000 by 1872. Useful information about *Putnam's* may be found in Ezra Greenspan, *George Palmer Putnam: Representative American Publisher* (University Park: Pennsylvania State University Press, 2000), especially ch. 12, "G. P. Putnam and Sons (and Daughters), 1867–72," where Greenspan corrects Mott's error to set average circulation at twelve thousand to fifteen thousand; also see Post-Lauria, "Magazine Practices"; Kent Ljungquist, "*Putnam's Monthly Magazine*," in Chielens, *American Literary Magazines*, 328–33; and Mott, *A History of American Magazines*, 2: 428–30. The *Galaxy* achieved a circulation high of over twenty-three thousand in 1871, according to Chielens's sketch in *American Literary Magazines*, 139–44; for additional coverage, see Robert J. Skolnick, "The *Galaxy* and American Democratic Culture, 1866–1878," *Journal of American Studies* 16 (1982): 69–80; Justus R. Pearson, "Story of a Magazine: New York's *Galaxy* 1866–1878," *Bulletin of the New York Public Library* 61 (1957): 217–37, 281–302; and Mott, *A History of American Magazines*, 3:361–81.

Philadelphia's *Lippincott's*, which refused to cite circulation figures during its early and unprofitable years, is discussed in Rayburn S. Moore, "Paul Hamilton Hayne and Northern Magazines, 1866–1886," in James Woodress, ed., *Essays Mostly on Periodical Publishing in America: A Collection in Honor of Clarence Gohdes* (Durham, NC: Duke University Press, 1993), 134–47; and Mott, *A History of American Magazines*, 3: 396–401.

8   Useful remarks about the *New National Era* appear in Roland E. Wolseley, *The Black Press, U.S.A.* (Ames: Iowa State University Press, 1990), 35; Martin E. Dann, ed., *The Black Press, 1827–1890: The Quest for National Identity* (New York: Putnam's, 1971), 91–99; Constance McLaughlin Green, *The Secret City: A History of Race Relations in the Nation's Capital* (Princeton, NJ: Princeton University Press, 1967), 94–113; and Mott, *A History of American Magazines*, 3: 283–84. Although Douglass eventually lost as much as $10,000 on the magazine, perhaps one reason why circulation reports remain unavailable, the weekly was recognized by Washington's *Daily Republican* as "a brave and forcible champion of the race for which it speaks." See "What the Press Say of the New Era," *New National Era* (3 February 1870): 2.

Further south, magazine circulations were likewise rarely discussed as magazines rarely succeeded for long and subscribers were often in arrears. The *Southern Monthly*, whose subscription agents were at least active throughout the South, is considered more fully in Sam G. Riley, *Magazines of the American South* (Westport, CT: Greenwood, 1986), 247–49; and Mott, *A History of American Magazines*, 2: 111. For the *New Eclectic*, which went on to absorb the *Land We Love* and become the *Southern Magazine*, see my "Home from the Theatre of War: The *Southern Magazine* and Recollections of the Civil War," in Price and Smith, *Periodical Literature in Nineteenth-Century America*, 183–201; Ray M. Atchinson's sketch in Chielens, *American Literary Magazines*, 395–99; and Mott, *A History of American Magazines*, 3: 46. For the *Southern Magazine* in the wider field of Southern periodicals, see Jay B. Hubbell, *The South in American Literature, 1607–1900* (Durham, NC: Duke University Press, 1954), 716–26; and Elisabeth Muhlenfeld, "The Civil War and Authorship," in Louis D. Rubin Jr., ed., *The History of Southern Literature* (Baton Rouge: Lousiana State University Press, 1985), 178–87.

To the west, the *Overland Monthly* in its postwar years is discussed in George Rathmell, "The *Overland Monthly:* California's Literary Treasure," *Californians* 8, no. 6 (1991): 12–21; Hank Nuwer's sketch in Sam G. Riley and Gary W. Selnow, eds., *Regional Interest Magazines of the United States* (Westport, CT: Greenwood, 1991), 241–46; William M. Clements's sketch in Chielens, *American Literary Magazines*, 308–13; Franklin Walker, *San Francisco's Literary Frontier* (New York: Knopf, 1939), 256–83; and Mott, *A History of American Magazines*, 3: 402–9, where the magazine's early peak circulation of ten thousand is noted. For the *Lakeside Monthly,* which reached a circulation of fourteen thousand in 1873 before that year's economic panic, see Michael Hackenberg's sketch in Chielens, *American Literary Magazines*, 199–203; Mott, *A History of American Magazines*, 3: 413–16; "The Life-Story of a Magazine," *Dial* 54 (16 June 1913): 489–92; and Herbert E. Fleming, "The Literary Interests of Chicago," *American Journal of Sociology* 11 (1906): 377–408.

9 The rates paid to Stowe and Hawthorne are discussed in Sedgwick, *Atlantic Monthly*, 74–76; particular attention to Stowe's market value may be found in Susan Coultrap-McQuin, *Doing Literary Business: American Women Writers in the Nineteenth Century* (Chapel Hill: University of North Carolina Press, 1990), 96–99. For Melville's success with short fiction in *Putnam's*, see Greenspan, *George Palmer Putnam*, ch. 9, "*Putnam's Magazine* and 'the Putnam Public' "; and Lea Bertani Vozar Newman, *A Reader's Guide to the Short Stories of Herman Melville* (Boston: G. K. Hall, 1986). The *Galaxy*'s continuing interest in Whitman is documented in Jerome Loving, *Walt Whitman: The Song of Himself* (Berkeley: University of California Press, 1999), 317–19. For general rates of payment to midcentury contributors, see Mott, *A History of American Magazines*, 2: 19–25, and 3: 12–17.

10 The reincarnation of "Ellen" and Davis's double life in *Peterson's* and the *Atlantic Monthly,* soon to be complicated by the *Galaxy* and *Lippincott's,* are discussed in Jane Atteridge Rose, *Rebecca Harding Davis* (New York: Twayne, 1993), 37–51; and Sharon M. Harris, *Rebecca Harding Davis and American Realism* (Philadelphia: University of Pennsylvania Press, 1991), 103–51. For fuller commentary on Davis's wartime writing for literary magazines, see Jean Pfaelzer, *Parlor Radical: Rebecca Harding Davis and the Origins of American Social Realism* (Pittsburgh: University of Pittsburgh Press, 1996), 76–106.

11 Young, *Disarming the Nation*, 94. As Young makes clear (329 n. 64), Alcott herself preferred "My Contraband" and reclaimed that title when her story

was reprinted in *Hospital Sketches and Camp and Fireside Stories* (1869); see 69–108 for her incisive discussion of Alcott's story in the context that later re-publication invited. The initial title change seems to have been the suggestion of *Atlantic* assistant Howard Ticknor, who wanted to avoid confusion with a story by Mary E. Dodge called "Our Contraband" that *Harper's Monthly* had published in August 1863; see Joel Myerson, Daniel Shealy, and Madeleine B. Stern, eds., *The Journals of Louisa May Alcott* (Boston: Little, Brown, 1989), 124 n. 31. Further discussion may be found in Sarah Elbert, introduction, to *Louisa May Alcott on Race, Sex, and Slavery* (Boston: Northeastern University Press, 1997), xl–xliv; Betsy Klimasmith, "Slave, Master, Mistress, Slave: Genre and Interracial Desire in Louisa May Alcott's Fiction," *ATQ* 11 (1997): 115–35; and Diffley, *Where My Heart Is Turning Ever,* 34–39. For the pervasive shiver of desire in such narratives, what Karen Sanchez-Eppler calls "anti-slavery fiction's fascination with miscegenation," see her *Touching Liberty: Abolition, Feminism, and the Politics of the Body* (Berkeley: University of California Press, 1993), 14–49. For Alcott's "The Brothers" as a step in her early magazine career, see Madeleine B. Stern, *Louisa May Alcott: From Blood & Thunder to Hearth and Home* (Boston: Northeastern University Press, 1998), 114–26; and Richard Brodhead, "Starting Out in the 1860s: Alcott, Authorship, and the Postbellum Literary Field," in *Cultures of Letters: Scenes of Reading and Writing in Nineteenth-Century America* (Chicago: University of Chicago Press, 1993), 69–106.

12   The publication history of Johnston's single story of the war is actually more complicated: before "Philemon Perch" published a revised version in the *New Eclectic,* the tale had appeared as "The Last Day of Mr. Williamson Slippey, Salt Merchant" in Augusta's *Southern Field and Fireside* (28 March 1863) but was not included the next year in *Georgia Sketches,* which thus remained in-souciantly antebellum. For the particulars of Johnston's kaleidoscopic career with the *Dukesborough Tales,* see Bert Hitchcock, *Richard Malcolm Johnston* (Boston: Twayne, 1978), 44–67, as well as his sketch in *DLB* 74 (1988): 232–37; Jimmy Ponder Voyles, "Richard Malcolm Johnston's Literary Career: An Estimate," *Markham Review* 4 (February 1974): 29–34; Hubbell, *The South in American Literature,* 777–82; and three related essays by Francis Taylor Long on "The Life of Richard Malcolm Johnston in Maryland, 1867–1898": "Pt. 1 Country Gentleman, Teacher, and Writer, 1867–1881," *Maryland Historical Magazine* 34 (December 1939): 305–24; "Pt. 2 Some Literary Friendships—The Lecture Platform, 1882–1889," *Maryland Historical Magazine* 35 (September 1940): 270–86; and "Pt. 3 The Closing Years, 1889–1898," *Maryland Historical Magazine* 36 (March 1941): 54–69.

13   Unlike Davis and Alcott, and certainly unlike Johnston, Twain was offered twice the normal rate for "A True Story" and more than the *Atlantic Monthly* paid anyone else, one measure of reputation's sure if bedeviling power. For discussion of a story that Tom Quirk calls "a vernacular tour de force," see his *Mark Twain: A Study of the Short Fiction* (New York: Twayne, 1997), 57–62; Diffley, *Where My Heart Is Turning Ever,* 44–53; and James D. Wilson, *A*

Reader's Guide to the Short Stories of Mark Twain (Boston: G. K. Hall, 1987), 267–73. To discover how much of Twain's story is "repeated word for word," see Herbert A. Wisbey Jr., "The True Story of Auntie Cord," *Mark Twain Society Bulletin* 4 (June 1981): 1, 3–5. For Twain's "Forty-Three Days in an Open Boat" (*Harper's Monthly*, December 1866) and his initial fumble with Eastern audiences, before *Innocents Abroad* (1869) and a scintillating humor department for the *Galaxy* (1870–1871), see Twain's own recollection in "My Debut as a Literary Person," *Century* 59 (November 1899): 76–88.

14 Gary W. Gallagher, *The Confederate War* (Cambridge, MA: Harvard University Press, 1997), 8.

15 Howard L. Sacks and Judith Rose Sacks, *Way Up North in Dixie: A Black Family's Claim to the Confederate Anthem* (Washington, DC: Smithsonian Institution Press, 1993).

◆○◆

TIME LINE

EVENTS	STORIES
1850s	
Compromise of 1850, including Fugitive Slave Act	
Kansas-Nebraska Act	
John Brown massacres settlers near Pottawatomie Creek in Kansas	"The Cabin at Pharaoh's Ford"
Dred Scott v. Sandford	
John Brown captured at Harper's Ferry in Virginia and hanged	
1860	
Lincoln elected (*November*)	
South Carolina secedes (*December*)	
1861	
Mississippi, Florida, Alabama, Georgia, and Louisiana secede (*January*)	
Texas secedes (*February*)	
Lincoln inaugurated (*March*)	
Fort Sumter falls (*April*)	
Lincoln calls out 75,000 state militia (*April*)	
Virginia secedes (*April*)	"Job and the Bug"
Blockade of the Confederacy begins (*April*)	
Arkansas and North Carolina secede (*May*)	

Tennessee formally secedes; U.S. Sanitary Commission approved (*June*)	
First Battle of Bull Run in Virginia (*July*)	"A True and Simple Tale of '61"
Jefferson Davis elected permanent president of the Confederacy (*November*)	"Ellen"

1862

Union takes Forts Henry and Donelson in Tennessee (*February*)	
Battle of Shiloh in Tennessee (*April*)	"Hopeful Tackett — His Mark"
New Orleans falls (*April*)	"Thomas Elliott's Speculations"
Memphis falls (*June*)	"Mrs. F.'s Waiting Maid" "Believe in Ghosts!"
Second Battle of Bull Run in Virginia (*August*)	"The Sergeant's Little Story"
Battle of Antietam in Maryland (*September*)	"On the Antietam"
Lincoln announces Preliminary Emancipation Proclamation (*September*)	"A Letter from the Country"
Battle of Corinth in Mississippi (*October*)	
Confederate draft exemptions expanded (*October*)	"T. J.'s Cavalry Charge"

1863

Emancipation Proclamation (*January*)	
Mosby's Rangers organized in Virginia (*January*)	
U.S. national draft enacted (*March*)	
	(*April*) "Colonel Charley's Wife"
Battle of Chancellorsville in Virginia (*May*)	
Siege of Vicksburg in Mississippi (*May*)	

Battle of Gettysburg in Pennsylvania (*July*)	"The Fourteenth at Gettysburg" "Lee at Gettysburg"
Vicksburg falls (*July*)	
New York City draft riots (*July*)	"Three Days of Terror"
Assault on Fort Wagner in South Carolina (*July*)	"The Brothers"
Battle of Chickamauga in Tennessee (*September*)	"The Case of George Dedlow"
Little Rock falls	"Robbed of Half a Million"
Battles of Lookout Mountain and Missionary Ridge in Tennessee (*November*)	
Spy Belle Boyd released from prison and sent to Richmond (*December*)	"In the Libey" "Mr. Williamson Slippey and His Salt"

1864

	(*January*) "A Night on the Mississippi"
Meridian, Mississippi falls (*February*)	"Mrs. Spriggins, the Neutral"
Confederates capture Fort Pillow in Tennessee (*April*)	"Buried Alive"
Battle of the Wilderness in Virginia (*May*)	
Battle of Spotsylvania in Virginia (*May*)	"A Night in the Wilderness"
Battle of Cold Harbor in Virginia (*June*)	
Atlanta falls (*September*)	
Battle of Cedar Creek in Virginia (*October*)	"The Freedman's Story"
Battle of Nashville in Tennessee (*December*)	"Road-Side Story"

1865

U.S. Congress passes 13th Amendment abolishing slavery (*January*)

Richmond falls (*April*)

Lee surrenders in Virginia at
Appomattox Courthouse (*April*)

Lincoln assassinated (*April*)

Jefferson Davis captured in Georgia
(*May*)   "The Skeleton in the Closet"

Kirby Smith's Western forces
surrender (*June*)   "Sentenced and Shot"

Lincoln conspirators executed (*July*)   "Wilhelmina"

POSTWAR

13th Amendment ratified

Force Acts passed to protect
civil rights   "A True Story, Repeated Word
for Word As I Heard It"

U.S. troops withdrawn to end
Reconstruction

28

Prelude

Political currents collided ominously in the West during the decade before Fort Sumter fell. In the Kansas Territory, open warfare broke out following the passage of the Kansas-Nebraska Act and the principle of squatter sovereignty in 1854. For the next five years, Kansas bled as the Emigrant Aid Society helped move in some two thousand New England settlers, who were met by increasingly violent advocates of slavery from Missouri. In 1857, after John Brown's massacre of settlers near Pottawatomie Creek, proslavery forces in the territorial legislature pushed through the "bogus" Lecompton Constitution that would help drive Northern and Southern Democrats apart while galvanizing the nascent Republican Party. For Parson Brewster in "The Cabin at Pharaoh's Ford," God's work then lies not only in moving Kansas toward entering the union as a free state but also in moving fugitive slaves quickly and quietly toward Canada. The underground railroad that he serves was particularly active just north of the upper tier of slave states, several of which (like Missouri) would become troubled border states during the war. Between 1855 and 1859, while John Brown moved deliberately toward the attack on Harper's Ferry, dozens of fugitive slaves were reported to have passed through secret Kansas "stations" on their way to Iowa and points north, good reason for border vigilantes to spy on "conductors" like Parson Brewster and for the parson's daughter to tremble.

◆○◆

Henry King

"THE CABIN AT PHARAOH'S FORD"

(*Overland Monthly*, December 1874)

It was not imposing; it was not pretty. It was hardly equal in either of these respects to the prevailing type of Kansas cabins in those days; and why Parson Brewster, a minister of the gospel and a man of more than average intelligence, should have made himself such a home in such a place was one of the ethical marvels of the settlement. But there it stood, or sat, on the bluff-slope, a few steps from the brink of the Neosho River, in sight of the ford, and surrounded on three sides by a stingy growth of hazel and dogberry bushes. It was constructed of unhewn logs, chinked with the most commonplace black soil, and roofed with clumsy slabs of cotton-wood, out of which sprouted singular little clusters of green and hungry twigs as the summer came on. The parson construed this last-named fact to be a sort of special providence and reverently thanked God more than once for touching his humble abode with "a sign that could be seen of all men"; but his neighbors, being better acquainted with the subtle chemistry of the tree-sap, knew that the parson had simply cut his slabs at the wrong time of the year. The cabin had one door, looking eastward, down the river-bottom, over clumps of stones and through narrow paths between the trees and decaying logs, to where the dim perspective was lost in the darkness of a sudden turn of the stream to the north. There was no window, because the parson had made no calculation for any in the plan of his dwelling, and the omission was not observed until the logs were all up and ready for the roof, and it was too late to introduce the necessary opening. There was a loose slab in one corner of the roof, however, which in pleasant weather partially did the office of a window, for, by pushing it aside, considerable light could be added from above to that which came in at the open door below. "It's just as well," the parson used to remark, "and there is an excellent precedent for it: the window in the ark was in the top, and looked straight up to Him who held the waters in the hollow of His hand." And so the quaint little cabin at Pharaoh's Ford came to be known in those parts as "Parson Brewster's ark."

In spite of its architectural oddity, this diminutive modern ark was sometimes a rather pleasing thing to look at. For instance, in the early dawn of that beautiful summer, after the spring rise of the river had been subdued to a conservative flow that felt its way carefully over the pebbles as if loth to disturb them, and the trees had taken on the deep and sultry green which was almost a glow in its peculiar richness, and the pent-up life at the heart of the cotton-wood slabs in the cabin's roof had begun to seek its way to the light in scores of little twigs bearing just leaves enough to hide their nakedness, there was something about the place that seemed to clothe it with a rude charm; and the wide-open door was at once an invitation and an interdiction to the sensitive passer-by. Nor was it much, if any, less alluring in the first stage of that succeeding autumn, when the rains, and winds, and early frost had washed and chilled the foliage into a crisped and jagged splendor, and the river was shuddering with apprehensions of ice and snow, and the languid twigs in the cotton-wood roof-slabs lay like tattered guidons about the awkward chimney and under the blue curl of smoke that ascended like incense to mingle with the haze and the clouds. It must be confessed, however, that the scrawny bushes which grew immediately about the cabin did not add any particular grace to the scene, at any season. But there they were, and had been from the first, and the parson resolutely refused to be persuaded that their removal was a thing to be desired. "When God appeared to Moses with a message," he used to say, "it was not in a great tree, but in a common little bush like one of these; and whenever God has anything to say to me, He will say it just as easily and as forcibly through these bushes as he would in a grove of cedars of Lebanon." There was no combating such an argument, and so the bushes remained.

The inside of the cabin was neat, but by no means gaudy, unless the piece of yellow calico that hung in front of the three shelves which held the household crockery, or the illuminated print of the crucifixion which was fastened to a log with a rusty nail at the top and pushed into a crevice between two logs at the bottom (and which had been torn through the loins of the Saviour and the head of the soldier with the spear, and fastened together with stitches of pale-blue thread), could be considered as coming within the meaning of the term. The furniture was mainly of the parson's own manufacture, and therefore not specially noticeable in the way of artistic design or finish; for, whatever might be said in praise of the parson's skill in constructing sermons and unraveling scriptural mysteries, he was an emphasized failure as a carpenter and furniture-maker. There was but one room, and a fire-place. I say "and a fire-place," because it was merely an adjunct of the house proper. In fact, it might be said that the house was a part of the fire-place, rather than that the fire-place was a part of the house; for the parson, having a horror of chimneys that would not draw, had built and tested his fire-place the first thing, and added the house to it afterward. There was a cellar beneath the floor, but no one would have suspected it, for the only entrance thereto was under the two flat stones that made the hearth; and, unlike most modern cellars, it had an underground passage connected with it, and the passage led off in the darkness to a rock, which, being rolled back, disclosed a manger filled with wild grass, in the parson's dug-out stable, only a step or two from the edge of the river. This passage ran under the parson's garden-plat — a little clearing in the hazel thicket — to which he had given, peculiarly enough, the name of "Gethsemane"; and the passage itself he had named "The Sepulchre" — "out of regard to the fact," he used to say to himself in his musings, "that the rolling away of that stone in the stable has so often been a resurrection." It can do no harm, at this remote day, to say that all this pertained to the concealment and flight of fugitive slaves.

So much for the appearance, appurtenances, and surroundings of the cabin at Pharaoh's Ford. I think I have mentioned everything of interest or strikingness that was ordinarily to be seen about there, with just a single exception; and I hesitate to complete the picture, for to do so I must introduce a young lady, and my unhandy pen makes but indifferent work with such objects. But it will not do to skip her, and indeed I have no inclination to be either ungallant to the young lady or neglectful of the duty I owe to my readers. Be it known, then, that Parson Brewster did not live entirely alone there in his cotton-wood ark by the Neosho. He had for a companion a daughter whom he called Hannah, and who looked to be about sixteen at the time of which I am writing. When I say that Hannah was handsome, in face and in form, I but state a fervent truth in a very flat way; albeit she usually dressed in a loose, short frock of coarse cotton cloth, did not possess a single piece of jewelry, had never seen a corset, and went bare-footed through half the summer. She sometimes twined a water-lily in her hair, or fastened a prairie-rose at her throat; but I am sure this was only a kind of involuntary manifestation of her femininity; and not an expression of personal vanity. There is still something of Eve in every one of the sex. Parson Brewster was accustomed to assert that the doctrine of innate depravity is fully proved every day in the crimes and trickeries of men; and is not the story of the fig-leaves reproduced more or less clearly in every feminine nature? But this has nothing specially to do with Hannah, whose shapely limbs and well-cut features were an integrant part of the ragged and tangled beauty of Pharaoh's Ford, like the statuesque sycamores that interlaced their boughs about the river-crossing, and the larkspurs and columbines that struggled up from beneath the stones and through the tufts of fragile grass in the background of hills and gullies. She rarely left the cabin, and as seldom talked with those who came there. Sometimes the passers-by would hear through the closed door a wild and tremulous singing — usually a fragment of some old hymn; and then such as were acquainted with the truth of the matter knew that poor Hannah was in "one of her spells," as the parson expressed it. For the unfortunate girl was subject to periodical aberrations of reason, during which she sung and cried almost constantly, and frequently became so crazed that it was necessary to chain her like a savage beast to her bed until the fever lulled and the brain was released from its consuming torture. Then her beauty, totally eclipsed for days and days by that great cloud of pain, would shine out again and touch her countenance with a fair lustre that was fresh and strong, and yet seemed just ready to fade away. All but the eyes — alas! all but the eyes. They retained and wore always a pitiful suggestion of the terrible glare that burned and flashed there in the periods of madness.

It was a very uncommon thing for any other of womankind than this strange girl to be seen about the cabin. The nearest house was several miles away, and the small sweet courtesies of tea-parties and afternoon-calls did not obtain in the neighborhood of Pharaoh's Ford to any marked extent. Possibly they never do in localities where millinery is only a vision or a memory, and corn-bread is a prosaic reality the year round. Occasionally, the wan features of a "mover's" wife would peer out from the lifted cover of a passing wagon on the way to some outlying settlement, or journeying back to "the States"; and there were a few instances of scared and hurrying Negro women wandering in after night to beg a few morsels of food and be piloted across the river. One of these came once in a raw storm of rain and sleet, with a half-clad babe in her arms; and Hannah remembered long afterward that her father took the queer little thing on his knee and bent his head over it as in prayer, and that then the woman went and laid with it overnight in the manger at the mouth of "The Sepulchre." And that was all. The visitors there were men, as a rule, and the coming of a woman was the exception. Hannah observed, too, with that keenness of instinct peculiar to her sex, that the conversations and discussions of these men related entirely to matters in which men alone seemed to be concerned, and that they rarely so much as mentioned the name of a woman. And yet she knew by their friendly allusions to one another's personal affairs, and by their tender kindness to her at all times, as well as by the warmth of the greeting which her father gave them whenever they came, that they could not at heart be cold or bad. Very likely they had no room in their natures just then for anything but a zealous sense of devotion to a single idea — the idea that had lodgment at the very core of their reflections, molding and moving them with all the heat and force of a great passion.

That was a memorable year in Kansas, and the councils and consultations that Hannah Brewster heard in the ark at Pharaoh's Ford were neither accidental nor purposeless. The Bogus Legislature, as it was called, had enacted a set of statutes for the Territory which actually made it a felony to so much as speak, write, or print a sentence in denial of the right to hold slaves therein, and disqualified as jurors in the trial of such cases all persons "conscientiously opposed to holding slaves"; while the enticing, persuading, or assisting of Negroes to escape from the Territory was declared to be grand larceny, for which the punishment provided was death! The acts of this legislature were indorsed by the Federal officials of Kansas, and ratified by the Federal authorities at Washington, and Federal troops were at hand to uphold and enforce them. The antislavery sentiment of the Territory was divided, and it had been from the start, on the point of respecting or defying laws forced upon the actual inhabitants by fraudulent elections and the menace of administration bayonets. The general feeling was probably in favor of making a virtue of what seemed to be a necessity by yielding a tacit obedience. But this feeling did not prevail, and never had prevailed, except in a feeble way, among those who were accustomed to take counsel together at Parson Brewster's; and these obnoxious laws, instead of dismaying or discouraging them, wrought their courage to a higher pitch, gave increased fervor to their enthusiasm, and apparently inspired them with renewed faith in the success of the work in which they were engaged. I fancy they were inclined to hail the bogus statutes as something akin to a blessing. In fact, the parson was heard to say "the finger of Providence was plainly visible in the matter," inasmuch as it was sure to bring on a crisis, and force men to take a stand on one or the other of the two sides of the controversy — "the sheep on this hand, the goats on that," as he put it.

The idea of openly resisting the laws, however, was something which even these men were not yet thoroughly persuaded to accept. Impulse favored it, but principle, as well as policy, argued against it. Such a step would be combating one wrong by committing another; and they could not quite reconcile their consciences to that kind of morals. Then, again, to precipitate a conflict of that character would be to place themselves in a treasonous attitude, and thus to furnish their adversaries with the coveted excuse for treating them as public enemies; and that prompting of worldly prudence, which is often a better monitor than the most exalted spirit of valor, made them hesitate to assume a position so emphatic in its meaning and so equivocal in the way of results. Parson Brewster alone declared for prompt and undisguised resistance, both as a duty and as an expedient; and he spent many a night trying to convert the others to his view of the situation. His arguments were mainly addressed to the moral perceptions, and his illustrations were usually drawn from the Scriptures. "This is God's work that we are engaged in," he would say; "and when God puts stumbling-blocks in our way He expects us to make stepping-stones of them." These bogus laws could not be obeyed or accepted, he urged, without at least a seeming betrayal of moral trust; and he would vehemently add: "Let us not play Jonah or Peter with this call to duty, but rather whet our knives and gather our fagots like Abraham, trusting God to raise up rams enough to save our Isaacs from the sacrifice." Then he would tell them the story of Phineas thrusting Zimri and the Midianitish woman through with a javelin, so turning away wrath from Israel, and winning for himself a perpetual covenant of peace from Jehovah — "he and his seed after him; even the covenant of an everlasting priesthood." All of which was but slightly to the purpose, perhaps, viewed from ordinary stand-points; but it was the parson's way of handling such things, and possibly it was more effective with that peculiar audience of his than a different course would have been. It is certain, anyway, that they usually listened to him with close attention, there being only one reported instance of real interruption, and that was when Copitt, from over on Gopher Creek, stopped him by venturing to say something about a Balaam going the wrong road without an ass to show him his error, to which the parson replied that he heard the bray distinctly, but did not see the flaming sword. An awkward pause ensued, and a stillness that was disturbed only by the creaking of a broken branch on the elm-tree under the cabin-eaves and a whisper of rustling in Hannah's frock as she turned on her stool in the corner to see what the silence meant. Then the parson slowly resumed his discourse, and Copitt seemed specially eager to catch every word. It is certain, also, that while his Scriptural illustrations may sometimes have tired his hearers just a little, he never failed to interest and inspirit them as he came to the close; for his perorations, apparently by accident, but really, I suspect, by design, always related to the wrongs and woes of those "held in bonds." More than once he made the stoutest listener tremble with compassion and indignation; and Hannah, often as she heard the story, invariably hid her face in the folds of her gown and sobbed through it all. He would picture the sinfulness of slavery and the sufferings of the enslaved like one who had himself been both slave and master. His pictures were not always true to nature, perhaps, but they were always striking and always touching, and he felt them to be possible, if they were not living realities. So he would show his little coterie of listeners the wounds and scars that came of overseers' scourgings, the inhuman selling apart of mother and child, the rude shelter and coarse food and coarser garments, the constant fear, the smothered longing for freedom. His words often held the very snap and sting of the whip in their intensity; and sometimes a whole volume of pathos and bitter agony would be crowded into half a dozen of his sentences—as when he would depict a man learning the alphabet at the peril of torture, or reading the Bible in dread apprehension of his life, and dying at last, alone and in squalor, without so much as the poor boon of a prayer. "And they tell us this is a divine institution!" he would exclaim, with a hiss and a sneer; and then, after a moment's pause, he would add: "So is hell a divine institution—but who wants to support it?"

I do not know exactly how or precisely when it came about, but before the summer was half gone Parson Brewster's view of the situation was the view of all those who frequented the ark. And not only in the neighborhood of Pharaoh's Ford, but throughout the whole Territory, the Free State settlers gradually came to a realization of the fact that they must either abandon their homes, their purposes, and their honest convictions of right and wrong, or defend them by a resort to force; and they very generally concluded to stay and "see it out." Then came the secret recruiting of companies of "guards" and "rangers" on one side, and the summoning of companies of sheriff's and marshal's "deputies" on the other; then the occasional burning of a house or the driving out of a troublesome abolitionist or an over-zealous operator of the contrary faith; then a formal skirmish at long range, here and there, in which there was more of tactics than shedding of blood; then the concentration of several squads of companies at a given point, and the throwing up of little earth-work forts; and finally, an actual state of war, with spies and scouting, and weary marches, and midnight ambuscades, and the clash and shock of substantial battle.

So the blue-and-green summer wore away into the bronzed pomp of October. The half-stripped trees no longer offered safe obscurity to lurking horsemen, and the report of a rifle woke an echo like a cannon-shot. But the horsemen were still abroad—ragged, grim, and quick of eye and ear; and there was yet a purple film of powder-smoke in the rim of the clouds that indolently floated over Pharaoh's Ford. The open country thereabout was a desolate waste of bleached grass and weeds, with here and there a stunted patch of corn or a few rows of absurd cabbages. There had been considerable planting done in the early spring, but little cultivation followed. Agriculture in Kansas that summer had been a mere diversion. The real business of the time was history-making. Not only were there no crops raised by the settlers living adjacent to the ford, but the road to the Missouri River had been blockaded for months by the pro-slavery forces, and no supplies could be obtained from "the States." They had contrived to subsist in a poor way during the summer on such stock and grain as they could gather and bring in when on their scouting expeditions up toward the Kansas River, where farming was a comparatively safe pursuit for those who were thoroughly loyal to the territorial government. But these forays had now not only become extremely hazardous, but also slenderly profitable in the way of booty, for on their last trip they had been able to "press" nothing better than a diminutive stack of not very good wheat, which they carried away in the sheaf, thrashed by hand-power, and ground in a couple of rheumatic old coffee-mills; and they tried to make themselves believe, no doubt, that the flat, speckled, and clammy cakes into which this primitive flour was baked—looking like huge linseed-poultices—were really fine eating. And then winter was fast approaching, too; and altogether the outlook was of a kind to induce some right sober thinking, and the speediest possible movements in the direction of meeting or averting what threatened to be a conquering calamity.

It may have been this matter which brought half a dozen of the settlement "captains" to the cabin in the waning of that reposeful autumn afternoon. That their business was of special importance, at least, was apparent when the parson requested Hannah to "go and stand in the yard a little while." This was an ordinary precaution there when questions of particular moment were to be considered—not that anyone doubted Hannah's fidelity, but the parson thought it best for her not to hear anything which might bring her trouble should she ever, by any chance, be called as a witness in a court of justice. Hannah herself did not exactly understand it; and sometimes she wondered, in her girlish way, as she stood out in the grass and the silence, gazing aimlessly up through the trees to the sky, what it was that they had to say or do that she might not hear or see it. But she made no complaints, and asked no questions.

They must have talked there together fully an hour, Hannah thought, and then they came out—all but her father, who stood by the half-open door and called her in; then taking her by the arm led her to her bed, and lifted the chain that lay always on the floor beneath it. She well knew what that meant. He was going away, and feared or fancied that the madness might come upon her during his absence. It was the work of only few moments; then he closed the door behind him and was gone; while she, securely shackled and left alone in the gloom and quietude of the cabin, leaned against the wall of logs, and peered out through a friendly chink into the whimsical fascinations of the twilight.

It was a lovely evening. The setting sun had left a rapture of amethyst in the heavens, and a dreamful mist hung like an enchantment over the river. A vagrant cloud moved leisurely out now and then above the trees, and drifted away and was lost in the shadow that crept up to meet it from the distant narrowness of the valley. There was no sound or sign of man, beast, or bird, and no louder noise than the loosing and falling of the stained leaves, save when a bit of dead bark dropped from the log on which Hannah leaned, or a shifting of her position disturbed the chain about her limbs. It was a scene to impress an emotional nature for a life-time. But Hannah's thoughts were busy with practical things, and probably the sense of utter aloneness that pervaded it all was the only poetical feature in it that reached her mind as she watched the light fade and the air grow thin and cool — for as the outlines of the landscape melted away, and the darkness came on, she shut her eyes and slept.

It was a sleep perplexed with visions — some beautiful, some ludicrous, some terrifying. One moment the dreamer would be sitting down at a table loaded with the choicest food, and the next she would be standing in the woods eating acorns and wild berries. Then a smooth and sunny river — so much clearer and brighter, she thought, than the sombre Neosho — would go gladly flowing past; and there were pleasure-boats on the bosom of it, filled with merry-faced boys and girls, who knelt in rich heaps of flowers and laughed. Then the river would sink swiftly into the earth out of sight, and tall trees would move by as in procession, with chains hanging from their branches, and blood oozing out on the crisp grass from their roots. Then a low level plain would appear, with groups of bearded men in grotesque costumes, dancing a confused quadrille, and stopping at intervals of a few seconds, with their hands to their ears, as if to catch the sound of some ghostly melody. Then the river would rise up again — a little darker than before, Hannah fancied, but still so limpid that she could count the toes on the blue-veined feet of the children who sat on the bank with their slender legs immersed to the knees, and swinging to and fro in the water. Then, as she watched, the river lost its sparkle; soon a sheet of ice was over it, and the feet of the children were frozen there close and stiff in the roughened edge of it. Then the ice rose slowly and steadily from the centre of the stream like a peak, and turned to stone, with little rills of water trickling out of yellow fissures in its sides, and on the summit stood a monster harp of gold, upright in a splendor of light and verdure. Then there was a flutter of invisible

wings in the air; spectral fingers struck a chord on the harp-strings, and a subdued and tender chorus of many voices was borne out above the world. And
then there came a sound of real singing from the profound hush of the cabin
where Hannah dreamed—faint at first as to the words, but not weak enough
in volume to quite disguise the air of that grand old hymn,

"From Greenland's icy mountains";

then a little fuller and a little louder; then a deep strain that the eager ear could
catch entire—

"Bows down to wood and stone";

then a pause as of pain or for breath; then a sustained clearness, strongly and
measuredly swelling into thorough distinctiveness—

"Till, like a sea of glory,
It spreads from pole to pole";

and then the harp disappeared in a dazzling gush of brightness, the peak tot-
tered and fell, the song was smothered, and nothing was left of it all but a few
deceitful echoes that lingered among the cobwebs and wasps'-nests in the slabs
of the cabin roof.

It must have been after midnight when Parson Brewster returned to "the ark,"
bringing with him two restless and shuddering Black men, whom he hastily
thrust under the hearth-stones and into the cellar. And, as he had feared or
foreseen, he found Hannah tossing and wailing in a fever of madness. She did
not know him when he spoke to her, and when he touched her hot head she
shrieked. As he stood watching her, and pitying her, and wondering what he
might do to soothe and relieve her, he heard a trampling of horses, then a halt,
and in a minute more the cabin-door was opened, and a crowd of ten or twelve
men entered without so much as the civility of rapping.

"Don't trouble yourself to offer us cheers," said the one who appeared to be
leader and spokesman of the party—"we don't mind standin'."

The parson was confused and alarmed, but he did not betray his real feelings
as he turned to the speaker and inquired, very pleasantly, "Is there anything I
can do for you?"

"Wall, yes, I 'low thar is," the spokesman answered. "We're kind o' cruisin'
round on the hunt of a gang o' cutthroat abolitionists as hes a nest in these parts,
and goes out at nights a-burnin' houses, an' a-runnin' off niggers, an' a-killin'
law-abidin' citizens. I say we're kind o' cruisin' round fur to git to fall in with
them cusses; an' we jest thought we'd trouble you to tell us whar they roost."

"I do not understand you," the parson replied, with the faintest possible quiver in his voice. But he did understand, and his blood ran cold as he thought of what was coming.

" 'Taint a bit o' use, you know," the spokesman continued, "to deal us any foolishness, 'cause we aint in no par*tic'lar* good condition fur to put up with it." As he said this, he drew a dragoon pistol from his belt, and put his finger to the trigger.

The parson was fully collected now, and he answered with perfect coolness and quite firmly: "If the laws have been violated, as you say, there is a way to vindicate them, decently and in order. There are judges and sheriffs ready-made, and witnesses of a certain kind are neither scarce nor expensive. As for me, I have all I can do to attend to my own business."

"Wall," said the spokesman, with significant emphasis, "I rayther *guess* thet's a kind o' waddin' as won't go down with this battalion. I tell ye what 'tis, old man, ef you keer anything par*tic'lar* about your health, you'd better not be sassy, 'cause these is mighty sickly times."

The parson looked him straight in the eye, without saying a word.

"Wall?" the man added, inquiringly.

"Well?" repeated the parson after him.

There was nothing more said. But two of the men stepped forward at the beck of the spokesman, and led the parson unresistingly out of the door, where his arms were rudely pinioned to a board placed across his shoulders in the fashion of a cross, and he was marched off up the road with the muzzles of five or six grim-looking pistols held unpleasantly near his head.

"Now, old man," said the leader of the party, as he called a halt in the margin of the wood at the top of the hill a few hundred yards south of the cabin, and carelessly threw his bridle-rein over a convenient sapling, "you've put us to consid'ble trouble; but we don't hold no malice agin ye on account o' that. Only we haint got no time fur to hev ye pester us much more, ye know. We want *you* fur to tell us whar we kin find them cusses as we're a lookin' fur, an' then *you* can *go*. Ef ye don't tell us, it's *bar*ly like as not we'll have to yank ye up to that limb."

The moon had gone down some time before, and the damp fog which had since been gathering was now so thick and so heavy that the expressionless sky seemed almost to reach the earth. But there was yet light enough to show the tall form and rugged features of the parson as he straightened the habitual stoop in his shoulders, and raising his bared head with a kind of scornful haughtiness, answered: "Whatever work your master, the devil, has for you to do, you must do without help from Jacob Brewster. I am not a Judas!"

There was a brief consultation between the leader and a few of the company who stood nearest to him, and then a lariat was unloosed from one of the saddle-bows and thrown over a limb of an adjacent tree.

"We've concluded to swing ye," said the leader with tantalizing unconcern, as he tied a noose in the end of the lariat, and looked questioningly toward the parson. The remark elicited no response.

It took little time to lead the parson under a limb and adjust the noose about his neck, and four stalwart fellows stood with their hands on the other end of the lariat, waiting for the word of command. They had not long to wait. "Pull!" said the leader, as he stepped back and glanced up at the limb, as if to measure its strength; and in a minute more the parson was dangling convulsively in the air, with his anguished face upturned to heaven like a reproach. Then they lowered him gently, and as his feet touched the ground again he fell limp and senseless, and lay groaning as if in the last agonies of death. But he was not dying, and the moist earth and cool breeze soon revived him; he sat upright, and would have stood erect but for the burdensome board across his shoulders, which swayed him to and fro, and would not let him rise.

There was another hasty consultation a few steps from where the parson sat looking uneasily around him, and three of the party started briskly down the hill toward the cabin and the river. There was not a word spoken while they were gone; and when two of them returned, they came leading Hannah between them. Then the noose was quickly re-fastened about the parson's neck, and he was drawn slowly and carefully up again, and swung and struggled there like a great blundering apparition. And Hannah clapped her hands, moved eagerly forward, and half laughing, half crying, sung, with trembling shrillness:

"Rock-a-by, ba-by,
In the tree-top;
When the wind blows
The cradle will rock."

As she sung, the swinging form was lowered, and there was a moment's pause in the lurid stillness; then it was raised again, faster and more violently than before. Suddenly a bright light burst out at the foot of the hill, pierced through the fog, and sent a pensive shimmer over the gray head up among the boughs.

"O, that's Jesus Christ!" shrieked Hannah; "take him down—take him down!" And she sunk on her knees, and covered her face with her hands.

The light paled, a cloud of smoke arose, and then the roof of the burning cabin fell with a crash, and a red sheet of flame rolled grandly up, blazed a moment like a meteor, then broke into sparks and was gone. But it lasted long enough to disclose to the strained eyes of the parson two crouching Black men

"NEGROES LEAVING THEIR HOME"

on the farther side of the river hurriedly pushing their way up the bluff. And it was no doubt the memory of this sight that possessed his fading senses when he feebly whispered, as they dropped him with a thud to the earth once more, "Thank God! That makes thirty-one—one for every State."

The fog still clung like a curse to the river, and obscured the white waste of ashes that lay where the cabin had stood. But out on the hill it was lifting a little now, and the discolored and distorted face that Hannah saw closely as she bent over it in the leaves, startled her to her feet, and she stood speechless and motionless as the dead man before her. Just for a moment, it was. Then she stooped and kissed the cold livid lips again and again, pressing the old gray head to her breast with piteous moaning, as the troopers mounted their horses and rode rapidly out of sight. And beyond it all, above the fog-banks, and the bluffs, and the tree-tops, in a cloud-rift away off to the north, was the glimmer of a star.

1861

"THE SPIRITS ABROAD — THE SPIRIT OF DISUNION"

The deepening crisis in the territories helped send Abraham Lincoln hundreds of miles across a divided continent to the White House. When he arrived in Washington during February 1861, after eluding an assassination attempt in Baltimore, he found a city that was as unfinished as the union was unsteady. The Capitol, where he was inaugurated in March, was covered with scaffolding, blocks of marble littered the grounds, a new iron dome was only partially built, and the crowning female statue of "Armed Freedom" had yet to be cast. With secession gathering momentum, military men abruptly relocated: Creole Pierre G. T. Beauregard left his new appointment as superintendent of West Point to command the attack on Fort Sumter, Virginian Joseph E. Johnston resigned as Quartermaster General to lead Confederate troops in the Shenandoah Valley, and Ohioan Irvin McDowell found himself in charge of the undisciplined Union volunteers assembled to defend the capital. On the cusp of war in "Job and the Bug," Washington is a miasma of questionable loyalties and thin disguises, a city whose poor boys and pawnshops quickly play a greater role than the Houses of Congress or Charleston's heavy guns.

◆०◆

Chauncey Hickox

"JOB AND THE BUG"

(*Lippincott's*, May 1871)

The old man looked like a beetle. He wore a black morning-gown tied tightly round the waist with a belt, a yard or more of black bombazine wound about his throat, a black cap set closely on his round head, and great goggles on his eyes. The round cap met the goggles from above, a grizzly beard met them from below; and it was difficult to tell what kind of face he carried beneath the cap and beard and goggles, or whether he had any real face at all. The belt and bombazine made him very small in the middle and the neck, his shoulders were full and round, and the loose gown made him large below the waist. Yes, he looked like a beetle, or some other great black bug, as he prowled among the dusty crannies under his shelves, and thrust his slender arms, like antennae, into all the doubtful corners of his desk.

His shop, or store, or office—bazaar, dépôt, emporium, repository, as an accomplished tradesman would call such a place of business—was an antiquarian bookstore, a pawnbroker's office and a junkshop generally. The establishment stood between Pennsylvania Avenue and that triumph of engineering and statesmanship, the great Washington Canal. Probably the old Bug's predecessor was in the "ring," and lobbied for the digging of this public work, on account of the junk business it would foster. This is certainly a more plausible reason for digging it than was ever made to appear to those who paid for it. For not all the judges in the departments round about—a clerk who has no other title is a judge in Washington—could compute the number of lame negroes and unfortunate women and scrub-headed boys who have earned their daily tobacco by gleaning tin, bones, iron, glass, rags, paper, old boots and Congressional speeches from the bottom of this ditch. Neither could all the government judges have taken an inventory of the Beetle's stock. He had all the second-hand school-books in use during the last sixty years; and if there was ever a book in the Greek or Hebrew line, in the Annual line, in the flash-novel line, in the theological line—if there was ever a book printed in these, or any lines at all, which could be found nowhere else, the Beetle had a dusty, mouse-eaten copy of it. If one wanted a flint for an ancient musket, a pod-auger, a coffin-plate, a dirty Masonic apron, a rusty Mexican spur, a leaky glue-pot, the long black antennae would go diving among the dark holes until they found it.

Among the oddities of this collection was the white surplice of a clergyman; and over it, on the same nail, hung a sword-belt and crimson sash. These had been wetted through the imperfect roof, until the coloring matter of the warlike trappings had run down and left a black mark, and a red stain like a blood-spot, on the bosom of the holy robe.

The accumulation of this stock must have been the work of a lifetime, and the "shebang," as Job called the establishment, was no doubt older than the canal. But the old black Bug did not appear until late in the winter of the year one thousand eight hundred and sixty. The original proprietor was a German Jew, who obtained, in consideration of the stock and good-will, a sum only twice as great as he would have asked had he not soon discovered that the Beetle, in spite of his mouldy and forbidding appearance, was not familiar with the sale of such trumpery. "Mine plessed fadders, sir! so sheap, so sheap, sir!" and the original proprietor gave a sigh to this successor and a chuckle to himself as he clinked the gold in his hand and surrendered the place to the old black Bug. And taking this transaction as evidence of his successor's commercial ability, the original proprietor muttered, "In von year I vill puy pack der place mit von 'alf der monish vot I now gits for him. Mine plessed fadders! Dat vill pe goot!"

Job was a hungry-looking boy, whose business it was to sweep the shebang, bring fuel, keep the Beetle's water-pitcher filled, brush the old man's desk and chair, wait on customers and make himself generally useful. He might have been anywhere from eight to fourteen years of age, for hunger will make small

48

boys old and old boys small. His chief garment was a pair of green trowsers, upheld by one twisted suspender of cotton cloth, the trowsers being very liberal in the seat and very conservative elsewhere; so that Job's legs, in color as well as shape, were like two cork-screws covered with verdigris. His legs were evidently made to accommodate those trowsers, and in doing it they resembled two little poles which had been overgrown by hop vines, and which had followed all the twistings and turnings of their spiral covers. His eyes were round, with yellow centres and pink borders, reminding one of china-asters; his face had the rich tint of a turkey's egg; and his hair was not unlike the husk of a cocoanut. He had great ability in making remarks entirely unsuited to his muscle. For instance, when he differed in opinion from the Beetle, that old gentleman — whose elegant diction and flowing periods assorted strangely with his dress and calling — would frequently call Job's statement a hollow falsehood, whereupon Job would unhesitatingly pronounce the statement of the Bug a solid lie. Strange to say, this ability was developed where muscle was the standard by which the propriety of all remarks was judged.

He was a Virginian by birth. And, to prevent any possible misapprehension, it may be well to add that his family was not one of the first in that State. His mother, at the close of her honey-moon of four days — if any moon can be so brief — became cook and washer on the new boat Josephine, which transported coal over the Chesapeake and Ohio Canal. The bridegroom, and subsequent father of our hero, was helmsman on the same vessel, which discharged her cargo at the port of Alexandria. Whisky being a slower poison then than it is now, Job's father continued for years to steer the Josephine successfully, until his family so increased that the small quarters of the boat could no longer accommodate the children.

The captain delicately stated the case to the helmsman thus: "Th' young uns ken go an' I'll keep you, er you mus' all go."

Genuine tears Job's mother shed when she bade the Josephine good-bye, for she knew the restraining influence of the domestic circle, and predicted the consequences of her husband being cut off from the elevating society of his family. "I know my ole man'll go bad," said she, "when me an' the young uns ain't with 'im."

But he could be induced to lead no other life, steer no other boat, and, unlike Napoleon, preferred his Josephine to a dozen children.

"I ken wash," said the appealing wife, "an' I's a-goin' to take in washin'; but what ken I do wi' 'em all?" pointing to her ragged multitude, of whom Job was the eldest and raggedest.

"Use 'em fer clo'es-pins, I reckon," was the father's answer as he hitched his trowsers, straddled the rudder and bore away for Alexandria.

And the theory that she did set little Job astride the line to hold unruly shirts in the wind is the only one that can explain the wonderful character of his legs.

So his mother occupied a whitewashed cabin under the steep bluffs above Georgetown and close to the bank of the canal. During the icy season her husband was with her at such odd hours as he was not hunting rabbits and opossums or lounging in the Georgetown grogshops. She was industrious, laboring hard to clothe her little ones and to fill her lord and protector twice a day with buckwheat cakes and bacon.

Every spring the Josephine and her helmsman came out of winter-quarters as good as new; and every summer day, before the whitewashed cabin, a line of sunburnt children gave the butterflies upon the roadside thistles and the chipmunks in the hollow rails a moment's peace, and ranged themselves along the bank of the canal to ask the mule-driver of some passing boat when and where he had met the Josephine. Every pleasant summer evening, after a day of hard work, the mother sat on her inverted washing-tub before her door, to smoke a pipe and watch the joy of her poor children as they played in the road and filled each other's hair with crowns of dust. Whenever a mule appeared around the curve she would tell the nearest child what boat was coming next, for she knew all the boats, and the men who manned them, and the mules that drew them.

Job, who desired to follow the occupation of his father, studied navigation about the Georgetown flumes and bridges and locks until he drifted into business with the Beetle. Having endeavored to deceive him as to weight in a certain transaction in the old-iron line, and the old black Bug having apparently endeavored to deceive Job in the same way during the same transaction, and each having failed in his endeavor, great confidence sprang up between them.

After ridding himself of the original proprietor, the Bug made some changes in the building which he occupied, and which was but a tumbledown shanty, wedged so closely between other shanties that it could not tumble down. It would have puzzled a looker-on to understand in what way the changes improved the Beetle's business facilities. Instead of enlarging his show-windows for a better display of the pawned trinkets, or his shelves for a better arrangement of the books, and instead of admitting more light into the gloomy hole, he had a dark and useless doorway made at the rear, leading out into the lumber-yards, negro-quarters and dumping-grounds, and toward a blind alley near the canal. It seemed to be a whim of the old man's — who apparently did business for the sole benefit of his customers — that some lame chiffonier, gathering his load along the canal, might be accommodated by this short cut to market. But a practical and less benevolent person would have smiled at the thought of a customer — especially a lame one — risking his legs and neck by attempting such an entrance.

Job was not reduced to the necessity of living in a Washington boarding-house, and continued to pass his nights comfortably in his mother's cabin by the canal in Georgetown. For the first three months he had but little to do. The Bug seldom asked a customer to buy, was not particular about prices, and made few sales. He busied himself very much, however, among the accounts and papers at his desk, and spent more time in writing than his dull trade seemed to require.

Job could not satisfy himself as to the reason why he was paid liberally for doing so little, and by an employer to whom he frequently gave the solid lie; for the youngster showed about the same respect toward his aged benefactor as he would have shown a mule-driver on the towing-path — or less, perhaps, if the mule-driver were larger than he. Yet the old Bug took little notice of the boy's impudence. The latter even fancied that he saw a twinkle of satisfaction through the old man's goggles, and a smile trying to get a foothold in the corner of his mouth, whenever the shebang became the scene of any new and very original exhibition of boyish deviltry. But the Beetle's face never really lost its gravity, nor betrayed that its possessor was other than the kind-hearted, simple-minded old creature he appeared to be, who might be easily imposed upon, and was altogether too slow to make a living in the junk business. When Job compared the treatment and pay he received with the treatment and pay he deserved, he was at times inclined to believe the old man a trifle insane. In fact, he regarded all disinterestedness as a mild form of insanity.

There was an old bedstead — of course — in the Beetle's stock, and some blankets that had been pawned; and on these it was supposed he slept after a late dinner at a neighboring restaurant. The shebang was opened late in the morning and closed early in the evening, and the proprietor never went to dinner nor to bed until after Job had left it for the night. Before he returned in the morning the Bug had breakfasted and was at his post.

One corner, less dusty and dismal than the others, contained a small table and several goblets. Sometimes Job was required, before going home, to fetch a bottle of wine and a little fruit, and leave them on this table. Occasionally he brought more substantial food than fruit, and in a quantity too great for the capacity of one virtuous old Bug. Job wondered how a junk-dealer of such poor business habits could afford to consume so many delicacies. With his usual modesty he pressed the Beetle for an explanation one morning while clearing away the remnants of quite a feast. He eyed the boy for a moment in a whimsical manner, turned his face partly away, and said with some feeling, "I sit at night, a lone old man, in this dark and still place, among the things that have found their way to me from so many broken homes and wretched people; and then I think that all the eyes which have read the mouldering books above me are looking at me from the dismal shelves. Over hundreds of these pages the tender eyes of women have been filled with tears. Hundreds of these leaves, faded and dusty, have been turned by hands as smooth and white and sweet as water-lilies. Children, with mouths like rosebuds, have bent their soft faces close to the many margins and fly-leaves on which they have scribbled. My poor old books are like myself—no longer welcomed in any prosperous home, nor sweetened by the breath of children, nor touched by lily hands, nor met by tender eyes. Each pawned article is a proof of want, and so of misery and despair and death. They remind me of my duty. So, when I sit down to my glass of wine at night, alone here in the gloom, I remember the blind girl who sells matches on the avenue, the lame negro who has the dog-cart across the street, the palsied old woman in the next block who can earn nothing. They all lodge within a step, and very often I bring them in. It's jolly to see them eat and drink. When Christmas comes, Job, we'll have a feast that will make them glad till they die. But that is doubtful too, for before Christmas comes again these streets will be red with blood, and we may be destroyed."

Ere the Bug ceased speaking, Job's attention was out at the window and on an unseasonable organ-grinder's monkey; yet his quick ear heard the closing sentences and his keen eye saw a strange smile vanishing from the old man's mouth. This discovery supplied another link in the chain of evidence that the Beetle was insane. How could such a benevolent being laugh while contemplating death and bloody streets? And did he smile at the prospect of more cripples to feed?

In February, one thousand eight hundred and sixty-one, when along the Border States some good men were watching the Northern sky and the Southern, like children overtaken by converging tempests, knowing not whither to fly from the whirlwind they knew must follow the meeting of the clouds, Abraham Lincoln ran up a flag at Independence Hall, and asked, without ostentation, if the descendants of Penn would sustain it. Then his sad eyes looked their last on a city of brotherly love, and he went on to his fate.

The day on which the flag was run up at Independence Hall was a wearisome one to the Beetle. He was busy with various small papers at his desk. There was more care than usual on his mind, and Job saw it. The disinterested youth was pained to see him so embarrassed with his accounts, for the sight suggested his failure and the loss of a situation where the disinterested youth was well paid for doing in most things as he pleased while occasionally giving the solid lie to his employer. More wine than ever was ordered for that night; and Job, who was sent home early, went away convinced that the old man's affairs were near a crisis, and that he was now about to go mad entirely and make a grand banquet for the vagabonds in honor of his failure.

The damp night closed over the dismal city. The mists from Murder Bay crept up about the White House, where a timid old man, drifting on the angry current of events like a withered leaf upon a river, thanked God that another day was gone. Legislators sat late beside their fires. To the taxed brains of new cabinet ministers their pillows brought no sleep.

At last the black, chill night turned gray and passed. A strange train swept into the outskirts of the foul city and neared the ghostly, uncertain Capitol, over which the derricks loomed like gibbets in the thick, raw air. A closed carriage rolled rapidly down the avenue, passed within a stone's throw of the Beetle's humble roof—and Mr. Lincoln's life was saved.

The Southern cloud grew blacker, rose higher, threatened to burst in fire and thunder on the capital. Troops were in motion through the South. Mail communication with it closed on the 31st of May. The North was called to war. The straggling city was a great camp. Couriers galloped through unfathomable mud. The avenues were noisy with braying mules, cracking whips, thundering wheels, drums, cheers and crowding feet. Across Long Bridge the raw troops tramped by thousands.

McDowell had to lead his unknown force against his unknown enemy. The first great battle was fought and lost—we knew not exactly why. No headway could be made, and what the cabinet was whispering in Washington was told aloud in Richmond.

During all this time the black Bug's face, or what little could be seen of it between his queer cap and grizzled beard, showed unwonted earnestness, and even satisfaction. From about the first of June, Job became more busy, the Bug a less indulgent master, and the crooked legs less eccentric in their movements. Job's regard for the Beetle was very much diminished, and relations between the two became less smooth. The boy was sent out to see what regiment had just arrived, whence it came, whither it appeared to be going. He ran to buy the daily papers. He ambled across the street to invite into the shebang a trio of stragglers from some passing company, and perhaps an officer of the line, that they might receive a second-hand revolver at half-price or a gift of moral books for the knapsack, and also gain assurances from the sympathizing remarks and kindly questions of the Beetle that in him, if in no other Washingtonian, the national soldier had a friend.

Mrs. Garrett, whose boarders did call her Mrs. Attic, and whose boarders do call her Mrs. Cockloft, was fortunately born on the right bank of the Potomac. She had qualities that could not have originated on the left bank of the Potomac. No other woman living could be so sublimely impervious to all the pestiferous facts and ideas which jeopard ancient society. No other woman living could utter "yer" in the place of "here" with equal elegance and unconsciousness; and no woman ever lived who was more determined in spelling public with a "k."

On a moonlight evening in August, one thousand eight hundred and sixty-one, a calm gentleman in gray and a dyspeptic lady in black sipped a late tea in Mrs. Cockloft's parlor, in company with that august keeper of boarders and preserver of ancient society.

In his youth the calm gentleman in gray had been known as Jacob F. Brown. He was "connected." Of course this fact had added to his difficulties in selecting a profession, his gentlemanly habits having early depleted the purse of his generous old father. After failing at West Point and proving too lazy for the law, he was sent to New England for an education in theology. He became the rector of a country parish in his native county, in time for a brief interposition of his example, his robes, his voice and similar unsubstantial things between the spirit of vandal iconoclasm and the institutions and traditions of his proud and historic Commonwealth — or something of that sort. He bade his flock an eloquent adieu, and accepted, as was said, a confidential foreign agency for the Confederacy. But instead of going abroad, he continued to tarry in Washington, in the society of Mrs. Cockloft. From the date of his consecration to spiritual things his name had been Rev. J. Fairfax Browne, which was a very different thing from Jacob F. Browne.

As the trio sipped their tea, the dyspeptic lady in black related, over her third cup, the lesson she had taught a Yankee officer that afternoon. It seemed she had been shopping, and in coming out of a storehouse had met a New York captain going in. It also appeared that he had been polite enough to remove his hat and open the door on her approach, and that she had been polite enough to drop a penny in his hat and sweep by in silent scorn.

A calm smile lighted the face of one listener, and a Cocklofty frown darkened that of the other. But both agreed that the hireling had been served right, while they sorrowed gently over the fact that he was not sufficiently a gentleman to fully appreciate the insult.

After a pause the dyspeptic lady in black remarked that the tea was elegant. The calm gentleman in gray added that the crackers were also elegant. The august keeper of boarders and preserver of ancient society still farther stated that nothing could exceed the elegance of the last hominy she had ordered.

Further conversation ensued, which took a physiological turn, and revealed two remarkable phenomena — that the governors of all the Northern States were insane, and that gentlemen were superior to gorillas. The Rev. J. Fairfax Browne also felt that nothing less than the success of the rebellion could relieve him from the painful necessity of doubting the wisdom and justice of Heaven.

As he arose to go he received a small package of manuscript from the dyspeptic lady in black.

In the mean time, Job was enjoying himself in Washington. He had not gone home at dark, as usual, for a regiment of Zouaves was arriving, whose gay uniforms and easy manners were so attractive that he had followed them to their bivouac in the Smithsonian grounds. His spirit had been so far roused by association with the passing troops that he had long cheered for the Union, and practiced tattoo on the head of every empty barrel he could find. On this evening he had made final arrangements, without consulting his employer, for joining a regiment as drummer on its march the very next morning.

After dining in a dry-goods box off the contents of a tipsy soldier's haversack, and drinking out of his felt hat at the street pump, he crossed the iron bridge on Seventh street and turned into Murder Bay, with a vague hope of reaching Georgetown in the course of the night. Passing near the shebang, he thought to astonish the old Beetle by a parting salute in the way of a "bang" against the door. But approaching for this purpose, he saw a glimmer of light shine through a single crack, and paused to first peep stealthily in and see whether the venerable Bug was entertaining the vagabonds or was going to bed. Job was a cool boy, especially when stating his opinions to his employer, but he was more astonished by what he saw now than the Bug could have been by any banging of the door. The Beetle was not there, and in his absence the place had evidently been entered by burglars, two of whom were making themselves at home among the old man's papers.

One of them was forty-five or fifty years of age, and his thin hair was sprinkled with gray. Many of the men marching through the capital that night became well acquainted with his spare face and form during the two succeeding years; and after hearing and buying his patriotic songs in the Potomac camps, were astonished, during the Gettysburg campaign, when they saw him hung up by the neck from the branch of a small tree near Frederick, in Maryland.

There sat also at the Beetle's desk the calm gentleman in gray who an hour before had been sipping tea in Mrs. Cockloft's parlor. A better boy might have called a policeman for the arrest of these interlopers and a search for the missing Beetle. But Job had suspected that something was going on about the place which he was not permitted to know; since the 31st of May his position had not been a sinecure; by daylight he would be marching with a drum on his back; and what better boys would do was generally just what Job would not do. So he silently looked and listened.

The elder of the two insisted that he must start for Port Tobacco, and could not go in the direction of Beauregard's or Johnston's lines; some third person, who should have been in Washington, had not arrived. While Job heard this, he saw the Rev. J. Fairfax Browne take up an ordinary walking-stick, unscrew the ferule protecting the lower end of it, stuff a tight little roll of French paper into the bottom of the cane and screw the ferule again into its place.

"So you'll try it on yourself?" said the other.

"I must. It's a part of the business that don't belong to me, but you see this news ought to go to-night. The weather is fine — rather too fine — and I'll have no trouble that I'm not prepared for. But I'm not clear about my character."

"Wear your graveyard toggery here just as usual, and be the same old mummy. Just what you want is to be recognized. You know there's but one dangerous point, and the regiment holding that is the very one that knows you best. Some of its officers have been in here, you remember, and half the men can identify you as a first-class old Abolitionist. Of course you'll have reasons enough for being among them. Bluff's your game."

"Well, I reckon you're right," replied the calm gentleman in gray as he took up a pocket mirror and began to touch his face with certain preparations known to every actor, by which his luxuriant black beard became mixed with gray, his fair skin assumed a faded hue and certain wrinkles crept into his cheeks. He now paused to take a parting drink at the Beetle's little table.

One of the men, as he drained the goblet, dropped his hand heavily upon the board, and down upon their heads fell the sash and sword-belt and the clergy-man's white surplice, with the bright red stain, like a blood-spot, on its bosom. The two men sprang to their feet, and Job vanished in a twinkling round the nearest corner.

An hour later he was prowling like a wharf-rat along Water street in George-town, inspecting all the mill-flumes and water-wheels between the canal bank and the river. A line of muskets flashed in the moonlight as a regiment filed across the Aqueduct — a common roadway now — on the way to Chain Bridge from Arlington. And following from the Virginia side — notwithstanding the Department order — was the usual squad of fugitive negroes, whom Job called "counterbands." As he passed the corner of a grist-mill, a few steps aside from the track of the disappearing regiment, he found an old slave on his knees, with clasped hands, trying to express his thanks in prayer. The moon shone on his uplifted face; his wrinkled cheeks were wet; in the dim light a narrow rim of white wool seemed like a halo encircling his bald head. Touching at last the left bank of the river, and thinking perhaps he had reached free soil, he knelt in Job's path to thank God. Yet this did not deter that young barbarian from stealing up in the shadow of the mill and startling the old slave from his prayer by tickling the bottoms of his bare feet. But when Job went to bed that night he said thoughtfully to his mother, "Mam, this yer fightin' 's fer niggers. I's made game right smart o' niggers, but I isn't gwine to make game of 'em no mo'."

Another figure emerged from another Georgetown street, and took the river-road ahead of Job—that of an old man who walked with a vigorous step. Job stopped in wonder, scratched his head and mechanically followed the apparition of the missing Beetle. The latter paused at the door of Job's mother, and gave her the superfluous information that her son might have a holiday, and need not go to Washington the next morning.

The black Bug failed in his attempt to cross Chain Bridge, the guard there having been re-formed that evening of soldiers who had never seen him; and a part of the same detachment was going forward at daylight to relieve the very outposts at which he expected his only trouble. Balked by them now, he feared a second meeting with some of the same men. They were cavalry, and would move fast enough to make this possible, even if he passed them at the bridge without delay. He must abandon the game of bluff.

He turned back toward Georgetown, made a detour through the underwood, and reached the canal and river again a short distance above the bridge. He waded the canal and disappeared behind a clump of bushes. A bundle of thin drapery, containing a black dressing-gown padded to roundness at the shoulders, tied by the belt, and enclosing a pair of goggles and a stone, was thrown into the canal; and in a moment more the old black Bug, the calm gentleman in gray, the Rev. J. Fairfax Browne, descended to the brink of the Potomac, washed the silver from his beard and the wrinkles from his face, and prepared to ford the river.

The moon was now setting. The Virginia shore had become but a black line, blending rapidly with the darkening sky beyond. Nothing was heard except the distant rumble of an ambulance, the muttering of the gloomy river and the cry of an owl in the near wood. The right bank, steep and wooded, was difficult of ascent, and during the intense darkness between the setting of the moon and the dawning of day, notwithstanding his knowledge of the country, the calm gentleman in gray became bewildered. This accident, and the greater caution now necessary, so delayed him that by noon the regiment in which Job had marched was passing him.

The next evening, Job's mother, hopeful, stolid, ignorant, who had never read a book, sat and smoked as usual before her door on her inverted washing-tub. The Josephine was due at Georgetown, where she now unloaded. "Yer, Izrul," she said, "jes' ye git roun' de curve dur 'n see if de Josephin's comin'."

Job's brother Israel ran on, and looked, in the waning light, far up the towing-path, but the black mules of his father's boat were not in sight. Still the woman sat and smoked. Her prime of life was passed. No garrulous neighbor was at hand: it was the close of day. A good memory was busy with the past. An imagination of some degree was busy with the future; and in it she saw nothing but her old unvarying toil and monotonous battle for life. The only child who could assist her was gone, perhaps for ever. So barbarous of speech as to be scarce intelligible in domestic talk, none but the Father in heaven could know what filled her mind and heart. But when Israel came back to her he saw a tear run down her face, and thought that some tobacco-smoke had got into her eyes.

She remembered how handsome her husband looked on her first trip in the Josephine, with his brown face and red shirt, as he stood up in the stern. She remembered what a happy tumult the blood made in her veins and heart when, a bride, she sat for the first time on the cabin-roof before him. She remembered the birth of little Job, and thought how fast the years had gone. The descending sun fringed with fire a low cloud which still hugged the horizon against a field of blood-red sky. The birds were seeking shelter. A raven rose along the river and flapped away toward the South.

She shook the ashes from her pipe, but lingered a moment longer and watched the Potomac, flushed with crimson and gold, sweep peacefully away below the Aqueduct, and the sun slide down behind the beautiful Virginia heights, soon to be engrailed with forts and trenches and redoubts.

At last the Josephine appeared through the dusk, and her helmsman, throwing ashore a bundle of black clothing that had become entangled with the tiller, exclaimed, "Yer, ole woman, work up this yer plunder fer the young ones."

As she took the bundle from the ground she kept her eyes fixed in the failing light on a portion of the trunk of a gray sycamore, or what she thought such, drifting by in the river. As the current rolled it over there were tossed above the surface the stiff arms of a dead man, as if he too were clutching for the clothes.

About three o'clock on the afternoon of the first day's march, Job's regiment halted for the night, and the first thing he did thereafter was to straggle toward a farm-house, passing through a jungle of laurel, oak and chinquopin bushes, sufficient to conceal whoever entered among them. His path was intersected at right angles by another, which at that point led down a slight declivity, and a large pine tree stood at the junction. This he had reached when he noticed a movement of the bushes on his left, and, pausing, he caught a glimpse of the same gentleman in gray he had watched through the chink of the shebang. Job crouched behind the tree. He had not forgotten the events of the last evening, and now for the first time the full truth flashed clearly across his mind. He instantly planned an act which a boy of gentler character and education might not have dared to attempt.

The late Beetle strode cautiously on, and as he rounded the tree, Job darted like a cat between his legs, caught his foot and tripped him so vigorously that the calm gentleman sprawled upon his face, while his walking-stick went spinning down the bank. Job sprang astride his victim, who rolled over, exhibiting a broken nose inquiringly between the drummer's bow legs, like red interrogation-point enclosed in blue parentheses.

A movement of the gentleman's arm, and Job also went spinning down the bank; but quick as thought he had seized the walking-stick, eluded several grasps and bounded toward his camp, whither the other dared not follow.

"Telegrab in the cane! telegrab in the cane!" That was the frantic shout of Job as he rushed into his colonel's presence, in spite of guards and military etiquette. "Telegrab in the cane!" was all he had breath to say, but before he could be ejected from head-quarters he had unscrewed the ferule, and spread out what he believed to be "telegrab" despatches.

A company of cavalry, followed by infantry, was turned back from outpost duty. A part of the former galloped across Chain Bridge to patrol the left bank of the river, toward which a half-moon of pursuers would soon force the gentleman in gray.

The semicircle of sabres and bayonets contracted with fatal rapidity. Should he attempt to either elude or break it, he would be hanged before dark. With just hope enough to make desperation great, he reached the stream, plunged under the surface, and attempted to cross without exposing more than his head, and that only at intervals. But the water was shallow.

A shot from the bridge told that he was discovered. He saw now that he was awaited on the opposite bank. He clung to one of the bare rocks that dot the water: it could not shelter him. To cross, to stop, to return, each was death. He hesitated; and as he looked up in despair to the sky, a single well-aimed carbine sent a bullet through his breast. He fell. The current took him. A red stain was in the water. A bloody bubble, inflated by the gasps of the dying, sailed bravely for a time and broke above the dead. The blue tide flowing from the North swept all before it.

When the facts, with Job's testimony, were reported that evening to the Department of War, it ordered secrecy, in the hope of securing others implicated in the nightly business of the shebang, and who would certainly not be caught there if Browne's fate were known. The newspapers, for once, were foiled, and many people of the District wondered why he had disappeared so suddenly from Washington society. Yet scores of them pass, every day, in the streets of the capital, a rough, unkempt young man, with rather crooked legs, who in his own patois is capable of telling the whole story, and whose mother lived to welcome him back to her whitewashed cabin on the bank of the canal.

By midsummer, when Union troops headed across the Long Bridge into Virginia, eleven states had left the Union. South Carolina was the first to go, just before Christmas in 1860; by the end of January, Mississippi, Florida, Alabama, Georgia, and Louisiana had followed. Texas joined the Confederacy in February, and Virginia seceded on the heels of Lincoln's call for seventy-five thousand volunteers from the states in April. The Confederate government moved from Montgomery to Richmond the next month, when Arkansas and North Carolina left the Union, just before Tennessee officially joined the Southern states in June. By July, the ninety-day volunteers under McDowell were picking berries on their way to the railroad junction at Manassas, where the war's first big battle would be fought. In no time, they would be swept into what Shelby Foote has called "a panorama of jetting smoke and furious movement," and they would meet the Confederate companies volunteering in "A True and Simple Tale of '61" with equal zeal. As an uneasy Ella Morton discovers when her lieutenant lover sends for her, the lives of Southern women were about to change dramatically. "In transforming governments, economies, and society," writes Drew Gilpin Faust, "the war necessarily challenged the very foundations of personal identity as well." For women like Ella Morton, there would be more than one way to defend the republic that Southerners believed they inherited and more than one mission for Confederate citizens that demanded courage.

◆◦◆

Izilda

"A TRUE AND SIMPLE TALE OF '61"

(*Southern Monthly*, December 1861)

The hospitable mansion of Mrs. K., in the capital of our State, was gleaming with lights, as carriage after carriage, filled with guests, drew up before her door. Diamonds glittered, and pearls gleamed in the scene. The front parlor was filled with joyous guests, all in a tremor of expectation, when the folding doors were suddenly thrown open, and standing under a canopy of evergreens and white roses was the lovely Julia (only daughter of the hostess), with her chosen one beside her, and her twelve attendants. The clergyman stepped forward from among the guests, and in a few moments more, amid the breathless silence, the "two were made one flesh." Congratulations followed, and then every one was free to enjoy himself as most congenial to him. All was hilarity and joy as they formed into groups, or strayed off in couples. Let us listen: "Is it not lovely? and how beautiful sweet Julia looks. Can she ever be unhappy? Oh, is not life very joyous?"

"Yes, to some; and would be to me could I always have you by me, and feel you were mine alone; but I feel a sad presentiment that, promised as we are, we shall not have a long life together."

"Oh, Charles, do not be gloomy; what can prevent in this highly favored land of ours, and our own good health, and we are to be united so soon; but see they are wondering what takes us away from them all."

"Yes, let us go back. But Ella, dear, you say this highly favored land; is it highly favored to be overrun with spies and incendiaries, and every right trampled on? No, to-morrow we vote on secession, and I shall vote for it, if I have to stand up to the cannon's mouth to sustain it."

"Pshaw! it will never come to that," said Ella Morton, "though I go for secession; but they will let us alone when we have seceded, for they are so anxious to get rid of us."

"Not so anxious as they pretend; only they think *we dare not do it,*" said Charles Loutrell, as they again joined the other guests.

The evening sped away, and it was growing late, when a friend arrived, who was expected earlier, but who said that he had just left the death-bed of one of their associates, who, four short weeks before, had brought a blooming bride from a neighboring town, and now, after a two-days' illness, lay in the arms of death. The intelligence threw a gloom over the company, causing the fair bride of the evening to cling closer to her new husband, wondering if aught on earth could part them *now;* and causing the party to break up, with a feeling that they would not meet under such pleasant circumstances soon again.

The morrow dawned: a second one of the States broke away from that government whose administrators were pledged to the destruction of the homes and rights of free-born men. There was much fear felt by the real lovers of the "sunny South," that it was a precipitate step with only one State pledged. But soon the cheering news came that one, and then another State had linked its destiny with hers; till, when noble old Virginia and gallant Tennessee were united in the sisterhood, all felt strength and courage. The call for 75,000 troops from the despot, called forth all the generous chivalry of the South to protect its homes from invasion, and preserve one spot on earth free from tyranny. Among the first, was our gallant friend, Charles Loutrell, who was bound, as he said, to stand up to the cannon's mouth to sustain his principles.

It was a lovely evening when he entered the wicket gate at Mrs. Morton's; spring roses shed their perfume around, and the moon was smiling on the scene as he took the vacant seat, beside Ella, on the gallery. Never to him had she seemed so lovely — dressed in snowy white, with a few white rose buds in her hair. How should he tell her of his determination, when a few more weeks would have united them for life?

"I hear that Capt. P. is getting up a company to go to Virginia," said Ella. "Do you think it necessary? Is there really to be fighting?"

"Yes, Ella, we have either to fight and maintain our independence, or be crushed out, our homes taken from us, and everything we value trampled upon; even now they are stealing the negroes and selling them in Cuba, when they profess to make war on us because we pay our money for our servants. Hypocrisy! Stealing better than lawful selling! and who does not know that a man would make any sacrifice rather than part with a servant that was attached to him."

"How can they be so blinded, or is it willful blindness," said Ella.

"It is willful, I think," said Charles, "and nothing but hot shot and cold steel will open their eyes, and I have come this evening to obtain your permission to defer our wedding a short time, till I go and help do it. Capt. P. wants me to be first lieutenant, and the company are unanimous for my election. But Ella, dear, my fate is in your hands, and I will not go without your consent."

"My consent! Oh Charles, do not ask *me* to decide; for how can I give you up? Oh never, never. Why this hard lot?"

"Ella, dear, would you have me stand back when my country needs her truest sons; when even your own precious life may be in danger, if we do not rally our utmost strength; but, as I said, you are controller of my fate. I leave it with you."

"I will not withhold you," said Ella, smiling through her tears, "though the thought is agony; and I will be brave, too. But what if you should meet a soldier's death?" and she shuddered at the thought.

"Would it not be better than to live the subject of a despot, worse than a monarch, and that under the name of republicanism, when a true republic consists in the hearty support of the people? and we could never give it to one who has so violated our dearest rights. And you will be proud of me yet; and if I should fall, who will treasure my memory more tenderly, or be more resigned that I fell in a good cause, trying to stem the tide of invasion."

And so it was settled that in three weeks he was to leave for Virginia.

Three weeks rolled quickly away, and Capt. P.'s fine company of volunteers were to leave for the seat of war. Most noble among them was lieutenant Loutrell, and even Ella seemed pleased to mark his soldier-like bearing as the company marched past her mother's cottage. The parting was over, for she could not trust her grief to say adieu in public. She had provided everything for his comfort, and proffered her own faithful Joe to be his servant, who said "he would take good care of Mas'r Charlie, and not let him forget Miss Ella."

"THE STAMPEDE FROM BULL RUN"

The faithful post brought many a message besides those by private hands, and Ella was weaving bright tissues of dreams when the war would be over, and happiness and love again smile upon them, when the telegraph brought the news of the memorable battle of Manassas. She knew that Capt. P.'s company were in the engagement, and carefully did she scan every name, but she did not see the one that she looked most earnestly for, and hope tried to rise in her heart, yet a heavy weight seemed resting there which she could not shake off. Soon a dispatch came, saying: "Ella, I am dying—come to me"; and before the sun had set, she was on her way to Virginia, accompanied by her father. She found her lover at Richmond, where he had been sent, very low, but able to give her his dying blessing, and to say he had done all for his country that he could, and he now bequeathed it to her hands.

"Yes," said Ella, "I accept the charge from you, and instead of giving way to my grief, I will renounce it as you did happiness and ease, and henceforth devote myself to the care of those that were your brothers. For their comfort will I toil, ever assured that you are watching over me with an angel's smile."

"My blessings on you, precious one; we have not lived in vain, and may we meet again where the wicked cease from troubling and the weary are at rest. My country—Ella—Heaven"; and all was over. Ella's grief was violent, but she remembered her promise; and soon after her lover was consigned to the silent earth, her father wished her to return home, but she told him Virginia's soil was dear to her, and as she had a fortune in her own right, she would stay with the family who had so kindly received her beloved Charlie when he was wounded, and keep Joe with her, and devote her time to the soldiers; and many brave hearts breathe blessings on her for delicacies prepared in sickness, and many comforts for those that brave the cold and sleety nights, with nothing but a blanket thrown on the cold ground; and here she intends to remain till the shout of victory is echoed from one end of this glorious Confederacy to the other.

Woman has a mission in this work as well as man, and while his strong arms are fighting, let her be brave, and thoughtful for the soldier's comfort, and if the shouts of victory come not as soon as wished for, still let them, with their sweet smiles, nimble fingers, and labors of love, find courage in their undertaking and they may be assured they will reap the reward of having done all for their country and the great cause of constitutional liberty that they could.

The homes from which volunteers were called were not left so far behind. In addition to the women who were summoned to the front by their men, sutlers soon followed the armies as local regiments sought domestic comforts, and smaller companies became the "substitute families" that Reid Mitchell has described. In camp, the most popular song on both sides of any picket line was "Home, Sweet Home," and the home front was no more remote than the letters and packages soldiers shared, the books and periodicals they read, the prayers they murmured, or the religious tracts (like "A Mother's Parting Words to Her Soldier Son") they received. On the march, however, soldiers could venture into territory so foreign that the trusting sister seeking an Ohio regiment in "Ellen" finds the kindness of strangers cannot banish the dangers of the road, especially a road that leads in 1861 to the border warfare south of Wheeling, the fight to control the Baltimore and Ohio Railroad, and the lure of nearby salt deposits in the Kanawha River Valley.

◆○◆

Rebecca Harding Davis

"ELLEN"

(*Atlantic Monthly*, July 1865)

If the publishers of the "Atlantic" will permit me, I should like to tell a little incident, growing out of the War, which came under my notice in the summer of 1861. I can give it only as a fragment, for I never heard the end of it, and that, to be candid, is my principal reason for telling it at all,—in the hope, slight enough, it is true, that some chance reader may be able to supply to me what is wanting. For this reason I shall give the true names of persons and places, and the dates also, as nearly as I can recollect them. It is only a simple story of a private in the Twenty-Fourth Ohio Volunteer Militia, and his sister, and may not touch others as it did me, for I can give but the bald facts; but I, seeing the reality, can remember nothing in the war which troubles me with such a sense of pain and simple pathos.

About thirty years ago, a family named Carrol, or Carryl, emigrated from the North of Ireland, and settled in Coldwater, a little fishing-village of Michigan.

They were sober and hard-working, but dull and ignorant, and in no way different from others of their class, except in their unusual strong affection for each other. Old Carrol, however, a rheumatic old man of sixty, with this weak, jealous pride in his "b'ys," working late and early to keep them clothed, to pay his wife's doctor's-bills, and trying to lay up enough to buy the two girls a feather-bed and a clock when they were married, stood in no need of whiskey or dances to keep him alive; this and his wife's ill health separated them from the fighting, rollicking Irish crew of the hamlet, — set them apart, so to speak, to act upon each other. Carrol, with one of his sons, worked in a saw-mill, and the other boys, as they grew old enough, easily found jobbing, being known as honest, plodding fellows. The little drama of their lives bade fair to be quiet, and the characters wrought out of it commonplace enough, had not Death thrust his grim face into the scene.

The youngest child was a girl, Ellen, born long after the others, and, like most children coming in the advanced age of their parents, was peculiar: the family traits had worn themselves out, new elements came in. The Irish neighbors, seeing how closely the girl was kept in-doors, and the anxious guard held over her by her father and brothers, thought her a "natural" or "innocent," whether she was or not. The Carrols kept their own counsel, and warded off gossip as best they could. It was from Ellen I heard how the change came among them first. "It was a fever," she said. "John took it, and little Phil, and then Jane. Jane was the oldest of us; it was she as nursed mother and kept the house. She looked as old as mother. Evenings she'd put on a white apron, and take me on her knee and sing for us. But she took the fever, and they're all three gone away"; which was always Ellen's phrase for death. She stopped there, adding afterwards quietly, that it was about that time the trouble in her head first came. Ellen took her sister's place in "keeping the house"; she had enough mind to learn the daily routine of cleaning and the little cooking. Her mother was a cripple for life, confined to her bed most of the time: a credulous, nervous woman, — the one idea in her narrow brain a passionate love for her husband and children.

After the three who had "gone away" were buried in the little Catholic grave-yard by the creek, the others crept closer together. Joe, nearest Ellen in age, was kept at home to help with the house- and yard-work, and, partly from being a simple-minded fellow, and partly to humor Ellen, fell into her girl's ways. "Joe and me," she said, "churned and cooked together, and then he'd bring his tools into mother's room and work. We liked that, he was so full of joking and whistling."

The old man was quieter after his children's death. One day the machinery at the mill, being old and rotten, broke; the hands were at work in it, underneath the beams which fell. An hour after, just as Ellen and Joe had put the chairs about the supper-table, and sat waiting for their father and Jim, the door was pushed open, and two heaps, shapeless, and covered closely with a quilt, were brought in upon a door. Whatever was the pain or loss of the widow or Joe, they had no time to indulge it; Ellen needed all their care after that for a year or two. She was "troubled," was all the satisfaction they gave to the neighbors' curiosity, who never saw her in that time.

In the second autumn of 1860, however, she began to go about again through the village; and Joe, after watching her anxiously for some time, found work as a hand on a schooner running to Sandusky, Ohio. Once in a while, during the winter, he came home to stay over-night. "Often," Ellen said, "when Joe came, we hadn't seen anybody cross the door-step since he went out of it, mother and I lived alone so much; but mother, in her worst days with pain, had a joking, laughing way with her that kept it pleasant in-doors."

The Carrols were noted as being a scrupulously clean folk; so it is probable that the little kitchen and bed-room were still the best idea Joe had of the world, — knowing nothing beyond, indeed, but the schooner and the deck of the wharf-boat in Sandusky. To understand what follows, you must remember the utter ignorance dominant in such fishing-stations as Coldwater. The poorer inhabitants, who stared at Ellen as she went down to the beach for water, were Irish and Dutch emigrants, forwarded there like cattle, who had settled down, sold their fish to the trading-vessels, and never had looked outside of that to know they were not naturalized. Ellen was little better; I do not suppose she ever read a newspaper in her life; yet, curiously enough, her language was tolerably correct, her manner quiet and thorough-bred, — even the inflections of her voice were low, and as composed as if she had learned self-poise in the hurly-burly of society. That belonged to her character, however, as much as to the solitude in which she had been brought up.

The mother sank rapidly this winter; but the two children, accustomed to her illness, were blind to the change.

When the States one by one seceded during the winter and spring, and the country was rife with war and the terror of it, the Coldwater people fished on dully as ever. Joe brought home stories of "fighting beyond there," and of men he had met on the Sandusky wharf who had gone, and then whittled and whistled as usual: the tale sounding to the two women fearful and far-off, as if it had been in the Crimea. "Though I *had* heard of the Virginians," said Ellen simply, when she told the story. "There was Mr. Barker, a Methodist preacher, told us once of the 'man-hunters,' as he called them, and how they chained their slaves and burned them alive, and hunted men with dogs. But I took him up wrong. I thought they all were black." Ellen's idea of them was as vague as ours is of the cannibals, and not very different, I suspect.

So far off did this country of the man-hunters seem, where "there was fighting," that, when Joe wandered about uneasily in one of his weekly visits, and told again and again, with furtive glances at his mother, how half the deck-hands on the schooner had gone into a regiment forming in Sandusky, and how it was a good chance to see the world, Ellen sewed quietly on, scarcely looking up. That Joe could have any interest in this dim horror of a war never crossed her poor brain.

The next day after the schooner sailed her mother grew suddenly worse, and began to sink, going faster every day for a week. It was the first time Ellen had been left alone to face danger. "If Joe was here!" the two poor creatures cried, through all their fright and pain. If Joe were there, Ellen thought all would be well again. But Thursday, his usual day for coming, passed without him. That night the mother died. Two women of the village, hearing the story from the doctor, came to the house in time to make the body ready for burial, — the "natural," as they called Ellen, sitting quietly by the bed, her face hid, not answering when they spoke.

There was a letter brought to her that night from Joe, a few lines only, written to his mother, saying he had enlisted and would not come back to say good-bye; he was going to do better for her and Ellen than he ever had done before. "I do not remember about that time," Ellen said afterward, when questioned. "My trouble came back when Joe left me." It brought the wild, wandering look into her eyes, even to refer to it in this way. I do not know if I spoke of the curious affection between this brother and sister. Father and brothers and sister had watched and cared for the girl, because of the great trouble which God had sent to her; and now all the love and gratitude she had given to them all, when living, was centred on this boy Joe. Joe absorbed all the world which her weak mind knew, — just at the age, too, when women's hearts open and are filling with thoughts of love and marriage. No matter how long Ellen had lived, "my brother," as she gravely, respectfully called him, would have been all, I think, she would ever have loved, and he would have satisfied all her cravings.

Her mother was buried before she became conscious again; then her reason came back to her; and when the woman who had stayed in the house returned, after a few hours' gossiping, she found Ellen, her old quiet self, going gently about the house, packing her clothes in a carpet-bag, and putting with great care in a little hand-basket, such as ladies carry knitting in, her Testament, their two or three silver spoons, Joe's box of Sunday collars, and what little money was left.

"Where are you going?" asked the woman, in some trepidation.

"To Joe," Ellen said, quietly, unconscious that there was anything unusual in the plan.

The woman speedily gathered a caucus of her cronies, with the doctor; but to all queries or remonstrances she returned the same quiet, unmoved answer.

She was going to Joe. What else should she do? There were only herself and her brother now: he would expect her. Who would cook for Joe, or keep his clothes straight, if she did not go? "My plan was," she said, gravely, long after, "that Joe would hire a little house for me near where the regiment stayed. He could have lived with me, and gone with them to fight when their turn came." Finally they allowed her her own way, partly because they were puzzled to know what else to do with her. Joe was in Sandusky with his regiment, the Twenty-Fourth Ohio, his letter had stated.

"It rained hard," she said afterwards, "that night, when I left Coldwater. Dr. S—— came down with me to the boat. He was very kind. We had to wait on the shore a bit, and it rained and was so dark you could only see the mud under foot and the great cold water beyond. When I looked at the mud, and the rain dripping, dripping through it, I couldn't but think of them as was lying under it up on the hill, — of them up on the hill. And there was a black line, Sir, where the water met the sky, and I thought I had to go beyond that, — I didn't know where. But Joe was beyond there. I kept saying, 'Joe, Joe,' over to myself, and 'Lord Jesus,' — thinking, if He stayed near me, I would not be afraid. For the boat rocked when I came on board, and the water underneath heaved up black. I never had been on the water before. But I sat down on deck with my little basket in my hand. Dr. S—— came back twice to speak to the Captain about me. He was very sorry for me; he said, 'God bless you, Ellen,' before he went away up the plank. I watched him as long as I could, but the night was dark and very wet. Then the shore seemed to go back from us, and he went with it; and Coldwater, and our old house, and them as were up on the hill went with it, and we were alone on the water in the rain. But I said 'Joe,' over and over to myself, trying to make believe he was near. I sat there until late. The night was very dark, and I was wet; but the boat kept heaving up and down, and there was a noise underneath like some great beast trying to get out. I did not know what they had down there. But the Captain came to me before morning. 'It's only the engine, Ellen,' he said. 'Go below, poor child!' He was very kind; he was kind all the time till we reached Sandusky. So were the boat-hands. There was no woman aboard but me; the men swore and cursed as I never heard before, but they always spoke respectful to me; they used to say, when they'd pass near where I sat with my basket, 'Keep heart, Ellen, you'll find your brother all right.' One of them said once, 'You needn't be feared: you've got a Friend as'll take care of *you*.' I said, 'Yes: Him and Joe.' "

It was noon of a clear day when the boat reached Sandusky City.

"I looked for Joe, quick, among the men that were on the wharf; but he was not there." (I prefer to let Ellen tell her own story as far as possible.) "I saw the Captain send a hand ashore, and when he came back, ask him a question;

then he came up to me; he looked anxious. 'Ellen,' he says, 'don't be troubled, but Joe is not here. The regiment went on to Columbus two days ago.' He said there'd be no trouble, that I could follow him on the railroad."

The Captain kept her on board until evening, when the train for Columbus started; then he went with her, secured her a seat, and arranged her comfortably. He had daughters at home, he told Ellen, bidding her keep quiet until she reached Columbus, then tell the name of her brother's regiment, and she would be with him in twenty minutes. "I am sure," he added, "Joe will get a furlough to attend to you."

The old boatman paid for her passage himself, his last charge being to "take care of her money," which made Ellen, when he was gone, remove it from her basket and carry it in a roll in her hand. There was a dull oil-lamp flickering in one end of the car, men's faces peering at her from every dusky corner, the friendly Captain's nodding a grave good-bye from the door, — and then, with a shrill cry, the train shot off into the night. It must be a lonesome, foreboding moment to any timid woman starting alone at night on a long journey, with the possible death waiting for her in every throb of the engine or coupling of the cars; so it was no wonder that the poor "natural," rushing thus into a world that opened suddenly wider and darker before her, "Joe," her one clear point, going back, back, out of sight, and withal a childish, unspeakable terror at the shrieking, fire-belching engine, should have cowered down on her seat, afraid to move or speak. So the night passed. "I was afraid to cry," said Ellen.

An hour or two after midnight the train reached Columbus; the depot dingy and dark; one or two far-off lamps bringing the only light out of the foggy night.

"The cars stopped with a great cry, and the people all rushed out. It seemed to me a minute and they were all gone. Nobody was left but me; when I got up and went to the car-door, they looked just like shadows going into the darkness, and beyond that there was a world of black houses. You've seen Columbus, Sir?"

"No."

"Then it would frighten you," — in her slow, grave way. "I suppose there are not so many people in all the world beside." (It was Ellen's only experience of a city.) "So I was there alone at the depot, waiting for Joe. I was so sure he would come. There was a crowd of men, with whips, calling out, and plucking at my shawl. I was very afraid, so I crept off into a dark corner and sat down on a box with my carpet-bag and basket. The men drove off with their carriages, but there were half a dozen others under a shed quarrelling. I sat there an hour, thinking surely Joe would be along. Then the clock struck two; I got up and went to the men under the shed. I said to them, 'Do you know Joseph Carrol?'"

"The men raised up from where they were lying, and stared at me. I'm afraid,

ON THE ROAD.

Sir, they had been drinking. So I said it again. They laughed and began to make jokes about me. I cried a little, — I couldn't help it, Sir. I knew the Lord Jesus was near me, but I couldn't help it. One of the men, whose clothes were the raggedest and whose face was very red, said —

" 'Boys, I guess you're mistaken. Who are you, my girl?'

"I told them I was Joseph Carrol's sister, and how it was I had come to find him.

" 'You'll have to help me, Sir,' I said to the red-faced man; 'for I have a trouble in my head often, and it seems as if it was a-coming soon.'

"Some of the men laughed again, but the man I had spoken to got up and buttoned his coat. He had to lean against the fence, he was so unsteady.

" 'You stop that jeering, Jim Flynn,' he says, swearing. 'Can't you see what the girl is? Where's your money, Ellen?'

"Then it was I found my money was gone. I remembered putting it on the seat beside me before we changed cars at Urbana. So I told him. He looked at me steady.

" 'I believe you,' he says. 'Come along. The Twenty-Fourth Ohio is out in Camp Chase, — four miles out. You come to an hotel to-night and go out to Joe in the morning.'

"So he took me up to a big house, and said to a man there that I was a decent girl, and gave him money to pay for my bed and breakfast, and bid me good-night."

Early in the morning Ellen dressed herself neatly, "to please Joe," and started out to the camp, carrying her basket, asking her way as she went. The girl had wrought herself up now to such a certainty of seeing him that a disappointment was sure to be a new and different shock from any that had gone before.

I suppose, too, the novel sight of the tents, the crowds of armed men, excited her feeble mind beyond its powers. She came to the gate and asked the sentry to tell Joseph Carrol of the Twenty-Fourth Ohio that his sister had come.

"It would need a long call to do that, my girl," said the man. "The Twenty-Fourth went off the active service yesterday."

"To where?"

"Virginia."

About a mile from the camp live two childless old people who then were keepers of the toll-gate on the road into town. I am ashamed to say that I have forgotten their name, it being a common one; but I remember what their lives were, and I am sure that they who carry the record of every man's hours to add to the Great Reckoning must find in their hackneyed name a meaning even to them of great truth and a rare charity. The old lady told me afterwards of her finding Ellen sitting on the roadside near her well, her mind quite gone, yet very gentle and grave even in her madness. They took her home to the toll-gate house, and kept her for two or three days, in which they learned her story.

"My husband," she said, "telegraphed to the Colonel of the regiment and found it was delayed at Bellaire; but as Ellen's health was in so critical a state, they thought it best to say nothing about her to the brother, and I was resolved that she should not go on. We offered (what we had never done before to any one) to adopt her, and treat her as our own child. People coming in and seeing the awkward country-body would wonder why we set such a sudden store by her, but in a little while they'd see as we did. I think her pure soul showed right through her homely face. Then she trusted people as free as a child; so everybody was kind to her. But I used to think there was but two people real to her in the world, — the 'Lord Jesus,' and 'Joe.' "

When Ellen was herself again, however, she insisted upon going on, and fell into so restless and wild a state that the gate-keeper and his wife were forced to yield. Her carpet-bag was repacked with all the additions which the old lady's motherly ingenuity could suggest, her pocket-book well filled, and then, having found her a companion to Bellaire, the Colonel was again telegraphed to, and Ellen herself was the bearer of letters from the Governor of Ohio and her new friends, in the hope of obtaining a furlough for Carrol. With a prudent after-thought, too, the gate-keeper's wife wrote Ellen's name and her own address upon a card which she fastened to the faithful little basket, in case of any accident; and then, with many anxious looks and blessings, Ellen again started on her journey.

At Zanesville, her companion, finding some unexpected business which would detain him in that place, left her to pursue her journey alone. It is but a

ON THE ROAD.

few hours' ride from Columbus to Bellaire (the terminus of the Central Ohio Railroad); but at Lewis's Mills this day a collision or some other accident occurred, by which the train was delayed until late that night; no other harm was done, except to give time for poor Ellen's chance again to fail her. Joe's regiment crossed the Ohio that night and went into Virginia.

Bellaire and Benwood, the opposite point on the other side of the river, are small railroad stations, which one or two iron-mills have rendered foul with ashes and smoke. The crossing of the river at that time was by a ferry, rendered purposely tedious by the managers of the Baltimore and Ohio Road, to force their passengers to the lower junction at Parkersburg. I mention this to account for the detention which ensued. When the train stopped at Bellaire, Ellen followed the crowd off the platform into a tavern consisting of a barn-like eating-room and a few starved little garret rooms over it. She stopped at the door uncertainly, while the passengers crowded about the eating-stands at the far end of the room. A fat, oily landlord came up with a hat driven down over his brows.

"Cross the river to-night, Ma'am? Slow work! slow work! Not get this train over till morning. Better take a bite."

Ellen managed to interpose her brother's name and that of the regiment.

"Twenty-Fourth Ohio? Gone over to-day and this evening. Government has the roads and ferries now, and that keeps passengers back. Troops must be transported, you know," — and then stopped suddenly, seeing Ellen's face.

"Where did you say he had gone?"

"Over," with a jerk of his thumb across the river, — "into Virginia. You are ill, young woman! I'll call Susan."

Virginia, the country of the man-hunters! A low moon lighted up the broad river and the hills beyond; they were mountains to Ellen, threatening and fierce. She looked at them steadily.

"All the stories I had heard of that country came up quick to me," she said, afterwards. "I thought it was death for me or Joe to venture there. Then he was gone! But I had a great courage, somehow, there at Bellaire. It came to me sudden. I said to the man it did not matter. I would have gone with Joe, and I could follow him. He spoke to me a minute or two, and then he went for 'Susan,' who was his wife. She was a sharp-faced woman, and she scolded her servants all the time; but she was very kind to me. When I told her about Joe, she brought me some tea, and made me lie down until it would be time to cross the ferry, which was not until near morning. She would take no money from me. She said, Sue Myers was no skin-flint to take money from the likes of me. Afterwards she said, if I found Joe and he did well, he could pay her some time again: these soldiers made money easy, lounging round camp. I was angry at that," Ellen said, reddening; "but she would not take the money from me. She told me not to be disappointed, if the regiment had left Benwood and gone out the Baltimore Road. She knew they were to camp at Piedmont, and to follow them up, for they had but a day's start of me. It was quite clear day before our turn came to cross the ferry, and then we had to wait for hours on the other side. When I came out of the ferry-house, I put my foot on the grass, and I thought, 'This is Virginia!' It was as if I had stepped on some place where a murder had been done. I was as silly as a half-witted person," blushing apologetically. "I have had great kindness done to me in Virginia since then."

Though Ellen said no more of this, as she was talking to Virginians, we readily understood the real terror which had seized her, added to the gnawing anxiety to see her brother. Caspar Hauser was not more ignorant of the actual world than this girl, brought up as she had been in such utter seclusion. The last few days had shattered whatever fancies she had formed about life, and given her nothing tangible in their stead. Even Coldwater and Joe, and "them that lay up on the hill," were beginning to be like dreams, cold and far-off. It was just a wild whirling through space, night-storms, strange faces crowding about her from place to place; undefined sights, sound that terrified her, and a long-drawn sickening hope to find Joe through all. No more warm rooms and comfortable evenings beside the fire with mother, no more suppers made ready for the boys, and jokes and laughing when they came home; there was no more a house to call home, no mother nor boys, only something cold and clammy under the muddy ground yonder.

"Ours had been a damp house on the lake-shore," Ellen said, "and we kept a fire always. Winter or summer, I always had seen a warm fire in the grate; but the morning I left Coldwater they put it out; and in all my travel, when I'd think of home, I'd go back to the thought of that grate, with a few wet ashes scattered over the hearth, and nobody to sweep them up, and the cold sun shining down the chimney on them. When I'd think of that, I'd say, 'It's all over!' It began to seem to me as if there was no more Ellen and no more Joe."

She had come, too, into the border region, where the war was breaking ground, with all its dull, gross reality of horrors, to which the farther South and North were strangers; the broken talk in the cars was even more terrifying to her, because half understood, — of quiet farmers murdered in cold blood, of pillaging and outrage, of anticipated insurrections among the slaves, and vengeance for their wrongs.

"I thought of the Lord Jesus and Joe, but they did not seem to be alive here," she said. "I would peep into my basket and look at the Testament and the spoons and Joe's collars, and that made things seem real to me." (Ellen's basket, by the way, was but another example of the singular habit which we find in persons of unsound intellect, the clinging to some one inanimate object as if it formed a tangible link to hold time and place together.)

When the train stopped at Littleton, the conductor, an old, gray-headed man, came up to Ellen as she sat alone.

"Simeon Myers told me your story," he said, gravely. "He crossed the river to tell me. I'll take the matter in hand myself; I telegraphed before leaving Benwood, in advance. The Twenty-Fourth Ohio, they say there, have gone on to camp at Piedmont; but the movements of the troops are so uncertain, we will wait until the answer comes to my despatch at the next station. You go to sleep, Ellen."

"Yes, Sir," humbly.

She sat with her hand over her eyes, until the name of the next station was called, then rose, and remained standing. The old conductor came in.

"Sit down," he said, gently. "Why, you shiver, and are as cold as if your blood was frozen!"

"My brother, Sir?"

"Tut! tut! Yes! Good news this time, Ellen. The Twenty-Fourth is at Fetterman, — has stopped there, I don't know why, — and" — pulling out his watch, but speaking slowly, and controlling her with his eye — "in two hours we will be there."

At this time (June, 1861) Government, striking at the Rebellion wildly, as a blind man learning to fence, was throwing bodies of raw, undisciplined troops into the Border States, wherever there was foothold, to their certain destruction, though with an ulterior good effect, as it proved. Camps of these men were stationed along the road as Ellen passed, — broad-backed and brawny-limbed Iowans and Indianians, clothed in every variety of militia military gear, riding saddleless horses, with a rope often for a bridle, sleeping on the ground with neither tents nor blankets. Near one of these straggling encampments the

long train stopped, with a trumpet-like shriek from the engine. "Here's Fetter-man, and here's Joe, Ellen," said the conductor, his old face in almost as bright a glow as hers, as he hustled her off on the platform.

"It was just a few low houses, not so large as Coldwater, and soldiers every-where, on the hills and in the fields and strolling along the road; and it was a clear, blue summer's day, and — oh, it did seem as the soldiers and the town and the sky were glad because I had got there at last, and were saying, 'Joe! Joe!' "

She went into the nearest house, a wide, wooden building, where two women sat shelling peas. Ellen propounded her usual question. The oldest woman took off her spectacles, and looked at her keenly.

"The Twenty-Fourth Ohio? How far did you say you had come? Michigan? Forgive me (Jinny, bring a chair), if I looked at you curiously; but I really fancied the people out yonder were savages."

Ellen laughed nervously.

"And you are Virginian? Yes! But my brother" —

The old lady's scrutiny grew graver.

"We are Virginians, in every sense of the word. So I know but little of the movements of the troops. But Captain Williams, the commandant of the post, occupies two of our rooms, and his wife is a gentle little body. Jinny, call Mrs. Williams."

So Jinny, a shy, kindly-faced little girl, disappeared, and speedily returned with the officer's wife (who had a dainty baby in her arms) and a glass of currant wine, which she pressed on Ellen. Mrs. Williams heard Ellen's story in silence, looking significantly at her hostess when it was finished.

"Yes, yes; of course you'll see Joe. Hold the baby, please, Jinny. Now let me take off your bonnet. But you won't mind, if there's a little delay, — a very little. I am not sure, but I am afraid. We'll send for Captain Williams, and know at once. But some detached companies went on to Grafton for special orders this morning, and I thought part of the Twenty-Fourth was with them. There! there! lie down a bit on my bed, or stay here with Mrs. Ford. Very well; it will all be right; only keep up heart."

So chattering, the little woman and the old one fussed about Ellen soothing, patting her, administering tea, comfort, and hope, all in a breath, as women do to the healing of soul and body, — while Jinny, baby in arms, made off and brought in a moustached young man, with a pleasant, cheerful face, not unlike his wife's.

"It is an unfortunate piece of work," he said. "Yes, the detachment included that company to which Carrol belonged. They are at Grafton now; and I cannot send a message, for official despatches will be going over the lines until night. In the morning, though, it shall be the first word to go. I know the colonel of that regiment, and I do not doubt we will have Joe here on furlough to-morrow."

"They were very careful of me," said Ellen. "Mrs. Ford made me sleep in her spare room; and Mrs. Williams brought me in my supper herself, and sat by me with baby all the evening. I couldn't believe they were all Virginians, and fighting against each other too. The next morning was clear and sunny. Jinny came in, and opened the window, and said, 'Isn't such a clear day a good omen?' But I hadn't courage to laugh with her, I was so tired; I had to lie still on a settee there was there. Captain Williams came in, and said, —

" 'By nine o'clock we will have an answer to my message, Ellen.'

"I said then, 'When it comes, if it is "No," will you just say, "No, Ellen," and no more, — not one word more, please?'

"He said, 'I understand,' and went out.

"I heard him tell them not to disturb me; so I lay quite still, with my hands over my eyes. He kept pacing up and down as if he was anxious; then I heard a man's step coming towards him. I knew he brought the message. Captain Williams came towards the door; his wife was there waiting. I heard him speak to her, and then he said, 'You do it, Mary.' So she came in, and kissed me, and she said, 'He is gone, Ellen,' — no more but that. I knew then I never should see my brother again. Mrs. Williams cried, but I did not. She told me, after a while, that he had gone by another road to the Kanawha Salines, where they were fighting that day. 'You *cannot* go,' she said. 'It is a wilderness of hills and swamps. You must stay with us; help me with baby, and presently Joe will be back.'

"I did not say anything. I lay there, and covered my face. She thought I was asleep presently, so rose softly and went away. I lay quiet all day. I could not speak nor move. They brought me some wine, and talked to me, but I did not understand. I knew I must go on, go on!"—with the wild look again in her eyes. "They would not disturb me, but let me lie still all night there. Early in the morning, before day, I got up softly, softly, I was so afraid they would hear me, and made a light. I wanted to bid Joe farewell before I started."

"Where were you going, Ellen?"

"On, you know,"—with that grave, secretive look of the insane. "I *had* to go. So I made a light. I wanted to write a letter to my brother, but my head was so tired I could not; then I took my little Testament, and I marked the four-teenth chapter of St. John. He knew that I liked that best, and I thought that would be my letter. I wrote alongside of the printing, 'Good bye, Joe.' Then I fastened it up, and directed it to Joseph Carrol, Kanawha Salines."

"That was a wide direction, Ellen."

"Was it, Sir?" indifferently. "So Joe has it now. I think all his life he'll look at that, and say, 'That was Sis's last word.' I went gently out of the door, and I put my book in the post-office, and then I went away."

She began, it appears, to retrace her way on the railroad-track on foot, leaving her money and clothes at Mrs. Ford's, but carrying the little basket carefully. The Williamses, thinking she had followed Joe, searched for her in the direction of Grafton, and so failed to find her. There are no villages be-tween Fetterman and Fairmount,—only scattered farm-houses, and but few of those,—the line of the railroad running between solitary stretches of moor-land, and in gloomy defiles of the mountains. Ellen followed the road, a white, glaring, dusty line, all day. Nothing broke the dreary silence but the whirr of some unseen bird through the forests, or the hollow thud, thud of a woodpecker on a far-off tree. Once or twice, too, a locomotive with a train of cars rushed past her with a fierce yell. She slept that night by the road-side with a fallen tree for a pillow, and the next morning began again her plodding journey.

I come now to the saddest part of the poor girl's story, gathered from her own indistinct remembrances. I mean to pass briefly over it. On the latter part of this day's travel, Ellen had passed several of the encampments which lined the road, but had escaped notice by making a detour through the woods. A mile or two east of Fairmount, however, coming near one, she went up to the first low shed; for the men had thrown up temporary huts, part wood, part mud.

"It was a woman who was there," she said, in apology; "and I was not very strong. I had eaten nothing but berries since the morning before."

The woman was a sutler. She listened to Ellen's explanations, incoherent enough probably, and then, bursting into a loud laugh, called to some of the soldiers lounging near by.

"Here's a likely tale," she said. "I half suspect this is the Rebel spy that's been

hanging round these two weeks, and kept Allan dodging you. See to her, boys, while I weigh out this sugar."

The regiment was made up of the offals of a large city; the men, both brutal and idle, eager for excitement; this sutler, the only woman in camp. The evening was coming on. Ellen was alone in the half-drunken, shouting crowd.

—Not alone. He was near who was real and actual to her always. When I think of Christ as the All-Wise and All-Merciful in this our present day, I like to remember Him as going step by step with this half-crazed child in her long and solitary journey. When I hear how her danger was warded back, how every rough face turned at last towards her with a strange kindness and tenderness, I see again the Hand that wrote upon the dust of the Temple, and clearer than in the storm or battle which I know He guides I see again the face of Him who took little children in His arms and blessed them.

When the sutler went down to the end of the field she found Big Jake, the bully of the regiment, holding the girl by the shoulder, her clothes covered with mud with which the men had pelted her. She had given one or two low cries of terror, and stood shivering weakly, her eye alone steady, holding the man at bay, as she might a brute. She held out her hands when she saw the woman. "I am no spy," she cried, shrilly.

"We'll soon test that," growled the camp-follower.

"Here, you Jake, unhand the girl! Yonder's Captain C——— looking this way. If she turns out as I say, it'll be a lucky stroke of work for you an' me."

Jake flung her back with a curse, and the woman led her to her shed. She searched Ellen. I saw the girl, when she told it, turn ashy white with terrible shame and anger. She was one of the womanliest women I ever knew.

"I would have killed her then," she said gravely.

"When she could not find that I was a spy, she fastened me in an open pen outside her shed. I tore off the clothes she had touched, they seemed so vile to me. I was so shamed that I held my hands to my throat so that I could die, but she came and fastened them with a cord. She kept me there all the evening, and the men looked over the pen and laughed at 'Mother

Murray's prisoner.' After a while I did not heed them. The moon came up, and I cried then thinking if mother or Joe could know what had come to me. *Then I made up my mind what to do.* I prayed to the Lord Jesus; but I thought, through all, what I would do. She brought me some food, but I would not touch it, though I was sick with hunger. When the drum had beat and the camp was all quiet, there was a sentry came walking up and down before the pen. He had a kind, good face: he whistled to keep himself awake. Afterwards he stopped it, and, leaning over the log-fence, said, 'Forgive me. I didn't think of your being a prisoner, or I would not have whistled.' It was so sudden, his kind way of speaking, that I began to cry, sitting back in the corner. He bade me never heed, for that I would be free in the morning. 'You're no spy,' he said, — 'only Captain Roberts heard Mother Murray's story, and put me here till he could see for himself in the morning.' Then he asked me questions, and somehow it did me good to tell all about Joe, and how I had not found him. He stood there when I had done, thinking, and whistling again, soft to himself. 'Just you wait, Ellen,' he says, — 'I know what you want.' And with that he takes out a little Testament, and, sitting down, he reads to me. Then he asked me what verses I liked, and talked of the chapters, till I began to forget all that had happened. Then he put the book in his pocket, and talked of other things, and made me laugh once or twice; and at last he took a card out of his pocket, and thought for a good while. Then he wrote a name on it, Mrs. Jane Burroughs, Xenia, Ohio, and gave it to me. 'That is my mother,' he said, very gravely, — 'as good a woman as God lets live. Do you go to her, Ellen, when you're out of this den, and tell her I sent you, and, if I should die in this bloody business, to remember I said to be good to you.' Soon after that another man came and took his place, and I saw him no more. He was very kind. But I knew what *I* would do," — with the same dropping of the voice.

In the morning Ellen was released, and the soldiers forbidden to molest her. She hurried along the road to Fairmount. There is a long bridge there, spanning the Monongahela. "I saw it when I was in the cars, and the sight of the water below it came back to me through all my trouble. It was noon when I came to it again. I don't think I stopped at all, to think about Joe, or to think good-bye to him. But," her eye wandering vaguely, "I said good-bye to my little basket. I had packed it at home for my journey, you know. I thought Joe would laugh when he saw some things I had there. But it was all over now. So I went down to the water's edge, and set it down; and then I went up, and climbed up on the parapet of the bridge, and then I heard a cry, and I was jerked down to the ground. When I came to myself, I was in a bed. They had ice on my head. They told me they had found my basket, and so knew my name. I laid there for several days. It was soldiers that found me. They paid for me at the tavern. But the regiment was going on. One day, when I was able to sit up, two of them said to me, they would take me to see Joe. They took me on the cars; all the way I had to lie down, with ice to my head. We came a long way; every time we stopped, they said we were going to Joe. I didn't know, my brain was like fire in my head."

Ellen was sent on by the officers of this regiment, and lodged by them for safe-keeping in the jail at Wheeling. The long-suspended brain-fever had set in. She was taken through the streets, her clothes ragged and muddy, her head bare, followed by a curious crowd of idlers, with just enough reason left to know what the house was in which they lodged her. Cruel as they were in act, it proved a kindness to the girl. The jailer and his family nursed her carefully, and gave her a large, airy room in the old debtors' prison.

After she had been there three weeks, a person who had accidentally seen Ellen that first day on the street went to the jail and asked to see her. A whim, perhaps, the fruit of idleness or curiosity. But Ellen thought otherwise. She was clothed and in her right mind now, and sat inside of the iron door, looking with her large, grave, blue eyes searchingly at her visitor. "God sent you," she said, quietly.

That night she told the jailer's wife that her new friend had promised to come the next morning and take her out.

"She may disappoint you, Ellen."

"No. I know God meant her to come, and I shall see my brother again."

She was strangely cheerful; it seemed as if, in that long torpor, some vision of the future had in truth been given to her.

"I shall see Joe," she would repeat steadily, a great glow on her face, "I know."

She carried her little basket, going to her friend's house. It was here I saw Ellen. She was not pretty,—with an awkward, ungainly build, and homely face; but there hung about her a great innocence and purity; and she had a certain trustful manner that went home to the roughest and gained their best feeling from them. Her voice, I remember, was low and remarkably sweet. It was curious to see how all, from the servants in the house to *blasé* young men of society, were touched by some potent charm, and tried in simple, natural ways to aid her. I used to think Ellen

was sent into the world to show how near one of the very least of these, His brethren, came to Him. She grew restless, — her disease working with her. "She must go on to Columbus, — to the gate-keeper and his wife. She would live with them as their child."

Meanwhile every effort had been made to communicate with her brother, or to gain a furlough for him. But all failed; the regiment was in the wilds of the Virginia border in active service. No message could reach him. There was no system then in the army.

What could be done for Ellen's comfort in the future her friends did anxiously, and then sent her on to Columbus. She remained with the old people but a week, however. "She was very happy with us," the gate-keeper's wife said. Governor Dennison promised to procure Joe a furlough, and, if possible, a dismissal, as soon as the regiment could be reached by letter. In the mean while she busied herself in making a dress and little useful things for housekeeping, to please her brother when he should come; used to talk all day of her plans, — how they would live near us in some quiet little house. Her trouble seemed all forgotten.

But one day she went out and saw the camp. The sight of the armed men and the uniforms seemed to bring back all she had suffered in Virginia. She was uneasy and silent that night, — said once or twice that she must go on, go on, — got her basket and packed it again. The next morning she went across the field without it, as if to take a walk. When an hour passed we searched for her, and found she had gone into town and taken passage on the Western Railroad.

My story ends here. We never could trace her, though no effort was left untried. I confess that this is one, though almost hopeless. Yet I thought that some chance reader might be able to finish the story for me.

Whether Joe fell in his country's service or yet lives in some "little house" for Ellen, or whether she has found a longer, surer rest, in a house made ready for her long ago by other hands than his, I may never know; but I am sure, that, living or dead, He who is loving and over all has the poor "natural" in His tenderest keeping, and that some day she will go home to Him and to Joe.

1862

"UPRISING OF THE NORTH"

The steady deployment that could elude wandering women was more often the experience of their men as hopes of a brief engagement faded. In Virginia, the early capture of the Kanawha Valley did not lead Union forces to many further victories, but the war in the West was gathering steam by February 1862, when Ulysses S. Grant's Army of the Tennessee was joined by a fleet of Union gunboats to take Forts Henry and Donelson just south of Kentucky. In March, Union troops moved to Pittsburg Landing on the Tennessee River, and the next month they met and defeated Confederate recruits in a confrontation that ended the war's first year with slaughter. "What like a bullet can undeceive!" Herman Melville would later write in his poem "Shiloh: A Requiem," and yet a backwoods cobbler in "Hopeful Tackett — His Mark" still volunteers to fight for "the lan dov the free-e-e" with enough "pure patriotism" to help explain why readers across the North continued to enlist.

◆○◆

Richmond Wolcott

"HOPEFUL TACKETT — HIS MARK"

(*Continental Monthly*, September 1862)

"An' the Star-Spangle' Banger in triump'
    shall wave
O! the lan dov the free-e-e, an' the ho mov
    the brave."

Thus sang Hopeful Tackett, as he sat on his little bench in the little shop of Herr Kordwäner, the village shoemaker. Thus he sang, not artistically, but with much fervor and unction, keeping time with his hammer, as he hammered away at an immense "stoga." And as he sang, the prophetic words rose upon the air, and were wafted, together with an odor of new leather and paste-pot, out of the window, and fell upon the ear of a ragged urchin with an armful of hand-bills.

"Would you lose a leg for it, Hope?" he asked, bringing to bear upon Hopeful a pair of crossed eyes, a full complement of white teeth, and a face promiscuously spotted with its kindred dust.

"For the Banger?" replied Hopeful; "guess I would. Both on 'em — an' a head, too."

"Well, here's a chance for you." And he tossed him a hand-bill.

Hopeful laid aside his hammer and his work, and picked up the hand-bill;

and while he is reading it, let us briefly describe him. Hopeful is not a beauty, and he knows it; and though some of the rustic wits call him "Beaut," he is well aware that they intend it for irony. His countenance runs too much to nose—rude, amorphous nose at that—to be classic, and is withal rugged in general outline and pimply in spots. His hair is decidedly too dingy a red to be called, even by the utmost stretch of courtesy, auburn; dry, coarse, and pertinaciously obstinate in its resistance to the civilizing efforts of comb and brush. But there is a great deal of big bone and muscle in him, and he may yet work out a noble destiny. Let us see.

By the time he had spelled out the hand-bill, and found that Lieutenant ———— was in town and wished to enlist recruits for Company ——, —— Regiment, it was nearly sunset; and he took off his apron, washed his hands, looked at himself in the piece of looking-glass that stuck in the window—a defiant look, that said that he was not afraid of all that nose—took his hat down from its peg behind the door, and in spite of the bristling resistance of his hair, crowded it down over his head, and started for his supper. And as he walked he mused aloud, as was his custom, addressing himself in the second person. "Hopeful, what do you think of it? They want more soldiers, eh? Guess them fights at Donelson and Pittsburg Lannen 'bout used up some o' them ridgiments. By Jing!" (Hopeful had been piously brought up, and his emphatic exclamations took a mild form.) "Hopeful, 'xpect you'll have to go an' stan' in some poor feller's shoes. 'Twon't do for them there blasted Seceshers to be killin' off our boys, an' no one there to pay 'em back. It's time this here thing was busted! Hopeful, you an't pretty, an' you an't smart; but you used to be a mighty nasty hand with a shot-gun. Guess you'll have to try your hand on old Borey's [Beauregard's] chaps; an' if you ever git a bead on one, he'll enter his land mighty shortly. What do you say to goin'? You wanted to go last year, but mother was sick, an' you couldn't; and now mother's gone to glory, why, show your grit an' go. Think about it, any how."

And Hopeful did think about it—thought till late at night of the insulted flag, of the fierce fights and glorious victories, of the dead and the dying lying out in the pitiless storm, of the dastardly outrages of rebel fiends—thought of all this, with his great warm heart overflowing with love for the dear old "Banger," and resolved to go. The next morning, he notified his "boss" of his intention to quit his service for that of Uncle Sam. The old fellow only opened his eyes very wide, grunted, brought out the stocking (a striped relic of the departed Frau Kordwäner), and from it counted out and paid Hopeful every cent that was due him. But there was one thing that sat heavily upon Hopeful's mind. He was in a predicament that all of us are liable to fall into—he was in love, and with Christina, Herr Kordwäner's daughter. Christina was a plump maiden, with a round, rosy face, an extensive latitude of shoulders, and a general plentitude and solidity of figure. All these she had; but what had captivated Hopeful's eye was her trim ankle, as it had appeared to him one morning, encased in a warm white yarn stocking of her own knitting. From this small beginning, his great heart had taken in the whole of her, and now he was desperately in love. Two or three times he had essayed to tell her of his proposed departure; but every time that the words were coming to his lips, something rushed up into his throat ahead of them, and he couldn't speak. At last, after walking home from church with her on Sunday evening, he held out his hand and blurted out:

"Well, good-by. We're off to-morrow."

"Off! Where?"

"I've enlisted."

Christina didn't faint. She didn't take out her delicate and daintily perfumed *mouchoir*, to hide the tears that were not there. She looked at him for a moment, while two great *real* tears rolled down her cheeks, and then — precipitated all her charms right into his arms. Hopeful stood it manfully — rather liked it, in fact. But this is a tableau that we've no right to be looking at; so let us pass by how they parted — with what tears and embraces, and extravagant protestations of undying affection, and wild promises of eternal remembrance; there is no need of telling, for we all know how foolish young people will be under such circumstances. We older heads know all about such little matters, and what they amount to. Oh! yes, certainly we do.

The next morning found Hopeful, with a dozen others, in charge of the lieutenant, and on their way to join the regiment. Hopeful's first experience of camp-life was not a singular one. He, like the rest of us, at first exhibited the most energetic awkwardness in drilling. Like the rest of us, he had occasional attacks of home-sickness; and as he stood at his post on picket in the silent night-watches, while the camps lay quietly sleeping in the moonlight, his thoughts would go back to his far-away home, and the little shop, and the plentiful charms of the fair-haired Christina. So he went on, dreaming sweet dreams of home, but ever active and alert, eager to learn and earnest to do his duty, silencing all selfish suggestions of his heart with the simple logic of a pure patriotism.

"Hopeful," he would say, "the Banger's took care o' you all your life, an' now you're here to take care of it. See that you do it the best you know how."

It would be more thrilling and interesting, and would read better, if we could take our hero to glory amid the roar of cannon and muskets, through a storm of shot and shell, over a serried line of glistening bayonets. But strict truth — a matter of which newspaper correspondents, and sensational writers, generally seem to have a very misty conception — forbids it.

It was only a skirmish — a bush-whacking fight for the possession of a swamp. A few companies were deployed as skirmishers, to drive out the rebels.

"Now, boys," shouted the captain, "after 'em! Shoot to kill, not to scare 'em!"

"Ping! ping!" rang the rifles.

"Z-z-z-z-vit!" sang the bullets.

On they went, crouching among the bushes, creeping along under the banks of the brook, cautiously peering from behind trees in search of "butternuts."

Hopeful was in the advance, his hat was lost, and his hair more defiantly bristling than ever. Firmly grasping his rifle, he pushed on, carefully watching every tree and bush. A rebel sharpshooter started to run from one tree to another, when, quick as thought, Hopeful's rifle was at his shoulder, a puff of blue smoke rose from its mouth, and the rebel sprang into the air and fell back — dead. Almost at the same instant, as Hopeful leaned forward to see the effect of his shot, he felt a sudden shock, a sharp, burning pain, grasped at a bush, reeled, and sank to the ground.

"Are you hurt much, Hope?" asked one of his comrades, kneeling beside him and staunching the blood that flowed from his wounded leg.

"Yes, I expect I am; but that red wamus over yonder's redder'n ever now. That feller won't need a pension."

They carried him back to the hospital, and the old surgeon looked at the wound, shook his head, and briefly made his prognosis.

"Bone shattered — vessels injured — bad leg — have to come off. Good constitution, though; he'll stand it."

And he did stand it; always cheerful, never complaining, only regretting that he must be discharged — that he was no longer able to serve his country.

And now Hopeful is again sitting on his little bench in Mynheer Kordwäner's little shop, pegging away at the coarse boots, singing the same glorious prophecy that we first heard him singing. He has had but two troubles since his return. One is the lingering regret and restlessness that attends a civil life after an experience of the rough, independent life in camp. The other trouble was when he first saw Christina after his return. The loving warmth with which she greeted him pained him; and when the worthy Herr considerately went out of the room, leaving them alone, he relapsed into gloomy silence. At length, speaking rapidly, and with choked utterance, he began:

"Christie, you know I love you now, as I always have, better'n all the world. But I'm a cripple now — no account to nobody — just a dead weight — an' I don't want you, 'cause o' your promise before I went away, to tie yourself to a load that'll be a drag on you all your life. That contract — ah — promises — an't — is — is — hereby repealed! There!" And he leaned his head upon his hands and wept bitter tears, wrung by a great agony from his loving heart.

Christie gently laid her hand upon his shoulder, and spoke, slowly and calmly: "Hopeful, your soul was not in that leg, was it?"

It would seem as if Hopeful had always thought that such was the case, and was just receiving new light upon the subject, he started up so suddenly.

"By jing! Christie!" And he grasped her hand, and—but that is another of those scenes that don't concern us at all. And Christie has promised next Christmas to take the name, as she already has the heart, of Tackett. Herr Kordwäner, too, has come to the conclusion that he wants a partner, and on the day of the wedding a new sign is to be put up over a new and larger shop, on which "Co." will mean Hopeful Tackett. In the mean time, Hopeful hammers away lustily, merrily whistling, and singing the praises of the "Banger." Occasionally, when he is resting, he will tenderly embrace his stump of a leg, gently patting and stroking it, and talking to it as to a pet. If a stranger is in the shop, he will hold it out admiringly, and ask:

"Do you know what I call that? I call that '*Hopeful Tackett—his mark.*' "

And it is a mark—a mark of distinction—a badge of honor, worn by many a brave fellow who has gone forth, borne and upheld by a love for the dear old flag, to fight, to suffer, to die if need be, for it; won in the fierce contest, amid the clashing strokes of the steel and the wild whistling of bullets; won by unflinching nerve and unyielding muscle; worn as a badge of the proudest distinction an American can reach. If these lines come to one of those that have thus fought and suffered—though his scars were received in some unnoticed, unpublished skirmish, though official bulletins spoke not of him, "though fame shall never know his story"—let them come as a tribute to him; as a token that he is not forgotten; that those that have been with him through the trials and the triumphs of the field, remember him and the heroic courage that won for him those honorable scars; and that while life is left to them they will work and fight in the same cause, cheerfully making the same sacrifices, seeking no higher reward than to take him by the hand and call him "comrade," and to share with him the proud consciousness of duty done. Shoulder-straps and stars may bring renown; but he is no less a real hero who, with rifle and bayonet, throws himself into the breach, and, uninspired by hope of official notice, battles manfully for the right.

Hopeful Tackett, humble yet illustrious, a hero for all time, we salute you.

At the mouth of the Mississippi, Union naval forces moved with equal audacity that April on New Orleans, the center of the international cotton trade. As the South's largest city, what Stephen Wise describes as "the only Confederate port of entry that could be rightfully called a major site of world commerce," New Orleans was the seat of Southern commercial opportunity and Northern commission envy, particularly for the New York merchants in "Thomas Elliott's Speculations" who vie over cargo and credit as the blockade of the South tightens. Throughout the war, New York would remain the economic heart of the North, with enough of an early murmur to speculate on leaving the Union as a duty-free port. Tom Elliott's impatience underlines the city's enthusiasm for the "barrels and bales and boxes" that kept soldiers and civilians alive for the duration, while the fortunes of New York's commission houses piled up.

◆○◆

Fred B. Perkins

"THOMAS ELLIOTT'S SPECULATIONS"

(*Harper's Monthly*, February 1863)

Thomas Elliott rang at the front door of Mr. Abijah Grigg, at five o'clock P.M. A livery-stable hostler meanwhile held, hard by, two very correct steeds, duly equipped with saddle and side-saddle. A curiously big, red, full-eyed Irish damsel, very frowzy about the hair, opened the door.

Thomas is an impatient man. As the door opened he said, "Come, Lily! Hurry! Every minute—"

"An' it's not Miss Lily that's in at all," said the Celtic lady, with a grin, and in a harsh, dry, rasping voice, as if her throat was lined with best double-B sand-paper. And there was a queer look in her big, bold, prominent eyes, as she added, "The misthress sez Miss Lily won't see yez thin." And therewithal she sedulously framed in her very solid person into the opening of the door. Thomas Elliott is a good young man certainly. But he certainly used a bad word at about this time—no matter what. He, however, speedily showed his self-control by extracting from his pocket a shining half-dollar, which he inserted into the hand of the Princess Margaret—for such, at least with him and Lily, was the lofty style and title of the damsel of the door. And withal he winked. A certain visible mollification might now be seen to pervade the hard face of the Princess Margaret, and she grinned. Then the enterprising Thomas, with barefaced assumption, said, in a loud voice, "Not ready yet? I'll wait in the hall." And thus pretending, he thrust forward in such wise that the Princess was in a manner obliged to make way, and he entered. But with a disagreeable sensation he said to himself, "There's something wrong." And there was.

What may be termed a simultaneous dialogue was in progress at the head of the stairs, executed in duetto by the strident soprano of Mrs. Grigg and the low-pitched, full, clear alto of Miss Lily; both earnest and half audible; in that smothered tone which we use when we are apprehensive that an inappropriate third party may hear us, but when we are too angry to care much if he does.

Tom stood, half-hearing and uncertain, in the pure receptivity of an unexpecting spectator. The Princess Margaret had disappeared to her depths. An angry beauty, in riding-habit and cap and feather, holding up her long skirts, tripped hurriedly down stairs, her face flushed and eyes sparkling and dewy with anger and tears; too exalted in mingled passions to care for forms.

"Come, Tom!" she said, and held out her hand, "I *will* see you once!"

And she led him into the parlor and shut the door. It is a mortification to be obliged to add that Mrs. Grigg came softly down stairs and listened at the key-hole; but a satisfaction to add further that, in spite of her listening, she could hear nothing at all.

Old Grigg — it would be in vain to deny that he is known in the street as Pig Grigg — is in the general commission business, and worth money; a big man, oldish, fat, with pendulous jowls, heavy of eyelid, bald of head, wigged, thick of neck, florid, full-blooded, as hot as ginger, as obstinate as a pyramid, harsh, vulgar, a greasy eater, uneducated, yet withal of shrewd, energetic, strong, large faculties, and successful in business. Mrs. Grigg shows the frame of a good face and figure; is dry and sharp and thin and pale as cheapest Rheinwein; a sad scold, I'm afraid; penurious and imperious. She and her husband are good bad examples of the American social and business life perversions of first-rate natural gifts, physical and mental.

But violets may grow in a barn-yard. These two pernicious elders certainly introduced into this world, and long maintained upon their premises, one of the most delightful daughters ever known — Lily Grigg. The daughter's graceful baptismal name was, perhaps, the last faint floweret of the romance of her poor, dried-up mother's departed youth. She is of middle size, plump; with long, abundant, wavy dark-brown hair, having a warm bright gleam in it where the light strikes it, as if it had dreamed of being a clear gold-red. Her skin is thin and fine and clear, and she has plenty of swift warm blood; so that her complexion is rosy, pure, translucent — like melted glass and red roses all mingled. It is a rare complexion. I never saw but two others like it; and one belonged to a Clerk of a Court, and the other to a strong-minded female lecturer. How inscrutable is the distribution of things! There never were such red perfect sculptured lips as Lily's—the mouth is most seldom beautiful of American features; nor such clear white pearls of teeth; nor such wonderful large, grand eyes, deep hazel, under eyebrows marked, but not heavy; and arched, but not too much—*that* indicates shallowness and fickleness; nor such a perfect arm and hand, down even to the minute finish of the finger-tips and the settings of the nails; nor such lithe, easy grace of figure and motion. She has all the perfection of step and form and gesture that belong to a splendid *physique,* perfect organisms, and strong, rich, pure, full-flowing vitality animating all. How the mischief those obnoxious old parents of hers— Well, never mind! she *is* their daughter, and that's enough.

But now, after all, it is somewhere here that I must have meant to begin— as thus:

In these present fearful times; in the midst of business troubles, war, taxation, and almost every thing else; in these hard, hard, times did Thomas Elliott win, as it were at the same moment, a most lovely wife and eke a most lovely sum of money. For it was done within the year 1862.

Elliott, please to understand, was clerk to Pig Grigg, and a very good clerk was he; with all his employer's business abilities, and a large supply of natural, good-natured politeness besides, and a good salary, and a few thousand dollars of his own by this time, and considerable musical talent, and very correct costume. A tall, good-looking chap is Master Thomas withal, with keen blue eyes and an intelligent look. So, in consideration of all this, and of his consequent convenience as a beau, and certain prepossessions in the bosom of Madam Grigg in favor of Tom's undeniable "good family," and since—as it appeared to the numskulls of parents—he certainly was not in danger of aspiring to the large wealth of the only child of the great commission-merchant!—in consideration of all this, I say, Elliott often escorted the old lady or the young one, or both, to public or private festivities, and sometimes passed an evening at the Griggish mansion.

But Master Tom, who often made Miss Lily laugh, and saw her splendid white teeth gleam between her red lips like a pearls' nest in the cleft of a ruby, notwithstanding all the proprieties, and "against the peace and contrary to the form of the statute in such case made and provided," made up his resolute masculine mind to become the proprietor of teeth, lips, and Lily altogether; and we hasten to add—for this is far from being a love-story—she was substantially consenting unto the same at this time.

Writing letters is always dangerous. Henry Clay lost the Presidency of the United States thereby; and Talleyrand would always agree to hang you if he could get one line of your handwriting. Thomas Elliott had not sufficiently laid these things to heart that fine morning when he indited that perhaps reprehensibly-enthusiastic note to Lily, which Mrs. Grigg seeing, and knowing the handwriting, could not resist the temptation to open — pleading to herself her duty to her daughter, and impelled by vague suspicions based on many minute signs, for some time past the cause of uneasiness to her and to her lean bosom's fat lord. So this little document, as Tom afterward observed, in what he said was Wall Street slang, "blew every thing higher than Gilderoy flew his kite" — a phrase suggestive of infinite queries about the diversions of that gentleman.

All this time Thomas and Lily are in the parlor, and Mrs. Grigg in a silent "feese" (it's a good word, but not in Webster) outside.

Lily said, softly, "Oh, Tom, you mustn't come any more!"

"What is it?" queried the gentleman.

"They read your note!" exclaimed Lily, coloring high with vexation at her parents, and shame for them too. "They are *so* angry!"

The young persons were silent for a moment. Lily's tones were fervent and resolute, and Tom was too much of a man to dispute her. And he felt besides that she meant "at present." Besides, did not his cunning man's instinct make him know surely that the beautiful girl was his own? Yes, indeed. A man knows the love that is his as surely and as quickly as a woman, and more so. But the passion and the fervid will of a strong man moved him to require and receive — none the less because it was not needed — an outward token before he departed. And he half lifted Lily, who was crying a little now, to a seat, and knelt close by her — and she did not resist at all. And he put his arms about her, and whispered,

"I will go, Lily. But you do not mean that I shall lose you, Lily? Kiss me once. You never gave me a kiss."

So she lifted her face to his, and lightly laid her arms around his neck and kissed him once. Then he rose quickly and departed, riding away with the hostler.

When, next morning — it was April 25, A.D. 1862 — Thomas Elliott entered the store of Abijah Grigg his usually bright face wore a somewhat resolved and preoccupied look. The eminent merchant gruffly greeted the obscure clerk. Like a true vulgarian, he did not administer with plain directness the awful and confounding admonition with which he felt himself charged, but transfused his ill-nature into the general texture of his conduct. He was sour of face and rude of manner. He found fault with the rate of commission which Tom had accepted on that last lot of guano; was inclined to charge upon Tom the non-return of a certain customer of yesterday; quite snarled over various letters; and, after sundry other nagglings, at last squarely charged that it was Tom's fault that the harbor-master had not berthed the *Sea Nymph* (with salted hides) right in front of the store, but had laid her across the end of a dock two blocks away.

Upon this Tom, who had answered him not a word, quietly wiped his pen, put up the blotter he had been writing in, turned down the lid of his inkstand, dismounted his Faber No. 2 from its clerkly perch over his right ear and put it on the rack, turned the key in his desk, took off and hung up his venerable office-coat, and put on a very neat "dress-sack," took his hat, and, turning to his respected and rather puzzled employer, said, not without a certain loftiness of manner,

"Mr. Grigg, let's not have any unnecessary difficulty. I have no particular expectation of coming to your house again that I know of."

Here the old merchant looked relieved, but his face clouded again as Tom added,

"I meant to have given you more notice, but things that have happened within a day or two have hurried me. I'm through with my work for you, Mr. Grigg. I'm to see a man at eleven this morning about a partnership. I can recommend William Waters for my place, if you don't think of any better man."

He held out his hand, saying, good-naturedly,

"Good-by, Sir! success to you."

Mr. Grigg shook hands without at all meaning to. He was badly upset. He had fully intended to administer a mild but firm reproof, and thought he had been paving the way to it very skillfully; and now he found himself suddenly thrown on the defensive by the manner and the language of the young man. Thus there jumbled about in his mind an incongruous mess of satisfaction at the discontinuance of Tom's visits, dissatisfaction at losing him, irritation at being "talked to," and that pompous, reproving state of mind that he had been nursing. And between the humbug sentiments which he had been meaning to express without feeling them, and these genuine sentiments which he had not expected to feel and did not mean to express, he mumbled and gobbled in his talk quite pitifully. The rich but vulgar New York merchant is seldom a great extempore orator of the feelings.

"Good-morning!" said he; "good-morning, then, Elliott!— Ah hem!— Ah'm!— I'm sorry — I'm glad — I hope that in future you — It's very proper — It's very improper — Well, just as you say — I'm sure — I was intending — Very well — very well!"

And with this lucid exposition of the moral bearing of things in general Tom left. After he was gone Pig Grigg very quickly and naturally heated up into

a great rage. Why should he not? He had been caused to look ridiculous —
to himself, at least; and in about fifteen minutes he agreed with himself, with
more heartiness of determination than accuracy in costume, that he would "sit
in that young puppy's skirts. Just as sure," he said, with a ludicrous habitual
asseveration of his, which wasn't meant to be true but sometimes was — "just
as sure as I'm a goose!"

"Young puppy," he said, and Tom was a well-grown fellow of twenty-four.
But he had risen up under the eyes of Pig Grigg for ten years, and we seldom see
the growth that goes on before our eyes. The old gentleman had, in fact, never
thought of Tom as a man, and had therefore felt toward him as toward an impertinent boy — a false position which had really exposed him to be outflanked,
as he actually was in the conversation just recited.

Tom felt the same state of things; indeed he had long felt it. As he left the
store he said to himself, "Can't an old man believe any body can be less than
fifty years of age and more than fifteen?"

Thomas Elliott, thus cast loose from the social and financial ties of so many
years, roamed meditatively along the bustling sidewalk of South Street, glid-
ing with the instinct of the experienced New Yorker through knots, tangles,
eddies, whirlpools of hurrying men that would have swamped a countryman,
with half-unconscious feet turned up Burling Slip, and by Liberty and Nassau
streets rambled into Wall Street — having no particular business before his appointment at eleven, when he was to meet his friend; intending to hold sweet
converse with him, if he could; and at any rate to have a good deliberate lunch
with him at noon, within the gastronomic retreat of the William Street Del-
monico. This friend was one Jaggles, a man of considerable culture, immense
business energy and shrewdness, and much good-nature too; a friend of Tom's
for some time, and already managing Tom's small means to the joint profit of
both. His business, in which Tom was to join, was "General Speculating" — If
you know what that is. The general speculator must have all his money ready
at any moment, and some credit; must be ready to say Yes instantaneously, and
No ten times quicker; must be ready to buy and sell any thing in the world
except his wife and children; and is equally likely, on any given day, to be the
exulting owner of a cargo of bananas and oranges, a monkey and barrel-organ,
a "job lot" of gilt-edged Bibles, a pile of calicoes "warranted fast colors," a new
patent, or of the ordinary commodities of real estate, stock, bonds, scrip, or
"good business paper."

As Tom, having turned eastward again, passed deliberately by that curious
silent *cul-de-sac,* or "vermiform process," known as Jauncey Court, he was met

by one in extreme haste, who seized him unceremoniously, and whispered, in an eager voice,

"Step in here a moment!"

"Ah! Mr. Wickwire," said Tom, "how goes it?"

But Wickwire—an old fellow in the broking line, a frequent coadjutor of Mr. Grigg in speculations—was in too much haste to be polite. He hauled Tom violently within the quiet precinct of the Court, and hurriedly whispered in his ear the words,

"New Orleans is open! They're past the forts!"

Tom stared. "How do you know?"

"Private dispatch through Pobbles at Richmond, *via* Baltimore," replied Wickwire. "Fully reliable! City taken yesterday! Be all over town to-morrow—perhaps this afternoon! We've just got to-day! See?"

Thomas Elliott thought he did. This dry old broker, with his score of hasty words, set up a great golden image in the young man's brain; whose glow, however, to do justice to him, did by no means obscure the rosy and more celestial light of that other lovelier figure hard by the yellow one! And no matter whether or not it would have been more chivalrous to run straightway back and tell Pig Grigg, as old Wickwire expected. Business is business. Every man for himself! Besides, Master Tom *may* have thought, "If I make it for Lily—" In fact, he undoubtedly did.

But all this flashed through his mind in one instant.

"I do see!" he cried. "Big thing, Mr. Wickwire!"

And he staid not upon the order of his going, but jumped forth out of Jauncey Court as if he had been shot out, and sped furiously eastward toward the Exchange, leaving old Wickwire to find out for himself why Mr. Grigg should fail to communicate with him. Past the Exchange flew Thomas, short round into Hanover Street, and headlong down into a small, dim, dingy, comfortless little cellar of an office, where wrote like lightning at a dirty desk a high-dried, hungry-faced man, all steel and whalebone.

"Howdo?" he snapped, as Elliott plunged in.

"All right!" replied Tom, as quickly. "Jaggles, I must have every cent! And there's an immense chance! Honor bright now; if you like it go in! Shall it be all on the square between us?"

Jaggles looked at him a moment, and seemed infected with the young man's enthusiasm. His level bushy eyebrows moved a little above his keen steel-gray eyes. He smiled, jumped up, struck his hand into Elliott's, and with the same intense swift utterance said,

"Allonthesquare! honorbright! how'llyouhaveit? Whatis't!"

"In bank—check it all out again. What's the figure?"

The speculator looked into his pocket-memorandum, and answered, "Eightfivetwentythreenaught."

That is, $8,523—all Elliott was worth.

"You'll go $15,000 or $20,000, if worth while, won't you, besides credits?" asked Tom.

Jaggles nodded, and Tom continued,

"Private news, and sure—*New Orleans is open!*"

Jaggles stared at Tom; but his stare quickly spread into a smile of intense satisfaction.

"I'm your man, Elliott! The *Superior* is not chartered. I'll secure her instantly. Flour and provisions. She'll carry—never mind; all we want to send. We must work like beavers, though. That cargo must be going in there all night. Grigg—?"

"Left him this morning," said Tom. "Got the news half an hour after."

"He'll be after us in short order," said Jaggles.

"Let him," said Tom.

They briefly conferred upon the character and nature of their respective purchases. That done,

"Jump now, you beggar!" cried Jaggles. "I'll see to the steamer. Come here at five."

Off they went; and a good deal of a stir they made that day among the flour and grocery men.

They met at five, as per agreement.

"All right!" sung out Jaggles. "The bread-stuffs are flying into the old *Superior* as if she had a real appetite. Tell you what! Betwixt buying one day in advance in the New York market, and selling in that empty New Orleans market, it's the neatest thing of the season!"

"Yes," said Tom. "And did you by chance meet Squire Grigg in your travels?"

"Some," answered the slangy speculator. "He has been flying about this burg after the manner of a bee in a tar-bucket." And Mr. Jaggles laughed. "It's unfortunate, but my charter-party was signed about two minutes before he came into the steamer office. He offered me $5,000 for my bargain. I was not at leisure to negotiate. He's got the *Sea Dragon*, though, he and Wickwire. But she can't finish discharging before to-morrow or next day morning."

"I met him up by the Corn Exchange," quoth Tom, demurely. "He turned so red! I think he can't have heard from Wickwire until one or two o'clock. Says he, 'Elliott, I'll pay you for using that news against me, you ungrateful

rascal, as sure as I'm a goose!'
I told him I should have stepped
round with the information, but
I had not time; and he grew too
angry to say one other word.
Let's go and get some dinner."

And they went.

It was four days later. The news
had rung all over the North of
that terrible glory of fire and
blood through which our brave
sailors bore the old Flag in
triumph back to its place over
New Orleans; and while it
thrilled and palpitated in the arteries of New York, the sons of commerce tried
with all their might to see the white gleam of dollars through the red glare of
victory. But Elliott and Jaggles were before Grigg and Wickwire, and they of
all the rest of the crowd of shippers to the new port. With triumphant swift-
ness the barrels and bales and boxes trundled down the wharves, and swung up
over the lofty black sides of the *Superior* and the *Sea Dragon,* and disappeared
in their great dark holds. The incessant labor of day and night gangs rapidly
filled up the steamers; and now the time draws nigh for the *Superior*'s clearance
to be granted by the scribes of the Custom-house, and Jaggles is writing like
lightning, as he always does, in his dreary shrine in Hanover Street. To him
enter Thomas Elliott in a blaze of unpleasant excitement, scarce able to keep
his feet on the floor for temper; all but dancing with disgust.

"Jag!" he sings out, "they've detained her on suspicion of contraband. Barney
says he's sorry; and I believe he is. But he says that, under the information he
has, she must discharge cargo. It's ruin, Jaggles! We're played out!"

At Elliott's first words the speculator sat bolt upright and stopped writing.
As Tom went on, his broad sallow forehead flushed faintly, his heavy eyebrows
gathered doom, his dull eyes grew brighter, and he replied,

"I perceive the hand of Joab in this thing. Grigg and Wickwire have done
that." Then he paused a moment, and added, "It certainly hurts us; but we can
save discharging, I think."

He hastily explained his plan to Tom. In pursuance of it they both went to
work like madmen; procured strong indorsements from three eminent commanders, who were influential politicians, just then in camp near by with their
brigades, and knew the Collector. They also procured full lists of each sepa-

rate purchase for shipment; and a memorandum of the politics and business-standing of every seller. Armed with this formidable mass of documents, they spent parts of a day and a half with good-natured Collector Barney, and at last succeeded in convincing him how unreasonable was the accusation that had wrought them so much woe. The clearance was granted; and, for various reasons, they spent no time in tracing out their slanderer. But when the fasts were cast loose, and the vast bulk of the *Superior* moved slowly away from the dock, the *Sea Dragon* had been rushing southward under a full head of steam for about thirty hours. Jaggles insisted on going out as supercargo, and on leaving Tom as his deputy at home.

It was four weeks and more before Tom heard a word about his venture. The letter that Jaggles wrote is too characteristic not to be given in full; besides, it contains certain information about our story not elsewhere to be found:

NEW ORLEANS, *May 30,* 1862.

"MY BOY, — Not to confound figures of speech with figures of arithmetic, see in the first place the sum-totals of the inclosed account-sales, as per which take notice that our speculation is a grand success. I get most; but I'm oldest. You get enough.

Such larks! as J. Gargery hath it. Also remember the case of the unprincipled gentleman in the Psalm:

'He digged a pit, he digged it deep,
He digged it for his brother;
But for his sin he tumbled in
The pit he made for t'other.'

"Such, my hearer, was the little fate of our brethren, Grigg and Wickwire. All the voyage out I groaned to think of their skimming the cream off that market. When we hauled up to the levee I spied gun-boats, 'darks,' Zouaves, secesh, blue uniforms, all sorts of things except *Sea Dragons*. It can't be possible, said I, that she's discharged and gone! But not a bit of it. We were first cargo. And if it hadn't been for that excessive tender-heartedness of mine, I really don't know but I should have sold the goods for their weight in specie. All the while I was gathering in the money I was saying, What's become of the *Sea Dragon*? for my kind heart was stirred within me. Well, after almost a week she came crawling along. She caught some heavy weather; and besides, gayest of all! she ran aground in one of those *blessed* keys up in the West Indies somewhere (overhaul your Atlas, and, when found, make a note of), and staid in that delightful and salubrious spot (to which I mean to make a

pilgrimage when I have time, with boiled pease in my shoes, *secundum artem*).
One Week! I was so tickled, and am yet, that I want you to run up at once and
kiss Grigg, and Wickwire too, and charge same to my account.

"Well, it's all right. Every thing comes out right, if you only wait long
enough! Another thing. I'm earning other moneys under the clause in the
charter-party about keeping the steamer six months, etc. I shall stay and come
back in her. Yours truly, JAGGLES"

When, a few days after the receipt of this letter, Thomas Elliott called upon
Pig Grigg, that worthy gentleman received him with considerable stiffness.
But business is business; and Tom had some business propositions to make.
Besides, it is a fact that if Abijah had realized that Tom was a man he would
have been far less uncivil. It required this squall of disagreement to clear up
the atmosphere of their relations to each other; and Tom's absence had proved
his value, and his successful speculation had shown him well able to "paddle
his own canoe." Neither of them raked up any past offenses, and the junior
gentleman first exhibited to the senior the state of his bank account, and then
proposed himself to him for a junior partnership. It is a fact that both interlocu-
tors thought of another proposition, involving a young lady; but they spoke
not of it. Mr. Grigg opened his eyes at Tom's cash account; said he would think
of the partnership plan; did think of it; agreed to it.

After all, Pig Grigg has a good deal of kindness in his old pecuniary heart —
to a successful business man. For he never said one word at home about the
matters in hand until one night, when it was all arranged, he took Tom home,
hauled him into the parlor, bawling out, with pretended gruffness,

"Here, mother! here, Lil! here's that impertinent Elliott again!" and heartily
enjoying the prim, cold, sour phiz of his spouse, and the blushing perplexity
of Lily. So did that mischievous Tom himself.

For all that Mrs. Grigg is a capital mother-in-law, because Tom keeps her in
good order when she comes to see Mrs. Lily Elliott.

Trade was more illicit in occupied New Orleans, where Benjamin Butler soon became military governor and where the corrupt traffic he encouraged earned him the name "Spoons" after the silverware that Union officers reportedly stole. For his notorious "Woman Order," which declared that any female insulting Union soldiers would be considered "a woman of the town plying her avocation," he was called "Beast" Butler and scorned. The brooding resistance of an occupied city that ensued puts a spy in the house that a colonel's family confiscates in "Mrs. F.'s Waiting Maid," a disquieting hint of the further risks that Southern women seemed peculiarly willing to take. Like the celebrated spy Belle Boyd, whose shifting disguise "personalizes the national and nationalizes the personal in subtle ways" for Sharon Kennedy-Nolle, the dispossessed Valerie Laudersmine suggests how malleable domestic norms might prove when homes were invaded and how resourcefully patriotic women might take their revenge.

◆○◆

Nora Perry

"MRS. F.'S WAITING MAID"

(*Harper's Monthly*, June 1867)

When General Butler was in New Orleans Colonel F. with his wife and family occupied the confiscated mansion of Mr. Chesang—a Frenchman by birth, and a rebel by principle. There was Mrs. F. and her two children, Tom and Eva— a boy and girl of fourteen and eleven, and Mrs. F.'s sister—a young lady of twenty. Besides these, two or three officers made it their home with them. It was a pleasant party, and Mrs. F. enjoyed it vastly, with one drawback, however. She was a New England woman, and accustomed to the domestic life of New England. Her house had always been a model of elegant nicety—her servants well trained and reliable, as a usual thing. To a person with her habits these slave-servants were almost intolerable. This, then, was the drawback— her *bête-noir* in the midst of so much that was delightful.

"The idea, Tom," she would say to her husband, "of being obliged to have six people to do what two could do at the North; and then of all the idle, careless, irresponsible creatures!"

The Colonel took it philosophically—laughed at their idleness, quoted the climate, their training, or want of training, and told Mrs. F. that in Rome she must expect to do as the Romans did. Mrs. F. knew all this, and a good deal more about it than Tom did, and she knew it was a trial.

But one day she came in to dinner radiant. I believe she thought the worst of her troubles were over.

"Tom!" she said, in an exultant undertone as she stood by the window with him waiting for Major Luce to come in — "Tom, I've discharged Rose, and engaged a perfect jewel of a waiting-maid."

"You don't say so! Let's send out at once and have a cannon fired and the bells rung."

"Now, Tom, be serious and listen. She is a creole, and belonged formerly in a French family up the river, and doesn't speak a word nor understand a word of English"; and Mrs. F. looked up in triumph as if the last item was the crowning virtue.

The Colonel laughed gayly. "That's the best of all is it, Kate?"

"It isn't the least, Colonel Tom. Do you remember how Rose used to be found at keyholes sometimes," answered Mrs. Tom, significantly.

Just here Major Luce came in, and the subject was dropped as they turned to the dinner-table; but when they rose the Colonel, who could never spare his fun, took Luce aside and said lowly, but not so lowly but that Mrs. Tom heard:

"Luce, I want you to go down to the General and communicate a bit of news to him — it's a bell-ringing, cannon-firing affair, Luce, and I've no doubt he'll give orders —"

"Now, Colonel, you're too bad"; and Mrs. Tom, interposing, told the story herself; but the Colonel had his laugh, and that was all he wanted.

Four or five days passed, and nothing more was said about the new waiting-maid until one morning the Major asked, "How does Rose's successor get on, Mrs. F.?"

"Admirably. She's a perfect treasure, Major Luce. I knew I should like her in the beginning, she was so quiet and deft. Ah, Major, if you had ever had your muslins torn, and your laces lost, and your best silk dresses borrowed without your leave, you would appreciate what it is to be served by this Mathilde," concluded Mrs. F., with mock gravity.

The Major laughed.

"I dare say I should, Mrs. F.; but my muslins and laces are warranted not to tear or lose, and my best silk dresses don't fit any body but myself."

Later on that same day they were all sitting in the drawing-room — Mrs. F. and the Colonel, and Miss Vescey — Mrs. F.'s sister, and Major Luce and two other officers who had dropped in for a call. It was getting late, and a wind had sprung up. Mrs. F. shivered with a little chill.

"Kate, you are taking cold; send for that paragon to bring your shawl," suggested the Colonel, in an aside.

When the paragon came in with the shawl he was busy talking again. Major Luce, who happened to be disengaged and looking that way, was probably the only person conscious of her personality as she entered. "How well she carries herself," he thought, vaguely. Then he glanced at her face. Below stiff folds of muslin, which concealed her hair, shone a pair of brilliant eyes, an olive cheek, and a mouth cut like Phene's, and curving beneath, a chin so firm, it was a trifle heavy.

"She looks like a picture; and where have I seen one like it?" mused the Major. "I know. In Valsi's studio at New York there's a Roman girl carrying a palm-branch, which she regards disdainfully. I used to think that Miss Laudersmine looked like it too sometimes. Valerie Laudersmine. I wonder where she is now. *She* was a Louisianian — used to spend her winters at New Orleans. Handsome, haughty creature — how she would lift that Greek head of hers if she knew I put her in comparison with a slave-girl! Heigh-ho! I suppose she's a rebel now. If she had been a man a pair of epaulets would have shone on her shoulders. And how soft she could be too, sometimes! I called her Valerie once — ah me!"

And in his recollection of Valerie Laudersmine he forgot Mathilde the waiting-maid.

The waiting-maid, however, as the days went on, continued to give unbounded satisfaction to her mistress. Nobody ever dressed hair like her; nobody was ever at once so deft and tasteful. Of course the Major forgot all about her; never thought of her again until again she recalled the picture in Valsi's studio, and so — Miss Laudersmine. He was playing backgammon with Miss Vescey in Mrs. F.'s little sitting-room up stairs one morning, and glancing over the board he could see Mathilde sitting sewing in the room beyond.

"Did you ever see that Roman girl in Valsi's studio, Miss Vescey?"

"Oh yes. It's a strange picture, I think."

"Did you ever notice that your new waiting-woman looks like it!"

"No, I never thought of it; but now you mention it, seems to me I do see the resemblance. But you needn't speak so low, Major Luce; she doesn't understand a word of English."

"Oh, she doesn't!"

Presently Mrs. F. came in, and presently after coming in she wanted something which Mathilde must bring.

"Mathilde!" and Mathilde came, quiet, soundless of foot, and prompt. She stood receiving the order, while the rest talked, oblivious of her. Major Luce was listening to Miss Vescey's description of the onyx ring she wore, and listening, was holding Miss Vescey's hand to look at the ring for the moment. He glanced up from the hand suddenly, and caught a pair of eyes that were not Miss Vescey's; dark, brilliant, and piercing, they startled him with an odd sensation, like peril; but as quickly as he met them they were withdrawn. As she left the room the influence seemed to pass, and he laughed at himself for it. He hardly thought of it again until the next day, as he was running up the stairs, he came upon her carrying a basket of flowers to her mistress's room. Two or three choice roses fell out at his feet, and he stooped involuntarily to pick them up. As he tossed them back he looked at her eyes again, but the lids were down, and her "*Je vous remercie*" was spoken in a swift nasal, and her whole air the very type of the class of slaves who are educated in the houses of the French planters up the river. As she went in he met Mrs. F. coming out. He could say to Mrs. F. what he couldn't to Miss Vescey, for besides being a great friend of his she was a married friend. Mrs. F. knew a good deal about his affairs, one way and another, and what he *hadn't* told her she had guessed from what he *had* told. She knew about Valerie Laudersmine. She knew, that is, that, as the phrase goes, Miss Laudersmine and Major Luce had had a great flirtation, and that at the end of the summer, when she waited to hear of their engagement, that Luce suddenly disappeared, and only came back when Miss Laudersmine had left, and then with a gloomy face, and two or three bitter words that once or twice dropped from his lips. She had guessed the story, for she knew Valerie Laudersmine well enough to know how proud she was, and how high she looked; and Everett Luce was not high enough for that looking. This was five years ago, and she supposed by this time that he had gotten over the whole affair, and perhaps forgotten Valerie Laudersmine.

In a moment she knew that he hadn't forgotten her when he stopped her and said:

"You remember Miss Laudersmine, Mrs. F.?"

"Oh yes." And Mrs. F. looked curiously up at his face. It was cool enough.

"Have you ever thought," he went on, "that your waiting-maid resembles her in some ways?"

"There!" And Mrs. F. struck her two hands together in the sudden shock of thought. "There! that is it! I knew there was something—some resemblance to somebody, I couldn't make out who."

They sat down together in the alcove of the bay-window in the hall, and by-and-by Luce said, with a wistful, grave simplicity that touched Mrs. F. greatly:

"I never quite got over Valerie Laudersmine, Mrs. F.?"

Mrs. F. said, in return, some kind, sympathetic, womanly things; and under her spell he told her more of the affair than she had ever known before, and she found that she had not guessed wrongly.

"It is a long while ago—five years, Mrs. F.; and I really thought the other day that I didn't care, you know, any more; but—just the turn of a girl's cheek and a pair of black eyes, and that old nerve I thought dead goes to vibrating again, and it aches confoundedly, Mrs. F., though I had the tooth drawn long ago."

He laughed, but it was a sad little laugh, sadder than any sigh to Mrs. F. And half ashamed of his confidence he resumed:

"I believe I am acting like a school-boy, or a fool, Mrs. F., but I am not going to say any thing about it after this."

Mrs. F. assured him that he might say just as much as he pleased about it to her, and that he was neither a school-boy nor a fool in her estimation for what he had told her. But *she* had something to say now.

"There's one thing you haven't thought of, Major Luce—perhaps you never knew the fact. Valerie Laudersmine, when she was at Cape May that summer, had a waiting-maid who bore quite a curious resemblance to herself."

Major Luce's face was all aflame in an instant. He wheeled round.

"Who knows—"

"Exactly, Major Luce. Who knows but this girl is the quondam waiting-maid of Miss Laudersmine? Shall I ask her now?"

"Yes, if you will, now and here."

Mrs. F. opened the door of her sitting-room and called "Mathilde!" Mathilde dropped the flowers which she was arranging and obeyed the call with her usual alacrity. And as Major Luce looked again at this face which recalled another face the nerve he had fancied dead began to thrill again; and it thrilled still more as he listened to the conversation that ensued. It was in French, and the girl's voice was as he had heard it a while before—nasal and a trifle shrill, like her class, not like the dulcet tones of Valerie Laudersmine, that soft-voiced siren who had sung his heart away five years ago.

"Mathilde," asked Mrs. F., "did you once belong to Miss Laudersmine?"

Mathilde looked open-eyed surprise as she answered, briskly, "*Oui, Madame.*"

"How long since?"

"Five years," after a minute's counting on her brown fingers, and with a stronger nasal than ever upon the *cinq*.

"And how came you to part from her?"

"Monsieur Laudersmine died, and Mademoiselle Valerie went to live with her uncle. It was an exchange, Madame. Madame Chesang wanted me, and offered Celie for me. Celie can not dress hair like me; but Mademoiselle Valerie is good-natured, so she took Celie for me, Madame."

"Do you mean to say, Mathilde, that Madame Chesang, who used to live in this house, was your mistress before you came to me?"

"Yes, Madame."

"And that Monsieur Chesang is uncle to Miss Laudersmine?"

"Yes, Madame."

"Did you come straight from Monsieur Chesang's here? and was Miss Laudersmine there?" broke in Luce, in a slightly nervous tone.

"Oh no, Monsieur. Mrs. Chesang died three years ago, and she gave me my freedom in her will; then I came down to the city and hired out as fine laundress. I haven't seen Mademoiselle Laudersmine since, and I couldn't tell where she is, Monsieur," with a curious, stealthy look at Luce from her piercing eyes.

There was no more to be learned from her after this, and as soon as possible Mrs. F. dismissed her back to her task. And after this Luce was no more at rest. He could never see the slim, straight figure, nor the olive curve of Mathilde's cheek, nor the flash of her dark, brilliant eyes beneath those folds of muslin, but it set his heart to beating with old memories. One night she passed him, unconscious of his presence, as he stood in that very bow-window. The poise of her head, the undulation of her movements was so like, so very, very like!

"Confound the resemblance!" he said, under his breath, and with an impatient stamp of his foot, a bitter, troubled, vexed face. And then he turned and looked after her. He saw her pass down the dim corridor. He saw her half turn the handle of a door, then pause, retrace her steps, and come swiftly, softly back. It flashed over him in an unreasoning sort of way, just then, that Mrs. F. and her sister were both away for the evening; at the same moment he shrank involuntarily within the embrasure. She came back and in that swift, soft-footed manner entered Mrs. F.'s room. And why not? He had seen her enter at that very door many and many a time. Why not now? There was no reason why not to be sure; but a curious sensation oppressed him as he watched her; a sensation that was compounded of suspicion and peril; and he remembered the same sensation once before when he had first seen her.

One, two, the seconds ticked by, in audible throbs from the great hall clock, and still he waited, watching now for her reappearance, yet half jeering at himself for the indefinable fancies that held him there.

One, two; it seemed an age. What was she about there so long? So long! Pshaw, it was but three minutes. Three minutes, in that time what might not be done?

"What a fool I am!" he muttered. "I believe I have been drinking too much Champagne; I dare say the girl is putting her mistress's finery in order."

But hark! the door opens; there she comes, the gay coral ear-rings sparkling and tinkling; a smile lurking about her lips, which parting, hum swiftly a bit of the Marseillaise. How like the maid is to her quondam mistress! The old pang strikes the watcher in his nook as he sees her; and he sees, too, one shapely hand thrust into an apron pocket, and hears the rustle of paper, and is half ashamed of himself for the suspicion that upon so slight a footing gains ground. But as she passes out of sight he says, with a certain dogged resolution:

"I'll keep an eye on her any way; if there's mischief I'll find it out—but I wish she wasn't so like, so very, very like."

And he did keep an eye on her. Twice that evening in the garden grounds he crossed her path with the careless pretext of smoking. Twice he cut off her egress from the private gateway. And at the last she turned with a gesture, and half an exclamation that was impatience and disappointment all in one—the impatience and disappointment simply of a foiled coquette.

"Possibly no deeper errand than to meet her lover"; but as he made this inward remark he sighed satisfaction as he saw her flit up the stairway before him. And by-and-by the Colonel and his wife and Miss Vescey came in. It was early yet, and a storm brooded in gusty sobs about the house; it brought damp and chill into the wide rooms, and Mrs. F., shivering under the influence, besought them to adjourn to her smaller boudoir, where Heckla should kindle a fire upon the hearth. Thither they went, and while Heckla, sable servitor, kindled a blaze which sent out aromatic odors of cypress and cedar, Miss Vescey brewed a beverage whose scents were of spices and wines. The scene so home-like and simple, dispelled all fancies and suspicions, but still there was the possibility, and the Major told his story. The Colonel, shrewd soldier, was alert at once, listening intently and gravely; but Mrs. F., nettled at any distrust of her favorite, made jest of the whole affair. It was only some little French love-mottoes Mathilde was after, probably; she herself had told Mathilde where to find them; or it might have been a recipe for a cosmetic Madame Droyer had bestowed upon her, a most wonderful recipe for the hands; and Mathilde had a passion for concocting messes; and very likely, too, it was the young creole who kept the drug-shop round the corner whom Mathilde was seeking at the gateways.

Major Luce felt excessively annoyed at Mrs. F.'s annoyance; annoyed and a trifle disturbed at this jest-making.

Miss Vescey, cognizant of all this, tried to dispel it with the breath of a little song, airily chanted over her foamy distillation. A little French song, whose English

> "Heart, heart of mine,
> Why dost repine?"

could scarcely give the impassioned aerial grace of the original, which he had heard before. But it was the same lovely tune; and he could imagine as he bent his head away from the singer, and dipped his mustache into the warm sparkle of the spiced wine frothing up in his glass—he could imagine Valerie Laudersmine singing to him one summer night as they rowed down the river for lilies. Five years, and the lilies were all dead long ago—and Valerie, perhaps she too had followed the lilies. A sharp pang pierced him. Dead! he had not thought of that. Dead—all that life and bloom and beauty!

He looked up suddenly; it was a whisper through the song that caught his ear—just a "My shawl, Mathilde," and there she stood, for once unconscious, for once rapt, away and apart—betraying herself. There was wistful depth in her eyes, there was melting sweetness on her lips, as if she might then be singing softly the old French song:

> "Heart, heart of mine,
> Why dost repine?"

A little tinkling crash, a start and exclamations, while Mrs. F. moved her violet silk from the scene of accident, and then they all fell to laughing over the Major's preoccupation.

"Or was it Julia's song?" bantered the Colonel.

"Yes, it was just that—Miss Julia's song," with a single glance at Miss Vescey, which cost Everett Luce all his self-command; for over it flashed another glance, startled, yet unafraid, as if—"I trust you: *you* will not betray."

And while they laughed and bantered he bent down from their gaze to the fragments of his glass upon the floor, unheeding the reminder of Mrs. F. that Mathilde could perform that service; and bending there, his hands touched hers, and he knew that perhaps he held her life—Valerie Laudersmine's life—in his keeping. Valerie Laudersmine! All this time it had been Valerie Laudersmine, and he had not known. At first a thrill of delight, swift and unreasoning, at her simple presence; then fear, anxiety, foreboding, and suspicion, which deepened into horror, at the fate that might be—that must be, closing around them. He drew a deep breath at the thought that he *had* betrayed her; for, knowing now that it was Valerie Laudersmine, he knew no step of hers was purposeless in that house, nor that, left alone, she did other work than her own. What thwarted purpose was that in the garden then? What noiseless errand in the room beyond? And he had betrayed her! Betrayal—what did it mean? And this betrayal was assuredly of wrong and misdoing, of treason and conspiracy! What did his loyalty command him to do but to betray all treason and conspiracy? His brain reeled with these questions, and his pulses throbbed dizzily, while still he bent there in such dangerous neighborhood, and still the laugh and bantering jest went on, and no one but they two conscious of the tragic undertone.

"Curious creature she is!" remarked the Colonel, as, the fragments gathered up, Mathilde moved stately from the room.

"A faithful creature!" interluded Mrs. F., with a little breath of malice. "See how she mends this old lace," holding up a web of Valenciennes.

"Lace? And how about that gold-lace on my coat, Mrs. F., which this 'faithful creature' was to rejuvenate with her wonderful fingers?" asked the Colonel.

"How about it? it's like new. You could never tell the broken thread; but look and see for yourself in the wardrobe in your room."

He came back with it on his arm, and looking at it, fell into praises which satisfied even Mathilde's mistress.

"And the papers in the inner pocket I told you of you put in my cabinet, I suppose, as I suggested?"

"No, not in the cabinet; it was that day I was ill in my room, and I dropped them in my writing-desk; or Mathilde did for me."

The eyes of Major Luce threw a startled, fearful glance across the table; and there was something in the answering glance of his superior that fully met it. Just a moment of waiting, then the Colonel rose again. Mrs. F. looked up from the contemplation of her slippers on the fender.

"Wait, and I'll send Mathilde for the desk, Tom." But the Colonel had disappeared, and presently returning, bore in his hands a little escritoir of gilt and inlaying.

"The key, Kate—underneath there. Don't you remember the small secret drawer outside for it?"

It was but a second that turning of the key, that lifting of the lid; but in the brief time what length of fear and dread, what fainting horror possessed him who watched and waited from the other side of the little table, where still Miss Vescey brewed her posset and hummed her song. But the song was coming to an end, no more to be resumed that night. It broke off suddenly in the turning of a note, at a new note in her brother-in-law's gay voice.

"Kate, Kate! what have you done?" It was not only displeasure, but it was the sharp, swift tone which bursts forth at only one crisis—that of peril or its anticipation. Then in an instant dismay seized upon the group there—in an instant they all knew what had happened, that Major Luce's suspicions had come true; but still in anxious voice Mrs. F. cried, "What is it? what have I done, Tom?"

"It was that plan of Gerritt's, Major, the whole line of attack, and the present disposition of our men in complete drawing"; but the Major, before the Colonel had spoken more than the first half dozen words, had disappeared.

He would save her yet from question or trial. If he reclaimed the lost paper, what more for all loyal purpose was needed? If he reclaimed it!

Down a wide hall, as he went out of Mrs. F.'s boudoir, he caught the echo of a footstep. Following it, the flutter of a light garment led him on, and on, still on, through a maze of doorways and passages until the fever of pursuit and delay nearly maddened him. Then a voice — was it Mrs. F.'s? — far off at first, then coming nearer, called "Mathilde, Mathilde!" — coming nearer, called "Mathilde, Mathilde!" — then other footsteps, other voices, when suddenly a breath of the storm blew coldly in from an opening door, and following on, he found himself in the garden-grounds, out in the wild tempestuous night. A late moon was struggling up through flying clouds, and by its fitful light he discerned what he sought. There she fled down the narrow, tortuous pathway which led to the river-gate. A moment more and he held her in his grasp — a moment more and he was speaking to her vehemently, almost incoherently, calling her "Valerie"; imploring, beseeching, commanding, in a breath. At the first words she knew her danger; yet the reckless adventurous spirit which had incited her on to the part she had undertaken still had possession of her. A strange exultant look gleamed from her eyes.

"Well!" she exclaimed, in the breathless pause.

"The papers! give me the papers, Valerie! then go free, and God help you!" he cried.

She seemed to start at the solemn passion of his tone; but immediately her voice rang steadily in answer:

"At the foot of the garden, by the river-gate, under the lion's head, there is a receptacle for letters — a cleft in the granite that will admit your hand. I dropped the packet there an hour ago — an hour hence it would have been beyond your reach, if you had not prevented my egress from the grounds; and so you checkmate me again, Sir." She stepped forward, as if to go, but still his detaining hand lingered on her arm.

"Well, am I to go free, Sir?" in haughty accents.

What Fate was it that held that moment? There was no shadow of doubt of her in his mind as she spoke; he believed she spoke only simplest truth, and that in the cleft of granite he should find what he sought; but some bitter pang of parting, some anxious fear for her welfare in the wild and dreary night made him hesitate perhaps.

"But how can you go, where can you go alone, Val — Miss Laudersmine, at this hour?"

Again his tone seemed to touch her; and she lifted wistful eyes a moment and answered gentler than before:

"I have friends who wait for me."

As she spoke, the wind rising in a fresh burst, a branch of the cypress under which she stood struck suddenly against her. Unprepared for the blow, she lost poise, reeled, and would have fallen but for her companion. As he caught her something slipped from her hold and rustled to the ground. The moon came sailing up and showed him what it was — a slender packet sealed with red wax. Good Heaven! how well he knew it! And how bitter the recognition now; yet what Providence! As he stooped to take it their eyes met.

"Yes, I deceived you," she exclaimed, bitterly, but with the bitterness of defeat solely. "I told you it was at the foot of the garden when I held it here in my hands. I meant to have gained time, as you see: an accident prevented me."

She stood as if waiting. She had deceived him. In how much more might she not even now be deceiving, misleading, and betraying? What was she to him? The woman whom he loved. But there was something else. There was his country and his honor! Suddenly his mind cleared, and a divine resolution possessed him.

"Valerie — Miss Laudersmine, you are my prisoner."

The next instant lights gleamed from the opening doors, footsteps and voices rang — a confusion of question and exclamation and wonder. It seemed an age to Major Luce that he stood there with his hand closed over Valerie Laudersmine's slight wrist, until the soldierly figure of Colonel F. stood before them. At the first glance the Colonel saw the whole — the double identity, the deep-laid thwarted purpose, and the pang of discovery. In another moment he saw, too, how much loyalty and honor meant with Everett Luce, as he noted the firm yet gentle hold of detention, and the stern sorrow of his face as he handed him the packet.

And Valerie Laudersmine was a prisoner in the house where she had fraudulently served. She uttered no complaint, she made no protest, she showed no sign of repentance, and none of anxiety through it all.

Quietly and even tenderly, for the sake of her youth and her sex, and perhaps, too, for the sake of the brave fellow who had so painfully proved his loyalty, the examination was carried on, and the final judgment awarded. It was certainly gentle judgment, that sentence of banishment up the river, upon an unwilling *parole d'honneur*. Gentle judgment for her sin; but she received it with the same cold, haughty apathy that had intrenched her from the first.

"I always thought her heartless — always," commented Mrs. F., with a pained, half-frightened face, after their last interview.

"And to think we should have been so deceived by a little disguising!" exclaimed Miss Vescey; "but there never was such an actress as Valerie Laudersmine. The first time I ever saw her she played in Mrs. Althorpe's private theatricals, and how Charlie Althorpe raved about her!"

Heartless and an actress! Perhaps they all judged her with this judgment except one, who might have been pardoned for even harsher judgment. But he, as those dark eyes lifted to his for the last time, realized what divine possibilities were lost in the warping realities of her education and associations, and what

"THE STARVING PEOPLE OF NEW ORLEANS"

she might have been if all her life had not been spent under an unnatural rule, where every selfish whim was fostered, and every idle wish indulged. Looking into her eyes, he said no word of reproach, but only with sad earnestness:

"Good-by, Valerie."

She dropped her hand in his; it was icy cold, and her haughty voice faltered a little in replying:

"You have done your duty, Major Luce, and I honor you for it."

In an instant, by that glance, by that faltering tone, he knew how near, yet how far apart they were; and he knew that when they parted it would be forever. But he had done his duty, and she honored him.

To Mrs. F. he said, one day:

"I suppose I shall overlive this, and perhaps at some time be a happy and contented man, with altogether another future than this that I thought possible once; for neither men nor women give up their lives at one disappointment, however great, unless they are weak or wicked."

This was good and true philosophy; but it sounded a little too matter-of-fact and cool to Mrs. F., who remembered so vividly the sad passion of love which had broken up into every word and look a little while since from this now quiet speaker. She had not fathomed Everett Luce yet.

"He isn't a fellow to make a fuss about any thing, but he is one to hold on to a feeling or a purpose a long time, Mrs. F.," commented that lady's husband.

And Mrs. F. realized how true this was as time went on, and found Major Luce untouched by all the bright eyes and winning smiles that lavished their sweetness upon him.

The war is over, and Valerie Laudersmine — now Valerie Laudersmine no longer, but the wife of one of her own race — released from that *parole d'honneur,* shows her handsome, haughty face at imperial fêtes and royal presentations. She achieved her destiny, and made a worldly, perhaps a loveless marriage; but that she was not altogether unworthy such love as Everett Luce had given her one little incident may serve to show. Meeting a fellow-countrywoman — none other than Miss Vescey — in a Paris salon one day, among other inquiries she asked, with a flushing cheek:

"And Major Luce, Miss Vescey? I hope the world goes well with him. He is a brave fellow — and a gentleman."

And this "brave fellow," this "gentleman," proves all his claims, and the world goes well with him. Men respect him, women trust him, and children welcome his approach. He has not made that other "future" for himself yet; but there is certainly nothing morbid in his mind, even though the only picture that hangs in his room is that Roman girl of Valsi's, whose aspect is that of Valerie Laudersmine.

Even the land seemed to begrudge the occupiers from the North, at least in the stories that Union pickets later told. The disappearing flutter of a maid's shawl in New Orleans could become for them the spectral shimmer of a blue light in Virginia, particularly on the road to a planter's decaying home. Midnight duty was often lonely; during an era when table rappings, seances, phrenology, and magnetoscopes were becoming commonplace, the flash of the inexplicable could be yet another reminder of the disembodied spirits that hovered over the nineteenth century, as Daniel Cottom has pointed out. What Union sentries see in "Believe in Ghosts!" suggests the malicious discontent of the Old Dominion as surely as a pair of lingering maid's eyes recalls the decided purposes of Southern rebellion.

◆○◆

"BELIEVE IN GHOSTS!

A REMINISCENCE OF VIRGINIA DURING

THE WAR — A TRUE STORY"

(*New National Era*, November 1870)

Believe in ghosts? Well, no; I can't say I do, and yet something I saw in Virginia, one night, during the war, somewhat staggered me, and I have never exactly known what to think about it. I know, though, that Tom Fairfax would swear to their ghosts, or at least one ghost, to his entire satisfaction on the subject.

Tell it to you? Certainly, I will; and maybe, as you are well versed in ghostly lore, you can explain what it was we saw — not Tom and I alone, but hundreds of the boys, for we were several days in the same place, and the whole picket line saw it repeatedly. See if any of your German metaphysical works will explain it. I ask, for it puzzles me.

We were camped on some old fields near the edge of a dense wood that was remarkable for the want of undergrowth; you could see way into the thick, cool woods, with nothing but the trunks of the trees to obstruct your vision as far as your sight could reach.

The first night we camped there I was off duty, being ill; we were on the alert, for we knew the enemy were not far off, and were expecting to see them at any moment, and our sentries were thrown out to avoid surprise. I heard the alarm during the night from the pickets, and the stir in the camp, but was too unwell to get up and see about it, as I found the alarm was not general, and the next

morning laughed heartily at the tale of a ghost having driven in the pickets; but when the thing was repeated the ensuing night, I began to think some one was playing practical jokes — either the men or some one who wanted to pass the line.

On the third night I was able to stand sentry myself, and Tom Fairfax and I requested the Colonel to put us on that road. He did so; and as Tom left me and went on ahead to the outer post, he laughingly said:

"Well, James, old boy, let's find out what material the ghost is made of if it comes tonight."

"All right; I'm with you," I replied. "If he's flesh and blood I'd not like to be in his shoes, for I don't intend he shall make a fool of me."

I forgot to mention that in the distance adjoining the field upon which we were encamped were the ruins of an old-time Virginia mansion that had evidently been built in the first settlement of the State. The main road running through the wood led past this house, but it was not on that road that the specter had been seen, but upon a by-road leading to an old mill on a rapid and deep, and yet very narrow stream of water.

It was a brilliant starlight night; the moon had sunk to rest, after showing her silver crescent to the admiring gaze of those who loved to look upon nature's beauties; and the light being steady and equal, one could see for a good distance. Fairfax was stationed near enough for me to hear his challenge, should any one come that way. In talking the matter over, we had both arrived at the conclusion that some one was trying to pass the lines, and we were determined to catch him, if possible. As time rolled by and nothing came, I gradually ceased to think of it; and my thoughts reverted to home and its loved ones, doubly dear to me, and the form of a dear little blue-eyed darling, who was waiting my return with anxious, prayerful heart, was very palpable to my mind's eye; and so deeply was I absorbed that Tom's challenge of "Who goes there? speak, or I'll fire on you!" fell upon my ear without drawing my attention to it till startled by the report of his gun, and, after a moment's dead silence, a yell so thrilling that it curdled my blood.

Looking down the road I saw running toward me on foot, to whose usual fleetness fear had added lightning speed, Tom Fairfax, the dauntless hero of a hundred hair breadth escapes, and closely following after him glided a singular-looking blue light that seemed in the distance to be a column of flame about six feet high.

As Tom reached me he exclaimed, "Great God, James, what is it?" and fell in a dead faint at my feet.

As the thing approached me it took the semblance of a headless man wrapped in a pale blue flame that flickered in the night air, looking just like little tongues of fire licking the shape. Though startled nearly out of my senses, I waited till it was within five feet of me, and fired my gun right into its breast. The flame waved and opened, spun up a foot or two, and then settled back into the flickering sheet of fire, and the evil thing sped steadily on past me toward the old mansion down the road.

I turned to help Tom, and, as I did so, some of the guard from the main road reached us: for, having heard the report of his gun and his yell, followed by my gun, they had not waited for orders, but hurried to our relief, and they saw the thing as it passed on toward the house. We carried Tom to camp, senseless, and a nice spell of brain fever was the result of his fright; and it would take more reasoning power than I ever heard of any one possessing to make Tom think there are not ghosts.

None of the men would stay alone on that post, and a squad was left there for the rest of the night. I fully determined to reach the old mansion and make inquiries about it; but we moved our quarters in a hurry next day, and I never knew the secret of the headless man and that road, or what scene of crime that old mill and the ruined mansion have shared between them.

The menace that unnerves camp sentries was a way of life for the war's couriers and scouts. In considerable numbers, they carried the army's dispatches, probed enemy lines, and gathered intelligence with a daring vulnerability. As Edwin Fishel has noted, spies may be the intelligence gatherers of choice for recent students of the war, but wartime field commanders were as likely to rely upon scouts, cavalry reconnaissance, prisoner interrogation, and the operations of both the Signal Corps and new balloons. In the late summer of 1862, when losses in the West and in the slaty hills that would become West Virginia were disturbing news in Richmond, the mounting successes of the Army of Northern Virginia bolstered Southern morale. To bring the war home to the North, Robert E. Lee moved his forces in August toward an invasion of Maryland. With his nephew Fitzhugh Lee and South Carolina's Wade Hampton joining J. E. B. Stuart to command the cavalry, Lee approached the winding Potomac north of Washington, D.C., where he awaited the late-night packets of scouts like the footsore rider in "The Sergeant's Little Story" who slips toward the river from Frederick. He would not be the only traveler on that moonlit road or the only soldier to reconnoitre a river crossing as the Potomac's banks filled with men.

◆◇◆

William H. Kemper

"THE SERGEANT'S LITTLE STORY"

(*Southern Magazine*, October 1873)

To our great surprise and commensurate gratification, the Sergeant was less reticent than usual, and seemed to be growing even autobiological. He was not a painfully handsome man: that odd-looking cavern, or sunken scar, in his leathery cheek was plainly not a dimple, nor could it in a spirit of the most elastic courtesy be regarded as a beauty-spot. The Sergeant sat next the decanter.

"Well, 'twas touch and go—a snap for him, a snap-shot for me; but the luck was mine. After catching the horse—a troublesome business—I went up to the man and inquired how he felt. He was lying on his face and made no answer. I turned him over. He seemed to be a fine-looking fellow, as well as I could judge in the deepening twilight, and about my own age. My ball had struck plumb-centre, a little above the line of his eyebrows; but as he'd fallen and bled face downward, he was not much disfigured. No time was lost in going through his pockets and haversack; the ford being not more than half a mile away, I was afraid they might have a double picket there, in which case they'd like enough be sending presently to see what the shot meant. Finding nothing about his person worth conveying, save his official dispatches, I hurriedly crammed them into my haversack along with a lot of late Washington and New York papers that I had got for General Lee's amusement from a lady friend near Frederick, then mounted the horse—a fine tight-built trotter, apparently of Morgan blood—and moved slowly and warily down toward the river. Two hundred yards from the ford I drew rein and listened. Everything seemed quiet. A solitary light shone in an upper window of the house at the canal-bridge—*you* ought to remember the house, Captain S——. The roaring of the water among the rocks ahead was the only sound that broke the silence of the night, until presently a big owl began his melancholy laughter in the wood behind me. Having been born in the woods, I didn't allow the solemn old cuss to frighten me, though I did wish he'd shut up, that's a fact. Dismounting, I pulled the horse up a steep bank into the dense shadows of the woods skirting the roadside, hitched him securely to a swinging limb, and limped along as best I might afoot to reconnoitre the ford. The coast was clear. This important discovery I effected by a simple little stratagem which had served my purpose on a previous occasion: without going dangerously near, or even crossing the canal, I merely brought my school-boy skill at yerking into play, and dropped a stone, like a shell from a miniature mortar, just where the vidette would be standing if about there at all. Having repeated the experiment without eliciting so much as a cuss-word in response, I advanced with confidence. The river was considerably lower than I had expected to find it. Groping along the water's edge I found a place where the mud was stiff enough to sit upon, then shucked my boots and peeled off my socks, bringing several square inches of blistered skin with them, and paddled my feet in the cool water. Dead beat as I was, the delightful sensation of relief from long agony almost sent me to sleep in spite of myself; but I thought of Uncle Bob's impatience, my own great danger, the importance of the dispatch I bore, the rest and refreshment and well-earned praise that awaited me at headquarters; in truth, I was thinking of too many things, and was nodding once more, but with a sudden exertion of will I straightened up like a Jack-in-the-box and drew on my boots, without socks, despite the pain, and limped back toward where I'd left the horse, resolved to get across the river at once. I found him all right; but that ominous old owl had taken advantage of my absence to come and perch himself in a tree right over him, where he was to-hoo-hooing at a great rate. Before mounting I thought of a good plan to secure the dispatch; for you must understand I didn't more than half like the outlook: things were a little *too* quiet. Somehow I began to fear that a rough road and danger still lay between me and camp. I took a little air-tight India-rubber bag in which I carried 'fine-cut' (when I had any) and put the dispatch, neatly folded, inside of that; then I poked the bag down the neck of my canteen, blew it up with my breath as tight as I could, and tied a string around the neck so as to keep the air in and the water out, or whiskey, as the case might be. You will observe now that by keeping the canteen about half-full of water, or whiskey, as I said before, the bag would float always out of sight, keeping always on top, no matter which way the canteen might be held, while it would make no noise if shaken.

"When mounted, I felt better, and struck into a brisk trot for the river. My feet stopped paining me for one thing, and on reaching the ford I was so gay and imprudent as to let off a rousing war-whoop which reverberated for a mile around. I instantly sobered down, regretting the senseless act on finding that I got no answer from the Virginia shore save the startling echo of my own voice; for I had hoped to find there a picket of Fitz Lee's or Hampton's men. If there, they were afraid to answer my challenge. I didn't comprehend the situation; in fact, I hardly had sense enough left to comprehend anything: I was emphatically a used-up man, so weary and sleepy that I swayed in the saddle like a drunken man as I forced the horse down the bank and into the river. Owing to my stupid condition, or the darkness of the night, for the clouds hung low and heavy, I missed the proper line of ford and struck too low down stream. Before getting forty feet from the bank the horse stumbled and scrambled over a large slippery rock, nearly pitching me out of the saddle, then plunged head down into almost swimming water, soaking the little round button on top of my Scotch cap and waking me up. Three or four plunges and desperate struggles brought us out to a little island—I reckon some of you recollect it?—about thirty-five or forty yards from the Maryland shore. It was covered with willow trees and thick undergrowth quite down to the water's edge, except on the Maryland side and around the lower end, where there was a strip of clean sandy beach some ten or fifteen feet in width. 'Humph!' says I, 'here's a nice berth for a fox-nap! Buck me! but I'll risk forty winks anyhow!'

"The fact is, gentlemen, human endurance has limits. I had now been on the trot for over two days and nights, and not even a sense of danger would make me hold up longer. So I rolled off the horse—leaving the saddle on him, but removing the bit from his mouth—fastened him to a willow-branch, crept round under cover of the thickest foliage at the lower point of the little island, and lay down to rest, using my well-stuffed haversack for a pillow. It was a dangerous chance I was taking. I knew it; but the night was so still, and everything seemed inviting me to snatch an hour's rest before continuing a perilous journey, the worst of which, for all I knew, might be still before me. Not a sound was to be heard betokening approach of danger—nothing save the rush and gurgle of the inky waters, the crunching of my horse's teeth leisurely chewing the willow-leaves, and the far-off whistle of the whippoorwill away up the river. Just before losing all sense in heavy slumber I noticed dreamily that the clouds broke away in the east, and I caught a glimpse of the crescent moon hanging by one horn in the top of a tall dead pine-tree high up on the Maryland bluff. It swung to and fro like a binnacle-light, and I remember thinking in a drowsy sort of way that if it wasn't careful it would drop off the limb and get broken. Just then the old owl opened again; only it seemed to me he had changed his base, and was now perched upon a leafless limb overhanging the roadside on the hill, and was talking to the poor fellow stretched out beneath, lying there so still and ghastly, the white face upturned to the moonlight, the wide-staring eyes, the purple spot in the pale forehead where the bullet went in and life came out. I seemed to be standing over him again, it was all so plain. Well, well, such is war—as the scout must wage it. There's no denying the fact though, it does make a man feel worse—more like a wild beast, like our elder brother Cain—to be obliged to slay his foe under such circumstances: alone, with no witness but his own conscience and the All-seeing Eye that pierces through the gathering gloom of night on the lonely forest road. But why it should be really worse than to do the same thing with the roar and crash and rattle of wholesale murder around you, I confess is not so plain to my mind. To single out your men—men not even aiming at you, neither—and pick 'em off one at a time, as some of us here have done, for an hour or two, that now appears to me— I beg pardon; where was I? Let's licker."

Having "lickered," the Sergeant proceeded.

"I must have slept like a Mississippi sawyer for I don't know how long, two or three hours perhaps, when *spi-yow! ʒweep!*—a shot from the Virginia shore, then three or four more in quick succession, answered by a rattling fusillade from the Maryland side. I was on my feet of course ere the second shot was fired and about to spring to saddle, but too late. The ford was crowded with Federal cavalry, cursing, yelling, stumbling and spurring furiously across the river, where our boys (a small picket from Hampton's command, as I afterwards learned) didn't stay to swop horses, as indeed there would have been no sense in doing; though why in thunder they didn't answer my challenge I never could discover. Now indeed I found myself entrapped and entangled in the meshes woven by my own folly. Although, as you remember, the island is not exactly in the line of ford, being some twenty-five or thirty yards down stream, it was impossible for my horse to long escape notice, standing, or rather plunging impatiently, in the full light of the moon, now high in the heavens. Luckily for me I was in deep shadow cast by overhanging willows, and had time to beat the assembly, so to speak, to collect my startled faculties and make them fall in line. My first thought was for the dispatch. Having gone through purgatory to get it and fetch it so far, you may safely bet I hadn't any notion of lightly losing it. Raising the canteen to my lips, I drained it of the last swallow of 'blue ruin,' somewhat improved by the flavor of India-rubber; then stooping down, I cautiously refilled it about half-way with Potomac water and corked it tightly. By this time they had seen the horse; and some had stopped and were pointing toward him, but seemed rather shy about coming down. An officer ordered 'three or four' of them to 'ride down there and see what it meant.' While they hesitated I took advantage of their timidity and delay to cast about for a chance of escape, and make a few little arrangements, such as strapping my belt outside of my haversack and canteen cords, so's to keep 'em down to my side in case I took water. And that same I meant to do too; for I had already discovered from their talk that they'd found the dead courier, and I knew mightily well what to expect if they found me too. I have been in and got out of some pretty rasping scrapes, but this was the only occasion save one during the entire war when I remember to have made up my mind deliberately to die rather than be caught. Bitterly I cursed my stupidity in not concealing the courier's body; and then, by way of change, I believe I tried my hand at praying, but couldn't get any further than 'now I lay me down to sleep,' when I remembered what a blamed fool I'd been to do that very thing, and that set me to cussin' again. Fact is, it was a little too late for either cussin' or prayin', and I soon came to that conclusion. Dropping silently on my hands and knees, I crept along under the willow-branches close to the water's edge and listened. Noticing just ahead of where I was, on the western side of the island, a long drooping branch of willow hung out almost touching the surface of what looked like pretty deep water, on the instant a vague undefined plan or hope of escape began to shape itself in my mind.

"By this time two or three of 'em had got round the horse on the other side of the bushes, talking. 'Why, how is this? What's this here on the saddle now?' 'Feels sorter wet and sticky, don't—' 'Blood, by jingo!' cries another. 'Can't you smell it, corp'ral? Then the corporal yells out, 'Ride down here, Kurnel! Dang me if this here ain't the courier's horse!' 'What the ——— should the horse be doing thar without a rider?' growled back a deep hoarse voice like the mate's of a three-master. 'Look alive there, blast yer block-heads, and ye'll mebby find the chap that rode him!'

"The devils now commenced shooting into the willow thicket, one of the balls grazing my right elbow: must get out of that some way. Sliding down into the water like a skilpot off a log, I found to my great joy that it was deep enough for my purpose; and so I lay low right under the overhanging limb, just keeping eyes, nose and ears out of water. Had hardly got settled comfortably (our ideas of comfort, you know, as of all else, are entirely relative) before the big Colonel himself was there, knocking, ripping and snorting around, poking his five-foot sabre into the bushes wherever he thought he spied something, and popping away every now and then with his revolver. Twice or three times the blamed officious old blunderbore came nigh hitting me, and I was getting right mad, when what should he do but come and stand on the limb, so's it pushed my head clean under water. Being taken unawares (I thought of course he was going to step over the limb, as anybody but a cussed old fool like him would have done), I couldn't help spluttering a little as my mouth went under. 'Aha!' says he, 'what's that?' I had worked my mouth and nose out, and was trying to draw my breath easy, but the strain on my lungs was terrible. He wasn't at all sure he had heard anything, but just out of downright deviltry and officiousness he gave point in tierce right down through the willow. Instinctively I ducked; but for all that I got the point of his confounded sabre through my cheek here, and have been trying ever since to digest a couple of big jaw-teeth. In making the thrust he lost his balance and came within an ace of piling in a-top of me. That was all that saved me: by the time he had gathered himself up I also had recovered in some degree my desperate composure, and was breathing as softly and steadily as a sleeping bull-frog. The limb knocked my cap off when he stumbled, and it was nearly floating out from under the willow; but I caught it in time and drew it down beneath me. I could feel that I was bleeding like a stuck pig, but it was no time for squealing. By this time a dozen or so, mostly officers, were crowding down to the island to see what the row was about; but the Colonel — God bless the old pudding-head! — ordered 'em all back, and away they went and he with them. Just as the last man was turning the corner, almost out of sight, he stopped, faced about, and I caught the click-click as he cocked his revolver. Says he, 'Thar's a big fish under that limb, and I knows it.' Down went my devoted head deep as I could get it. I heard no report; but the peculiar metallic ripping sound of the ball as it cut the water just above my ear I shall not soon forget. It sounded like tearing sheet-iron.

"That appeared to satisfy them. When I ventured to raise my head and look about me, they had taken my horse and were hurrying on to overtake their command. The long line of horsemen, riding by twos, still stumbled and splashed and clattered across the moonlit river, and plunging up the steep bank, disappeared in the silent shadows beyond. How long I remained in the water I cannot tell; it seemed to me many hours. I was growing sensibly weaker from the loss of blood, while the water chilled me to the very marrow; yet still I kept my position, kneeling in the water beneath the sheltering willow. At length, as the moon forged slowly down the western skies, fleecy clouds began to gather and obscure her light once more. At length too the cavalry had all passed by; some ambulances and a light wagon or two followed, and I was just crawling out from my hiding-place, bracing my resolution for a bold push toward the old Virginia shore, when the head of a column of light artillery appeared. Here was a go! I had seen some crossing of artillery at this ford before: easy enough going in, but the very old Tommy to get out. If it should chance to be a large battalion, at all commensurate with the force of cavalry which had preceded it, there was very great probability that they wouldn't get over till long after daylight, in which event, you will understand, it was likely to be quite interesting for me. Pass the decanter, if you please.

"Still I felt quite confident of getting out of the trap in some way, particularly since the moon now shed so feeble a light that I could venture to stand up and shake myself—a very primitive, Newfoundland mode of making the toilette, but quite refreshing and satisfactory under some circumstances. Well, just as I feared, the leading carriage stalled at the steep and slippery bank on the Virginia side. No use to hitch in more horses: only a certain number— not more than four—had room to pull to advantage. Hearing the word passed back for picks and shovels and axes, I knew well what was to be done: while some were grading the ascent, others would be set to work cutting branches to throw under the horses' feet. To leave the island at the lower end and attempt to make the Virginia shore by wading and swimming in the rapids among the big boulders below the ford, I felt would be sheer madness in my exhausted condition. I was so wrapped in thought, striving to strike out some plan of escape from the perils thickening around me, that I failed to notice two men who had left the column near the Maryland side and were riding down toward the island, till the foremost one was nearly upon me. I drew back farther behind the willows, crouched, watched, listened. Never dog with hydrophobia dreaded water more than I did then; but I slowly edged off toward my former hiding-place, ready to take another plunge if it should prove necessary. The leading man was plainly drunk in the first degree, and when the other joined him there was a pair of 'em. From their thick-tongued talk about wagons, chests and such matters, it seemed they belonged to the bomb-proof departments. There was a rattling of canteens; the first comer handed his companion a key which he swore 'was the one t' th' blue ch-chist, 'n' the d-dimijohn was the one in th' lef'-han' corner.' He enjoined upon him to 'fill both canteens ch-chunk-full, 'n' not to g-guzzle it 'fore he g-got back, neither'; meantime he (the speaker) would 'knock it off' there. While giving his directions he had managed to roll off the saddle and fasten his horse to the very limb which I had used for the same purpose. The other chap rode off toward the rear, declaring he 'wouldn't be gone more'n half an hour.' My man then staggered to the lower end of the island, worked himself out of his overcoat, bundled it up awkwardly for a pillow, and laid himself out to 'knock it off.' Here was my chance: I was saved!

Stealthily and slowly I grasped the handle of my trusty bowie-knife — the only friend I could depend on now, and the better for being a silent one, not given to noisy demonstrations — and drew him gently from the modest retirement and obscurity of my dexter boot-leg, where he had so long lain *perdu*, biding his time. Stand by me now, if ever, old 'Buck-Horn,' friend and mess-mate! Let but this one stroke be straight, sure and deadly, and never again shall thy glittering blade be condemned and degraded to the ignominious office of slicing mess-pork! A sword, a battle-axe, and perchance a razor shalt thou be all the days of thy — life I was going to say, but changed my mind and substituted existence, as being more correct."

"You did, did you?" here broke in Sammy G——, a pert young nephew of the Sergeant, who believed in "turning things around and looking at 'em both ways," as he said. Then I put in. "Sergeant," said I, "you should remember that you are not telling this story for publication in the *Scribbler's Scrap-Book*. Do you mean to assert that you really were going to murder that person in cold blood, and that you really did apostrophise your bowie-knife in those terrible, awe-inspiring words, or words to that effect?"

"Sir," said he, with dignity slightly marred by a manifestation of temper, "I don't wish to be criticised in this way. If I didn't use precisely those words, 'those words,' as you style them, would have admirably expressed my senti-ments, and would have been appropriate to the occasion. That should suffice. As to murdering people in cold blood, you should consider that I was about as cold and bloody as a man can well be, and laboring under heavy provocation besides; but if any of you gentlemen think you can tell the story, that is to say if you imagine that you can narrate the circumstances better than I can, why just push ahead and do it."

Here Sammy thought it high time for him to say something again, and he cried out: "That's all in my eye! Them calvary was Hampton's men, an' I heard Kurnel Toliver say 'at he ketched Uncle Tom [that's the Sergeant] on a island, and all wet, and give him a drink, *I* did!"

"O you be durned!" said the Sergeant, and immediately proposed a game of euchre.

During the first week of September 1862, Lee began moving Southern troops across the upper Potomac, while Thomas J. Jackson and James Longstreet were directed to converge on Harper's Ferry and thereby protect his supply line to the Shenandoah Valley. Before they returned, a copy of Lee's orders for his divided army was left behind and discovered by Union soldiers. With reason for confidence, George B. McClellan hastened Union troops to South Mountain passes, and Confederate forces were pushed toward the village of Sharpsburg. On September 17, after the Army of the Potomac took up positions along Antietam Creek and the Army of Northern Virginia was reunited, tens of thousands of soldiers would meet as they do in "On the Antietam" for what would be the bloodiest single day of the war, a day so horrific that even the birds would vanish until the following spring. For well-to-do sons like Drake Porter and tenement boys like Jack Middleton, who first meet bitterly in New York's back streets, the day would have a long foreground and yet take a peculiar turn.

◆◦◆

"ON THE ANTIETAM"

(*Harper's Weekly*, 3 January 1863)

"I'll make you sorry for that! The fighting's fair enough; but I'm no more a dog than you are, and you shall pay for it if it takes years to do it—see if you don't!"

It was Jack Middleton who yelled out this, as, bruised and bleeding, he reeled away from Drake Porter, who had let him up with some contemptuous remark about "soiling his hands," seconded by our insulting laughter, for boyish sense of justice is not keen, and I doubt if it ever occurred to any of us that any thing from the "back street" had feelings and passions like unto ourselves. Feud had long existed between what was known in boys' parlance as the "back-streeters" and "ours"; the "back-streeters" pouring forth from two or three wretched tenement buildings in our rear, and "ours" being represented by the children of the well-to-do row of houses between ——d and ——th Avenues in ——th Street.

Extremes met here indeed, but only with blows; the "back-streeters" evidently regarding overcoats and whole pairs of shoes as so many direct injuries, while we considered their very unkempt existence as an impertinence, and with sticks and fists and stones, at every corner, and in every alley, whenever and wherever we were unlucky enough to meet, fought our Society's old quarrel.

At such times Drake acted as our leader, fighting with an earnest fury that made all fly before him, unless I except Jack Middleton, the back-street leader, and opposite type of Porter; olive-skinned, black-eyed, squarely built, opposing steady, dogged resistance to Drake's *élan*, and undismayed by the fact of being whipped seven times out of nine, coming up to every battle with a cold perseverance that I never saw warmed to fury but on the occasion above quoted.

The threat, however, was but little regarded — hardly remembered, except as a jest; and soon after, being sent off to school, the back street and its brawls were fast being forgotten, when, oddly enough, Middleton turned up in our very midst — no longer as a New York Bedouin, but as the nephew of a wealthy South Carolinian, who had traced, found him out, and adopted him. Rid of his rags and his hang-dog manner, I have really never seen a finer-looking boy; and gradually sprung up between him and Drake a curious rivalry (the result, doubtless, of a nearly equal balance of faculties), developing itself in the lecture-room, the gymnasium, with the girls of the neighboring seminary, wherever they came in contact; and daily growing in bitterness till we were again separated, he going to a Southern university, and we living very much after the ordinary New York fashion, till the war broke out.

Nearly all the —— th Street boys were in our regiment — Spaulding, Elliott, Davis, and, best of all, Drake Porter, Captain of our Company, and on the high-road to a well-deserved promotion. It was the 17th of September, the day of the battle of Sharpsburg. Already Monday and a part of Tuesday we had spent facing the enemy, talking to them occasionally with our guns, and answered emphatically by their batteries. As usual, they had the chronic advantage of position, being stationed behind the crest of a hill, and separated from us by the Antietam, sweeping along at their base, and too deep to be forded except in one or two places. The country between was broken, mostly plowed land, sometimes covered with high, growing corn, and terribly cut up with ravines and passes; and, with their usual touching faith in "the strongest battalions," the rebels were assembled in force, having brought troops from Hagarstown and Harper's Ferry. We had crossed the creek about four o'clock, and after some tolerably sharp skirmishing had fairly carried and taken possession of the woods from whence they had first fired at us. So we were all in famous spirits, with the exception of Drake, who was curiously grave and silent. Before lying down for the night he gave me a little packet.

"There are letters for Belle and mother, a ring, and some other trifles. If any thing happens to me you will see to them."

To which I assented briefly enough, I fancy, being much too careful of my sleeping-time to waste any of it in talking. It was midnight already, and every few minutes there was an alarm of some sort: one time it was the rebels shooting each other—by way of practice, I suppose; at another it was picket-fighting; again they were bringing in half a dozen sulky Confederates; altogether it hardly seemed that we had slept half an hour when the battle began.

As the rebel fire slackened the first line went on to the woods with a cheer and a rush, only to be beaten back by the heaviest volleys with which they had favored us yet; and then out poured the rebels, swarming like bees, in masses, not in columns, flowing out over the field, and forcing back the second brigade by sheer superiority of numbers. We could see it all plainly enough; and let me tell you, reading lists of names and seeing the men with whom you have lived familiarly shot down before your eyes stirs the blood in a widely different way.

And it was with a "Thank God!" that we heard the signal to advance. Down the hill we went on a run, making straight for the corn-field. Half way there Spaulding fell; a little further on Elliott and Manvers. Manvers was Drake's cousin; Elliott was to have married my sister Jessie—but there was no time for mourning then. We were close upon the rebels, fighting hand to hand; and they fought us like tigers, and held to every inch of ground with a stubbornness unequaled. When we took our stand on the ridge they came at us again and again, with such a dash as seemed as if it must carry all before them. Our guns thundered away nobly on our right; but they had a battery that the archfiend himself couldn't have planted so as to rake us more effectually, while their sharp-shooters picked us off from the woods beyond very much at their ease. We saw nothing of the promised assistance, and our ammunition was giving out, and, tired of waiting, we began to go down into the corn; and just then Doubleday had stopped that confounded battery, and the rebels giving back as we pressed on after them into the woods, and with Crawford and Gordon coming close behind us, things looked like success.

All this time Drake fought steadily, and, as usual, in the hottest of the fire, but escaping, as by a miracle, unharmed. In our downward rush we had carried all before us, but we found the woods a perfect hornet's nest. The ——th, that had never faltered once, broke and fell back now; and Drake, fighting hand to hand, was separated and carried far on in advance of the rest, but being a good swordsman, managed before long to give his quietus to his opponent, who was in a little too much of a hurry. In the struggle they had insensibly gotten out of the thickest of the fight into comparative quiet and seclusion; and Drake, thankful for even a moment's breathing-time, was trying to wipe away some of the blood and grime from his face, when his quick ear caught an ominous click. He looked about, behind him, finally overhead, and there, showing among the leaves, a rifle-barrel glinted in the sun, and a pair of fiery eyes glowed above it. To start or run was simply almost inevitable death, and Drake, unwilling even to die in a hurry, folded his arms, saying, coolly,

"My friend, if you are so long in sighting you will be behindhand in your count."

"I have been longer in sighting than you think, perhaps, Captain Porter," was the reply, in a not unfamiliar voice, while a series of cautious movements showed from among the leaves a face at which Drake stared in utter perplexity and amazement. Suddenly light broke in upon him.

"Why, it is Jack Middleton!"

"Precisely! though your memory is not so good as mine. I recognized you on the instant, perhaps because I was so anxious to meet you."

"I have been fighting since daybreak, and don't feel too clear-headed. Do you think you could explain?"

"With pleasure. I could have killed you twice over, only that I was anxious to make this very explanation. I remember that at school you were always sharp-set after the reason of every thing. It would be a pity that you should die without knowing why."

Middleton dropped out these cruel words slowly, watching his victim's face the while for their effect, but no matter what thoughts of Belle and mother were trying at his heart-strings, he only answered,

"You are so tedious that I begin to think you have only a woman's reason, 'Because.'"

"You shall see. You remember that some years ago you called me a dog; that was the beginning of the debt I owe you. When we were at school you put it out at interest. You no longer called me a dog, but you treated me as one. You thought I would have been glad to crawl to your feet, and lick your hand, in return for your condescension. You would never let me alone. You would not be repulsed. I was not worth your disliking. At every step you crossed my path.

You took my honors, you stole the hearts that would have been mine. I kept account of all these items; and, do you remember Virginia Brush?"

"A little girl with yellow curls—splendid ones? Yes, I think I do."

Middleton made a hasty movement, as if to fire, but checked himself.

"Drake Porter, I loved that girl, and would have won her but for you. You crossed me there in sheer wantonness. You cared nothing for her; I would have given my soul for her. From that time I swore to have your life. I was sure at last of—"

His hand was on the trigger, waiting the completion of the sentence, his body bent in the very act of firing, and Porter was calculating the chances of a jump at the last moment, when whir! went something over his head, and Middleton fell crashing through the limbs to the ground dead, shot through the heart by a chance bullet, if it is not profane here to speak of chance.

Drake told me the story after, and—

"I tell you what, old fellow," he concluded, "it was about as peculiar a predicament as I ever caught myself in. There wasn't an atom of feeling in my body, except in the spot that the devil's rifle covered; and when that blessed bullet sent him heels over head, I think if there hadn't been a party of our boys close at hand I should have knelt down and made a baby of myself. On the whole, I am not anxious to try it again."

To which I answered, as in duty bound,

"I should think not."

The ghastly heaps of the Antietam dead kept McClellan from pressing for a decisive victory. His hesitation cost him his command, but Lincoln also seized the moment of Lee's thwarted invasion to announce the Emancipation Proclamation in preliminary form on September 22, 1862. Signed on January 1, 1863, the act liberated slaves selectively in rebelling states while enabling black enlistments in the Union cause. Although the border states of Maryland, Delaware, Kentucky, and Missouri were excluded along with some Union-controlled territory, the Emancipation Proclamation nonetheless meant that Lincoln's armies were now fighting for liberty as well as the Union and that Confederates risked social disintegration as well as defeat. "Emancipation," writes Phillip Shaw Paludan, "pushed whites to new definitions of what the nation stood for and of the type of people they were." As Charity Grimes reveals in her letter to the "edditer," opinion in the North was divided enough that autumn for friends to disagree and to go at each other with whatever was handy.

◆○◆

Charity Grimes

"A LETTER FROM THE COUNTRY"

(*Harper's Weekly*, 8 November 1862)

To the Edditer of Harper's Weekly:

DEAR MR. EDDITER— Sarah Blue is a woman, and I bein' a person ov the same secks, yu see it's nateral we shouldn't allways agree.

I call myself a thorrough administratrix—I go fur the administrashun, thet is, fur the present one. None ov yure sham demockracys fur me!

Sarah says the same; but, between yu and me, it ain't true. Sarah is a good administratrix jest as long as affares go on tu suit her, but jest the eyedentical minit things go against the grain, she's off on the other side like a roket.

But I don't wunder at her idees bein' sumwhat fuddled on pollytics, for her father was the gratest turn-coat yu ever did see. He was brot up a method-ist—then turned dimmycrat, and was made hog-reeve the same yeer, and evry one said that he intered inter pollytical life for the sake ov gittin' that office. Bimeby he jined the odd fellus (he was odd enuff then, in all konshunce!), and putty soon arter that he gut married and dyed his whiskers, fur which latter offense he was expelled frum the methodists, on the charge ov pervurtin' the Scripture, which says, thou canst not make one hair white or black. Then he bort a small farm (he was a blacksmith before), and settled daown near us, and has voted reggerlarly on the dimmycratic ticket ever sense, but twise—once in Harrison's time, and agin Taylor's; and ef aour State elecshun had come befour Pennsilvany, so he'd a known old Abe was baound tu win, he'd have voted for him.

Sense the war broke aout he's jined the Quakers, and every time he hears ov a draft bein' spoken of he quakes like a piece o' crab-apple jelly when yu fust turn it ker slap aout of the mold.

Naow there's one thing where Sarah is as like her father as two peas. She is fond ov pollytics. She reeds the New York *Herald* reggerlarly, so's tu be on all sides tu once; and don't hardly touch a novel, except the hisstorical novels in the Sunday papers. She don't reed menny works of fickshun, except ockashun-ally storys rit by the reliable correspondents of some of the newspapers. She nevver plays whist, becawse her father was a methodist; but she cheets awful in old maid and slap-jack, and sumtimes tells fokeses fortunes with the kards. But they don't many of 'em cum true. Tho' once she told Sam Jennings thet he would be choked tu death sum day eeting flap-jacks; and sure enuff, one nite, jest after supper, when his mouth was full of cakes and molasses, he slipped daown the sellar stares and broke his neck. They had a corrowner's jury on the boddy, and the verdick was he died from flap-jacks, as he had so menny in his maouth thet it removed the senter of gravety, and made him top-heavy, which cawsed him tu fall daown seller.

Wa'al, as I was goin' tu remarc, the larst conversashun I had with Sarah was abaout pollytics.

I was doin' aour ioning—we don't keep no hired gurl, and I du the work mostly—when in rushed Sarah Blue, as mad as a march hair, and sot rite daown on my pile ov hankerchefs, thet I'd put on the settle bench after ioning of 'em till they was as slick as a whistle.

"Charity! What *du* you think?" says she, as pail as a gost.

"Why, for the land's sake, what's the matter?" says I.

"Matter enuff!" she ansered, looking the very picture of skorn. "Old Abe Lincon has made a nu proclamashun!"

"Wa'al naow," says I, "I'm glad on't!—is it good?"

Yu see I didn't know exackly what it was—I didn't know but it was sum nu kind of cake he'd maid. Yu know we hev Washingtun Cake, and 'Lecshun Cake, and why shuldn't we hev Lincun Cake? Haowever, I didn't tell Sarah what I thort it was, and I was glad I didn't arterwards.

"Good! there ain't no good tu it," she replyed; "don't yu think he's gorne and told all the niggers tu cut sticks and run from there marsters as farst as thay kan; and he is trying tu aggeravate aour Suthern brethren [thet's what she kalls the rebels], and I'm afrade they wun't like it!"

"LINCOLN'S LAST WARNING"

"Du tell!" said I.

"Oh Abe, *dear* Abe!" says she, agoin' rite daown on her nees tu the picture of the present ockupent ov the White Haouse, "du evry thing else but that! Kill the Saouth with yure bagonets, run 'em thro' with sords, shute 'em with pistuls, and knock 'em over with the cannon's rore, but spare, oh! spare thare pockets! Skin 'em alive, but don't tutch their niggars!"

"Don't yu mind a wurd she says!" cried I, impashuntly. "She don't know what she's a saying! Go it, Farther Abraham, and I'll sustane yu!"

"Grimes and liberty!" "Glory halleuyah!"

Don't yu think, Mister Edditer, that kritter gut so mad, she up and took one of my own flat ions and kum at me like a wild-cat!

I immejitly seesed hold of the tongs, and twe fit thare in the kitchen till her face looked as if she'd hed the small-pox, and mine was puffed up as 'tis when I hev the tooth-ake, and all my kleen close that I'd ioned hed tu be put inter the wash agin.

I hev'nt bin aout ov the haouse sence.

But I had my reevenge, fur I rit a poim—a sarkastical poim, ov coarse—abaout the abolishun ov nigger slavery, and sent it tu Sarah Blue, and sined it Trooth, so she'd know who rit it. She hasn't spunk anuff tu anser it, tho'. Here it is, deer reeder:

POIM.

Abram, spair the Saouth!
Tutch not a single nigger;
They'll bee daown in the maouth
Ef yu cut such a figgar!
'Twas England's forstring hand
The niggers here that brot;
Here Abram, let 'em stand!
Yure acks shall harm 'em not.

When but a pickaninny
They're wuth a lot ov tin;
Naow, good as gold frum Ginny,
A fust-rate price they'd win.
The Saouth wants mony orful,
And fites us, tooth and nale;
But oh! kan it be lorful
Tu give thare niggs leg-bail?

Who fired rite on aour flag—
Dragged freemen tu thare graves?
Who luv tu boast and brag
Thet we shall bee thare slaves?
Who cum upon aour track,
And scatter ruin threugh it?
And ef we kan strike back,
For pity's sake, let's *du it!*

Yes! By our martyred dead,
We'll follow Abram's plan;
On tu thare soil we'll tread,
And hit 'em whare we kan!

CHARITY GRIMES

[We shall be glad to hear from Mrs. GRIMES again. —*Ed. Harper's Weekly*]

136

In the "Saoth" as 1862 waned, enlistments had become as acute a problem as the fate of the slaves. When bounties and furloughs did not entice enough one-year volunteers to return to their regiments, the Confederate Congress instituted the first draft in American history, with the provision that volunteers could join a new regiment, as those enlisting in the infantry or the artillery or the cavalry had the year before. Unquestionably, the battlefield still belonged to foot soldiers; the Civil War was, in the words of James Robertson, "from first to last an infantryman's contest." But there was honor in artillery service and prestige in riding with the cavalry, especially in the war's earlier years, before trenches and breastworks had curtailed mounted charges. For a one-time lawyer like T. J. McSnorter, the ring of spurs and sabers is almost as enchanting as the routine dazzle of words and the gathering crowd on a mountain street.

◆○◆

Confederate Gray

"T. J.'S CAVALRY CHARGE"

(*New Eclectic Monthly*, April 1870)

It was on a bright morning in the Fall of 1862, that a man clad in a soiled and tattered suit of Confederate gray might have been seen astride a fiery, though somewhat jaded steed, on the principal street of a straggling village situated in the mountains of Western North Carolina. He was surrounded by a dozen hardy mountaineers on foot, who were listening with intense interest to what he was saying. Our hero was one Timothy J. McSnorter, known in all that region of country as "T. J." His hearers were his old companions in many a well-contested game of "Seven Up," many a drunken carousal, and many a vigorous "stag-dance."

T. J. was an "original" character. Previously to the war, an extra quantity of "brass," a rude kind of eloquence, a stentorian voice, and certain peculiarities of oratorical style, had won for him among his unsophisticated neighbors and acquaintances the reputation of a "powerful" lawyer. He was a first-class "ranter" and an accomplished demagogue. He knew that a majority of men, at least in his section, were wont to measure the mental ability of an orator by the strength of his lungs and the length of his speeches, and he pushed his advantages in these respects to the uttermost limit. He belonged to what may be styled the stripping class of public speakers. He invariably began his harangues by taking off his coat, tossing it disdainfully from him, and rolling up the sleeves of his shirt. These movements were always accompanied by a peculiar look and toss of the head that seemed to say, "Now I have a big job on hand, so look out for lightning, thunder, and a respectable earthquake!" As he warmed with his subject, his vest would follow his coat, then his neck-tie, then his shirt-collar would follow his neck-tie, then his shirt-bosom would be unbuttoned and thrown open with a sort of spasmodic jerk; and it is said that on one occasion his shirt followed the articles of clothing already named, so that his peroration found him divested of everything except his trousers and boots.

Tall, raw-boned, angular, and cadaverous, with eyes large, white, and turning almost over in their sockets, a mouth so wide that it seemed as if it had been made by a transverse blow with the edge of a hatchet, his cheek bulged with a quid of mountain "cut and dried" as large as a hen's egg, a voice as harsh as the cry of a hungry raven and so loud as to have silenced from very shame the bellowing of the biggest bull of Bashan, T. J. now presented an object of side-splitting interest, as with unkempt hair, slouched hat, and an old fashioned horse-pistol at his left side, and his left knee resting on the pommel of his saddle, he thus let off to his gaping admirers the pent-up eloquence of eighteen months: —

"Gentlemen, you have asked where I have been and where I am going. I have been to the tented field, where banners wave, where sabres gleam, where bayonets shimmer, where muskets rattle and where cannons peal! I need not remind you that I once thought the Bar the fittest place for the display of the remarkable talents with which my Creator, in His unerring wisdom, was pleased to endow me. And I was 'some' at the Bar; yes, a 'whole team,' with the tar-bucket hung on the coupling-pole and a big 'yaller' dog under the wagon. Bill Simmons, you know I was, for who saved you from the damning infamy of the whipping-post? You know it too, Tom Snickers, for had it not been for my profound legal acquirements and Demosthenean eloquence, you would be, at this very hour, with cropped hair and zebra pants, making yourself useful in the public jail and penitentiary of the State, Sir! And you, Dave Wilkins, cannot be ignorant on this subject, for it was my legal acumen and my pathetic appeals to the sympathies of a brainless jury composed of such sap-headed men as you, Sam Jones, and you, John Smith, that sent Dave forth, not as a convicted felon to the scaffold, where he ought to have gone, but to the enjoyment of a worthless existence and an unappreciated liberty, Sir!"

Each of the gentlemen thus courteously appealed to bowed acquiescence as he was individually addressed, and when T. J. finished they all bowed together.

"Yes," he continued, "that's so, Gentlemen; but, as I was about to remark, there was reserved for me a still more appropriate and exalted sphere of action.

That sphere is the theatre of war—war, the noblest of sciences—war, the mightiest and the grandest of all the games of chance—war, a game in which steel-panoplied battalions are the cards, and empires the stakes, Sir! Yes, Gentlemen, war is T. J.'s natural element, Sir!

"At first I joined the infantry, and a grand arm of the service it is too. Hoosiers, like you, reared in these mountain gorges, have no conception of the part played by infantry during an engagement. Well, I will tell you how the thing works, Sir! First, a line of crack shots is thrown to the front to feel the enemy and to gain time for the formation of the grand line of battle. These men are called skirmishers. When they see the enemy they begin to pop at them at 'long taw,' but, by-and-by they are forced back by superior numbers, and then the main column begins to play its part. It is not 'pop, pop, pop,' as it was with the skirmishers, but at first the united fire of a company here and there, then of a regiment; and then, all of a sudden, a deafening roar from battalions, regiments, brigades, divisions, and whole corps, rends the air, Sir! Soon comes the thrilling order, 'Charge bayonets!' and then, with death playing on ten thousand slanting points of steel, the mighty enginery emerges from its curtain of smoke and flame, and sweeps onward to grapple in fearful embrace with the eager and on-rushing foe, Sir!

"Gentlemen, the infantry service is glorious, yes, glorious, Sir! But it has its drawbacks, Sir, its drawbacks! Tired going through the mud from daylight until dark, and often far into night; weighted down with knapsack and musket and cartridge-box; sometimes double-quicking for miles, sometimes standing still for hours in the drenching rain or driving snow, bespattered with mud by the dashing cavalry, and always expected to do the hardest fighting, I found that the infantry did not suit T. J., no, not by a long sight, and I quit it, and joined the artillery, Sir!

"Artillery means cannon, Gentlemen! Do you want to know what a cannon is, Sir? A cannon is a big gun, Sir; so big that it has to be pulled by horses, Sir! And it shoots a ball as big as Dave Wilkins's sugar kettle; and so far that you can't get away from it; and it cracks louder than all the rifles and shotguns in this county put together would; and it tears a hole big enough for a three-year-old bear to crawl into. That's what it is, Sir; that's what it is!

"Infantry is a grand arm of the service, Gentlemen, but it won't compare with the artillery. Boom! boom! boom! and then, from an hundred brazen, belching throats, comes a simultaneous crash, shaking earth and heaven, and rolling through the firmament like the voice of doom through the caverns of the damned! And such execution! The solid shot tear through the forests like a tornado; the shell shriek through the air like distracted fiends; grape and canister mow down companies and regiments as a first-class McCormick's Reaper

lays wheat in a harvest field; while with each discharge the grim monsters leap high in air, as if exulting in their capacity for the destruction of our race! Ah, the artillery is indeed sublime! But I soon got tired of it. It is very convenient and comfortable to ride along on a caisson while on a march; but in action there is too much hard work lifting those heavy guns, and just a little too much danger for T. J. I tell you, Gentlemen, a battery with the concentrated fire of three or four of the enemy's batteries upon it, is not the healthiest place in the world, Sir! So I concluded to quit the artillery and join the cavalry.

"You may talk about infantry and about artillery, but after all the cavalry is just the thing for a man of spirit like T. J. It is after the infantry and artillery have broken and shattered the columns of the enemy, that the cavalry arm of the service is brought into play. First, you hear a rumbling sound as of an earthquake rapidly approaching. Clear the track, it is a cavalry charge! Here they come, column upon column, horses and riders; a thousand spurs pressed to a thousand quivering flanks; a thousand streaming plumes on a thousand helmeted heads; a thousand sabres raised in air! The very horses seem infused with the spirit of their riders. With fiery eyes, expanded nostrils, and every nerve and muscle in full play, they thunder down upon the affrighted, dying, shrieking foe, while pistol-shot and sabre-stroke are doing their work of carnage and of death!

"But, Gentlemen, why try to describe that which, in itself, is indescribable? I will show you how the thing is done!"

So, fixing his feet firmly in his stirrups, T. J. rode proudly down the street some two hundred yards. Here he halted, about faced, and drew his pistol. By this time, every man, woman, and child in the village, attracted by the well-known voice, had collected on the sidewalk. Straightening himself up, grasping the reins with his left hand, and inclining his body forward at an angle of about forty-five degrees, T. J. drove his spurs into the flanks of his horse. The animal responded to the touch of the steel, and up street they came, the sparks flying from the heels of the steed at every maddening bound. Having passed over about half the distance, T. J. suddenly levelled his pistol directly to the front, and as he shouted "Fire!" pulled trigger, and in an instant horse and rider rolled in the dust. The horse, shot directly through the back of his head, gave one groan and was dead.

As T. J. slowly gathered himself up, he cast a rueful glance at his horse; then with "*There now, won't Betsy give me particular fits!*" he slowly hobbled to the sidewalk.

Reader, if you wish to avoid a personal difficulty, never say a single word to T. J. about his grand cavalry charge. He now swears that the cavalry is a humbug — "an unmitigated humbug, Sir!"

1863

Women raised more than flatirons during the years of the war. Elizabeth Leonard estimates that between 500 and 1,000 women enlisted as men and fought as soldiers before the war ended, including some 250 that DeAnne Blanton has discovered in the Confederate armies. Although their service is often difficult to trace, it is likely that some were stationed across Virginia and up along the Potomac to the north, where Union troops patroled the river fords. Particularly after John Singleton Mosby organized a company of partisan rangers in January 1863, guerrilla warfare increased north of Washington so markedly that communications were threatened, army detachments were harassed, and loaded supply wagons were in constant danger of attack. Among the hills of northern Virginia and neighboring Maryland, Mosby's squads were venturesome and ruthless, a plaguing worry for Union companies like Captain Charley's that were sent out to reconnoiter.

◆○◆

"COLONEL CHARLEY'S WIFE"

(*Harper's Weekly*, 8 October 1864)

"Yes, they *are* a splendid pair! There's no discount on that. There ain't a braver man in the Army of the Potomac than Colonel Charley; and as for 'Mother Jane,' as the boys call her (because you see she's *like* a mother to us although she's only a chick in age compared to some of us), *she* deserves a fighting man for a husband, for she's just the gamest woman that ever *I* see. Tell you what, if you fellows had seen what she done one day when she pulled a party of us Forty-ninth boys out of the tightest place ever *I* was in (and that's saying something, too), you'd take your oath that she'd *ought* to be a soldier's wife."

Sergeant Blake was convoying a squad of new recruits for the Forty-ninth. They had got within the lines of the Army of the Potomac, and were making their last halt before joining the regiment at Falmouth. The Sergeant had just been greeted warmly by a noble-looking officer, who rode up while they were boiling their coffee, accompanied by a handsome woman with a pleasant brown face and short, thick, black curls, which made a glossy fringe for a bewitching little jockey-hat, whose jaunty scarlet feather, held in place by a silver eagle, gave her a military air charmingly in keeping with the martial surroundings. The lady had also greeted the Sergeant with great cordiality, while the officer, whose shoulder-straps marked him as a Colonel, addressed a hearty "Glad to see you, my lads!" to the admiring squad.

"Sergeant," said one of the men, as the subjects of the former's eulogy cantered off, the lady sitting her spirited bay mare with the greatest ease and grace, "would you mind telling us the story?"

"Well, I don't care if I do. It'll show you fellows what *you* may have to come to some day yourselves; and it'll teach you the value of keeping a stiff upper lip when you are hard pushed." And, as the Sergeant took up an easy position against the trunk of a huge pine-tree, the men lit their pipes and gathered around him to hear his story.

"Well, you see, Colonel Charley was only a Captain then; that day's work sewed a Major's straps upon his shoulders. Little Williams ('Matches,' the boys used to call him, because his legs looked like a couple o' lucifers), who was appointed Major because he was first cousin or something to somebody that had *influence*, although he didn't know a ramrod from a cartridge-box when he joined, got a hint shortly after the circumstances I am going to tell you about that he had better resign, and Captain Charley got the place, and then the Lieutenant-Colonel took sick and resigned, and when poor Clark got his finish at Chancellorsville Captain Charley got to be Colonel. But he was only a Captain then, as I told ye.

"You see, the Captain had been ordered to take two companies of the old Forty-ninth and make a reconnaissance down the railroad (I didn't tell you that we were guarding one of the Potomac fords); for it was said that a gang of Mosby's men had been seen in the neighborhood, and it was thought they were trying to cut the road. We scouted for about six miles down without seeing a sign of a grayback, and had about made up our minds it was a false alarm. About three o'clock in the afternoon we turned and started for camp. We had just halted to rest a bit at a spring that ran out of the side-hill, where the railroad makes a deep cut through a long, narrow ledge, when we heard half a dozen shots in our rear, followed by a loud yell, and then Gus Lynch, one of our fellows who had lagged a little behind, came kiting 'round the point of the hill as if the old boy had kicked him. Gus sung out as he came up, 'Look out boys, Mosby is after us full chisel!'

"We had barely time to obey Captain Charley's order to fix bayonets and form when the first of the ragamuffins hove in sight around the curve. There were about three hundred of 'em in all; and mean, dirty, sheep-stealin' looking rascals they were. They didn't charge on us right away, as we expected, but pulled up when they got in sight, probably not knowing how strong we were.

"Now in numbers they greatly overmatched us, for we had only about forty muskets all told. But we had much the best of them in our position. If we had expected them we couldn't have picked out a stronger place to make a stiff fight. Captain Charley saw this at a glance. It was, of course, impossible for us to retreat, for they, being mounted, could have ridden us down in a minute. But we could hold the cut easy enough.

"You see the cut was narrow — just wide enough for the track — and as luck would have it there was a pretty deep drain-way running across the line between us and the rebs, which was uncovered, and about fifteen feet over. It was easy enough to cross it on the trussels, but it was a stumper for a horse. Our rear was open, but we knew well enough that they couldn't get at us there without dismounting or riding several miles around, for the side of the ledge they were on was like a wall almost. But it was an ugly trap, after all; for if they couldn't get *in,* we couldn't get *out;* and if they could hold us there until night it would be pretty easy for them to swarm up the bank and pop us over from the top, while we couldn't get a sight at them at all. But we stood and made ready for 'em, and made up our minds to trust in Providence, and to charge them five graybacks for every blue-jacket they knocked over.

"And let me tell you, boys," said the Sergeant, knocking the ashes out of his pipe, "that this trust in Providence that the dominies tell about is no humbug, as you'll find out when you get under fire. A soldier may get kind of reckless and devil-may-care sometimes, from often looking death in the eye and escaping; but you may be sure that few men go in where the bullets fly, and the shells howl like blood-thirsty devils, and their comrades are struck down right and left, without feeling that they are in the hands of a merciful God. I tell you, comrades, there are no truer prayers spoken than those which go out from soldiers' hearts, though you may not see a movement of the close-shut lips along the lines of battle."

The Sergeant here paused to fill and light his pipe, while a solemn look fell upon the rough faces around him, and more than one emphatic "That's so!" and "Three for you!" went up from the veterans of the circle.

"Well," resumed the Sergeant, "as I was saying, Mosby's men had a bad job before 'em; worse, a good deal, than they were aware of. It was a good half-hour before they undertook to disturb us, although a couple of the dirty critters *did* ride toward the mouth of the cut as if to reconnoitre; but a shot or two sent them to the right-about in quick time. It was policy in us not to waste any powder, for we only had ten rounds apiece, so, although we might have picked off some of 'em as they stood, we just held our fire and kept our eyes peeled.

"By-and-by we could see that they were getting ready for a charge; so it was certain they didn't know any thing of the gully in the road, as it would have been madness to have charged with that in front of 'em. They came on first at a slow trot in single file, which was the best they could do, on account of the narrow track. Captain Charley had, before this, picked out ten of his best shots, boys that could take the spark out of a squirrel's eye at a hundred yards. This detail he now moved to the front, and on the further side of the gully. As they stood close the rebs couldn't see the ditch. Then says the Cap, 'Men, count from right to left, *one, two, three,* and so on.' They counted up to *ten.* 'Now when these fellows yonder get on the curve they will be out of line, and I want every one of you to cover his man. Number *one* take the first, number *two* the second, and so on; and when I give the word pelt the scoundrels.' So there our fellows stood, ten men to stop three hundred.

"Well, when they got within about three hundred yards of us they set up one of their devilish yells, and came on at hot jump. They thought they could stampede us; but we belonged to the Army of the Potomac," said the Sergeant, with a gleam of pride in his honest gray eye.

"As soon as they got well strung out around the curve Captain Charley sung out, 'Fire!' and those ten pieces cracked pretty much together, and, as I'm a living sinner, six of the Johnnies were tumbled off their horses dead, and two more were badly hurt. *That* charge was done for. They brought up all standing, and were in a panic in no time, turning tail without stopping to pick up their killed.

"We hoped this would put a finish to their operations; but it seems they were determined to have one more crack at us; and this time they showed us a trick that I never saw before, although I've read of something like it in accounts of Injun fights. It was a pretty 'cute dodge, and if it hadn't been for the ditch in front of us it would have fetched us, sure pop. They came on in the same way as they did before, but, just as they got fairly on the wind around the turn, we heard their officer sing out some order, and quick as a flash down went every man's head and the best part of his body behind his horse, so that they were pretty well covered by the necks of the animals. The thing was done so sudden and unexpected that it threw our fellows off their sight; and, although two or three horses were badly hurt, not a man, so far as we could judge, was hit.

"Of course there was no time to pick out another detail. The men had been formed four front, and the orders were to fire at the word, the front rank to fire and kneel, the second rank the same, and so on. Captain Charley kept the men in front of the ditch as long as it was safe, and then gave them the order to fall back, the ranks opening to let them pass to the rear. They all came off safe but one, Reuben Banks, who was shot dead by the rebel Captain. Well, of course as soon as our fellows jumped back the rebs saw the ditch, and the foremost of 'em pulled up sharp with a loud yell. But those in the rear came tearing on, and in a second the cut was jammed full of plunging horses and cursing men — and *such* cursing I never heard before nor since. It seemed to make the very air thick and blue. Now was our chance, and the way we pelted 'em with cold lead was a caution. 'Twasn't five minutes before the whole pack was running like hounds. Our fellows gave three rousing cheers as they went off; and felt good just then for any number of graybacks Mosby could send along.

"We now thought, most of us, that we had whipped them off for good and all, and wondered why Captain Charley didn't give us the order to fall in and march to camp, for we were by this time about used up and as hungry as wolves. But he was wiser than we were. He knew very well that they had got their *mad* up, and that they would hang on to us now for revenge. The moment we marched out of that cut we were doomed; our only safety was in the gully, and we must by all means cover that with our pieces.

"But it was certain that *something* must be done and very quickly. Our camp was only three miles off by the road. Some of us were sure that our firing must have been heard, and would bring out a rescue party; but Captain Charley thought that most likely the sound being pent up in the cut would prevent its reaching any distance, and the result proved that he was right. A man might be sent round by the road, and it was probable he could slip off without being seen by the Johnnies. But the best he could do he couldn't get to camp and a party get out to us in less than two hours, and it was now five o'clock. By seven it would be dark, and our flints would be fixed. Captain Charley was familiar with the ground, for he had often scouted over it, and he knew that a short cut along the crest of the ridge would carry a man to our lines in half an hour. The mischief of it was that a fellow couldn't get away without the rebs sighting him, and he would have to run for it sure, and trust to luck and his legs for his life. It was a risky thing for any man to attempt, but Cap determined to try it on. He first sent off a man by the road to take advantage of the chances of help coming in time that way; and then, says he to the boys, 'Men,' says he, 'I want a volunteer to go to camp along the top of that ridge. It'll be a dangerous job; for the man that does it will have to dodge bullets and to race with some of those rascals yonder: afoot though, for they can't ride up yon bank, and it'll be a pretty long start. If he gets off safe this command is saved, and if I can get him made a lieutenant I pledge my word to do it!'

"Now, boys, there were just as brave fellows in that party as ever bit a cartridge, and yet for a minute there wasn't a foot budged. I tell you what, it's one thing to face death in company with other good men—*the touch of the elbow* is a wonderful thing to brace a man's heart—but when you are asked to cut loose from your comrades and make a target of yourself for you don't know how many bullets, it's no use talking; not many men *would* jump to do it. You'll read a good deal in the newspapers about 'gallant actions' and 'daring deeds' of individuals; but I tell you, boys—and it's no disgrace in an old soldier like me to own it—life is just as precious to a soldier as to any man, and he is no more eager to expose himself in cool blood to the danger of death than if he had never smelt gunpowder. I've seen things done *in action* that you would talk about as long as you live; but in a fight I hold that a man isn't himself. There is a kind of intoxication in the smell of burnt powder, the banging of the guns, the shout and tumult around, and, more than all else, a sense of *power* that comes over a man in the mere handling and sighting of that cold, hard, bright thing that can *kill*—that carry men on to do great things in spite almost of themselves.

"But I must get on with my story. As I was a saying, at first not a man budged; but just as we all began to feel so cruelly ashamed of ourselves that, I think, in another minute we should have been ready to fight for the honor of going, out steps a young fellow belonging to Company H, and said he was ready to go.

"This lad was called Mark Wilson. He was a slim, good-looking chap, who had never been considered of much account in the regiment. The truth was that the boys suspected that he considered himself too genteel to be a soldier. Camp is a poor place to put on airs or play gentility, and Mark wasn't popular in his company. But he rather seemed to like to be avoided, and was in the habit of keeping to himself as much as possible, and never joining in the sports of the boys. We all noticed that he never got any letters nor wrote any; never spoke of home or friends; in fact, didn't seem to have any, or any body to care for him. Sometimes the boys would be curious, and try to pump him; but they never got any satisfaction; and once or twice, when they pressed him pretty hard, he actually burst out crying. The theory about him was that he was some rich man's son who had run away from home, and was too proud to let his folks know where he was.

"Well, when Mark stepped out, I suppose at least a score of vets jumped to the front and wanted to go; but, to every body's surprise, Mark wouldn't back down. He insisted that, as he was first to volunteer, it was his *right* to go. The Cap says to him: 'Well, Mark, you're a plucky boy, and you certainly shall go if you wish it; but it seems to me you had better let me pick out a stronger and tougher man.' But the little chap wouldn't yield. He said, 'No, Captain. If I am killed I have nobody to grieve for me; and I suppose I am the only one in the regiment who hasn't got *some* friend.' The poor little fellow looked as if he was going to cry, and some of *us* felt like crying too.

" 'Well, Mark,' said Captain Charley, 'go you shall; but you mustn't say you haven't got any friends. A brave boy like you will make friends every where, and if we come out of this safe you shall never want a friend as long as Charley Heming is alive.'

"There was a tree growing out of the side of the cut just a little ways back, and its top reached above the top of the bank. Captain Charley gave Mark a few directions, and handed him his revolver, and told him to be off as quick as he could. We all of us stared to see Mark, as the Captain put out his hand to shake hands, seize it, and press it to his heart, and kiss it, turning as red at the same time as a ripe strawberry. Then the little fellow ran to the tree, climbed it like a monkey, and jumped off on to the bank. Captain Charley, after a couple of minutes, couldn't keep quiet any longer, so he shinned up the tree too to take observations. 'They haven't seen him yet,' he sung out to us below. 'Ah! there come three of the scoundrels up the bank, and put after him. By George! the boy runs like a deer. He has got a fine start too; but one of the graybacked villains has got the longest legs, and gains on him. There, the leading man halts and fires his carbine. Curse it, he's hit; he's down. No, he only tripped, or fell on purpose. He's up and off again. But Long Legs is coming to close quarters. Ha! Mark wheels and gives Mr. Reb a barrel of his revolver; another. By Jove, he has tumbled him! And he don't get up. I guess he's done for, thank God! The other two have come up and stopped.' The Captain now said nothing for another minute, and then he flung down his cap with a yell of delight, which was answered right heartily by us fellows below, for we knew before he said it that Mark had got off safe. The two graybacks didn't chase him any further, and soon returned to their command carrying the dead man with them.

"Well, the rebs stuck to us as long as they dared; but about six o'clock a rattle of musketry and a Union cheer told us that our men had come up and taken the rascals in the rear. There was a round or two, and then the cavalry skedaddled in every direction. Several were killed and wounded, and about forty taken prisoners. We got back to camp in high spirits about eight o'clock.

"And now, boys, I come to the most curious part of the story. As soon as we got in Captain Charley was told that Mark was in the hospital badly wounded. He had really been hit when the Captain saw him fall, the ball breaking his left arm badly; but the plucky chap had kept right on, although he fainted dead away the minute he had given Captain Charley's message to the Colonel. And when they came to dress his arm they found that they had a *woman* on their hands!"

"Sho!" "You don't say so!" "Holy Mother!" "Sho!" "Bully gal!" A chorus of ejaculations of astonishment arose from the many-blooded group as the Sergeant came to this *dénouement*.

"Yes, a woman; and, what's more, dead in love with Captain Charley. You see I heard the rest of the story from Jake Downing, who was nursing in the hospital at the time. It seems that when she came to, and saw she was found out, she cried fit to break any one's heart, and begged them not to expose her, and, above all, not to tell Captain Heming. They comforted the poor thing as well as they could, and promised to keep her secret for her. Before we got in she was delirious from the pain and excitement. It was while she was out of her head this way that they found out that she thought so much of the Captain. When he came in the surgeon thought best under all the circumstances to give him a hint of how matters stood, and he had the girl taken to a private house in the neighborhood, and nursed until she got well. It came out that she was the daughter of a farmer in Erie County, New York, and had a step-mother who was a perfect she-devil. Jane—for that was her name—and a brother, a little younger than herself, led the life of niggers. Finally, the boy ran away, enlisted, and was shot at Pea Ridge. The girl then had nobody left to care for, but she stood her step-mother's bad treatment as long as she could, until one night the old termagant beat her like a dog for what she called her 'impudence,' and actually shut her up in an outhouse, and kept her there all night. The next night Jane dressed herself in a suit of her brother's clothes, cut off her hair, and slipping out of the house, ran away. How she got into the Forty-ninth I never heard, but I know she *did* serve with us two years, and we never suspected her. Well, the upshot was that when Captain Charley found the plucky little girl had taken a fancy to him, and no blame to her—you saw him a bit ago—and when he found, too, that she was, when her natural self, a right pretty girl, and a *good* girl, too, it was natural enough that he should fall in love with *her*, and he did. I tell you, boys, we had a bully time when they got married, which they did in camp as soon as Jane got about again. We fixed up a bower of ever-greens, and made it gay with flags; then we took the drums of the regimental corps, and built up an altar for the chaplain; and every body said they never saw a handsomer couple than our chaplain tied that day. Old General H—— gave away the bride, and he gave her a buss when it was over that the boys swore was like the crack of a 6-pounder rifle. Then we had the brigade band for music, and the jolliest spread and dance that ever you saw. We had lots of ladies down from Washington, and several officers' wives and daughters, and our Jane was just as much of a lady as any of 'em.

"That was the Colonel and his wife you saw a bit ago. They've got a nice place near Alexandria, and it's a regular soldiers' hotel. No fellow in the Union blue ever passes there without being hailed to stop in; and if one of the Forty-ninth gets astray in that neighborhood his own mother couldn't use him better than does Mother Jane. She can't keep away from camp long, though; and her boy, the pet of the regiment, has learned to sleep under fire. The boys would rather see her pretty face than the paymaster's any day. Fall in! March!"

"THE BATTLE OF GETTYSBURG — LONGSTREET'S ATTACK"

In the larger Eastern theater, Union fortunes were taking a turn for the worse. After Ambrose Burnside replaced McClellan in November 1862, he led the Army of the Potomac the following month on an ill-planned attack of Fredericksburg that left thousands of bluecoats dead at the foot of Marye's Heights and put Union forces no closer to taking Richmond. When Joseph Hooker assumed command in January, he reorganized the army, only to see Lee triumph again in early May at nearby Chancellorsville, where Hooker was knocked unconscious by a cannonball and ultimately retreated in nighttime rain. Before he resigned in June, Hooker did follow Lee northward toward Pennsylvania, but the Union forces that engaged the Army of Northern Virginia at Gettysburg looked to George Gordon Meade as the commander to halt the July invasion. He would have help. Pennsylvanian John Reynolds saw the wisdom of claiming the high ground of Cemetery Ridge before he was picked off by a sharpshooter on the battle's first day. Winfield Scott Hancock, also from Pennsylvania, made the ridge line blue and held on. By the afternoon of the third day, when Connecticut volunteers in "The Fourteenth at Gettysburg" look down from the heights, Confederate guns would be opening a major artillery barrage to clear the way for the panoply of frontal assault. As Carol Reardon has noted, "Union veterans of many firefights in the wooded Virginia countryside seldom had seen so many soldiers at any one time as they now saw marching across that open field." What the 14th Connecticut would see advancing in the afternoon sun were the gathering brigades and battle flags of Pickett's famous charge.

◆◇◆

"THE FOURTEENTH AT GETTYSBURG"*

(*Harper's Weekly*, 21 November 1863)

"Come, Fred, tell me all about that glorious fight which, you know, it was just my ill-luck to miss. If it had been such another whipping as we had at Fredericksburg, the Fates would probably have let me be there. I have heard several

---

*REBEL BATTLE-FLAGS CAPTURED. First Tennessee, captured by the Fourteenth Connecticut Volunteers at Gettysburg, July 3, 1863. Fourteenth Tennessee, captured by the Fourteenth Connecticut Volunteers at Gettysburg, July 3, 1863. Sixteenth North Carolina Regiment, captured by the Fourteenth Connecticut Volunteers at Gettysburg, July 3, 1863. Battle-flag, State not given, captured by the Fourteenth Connecticut Volunteers at Gettysburg, July 3. Battle-flag, State not given, captured by the Fourteenth Connecticut Volunteers.

accounts, and know the regiment did nobly; but the boys all get so excited telling about it that I have not yet a clear idea of the fight."

"Here goes, then," said the Adjutant, lighting a fresh cigar. "It will serve to pass away time, which hangs so heavy on our hands in this dreary hospital.

"We were not engaged on the first day of the fight, July 1, 1863, but were on the march for Gettysburg that day. All the afternoon we heard the cannonading growing more and more distinct as we approached the town, and as we came on the field at night learned that the First and Eleventh corps had fought hard, suffered much, and been driven back outside the town with the loss of Major-General Reynolds, who, it was generally said, brought on an engagement too hastily with Lee's whole army. We bivouacked on the field that night.

"About nine o'clock the next morning we moved up to the front, and by ten o'clock the enemy's shells were falling around us. Captain Coit had a narrow escape here. We had just stacked arms and were resting, when a runaway horse, frightened by the shelling, came full tilt at him; 'twas 'heavy cavalry' against 'light infantry'; but Coit had presence of mind enough to draw his sword, and bringing it to a point it entered the animal's belly. The shock knocked Coit over, and he was picked up senseless with a terribly battered face, and carried to the rear."

"By-the-way, Fred, is it not singular that he should have recovered so quickly and completely from such a severe blow?"

"Indeed it is. He is as handsome as ever; but to go on. At four o'clock in the afternoon we moved up to support a battery, and here we lay all night. About dark Captain Broatch went out with the pickets. Though under artillery fire all day we were not really engaged, as we did not fire a gun. Some of our pickets, unfortunately going too far to the front, were taken prisoners during the night.

"At about five o'clock on the morning of the 3d Captain Townsend went out with companies B and D and relieved Broatch. As soon as he got out Townsend advanced his men as skirmishers some three hundred yards beyond the regiment, which moved up to the impromptu rifle-pits, which were formed partially by a stone-wall and partially by a rail fence. Just as soon as our skirmishers were posted they began firing at the rebel skirmishers, and kept it up all day, until the grand attack in the afternoon. Before they had been out twenty minutes, Corporal Huxham, of Company B, was instantly killed by a rebel bullet. It was not discovered until another of our skirmishers, getting out of ammunition, went up to him, saying, 'Sam, let me have some cartridges?' Receiving no answer, he stooped down and discovered that a bullet had entered the poor fellow's mouth and gone out at the back of his head, killing the brave, Chancellorsville-scarred, corporal so quickly that he never knew what hurt him. Presently Captain Moore was ordered down with four companies into a lot near by, to drive the rebel sharp-shooters out of a house and barn from whence they were constantly picking off our men. Moore went down on a double-quick, and, as usual, ahead of his men; he was first man in the barn, and as he entered the Butternuts were already jumping out. Moore and his men soon cleared the barn and then started for the house. Here that big sergeant in Company J (Norton) sprang in at the front door just in time to catch a bullet in his thigh, from a reb watching at the back; but that reb did not live long to brag of it, one of our boys taking him 'on the wing.' Moore soon cleared the house out and went back with his men. Later in the day the rebs again occupied the house, and Major Ellis took the regiment and drove them out, burning the house, so as not to be bothered by any more concealed sharp-shooters in it."

"Yes, I know the Major don't like to do a thing but once, so he always does it thoroughly the first time."

"It was in these charges for the possession of that house we lost more officers and men than in all the rest of the fight.

"About one o'clock in the afternoon the enemy, who had been silent so long that the boys were cooking coffee, smoking, sleeping, etc., suddenly opened all their batteries of reserve artillery upon the position held by our corps (the Second). First one great gun spoke, then, as if it had been the signal for the commencement of an artillery conversation, the whole hundred and twenty or more opened their mouths at once and poured out their thunder. A perfect storm of shot and shell rained around and among us. The boys quickly jumped to their rifles and lay down behind the wall and rail barricade. For two hours this storm of shot and shell continued, and seemed to increase in fury. Good God! I never heard any thing like it, and our regiment has been under fire 'somewhat,' as you know. The ground trembled like an aspen leaf; the air was full of small fragments of lead and iron from the shells. Then the sounds — there was the peculiar *'whoo? — whoo? — whoo-oo?'* of the round shot; the *'which-one?'* — *'which-one?'* of that fiendish Whitworth projectile, and the demoniac shriek of shells. It seemed as if all the devils in hell were holding high carnival. But, strange as it may seem, it was like many other 'sensation doings,' 'great cry and little wool,' as our regiment, and, in fact, the whole corps lost very few men by it, the missiles passing over beyond our position, save the Whitworth projectiles which did not quite reach us, as their single gun of that description was two miles off. Had the enemy had better artillerists at their guns, or a better view of our position, I can not say what would have been the final result; but certain it is, nothing mortal could have stood that fire long, had it been better directed, and if our corps had broken that day, Gettysburg would have been a lost battle, and General Lee, instead of Heintzelman, the commanding officer in this District of Columbia to-day.

"About three P.M. the enemy's fire slackened, died away, and the smoke lifted to disclose a corps of the rebel 'Grand Army of Northern Virginia,' advancing across the long level plain in our front, in three magnificent lines of battle, with the troops massed in close column by division on both flanks. How splendidly they looked! Our skirmishers, who had staid at their posts through all, gave them volley after volley as they came on, until Captain Townsend was ordered to bring his men in, which he did in admirable order; his men, loading and firing all the way, came in steadily and coolly — all that were left of them, for a good half of them were killed or wounded before they reached the regiment.

"On, on came the rebels, with colors flying and bayonets gleaming in the sunlight, keeping their lines as straight as if on parade: over fences and ditches they come, but still their lines never break, and still they come. For a moment all is hush along our lines, as we gaze in silent admiration at these brave rebs; then our division commander, 'Aleck Hayes,' rides up, and, pointing to the last fence the enemy must cross before reaching us, says, 'Don't fire till they get to that fence; then let 'em have it.'

"On, on, come the rebs, till we can see the whites of their eyes, and hear their officers command, 'Steady, boys, steady!' They reach the fence, some hundred yards in front of us, when suddenly the command 'Fire!' rings down our line; and, rising as one man, the rifles of the old Second Army Corps ring a death-knell for many a brave heart, in butternut dress, worthy of a better cause — a knell that will ring in the hearts of many mothers, sisters, and wives, on many a plantation in the once fair and sunny South, where there will be weeping and wailing for the soldier who never returns, who sleeps at Gettysburg. 'Load and fire at will!' Oh Heaven! how we poured our fire into them then — a merciless hail of lead! Their first line wavers, breaks, and runs; some of their color ser-geants halt and plant their standards firmly in the ground: they are too well disciplined to leave their colors yet. But they stop only for a moment; then fall back, colors and all. They fall back, but rally, and dress on the other lines, under a tremendous fire from our advancing rifles: rally, and come on again to meet their death. Line after line of rebels come up, deliver their fire, one volley, and they are mown down like the grass of the field. They fall back, form, and come up again, with their battle-flags still waving; but again they are driven back.

"On our right is a break in the line, where a battery has been in position, but, falling short of ammunition, and unable to move it off under such a heavy fire, the gunners have abandoned it to its fate. Some of the rebels gain a footing here. One daring fellow leaps upon the gun, and waves his rebel flag. In an instant a right oblique fire from 'ours,' and a left oblique from the regiment on the left of the position, rolls the ragged rebel and rebel rag in the dust, rolls the determined force back from the gun, and it is ours.

"By-and-by the enemy's lines come up smaller and thinner, break quicker, and are longer in forming. Our boys are wild with excitement, and grow reckless. Lieutenant John Tibbetts stands up yelling like mad, 'Give it to 'em! give it to 'em!' A bullet enters his arm — that same arm in which he caught two bullets at Antietam: Johnny's game arm drops by his side; he turns quickly to his First Lieutenant, saying, 'I have got another bullet in the same old arm, but I don't care a d——n!' Heaven forgive Johnny! rebel lead will sometimes bring rebel words with it. All of 'ours' are carried away with excitement; the Sergeant-Major leaps a wall, dashes down among the rebs, and brings back a battle-flag; others follow our Sergeant-Major; and before the enemy's repulse becomes a rout we of the Fourteenth have six of their battle-flags.

"Prisoners are brought in by hundreds, officers and men. We pay no attention to them, being too busy sending our leaden messengers after the now flying hosts. One of our prisoners, a rebel officer, turns to me, saying, 'Where are the men we've been fighting?' 'Here,' I answer, pointing down our short thin line. 'Good God!' says he, 'is that all? I wish I could get back.' "

"Yes," I interrupted, "Townsend told me that when he fell back with his skirmishers and saw the whole length of our one small, thin, little line pitted against those then full lines of the rebels, his heart almost sank within him; but Meade had planned that battle well, and every one of our soldiers told."

"Yes," said Fred, "Meade planned the fight well, and Hancock, Hayes, and in fact all of them fought it well. All through the fight General Hancock might be seen galloping up and down the lines of our bully corps, regardless of the leaden hail all about him; and when finally severely wounded in the hip he was carried a little to the rear, where he lay on his stretcher and still gave his orders.

"The fight was now about over; there was only an occasional shot exchanged between the retreating rebel sharp-shooters and our own men, and I looked about me and took an account of stock. We had lost about seventy killed and wounded and taken prisoner, leaving only a hundred men fit for duty. We had killed treble that number, and taken nearly a brigade of prisoners; six stands of colors, and guns, swords, and pistols without number. For the first time we had been through an action without having an officer killed or fatally wounded, though Tibbetts, Seymour, Stoughton, Snagg, Seward, and Dudley were more or less seriously wounded, and Coit disabled.

"Hardly a man in the regiment had over two or three cartridges left. Dead and wounded rebels were piled up in heaps in front of us, especially in front of Companies A and B, where Sharpe's rifles had done effective work.

"It was a great victory. 'Fredericksburg on the other leg,' as the boys said. The rebel prisoners told us their leaders assured them that they would only meet the Pennsylvania militia; but when they saw that d——d ace of clubs (the trefoil badge of the Second Corps), a cry went through their lines—'the Army of the Potomac, by Heaven!'

"So ended the battle of Gettysburg, and the sun sank to rest that night on a battle-field that had proved that the Army of the Potomac could and would save the people of the North from invasion whenever and wherever they may be assailed.

> 'Long shall the tale be told,
> Yea, when our babes are old.'"

"Pshaw, Fred! you are getting sentimental. Let's go out in the air and have another cigar."

There was less hearty sparring in Confederate camps as the battle of Gettysburg unfolded. There had been signs of imminent glory: not only were Lee's victories accumulating, but Southern success elsewhere in the East had been noteworthy. In the late spring of 1862, Jackson had ridden his modest force of seventeen thousand up and down Virginia's Shenandoah Valley to best one Union general after another, while he collected the military and medical supplies that would give his cavalry and Southern troops a continuing edge. When Jackson died at Chancellorsville, his place as Lee's nimble arm was taken by James Ewell Brown Stuart, whose restless and far-flung reconnaissance was already a matter of legend. In June, Longstreet advanced his corps to plunder the Pennsylvania countryside as Virginia had been plundered and, in July, George Pickett arrived late at Gettysburg to make a name for himself at last. The fame he won and the battle they lost would be the war's turning point in more ways than one: not only was Gettysburg the high tide of Lee's Northern invasions, but his fate in Pennsylvania meant that hundreds of army wagons filled with the wounded would have to make their awkward way south in heavy rain. Those unequipped wagons, what John Billings called "heavy, lumbering affairs at best," would be entrusted to John D. Imboden, whose "Lee at Gettysburg" describes their tortured progress toward the Maryland hills as well as Lee's despondent care.

◆◦◆

J. D. Imboden

"LEE AT GETTYSBURG"

(*Galaxy*, April 1871)

The recent death of the commander of the Confederate armies, General Lee; the uncertainty which exists in the public mind of the South whether he had prepared since the war any record of his military operations to supply the loss in the burning of Richmond of so many of the official papers of the Confederacy; and the desire that all fair-minded men feel, that the materials for a true and complete history of the great conflict in all its details shall be collected and preserved for the use of the future dispassionate and impartial historian of the war, are sufficient reasons, it seems to me, for the publication of the following incidents of General Lee's invasion of Pennsylvania in the summer of 1863, and of his retreat from Gettysburg.

For convenience of narration, and to give authenticity to the facts stated, I write under my own signature, and as an eye-witness of all that is related.

This, I am aware, exposes me to the charge of egotism and a desire for notoriety, apparently strengthened by confining myself to the narrow field of operations in which I was an humble actor. But so many others, far more competent than myself, have furnished the reading world with a comprehensive history of the general movements of the contending armies that culminated at Gettysburg — *the* decisive battle of the war — that for me at this late day to undertake a repetition of what has been so often and so well done would indeed appear a vainglorious task. I therefore prefer confining myself to a simple statement of hitherto unpublished facts that came under my personal observation, as a modest contribution to the annals of the period; some of them of little importance in themselves, but forming a part of the history of the great event that probably decided the fate of the country.

To understand properly how I came to occupy the important position assigned me by General Lee in his retreat from Gettysburg, and which gave me the opportunity of seeing and hearing what I am about to narrate, it is necessary to state that during the whole of the preceding winter and spring I had a somewhat independent and mixed command of infantry, artillery, and cavalry, which I had raised and organized in my native mountains of Virginia, after "Stonewall" Jackson's famous campaign in 1862 in the Shenandoah Valley, in which, with less than 15,000 men, he in about thirty days encountered and defeated successively Generals Milroy, Banks, Fremont, and Shields, and, having relieved the valley of their presence, moved to the Chickahominy to assist in the operations against General McClellan.

In May, 1863, with the mountaineers I had enlisted and organized during the nine preceding months, strengthened by some temporary reinforcements, amounting altogether to about 3,300 men, I was ordered by General Lee on an expedition through the northwestern counties beyond the Alleghanies, to break up the military posts at Beverly, Buckhannon, Philippi, Weston, Bulltown, Sutton, Big Birch, and Summersville, and, if possible, with the coöperation of Generals William E. Jones and Samuel Jones, to destroy the Baltimore and Ohio Railroad in the mountains, and then drive the Federals out of the Kanawha Valley. This raid occupied thirty-seven days, and was in the main successful. Within a week after our return to the vicinity of Staunton in the Shenandoah Valley, I received a long confidential letter from General Lee, informing me of his purpose to cross the Blue Ridge from the Rapidan into the valley, to capture Winchester, and cross the Potomac; and directing me to move independently and at once through the mountains against Cumberland, Maryland, to break up the small posts along the Baltimore and Ohio Railroad, and destroy all the bridges eastward as far as Martinsburg, communicating to him as often as practicable my progress. This order was rapidly executed, and by the time we had destroyed the bridges, depots, and canal-boats, and cut the canal between Cumberland and Martinsburg, General Lee had driven Milroy out of Winchester and was crossing the Potomac. He again confidentially advised me of his contemplated movements, and ordered me to go into Pennsylvania as far as I deemed it prudent, west of the North Mountain, and to keep an eye upon Milroy, who was reported to be collecting his scattered troops at Bloody Run. This duty took us as far as McConnellsburg, where we crossed the mountains eastward to Mercersburg. There, on the night of the 30th of June, we were ordered to Chambersburg to relieve General Pickett's division, which held the place. Arriving about 4 P.M. on the 1st of July, General Pickett at once moved off to join the army, then near Gettysburg.

That night I received a brief note from General Lee, expressing the apprehension that we were in some danger of being cut off from communication with him by the Union cavalry, and directing us to move next morning as far as the South Mountain on the road toward Gettysburg, and keep it open for Generals William E. Jones and Beverly Robertson, whose brigades of cavalry were in the direction of Shippensburg. About midnight of the 2d, after a good deal of harassment from detachments of the hostile cavalry, we gained the top of the mountain, east of the Hon. Thad. Stevens's iron works, then in ruins. Before daybreak on the 3d Robertson and Jones passed us, and about sunrise we followed them. I belonged to no division or corps in our army, and therefore on arriving near Gettysburg about noon, when the conflict was raging in all its fury, I reported directly to General Lee for orders, and was assigned a position to aid in repelling any cavalry demonstration that might occur on his flanks or rear. None being made, my little force took no part in the battle. I then had only about 2,100 effective mounted men and a six-gun battery.

When night closed upon the grand scene our army was repulsed. Silence and gloom pervaded our camps. We knew that the day had gone against us, but the extent of the disaster was not known except in high quarters. The carnage of the day was reported to have been frightful, but our army was not in retreat, and we all surmised that with to-morrow's dawn would come a renewal of the struggle; and we knew that if such was the case those who had not been in the fight would have their full share in the honors and the dangers of the next day. All felt and appreciated the momentous consequences of final defeat or victory on that great field. These considerations made that, to us, one of those solemn and awful nights that every one who fought through our long war sometimes experienced before a great battle.

Few camp fires enlivened the scene. It was a warm summer's night, and the weary soldiers were lying in groups on the luxuriant grass of the meadows we occupied, discussing the events of the day or watching that their horses

"THE HARVEST OF DEATH — GETTYSBURG, JULY 4, 1863"

did not straggle off in browsing around. About eleven o'clock a horseman approached and delivered a message from General Lee, that he wished to see me immediately. I mounted at once, and, accompanied by Lieutenant McPhail of my staff, and guided by the courier, rode about two miles toward Gettysburg, where half a dozen small tents on the roadside were pointed out as General Lee's headquarters for the night. He was not there, but I was informed that I would find him with General A. P. Hill half a mile further on. On reaching the place indicated, a flickering, solitary candle, visible through the open front of a common tent, showed where Generals Lee and Hill were seated on camp stools, with a county map spread upon their knees, and engaged in a low and earnest conversation. They ceased speaking as I approached, and after the ordinary salutations General Lee directed me to go to his headquarters and wait for him. He did not return until about one o'clock, when he came riding alone at a slow walk and evidently wrapped in profound thought.

There was not even a sentinel on duty, and no one of his staff was about. The moon was high in the heavens, shedding a flood of soft silvery light, almost as bright as day, upon the scene. When he approached and saw us, he spoke, reined up his horse, and essayed to dismount. The effort to do so betrayed so much physical exhaustion that I stepped forward to assist him, but before I reached him he had alighted. He threw his arm across his saddle to rest himself, and fixing his eyes upon the ground leaned in silence upon his equally weary horse; the two forming a striking group, as motionless as a statue. The moon shone full upon his massive features, and revealed an expression of sadness I had never seen upon that fine countenance before, in any of the vicissitudes of the war through which he had passed. I waited for him to speak until the silence became painful and embarrassing, when to break it, and change the current of his thoughts, I remarked in a sympathetic tone, and in allusion to his great fatigue:

"General, this has been a hard day on you."

This attracted his attention. He looked up and replied mournfully:

"Yes, it has been a sad, sad day to us," and immediately relapsed into his thoughtful mood and attitude. Being unwilling again to intrude upon his reflections, I said no more. After a minute or two he suddenly straightened up to his full height, and turning to me with more animation, energy, and excitement of manner than I had ever seen in him before, he addressed me in a voice tremulous with emotion, and said:

"General, I never saw troops behave more magnificently than Pickett's division of Virginians did to-day in their grand charge upon the enemy. And if they had been supported, as they were to have been — but, for some reason not yet fully explained to me, they were not — we would have held the position they so gloriously won at such a fearful loss of noble lives, and the day would have been ours."

After a moment he added in a tone almost of agony:

"Too bad! *Too bad!!* OH! TOO BAD!!!"

I never shall forget, as long as I live, his language, and his manner, and his appearance and expression of mental suffering. Altogether it was a scene that a historical painter might well immortalize had one been fortunately present to witness it.

In a little while he called up a servant from his sleep to take his horse; spoke mournfully, by name, of several of his friends who had fallen during the day; and when a candle had been lighted invited me alone into his tent, where, as soon as we were seated, he remarked:

"We must return to Virginia. As many of our poor wounded as possible must be taken home. I have sent for you because your men are fresh, to guard the trains back to Virginia. The duty will be arduous, responsible, and dangerous, for I am afraid you will be harassed by the enemy's cavalry. I can spare you as much artillery as you require, but no other troops, as I shall need all I have to return to the Potomac by a different route from yours. All the transportation and all the care of the wounded will be intrusted to you. You will recross the mountain by the Chambersburg road, and then proceed to Williamsport by any route you deem best, without halting. There rest and feed your animals, then ford the river, and make no halt till you reach Winchester, where I will again communicate with you."

After a good deal of conversation he sent for his chiefs of staff and ordered them to have everything in readiness for me to take command the next morning, remarking to me that the general instructions he had given would be sent to me next day in writing. As I was about leaving to return to my camp, he came out of his tent and said to me in a low tone: "I will place in your hands to-morrow a sealed package for President Davis, which you will retain in your own possession till you are across the Potomac, when you will detail a trusty commissioned officer to take it to Richmond with all possible despatch, and deliver it immediately to the President. I impress it upon you that whatever happens this package must not fall into the hands of the enemy. If you should unfortunately be captured, destroy it."

On the morning of the 4th my written instructions and the package for Mr. Davis were delivered to me. It was soon apparent that the wagons and ambulances and the wounded could not be ready to move till late in the afternoon. The General sent me four four-gun field batteries, which with my own gave me twenty-two guns to defend the trains.

Shortly after noon the very windows of heaven seemed to have been opened. Rain fell in dashing torrents, and in a little while the whole face of the earth was covered with water. The meadows became small lakes; raging streams ran across the road in every depression of the ground; wagons, ambulances, and artillery carriages filled the roads and fields in all directions. The storm increased in fury every moment. Canvas was no protection against it, and the poor wounded, lying upon the hard, naked boards of the wagon-bodies, were drenched by the cold rain. Horses and mules were blinded and maddened by the storm, and became almost unmanageable. The roar of the winds and waters made it almost impossible to communicate orders. Night was rapidly approaching, and there was danger that in the darkness the "confusion" would become "worse confounded." About four P.M. the head of the column was put in motion and began the ascent of the mountain. After dark I set out to gain the advance. The train was seventeen miles long when drawn out on the road. I was moving rapidly, and from every wagon issued wails of agony. For four hours I galloped along, passing to the front, and heard more — it was too dark to see — of the horrors of war than I had witnessed from the battle of Bull Run up to that day. In the wagons were men wounded and mutilated in every conceivable way. Some had their legs shattered by a shell or Minié ball; some were shot through their bodies; others had arms torn to shreds, some had received a ball in the face, or a jagged piece of shell had lacerated their heads. Scarcely one in a hundred had received adequate surgical aid. Many had been without food for thirty-six hours. The irragged, bloody, and dirty clothes, all clotted and hardened with blood, were rasping the tender, inflamed lips of their gaping wounds. Very few of the wagons had even straw in them, and all were without springs. The road was rough and rocky. The jolting was enough to have killed sound, strong men. From nearly every wagon, as the horses trotted on, such cries and shrieks as these greeted the ear:

"O God! why can't I die?"

"My God! will no one have mercy and kill me and end my misery?"

"Oh! stop one minute and take me out and leave me to die on the road-side."

"I am dying! I am dying! My poor wife, my dear children! what will become of you?"

Some were praying; others were uttering the most fearful oaths and execrations that despair could wring from them in their agony. Occasionally a wagon would be passed from which only low, deep moans and sobs could be heard. No help could be rendered to any of the sufferers. On, on; we *must* move on. The storm continued and the darkness was fearful. There was no time even to fill a canteen with water for a dying man; for, except the drivers and the guards disposed in compact bodies every half mile, all were wounded and helpless in that vast train of misery. The night was awful, and yet in it was our safety, for no enemy would dare attack us when he could not distinguish friend from foe. We knew that when day broke upon us we would be harassed by bands of cavalry hanging on our flanks. Therefore our aim was to go as far as possible under cover of the night, and so we kept on. It was my sad lot to pass the whole distance from the rear to the head of the column, and no language can convey an idea of the horrors of that most horrible of all nights of our long and bloody war.

Daybreak on the morning of the 5th found the head of our column at Greencastle, twelve or fifteen miles from the Potomac at Williamsport, our point of crossing. Here our apprehended troubles from the Union cavalry began. From the fields and cross-roads they attacked us in small bodies, striking the column where there were few or no guards, and creating great confusion.

To add still further to our perplexities, a report was brought that the Federals in large force held Williamsport. This fortunately proved untrue. After a great deal of harassing and desultory fighting along the road, nearly the whole immense train reached Williamsport a little after the middle of the day. The town was taken possession of; all the churches, school-houses, etc., were converted into hospitals, and proving insufficient, many of the private houses were occupied. Straw was obtained on the neighboring farms; the wounded were removed from the wagons and housed; the citizens were all put to cooking and the army surgeons to dressing wounds. The dead were selected from the train—for many had perished on the way—and were decently buried. All this had to be done because the tremendous rains had raised the river more than ten feet above the fording stage, and we could not possibly cross.

Our situation was frightful. We had over 10,000 animals and all the wagons of General Lee's army under our charge, and all the wounded that could be brought from Gettysburg. Our supply of provisions consisted of a few wagon loads of flour and a small lot of cattle. My effective force was only about 2,100 men and twenty-odd field pieces. We did not know where our army was; the river could not be crossed; and small parties of cavalry were still hovering around. The means of ferriage consisted of two small boats and a small wire rope stretched across the river, which owing to the force of the swollen current broke several times during the day. To reduce the space to be defended as much as possible, all the wagons and animals were parked close together on the river bank.

Believing that an attack would soon be made upon us, I ordered the wagoners to be mustered, and, taking three out of every four, organized them into companies, and armed them with the weapons of the wounded men found in the train. By this means I added to my effective force about five hundred men. Slightly wounded officers promptly volunteered their services to command these improvised soldiers; and many of our quartermasters and commissaries did the same thing. We were not seriously molested on the 5th; but next morning about nine o'clock information reached me that a large body of cavalry from Frederick, Maryland, was rapidly advancing to attack us. As we could not retreat further, it was at once frankly made known to the troops that unless we could repel the threatened attack we should all become prisoners, and that the loss of his whole transportation would probably ruin General Lee; for it could not be replaced for many months, if at all, in the then exhausted condition of the Confederate States. So far from repressing the ardor of the troops, this frank announcement of our peril inspired all with the utmost enthusiasm. Men and officers alike, forgetting the sufferings of the past few days, proclaimed their determination to drive back the attacking force or perish in the attempt. All told, we were less than 3,000 men. The advancing force we knew to be more than double ours, consisting, as we had ascertained, of five regular and eight volunteer regiments of cavalry, with eighteen guns, all under the command of Generals Buford and Kilpatrick. We had no works of any kind; the country was open and almost level, and there was no advantage of position we could occupy. It must necessarily be a square stand-up fight, face to face. We had twenty-two field guns of various calibre, and one Whitworth. These were disposed in batteries, in semicircle, about one mile out of the village, on the summit of a very slight rising ground that lies back of the town. Except the artillery, our troops were held out of view of the assailants, and ready to be moved promptly to any menaced point along the whole line of nearly two miles in extent. Knowing that nothing could save us but a bold "bluff" game, orders had been given to the artillery as soon as the advancing forces came within range to open fire along the whole line, and keep it up with the utmost rapidity. A little after one o'clock they appeared on two roads in our front, and our batteries opened. They soon had their guns in position, and a very lively artillery fight began. We fired with great rapidity, and in less than an hour two of our batteries reported that their ammunition was exhausted. This would have been fatal to us but for the opportune arrival at the critical moment of an ammunition train from Winchester. The wagons were ferried across to our side as soon as possible, and driven on the field in a gallop to supply the silent guns. Not having men to occupy half our line, they were moved up in order of battle, first to one battery, then withdrawn and double-quicked to another, but out of view of our assailants till they could be shown at some other point on our line. By this manoeuvring we made the impression that we had a strong supporting force in rear of all our guns along the entire front. To test this, Generals Buford and Kilpatrick dismounted five regiments and advanced them on foot on our right. We concentrated there all the men we had, wagoners and all, and thus, with the aid of the united fire of all our guns directed at the advancing line, we drove it back, and rushed forward two of our batteries four or five hundred yards further to the front. This boldness prevented another charge, and the fight was continued till near sunset with the artillery. About that time General Fitzhugh Lee sent a message from toward Greencastle, that if we could hold out an hour he would reinforce us with 3,000 men. This intelligence elicited a loud and long-continued cheer along our whole line, which was heard and understood by our adversaries, as we learned from prisoners taken. A few minutes later General J. E. B. Stuart, advancing from Hagerstown, fell unexpectedly upon the rear of their right wing, and in ten minutes they were in rapid retreat by their left flank in the direction of Boonsborough. Night coming on enabled them to escape.

By extraordinary good fortune we had thus saved all of General Lee's trains. A bold charge at any time before sunset would have broken our feeble lines, and we should all have fallen an easy prey to the Federals. This came to be known as "the wagoners' fight" in our army, from the fact that so many of them were armed and did such gallant service in repelling the attack made on our right by the dismounted regiments.

Our defeat that day would have been an irreparable blow to General Lee, in the loss of all his transportation. Every man engaged knew this, and probably in no fight of the war was there a more determined spirit shown than by this handful of cooped-up troops. The next day our army from Gettysburg arrived, and the country is familiar with the manner in which it escaped across the Potomac on the night of the 9th.

It may be interesting to repeat one or two facts to show the peril in which we were until the river could be bridged. About 4,000 prisoners taken at Gettysburg were ferried across the river by the morning of the 9th, and I was ordered to guard them to Staunton. Before we had proceeded two miles I received a note from General Lee to report to him in person immediately. I rode to the river, was ferried over, and galloped out toward Hagerstown. As I proceeded I became satisfied that a serious demonstration was making along our front, from the heavy artillery fire extending for a long distance along the line. I overtook General Lee riding to the front near Hagerstown. He immediately reined up, and remarked that he believed I was familiar with all the fords of the Potomac above Williamsport, and the roads approaching them. I replied that I knew them perfectly. He then called up some one of his staff to write down my answers to his questions, and required me to name all fords as high up as Cumberland, and describe minutely their character, and the roads and surrounding country on both sides of the river, and directed me to send my brother, Colonel Imboden, to him to act as a guide with his regiment, if he should be compelled to retreat higher up the river to cross it. His situation was then very precarious. When about parting from him to recross the river and move on with the prisoners, he told me they would probably be rescued before I reached Winchester, my guard was so small, and he expected a force of cavalry would cross at Harper's Ferry to cut us off; and he could not spare to me any additional troops, as he might be hard pressed before he got over the river, which was still very much swollen by the rains. Referring to the high water, he laughingly inquired, "Does it ever quit raining about here? If so, I should like to see a clear day."

These incidents go to show how near Gettysburg came to ending the war in 1863. If we had been successful in that battle, the probabilities are that Baltimore and Washington would at once have fallen into our hands; and at that time there was so large a "peace party" in the North, that the Federal Government would have found it difficult, if not impossible, to carry on the war. General Lee's opinion was that we lost the battle because Pickett was not supported, "as he was to have been." On the other hand, if Generals Buford and Kilpatrick had captured the ten thousand animals and all the transportation of Lee's army at Williamsport, it would have been an irreparable loss, and would probably have led to the fall of Richmond in the autumn of 1863. On such small circumstances do the affairs of nations sometimes turn.

The dirt had hardly fallen on the bodies left at Gettysburg when violence broke out in the streets of New York. On Saturday, July 11, 1863, names were drawn to meet district quotas for the national draft that Congress had enacted in March, a Union effort to fill diminished ranks that had previously depended on volunteer state regiments and local recruiting. All men between twenty and thirty-five were eligible for the drawing, as were all unmarried men up to ten years older. Few whose names were called actually served: some disappeared, some were excused because of their health or family obligations, and some paid substitutes $300 to go in their place, a practice that by fall would encourage higher enlistments when such commutation fees became federal bounties. But during July, the tenement laborers who could not pay rose up against the black workers they feared and the white upper classes they despised. "The draft riots," notes Iver Bernstein, "encompassed both neighborhood and workplace, and were in a sense both mob action and strike." For several days rioters would attack draft offices, Protestant churches, the premises of Horace Greeley's Republican Tribune, *the homes of abolitionists, and the Colored Orphan Asylum. New York's draft riots were the country's worst urban clash, and they would leave over a hundred people dead. During those feverish days in July, many more would lock their doors in vain against the war in the streets, as two New England women visiting family in "Three Days of Terror" would find out.*

•◦•

Ellen D. Larned (Ellen Leonard)

"THREE DAYS OF TERROR"

(*Harper's Monthly,* January 1867)

On the tenth of July, 1863, my mother and myself arrived in the city of New York. We had set out on a grand tour of visitation. After vegetating year after year in a New England village, we had sallied forth in genuine country fashion to hunt up our kinsfolk in various parts of the land. We were in no hurry. We had the whole summer before us. We wished to avoid crowds, noise, and excitement, to stop whenever we pleased, as long as we chose, and have a slow, old-fashioned, sociable, sensible journey. Thus far our tranquil visions had been more than realized. For three weeks we had been loitering placidly along our way, and nothing had occurred to mar our tranquility. We hoped now to spend a few days quietly with my brother J., call on various friends and relatives, visit Central Park and a lion or so, shop a little, and move onward at our leisure.

But man proposes and Fate *disposes*, and nothing in New York turned out as we expected. Instead of visiting our friends and meandering leisurely about the city, we were caught in a mob and penned up in our first stopping-place. From the first moment of our arrival every thing went wrong. J. did not meet us at the boat as he had promised, and we had to find our way without him in a drizzling rain. The streets were dark, dirty, and crowded with ill-looking people. The whole city was enveloped in fog and gloom. The home regiments had gone to drive the rebels from Pennsylvania, and many hearts were trembling. The household which received us had its full share of anxiety. Its youngest member, a youth of seventeen, had gone with the volunteers, and other friends were in the Army of the Potomac. The disappointing brother, too, was employed on a sad mission, helping a friend to Gettysburg to find the body of a slain brother; so that within doors we found it as dismal as without, and our first impressions of the great city were any thing but cheering.

Our prospect was limited to two rows of brick-houses and a broad expanse of house-roofs from our room in the upper story. "Nobody was in town," but the streets were jammed with carts and children, and the noise and clatter were incessant and deafening. The weather continued most oppressive. Low, dingy clouds possessed the sky, and not a breath of fresh air was attainable. I thought New York a most detestable summer residence, and resolved to leave it as soon as possible.

On the third morning of our sojourn, however, the sky brightened. The sun attempted to shine, and the papers brought good tidings. Lee was retreating, Meade pursuing, the Potomac rising, and our spirits rose with it. At breakfast Central Park was moved and carried by acclamation; but soon some pattering rain-drops brought out an opposition, which induced us to defer our jaunt till settled weather. So we scattered in various directions — J. down town, and I to Broadway. But even there I could see nothing attractive. Every thing looked hot, glaring, and artificial, and every body looked shabby, jaded, and care-worn. An overworked horse dropped dead in the street before me, and I was glad to take refuge for a time in the Astor Library.

Returning thence at mid-day I first saw signs of disturbance. A squad of policemen passed before me into Third Avenue, clerks were looking eagerly from the doors, and men whispering in knots all up and down the street; but I was too much a stranger to be certain that these appearances were unusual, though they annoyed me so much that I crossed at once to Second Avenue, along which I pursued my way peacefully, and once at home thought no more of it. We were indulging ourselves in siestas after our noonday lunch, when a great roaring suddenly burst upon our ears — a howling as of thousands of wild Indians let loose at once; and before we could look out or collect our thoughts at all the cry arose from every quarter, "The mob! the mob!" "The Irish have risen to resist the draft!"

In a second my head was out the window, and I saw it with my own eyes. We were on a cross-street between First and Second avenues. First Avenue was crowded as far as we could see it with thousands of infuriated creatures, yelling, screaming, and swearing in the most frantic manner; while crowds of women, equally ferocious, were leaning from every door and window, swinging aprons and handkerchiefs, and cheering and urging them onward. The rush and roar grew every moment more terrific. Up came fresh hordes faster and more furious; bareheaded men, with red, swollen faces, brandishing sticks and clubs, or carrying heavy poles and beams; and boys, women, and children hurrying on and joining with them in this mad chase up the avenue like a company of raging fiends. In the hurry and tumult it was impossible to distinguish individuals, but all seemed possessed alike with savage hate and fury. The most dreadful rumors flew through the street, and we heard from various sources the events of the morning. The draft had been resisted, buildings burned, twenty policemen killed, and the remainder utterly routed and discomfited; the soldiers were absent, and the mob triumphant and increasing in numbers and violence every moment.

Our neighborhood was in the greatest excitement. The whole population turned out at once, gazing with terror and consternation on the living stream passing before them, surging in countless numbers through the avenue, and hurrying up town to join those already in action. Fresh yells and shouts announced the union of forces, and bursting flames their accelerated strength and fury. The armory on Twenty-second Street was broken open, sacked, and fired, and the smoke and flames rolled up directly behind us.

With breathless interest we watched their rapid progress till diverted by a new terror. Our own household had been invaded. My brother's wife was gone; no one knew whither. Above and below we looked in vain for her. We could only learn that a note had been brought to her just before her disappearance. What could have happened? At such times imagination is swift and mystery unsupportable. We were falling into a terrible panic, and devising all manner of desperate expedients, when the wanderer appeared, looking very heroic, accompanied by J., all bloody and wounded. He had been attacked by the mob while passing a little too near them, knocked down, terribly beaten, and robbed of watch and pocket-book. Reality for once had outstripped imagination. For a time all our attention was absorbed in him. The wounds, though numerous, were happily not of a dangerous character. The gang which attacked him, attracted by his little tri-colored badge of loyalty, were fortunately only armed with light fence-pickets; so that, though weak from loss of blood, and badly cut and bruised in head, limbs, and body, no serious consequences seemed likely to result from his injuries.

Outdoors, meanwhile, all was clamor and tumult. Bells were tolling in every quarter. The rioters were still howling in Twenty-second Street, and driving the firemen from the burning armory. The building fell and the flames sunk, and then darkness came all at once and shut out every thing. We gathered gloomily around my brother in the back-parlor. An evening paper was procured, but brought no comfort. It only showed more clearly the nature and extent of this fearful outbreak. It only told us that the whole city was as helpless and anxious as ourselves. Many were in far greater danger, for obscurity is sometimes safety; but the black, lowering night, and the disabled condition of our only male protector, oppressed us heavily. Our neighborhood was all alive. Men tramped incessantly through the street, and women chatted and scolded in the windows; children cried and cats squalled; a crazy man in the rear raved fiercely for Jeff Davis and the Southern Confederacy; but over every other sound every few moments the bells rang out the alarm of some new fire. Some were very near; some at a distance. We would start and count the district, and tremble for the *Tribune* or the Arsenal.

Thus passed the eve, till at last we separated and tried to compose ourselves to rest; but who could sleep with such terrors around them? That fiery mass of frenzied creatures which had passed so near us in the afternoon was raging somewhere in the city, and that frightful roar and rush might any moment burst again upon our ears. They might sweep through our street and scatter every thing before them. Fires kindled by them illumined many parts of the city.

As the clocks struck twelve a great shout startled me, and a light flamed right up before me. A huge bonfire had been kindled in the middle of the street not far below us. Wild forms were dancing about it, and piling on fresh fuel. Great logs and beams and other combustibles were dragged up and heaped upon it. Sleep, now, was of course impossible. From a seat in an upper window I saw it rise and fall, flame up and fade. Was it a plaything or a signal? In either case I dared not leave it. A gang of noisy boys gathered around it. "Bring out Horace Greeley!" once was called. At last, after two hours' watching and wondering, a heavy shower put out the fires and drove the rioters homeward. Dark figures slunk to darker lanes and hovels, and rest and quiet fell on the distracted city.

At break of day it roused again. Another cloudy, foggy, warm, oppressive morning. Very early I resumed my post of observation. A black, charred mound loomed up below, and cinders, smoke, and soot filled the air and encrusted every object. Rough-looking men were already astir. A car passed down the avenue crowded inside and out; another passed; another, and no more. No rattling carts were heard, no shrieking milkmen. All ordinary sights and sounds were

"THE RIOTS AT NEW YORK"

missing. Soon hordes of ragged children attacked the heap of rubbish in the street. Little fair-haired girls and toddling boys bore off great armfuls of sticks and brands. Meanwhile the larger children, great boys, grown women, had hurried off to the smoking ruins in Twenty-second Street, and returned laden with spoils. Charred beams, baskets of coal, iron rails, muskets, and musket-barrels were carried by in vast quantities. The "dangerous classes" were evidently wide awake.

Our household meanwhile bestirred itself slowly. J. had rested little, but was free from fever or any alarming symptoms. Much time was spent in dressing his wounds, and some in preparing breakfast. There was no milk, no ice to be had, and meat and bread were on the wane; and so I ventured out with my sister H. for supplies. We found our street full of people, excitement, and rumors. Men and boys ran past us with muskets in their hands. We heard that a fight was in progress above Twenty-second Street. The mob had seized a gun-factory and many muskets; but the police had driven them off and taken back part of their plunder. It was cheering to find that the police were still alive. Second Avenue was densely thronged, but no cars were running. A great crowd surrounded the ruins of the Armory and blackened the Twenty-second Street crossing. Men talked in low, excited tones, and seemed afraid of each other. The stores were mostly closed and business suspended. With difficulty we procured supplies of provisions and a newspaper; but percussion caps and ammunition were stoutly denied us. No one dared to admit that they kept any such articles lest the rioters should take them away by force. A friendly bookseller at last supplied us. He had been out in disguise, he said, and heard the rioters boasting among themselves. One said he had made a hundred dollars already, and now he had arms and meant to  use them. All the shops on the avenue had been threatened. The mob were gathering in great force in our vicinity, and things looked every moment more threatening; so we hurried home as fast as possible, and I took my post again at the window.

New and strange sights met my eyes. Such multitudes of people every where: filling street and sidewalks, crowding all the doors and windows, the balconies and roofs of the houses. Many were merely spectators; some not far distant were *actors*. In the First Avenue the crowd was now very dense and clamorous. The liquor store on the corner was thronged with villainous-looking customers, and the women who had welcomed the mob on their first appearance were again talking loudly as if urging them on to action. "Die *at home!*" was the favorite watch-word which often reached our ears. Every thing indicated that a collision was approaching. We caught, after a time, a glimpse of soldiers, and heard the welcome rattle of musketry, distant at first, then nearer and nearer. The soldiers marched to and through Twenty-second Street and turned down First Avenue. The mob yelled and howled and stood their ground. Women from the roofs threw stones and brickbats upon the soldiers. Then came the volleys; the balls leaped out and the mob gave way at once and fled in every direction. A great crowd rushed through our street, hiding in every nook and corner. We closed doors and blinds, but still peeped out of the windows. The soldiers marched slowly back up the avenue, firing along the way; crossed over into Second Avenue, marched down opposite our street and fired again. Again the mob scattered, and scampered in droves through the street. Yet another volley, and balls came tearing down the centre of our street right before us, dashing along the pavements and carrying off frames from the trees. A boy on the sidewalk opposite was struck; he fell in a pool of blood, and was carried away to die. The streets were now cleared, the crowds had vanished, the soldiers withdrew, and the mob was quelled. For two hours peace and quiet prevailed. Our neighbors retired to their several abodes. We took dinner by gas-light with closed blinds, and flattered ourselves that the worst was over.

But as night came on the sun came out, and men crawled out into sight again. A stranger on horseback rode slowly up the street. Crowds quickly gathered around him. Swarms rushed out of the old liquor store and from all the neighboring alleys, and greeted him with shouts and cheers. We saw him waving his hat and haranguing the multitude, and heard their storm of response, but could catch no words. Great bustle and preparation followed. Women were foremost among them, inciting and helping. The rider slunk off again eastward as he came, while men formed in bands and marched off down the avenue. A squad of lads, decently clad and armed, marched down our street and joined those on the corner, were received with loud cheers, and sent on after the others.

The sun set clear, and a beautiful night came on; a radiant midsummer night, but darker to us than the preceding. Dark skies seemed more in harmony with the scenes around us, and the contrast only deepened the gloom. The papers brought no encouragement. Fearful deeds of atrocity were recorded. The mob were increasing in power and audacity, and the city was still paralyzed and panic-struck. The small military force available could only protect a few important positions, leaving the greater part defenseless. Our inflammable neighborhood was wholly at the mercy of the mob. Again with heavy hearts we assembled in the back-parlor and discussed probabilities and contingencies. Our position on the very edge of one of the worst of the "infected districts" had in it, after all, one element of security: the mob could not touch us without endangering some of their friends. The incessant din and clamor without were little calculated to strengthen our courage. The warm, bright night set every evil thing in motion, and man and beast conspired to fill the air with all manner of hideous and discordant sounds. The tramping, scolding, screaming, squalling, and raving of the preceding night were repeated and intensified. Cats and dogs squalled and howled, bells rang incessantly, and mingled with all these sounds came at intervals the most mournful of all, the long-drawn piercing wails of Irishwomen bemoaning their dead.

Worn out with listening we resolved at last to try to rest. I made up a bundle, put my clothes in running order, read the most comforting Psalms I could find, and laid myself down to sleep. Scarcely had my head touched the pillow when a new alarm of fire sounded. Lights streamed through the door of my room and illumined the houses opposite. "Another fire in Twenty-second Street!" was the cry. The police station had been set on fire, and volumes of smoke and flame were rising again very near us. From the rear windows we saw it all with the utmost distinctness; heard the roaring and crackling, and felt the heat of the flames. Soon they wrapped the house and caught the adjacent fire-tower, whose bell was clamoring even now for aid. The mob yelled with delight, and drove off the eager firemen. The flames soon wreathed the tower and rose in majestic columns. The whole neighborhood was flooded with light. Thousands of spectators gazed upon the scene, crowning the house-tops as with statues of living fire. The blazing turret shook and reeled, beams snapped and parted, and the bell plunged heavily downward, "tolling the death-knell of its own decease"; but its dying notes were lost in the triumphant shouts of the mob maddened by their success. We heard them hurrying on to the gas-works, leaving the waning fires at last to the firemen. We could hear them pounding and shaking the gates, swearing at their inability to force them, and then rushing off again for some easier prey.

The fires were now quite subdued, and we ventured to return to our several rooms. It was past midnight, but the city was still wide awake. The streets were thronged, and the opposite houses were all open and brilliantly lighted. They belonged to the better class of tenement houses; and their occupants, though not themselves rioters, so far sympathized with them as evidently to feel no fear of them. Many were chatting at this time about the doors and windows with a careless merriment which I could not but envy. I gave a parting look up and down the street, and again sought my pillow. The tramping in the street gradually subsided, the din and discord slowly died away, and a slight stupor was stealing gently over me, when a sudden rush and scream brought me again in an instant to my window. There was a spring and a chase, and then such piercing, thrilling cries as words can not describe. I could see nothing. Not a person was in sight; but from the vicinity of that wretched liquor store I distinctly heard dreadful cries, and caught these broken words: "Oh, brothers! brothers! Save me! save me!"

The sounds thrilled through the opposite and nearer houses. Lights quivered and wavered, and doors were shut hastily. The cries and groans continued. There were confused sounds as of dragging and lifting, and then silence. A mist had veiled the stars, and darkness fallen upon the street. Our noisy neighbors were struck dumb. Every door and window was closed, and every light extinguished. I trembled from head to foot, and could scarcely grope my way to the back chamber. Part of our household were still watching there, more bells were tolling, and three new fires were raging. Destruction and death were on every side.

Again I returned to my old position in the window, and peered out into the darkness. All things looked ghostly and ghastly. The houses opposite were dissolved in mist. I seemed to see through them far down into the heart of the city, and heard in the distance the roar as of great multitudes in commotion.

What was passing I could not tell, but any thing and every thing seemed possible at this hour. Would the night ever end, or any thing be left should morning come? Once only the welcome report of musketry reached my ears. At last the glimmering of dawn appeared. The mist dissolved; the wandering houses came back to position; the street resumed its old familiar look, and men and boys their ceaseless tramp, tramp, tramp.

One of these men stopped across the way, and said, in a low, scared tone to some one in the house: "They hung a Massachusetts ——— over there last night." One word was lost to me—what it was I can only conjecture; but whether citizen, soldier, or negro, I do not doubt that some poor fellow very near us met the fate of so many others in those days of terror; and though his name and story may never be known on earth, his cries for help will surely rise up in judgment against his murderers.

But another day had come, Wednesday, July 15th. A long, bright, blazing midsummer day was before us. There was little change in the aspect of affairs without. The city was not all burned down, we found. The newspapers were still alive, and insisting that more troops were on hand and the mob checked; but we saw no signs of it. The morning indeed passed more quietly. The rioters were resting from the labors of the night; but business was not resumed, and swarms of idle men still hung about the streets and stores. No cars were running in the avenues, no carts in the streets. No milkmen came, and no meatmen, and not a soldier or policeman showed his head.

The day dragged on heavily. There was little to be seen, and nothing to be done but write letters that could not be sent, and wonder at our situation. Little had we thought that our quiet pilgrimage would lead us to such turbulent and tempestuous scenes. All our plans had been brought to naught. Visiting, shopping, sight-seeing, were not even to be considered. All ordinary pursuits and pleasures had ceased, social intercourse was given up, and nothing remained but chaos and confusion. We heard but the vaguest reports of the doings of the city, and still less of the outer world. The war at the door drowned the battle afar off.

It was most humiliating, it was almost incredible, that such a state of things should exist in the heart of a civilized and Christian community. "Was this your joyous city, whose merchants were princes, whose traffickers were among the honorable of the earth?" Could it be that this great city, the pride and boast of the nation, was trampled down and held under the feet of these mad rioters? She seemed utterly prostrate and helpless. Her vast treasures, her immense storehouses, her long lines of palaces, her great multitudes of citizens, were bound and offered up for sacrifice. The whole nation was trembling and terror-struck. No one could see when and where it would terminate.

Flight seemed the only refuge. Could not we, wearied travelers, at least steal away to some green nook and be at rest? We discussed plans and dismissed them. Nothing seemed feasible. There were no cars and no carriages, and no one to help us to them. J., though improving, was still unable to go out, and we were unwilling to leave him and his family in such circumstances. We were bound, hand and foot, in this miserable neighborhood, unable to stir out of doors, and with the prospect of another night of horrors.

The day, though quieter than the preceding, was far more irksome. The brick walls and glaring streets, the heat, confusion, and confinement were intolerably wearisome. The sun blazed more and more fiercely. The stillness was oppressive and ominous. It seemed the calm before a storm. Already clouds were gathering in the horizon. As night approached we heard drums beating, and gangs of rioters marched up their favorite avenue. The whole population bestirred itself at once. Men, women, and children rushed out cheering and clamoring, some hurrying on with the crowd, some hanging around the corner. Many soon returned, laden with spoil — bedding, clothing, and furniture. The crowd increased rapidly in the street and around the liquor store. Great excitement prevailed. There was loud talking with fierce gestures. Some ran thither with fire-arms, some with poles and boards. Then some one shouted, "They are coming!" and a small band of soldiers appeared marching up our street. The mob seemed to swell into vast dimensions, and densely filled the whole street before them. Hundreds hurried out on the house-tops, tore up brick-bats, and hurled them with savage howls at the approaching soldiers. Shots were fired from secret ambushes, and soldiers fell before they had fired. Then they charged bravely into the mob, but their force was wholly inadequate. One small howitzer and a company of extemporized militia could do little against those raging thousands. A fierce conflict raged before our eyes. With breathless interest we watched them from door and windows. We feared the soldiers would be swallowed up and annihilated. Some now appeared in sight with a wounded officer and several wounded men, looking from side to side for shelter. Their eyes met ours with mute appeal. There was no time to be lost; the mob might any moment be upon them. There was a moment's consultation, a hasty reference to J., an unhesitating response: "Yes, by all means"; we beckoned them in, and in they came. Doors and windows were at once closed, and the house became a hospital, and seemed filled with armed men. The wounded men were carried into my brother's room; the Colonel was laid on the bed, and the others propped up with pillows. There were a few moments of great commotion and confusion. We flew for fans, ice water, and bandages. Some of the soldiers went out into the fight again, and some remained with the wounded. A surgeon, who had volunteered as a private under his old commander, dressed the wounds of the sufferers. The Colonel was severely wounded in the thigh by a slug made of a piece of lead pipe, producing a compound fracture. The wounds of two others, though less dangerous, were severe and painful.

Twilight was now upon us, and night rapidly approaching. The soldiers had been forced to retreat, leaving the mob in great force and fury. We heard them shouting and raving on the corner, and knew that we were in great danger. Already they were clamoring for the wounded soldiers who had escaped them. We thought of Colonel O'Brien's fate, and could not suppress the thought that our own house might be made the scene of a like tragedy. Could we defend ourselves if attacked? A hurried consultation was held. We had arms and ammunition, and, including J. and the slightly wounded soldiers, half a dozen men able and willing to use them. But we could not "man our lines." We were open to attack at once from the front and rear, the roof, the front basement, and the balcony above it. We might, indeed, retreat to the upper stories, barricade the stairway, and hold it against all the assailants that could crowd into the hall. But if they chose to fire the house below we could not prevent it, and then there would be no escape either for our wounded or ourselves.

The Colonel promptly decided the question; resistance was hopeless, could only make the case worse, and must not be attempted. Not only so, but all signs of the presence of soldiers must be removed. Arms, military apparel, and bloody clothing were accordingly concealed. The Colonel was conveyed to the cellar and placed on a mattress. The young soldier, next to him most severely wounded, was assisted up the rear apartment on the upper floor and placed in charge of my mother and myself. The soldiers who had remained were then ordered to make their escape from the house as they best could, and to hasten to head-quarters with an urgent request that a force might be sent to our relief. The surgeon was also requested to go, but would not listen to the suggestion. He had been regimental surgeon for two years under the Colonel, and insisted on remaining by his side, to take care of him, and to share his fate whatever it might be. He took his post, therefore, in the cellar, extemporizing as well as he could some scanty means of concealment for both from the boxes and bins which it contained. The remaining soldier, though severely wounded in the foot, could yet walk with pain and difficulty; and it was decided that, as soon as it should be safe or necessary, he should try the chances of escape through the scuttle and over the roofs of the adjoining buildings.

J., with his bandaged head and disabled arm, was liable to be taken for a wounded soldier, and his wife, and her sister Mrs. P——, insisted that he also should betake himself to the roof. He could render no material assistance if he remained; on the other hand, his presence might precipitate a scene of violence which would not be offered to ladies alone. They did not feel that they were personally in danger—so far there was no report that the lawless violence of the rioters had been directed against women; and if he could get away he might be the means of bringing speedier relief. Very reluctantly he yielded to these considerations, and prepared to accompany the wounded soldier. The mother of the household took refuge in her room on the second-floor. To her daughter-in-law, wife of an absent son, was assigned a post of observation at a front window. The two heroic women, H. and her sister, remained below to confront the mob.

Of all these arrangements, made mostly after we had assumed the charge assigned us, we at the time knew nothing. In utter darkness and desolation we sat above by the bedside of our young soldier, receiving his farewell messages for his mother and friends, and knowing not how soon he might be torn from us. There was no human power to help us in this extremity; we could only trust in Him "who stilleth the madness of the people." The suspense was terrible. In the rear, as we stole an occasional out-look through our closed blinds, we could see men here and there climbing the fences; they might be rioters breaking in, or residents breaking out. All was confusion and uncertainty. We knew not friends from foes.

In front the demonstrations were still more alarming. The rioters had taken possession of the street, stationed a guard on both avenues, and were chasing up and down for the soldiers. Then they were seen searching from house to house; beginning, fortunately for us and ours, on the opposite side, proceeding toward Second Avenue, then crossing the street and coming back gradually toward us. At last they reached the house next to ours. A few moments we waited in breathless silence. Then came a rush up the steps, and the bell rang violently. Not a sound was heard through the house. Again and yet again the bell rang, more and more furiously. Heart throbbed, nerves quivered, but no one stirred. Then came knocks, blows, kicks, threats, attempts to force the door. Come in they must and would; nothing could stay them.

Having gained for the retreating party all the time she could, Mrs. P—— at length unlocked the door, opened it, passed out, and closing it behind her, stood face to face with the mob, which crowded the steps and swarmed on the sidewalk and the adjacent street. What could she do? She knew that they would come in, that they would search the house, that they would find the men; but she was determined not to give them up without an effort to save them. Possibly, in parleying with them, she might at least calm somewhat the fury of the passion that swayed that howling mob; possibly in that brutal and maddened throng there might be a few with human hearts in their bosoms to which she might find a way, win them to her side, and enlist their aid in saving the lives of the intended victims. That was her only hope.

"What do you want?" she asked, while the air was yet ringing with the cry that came up from the crowd, "The soldiers! the soldiers!" "Bring out the soldiers!" One who stood near and seemed to be a leader replied, "There were two soldiers went into this house, and we must have them. You must give them up."

"There *were* two that came in, but went out again. They are not here now."

She spoke in a low but perfectly clear and steady voice, that compelled attention, and the crowd hushed its ravings to catch her words.

"Let us see; if they are not here we will not harm you; but we must search the house."

"We can not let you in; there are only women here—some that are old and feeble, and the sight of such a crowd will frighten them to death."

"They shall not all come in," was the reply; and after some further parley it was agreed that half a dozen only should enter and make the search. The leader gave his orders, the door was opened, and the men detailed came in; but before it could be closed the mob surged up, pressed in, and filled the hall. Many of them were armed with the stolen carbines.

"Light the gas!" was the cry.

"My sister has gone for a light."

It came, and the parley was renewed. The leader again demanded the soldiers; insisted that they were there, and said it would be better for themselves if they would give them up. She persisted in the statement she had made.

"She is fooling us, and using up the time while they are getting away by the roof!" cried one, and pressing forward with his musket pointed at her, endeavored to pass her. Very deliberately she took hold of the muzzle and turned it aside, saying, "Don't do that. You know I am a woman, and it might frighten me."

The leader returned to the charge. "We know the men are here, and if you give them up to us you shall not be harmed. But if you do not, and we find them, you know what a mob is. I can not control them; your house will be burned over your heads, and I will not guarantee your lives for five minutes."

"You will not do that," was the reply. "We are not the kind of people whose houses you wish to burn. My only son works as you do, and perhaps in the same shop with some of you, for seventy cents a day."

She did not tell them that her amateur apprentice boy had left his place to go to Pennsylvania and fight their friends the rebels. A young man, whom she had noticed as one of the few of decent appearance, stepped to her side and whispered to her, advising her compliance with the demand, assuring her that the men could not be controlled. The tone more than the words indicated to her that she had made one friend; and she found another, in the same way, a moment later.

Meantime the leaders were consulting whether they should go first above or below, and decided on the latter. Stationing one man with a musket at the door, and one at the stairs, they proceeded, pioneered by H., first to the parlors, and then to the basement, thoroughly examining both. Most fortunately the sentinels were the two young men in whom Mrs. P—— felt she had found friends, and she was not slow to improve the opportunity to deepen the impression she had made. But now the crowd outside, thundering at the basement door, burst in the panels, and forcing it open, with terrible oaths and threats rushed in and filled the lower hall. Part joined the searching party, and some hurried up the first-floor. One, crowding past the sentinel, was striding up the stairs. We heard his call to his comrades, "Come on up stairs!" and our hearts sunk within us. But the sentinel's stern command, enforced by his leveled piece, brought him back.

The main party, having ransacked the basement rooms, now turned to the cellar. In a moment a loud shout announced that they had found a victim. The surgeon was dragged up, forced out at the lower door, and delivered over to the crowd outside. A blow from a bludgeon or musket felled him to the earth, inflicting a terrible wound on the head. "Hang him, hang him!" "To the post at the Twenty-second Street corner!" were the cries as they hurried him off. The search within proceeded; a moment more and they had found the Colonel. A new and fiercer shout was sent up. An order from a leader thrilled through the hall. "Come down here some of yees wid yer muskets!"

At the first cry from the cellar Mrs. P—— sprung for the basement, intending to make her way at any hazard. A sentinel stood at the head of the stairway; a stalwart brute, reeking with filth and whisky. He seized her, with both arms about her waist, with a purpose of violence quite too evident. She struggled to free herself without raising an alarm, but in vain; then a sudden and piercing shriek, which rung through the house, made him for an instant relax his hold, and, wrenching herself away, she hurried back and sought the protection of the friendly sentinel.

"He will not let me pass; I must go down."

"You must not," he replied; "it is no place for you." And then he added, looking sternly at her, "You have deceived us. You said there was no one here, and there is."

"I would have done the same thing for you if you had been wounded. Look at me; do you not believe me?"

He did look, full in her eye, for an instant; then said: "Yes, I do believe it. You have done right, and I admire your spirit."

"But I must go down. Go with me."

"No; it is no place for you."

"Then go yourself, and save his life."

And turning over his charge to the sentinel at the door, he did go. Meantime the searching party, having found the Colonel, proceeded to question him. He said he was a citizen, accidently wounded, and had been obliged to seek refuge there.

"Why did you hide, if you are a citizen?"

Because, he said, he was afraid he should be taken for a soldier. They would not believe, but still he insisted on his statement. Then the muskets were sent for, and four pieces leveled at his head, as he lay prostrate and helpless.

"Fire, then, if you will, on a wounded man and a citizen. I shall die, any how, for my wound is a mortal one. But before you fire I wish you would send for a priest."

"What, are you a Catholic?"

"Yes."

This staggered them; and while they were hesitating the sentinel joined the group, and as soon as he looked on the Colonel exclaimed: "I know that man. I used to go to school with him. He is no soldier."

This turned the scale. The leaders were satisfied, and decided to let him go. But before leaving him they rifled his pockets; and here he narrowly escaped falling into renewed danger. While the parley was in progress his fingers had been busily occupied in quietly and coolly removing from his pocket a quantity of bullets which he had forgotten, and which, if they had been found, would certainly have betrayed him.

Those of the mob who had remained above, disappointed of their prey, with oaths and execrations protested against the action of their leaders, and sent the ruffian at the head of the stairway down to see if it was all right. But the positive statements of the friendly sentinel, which Mrs. P —— had the satisfaction of hearing him rehearse, as the two met in the lower hall, disarmed even his suspicions, and the rest could do no otherwise than acquiesce. So well satisfied, indeed, were the leaders, and, as it is not unreasonable to suppose, so impressed with the resolute bearing of the two ladies, that they volunteered to station a guard before the door to prevent the annoyance of any further search. As they had found the two men who had been reported to them as having entered the house, it did not seem to occur to them that there might be still others concealed; and so they took their departure, leaving the upper stories unvisited.

The surgeon in the mean time had been no less fortunate. In the crowd which hurried him off to death there happened to be one or two returned soldiers who had served in the same regiment with him, and when he came where it was light recognized him. They insisted on saving him, and, raising a party in their favor, finally prevailed, and having rescued him escorted him in safety to his home.

While these events were passing below our alarm and anxiety were beyond all expression. Our poor charge especially was in the greatest distress; ignorant of the fate of his Colonel and comrades, and apprehending every moment that he might himself be found and dragged out by the mob. Of course we knew but imperfectly at the time of it what was going on. We knew that the soldiers were in the house, and that men bent on their destruction were seeking for them. We heard the clamor without, the cry for "The soldiers!" the rush into the hall. Then we heard the calm, steady tones of the ladies, holding the mob in listening attention, and took courage. We heard the movement through the parlors and downward to the basement. Then came the irruption of the fierce crowd into the lower hall; and very soon loud cries from below told us that some one was found. It might be the surgeon or the Colonel; it might be my brother, for we did not then know that he had effected his escape.

Again came up screams from below, ejaculations, loud words. Could it be that another was found? Again the heavy tramp of many men, this time moving upward and talking eagerly and rapidly. They paused in the hall; we dared not move or breathe; would they come up the stairs? No! The door is opened, men pass out, it is closed after them, and all is silent. Have they gone for others to complete the search, or to murder those already carried out?

Venturing at last below, as the stillness continued, I learned how favorable a turn affairs had taken. But though relieved for the moment, we were still in great anxiety, and in not a little peril. No one knew certainly what had become of J. The Colonel was greatly in need of immediate surgical attendance, and removal from the damp, chilly cellar. Our poor young soldier, too, was suffering much, both in mind and body. He was a volunteer of a day's service only, and this first experience of civil war was very painful. The rioters might learn or suspect that they had been deceived, and return to the search. He could bear to be shot in open fight, but not to be so hunted down. Help seemed to him impossible. The whole military force in the city, he knew, was already detailed on special duty, and none could be spared for us. If the rioters should come again nothing could save him; any further attempt at concealment would be worse than useless, and flight in his condition was impossible. We tried our best to cheer him, and to wait in patience, trusting to Him who had thus far kept us in safety. The weary hours dragged heavily onward. My mother and myself still sat in the dark with our young soldier, while the other ladies attended to the Colonel in the cellar.

The continued absence of J. gave us now much uneasiness. What had become of him we could not conjecture. From time to time I looked out from my old loop-hole in the front window. All was dark and desolate. Not a light in the opposite houses; not a person in sight but the men stationed before our house by the rioters. These marched back and forth in silence while a large body were carousing around the old liquor stand. "Come on," I heard one call, "and bring eight or ten with you!" They might come on again any moment, maddened with drink and disappointed vengeance. As time went on they grew more and more uproarious, singing, dancing, swearing, and yelling.

Anxious and troubled, I wandered from front to rear, now leaning out of the window to catch every movement without, and carrying back reports to my still more anxious and troubled soldier.

It was now, we thought, past midnight. We had no hope of relief, no thought or expectation but of struggling on alone hour after hour of distress and darkness; but as I was listening in my window to some unusually threatening demonstrations from the mob, I heard the distant clank of a horse's hoof on the pavement. Again and again it sounded, more and more distinctly; and then a measured tread reached my ears, the steady, resolute tramp of a trained and disciplined body. No music was ever half so beautiful! It might, it must be, our soldiers! Off I flew to spread the good news through the household, and back again to the window to hear the tramp nearer and fuller and stronger, and see a long line of muskets gleam out from the darkness, and a stalwart body of men stop at our door. "Halt!" was cried; and I rushed down stairs headlong, unlocked the door without waiting for orders, and with tears of joy and gratitude which every one can imagine and nobody describe, welcomed a band of radiant soldiers and policemen, and in the midst of them all who should appear but my brother, pale and exhausted, who had gotten off the house-top in some mysterious way and brought this gallant company to our rescue!

There was no time for inquiries or felicitations. The wounded men were our first care. Our young soldier in his delight had hobbled to the stairway, and was borne down in triumph by his sympathizing comrades, while a larger company brought the Colonel from the cellar. A pitiful sight he was, all bleeding and ghastly, shivering with cold and suffering great pain. Both soldiers were placed carefully in the carriage brought for their conveyance, and then we ladies were requested to accompany them immediately. It was unsafe to remain in the house, soldiers could not be spared to protect it, and it was best for us to go at once to the Central Police Station.

There was no time for deliberation or preparation, with two wounded men waiting. My mother was stowed away in a corner of the carriage, the other mother of the household perched up with the driver, and the remainder straggled along with my brother in various stages of dilapidation — some without bonnets, and some without shawls, and some in the thinnest of mus-

"THE RIOTS AT NEW YORK"

lins and slippers. My own clothes were locked up and the keys unattainable; so I snatched what I could and ran with the others. Our military escort soon brought us into subordination. While we had been preparing, one of the two companies had been fighting, and had utterly dispersed the mob on the corner; but this we had hardly noticed, so intently had we been occupied. They were now ready to resume their march. We were formed into column with the utmost formality and precision. One piece of artillery and one company of infantry preceded, and another of each followed the carriage, marching slowly and majestically along the middle of the street; while we ladies moved as slowly along the sidewalks, surrounded by officers, policemen, and newspaper reporters.

The change was so sudden, so unexpected, so magical, that it was difficult to believe that we were really in the body. We, who had been so lately in the depths of darkness and desolation, were now encompassed by armed bands eager to help and serve us. Dangers, seen and unseen, were still around us; great fires illumined the southern sky; house, furniture, and clothing were left behind as unprotected, but still we could only exult in the rescue of our hunted soldiers and our own blissful release from suspense and terror. With joyful hearts we followed our martial guard. This midnight flitting was full of romantic interest. The streets were silent and dark, lighted only by distant lurid flames. Slowly and solemnly the long, black procession moved onward down the broad avenue, through narrow and winding streets, stopping only from time to time for water for the wounded soldiers, or to scatter the foes lurking around us. Sometimes the skirmishers in advance charged out into the darkness, sometimes fired down the cross-streets, but no serious interruption occurred; and at last, after a weary march, the steady light of the Central Police Station gladdened our waiting eyes.

All now was life and animation. Well-dressed citizens were hurrying to and fro. Stalwart soldiers lined the street and guarded the steps and entrance, through which we were conducted to an inner apartment, and with much state and ceremony presented to the chieftains of civic power. Three days' experience of anarchy had made us feel the blessedness of lawful restraint, and surely no body of men ever looked so beautiful as these executives of law and government. Such fresh, radiant, energetic, clear-headed, and strong-hearted leaders looked able to conquer all the rioters in the land. Every body was wide-awake, dispatches coming and going, messengers flying about in all directions.

We were received with great civility and offered every possible accommodation, but the best attainable were somewhat scanty. The two rooms had each a table, a writing-desk, and a stack of arms, but no sofa or rocking-chair, no chance for napping or lounging. We saw at once that it was no resting-place for us, and after a brief council resolved to follow the fate of our Colonel; and so, leaving a spot which shines brightly in my remembrance, we continued our march to the St. Nicholas Hotel, obtaining admittance, ascended four flights of stairs, parted with our kind and gentlemanly escort, and sat down to rest at half past two Thursday morning!

Sleep was of course still impossible. The exciting scenes of the night, and the incessant roar and rumble of Broadway, kept all awake; and at four o'clock loud cheers brought us to the window to see the glorious returning "Seventh" marshaled before us, and with all our hearts and voices we joined in the welcome which greeted them. A brighter morning dawned upon the city; other regiments had arrived in the night, and we knew that it was now safe. Broadway was busy and noisy. Business was resumed, and the mob much subdued, though still rampant in our old neighborhood. A reconnaissance showed that it was still unsafe to venture there. We passed the morning comparing notes and considering what to do with ourselves. My only desire was to quit the city — to beat a retreat as soon as possible. Our quiet tour had been rudely interrupted, our plans and purposes brought to naught; we had suffered great fatigue and anxiety, and we were unwilling to stay a moment longer. It was humiliating to leave our luggage in the enemy's country; but what were clothes to rest and quiet? A place for our heads was of more consequence than *bonnets!* Our friends were compelled to stay, but we could go; and most happy were we, now that we were sure of their safety, to improve that privilege. And so at three o'clock on Thursday afternoon, just three days from our first glimpse of the rioters, we shook the dust of New York from our slippers, and, trunkless and bonnetless, sped up North River.

Across the North, New York's civil unrest revealed the anger of those who could not escape the new draft, but the reported damage also stirred a growing concern for the black people and Republican property that the Democratic Irish had attacked. Public perceptions of the war's purpose were changing. As slaves emancipated themselves from Southern households in 1863, they began to join freeborn black men in volunteering for Union service, most notably in Boston. The 54th Massachusetts under Robert Gould Shaw, who had been raised in a prominent abolitionist family, would be the first black regiment sent south and would lead the assault on Charleston's Fort Wagner in mid-July. Championing emancipation, Louisa May Alcott called such efforts the "great struggle for the liberty of both the races." Certainly, where New York's rioters brought the war into the homes of women, battlefield casualties like those in Charleston brought women into the war's hospitals as early as 1861, when the United States Sanitary Commission was founded as the forerunner of the American Red Cross. Both permanent and makeshift facilities were set up over the next four years, one reason why Nurse Dane in "The Brothers" only begins her wartime service in Washington. She begins to question her sympathies as "mistress" when a wounded rebel captain is brought in with a servant, who has the unmistakable look of his master.

◆◇◆

Louisa May Alcott

"THE BROTHERS"

(*Atlantic Monthly*, November 1863)

Doctor Franck came in as I sat sewing up the rents in an old shirt, that Tom might go tidily to his grave. New shirts were needed for the living, and there was no wife or mother to "dress him handsome when he went to meet the Lord," as one woman said, describing the fine funeral she had pinched herself to give her son.

"Miss Dane, I'm in a quandary," began the Doctor, with that expression of countenance which says as plainly as words, "I want to ask a favor, but I wish you'd save me the trouble."

"Can I help you out of it?"

"Faith! I don't like to propose it, but you certainly can, if you please."

"Then give it a name, I beg."

"You see a Reb has just been brought in crazy with typhoid; a bad case every way; a drunken, rascally little captain somebody took the trouble to capture, but whom nobody wants to take the trouble to cure. The wards are full, the ladies worked to death, and willing to be for our own boys, but rather slow to risk their lives for a Reb. Now you've had the fever, you like queer patients, your mate will see to your ward for a while, and I will find you a good attendant. The fellow won't last long, I fancy; but he can't die without some sort of care, you know. I've put him in the fourth story of the west wing, away from the rest. It is airy, quiet, and comfortable there. I'm on that ward, and will do my best for you in every way. Now, then, will you go?"

"Of course I will, out of perversity, if not common charity; for some of these people think that because I'm an abolitionist I am also a heathen, and I should rather like to show them, that, though I cannot quite love my enemies, I am willing to take care of them."

"Very good; I thought you'd go; and speaking of abolition reminds me that you can have a contraband for servant, if you like. It is that fine mulatto fellow who was found burying his Rebel master after the fight, and, being badly cut over the head, our boys brought him along. Will you have him?"

"By all means, — for I'll stand to my guns on that point, as on the other; these black boys are far more faithful and handy than some of the white scamps given me to serve, instead of being served by. But is this man well enough?"

"Yes, for that sort of work, and I think you'll like him. He must have been a handsome fellow before he got his face slashed; not much darker than myself; his master's son, I dare say, and the white blood makes him rather high and haughty about some things. He was in a bad way when he came in, but vowed he'd die in the street rather than turn in with the black fellows below; so I put him up in the west wing, to be out of the way, and he's seen to the captain all the morning. When can you go up?"

"As soon as Tom is laid out, Skinner moved, Haywood washed, Marble dressed, Charley rubbed, Downs taken up, Upham laid down, and the whole forty fed."

We both laughed, though the Doctor was on his way to the dead-house and I held a shroud on my lap. But in a hospital one learns that cheerfulness is one's salvation; for, in an atmosphere of suffering and death, heaviness of heart would soon paralyze usefulness of hand, if the blessed gift of smiles had been denied us.

In an hour I took possession of my new charge, finding a dissipated-looking boy of nineteen or twenty raving in the solitary little room, with no one near him but the contraband in the room adjoining. Feeling decidedly more interest in the black man than in the white, yet remembering the Doctor's hint of his being "high and haughty," I glanced furtively at him as I scattered chloride of lime about the room to purify the air, and settled matters to suit myself. I had seen many contrabands, but never one so attractive as this. All colored men are called "boys," even if their heads are white; this boy was five-and-twenty at least, strong-limbed and manly, and had the look of one who never had been cowed by abuse or worn with oppressive labor. He sat on his bed doing nothing; no book, no pipe, no pen or paper anywhere appeared, yet anything less indolent or listless than his attitude and expression I never saw. Erect he sat, with a hand on either knee, and eyes fixed on the bare wall opposite, so rapt in some absorbing thought as to be unconscious of my presence, though the door stood wide open and my movements were by no means noiseless. His face was half averted, but I instantly approved the Doctor's taste, for the profile which I saw possessed all the attributes of comeliness belonging to his mixed race. He was more quadroon than mulatto, with Saxon features, Spanish complexion darkened by exposure, color in lips and cheek, waving hair, and eye full of the passionate melancholy which in such men always seems to utter a mute protest against the broken law that doomed them at their birth. What could he be thinking of? The sick boy cursed and raved, I rustled to and fro, steps passed the door, bells rang, and the steady rumble of army-wagons came up from the street, still he never stirred. I had seen colored people in what they call "the black sulks," when, for days, they neither smiled nor spoke, and scarcely ate. But this was something more than that; for the man was not dully brooding over some small grievance; he seemed to see an all-absorbing fact or fancy recorded on the wall, which was a blank to me. I wondered if it were some deep wrong or sorrow, kept alive by memory and impotent regret; if he mourned for the dead master to whom he had been faithful to the end; or if the liberty now his were robbed of half its sweetness by the knowledge that some one near and dear to him still languished in the hell from which he had escaped. My heart quite warmed to him at that idea; I wanted to know and comfort him; and, following the impulse of the moment, I went in and touched him on the shoulder.

In an instant the man vanished and the slave appeared. Freedom was too new a boon to have wrought its blessed changes yet, and as he started up, with his hand at his temple and an obsequious "Yes, Ma'am," any romance that had gathered round him fled away, leaving the saddest of all sad facts in living guise before me. Not only did the manhood seem to die out of him, but the comeliness that first attracted me; for, as he turned, I saw the ghastly wound that had laid open cheek and forehead. Being partly healed, it was no longer bandaged, but held together with strips of that transparent plaster which I never see without a shiver and swift recollections of the scenes with which it is associated in my mind. Part of his black hair had been shorn away, and one eye was nearly closed; pain so distorted, and the cruel sabre-cut so marred that portion of his face, that, when I saw it, I felt as if a fine medal had been suddenly reversed, showing me a far more striking type of human suffering and wrong than Michel Angelo's bronze prisoner. By one of those inexplicable processes that often teach us how little we understand ourselves, my purpose was suddenly changed, and though I went in to offer comfort as a friend, I merely gave an order as a mistress.

"Will you open these windows? this man needs more air."

He obeyed at once, and, as he slowly urged up the unruly sash, the handsome profile was again turned toward me, and again I was possessed by my first impression so strongly that I involuntarily said,—

"Thank you, Sir."

Perhaps it was fancy, but I thought that in the look of mingled surprise and something like reproach which he gave me there was also a trace of grateful pleasure. But he said, in that tone of spiritless humility these poor souls learn so soon,—

"I a'n't a white man, Ma'am, I'm a contraband."

"Yes, I know it; but a contraband is a free man, and I heartily congratulate you."

He liked that; his face shone, he squared his shoulders, lifted his head, and looked me full in the eye with a brisk—

"Thank ye, Ma'am; anything more to do fer yer?"

"Doctor Franck thought you would help me with this man, as there are many patients and few nurses or attendants. Have you had the fever?"

"No, Ma'am."

"They should have thought of that when they put him here; wounds and fevers should not be together. I'll try to get you moved."

He laughed a sudden laugh,—if he had been a white man, I should have called it scornful; as he was a few shades darker than myself, I suppose it must be considered an insolent, or at least an unmannerly one.

"It don't matter, Ma'am. I'd rather be up here with the fever than down with those niggers; and there a'n't no other place fer me."

Poor fellow! that was true. No ward in all the hospital would take him in to lie side by side with the most miserable white wreck there. Like the bat in Aesop's fable, he belonged to neither race; and the pride of one, the helplessness of the other, kept him hovering alone in the twilight a great sin has brought to overshadow the whole land.

"You shall stay, then; for I would far rather have you than my lazy Jack. But are you well and strong enough?"

"I guess I'll do, Ma'am."

He spoke with a passive sort of acquiescence, — as if it did not much matter, if he were not able, and no one would particularly rejoice, if he were.

"Yes, I think you will. By what name shall I call you?"

"Bob, Ma'am."

Every woman has her pet whim; one of mine was to teach the men self-respect by treating them respectfully. Tom, Dick, and Harry would pass, when lads rejoiced in those familiar abbreviations; but to address men often old enough to be my father in that style did not suit my old-fashioned ideas of propriety. This "Bob" would never do; I should have found it as easy to call the chaplain "Gus" as my tragical-looking contraband by a title so strongly associated with the tail of a kite.

"What is your other name?" I asked. "I like to call my attendants by their last names rather than by their first."

"I've got no other, Ma'am; we have our masters' names, or do without. Mine's dead, and I won't have anything of his about me."

"Well, I'll call you Robert, then, and you may fill this pitcher for me, if you will be so kind."

He went; but, through all the tame obedience years of servitude had taught him, I could see that the proud spirit his father gave him was not yet subdued, for the look and gesture with which he repudiated his master's name were a more effective declaration of independence than any Fourth-of-July orator could have prepared.

We spent a curious week together. Robert seldom left his room, except upon my errands; and I was a prisoner all day, often all night, by the bedside of the Rebel. The fever burned itself rapidly away, for there seemed little vitality to feed it in the feeble frame of this old young man, whose life had been none of the most righteous, judging from the revelations made by his unconscious lips; since more than once Robert authoritatively silenced him, when my gentler hushings were of no avail, and blasphemous wanderings or ribald camp-songs made my cheeks burn and Robert's face assume an aspect of disgust. The captain was a gentleman in the world's eye, but the contraband was the gentleman in mine; — I was a fanatic, and that accounts for such depravity of taste, I hope. I never asked Robert of himself, feeling that somewhere there was a spot still too sore to bear the lightest touch; but, from his language, manner, and intelligence, I inferred that his color had procured for him the few advantages within the reach of a quick-witted, kindly treated slave. Silent, grave, and thoughtful, but most serviceable, was my contraband; glad of the books I brought him, faithful in the performance of the duties I assigned to him, grateful for the friendliness I could not but feel and show toward him. Often I longed to ask what purpose was so visibly altering his aspect with such daily deepening gloom. But I never dared, and no one else had either time or desire to pry into the past of this specimen of one branch of the chivalrous "F.F.V.S."

On the seventh night, Dr. Franck suggested that it would be well for some one, besides the general watchman of the ward, to be with the captain, as it might be his last. Although the greater part of the two preceding nights had been spent there, of course I offered to remain, — for there is a strange fascination in these scenes, which renders one careless of fatigue and unconscious of fear until the crisis is passed.

"Give him water as long as he can drink, and if he drops into a natural sleep, it may save him. I'll look in at midnight, when some change will probably take place. Nothing but sleep or a miracle will keep him now. Good night."

Away went the Doctor; and, devouring a whole mouthful of gapes, I lowered the lamp, wet the captain's head, and sat down on a hard stool to begin my watch. The captain lay with his hot, haggard face turned toward me, filling the air with his poisonous breath, and feebly muttering, with lips and tongue so parched that the sanest speech would have been difficult to understand. Robert was stretched on his bed in the inner room, the door of which stood ajar, that a fresh draught from his open window might carry the fever-fumes away through mine. I could just see a long, dark figure, with the lighter outline of a face, and, having little else to do just then, I fell to thinking of this curious contraband, who evidently prized his freedom highly, yet seemed in no haste to enjoy it. Doctor Franck had offered to send him on to safer quarters, but he had said, "No, thank yer, Sir, not yet," and then had gone away to fall into one of those black moods of his, which began to disturb me, because I had no power to lighten them. As I sat listening to the clocks from the steeples all about us, I amused myself with planning Robert's future, as I often did my own, and had dealt out to him a generous hand of trumps wherewith to play this game of life which hitherto had gone so cruelly against him, when a harsh, choked voice called, —

"Lucy!"

It was the captain, and some new terror seemed to have gifted him with momentary strength.

"Yes, here's Lucy," I answered, hoping that by following the fancy I might quiet him, — for his face was damp with the clammy moisture, and his frame shaken with the nervous tremor that so often precedes death. His dull eye fixed upon me, dilating with a bewildered look of incredulity and wrath, till he broke out fiercely, —

"That's a lie! she's dead, — and so's Bob, damn him!"

Finding speech a failure, I began to sing the quiet tune that had often soothed delirium like this; but hardly had the line, passed my lips, when he clutched me by the wrist, whispering like one in mortal fear, —

"Hush! she used to sing that way to Bob, but she never would to me. I swore I'd whip the Devil out of her, and I did; but you know before she cut her throat she said she'd haunt me, and there she is!"

He pointed behind me with an aspect of such pale dismay, that I involuntarily glanced over my shoulder and started as if I had seen a veritable ghost; for, peering from the gloom of that inner room, I saw a shadowy face, with dark hair all about it, and a glimpse of scarlet at the throat. An instant showed me that it was only Robert leaning from his bed's-foot, wrapped in a gray army-blanket, with his red shirt just visible above it, and his long hair disordered by sleep. But what a strange expression was on his face! The unmarred side was toward me, fixed and motionless as when I first observed it, — less absorbed now, but more intent. His eye glittered, his lips were apart like one who listened with every sense, and his whole aspect reminded me of a hound to which some wind had brought the scent of unsuspected prey.

"Do you know him, Robert? Does he mean you?"

"Lord, no, Ma'am; they all own half a dozen Bobs: but hearin' my name woke me; that's all."

He spoke quite naturally, and lay down again, while I returned to my charge, thinking that this paroxysm was probably his last. But by another hour I perceived a hopeful change, for the tremor had subsided, the cold dew was gone, his breathing was more regular, and Sleep, the healer, had descended to save or take him gently away. Doctor Franck looked in at midnight, bade me keep all cool and quiet, and not fail to administer a certain draught as soon as the captain woke. Very much relieved, I laid my head on my arms, uncomfortably folded on the little table, and fancied I was about to perform one of the feats which practice renders possible, — "sleeping with one eye open," as we say: a half-and-half doze, for all senses sleep but that of hearing; the faintest murmur, sigh, or motion will break it, and give one back one's wits much brightened by the brief permission to "stand at ease." On this night, the experiment was a failure, for previous vigils, confinement, and much care had rendered naps a dangerous indulgence. Having roused half a dozen times in an hour to find all quiet, I dropped my heavy head on my arms, and, drowsily resolving to look up again in fifteen minutes, fell fast asleep.

The striking of a deep-voiced clock woke me with a start. "That is one," thought I, but, to my dismay, two more strokes followed; and in remorseful haste I sprang up to see what harm my long oblivion had done. A strong hand put me back into my seat, and held me there. It was Robert. The instant my eye met his my heart began to beat, and all along my nerves tingled that electric flash which foretells a danger that we cannot see. He was very pale, his mouth grim, and both eyes full of sombre fire, — for even the wounded one was open now, all the more sinister for the deep scar above and below. But his touch was steady, his voice quiet, as he said, —

"Sit still, Ma'am; I won't hurt yer, nor even scare yer, if I can help it, but yer waked too soon."

"Let me go, Robert, — the captain is stirring, — I must give him something."

"No, Ma'am, yer can't stir an inch. Look here!"

Holding me with one hand, with the other he took up the glass in which I had left the draught, and showed me it was empty.

"Has he taken it?" I asked, more and more bewildered.

"I flung it out o' winder, Ma'am; he'll have to do without."

"But why, Robert? why did you do it?"

"Because I hate him!"

Impossible to doubt the truth of that; his whole face showed it, as he spoke through his set teeth, and launched a fiery glance at the unconscious captain. I could only hold my breath and stare blankly at him, wondering what mad act was coming next. I suppose I shook and turned white, as women have a foolish habit of doing when sudden danger daunts them; for Robert released my arm, sat down upon the bedside just in front of me, and said, with the ominous quietude that made me cold to see and hear, —

"Don't yer be frightened, Ma'am; don't try to run away, fer the door's locked an' the key in my pocket; don't yer cry out, fer yer'd have to scream a long while, with my hand on yer mouth, before yer was heard. Be still, an' I'll tell yer what I'm goin' to do."

"Lord help us! he has taken the fever in some sudden, violent way, and is out of his head. I must humor him till some one comes"; in pursuance of which swift determination, I tried to say, quite composedly, —

"I will be still and hear you; but open the window. Why did you shut it?"

"I'm sorry I can't do it, Ma'am; but yer'd jump out, or call, if I did, an' I'm not ready yet. I shut it to make yer sleep, an' heat would do it quicker 'n anything else I could do."

The captain moved, and feebly muttered, "Water!" Instinctively I rose to give it to him, but the heavy hand came down upon my shoulder, and in the same decided tone Robert said, —

"The water went with the physic; let him call."

"Do let me go to him! he'll die without care!"

"I mean he shall; — don't yer interfere, if yer please, Ma'am."

In spite of his quiet tone and respectful manner, I saw murder in his eyes, and turned faint with fear; yet the fear excited me, and, hardly knowing what I did, I seized the hands that had seized me, crying, —

"No, no, you shall not kill him! it is base to hurt a helpless man. Why do you hate him? He is not your master?"

"He's my brother."

I felt that answer from head to foot, and seemed to fathom what was coming, with a prescience vague, but unmistakable. One appeal was left to me, and I made it.

"Robert, tell me what it means? Do not commit a crime and make me accessory to it. There is a better way of righting wrong than by violence; — let me help you find it."

My voice trembled as I spoke, and I heard the frightened flutter of my heart; so did he, and if any little act of mine had ever won affection or respect from him, the memory of it served me then. He looked down, and seemed to put some question to himself; whatever it was, the answer was in my favor, for when his eyes rose again, they were gloomy, but not desperate.

"I *will* tell you, Ma'am; but mind, this makes no difference; the boy is mine. I'll give the Lord a chance to take him fust; if He don't, I shall."

"Oh, no! remember, he is your brother."

An unwise speech; I felt it as it passed my lips, for a black frown gathered on Robert's face, and his strong hands closed with an ugly sort of grip. But he did not touch the poor soul gasping there behind him, and seemed content to let the slow suffocation of that stifling room end his frail life.

"I'm not like to forget that, Ma'am, when I've been thinkin' of it all this week. I knew him when they fetched him in, an' would 'a' done it long 'fore this, but I wanted to ask where Lucy was; he knows, — he told to-night, — an' now he's done for."

"Who is Lucy?" I asked hurriedly, intent on keeping his mind busy with any thought but murder.

With one of the swift transitions of a mixed temperament like this, at my question Robert's deep eyes filled, the clenched hands were spread before his face, and all I heard were the broken words, —

"My wife, — he took her" —

In that instant every thought of fear was swallowed up in burning indignation for the wrong, and a perfect passion of pity for the desperate man so tempted to avenge an injury for which there seemed no redress but this. He was no longer slave or contraband, no drop of black blood marred him in my sight, but an infinite compassion yearned to save, to help, to comfort him. Words seemed so powerless I offered none, only put my hand on his poor head, wounded, homeless, bowed down with grief for which I had no cure, and softly smoothed the long neglected hair, pitifully wondering the while where was the wife who must have loved this tender-hearted man so well.

The captain moaned again, and faintly whispered, "Air!" but I never stirred. God forgive me! just then I hated him as only a woman thinking of a sister woman's wrong could hate. Robert looked up; his eyes were dry again, his mouth grim. I saw that, said, "Tell me more," and he did, — for sympathy is a gift the poorest may give, the proudest stoop to receive.

"Yer see, Ma'am, his father, — I might say ours, if I warn't ashamed of both of 'em, — his father died two years ago, an' left us all to Marster Ned, — that's him here, eighteen then. He always hated me, I looked so like old Marster: he don't, — only the light skin an' hair. Old Marster was kind to all of us, me 'specially, an' bought Lucy off the next plantation down there in South Car'lina, when he found I liked her. I married her, all I could, Ma'am; it warn't much, but we was true to one another till Marster Ned come home a year after an' made hell fer both of us. He sent my old mother to be used up in his rice-swamp in Georgy; he found me with my pretty Lucy, an' though young Miss cried, an' I prayed to him on my knees, an' Lucy run away, he wouldn't have no mercy; he brought her back, an' — took her, Ma'am."

"Oh! what did you do?" I cried, hot with helpless pain and passion.

How the man's outraged heart sent the blood flaming up into his face and deepened the tones of his impetuous voice, as he stretched his arm across the bed, saying, with a terribly expressive gesture, —

"I half murdered him, an' to-night I'll finish."

"Yes, yes, — but go on now; what came next?"

He gave me a look that showed no white man could have felt a deeper degradation in remembering and confessing these last acts of brotherly oppression.

"They whipped me till I couldn't stand, an' then they sold me further South. Yer thought I was a white man once; — look here!"

With a sudden wrench he tore the shirt from neck to waist, and on his strong brown shoulders showed me furrows deeply ploughed, wounds which, though healed, were ghastlier to me than any in that house. I could not speak to him, and, with the pathetic dignity a great grief lends the humblest sufferer, he ended his brief tragedy by simply saying, —

"That's all, Ma'am. I've never seen her since, an' now I never shall in this world, — maybe not in t'other."

"But, Robert, why think her dead? The captain was wandering when he said those sad things; perhaps he will retract them when he is sane. Don't despair; don't give up yet."

"No, Ma'am, I guess he's right; she was too proud to bear that long. It's like her to kill herself. I told her to, if there was no other way; an' she always minded me, Lucy did. My poor girl! Oh, it warn't right! No, by God, it warn't!"

As the memory of this bitter wrong, this double bereavement, burned in his sore heart, the devil that lurks in every strong man's blood leaped up; he put his hand upon his brother's throat, and, watching the white face before him, muttered low between his teeth, —

"I'm lettin' him go too easy; there's no pain in this; we a'n't even yet. I wish he knew me. Marster Ned! it's Bob; where's Lucy?"

From the captain's lips there came a long faint sigh, and nothing but a flutter of the eyelids showed that he still lived. A strange stillness filled the room as the elder brother held the younger's life suspended in his hand, while wavering between a dim hope and a deadly hate. In the whirl of thoughts that went on in my brain, only one was clear enough to act upon. I must prevent murder, if I could, — but how? What could I do up there alone, locked in with a dying man and a lunatic? — for any mind yielded utterly to any unrighteous impulse is mad while the impulse rules it. Strength I had not, nor much courage, neither time nor wit for stratagem, and chance only could bring me help before it was too late. But one weapon I possessed, — a tongue, — often a woman's best defence; and sympathy, stronger than fear, gave me power to use it. What I said Heaven only knows, but surely Heaven helped me; words burned on my lips, tears streamed from my eyes, and some good angel prompted me to use the one name that had power to arrest my hearer's hand and touch his heart. For at that moment I heartily believed that Lucy lived, and this earnest faith roused in him a like belief.

He listened with the lowering look of one in whom brute instinct was sovereign for the time, — a look that makes the noblest countenance base. He was but a man, — a poor, untaught, outcast, outraged man. Life had few joys for him; the world offered him no honors, no success, no home, no love. What future would this crime mar? and why should he deny himself that sweet, yet bitter morsel called revenge? How many white men, with all New England's freedom, culture, Christianity, would not have felt as he felt then? Should I have reproached him for a human anguish, a human longing for redress, all now left him from the ruin of his few poor hopes? Who had taught him that self-control, self-sacrifice, are attributes that make men masters of the earth and lift them nearer heaven? Should I have urged the beauty of forgiveness, the duty of devout submission? He had no religion, for he was no saintly "Uncle Tom," and Slavery's black shadow seemed to darken all the world to him and shut out God. Should I have warned him of penalties, of judgments, and the potency of law? What did he know of justice, or the mercy that should temper that stern virtue, when every law, human and divine, had been broken on his hearth-stone? Should I have tried to touch him by appeals to filial duty, to brotherly love? How had his appeals been answered? What memories had father and brother stored up in his heart to plead for either now? No,—all these influences, these associations, would have proved worse than useless, had I been calm enough to try them. I was not; but instinct, subtler than reason, showed me the one safe clue by which to lead this troubled soul from the labyrinth in which it groped and nearly fell. When I paused, breathless, Robert turned to me, asking, as if human assurances could strengthen his faith in Divine Omnipotence,—

"Do you believe, if I let Marster Ned live, the Lord will give me back my Lucy?"

"As surely as there is a Lord, you will find her here or in the beautiful hereafter, where there is no black or white, no master and no slave."

He took his hand from his brother's throat, lifted his eyes from my face to the wintry sky beyond, as if searching for that blessed country, happier even than the happy North. Alas, it was the darkest hour before the dawn!—there was no star above, no light below but the pale glimmer of the lamp that showed the brother who had made him desolate. Like a blind man who believes there is a sun, yet cannot see it, he shook his head, let his arms drop nervelessly upon his knees, and sat there dumbly asking that question which many a soul whose faith is firmer fixed than his has asked in hours less dark than this,— "Where is God?" I saw the tide had turned, and strenuously tried to keep this rudderless life-boat from slipping back into the whirlpool wherein it had been so nearly lost.

"I have listened to you, Robert; now hear me, and heed what I say, because my heart is full of pity for you, full of hope for your future, and a desire to help you now. I want you to go away from here, from the temptation of this place, and the sad thoughts that haunt it. You have conquered yourself once, and I honor you for it, because, the harder the battle, the more glorious the victory; but it is safer to put a greater distance between you and this man. I will write you letters, give you money, and send you to good old Massachusetts to begin your new life a freeman,—yes, and a happy man; for when the captain is himself again, I will learn where Lucy is, and move heaven and earth to find and give her back to you. Will you do this, Robert?"

Slowly, very slowly, the answer came; for the purpose of a week, perhaps a year, was hard to relinquish in an hour.

"Yes, Ma'am, I will."

"Good! Now you are the man I thought you, and I'll work for you with all my heart. You need sleep, my poor fellow; go, and try to forget. The captain is still alive, and as yet you are spared that sin. No, don't look there; I'll care for him. Come, Robert, for Lucy's sake."

Thank Heaven for the immortality of love! for when all other means of salvation failed, a spark of this vital fire softened the man's iron will until a woman's hand could bend it. He let me take from him the key, let me draw him gently away and lead him to the solitude which now was the most healing balm I could bestow. Once in his little room, he fell down on his bed and lay there as if spent with the sharpest conflict of his life. I slipped the bolt across his door, and unlocked my own, flung up the window, steadied myself with a breath of air, then rushed to Doctor Franck. He came; and till dawn we worked together, saving one brother's life, and taking earnest thought how best to secure the other's liberty. When the sun came up as blithely as if it shone only upon happy homes, the Doctor went to Robert. For an hour I heard the murmur of their voices; once I caught the sound of heavy sobs, and for a time a reverent hush, as if in the silence that good man were ministering to soul as well as sense. When he departed he took Robert with him, pausing to tell me he should get him off as soon as possible, but not before we met again.

Nothing more was seen of them all day; another surgeon came to see the captain, and another attendant came to fill the empty place. I tried to rest, but could not, with the thought of poor Lucy tugging at my heart, and was soon back at my post again, anxiously hoping that my contraband had not been too hastily spirited away. Just as night fell there came a tap, and, opening, I saw Robert literally "clothed and in his right mind." The Doctor had replaced the ragged suit with tidy garments, and no trace of that tempestuous night remained but deeper lines upon the forehead and the docile look of a repentant child. He did not cross the threshold, did not offer me his hand, — only took off his cap, saying, with a traitorous falter in his voice, —

"God bless you, Ma'am! I'm goin'."

I put out both my hands, and held his fast.

"Good bye, Robert! Keep up good heart, and when I come home to Massachusetts we'll meet in a happier place than this. Are you quite ready, quite comfortable for your journey?"

"Yes, Ma'am, yes; the Doctor's fixed everything; I'm goin' with a friend of his; my papers are all right, an' I'm as happy as I can be till I find" —

He stopped there; then went on, with a glance into the room, —

"I'm glad I didn't do it, an' I thank yer, Ma'am, fer hinderin' me, — thank yer hearty; but I'm afraid I hate him jest the same."

Of course he did; and so did I; for these faulty hearts of ours cannot turn perfect in a night, but need frost and fire, wind and rain, to ripen and make them ready for the great harvest-home. Wishing to divert his mind, I put my poor mite into his hand, and, remembering the magic of a certain little book, I gave him mine, on whose dark cover whitely shone the Virgin Mother and the Child, the grand history of whose life the book contained. The money went into Robert's pocket with a grateful murmur, the book into his bosom with a long look and a tremulous —

"I never saw *my* baby, Ma'am."

I broke down then; and though my eyes were too dim to see, I felt the touch of lips upon my hands, heard the sound of departing feet, and knew my contraband was gone.

When one feels an intense dislike, the less one says about the subject of it the better; therefore I shall merely record that the captain lived, — in time was exchanged; and that, whoever the other party was, I am convinced the Government got the best of the bargain. But long before this occurred, I had fulfilled my promise to Robert; for as soon as my patient recovered strength of memory enough to make his answer trustworthy, I asked, without any circumlocution, —

"Captain Fairfax, where is Lucy?"

And too feeble to be angry, surprised, or insincere, he straightway answered, —

"Dead, Miss Dane."

"And she killed herself, when you sold Bob?"

"How the Devil did you know that?" he muttered, with an expression half-remorseful, half-amazed; but I was satisfied, and said no more.

Of course, this went to Robert, waiting far away there in a lonely home, — waiting, working, hoping for his Lucy. It almost broke my heart to do it; but delay was weak, deceit was wicked; so I sent the heavy tidings, and very soon the answer came, — only three lines; but I felt that the sustaining power of the man's life was gone.

"I thought I'd never see her any more; I'm glad to know she's out of trouble. I thank yer, Ma'am; an' if they let us, I'll fight fer yer till I'm killed, which I hope will be 'fore long."

Six months later he had his wish, and kept his word.

Every one knows the story of the attack on Fort Wagner; but we should not tire yet of recalling how our Fifty-Fourth, spent with three sleepless nights, a day's fast, and a march under the July sun, stormed the fort as night fell, facing death in many shapes, following their brave leaders through a fiery rain of shot and shell, fighting valiantly for "God and Governor Andrew," — how the regiment that went into action seven hundred strong came out having had nearly

"A NEGRO REGIMENT IN ACTION"

half its number captured, killed, or wounded, leaving their young commander to be buried, like a chief of earlier times, with this body-guard around him, faithful to the death. Surely, the insult turns to honor, and the wide grave needs no monument but the heroism that consecrates it in our sight; surely, the hearts that held him nearest see through their tears a noble victory in the seeming sad defeat; and surely, God's benediction was bestowed, when this loyal soul answered, as Death called the roll, "Lord, here am I, with the brothers Thou hast given me!"

The future must show how well that fight was fought; for though Fort Wagner still defies us, public prejudice is down; and through the cannon-smoke of that black night the manhood of the colored race shines before many eyes that would not see, rings in many ears that would not hear, wins many hearts that would not hitherto believe.

When the news came that we were needed, there was none so glad as I to leave teaching contrabands, the new work I had taken up, and go to nurse "our boys," as my dusky flock so proudly called the wounded of the Fifty-Fourth. Feeling more satisfaction, as I assumed my big apron and turned up my cuffs, than if dressing for the President's levee, I fell to work on board the hospital-ship in Hilton-Head harbor. The scene was most familiar, and yet strange; for only dark faces looked up at me from the pallets so thickly laid along the floor, and I missed the sharp accent of my Yankee boys in the slower, softer voices calling cheerily to one another, or answering my questions with a stout, "We'll never give it up, Ma'am, till the last Reb's dead," or, "If our people's free, we can afford to die."

Passing from bed to bed, intent on making one pair of hands do the work of three, at least, I gradually washed, fed, and bandaged my way down the long line of sable heroes, and coming to the very last, found that he was my contraband. So old, so worn, so deathly weak and wan, I never should have known him but for the deep scar on his cheek. That side lay uppermost, and caught my eye at once; but even then I doubted, such an awful change had come upon him, when, turning to the ticket just above his head, I saw the name, "Robert Dane." That both assured and touched me, for, remembering that he had no name, I knew that he had taken mine. I longed for him to speak to me, to tell how he had fared since I lost sight of him, and let me perform some little service for him in return for many he had done for me; but he seemed asleep; and as I stood reliving that strange night again, a bright lad, who lay next him softly waving an old fan across both beds, looked up and said,—

"I guess you know him, Ma'am?"

"You are right. Do you?"

"As much as any one was able to, Ma'am."

"Why do you say 'was,' as if the man were dead and gone?"

"I s'pose because I know he'll have to go. He's got a bad jab in the breast, an' is bleedin' inside, the Doctor says. He don't suffer any, only gets weaker 'n' weaker every minute. I've been fannin' him this long while, an' he's talked a little; but he don't know me now, so he's most gone, I guess."

There was so much sorrow and affection in the boy's face, that I remembered something, and asked, with redoubled interest,—

"Are you the one that brought him off? I was told about a boy who nearly lost his life in saving that of his mate."

I dare say the young fellow blushed, as any modest lad might have done; I could not see it, but I heard the chuckle of satisfaction that escaped him, as he glanced from his shattered arm and bandaged side to the pale figure opposite.

"Lord, Ma'am, that's nothin'; we boys always stan' by one another, an' I warn't goin' to leave him to be tormented any more by them cussed Rebs. He's been a slave once, though he don't look half so much like it as me, an' I was born in Boston."

He did not; for the speaker was as black as the ace of spades,—being a sturdy specimen, the knave of clubs would perhaps be a fitter representative,—but the dark freeman looked at the white slave with the pitiful, yet puzzled expression I have so often seen on the faces of our wisest men, when this tangled question of Slavery presents itself, asking to be cut or patiently undone.

"Tell me what you know of this man; for, even if he were awake, he is too weak to talk."

"I never saw him till I joined the regiment, an' no one 'peared to have got much out of him. He was a shut-up sort of feller, an' didn't seem to care for anything but gettin' at the Rebs. Some say he was the fust man of us that enlisted; I know he fretted till we were off, an' when we pitched into old Wagner, he fought like the Devil."

"Were you with him when he was wounded? How was it?"

"Yes, Ma'am. There was somethin' queer about it; for he 'peared to know the chap that killed him, an' the chap knew him. I don't dare to ask, but I rather guess one owned the other some time, — for, when they clinched, the chap sung out, 'Bob!' an' Dane, 'Marster Ned!' — then they went at it."

I sat down suddenly, for the old anger and compassion struggled in my heart, and I both longed and feared to hear what was to follow.

"You see, when the Colonel — Lord keep an' send him back to us! — It a'n't certain yet, you know, Ma'am, though it's two days ago we lost him — well, when the Colonel shouted, 'Rush on, boys, rush on!' Dane tore away as if he was goin' to take the fort alone; I was next him, an' kept close as we went through the ditch an' up the wall. Hi! warn't that a rusher!" and the boy flung up his well arm with a whoop, as if the mere memory of that stirring moment came over him in a gust of irrepressible excitement.

"Were you afraid?" I said, — asking the question women often put, and receiving the answer they seldom fail to get.

"No, Ma'am!" — emphasis on the "Ma'am," — "I never thought of anything but the damn' Rebs, that scalp, slash, an' cut our ears off, when they git us. I was bound to let daylight into one of 'em at least, an' I did. Hope he liked it!"

"It is evident that you did, and I don't blame you in the least. Now go on about Robert, for I should be at work."

"He was one of the fust up; I was just behind, an' though the whole thing happened in a minute, I remember how it was, for all I was yellin' an' knockin' round like mad. Just where we were, some sort of an officer was wavin' his sword an' cheerin' on his men; Dane saw him by a big flash that come by; he flung away his gun, give a leap, an' went at that feller as if he was Jeff, Beauregard, an' Lee, all in one. I scrabbled after as quick as I could, but was only up in time to see him git the sword straight through him an' drop into the ditch. You needn't ask what I did next, Ma'am, for I don't quite know myself; all I'm clear about is, that I managed somehow to pitch that Reb into the fort as dead as Moses, git hold of Dane, an' bring him off. Poor old feller! we said we went in to live or die; he said he went in to die, an' he's done it."

I had been intently watching the excited speaker; but as he regretfully added those last words I turned again, and Robert's eyes met mine, — those melancholy eyes, so full of an intelligence that proved he had heard, remembered, and reflected with that preternatural power which often outlives all other faculties. He knew me, yet gave no greeting; was glad to see a woman's face, yet had no smile wherewith to welcome it; felt that he was dying, yet uttered no farewell. He was too far across the river to return or linger now; departing thought, strength, breath, were spent in one grateful look, one murmur of submission to the last pang he could ever feel. His lips moved, and, bending to them, a whisper chilled my cheek, as it shaped the broken words, —

"I would have done it, — but it's better so, — I'm satisfied."

Ah! well he might be, — for, as he turned his face from the shadow of the life that was, the sunshine of the life to be touched it with a beautiful content, and in the drawing of a breath my contraband found wife and home, eternal liberty and God.

A more covert danger was provoked by partisan guerrilla warfare in western Tennessee, which Union troops had occupied since Memphis fell in June 1862. For soldiers on patrol, a backroad mission could be both essential and unwise, as a hapless lieutenant discovers in "The Case of George Dedlow." Compounding the threat of moonlit interference was the growing struggle during the summer of 1863 to control the rest of the state. After Vicksburg finally surrendered to Grant on July 4, the day Lee retreated from Gettysburg, Union forces pushed east toward the railroad junction at Chattanooga, first for the costly melee at Chickamauga in mid-September and then for the breathtaking assaults on Missionary Ridge and Lookout Mountain in the battle of Chattanooga two months later. Whether on lonely roads or crowded slopes, the expense of possession was borne by those who fell, particularly if they did not die outright. At a time when ether was often in short supply, when bacteria was poorly understood and gangrene could be epidemic, even surgeons like George Dedlow were not prepared for what could happen with gunshot wounds. Assessing Silas Weir Mitchell's research into wartime amputations, Lisa Long writes that "we need the physical boundaries of sensation to create an illusion of individuality, of self. Without that sense, the individual is smudged, erased." For George Dedlow, the psychic wounds prove so deep, even at war's end, that he has only a ghost of a chance.

⁕⚬⚬⁕

Silas Weir Mitchell

"THE CASE OF GEORGE DEDLOW"

(*Atlantic Monthly*, July 1866)

The following notes of my own case have been declined on various pretexts by every medical journal to which I have offered them. There was, perhaps, some reason in this, because many of the medical facts which they record are not altogether new, and because the psychical deductions to which they have led me are not in themselves of medical interest. I ought to add, that a good deal of what is here related is not of any scientific value whatsoever; but as one or two people on whose judgment I rely have advised me to print my narrative with all the personal details, rather than in the dry shape in which, as a psychological statement, I shall publish it elsewhere, I have yielded to their views. I suspect, however, that the very character of my record will, in the eyes of some of my readers, tend to lessen the value of the metaphysical discoveries which it sets forth.

I am the son of a physician, still in large practice, in the village of Abington, Scofield County, Indiana. Expecting to act as his future partner, I studied medicine in his office, and in 1859 and 1860 attended lectures at the Jefferson Medical College in Philadelphia. My second course should have been in the following year, but the outbreak of the Rebellion so crippled my father's means that I was forced to abandon my intention. The demand for army surgeons at this time became very great; and although not a graduate, I found no difficulty in getting the place of Assistant-Surgeon to the Tenth Indiana Volunteers. In the subsequent Western campaigns this organization suffered so severely, that, before the term of its service was over, it was merged in the Twenty-First Indiana Volunteers; and I, as an extra surgeon, ranked by the medical officers of the latter regiment, was transferred to the Fifteenth Indiana Cavalry. Like many physicians, I had contracted a strong taste for army life, and, disliking cavalry service, sought and obtained the position of First-Lieutenant in the Seventy-Ninth Indiana Volunteers, — an infantry regiment of excellent character.

On the day after I assumed command of my company, which had no captain, we were sent to garrison a part of a line of block-houses stretching along the Cumberland River below Nashville, then occupied by a portion of the command of General Rosecrans.

The life we led while on this duty was tedious, and at the same time dangerous in the extreme. Food was scarce and bad, the water horrible, and we had no cavalry to forage for us. If, as infantry, we attempted to levy supplies upon the scattered farms around us, the population seemed suddenly to double, and in the shape of guerillas "potted" us industriously from behind distant trees, rocks, or hasty earthworks. Under these various and unpleasant influences, combined with a fair infusion of malaria, our men rapidly lost health and spirits. Unfortunately, no proper medical supplies had been forwarded with our small force (two companies), and, as the fall advanced, the want of quinine and stimulants became a serious annoyance. Moreover, our rations were running low; we had been three weeks without a new supply; and our commanding officer, Major Terrill, began to be uneasy as to the safety of his men. About this time it was supposed that a train with rations would be due from the post twenty miles to the north of us; yet it was quite possible that it would bring us food, but no medicines, which were what we most needed. The command was too small to detach any part of it, and the Major therefore resolved to send an officer alone to the post above us, where the rest of the Seventy-Ninth lay, and whence they could easily forward quinine and stimulants by the train, if it had not left, or, if it had, by a small cavalry escort.

It so happened, to my cost, as it turned out, that I was the only officer fit to make the journey, and I was accordingly ordered to proceed to Block House No. 3, and make the required arrangements. I started alone just after dusk the next night, and during the darkness succeeded in getting within three miles of my destination. At this time I found that I had lost my way, and, although aware of the danger of my act, was forced to turn aside and ask at a log-cabin for directions. The house contained a dried-up old woman, and four white-headed, half-naked children. The woman was either stone-deaf or pretended to be so; but at all events she gave me no satisfaction, and I remounted and rode away. On coming to the end of a lane, into which I had turned to seek the cabin, I found to my surprise that the bars had been put up during my brief parley. They were too high to leap, and I therefore dismounted to pull them down. As I touched the top rail, I heard a rifle, and at the same instant felt a blow on both arms, which fell helpless. I staggered to my horse and tried to mount; but, as I could use neither arm, the effort was vain, and I therefore stood still, awaiting my fate. I am only conscious that I saw about me several Graybacks, for I must have fallen fainting almost immediately.

When I awoke, I was lying in the cabin near by, upon a pile of rubbish. Ten or twelve guerillas were gathered about the fire, apparently drawing lots for my watch, boots, hat, etc. I now made an effort to find out how far I was hurt. I discovered that I could use the left forearm and hand pretty well, and, with this hand I felt the right limb all over until I touched the wound. The ball had passed from left to right through the left biceps, and directly through the right arm just below the shoulder, emerging behind. The right hand and forearm were cold and perfectly insensible. I pinched them as well as I could, to test the amount of sensation remaining; but the hand might as well have been that of a dead man. I began to understand that the nerves had been wounded, and that the part was utterly powerless. By this time my friends had pretty well divided the spoils, and, rising together, went out. The old woman then came to me and said, "Reckon you'd best git up. They'uns is agoin' to take you away." To this I only answered, "Water, water." I had a grim sense of amusement on finding that the old woman was not deaf, for she went out, and presently came back with a gourdful, which I eagerly drank. An hour later the Graybacks returned, and, finding that I was too weak to walk, carried me out, and laid me on the bottom of a common cart, with which they set off on a trot. The jolting was horrible, but within an hour I began to have in my dead right hand a strange burning, which was rather a relief to me. It increased as the sun rose and the day grew warm, until I felt as if the hand was caught and pinched in a red-hot vice. Then in my agony I begged my guard for water to wet it with, but for some reason they desired silence, and at every noise threatened me with a revolver. At length the pain became absolutely unendurable, and I grew what it is the fashion to call demoralized. I screamed, cried, and yelled in my torture, until, as I suppose, my captors became alarmed, and, stopping, gave me a handkerchief, — my own, I fancy, — and a canteen of water, with which I wetted the hand, to my unspeakable relief.

It is unnecessary to detail the events by which, finally, I found myself in one of the Rebel hospitals near Atlanta. Here, for the first time, my wounds were properly cleansed and dressed by a Dr. Oliver Wilson, who treated me throughout with great kindness. I told him I had been a doctor; which, perhaps, may have been in part the cause of the unusual tenderness with which I was managed. The left arm was now quite easy; although, as will be seen, it never entirely healed. The right arm was worse than ever, — the humerus broken, the nerves wounded, and the hand only alive to pain. I use this phrase because it is connected in my mind with a visit from a local visitor, — I am not sure he was a preacher, — who used to go daily through the wards, and talk to us, or write our letters. One morning he stopped at my bed, when this little talk occurred.

"How are you, Lieutenant?"

"O," said I, "as usual. All right, but this hand, which is dead except to pain."

"Ah," said he, "such and thus will the wicked be, — such will you be if you die in your sins; you will go where only pain can be felt. For all eternity, all of you will be as that hand, — knowing pain only."

I suppose I was very weak, but somehow I felt a sudden and chilling horror of possible universal pain, and suddenly fainted. When I awoke, the hand was worse, if that could be. It was red, shining, aching, burning, and, as it seemed to me, perpetually rasped with hot files. When the doctor came, I begged for morphia. He said gravely: "We have none. You know you don't allow it to pass the lines."

I turned to the wall, and wetted the hand again, my sole relief. In about an hour, Dr. Wilson came back with two aids, and explained to me that the bone was so broken as to make it hopeless to save it, and that, besides, amputation offered some chance of arresting the pain. I had thought of this before, but the anguish I felt — I cannot say endured — was so awful, that I made no more of losing the limb than of parting with a tooth on account of toothache. Accordingly, brief preparations were made, which I watched with a sort of eagerness such as must forever be inexplicable to any one who has not passed six weeks of torture like that which I had suffered.

I had but one pang before the operation. As I arranged myself on the left side, so as to make it convenient for the operator to use the knife, I asked: "Who is to give me the ether?" "We have none," said the person questioned. I set my teeth, and said no more.

I need not describe the operation. The pain felt was severe; but it was insignificant as compared to that of any other minute of the past six weeks. The limb was removed very near to the shoulder-joint. As the second incision was made, I felt a strange lightning of pain play through the limb, defining every minutest fibril of nerve. This was followed by instant, unspeakable relief, and before the flaps were brought together I was sound asleep. I have only a recollection that I said, pointing to the arm which lay on the floor: "There is the pain, and here am I. How queer!" Then I slept, — slept the sleep of the just, or, better, of the painless. From this time forward, I was free from neuralgia; but at a subsequent period I saw a number of cases similar to mine in a hospital in Philadelphia.

It is no part of my plan to detail my weary months of monotonous prison life in the South. In the early part of August, 1863, I was exchanged, and, after the usual thirty days' furlough, returned to my regiment a captain.

On the 19th of September, 1863, occurred the battle of Chickamauga, in which my regiment took a conspicuous part. The close of our own share in this contest is, as it were, burnt into my memory with every least detail. It was about six P.M., when we found ourselves in line, under cover of a long, thin row of scrubby trees, beyond which lay a gentle slope, from which, again, rose a hill rather more abrupt, and crowned with an earthwork. We received orders to cross this space, and take the fort in front, while a brigade on our right was to make a like movement on its flank.

Just before we emerged into the open ground, we noticed what, I think, was common in many fights, — that the enemy had begun to bowl round-shot at us, probably from failure of shell. We passed across the valley in good order, although the men fell rapidly all along the line. As we climbed the hill, our pace slackened, and the fire grew heavier. At this moment a battery opened on our left, — the shots crossing our heads obliquely. It is this moment which is so printed on my recollection. I can see now, as if through a window, the gray smoke, lit with red flashes, — the long, wavering line, — the sky blue above, — the trodden furrows, blotted with blue blouses. Then it was as if the window closed, and I knew and saw no more. No other scene in my life is thus scarred, if I may say so, into my memory. I have a fancy that the horrible shock which suddenly fell upon me must have had something to do with thus intensifying the momentary image then before my eyes.

When I awakened, I was lying under a tree somewhere at the rear. The ground was covered with wounded, and the doctors were busy at an operating-table,

improvised from two barrels and a plank. At length two of them who were examining the wounded about me came up to where I lay. A hospital steward raised my head, and poured down some brandy and water, while another cut loose my pantaloons. The doctors exchanged looks, and walked away. I asked the steward where I was hit.

"Both thighs," said he; "the Doc's won't do nothing."

"No use?" said I.

"Not much," said he.

"Not much means none at all," I answered.

When he had gone, I set myself to thinking about a good many things which I had better have thought of before, but which in no way concern the history of my case. A half-hour went by. I had no pain, and did not get weaker. At last, I cannot explain why, I began to look about me. At first, things appeared a little hazy; but I remember one which thrilled me a little, even then.

A tall, blond-bearded major walked up to a doctor near me, saying, "When you've a little leisure, just take a look at my side."

"Do it now," said the doctor.

The officer exposed his left hip. "Ball went in here, and out here."

The Doctor looked up at him with a curious air,—half pity, half amazement. "If you've got any message, you'd best send it by me."

"Why, you don't say it's serious?" was the reply.

"Serious! Why, you're shot through the stomach. You won't live over the day."

Then the man did what struck me as a very odd thing. "Anybody got a pipe?" Some one gave him a pipe. He filled it deliberately, struck a light with a flint, and sat down against a tree near to me. Presently the doctor came over to him, and asked what he could do for him.

"Send me a drink of Bourbon."

"Anything else?"

"No."

As the doctor left him, he called him back. "It's a little rough, Doc, isn't it?"

No more passed, and I saw this man no longer, for another set of doctors were handling my legs, for the first time causing pain. A moment after, a steward put a towel over my mouth, and I smelt the familiar odor of chloroform, which I was glad enough to breathe. In a moment the trees began to move around from left to right, — then faster and faster; then a universal grayness came before me, and I recall nothing further until I awoke to consciousness in a hospital-tent. I got hold of my own identity in a moment or two, and was suddenly aware of a sharp cramp in my left leg. I tried to get at it to rub it with my single arm, but, finding myself too weak, hailed an attendant. "Just rub my left calf," said I, "if you please."

"Calf?" said he, "you ain't none, pardner. It's took off."

"I know better," said I. "I have pain in both legs."

"Wall, I never!" said he. "You ain't got nary leg."

As I did not believe him, he threw off the covers, and, to my horror, showed me that I had suffered amputation of both thighs, very high up.

"That will do," said I, faintly.

A month later, to the amazement of every one, I was so well as to be moved from the crowded hospital at Chattanooga to Nashville, where I filled one of the ten thousand beds of that vast metropolis of hospitals. Of the sufferings which then began I shall presently speak. It will be best just now to detail the final misfortune which here fell upon me. Hospital No. 2, in which I lay, was inconveniently crowded with severely wounded officers. After my third week, an epidemic of hospital gangrene broke out in my ward. In three days it attacked twenty persons. Then an inspector came out, and we were transferred at once to the open air, and placed in tents. Strangely enough, the wound in my remaining arm, which still suppurated, was seized with gangrene. The usual remedy, bromine, was used locally, but the main artery opened, was tied, bled again and again, and at last, as a final resort, the remaining arm was amputated at the shoulder-joint. Against all chances I recovered, to find myself a useless torso, more like some strange larval creature than anything of human shape.

Of my anguish and horror of myself I dare not speak. I have dictated these pages, not to shock my readers, but to possess them with facts in regard to the relation of the mind to the body; and I hasten, therefore, to such portions of my case as best illustrate these views.

In January, 1864, I was forwarded to Philadelphia, in order to enter what was then known as the Stump Hospital, South Street. This favor was obtained through the influence of my father's friend, the late Governor Anderson, who has always manifested an interest in my case, for which I am deeply grateful. It was thought, at the time, that Mr. Palmer, the leg-maker, might be able to adapt some form of arm to my left shoulder, as on that side there remained five inches of the arm bone, which I could move to a moderate extent. The hope proved illusory, as the stump was always too tender to bear any pressure. The hospital referred to was in charge of several surgeons while I was an inmate, and was at all times a clean and pleasant home. It was filled with men who had lost one arm or leg, or one of each, as happened now and then. I saw one man who had lost both legs, and one who had parted with both arms; but none, like myself, stripped of every limb. There were collected in this place hundreds of these cases, which gave to it, with reason enough, the not very pleasing title of Stump-Hospital.

I spent here three and a half months, before my transfer to the United States Army Hospital for nervous diseases. Every morning I was carried out in an arm-chair, and placed in the library, where some one was always ready to write or read for me, or to fill my pipe. The doctors lent me medical books; the ladies brought me luxuries, and fed me; and, save that I was helpless to a degree which was humiliating, I was as comfortable as kindness could make me.

I amused myself, at this time, by noting in my mind all that I could learn from other limbless folk, and from myself, as to the peculiar feelings which were noticed in regard to lost members. I found that the great mass of men who had undergone amputations, for many months felt the usual consciousness that they still had the lost limb. It itched or pained, or was cramped, but never felt hot or cold. If they had painful sensations referred to it, the conviction of its existence continued unaltered for long periods; but where no pain was felt in it, then, by degrees, the sense of having that limb faded away entirely. I think we may to some extent explain this. The knowledge we possess of any part is made up of the numberless impressions from without which affect its sensitive surfaces, and which are transmitted through its nerves to the spinal nerve-cells, and through them, again, to the brain. We are thus kept endlessly informed as to the existence of parts, because the impressions which reach the brain are, by a law of our being, referred by us to the part from which they came. Now, when the part is cut off, the nerve-trunks which led to it and from it, remaining capable of being impressed by irritations, are made to convey to the brain from the stump impressions which are as usual referred by the brain to the lost parts, to which these nerve-threads belonged. In other words, the nerve is like a bell-wire. You may pull it at any part of its course, and thus ring the bell as well as if you pulled at the end of the wire; but, in any case, the intelligent servant will refer the pull to the front door, and obey it accordingly. The impressions made on the cut ends of the nerve, or on its sides, are due often to the changes in the stump during healing, and consequently cease as it heals, so that finally, in a very healthy stump, no such impressions arise; the brain ceases to correspond with the lost leg, and, as *les absents ont toujours tort,* it is no longer remembered or recognized. But in some cases, such as mine proved at last to my sorrow, the ends of the nerves undergo a curious alteration, and get to be enlarged and altered. This change, as I have seen in my practice of medicine, passes up the nerves towards the centres, and occasions a more or less constant irritation of the nerve-fibres, producing neuralgia, which is usually referred to that part of the lost limb to which the affected nerve belongs. This pain keeps the brain ever mindful of the missing part, and, imperfectly at least, preserves to the man a consciousness of possessing that which he has not.

Where the pains come and go, as they do in certain cases, the subjective sensations thus occasioned are very curious, since in such cases the man loses and gains, and loses and regains, the consciousness of the presence of lost parts, so that he will tell you, "Now I feel my thumb, — now I feel my little finger." I should also add, that nearly every person who has lost an arm above the elbow feels as though the lost member were bent at the elbow, and at times is vividly impressed with the notion that his fingers are strongly flexed.

Another set of cases present a peculiarity which I am at a loss to account for. Where the leg, for instance, has been lost, they feel as if the foot was present, but as though the leg were shortened. If the thigh has been taken off, there seems to them to be a foot at the knee; if the arm, a hand seems to be at the elbow, or attached to the stump itself.

As I have said, I was next sent to the United States Army Hospital for Injuries and Diseases of the Nervous System. Before leaving Nashville, I had begun to suffer the most acute pain in my left hand, especially the little finger; and so perfect was the idea which was thus kept up of the real presence of these missing parts, that I found it hard at times to believe them absent. Often, at night, I would try with one lost hand to grope for the other. As, however, I had no pain in the right arm, the sense of the existence of that limb gradually disappeared, as did that of my legs also.

Everything was done for my neuralgia which the doctors could think of; and at length, at my suggestion, I was removed to the above-named hospital. It was a pleasant, suburban, old-fashioned country-seat, its gardens surrounded by a circle of wooden, one-story wards, shaded by fine trees. There were some three hundred cases of epilepsy, paralysis, St. Vitus's dance, and wounds of nerves. On one side of me lay a poor fellow, a Dane, who had the same burning neuralgia with which I once suffered, and which I now learned was only too common. This man had become hysterical from pain. He carried a sponge in his pocket, and a bottle of water in one hand, with which he constantly wetted the burning hand. Every sound increased his torture, and he even poured water into his boots to keep himself from feeling too sensibly the rough friction of his soles when walking. Like him, I was greatly eased by having small doses of morphia injected under the skin of my shoulder, with a hollow needle, fitted to a syringe.

As I improved under the morphia treatment, I began to be disturbed by the horrible variety of suffering about me. One man walked sideways; there was one who could not smell; another was dumb from an explosion. In fact, every one had his own grotesquely painful peculiarity. Near me was a strange case of palsy of the muscles called rhomboids, whose office it is to hold down the shoulder-blades flat on the back during the motions of the arms, which, in themselves, were strong enough. When, however, he lifted these members, the shoulder-blades stood out from the back like wings, and got him the soubriquet of the Angel. In my ward were also the cases of fits, which very much annoyed me, as upon any great change in the weather it was common to have a dozen convulsions in view at once. Dr. Neek, one of our physicians, told me that on one occasion a hundred and fifty fits took place within thirty-six hours. On my complaining of these sights, whence I alone could not fly, I was placed in the paralytic and wound ward, which I found much more pleasant.

A month of skilful treatment eased me entirely of my aches, and I then began to experience certain curious feelings, upon which, having nothing to do and nothing to do anything with, I reflected a good deal. It was a good while before I could correctly explain to my own satisfaction the phenomena which at this time I was called upon to observe. By the various operations already described, I had lost about four fifths of my weight. As a consequence of this, I ate much less than usual, and could scarcely have consumed the ration of a soldier. I slept also but little; for, as sleep is the repose of the brain, made necessary by the waste of its tissues during thought and voluntary movement, and as this latter did not exist in my case, I needed only that rest which was necessary to repair such exhaustion of the nerve-centres as was induced by thinking and the automatic movements of the viscera.

I observed at this time also, that my heart, in place of beating as it once did seventy-eight in the minute, pulsated only forty-five times in this interval, — a fact to be easily explained by the perfect quiescence to which I was reduced, and the consequent absence of that healthy and constant stimulus to the muscles of the heart which exercise occasions.

Notwithstanding these drawbacks, my physical health was good, which I confess surprised me, for this among other reasons. It is said that a burn of two thirds of the surface destroys life, because then all the excretory matters which this portion of the glands of the skin evolved are thrown upon the blood, and poison the man, just as happens in an animal whose skin the physiologist has varnished, so as in this way to destroy its function. Yet here was I, having lost at least a third of my skin, and apparently none the worse for it.

Still more remarkable, however, were the physical changes which I now began to perceive. I found to my horror that at times I was less conscious of myself, of my own existence, than used to be the case. This sensation was so novel, that at first it quite bewildered me. I felt like asking some one constantly if I were really George Dedlow or not; but, well aware how absurd I should seem after such a question, I refrained from speaking of my case, and strove more keenly to analyze my feelings. At times the conviction of my want of being myself was overwhelming, and most painful. It was, as well as I can describe it, a deficiency in the egoistic sentiment of individuality. About one half of the sensitive surface of my skin was gone, and thus much of relation to the outer world destroyed. As a consequence, a large part of the receptive central organs must be out of employ, and, like other idle things, degenerating rapidly. Moreover, all the great central ganglia, which give rise to movements in the limbs, were also eternally at rest. Thus one half of me was absent or functionally dead. This set me to thinking how much a man might lose and yet live. If I were unhappy enough to survive, I might part with my spleen at least, as many a dog has done, and grown fat afterwards. The other organs, with which we breathe and circulate the blood, would be essential; so also would the liver; but at least half of the intestines might be dispensed with, and of course all of the limbs. And as to the nervous system, the only parts really necessary to life are a few small ganglia. Were the rest absent or inactive, we should have a man reduced, as it were, to the lowest terms, and leading an almost vegetative existence. Would such a being, I asked myself, possess the sense of individuality in its usual completeness, — even if his organs of sensation remained, and he were capable of consciousness? Of course, without them, he could not have it any more than a dahlia, or a tulip. But with it — how then? I concluded that it would be at a minimum, and that, if utter loss of relation to the outer world were capable of destroying a man's consciousness of himself, the destruction of half of his sensitive surfaces might well occasion, in a less degree, a like result, and so diminish his sense of individual existence.

I thus reached the conclusion that a man is not his brain, or any one part of it, but all of his economy, and that to lose any part must lessen this sense of his own existence. I found but one person who properly appreciated this great truth. She was a New England lady, from Hartford,—an agent, I think, for some commission, perhaps the Sanitary. After I had told her my views and feelings, she said: "Yes, I comprehend. The fractional entities of vitality are embraced in the oneness of the unitary Ego. Life," she added, "is the garnered condensation of objective impressions; and, as the objective is the remote father of the subjective, so must individuality, which is but focused subjectivity, suffer and fade when the sensation lenses, by which the rays of impression are condensed, become destroyed." I am not quite clear that I fully understood her, but I think she appreciated my ideas, and I felt grateful for her kindly interest.

The strange want I have spoken of now haunted and perplexed me so constantly, that I became moody and wretched. While in this state, a man from a neighboring ward fell one morning into conversation with the chaplain, within ear-shot of my chair. Some of their words arrested my attention, and I turned my head to see and listen. The speaker, who wore a sergeant's chevron and carried one arm in a sling, was a tall, loosely made person, with a pale face, light eyes of a washed-out blue tint, and very sparse yellow whiskers. His mouth was weak, both lips being almost alike, so that the organ might have been turned upside down without affecting its expression. His forehead, however, was high and thinly covered with sandy hair. I should have said, as a phrenologist, Will feeble,—emotional, but not passionate,—likely to be enthusiast, or weakly bigot.

I caught enough of what passed to make me call to the sergeant when the chaplain left him.

"Good morning," said he. "How do you get on?"

"Not at all," I replied. "Where were you hit?"

"O, at Chancellorsville. I was shot in the shoulder. I have what the doctors call paralysis of the median nerve, but I guess Dr. Neek and the lightnin' battery will fix it in time. When my time's out I'll go back to Kearsage and try on the school-teaching again. I was a fool to leave it."

"Well," said I, "you're better off than I."

"Yes," he answered, "in more ways than one. I belong to the New Church. It's a great comfort for a plain man like me, when he's weary and sick, to be able to turn away from earthly things, and hold converse daily with the great and good who have left the world. We have a circle in Coates Street. If it wa'n't for the comfort I get there, I should have wished myself dead many a time. I ain't got kith or kin on earth; but this matters little, when one can talk to them daily, and know that they are in the spheres above us."

"It must be a great comfort," I replied, "if only one could believe it."

"Believe!" he repeated, "how can you help it? Do you suppose anything dies?"

"No," I said. "The soul does not, I am sure; and as to matter, it merely changes form."

"But why then," said he, "should not the dead soul talk to the living. In space, no doubt, exist all forms of matter, merely in finer, more ethereal being. You can't suppose a naked soul moving about without a bodily garment. No creed teaches that, and if its new clothing be of like substance to ours, only of ethereal fineness,—a more delicate recrystallization about the eternal spiritual nucleus,—must not it then possess powers as much more delicate and refined as is the new material in which it is reclad?"

"Not very clear," I answered; "but after all, the thing should be susceptible of some form of proof to our present senses."

"And so it is," said he. "Come to-morrow with me, and you shall see and hear for yourself."

"I will," said I, "if the doctor will lend me the ambulance."

It was so arranged, as the surgeon in charge was kind enough, as usual, to oblige me with the loan of his wagon, and two orderlies to lift my useless trunk.

On the day following, I found myself, with my new comrade, in a house in Coates Street, where a "circle" was in the daily habit of meeting. So soon as I had been comfortably deposited in an arm-chair, beside a large pine-table, the rest of those assembled seated themselves, and for some time preserved an unbroken silence. During this pause I scrutinized the persons present. Next to me, on my right, sat a flabby man, with ill-marked, baggy features, and injected eyes. He was, as I learned afterwards, an eclectic doctor, who had tried his hand at medicine and several of its quackish variations, finally settling down on eclecticism, which I believe professes to be to scientific medicine what vege-tarianism is to common sense, every-day dietetics. Next to him sat a female,— authoress, I think, of two somewhat feeble novels, and much pleasanter to look at than her books. She was, I thought, a good deal excited at the prospect of spiritual revelations. Her neighbor was a pallid, care-worn girl, with very red lips, and large brown eyes of great beauty. She was, as I learned afterwards, a magnetic patient of the doctor, and had deserted her husband, a master me-chanic, to follow this new light. The others were, like myself, strangers brought hither by mere curiosity. One of them was a lady in deep black, closely veiled. Beyond her, and opposite to me, sat the sergeant, and next to him, the medium, a man named Blake. He was well dressed, and wore a good deal of jewelry, and had large, black side-whiskers,—a shrewd-visaged, large-nosed, full-lipped man, formed by nature to appreciate the pleasant things of sensual existence.

Before I had ended my survey, he turned to the lady in black, and asked if she wished to see any one in the spirit-world.

She said, "Yes," rather feebly.

"Is the spirit present?" he asked. Upon which two knocks were heard in affirmation.

"Ah!" said the medium, "the name is—it is the name of a child. It is a male child. It is Albert,—no, Alfred!"

"Great Heaven!" said the lady. "My child! my boy!"

On this the medium arose, and became strangely convulsed. "I see," he said, "I see—a fair-haired boy. I see blue eyes,—I see above you, beyond you—" at the same time pointing fixedly over her head.

She turned with a wild start. "Where,—whereabouts?"

"A blue-eyed boy," he continued, "over your head. He cries,—he says, Mamma, mamma!"

The effect of this on the woman was unpleasant. She stared about her for a moment, and, exclaiming, 'I come,—I am coming, Alfy!" fell in hysterics on the floor.

Two or three persons raised her, and aided her into an adjoining room; but the rest remained at the table, as though well accustomed to like scenes.

After this, several of the strangers were called upon to write the names of the dead with whom they wished to communicate. The names were spelled out by the agency of affirmative knocks when the correct letters were touched by the applicant, who was furnished with an alphabet card upon which he tapped the letters in turn, the medium, meanwhile, scanning his face very keenly. With some, the names were readily made out. With one, a stolid personage of disbelieving type, every attempt failed, until at last the spirits signified by knocks that he was a disturbing agency, and that while he remained all our efforts would fail. Upon this some of the company proposed that he should leave, of which invitation he took advantage with a sceptical sneer at the whole performance.

As he left us, the sergeant leaned over and whispered to the medium, who next addressed himself to me. "Sister Euphemia," he said, indicating the lady with large eyes, "will act as your medium. I am unable to do more. These things exhaust my nervous system."

"Sister Euphemia," said the doctor, "will aid us. Think, if you please, sir, of a spirit, and she will endeavor to summon it to our circle."

Upon this, a wild idea came into my head. I answered, "I am thinking as you directed me to do."

The medium sat with her arms folded, looking steadily at the centre of the table. For a few moments there was silence. Then a series of irregular knocks began. "Are you present?" said the medium.

The affirmative raps were twice given.

"I should think," said the doctor, "that there were two spirits present."

His words sent a thrill through my heart.

A double rap.

"Are there two?" he questioned.

"Yes, two," said the medium. "Will it please the spirits to make us conscious of their names in this world?"

A single knock. "No."

"Will it please them to say how they are called in the world of spirits?"

Again came the irregular raps, — 3, 4, 8, 6; then a pause, and 3, 4, 8, 7.

"I think," said the authoress, "they must be numbers. Will the spirits," she said, "be good enough to aid us? Shall we use the alphabet?"

"Yes," was rapped very quickly.

"Are these numbers?"

"Yes," again.

"I will write them," she added, and, doing so, took up the card and tapped the letters. The spelling was pretty rapid, and ran thus as she tapped in turn, first the letters, and last the numbers she had already set down:

"UNITED STATES ARMY MEDICAL MUSEUM, NOS. 3486, 3487."

The medium looked up with a puzzled expression.

"Good gracious!" said I, "they are *my legs! my legs!*"

What followed, I ask no one to believe except those who, like myelf, have communed with the being of another sphere. Suddenly I felt a strange return of my self-consciousness. I was re-individualized, so to speak. A strange wonder filled me, and, to the amazement of every one, I arose, and, staggering a little, walked across the room on limbs invisible to them or me. It was no wonder I staggered, for, as I briefly reflected, my legs had been nine months in the strongest alcohol. At this instant all my new friends crowded around me in astonishment. Presently, however, I felt myself sinking slowly. My legs were going, and in a moment I was resting feebly on my two stumps upon the floor. It was too much. All that was left of me fainted and rolled over senseless.

I have little to add. I am now at home in the West, surrounded by every form of kindness, and every possible comfort; but, alas! I have so little surety of being myself, that I doubt my own honesty in drawing my pension, and feel absolved from gratitude to those who are kind to a being who is uncertain of being enough himself to be conscientiously responsible. It is needless to add, that I am not a happy fraction of a man; and that I am eager for the day when I shall rejoin the lost members of my corporeal family in another and a happier world.

Sustaining an army was an intricate undertaking, even when soldiers did not need ambulance wagons or protracted hospital care. Logistics were perennially as complex as the treatment of nerves. Throughout the war, regiments needed to be paid, for instance, regardless of where they were camped or how far paymasters had to travel. In "Robbed of Half a Million," that could be hundreds of miles from the Sub-treasury building in St. Louis and still a fair distance from the nearest railhead at Rolla. Until 1864, Union infantry soldiers were paid $13 a month in pulpy greenbacks, and they were often paid sporadically so that back pay accumulated. Traveling paymasters were thus likely targets in the dangerous border country of the Ozarks. Wartime Missouri, as Michael Fellman describes it, was "a place where civilians as well as soldiers, women as well as men were sucked into a general catastrophe which became immediately personal." Among the rocky backwoods of southern Missouri and northern Arkansas, even Army recruits were hard to read. In treacherous pockets like Horse Creek, where bushwhackers had long preyed on the unwary, homes were scattered and a Union paymaster hesitated to trust their safety.

◆◎◆

J. O. Culver

"ROBBED OF HALF A MILLION"

(*Harper's Monthly*, October 1866)

So you want to hear that little story about how I lost half a million, do you? Now, to begin with, you must know that I actually lost half a million. There should not be any doubt about *that* fact. My report, telling just how I lost it, is on file in the War Department, carefully drawn up. The troops in our Department were generally paid bi-monthy, according to the Regulations, but on this particular forenoon in the summer of 1863, when I was summoned to headquarters, four months' pay was due. For this reason the check handed me was several hundred thousand dollars larger than usual. The order read:

"You will proceed, with five other paymasters, without delay, by the shortest and safest route, to pay the army lying at, or near—"

"Without delay," said I, folding the order, "means to-morrow morning, Colonel. But the army lies three hundred miles from here, scattered along at various points. It is a rough region, tumbled into wooded hills, mountain spurs, and tangled ravines, swarming with outlaws. There are few cavalrymen that can be spared to escort us, and I fear a raid."

"Raids, Sir," said the Colonel, swelling with the importance of the announcement, "are like ocean storms. No good shipmaster delays sailing because storms may cross his path. He fights them out when he meets them, and that's the way you must do with raiders."

Of course there was nothing to be said against this display of Grand Tactics.

"But," said I, still anxious to delay, "I don't see how we are to get the blanks and money ready. The Sub-treasury clerks say that the last two millions were in thousand and hundred dollar notes. We must have at least a million in as small bills as fifties."

"Yes, they always send us whales when we want mackerel and sardines," he replied; "but you must change off large for small bills at the banks, and with sutlers in the field."

It was hard work, with no time for dinner or supper, but we got together, from the various money dens, several bushels of small bills: ragged and rotten, and emitting a very offensive smell. Some officers counted only large bills, and took the others for what the packages were marked; but my clerk, Wooddie, was very careful and patient, so we counted every piece of our share.

"Too much money is a 'weariness of the flesh,' an endless grind and bore," said poor Wooddie, as he crept into bed. "I hate every thing under a hundred-dollar bill, and I can't for the soul of me see how people become so miserly as to hoard up the vile stuff."

He roused up at intervals all night to vent his spleen in similar speeches. I tried in vain to sleep, but the night was feverish, and seemed groaning with internal agony, as if it had swallowed a whirlwind and was trying to throw it up. It was thick, black, and foreboding. The wind came in fitful gusts from the southwest, sounding like the advance skirmishers of a severe storm. No wonder that daylight found Wooddie sick and unable to move; it was some time before I could be convinced that I wasn't down sick myself. But there was no escaping the trip now, so I hastened to the Sub-treasury building.

On the window-sill, inside, looking through the round iron bars, sat old Toby, the watch-dog, and behind him stood Uncle Daniel, his master and companion. They looked exactly alike. Uncle Daniel had been vault-porter twenty years, and had lugged so many tons of gold into the vault and out, and shoveled it up into bags, and weighed and watched it so long that he and the dog had grown very yellow, and that is why I noticed that they were a thought paler than usual this morning. I nodded, but they paid no attention to me. They were looking across the way at a very old building, so I looked too. Its iron blinds sagged heavily on hinges; the walls were black with smoke, and every window was hung with festoons of dusty spiders' webs.

It had been a stanch fire-proof dwelling-house in its day, with marble cornice and carved window-caps, but since its coarse burly neighbors, the business-houses, had encroached on its yard; and especially since a big-throated chimney near by had commenced puffing smoke into its eyes, ears, and nose, day and night, the respectable mansion had fallen into a decline, and gone to entertaining all sorts of characters for money. As the necessary consequence of absorbing so much unwholesome matter, its face had become pimpled with an eruption of signs, and the door-posts had broken out into yellow blotches, inscribed "Rooms to Let." One room, however, was not to be let, evidently, and that was the one at which old Toby and Uncle Daniel were looking. The first thing visible, through the raised window, was a pair of patent-leather boots, and the next thing was the wearer, sitting in a chair smoking. He didn't look like a photographer or dentist (half the tenants in such buildings usually are one or the other); besides, *their* days don't begin till about ten o'clock. I had no time to puzzle longer, for the balance of the party had come up; the door was opened, our safes, cots, and chests loaded on the dray, and started for the dépôt.

Uncle Daniel called me behind the door, where old Toby eyed me with grim tolerance, evidently reserving the right (after our two years' acquaintance) to take me by the throat at any time he chose, without violating past pledges.

"Now, Major," said Uncle Daniel, shaking his head, "I'm afraid you'll have trouble."

"What's the matter? Any packages short, Uncle?" said I.

"No, nothing of that kind," said he; "but you start on an unlucky day, and that man over the way is a spy, *I* think. The city is overrun with rogues. I see 'em walk past here, looking in at the money with their robber faces. The country is full of bushwhackers where you're going. I hate to spare him, Major, but I believe I'll let Toby go with you."

"Thank you," said I, "but I guess it would be a little safer for me to take a basket of torpedoes on my arm as a protection. I'm afraid I'd have to be iron-clad if he was along."

"Oh no," said Uncle Daniel, "you'd get along if I only told him to mind you. He hasn't had orders to mind any body but me yet, you see. Here!" said he to the dog, "go with the Major, *go!*"

Toby followed me out, and the door clanged behind us. I noticed that the window across the way was closed. As I hurried up the street, and turned down toward the dépôt I glanced back at Toby. He was close by and didn't look amiable; it was rather unpleasant, in fact, to see how that dog tried to hold me "with his glittering eye." He didn't act to me like a dog who was conscious of having a master quite so close to him as I was. The farther I went, and the faster I walked, the plainer it became that Toby was guarding me instead of obeying my behests. I whistled to him and he growled; I said "Get out," in a modified way, and he showed his teeth rather closer to my legs than was pleasant. I called him "Good doggie," which he resented as much as a boy resents being called "Bub."

I found him determined to hasten hostilities, and, as I had no iron armor, I went to a tree-box to tear off the top slat for a club. He discovered this overt act, and made such a ferocious attack that I was forced up the tree. Confound the dog! if you've never been treed you have no idea how much he had grown in the last few seconds, and how unnatural his neck looked. It was impossible to coax or compromise. He had misunderstood his master, and only his master could set him right. I should certainly miss the train and lose my money. I called to a German for help, but he turned and hurried down the street for a policeman, under the impression that I was a burglar.

Just as I was getting ready to leap down and take my chances a large man, wearing a slouched hat, came down the street in haste, evidently going to the train. He stopped, greatly surprised at seeing the dog; and old Toby seemed to instantly recognize the stranger as a natural enemy, and started for him. I jumped down, and ran for the dépôt—we all ran—the slouched-hat fellow being just enough ahead of the dog to shut the car door between them. Old Toby licked his lips, looked about, then went and lay down on our safes by the baggage-car, "the monarch of all he surveyed."

The fellow in the slouched hat, having taken a good survey of matters from the window, passed cautiously into the baggage-car, and taking a lasso he threw it over Toby's head, and pulled him up to the door.

"Taken a spite at *me*, eh?" said he to the dog, kicking him. "Perhaps you'll know me next time," snarled the man, still kicking his head; and at each kick old Toby snapped at his boots and trowsers, and the side of the car—he was so blind with rage. "Perhaps you'll want to follow me up stairs *again*," continued the man, still choking and kicking him. "Perhaps you don't like my looks. Maybe my hair isn't parted to suit you."

"There, I guess that will do," said I, stepping up to him and taking hold of the rope.

"He's a particular friend of *yours*, is he?" said the man, savagely, looking down as if he intended to lasso me too.

"No," said I, "but you needn't kill the dog because he don't like your looks. You are not so handsome that you need be jealous of a dog's opinion."

He looked at me as Toby did when I was up the tree, then walked back into the car, and I told a policeman to deliver the dog to Uncle Daniel.

We were all day riding the hundred and twenty miles, and I had time to examine the passengers' faces. Uncle Daniel's spy was not on board, unless he was the man who wore the slouched hat. I could not believe he was the one. His clothes were coarse and his boots heavy. But I had never before seen such a restless, hungry, leaping eye. A Grand Jury of physiognomists would have found a bill of indictment against him without other evidence than his face. He seemed to know that I knew he was a rogue; and sometimes he looked at me with defiance, and sometimes furtively, as if he suspected I was on his track. I was, and had made up my mind to continue the healthy prejudice against him that old Toby seemed to entertain.

Five o'clock brought us to the railroad terminus — a sea of mud, navigated by six mule-teams and covered army wagons. The sutlers' shops had drifted in irregular rows on to a shoal of oyster cans, and the proprietary Jew inhabitants had red shirts hung out in front as signals of distress. Every body seemed to be away from home and hungry for oysters; but the great and reigning monsters of this miry ocean were the mule-drivers — a vicious, obstinate, and profane race; embodied lawlessness; migratory insurrections; beings about as much like men as mules are like horses. While looking at one of these teams I saw the man with the slouched hat getting into a wagon, and he had a pair of patent-leather boots in his hands. I followed him, clambering over bales of hay, barrels of pork, and boxes of crackers, scattered along the shore of mud, winding about among great, rough-boarded warehouses crammed with army blankets, clothing, boxed arms, gun-carriages, hospital cots, trenching spades, and axes mixed in endless profusion and confusion, to the Quarter-master's office.

"Who is that?" I asked of the Quarter-master, pointing to the man I had seen get on the wagon.

"He's an M.D.," said the Captain.

"An M.D.? What regiment is *he* surgeon of?"

The Captain laughed immoderately. His six clerks looked up from their writing and laughed too, but quite respectfully. "Why, M.D. means Mule Driver," said the Captain.

"You don't pretend to say that he is one of *your* drivers?"

"Yes, Major, I do say just that," replied the Captain.

"But who is he? Where did he come from? Is his character good?" said I.

At these questions every body in the room laughed, and this time without the slightest respect. Asking about a mule driver's character was too good a joke to be resisted.

"We can't be particular, Major," said the Captain, "and the less I know about their histories the better I like 'em. I generally ask two questions: Can you drive? Did you ever get stalled so you couldn't get out yourself and nobody could help you out? If they answer these questions right I hire 'em, no matter if they've got shackles and State's prison clothes on. I believe our best driver is an ex-burglar. He's strong, and takes pride, as most men will, for a time, in doing a new business well. Some of our worst drivers are horse-thieves. You see they naturally like horses, and of course they hate mules and won't feed 'em. Mules must be fed and watered, and that's about all *they* want. Now all this is business. When it comes to pleasure, like marrying into this fellow's family; or private matters, like having him for partner in trade, I'd object. I wouldn't like to meet him alone in a dark night. But he knows all this country; the fords, springs, and foraging places, and is on that account very valuable to a train. He calls himself Beaumont. He's off and on, and don't drive regular."

"By-the-way, Captain," said I, willing to change the subject, "my clerk is sick; can't you spare one out of your office?"

"No," he replied, "a good one can't be spared, and a poor one you don't want; but I think you can get a fellow named Hickey—nephew of the post commander at ———, right where you are going. He came down on the train with you; was dressed in military clothes. You can talk with him; *that* won't hurt any body."

"Well," I replied, "I will look into the Provost Marshal's office for a clerk, and then come around."

Such an ignorant and hopeless crowd I never saw before. "Nobody among these refugees fit for a clerk, have you?" said I to the Provost.

"No, Sir," he replied, emphatically, "fit for nothing, not even fit food for powder. They don't know how to do any thing, and they are too lazy to work if they did know how."

I met Hickey as I went down the steps, and promised to take him if I didn't hear from Wooddie in the morning.

As I sat in the ambulance next morning ready to start, knitting my brows with vexation, trying to avoid my fate, I suddenly raised the curtain, and putting out my head told Hickey to get in. He had been about head-quarters long enough to get poisoned by its bad atmosphere. A perfect flunky is not an American production, but Hickey had all of the natural and most of the acquired qualifications. He was devoid of honor, subservient to power, and merciless to weakness or misfortune. He was not a safe man to help handle half a million of money. I found that he was a Southerner, and had been in the enemy's country till 1863. All these things came out, and all these doubts were raised, before we had gone ten miles. I was thinking of Uncle Daniel's warning, and looking ahead, when

I was startled by seeing the eyes of Beaumont looking back at me under his slouched hat.

"Hallo there! Who are you?" said I, in my first surprise. He did not reply, or turn his head. "You driver, there!" I continued, "I mean *you*. Who are you? Where did you come from?"

He made no answer.

"I'd have him arrested," said Hickey.

"You can't," growled an old clerk named Stretcher.

"Can't? I'd like to know why not," said Hickey.

"Because," said Stretcher, "he ain't an enlisted man, and ain't obliged to answer any questions. He hired out to drive mules, and so long as he does that right he's safe."

"Well," said Hickey, "I know the Colonel, my uncle, arrested a driver one day for not saluting him."

"Yes," retorted old Stretcher, who had been for twenty-five years a clerk in the regular service, and consequently despised every thing that wasn't regular — "I suppose your uncle, the Colonel, would arrest a mule for he-hawing in his presence; that's all you volunteers know. Now you might just as well ask the driver to answer a conundrum or a problem in mathematics as ask him where he came from. It don't make any difference where he came *from* if he only goes *to* the right place."

"That's true of humanity generally," said I, to turn the conversation.

"It's true of mule-drivers any how," growled Stretcher.

"But maybe he came from State's prison," said Hickey.

"Probably," replied Stretcher; "but that's no matter, so long as the mules don't find it out and become demoralized."

Hickey couldn't talk much with this splenetic old veteran, and we all fell to discussing the deep fords, heavy hills, and horrible roads. Old Stretcher declared the country wasn't worth conquering, and wouldn't pay for what it cost monthly to scout it over; and as for the inhabitants, they wasn't half so good as we could get by the hundred thousand every year for nothing from emigrant ships.

I noticed that neither Hickey nor Beaumont liked this kind of talk, and I saw also that they seemed to recognize each other. We camped at the mouth of a gorge on the bank of a river that night, and while I sat in a bushy cover overlooking the little valley where we lay Hickey and Beaumont came up to the spring below me for water.

"Don't you know you ought to be arrested?" said Hickey.

"Don't you know you dare not do it?" replied Beaumont.

"I can *have* it done though," said Hickey.

"So I *can have* something done," retorted Beaumont; "but that's no sign I *will have* it done. You let me alone, and I'll let you alone; that's fair for both."

A knot of cavalrymen of the escort coming to fill their canteens drove this precious pair away. It was plain that they were a couple of rogues from the enemy's country. So long as they quarreled I was all right.

In the morning we found the ragged skirts of a storm dragging over our heads; the landscape soaked with last night's rain; the trees hanging their arms down hopelessly; and nothing but a canal of mud wending its snaky way over the hills where the road should be. We started up this canal and got stalled; we struggled and fought; we waded on foot along its sides, and finally camped thirteen miles from our last stopping-place. I had noticed that when we got out to lighten the ambulance Hickey had staid in and talked with the driver. That night the driver had Hickey's blanket—they had compromised—and I must look out. Our pickets were driven in, and we stumbled about in mud and darkness getting ready for an enemy that never came, all night.

Eight days of the same roads brought us to the last permanent post, three days' march from the main army.

I had resolved to discharge Hickey, and the Colonel commanding was resolved that I should not discharge him. This patriot divided his duty up into five parts, so he could be sure and attend to it. The first one served was old Colonel Hickey himself. If it was necessary to take all day for that purpose he took it. After Colonel Hickey came his family (he kept a distinction in his own favor there); next followed his friends; then his State; and, lastly, the United States.

Wooddie telegraphed me asking if the roads were passable; and as all dispatches went through the Commandant's hands, he replied that the roads were *im*passable. He did many small things to secure his nephew a place. But late one night Wooddie rode up in a dispatch ambulance. Head-quarters was offended, out of humor, and frowned. A frown from there passes down through a camp or garrison like a pestilence. The Quarter-master was impudent, the escort was glum, the drivers sour, and the very mules seemed more obstinate than ever. I had determined to go alone, with half a million of dollars, and pay some regiments lying on the extreme right wing, leaving the balance of the party at the post to figure up the rolls of the main army.

Hickey and Beaumont were the only ones who knew the road, and though I had once determined not to have them, I thought, on reflection, it would be better to keep them with me than have them away plotting. I told Hickey that I wanted him to go, and Beaumont to drive. He turned red, and said he believed Beaumont was sick and out in the country with some friends. I knew that was false, for I had seen them both drinking together an hour before. He returned at noon to say that Beaumont *was* sick, and could not go. Before night he sent word that he was sorry that even he would be unable to go. My only way now was to get a large escort and a guide, and push through at once. I called on the Colonel and asked for 100 picked men and a guide.

"Of course! you Paymasters always want big escorts," said he, testily, "but I can't spare men, and you don't need 'em either. There's nothing on the road to hurt you. You'd understand this if you were in the field fighting. The enemy is getting ready to attack us, and their forces are all drawn in. I wish," he continued, "Government would put none but military men in the disbursing department, instead of appointing from civil life."

"I suppose a few appointments from *un*civil life would help matters," I replied.

"Yes, Sir"; said he, flushing up and scowling.

"I don't think," continued I, coolly, "that our department could absorb *all* the uncivil office-seekers."

"Adjutant," said he, "have twenty-five men ordered for an escort to start to-morrow; tell the Quarter-master to furnish a guide." And he paced the floor as if he felt the faces of his enemies beneath his boots.

"Thank you, Colonel; good-day;" and I sauntered out.

That night my ambulance axle-tree was sawed off, and it took all next day to fix it; but we were ready for the next morning, and I got up very early. I met old Stretcher hunting for something to drink.

"I can't sleep, Major," he said, "and I must have a thimbleful of something to kill this morning fever-fog. I wish I was going with you out of this filthy hole, only that ain't a very likely strip of country you are going through. It's where the Horse Creek gang used to range. Fifteen years ago a stranger's life wasn't worth sixpence there. I don't believe there ever was a time when it would be safe for a man to ride a good horse through that region. We've got a specimen of the inhabitants. Your driver, Beaumont, came from there, and he ain't a man calculated to call in emigrants, is he?"

"How do you know he lived there?" I asked.

"Because I heard him and Hickey talking about it. I don't know exactly what they said. I saw Beaumont riding out of town yesterday morning early."

"On which road?" said I.

"North road," he replied.

"North road? All right. I hope he won't stop till he gets to the Russian Possessions," said I, relieved to hear that it wasn't the west road, which I was to take.

The escort was late and no guide could be had. The Quarter-master thought the road was plain; the Colonel had no doubt I could inquire the way; and the commander of the escort didn't apprehend any trouble, so we were off on the west road at a trot, and found every thing the first day as we desired. By the next noon we were at fault, and wallowing along till three o'clock, we came to a better road, which we passed down as fast as we could, anxious to find a good camp. The farther we went the more forbidding the surrounding country appeared.

Along the river bottoms the thickets were almost impenetrable, and the open upland was entirely uncultivated. No houses any where; no fences; no sign of civilization except horses' tracks. Grass grew in the middle of the road, and in many places clear across it. At last we reached a scrub-oak plain, and, passing down out of that country, we came to a ford, trampled by horses, but clear, and beyond that, on a ridge of beautiful timber, where the woods stretched up into a growth of tall trees and there was no underbrush, we found a large log-house with a yard fenced in by rails. One white man and an old colored woman lived here. The man said we were half a day's ride from the right road.

"What is this mud-hole back here?" said I.

"That is Horse Creek, and this is called Horse Creek Crossing," said he, looking as if he didn't expect us to be pleased with the name.

"Is it a good lively country for bushwhackers?" said I, getting out.

"Wa'al, I don't know exactly," he drawled. "I wouldn't be surprised if there was *some* scattered around."

"I wouldn't either," said the commander of the escort, riding up, "but I guess they won't trouble us to-night. We must stay here any how, the horses are tired out."

It was a delicious place: shady and silent, with only a few shy wood birds flying occasionally from tree to tree, high up from the ground, their strange notes adding to the hermit-like seclusion of the forest. Grand rooms these, with extra high ceilings.

Nothing in this quiet nook had been disturbed by the war. The cattle were untouched, the granary full, and the cellar supplied. I was surprised, however, to find so many evidences of woman's presence, but no woman except Aunt Sarah the colored cook.

After supper, in walking about, I noticed that the top rails of the fence, and the trees in the road had been gnawed by horses. I showed these signs to the commander of the escort, and told him I feared we might be attacked. He said he didn't fear any *men* who fought in the woods. They were cowards, and we might as well laugh as cry; we couldn't do better than wait.

It was a beautiful night, so Wooddie and I put our cots under a large tree in the front-yard.

As the shadows deepened the whip-poor-wills commenced their songs; now startling the listener with their sudden sharp cry near at hand, then calming us with the faintest reply in the distance, sounding as soft as a fading echo. The night-hawks darting above the tree tops sent down their clear, deep voices, saying, "Sleep, sleep!" and the crickets, from every crevice of the log-house, and the leaves in the woods, chirped, "Peace! peace! peace!" as though men knew no more of brimstone than Adam did in Eden. Out of the reach of hunger, and orders, and brass buttons; here in the woods, with the birds, we found the first real rest since we had entered service.

"In such a place as this, Wooddie," said I, "under the shade of melancholy boughs, I would lie down at last and sleep, beneath the roots of these old storm-fighters."

"You'll excuse me," he replied, "but I wouldn't like to enter into the matter so deep as that yet, though I'm awful sleepy; so good-night," and he was soon in dream-land.

I lay listening to the birds, and I thought, after a long time, that I noticed a peculiarity in one whip-poor-will's note, and that the bird seemed to be slowly approaching the camp.

"Wooddie! Wooddie!" said I, shaking his cot, "get up, old fellow!"

"Eh?" said he, sitting up, rubbing his eyes, and looking over — "I dreamed you called me."

"So I did; listen to that whip-poor-will."

"Listen! why," said he, "there's a thousand of 'em. I might as well listen to the rustle of a single leaf in these woods."

"But there is a particular one," said I, "over beyond the well, and some distance off."

"I hear the scabbard and spurs of the guard," said he; "and, now I think of it, can you tell me why every guard we have placed over our safe has spurs with bells on 'em?"

"Perhaps to keep them awake," said I; "but don't you hear my whip-poor-will now?"

"No, I hear one in the other direction, exactly opposite," he replied.

I heard this, and the two seemed to be answering each other. Wooddie laughed at this, and fell asleep again. The birds had stopped. It was getting past midnight, when two birds in opposite directions took up the song; then all four joined in, one after another.

I had just reached over to wake up Wooddie when the pickets fired their guns; there was a thunder of horses' feet coming each way along the road, a scrambling rush through the trees, and the yard was black with horsemen. I had been knocked down and trampled upon. I remembered seeing Wooddie running toward the well. I wonder now how I could have been so cool, as I crawled up to a tree and sat there with a burning sensation in my back, saying to myself, as I rubbed my hands over the bruised spot, "This is a bad job—a very bad job, old boy, and you ain't quite equal to it!" Then I fell over on my side, oblivious of this world's tricks upon travelers.

The next thing I knew it was late in the morning; the sun shone, the birds were singing, and I could see the shadows slowly moving to and fro in the woods as I lay on my cot, in the log-house, unable to move.

"This *is* cool," said I to the post-surgeon, who was present; "but how did it all happen, doctor?"

"Well, the old Colonel got scared about you, fearing that he had not given you enough of an escort," said the Doctor; "so he sent out two hundred men, and an ambulance for the wounded! We got to Horse Creek late, and were just dismounting when we heard firing over here, and pushed on, to find you in possession of four or five hundred guerrillas, who fell back, and our party followed up, leaving me here."

"But where is the money? Where is Wooddie?" said I.

"Brushed and gone," replied the Surgeon; "and there's what's left of the wagon!"

I looked through a chink in the logs and saw a heap of ashes; but among the tires, hub-rings, braces, and bolts, I could see nothing looking like a safe.

"So the hounds have chosen my better part and taken it away, eh? Well, Doctor," said I, "that ruins me!"

"There's nothing that time won't cure," he replied.

The troops came back that day, bringing no safe, no Wooddie, no news.

Alone at last, with the blessed rain pattering down through the high halls of these woods on to the log-house roof. Blessed the delicious night, bringing sleep and forgetfulness! and twice blessed the sunshine and the womanly face that I found bending over me next morning! Maybe she wouldn't have been much of a woman on Broadway; but she was a great deal of a woman there in the woods at that time.

"Are you badly wounded?" she asked, in a low voice.

"Not bodily," I replied; "but I've lost half a million dollars, and that hurts me."

"But," said she, "was it *your* money?"

"No, Madam," I replied, "but a trust-fund from those who relied on my discretion and courage; and though not criminally negligent, nevertheless I am stung with regret that I was not over-careful. I should have staid at the post, and insisted on a larger escort and a guide."

I turned over, conscious that my head was getting light, and awoke to find the insects droning the drowsy afternoon away.

"Who is the lady?" said I, to Aunt Sarah, the cook.

"Missus Adeline I call her," said she. "Missus Adeline Danton is her name."

"Is the man we found here her husband?"

"Bless us, no!" she replied. "He ain't nobody here. He was just staying. He's gone *now,* sure enough. Missus is a kind of widow."

"A *kind* of widow!" said I. "What kind?"

"Why, them kind," said she, "where their husbands ain't dead."

"Her husband must have been a great villain to have left her," said I.

"Bless you, chile," she replied, "he's chief of the Horse Creek gang, and she got a divorce from him, or some kind of a paper breaking up their wedding; but he or some of his gang killed the old Judge that wrote out the paper, so they say poor Missus is just the same again as she was afore."

I was smiling at this novel notion when Mrs. Danton came in, glad to see me better.

In two days I was able to have my cot moved under the trees. Of course I thought of the half million. It was the ghost that came out of the woods to haunt me at midnight. I dreamed once of being in prison, and on the black walls of my narrow cell were the figures $500,000 written in fire.

But while I dreamed in the woods old Hickey worked against me outside. An exaggerated statement of my loss had been telegraphed to head-quarters, and on the seventh day came this order:

HEADQUARTERS DEPARTMENT, *July*—, 1863.

"MAJOR ——— having been, as is reported, robbed of a large amount of Government funds, is ordered to report at these head-quarters, in person, immediately.

"By Order," etc.

It took ten men and an ambulance to bring this down. As I could not go in person over the whole road, Mrs. Danton wrote a report, in detail, of my loss, and drew up a certificate in due and ancient form, stating that it was impossible for me to report in person without great danger to life, and that this certificate was given because there was no surgeon to certify. I signed these, and they were handed to the Lieutenant commanding, and he started off.

"Do you intend to leave the ambulance?" asked Mrs. Danton, with a look of alarm and distress.

"Yes, that waits for the Major," said he, touching his hat and riding away through the woods, with his men clanking at his heels.

I raised my head, and, sure enough, there was that scoundrelly driver, Beaumont, sitting under a tree smoking. This it was that had so distressed Mrs. Danton—she feared to have me alone in the woods with that villain, after my description of him to her. I tried to console her, but to little purpose. I had never seen her so downcast before. The matter was getting too serious for me to lie there still, so I determined to get up and test my strength.

Toward evening I made my way by aid of a stick to a shady place near the brook where Auntie usually washed, and sat down on a log to watch the minnows play.

"I will do any thing you ask," said a man.

"Then leave me," replied Adeline.

"No, never till I have him safe in my hands," said he.

"You know I can not consent," she replied.

"You *must*," said he, savagely. "I am a ruined and desperate man, and will not be trifled with. When I leave this spot he must go too. He shall go."

I stood up, and through the branches saw the driver Beaumont. His wig was thrown aside, disclosing a high, white forehead, contrasting strangely with his bronzed cheeks and face distorted with passion. At sight of me his eyes flashed with hate, and springing into the open space where I stood he snapped a pistol at my head. It missed fire, and I managed to strike a stinging blow on his hand with the stick I held, and knocked the pistol down. He turned, and, leaping into the bushes, was gone; and well for him too, for we heard the tramp of horses by the house. Twenty men, booted, spurred, and dusty, brought an order to take me to the post. I was arrested! On what charge think you? Why, conspiring with the enemy, to wit, a certain spy named Beaumont, whereby the United States lost a large sum, to wit, half a million dollars. "Wasn't this a dainty dish to set before a king?" To spice the entertainment Mrs. Adeline Danton was subpoenaed as a witness.

In preparing the ambulance for me with pillows, so I could ride easy, Aunt Sarah found a small water-proof satchel, which she handed me, saying: "These are *his* duds, I reckon."

They belonged to Beaumont, and I put them deep down in a safe corner of my valise, and next morning early a cavalcade crossed Horse Creek going toward the post, and near the head of the procession rode Adeline Danton and the man who lost the money.

The charges and specifications were so long and formal that the reading of them produced a sensation of doubt and guilt in my mind. It took much telegraphing and many orders to get up a court-martial. They are queer contrivances, being good or bad according to the humor of the man making the detail. I had little to hope from old Colonel Hickey, and still less from his tools, composed of the scum which had drifted back from the main army and lodged about his post. He was allowed to manage matters as he pleased.

After four weeks of fussing, one afternoon in August the court convened;

principal witness for the prosecution, F. Hickey Esq., civilian. If there was any thing tending to elevate Hickey, or his uncle, or friends, and to depress me and my clerk and friends, that wasn't sworn to by said F. H., it must have been an oversight on his part; "an error of the head and not the heart." I found from his testimony, and the Judge-Advocate's remarks, that my design had been to divide the money, share and share alike, to Beaumont, Wooddie, and myself. He believed I had consummated that plan in part, and that no money had been taken by the enemy. The money would probably now be found concealed in the woods; perhaps I had left it at the post before starting. In proof he introduced several dozen witnesses who knew nothing about me or my money; and still others who didn't know much about any thing, and a note from Wooddie, which ran thus:

> DEAR MAJOR, — I'm in the enemy's hands. The rations are good, but you know money is almost indispensable to an invalid in the condition I am. To be well I must have delicacies — send some. Please forward this note to my mother. She told me that I must beware of strong drink. I think constantly of her words. Remember me to Mr. Hickey; remember me also to our old driver.
> Love to Adeline.
>
> "WOODDIE."

"Here," said the Judge Advocate, "he asks for money. How can the defendant have money if he has been robbed? If he has money it must be stolen." As to this clerk being remembered to Mr. Hickey, Mr. H. repudiates him; but that he should send his regards to a co-conspirator — Beaumont, is natural, and so with regard to Adeline Danton, who might, for aught he knew, be a conspirator too. He relied much on that letter, and would submit the case on the part of the Government.

I was to put in my defense the next day. I thought Wooddie's letter contained a secret dispatch, and so I took a copy by permission. It was neither blank verse nor poetry. I read every other word, and so on up to every ninth word, which last made this sentence: "Rations indispensable. To please me think Hickey to."

Only one thing was clear; he was living on Andersonville fare, poor fellow! and had feared to say so in his letter lest it should be suppressed. I divided my money and sent him half. The next day I put in my defense. It wasn't much. I was sick and discouraged, careless and impudent. The Court's dignity was offended. I was thought hardened, and found guilty. I was glad to know the worst, and have Mrs. Danton permitted to return to her home. On the morning of her departure I showed her Wooddie's note, and asked her how she came to know him.

"I don't know him," said she.

"But he sends you his love," I replied.

"It must be some more favored Adeline," said she.

"But there is no other in the world that I know," I replied.

"Well," said she, "I'm glad some one loves me, and I can't do less than send mine in return; and if he or you will come to my house again, I hope you'll meet not quite so warm but a much more hospitable reception than you did the first night."

"Well," said I, forcing a smile, "expect us when I have finished my time at the 'Dry Tortugas.' Good-by." She shook her head as the ambulance rolled away, and I saw her handkerchief up to her face—thinking of my sentence, poor girl! It might yet be disapproved, and I restored to duty, so I went back to study over the note. Adeline must be the key. It had seven letters, but every seventh word meant nothing. Finally, I transcribed it into lines of seven words:

"DEAR MAJOR,—I'm in the enemy's hands.
The rations are good, but you know
money is almost indispensable to an invalid
in the condition I am. To be
well I must have delicacies; send some.
Please forward this note to my mother.
She told me that I must beware
of strong drink. I think constantly of
her words. Remember me to Mr. Hickey.
Remember me also to our old driver."

Eureka! An acrostic dispatch! The first two words, then the first; the first two twice, then the first read: "*Dear Major,—The money is in the well.*" The good and faithful boy had run to the wagon and thrown the safe into the well when the first gun was fired almost, and was captured there. The last words of the last four lines read: "*Beware of Hickey, driver.*"

I showed the dispatch to no one. It was blowing hot through the War Department in those days, and healthy blasts they were too. One of them swept away our old General, and a new one came riding down—a gentleman fit to command. He looked at the epaulets nature put on men instead of the straps of the tailors. I saw him, and he trusted me at once. He said Wooddie should be exchanged; and the next day I was riding down to Horse Creek Crossing with a hundred men at my heels. Adeline looked pale and frightened, then very red and glad when I rode up. I soon had hooks in the well, and an hour afterward the safe was up and opened, showing a mass of pulpy green—a visible, rich green—worth half a million to me. I returned to the post and telegraphed my success. The court-martial finding came back "Disapproved," and I was restored to duty.

Wooddie had returned, and Colonel Hickey had been ordered to the front. Now came my turn. I had evidence sufficient to convict young Hickey of the charge against me; to wit, conspiring with the enemy, one Beaumont, a spy, to rob the United States of half a million of dollars. He was arrested, and the papers belonging to Beaumont (given me by Aunt Sarah), with others found near the house, were put in evidence.

Indeed, Aunt Sarah herself came forward and swore to some very curious and stunning things. Hickey and Beaumont had been engaged in a robbery some time before, and Beaumont having done most of the work claimed most of the money. They had quarreled; Beaumont keeping all the money. Hickey, hearing that his uncle was an officer, had come through the lines to get a place under him. Beaumont had been a doctor and a gentleman. He married Adeline Danton six years before, and they had a boy, the very image of Adeline. The Doctor drank, gambled, and finally became such a villain in many ways that she got a divorce from him, and sent her boy inside our lines. His father was roaming up and down the country as a driver, looking for the child, and picking up booty, when he fell in with a rogue in the city, who put him to watching the paymasters from the old, dingy building where I first saw him. He found Hickey. They made up the old quarrel on the road with us. They agreed to rob me and divide the spoil; but as Hickey got no booty he thought Beaumont had been false again, and accused me of conspiring with him as a spy—thus revenging himself on Beaumont and injuring me. It came out that Hickey had actually furnished Beaumont the pass, stolen from his uncle, to go outside our lines and gather a band the day previous to my leaving; that Hickey was the one who sawed off the ambulance axle-tree; and that Beaumont was close by when I was attacked. Hickey was sentenced to imprisonment during the war.

Beaumont roamed the woods—a fiend incarnate—with an outcast and desperado gang, ready to do his bidding. He was sworn to kill a great many good and loyal citizens of the United States, and, among others, myself. This, of course, he was to do "at sight," as all such oaths ran.

Well, in the merry month of October, I went down into the Horse Creek region with plenty of money and plenty of men. We smoked, we shouted, we sang, and reveled in the sunshine and bracing air like boys let loose from school.

Not two hundred rods from Horse Creek Crossing we were popped at from the bush. In a moment after a powerful black horse bounded into the road ahead of us and disappeared. His saddle was empty and bridle broken. We searched the woods and found where the horse had stood under a tree, and not three rods off lay Beaumont with his neck broken. His head had been dashed against a lower limb when the horse started. We buried him where he lay.

The fences about the old house were burned, and the ground trampled into mud by horses' feet. It looked gloomy enough. Adeline had gone North.

"See here," said the Major, who had been relating this story, pointing to the garden behind his office, "*The Sequel.*"

There was Aunt Sarah, and the handsome boy, who looked so much like his mother; and the beautiful bright face of the woman who used to be Adeline Danton was turned toward the office. Wooddie was junior partner, in the front-room smoking, with old Toby under the table as deaf as a *post* — military or otherwise.

Solutions came less readily to those who fell into the hands of the enemy as prisoners, particularly as their numbers grew. Initially, officers were paroled and enlisted men were confined briefly as informal exchanges were negotiated, especially after a cartel was signed in July 1862. But when negotiations broke down in mid-1863, just as battlefield captures soared, thousands were assigned to burdened facilities for longer terms that bred near squalor. In the North, Confederate officers were regularly sent to Johnson's Island in Lake Erie or Fort Delaware near Philadelphia, while enlisted men were held in prisons like Maryland's Point Lookout or the cheap barracks constructed in Elmira, New York. In the South, nearly all Union prisoners were funneled through a Richmond warehouse once belonging to Libby & Son, but as numbers climbed only the officers were likely to stay. Union enlisted men were generally sent to Belle Isle in the James River, where nearly ten thousand were consigned to tents and shacks so crowded in 1863 that prisoners were eventually moved to new makeshifts and harsher conditions in Georgia's Andersonville. Without the more varied diet that officers generally managed, the rank and file could not digest the scraps they had and grew emaciated, like the walking shadows of "In the 'Libey.' " As Frank Byrne has pointed out, "It was less an absolute absence of food than dysentery and diarrhea that killed the bulk of those who died in the South from 1863 to 1865 and turned so many of the survivors into living skeletons." Like the captured surgeon in search of his brother Jem lost at Gettysburg, ailing prisoners were both bound to those who shared their misery and likely to brood on their escape.

"IN THE 'LIBEY' "

(*Harper's Weekly*, 20 February 1864)

I could never think of Jem as dead, though I certainly had no definite grounds for my belief to stand on — in the very teeth, too, of the formidable fact that all effort to find him — and many and strenuous ones had been made — had thus far proved futile. He had enlisted as a private — Jem had always a dash of romance about him — and had thereby nothing to distinguish him in that awful mangled heap at Gettysburg; and yet I could never fancy his poor body lying under that mournful slab raised for "the unknown," though bankrupt of reasons for my conviction.

So when I found myself at Richmond, with that curious aptness of the soul for winnowing out the few grains of good *perdue* in a whole harvest of evil, my heart gave a quick upward bound at the thought, "Perhaps I shall find Jem here" — Jem was my younger brother, and my pet from petticoats up — otherwise the outlook wasn't too bright.

The rebels had made a dash on our hospital, which was in about as good fighting condition as the general run of hospitals, took fifty of our boys out of their beds, among them one poor fellow, Simms I think, with his leg just off, and their surgeons; probably by way of padding for an article in the *Examiner* — I know of no other reason, as we were all non-combatants, and they had already mouths enough to feed — and there we were, huddled together in the street, Eugene Delacroix, a cool, resolute fellow, Robert Allan, and myself, with our poor men lying all about, some groaning and ghastly with pain, and the most merciless sun beating down upon us, scorching out our very lives as we stood there three mortal hours. Probably some red tape was to be unwound somewhere — but at last they brought carts into which they huddled our sick and wounded and dashed off, jolting and jostling them as they drove recklessly over the rough pavement very much after the manner of a butcher with a load of calves.

Allan said something about it and was immediately overhauled by the Chief of Police, the Provost Marshal, and Heaven knows what all; and then we were relieved by the Richmond authorities of whatever money we were so unfortunate as to have about us, and marched with lighter pockets, if not hearts, to Libey Prison. Then I began to look out for Jem and got my first sup of disappointment. They had placed us of course in the officers' room. Jem was a private, and might be one of the hundred and fifty tramping noisily over our heads, or in some of the rooms below, or in some other prison; and in either case he might almost as well have been in Soudan for all hope of meeting him; or, and it was my last hope, he might be in the hospitals, where it was possible that we should be allowed to do service. Delacroix suggested that.

The room, our future prison, was in the third story and crowded, for there were already some two hundred officers confined there. The air was stifling, loaded with so many breaths; the hot glaring sun beat in pitilessly at the broken unshaded windows, added to which, at that moment, were the fumes of the single stove allowed for the cooking of the rations. Ah! if the tender, white-handed mothers and wives, if the gay girls dancing in Northern ball-rooms could but have looked in this bare, cheerless, unceiled room, with unglazed panes at best, and frequently only bits of canvas and strips of boards nailed over the openings, unplastered walls, unevery thing belonging to common decency or comfort, I think their merriment would have grown half-terrible to them, and, through the sweet delirious waltz-music, would sound out something like a wail! Each day a certain number among us were detailed for cooking and

"THE UNION PRISONERS AT RICHMOND, VIRGINIA"

scrubbing service, and in due course of time I had my turn at both, and fell into it, I think, quite naturally; but I could never get over my secret wonder at Delacroix when similarly employed, he was so precisely the man that it was impossible to imagine in any such predicament—I had always an undefined notion that the laws of nature contained a special clause for his benefit, and that no dilemma would ever dare face him, much less offer him its horns.

As for poor Allan he succumbed at once, and went about in a very miserable way indeed, though men of more calibre might be pardoned for being a little down on their luck. There were put up bare wooden bunks for about half of us; the rest must sleep on the floor: pillows and mattresses there were none— a blanket you might have if you were fortunate enough to have brought one with you—otherwise none. The rations were scanty; but water, the muddy, brackish water of the James River, was even more sparingly dealt out. I thought of the old border-riders vowing candles as long as their whingers to St. Mary when in a scrape. I would have given one as long as the Bunker Hill monument to St. Croton could he have interfered in our behalf. Not specially heroic this, but still I maintain worth the chronicling; for to keep up good heart and firm courage, as the majority of our men did, unwashed, unrested, half-starved, as we soon were, and treated like dogs through long monotonous days of a dreary

"THE PRISONS AT RICHMOND — UNION TROOPS PRISONERS AT BELLE ISLE"

and cheerless captivity, needs more pluck — enduring pluck of the kind that will bear a strain on it, than ever was required for a forlorn hope.

Meanwhile the days crawled on — dragged is too fast a word for prison time — and constantly I was on the sharp look-out for fun. As Delacroix had said, we soon obtained access to the hospitals for Union soldiers, visiting them daily. They were three in number, and from the first hour of our entrance I should have thought complaint a blasphemy. They used to bring there the poor wretches from the tobacco factories and Belle Isle, worn almost to skeletons, sometimes with the skin literally dried on the bone, moving masses of filth and rags, snatching at any article of food as they passed, groveling and struggling weakly for it like dogs, many of them actually in the agonies of death, taken there that they might be said to have died in hospital. In one day the ambulance brought us eighteen, and eleven out of them died; in fact, we saw little but such sombre processions. We had little medicine to give them, and no food but a scanty measure of corn-bread and sweet potatoes; and this for men down with dysentery and typhoid pneumonia. These, too, were men in the last stages of disease; hundreds more, fit subjects for hospital treatment, were left on the island and in the prisons for lack of hospital accommodation. In the three Union hospitals the average of deaths was forty a day. We lived in an atmosphere of death; corpses were on every side of us. We did what we could; but after all it was little more than standing with our hands fast bound to witness sufferings that we could not alleviate. I had done looking for Jem. I hoped now that he was dead. Better that his handsome head lay low among a heap of unknown slain than to have been tortured all these months in a Richmond prison.

Our own condition was not improving. The weather was growing colder, and the wind whistled most unpromisingly through our broken windows. Stoves were put up, but no fuel was given to burn in them; and sleeping on bare planks, without mattress or covering, was getting to be a problem. There was a falling off also in the matter of rations — corn-bread and two ounces of rice now was our daily allowance; added to this, daily brutality and insolence on the part of the under-keepers, dead silence from home, and the long, hopeless winter setting in; but the edge of all this was blunted for me by the hospital horrors. My very sleep was dreadful with dying groans and pitiful voices calling on those who, thank God! will never know how they died.

One morning the ambulance had brought a load of fourteen from the island, and when I came to the hospital, a little later than usual, I found Delacroix standing by the side of one of them — a young man, judging from the skeleton-like but still powerful frame — an old one, from the pinched and ghastly face — a dying one, at all events. Used as we were to horrors, I saw that Delacroix was laboring under some unusual emotion. He was white to the very lips. I understood why when he muttered in my ear the word "Starving!" Low as it was uttered, the poor boy caught the word.

"Yes," he said, feebly. "It is quite useless, gentlemen — no," turning from the bread that Delacroix offered, "I loathe it now. For days and days I have been mad for it. I have had murder in my heart. I thought if one died the rest might live. Once we caught a dog and roasted him, and quarreled over the bits. We had no cover; we lay on the scorching sand, and when the terrible heats were over came the raw fogs and bitter wind."

He stopped, seemingly from exhaustion, and lay a few moments silent; then the pitiful voice commenced again.

"We were very brave for a while; we thought help was coming. We never dreamed they could go on at home eating, lying soft, and making merry while we were dying by inches. I think if my brother knew — If ever you get back I charge you, before God, find out Robert Bence, surgeon of the —— Maine. Tell him that his brother Jem starved to death on Belle Isle, and that thousands more are — Ah! just Heaven! the pain again! O Christ! help me! have —"

The words died away in inarticulate ravings. He tossed his arms wildly over his head; his whole frame racked with the most awful throes. And this was my poor boy; so wasted, so horribly transformed, that I had not known him. His glazing eyes had not recognized me. His few remaining hours were one long, raving agony. He never knew that his brother was by his side. I died over and

247

over again, standing there in my utter helplessness. I had never so thanked God as when his moaning fell away into the merciful silence of death.

Delacroix, who had remained with me, vented his grief and wrath in the bitterest curses; but I was stunned. My grief was so vast that I could not then fully comprehend it. There were in store for me days of future horror, hours of sickening remembrance of his agony, of maddening thought of that most awful and protracted torture; cold, hunger, disease, despair, all at once; but then I waited in silence till they had taken him away, with the nine others dead out of the fourteen brought there in the morning, and then went mechanically back with Delacroix. It was after sundown, but the first sight that saluted us in the prison was a row of pails and brushes, and the keepers detailing the officers for the duty of scrubbing. At that Delacroix burst out, angrily,

"How the devil do you think we are going to sleep on these floors after they are scrubbed, and without fires to dry them? Is your Government trying to kill us with sleeplessness, since it can't starve us out? Already we have walked all one night this week, because lying down was impossible."

The keeper turned, with an ugly grin on his brutal face:

"Since you are so delicate you can try the dungeons for a day or two. You won't be troubled with scrubbing there; and you will find the company that is fit for a Yankee — in the vermin."

So Delacroix was marched off to the dungeons, as poor Davies had been the week before, though scarcely over the typhoid fever — as Major White and Colonel Straight have since been, and many another hapless officer, for a trivial offense or none at all. They kept him there three days in that noisome hole. He came out looking a little pale, but plucky as ever. The spite of a brutal man is a hound that never tires. The keeper watched his opportunity, swore that he saw Delacroix looking out at window (this high offense was punishable with death), and put him down again — for four days, this time. Then we got another turn of the hand-screw. We were no longer allowed to attend the hospitals. Delacroix's eyes flashed.

"There goes the last obstacle to escape. While I thought I could be of use to our poor fellows here I would not go; but now — I have had plenty of time to think down there, and I have thought to purpose. I have a plan. If you like you can try it with me; if not, I go alone."

To know how sounded that word "escape" one must first have realized a prison. The risk was enormous, and failure meant the damp dungeons of the Libey, of which Delacroix gave no alluring description. The plan, however, was feasible. By agreement each managed to secure a sleeping-place near the door, and when all was quiet stole out, shoes slung about our necks, to the upper story, where was a sky-light, through which we were soon out on the roof, and in present possession of our freedom, though it was to be regretted that it was so many stories high. We went straight to the end of our roof, Delacroix, in his walks, having noted that the second building above us was empty; but the adjoining house, unfortunately, was a two-story building, so that we were forced to descend by help of the lightning-rod, which Delacroix did well enough, going down hand over hand with the ease of a cat; while I, less agile, met with one or two slips, and came down with a final thump, which should have startled the guards below, but did not, luckily for us. Then we found ourselves on a level with the third-story window of the next house—the empty one.

"But how if it shouldn't be empty?" I whispered.

"It is empty," returned Delacroix, energetically, leaning across the little chasm of division to open the sash. "Now, will you go first?"

In I went—bare floor—empty rooms—open doors; that looked uninhabited, at any rate. Delacroix followed; and then we began to make our way down in the Egyptian darkness, getting several stumbles, and nearly breaking our necks on the last flight of stairs—a most villainous one. The lower door was bolted, but, being on the inside, it proved no such mighty matter to open it. Then there was a cold, damp rush of air, and we dimly made out that we were in a small back yard, over-looked by tall buildings, showing ghost-like against the sky. The gate was locked, and we did not stop to pry it open, but took the fence in gallant style, and away! Scarce any one was stirring, and walking leisurely through the dark and quiet streets, by morning light we were well out of Richmond; and now commenced the real perils of our journey; first the brightning light, which urged us to all possible speed in finding a cover. Delacroix had a pocket-compass, and by it we struck a northeasterly course, going on bravely till presently we came plump on a fort—peril number two. "Down!" whispered Delacroix, dropping on hands and knees in the grass. I followed his example in all haste, and so we wormed our way some hundred yards onward. Suddenly Delacroix clutched my wrist. Something was vibrating in the air— a dull, heavy, regular sound, caught all the more readily from our nearness to the ground, and with it a curious, faint tinkle, growing nearer, sounding out loudly now on the raw air. Both exclaimed, at the same instant, "Cavalry, by George!" It was an even chance whether they would ride us down or miss us; but there was nothing left save to crouch lower in the grass, and crouch we did. Doubtless some sweet saint at home was praying for us, for the chance proved in our favor. On they came, at an easy gallop, spurs and sabres jingling, and chatting carelessly; passed us, little dreaming who were their neighbors for that moment; died away into silence the echo of hoofs and tinkle of spurs. But now daylight was a very positive affair indeed, further travel too dangerous, and even Delacroix admitted, with a groan, that remaining where we were was our only safety.

"Remaining where we were" sounds like ease and rest—a peaceful phrase, in fact, conveying a notion of repose; but it was a marvelously hard thing to do. There was the probability of discovery; then, spite of peril, we were in a very desperation of sleepiness, and dropping off continually, to wake up in a panic, fancying that our foes were upon us. We were chilled to the heart; what with night-dews, and raw air, the dampness of the earth, and the enervation of our imprisonment; and as the day wore on we grew ravenous as wolves. Surely night was never before half so welcome, though words have not in them an expression of the difficulties of our way. The sacred soil stuck to our tired feet as if it had been in the Secession interest, and were all the briers sworn rebels they could not have caught and torn us more persistently. Once we floundered into a morass. "Courage," quoth Delacroix, "the Libey dungeons are worse." Twenty times over I should have lain down in a sullen despair, had it not been for his undaunted courage, pushing on spite of every thing, himself included.

Daybreak found us in the "open" quite out of reach of any cover. A little ahead the road turned sharply, cutting off our view, but both heard a sound of singing, to which quick steps sounding out in the frosty air kept time, and the singing and walking grew every moment plainer. It was coming toward us. Delacroix laid a hand on his pistols, but I had already caught the words,

"Berry early in de mornin', when de Lor' pass by,
When de Lor' pass by, and invite me to come,"

chanted to one of the barbaric refrains, so often heard on the plantations, and stayed his hand. The next moment the singer came in sight—a negro, as I had thought. He would have passed us without seeming notice, but Delacroix stopped him, saying, briefly,

"We are Union officers, runaways from Richmond; weary, starving, and in want of a hiding-place. Will you help us?"

A sudden gleam lighted up the man's dark face.

"Sartain, mas'r. De Linkum men fight for poor nigga—nigga help when he kin. Dis chile hide mas'r safe as ef he be in Washington."

"And if he betrays us—"

"I'll blow his brains out," returned Delacroix, promptly.

"Small consolation that."

"It is our only chance, at any rate, and besides the sky *won't* fall. He is honest."

But for all that he watched him like a cat. At the first suspicious move our colored friend would have found short shrift. I had my hand on my knife, and Delacroix's revolver was in dangerous readiness. As yet, however, there was no need for action. We met not a soul, and guiding us to a fodder-house, he assured us that we might rest there at ease till dark.

We were so dead tired that we scarcely waited for the end of his assurance before we threw ourselves on the floor and were off asleep. From a rest as deep and sweet as the peace of Heaven I was startled by a hand on my shoulder. My knife was out on the instant.

"Cut de pone, mas'r, not me," cried our negro guide, retreating in some alarm. He had brought us some corn pones. We fell on them like starved wolves, and then off to sleep again, till the dark made it safe to recommence our journey. Our guide did not take the road, however, but struck across toward what we recognized as the colored quarters of a plantation. "Supper first," he observed, sententiously, ushering us into one of the low wooden buildings. We had expected solitude and silence, and got a shock. The room was crowded, and fresh comers pouring in every moment.

"It is a trap!" cried Delacroix. "We are betrayed."

"Mas'r too quick," answered our guide; "dis am a 'spression ob de feelin' in de cullud brest, dat all. Ebery one, big and little, come to bress de Lor' and de brave Linkum ossifers. Hercules, gib de gemmen seats; you, Cesar," to a little grinning twelve-year-old imp, "quit dat yer. Git de oder little chaps and deflect youselves as pickets. Sojer march roun' and roun', gun on he shoulder: hold he head so high. Can't eben see poor nigga, he sech great man. O Lor'! tink de nigga no 'count; neber tink we hab pickets too, and de Linkum men right under he nose, he! he! Sue, push dat yer chicken dis way. Lizy, gib us de pone and milk. Don' stan' nudgin' and winkin'. Step about gals, be spry."

It was plain that this was a man in authority, though how much was due to calibre, and how much to a ragged military coat, minus the buttons, and a hat, curiously jammed and broken, was too delicate an analysis for men in our condition. The room was crowded, for the news of our hiding had gone from mouth to mouth through the entire plantation, and every soul was there to welcome us. There was little or no noise; but the intense, thrilling excitement on every dusky face was a thing not soon to be forgotten.

"Telled ye so!" cried one old woman; "allers said de good Lor' hear de groanin' and sighin' sometime. Oh! chil'en, I pray night and day all dese yer years since dey sell away my little Sue. 'O Lor', make dem like a wheel'; and ole Sam, he say dat a debil's prayer; but I hearn it in de Bible — hearn Mas'r Arnold read it he ownself; and now, sure enuf, de Lor' hab make 'em no 'count — jest like a wheel rollin', rollin', can't fin' no rest till dey roll straight down to eberlastin' ruin; and de jubilee's comin' and de Lor' bress dese men dat bring it. De Lor' ob glory keep 'em safe; and oh! mas'r, tell de good Linkum men strike hard—he's groanin' sech a weary time."

She was interrupted by our guide, who plainly thought his prerogative in danger.

"Dat's enuf, ole Susan. Curus how women's tongues kin run. Time to sperse, ladies and gemmen, and, 'member now, no noise. Now ef mas'r's ready—"

The sentence was completed by a sudden dropping of his military coat and dignity together, placing him at once in his former light of an everyday member of society. The remainder of our journey had in it little of adventure. Our guide led us around the pickets, moralizing all the way on, "He hold he head so high—tink nigga no 'count," and ferried us across the Mattapony. Here we were given into the keeping of another negro, passed a damp but monotonous day in the woods, were treated to another plantation supper; then another day hiding, another night in pushing through morass and forest, another guide. As good old Bunyan has it, "we were bemired to purpose"—were torn and footsore; but at last we reached the Rappahannock. There our guide left us, and there we passed a day watching men oystering in the river, and wishing for a few of them on shore. The programme was simple now. We had only to wait till midnight, take one of the boats, and drop down the river to the gun-boats; but oh! those hours of chilled and aching waiting!

The friends who welcomed us with open arms gazed at us with a sort of terror, so wan, ragged, haggard, ghastly, was our appearance. Delacroix looked at least five years older; while I—but small marvel if I have changed—I have always in my ears that moaning vice, "Tell him that his brother Jem starved to death on Belle Isle!" I have the vision before me night and day of that writhing frame, that lone, raving agony; and there are thousands more to freeze and starve! God help them!

The sharp edge of want was not always nature's doing. New York speculators and commission merchants in 1862 were easily rivaled by Southern middlemen thriving on goods that grew increasingly scarce. Although the Northern blockade along the Southern coast had been spotty in the months after warships appeared in April 1861, Union victories in Southern harbors during the war's first year made the blockade effective enough to pinch Confederate households and render the trade in tea and blankets, medicines and hoopskirts even more lucrative. Especially dire were shortages of salt, which was essential for preserving meat; in some places, prices rose from $2 a bag before the war to $60 a bag as early as 1862. As hardships multiplied, Atlanta prospered. "From a modest commercial town of nine thousand inhabitants," Mary DeCredico has noted, "Atlanta metamorphosed into the single most important distribution center in the Deep South." So crucial did the city become that acute deprivation would choke northern Georgia after William Tecumseh Sherman took Atlanta in September 1864. Two months later, he set fire to the city and moved out with his army of foragers for Savannah and the sea. But even before Atlanta burned, there was such a demand for salt, as Confederate control of saline deposits dwindled and transportation costs shot up, that a calculating merchant like Williamson Slippey might hoard what he had, watch prices climb, and indulge a secret habit of an evening as winter came on.

◆○◆

Richard Malcolm Johnston (Philemon Perch)

"MR. WILLIAMSON SLIPPEY AND HIS SALT"

from the *Dukesborough Tales*

(*New Eclectic Monthly*, October 1870)

"Sale omnes superare." —CICERO

The Slippeys had never been any great things. The Dukesborough people as a general thing used to look down upon the Slippeys. Somehow all of them did poorly. Poorly in their raising; and when they grew up, they all, boys and girls, married poorly. Anything like improvement seemed to be impracticable to any of the name. This was the way with the first set. Old Jimmy Slippey, the father of the family, all of whom were extremely like him, persuaded himself in his old age that he had been a model of a parent; and he became disgusted with his children for having fallen so far short of his great example. Quite late in life, however, Mrs. Slippey, the last Mrs. Slippey (for she was the second who had enjoyed the honor of that name), who was much younger than her husband, gave birth unexpectedly to another son. He was named Williamson.

Even while yet a baby, Williamson seemed to give such uncommon promise that his father, although he said that he should never live to see it, used to foretell that this son of his old age would make such a career as would lift up the Slippeys in good time out of their obscurity, and be an honor to his family when he himself should be in his grave. Among other evidences of precocity was that afforded by the surprising speed and facility with which he cut his teeth. On one occasion in particular, when he was only a few months old, while his father was fondly caressing the three which had appeared in front, he slyly, as it were, sucked his finger off, and with another quite away to one side bit it with such violence that Mr. Slippey cried out with mingled pain and delight. And not only so, but as the latter ever afterwards declared, he smiled and even winked when he did it. Now, the question was if he did these things in infancy and with his own folks, what would he do at manhood and with the world at large? The old gentleman pondered on these things, and in the fulness of assurance he was often heard to say that people need not be surprised if Williamson should some day become a public man.

The fond parent was right in saying that he should not live to see these things. Indeed, Dukesborough itself was destined to fall before the time of Williamson Slippey's highest greatness. Yet the old gentleman, even in dying, adhered to his hopes and opinions; and bequeathed to his favorite child, who was yet in his shirt, the bulk of his estate. This consisted mainly of a small, brown, aged, short-tailed pony named Bull.

Interesting as his boyhood and youth and young manhood may have been, yet I cannot linger among them. If it would not have done to begin with the history of Diomede from the death of Meleager, nor with the Trojan war from the double egg of Leda (*vide Epistola ad Pisones*), neither will it now do to narrate all the events in the life of Mr. Williamson Slippey that were preliminary to that high career which, at a later period and in an unusually excited state of society, he was destined at least for a short time to lead. The facts are, however, that he had had some few ups and many downs in the interim between childhood and the period which I propose to select for the purpose of holding him and his business up to the public view.

This was in the winter of 1863–4. At this time, Mr. Slippey was in the city of Atlanta. Indeed, it seemed to me that there were very few persons (at least among those who were old enough and not too old to travel) who were not in the city of Atlanta at some time or other during the late war. In those days, if you wanted to see specially and soon any particular person whose whereabouts you did not certainly know, your best plan was to go to Atlanta and walk about the railroad dépôt. If you did not see him at once, the chances were that he would arrive by the next train. We had never expected, it is true, to see Sherman. And, indeed, many persons did not see him, for they had to leave before he reached there, and did not return until after he was gone.

As for Mr. Williamson Slippey, he had been residing there for five or six years before the war, and had kept a little store, of which he was very proud. If old Jimmy Slippey, when he was prophesying such great things of this son, foresaw thus far into the future, he must have been right in feeling that this last paternity had already made amends for the disappointments of all the preceding ones.

In politics, Mr. Slippey had been an original secessionist. The fact was, Yankees were settling in Atlanta too fast. Then Mr. Slippey had no idea that there would be any war; and even if there should be one, he reflected that, according to the best of his recollection (although he looked younger), he was over or very nearly over forty five years of age. Besides, furthermore, there was no doubt that in times of war people came to town oftener than in times of peace, they bought and consumed more merchandise, and, upon the whole, such times were better for the mercantile business. So Mr. Slippey became a secessionist out and out, saying loudly, often and often, that consequences might be consequences.

Although his business was avowedly and mainly grocery, yet he watched the general market, and was in the habit of keeping a few other things besides: a small lot of cutlery, mostly pocket knives; a few saddles and grindstones; some tubs and wagon whips; and even a trifling supply of assorted candy and nails. For having caught a customer in the general line, Mr. Slippey seemed to feel it to be his duty to accommodate him in these special articles instead of sending him all over town for them. By such and like means he was making a little more and more every year; and when the war broke out, Mr. Slippey might have been said to be a growing man.

"Williamson Slippey *is* a growin' man, certing shore," used, in point of fact, to say Elias Humphrey, a small farmer in the neighborhood. He had backed up Mr. Slippey as well as he could ever since he had been at Atlanta, and carried him many a customer in a small way. Mr. Humphrey had predicted that Mr. Slippey would grow after a while, and sure enough here he was growing.

"Jest as I said he would," Mr. Humphrey often remarked triumphantly.

At a very early period in our late struggle, which I am sure every Southern man and woman, boy and girl, of this generation is likely to remember as long as they live, the attention of the Southern public began to be directed to the subject of salt. And I must remark in passing, that probably at no time in the history of commerce has that one subject received greater attention than during our late struggle. Old as I was at the time, and having been a considerable reader of books for one of my age, yet I found that I had had no idea of how much general attention would or could be bestowed upon the single article of salt as was the case in our late struggle. Of course that is all over now. I know that very well; and it is not my intention now to bring up the heart-rending scenes which I often witnessed, and which were caused mainly by the want of salt; and I will end what I had to say upon the general principles, appertaining to that subject, by expressing the sincere hope that never again in what time is left for me to live, may I, and my friends and neighbors and countrymen of the South generally, be so pinched for salt for ourselves and our cattle, our sheep and hogs, and even our goats (what few we had), as was the case in our late unfortunate struggle. We may have war again. I am well aware of that. The universal Yankee nation have grown lately to be a mighty nation for fighting; and therefore I think it is highly probable that we shall have other wars. But I do think that an old man like me, who has seen more than one war (although all former ones were as nothing when compared with the last), and who may be said to be disgusted with wars in general, may be allowed, even in this connection, to express the hope that if other wars are to come, some arrangements will somehow be made by somebody by which the people everywhere can be supplied with salt at living prices, and man and beast will not be so put to it in order to obtain it as was the case in our late unfortunate struggle. There was probably not a single old smoke-house in the whole Confederate States whose floor was not dug up for at least three feet, thereby rendering it yet more accessible to thieves and rats. I remember well in the case of my own — however, I forgot that I was to stop. I will stop, and merely remark in conclusion that the disposition to talk overmuch, which I sometimes suspect to be coming upon me, as I have often noticed in men of my age and even younger, and which I have thus far been careful to avoid — this disposition, I say, I never feel more sensibly than when I am thinking of how we of the South were cramped about salt during the time of our late most unfortunate struggle.

Mr. Slippey had always managed, even before the war, to make a little something upon salt. He had usually cleared from eighteen and three quarters to thirty-seven and a half cents a sack. Bagging, Mr. Slippey had grown to be a little afraid of. He had been "burnt" once, as he expressed it, by bagging. But salt, he used to boast that he understood through and through. Now it so happened that when we were into the war for good, he had about a hundred sacks on hand. Salt went up with such rapidity that it soon reached ten dollars a sack. It would seem that now was a good time for Mr. Slippey to sell out. But did he do it? Not he. Not the first sack. Instead of this Mr. Slippey went about buying

"DESTRUCTION OF A REBEL SALT FACTORY"

more salt. Indeed, he sold out everything he had *but* salt. He seemed determined to stake everything, even to his reputation as a merchant, upon salt. For
he had predicted that if this war should continue, salt would go a great deal
higher yet. Indeed there was no telling where salt would go. Thus things went
on until the summer of 1863, when Mr. Slippey, yet holding on to his stock,
prophesied publicly and above board that salt would go up to one hundred and
fifty dollars. True, he was laughed at, and by some persons abused. But having
said it, Williamson Slippey stuck to it.

Like all other prophets (mere uninspired prophets, I mean) he wished his
predictions verified. When the summer had passed, and while the fall was passing, Mr. Slippey was excited to a degree probably beyond anything that had
ever been noticed in the town in similar circumstances. It seemed as if we were
going to have a late fall. Mr. Slippey had rather hoped that winter, his business
season, was going to set in sooner than usual. Instead of this, he thought there
had never been such a late fall!

Meanwhile, our public troubles seemed rather to promise an early adjust-
ment, and most persons were highly gratified by the prospect. As it interfered
with his predictions and his business, Mr. Slippey was not. He was not the man
to be willing to be made a fool of. Conscription had taken all the men below
thirty five. Like other men over that age, he thought that was a very fine thing,
and though this business might be carried yet further, still, according to the

best of his recollection as to his own age, it was not likely to reach him. Yet the fall lingered, and while it lingered he came near selling off his stock. But the idea of eating his own words in that way was so revolting to his feelings, and he thought he knew the universal Yankee nation so well, that he concluded to hold on.

Didn't he say so? A winter campaign is decided on. Didn't he say so? The salt-works will not be competent to supply the necessary demand. Didn't he say so? The railroads will not be able to afford transportation for what the salt-works can furnish. Now, watch the figures if you like. Salt, sixty dollars a sack! Seventy! Eighty-five! One hundred! That will do. Everybody gets hopeless, and nobody cares a red where it goes now. So, without anybody's remonstrance, it went on up to one hundred and fifty dollars, and Williamson Slippey was numbered among the prophets.

Now Mr. Slippey thought he might afford to sell. During the year he had done but a small business in that way, and that mostly by way of barter for his family expenses. These were extremely moderate in spite of the high price of everything. He had economised while accumulating his stock to a degree that showed genius. He carried matters to such extremes that his wife, who was by no means an extravagant woman, and some grown-up daughters tried to hold him back by representing that unless they could do so, he and they must all perish together. These ladies did not suppose, nor did the public, that he ever treated himself to any luxury. They did not dream that every night of his life he was in the habit of making, at his store where he slept, a whiskey-stew, and then drinking it up alone.

It was about the middle of December. A cold spell had set in. Salt was in high demand. Mr. Slippey had been selling briskly for some days. Late one afternoon, Mr. Elias Humphrey, his old friend, came into the store. Lately, Mr. Humphrey had not been much about there. The fact is, Mr. Slippey had grown so far above him that his society was not as welcome as formerly. Mr. Humphrey had noticed this, and governed himself accordingly. But he wanted a sack of salt, and, like the rest of his neighbors, had put off buying until his little pen of hogs was ready to be killed. He had not made any cotton, and the summer drought had cut short his crop of corn. He had therefore but little money. You think that man did not have the effrontery, trusting to old friendship, to try to borrow a sack from Mr. Slippey? He stated his case. He spoke with the earnestness of a man who felt that it was needed to ensure success. He looked around at the great heaps of salt-bags (and he knew that there were many others in the cellar or elsewhere), and wound up with an effort to convince Mr. Slippey that one single sack would hardly be missed from such a vast pile.

"Jest one leetle bit of a sack, Slippey."

Mr. Slippey at first believed that Mr. Humphrey was joking. But he looked closely at him and saw that he was in earnest.

"Have you any peach brandy, 'Lias?"

"No."

"But you know who has some?"

"Yes; some of the neighbors has some, but they ask a mighty big price for it."

"What?"

"Twelve dollars a gallon."

"Gracious! that *is* high. But you can get it cheaper. You can get it for ten."

Mr. Humphrey did not think he could; but supposing he could?

"Well then, if you can, you can make thirty dollars."

"How?" inquired Mr. Humphrey doubtingly.

"If you will bring me twelve gallons of good peach brandy (I want it in case of sickness, you know) I will let you have a sack of salt. That is thirty dollars less than the price of salt to-day, and the price will be twenty dollars higher next week."

"But I can't raise the money. You won't lend me a sack then?"

Mr. Slippey could not quite do that. It would not—ah—be treating his brother merchants right. If it wasn't for treating his brother merchants wrong, he would do it. Positively he would, but for that.

Mr. Humphrey looked hard at his old friend, and it was on his mind to say some bitter things. His lip trembled in the effort to repress his feelings. But he did repress them, and walked quietly away. Mr. Slippey was troubled somewhat. To turn off in that way a man that had befriended him looked hard. He watched him as he went in and came out of several stores. Once or twice he thought of calling him back and putting a sack down to him at half price. He did try to do it. But he could not; and when he found that he could not, he quit trying.

Oh what a glorious stew Mr. Slippey had that night! It was about nine o'clock when he began it. He was not in the habit of beginning until about half-past nine; mostly because he would not have liked to be interrupted in a matter that was not one of business, and in which he needed and desired no companion. But all the time during the afternoon and in the evening he had been troubled by thoughts of Elias Humphrey, and he wanted to think of a more agreeable subject. Salt was such a subject; but somehow Mr. Humphrey had become mixed up with that. So he turned away from it and set his mind upon whiskey-stew.

The night was cold and he had a splendid fire. Still he mended it a little, and after carefully closing, as he believed, the door of his store, he presently brought out from a corner where they stayed, and where nobody suspected that such things were, a demijohn, a pewter mug and spoon, a tea-kettle, and a little round sugar box. Mr. Slippey had taken to stew only since the war began. Yet no man of the largest experience knew better how to mix things than he did. He took pains, I tell you. He stirred and tasted even the sugar and water before he poured in the whiskey. For he had ever been a dear lover of sugar, owing partly, as he used to confess, to the fact of how little of that article he was accustomed to get when he was a boy.

"Nobody," he would often say blandly, after he had become great, "nobody loved it better than I did, and got it sildomer."

When he had gotten the sugar and water right, then he poured in the whiskey. He stirred and tasted, and stirred and tasted, until it was exactly right. By the time it was finished it was capital! He would stir and taste even while it was simmering over the coals. Just at the instant when it would have boiled, he took it off the fire. Hot as it was he took a little sip immediately, gave a slight cough, smiled, and ejaculated "Hah!" He then filled the mug, put it on the table, drew up his arm-chair, and stroking gently the leg which was next the fire, and throwing the other across the table, he began to sip with the deliberation of a man who feels that he has something good which he wishes to last a long time.

Mr. Slippey sipped and thought how good it was. He sipped and surveyed the vast piles before him, as they lay in the rear part of his store. He sipped and wondered why he had not taken to stew before. He had once been a great temperance man, even a Knight of Jericho. Nay, that man used to make speeches in a small but violent way, especially against moderate drinkers, whom he used to style, every single one of them, first-lieutenants of the devil. But he now believed that of all the things that he had ever done this was the most foolish. The fact was, Mr. Slippey had had no idea how good whiskey-stew was until he had tried it.

"My opinion is," said Mr. Slippey then and there to himself, yet in audible tones, "my opinion is that there ain't nary man, nor nary woman in the world that wouldn't love a sweetened dram."

Whereupon he took a whole mouthful, and his very eyes seemed to cry with delight.

Again Mr. Slippey surveyed the heaps of salt, and by this time all unpleasant thoughts of Mr. Humphrey having departed, he began to make all sorts of inward speculations upon the salt question and upon the war. For he had studied both these subjects closely; the former for its own sake, and the latter for the sake of the bearing it might have upon the former. He had read everything he could find upon the subject, even to allusions to it in the Bible, and had come to the conclusion that salt was a much more important article than he had once supposed. He began away back at the salt-mines of Lymington. Wasn't that a slim business? And wasn't the same thing here a slim business? He laughed scornfully at the pitiful turn-out the salt companies were making. Pshaw! they never can do anything. Fossil-beds and brine-springs are the things for salt. Cheshire and Worcestershire are the places for salt. If you want *salt*, go to Cheshire and Worcestershire. But the question is, how will you get there? And then the question will be, how will you ever get back again with your salt? Only to think now of how much Mr. Slippey would be worth if he had a monopoly of those fossil-beds and brine-springs for one year, and then could run the blockade! Five hundred thousand tons of salt! Not sacks! TONS! How many sacks make a ton? What would it all amount to at present prices? Why, it went far up into the billions! He wouldn't take time to work it up just now; but he shouldn't be surprised if it went up somewhere among the trillions. Goodness alive! Mr. Slippey could buy out the Rothschilds and own them every one. Blame them old Jews! They shouldn't hold up their heads in the presence of Mr. Slippey.

But then if that amount of salt were here, the price might fall. No, upon reflection it should not. He would keep it in different places and make it look scarce, and by Gracious! he wouldn't sell a sack without getting his price. Everything and everybody, people and cattle, might die of the murrain before he would fall in his price after going to the expense and risk of working the fossil-beds and brine-springs of Cheshire and Worcestershire for one whole blessed year, and then running the blockade. Mr. Slippey was indignant at the bare idea of lowering the price. Fool with him much about it and he would raise it higher yet!

But the Governor might seize it.

"There now!" exclaimed Mr. Slippey aloud. "Old Brown *is* a mighty seizer, that's a fact; and he is sot on gettin' salt wharsomever he can for them miserable old poor people up in Cherokee."

He took another sip and reflected.

Let him see now. How would it do to take the Governor into — ah — a sort of partnership? Oh the mischief! That won't do. Old Brown was born with a prejudice against merchants. By gracious! he would seize the salt and Mr. Slippey too, and lock them both up in the Penitentiary.

But let him see again. How would it do to put salt to the Georgia people at half price, and compel the rest of the Confederacy to make up the loss?

But wouldn't the Confederate Government seize? The Confederate Government! Thunder! No. It had more money now than six yoke of oxen could pull down a mountain, and was still grinding out more every day and every night. Pshaw! if he could keep old Brown down he could manage the Confederate Government easy enough.

But a speedy peace would cut these profits down? A speedy peace, indeed! Mr. Slippey had no fears on that subject. He would take all them chances.

Mr. Slippey was a happy man as he rubbed his leg and sipped his stew. While going again over his calculations as to the value of one year's product of the fossil-beds and brine-springs, his mind became a little fatigued, and he thought he would rest a moment and take another sip. It was near the bottom, and the undissolved sugar had made a sort of mush that seemed the very perfection of earthly sweets. As he sat there leaning back in his chair, resting, and sipping and sucking, he was fast getting to the conclusion that he was the happiest of mankind.

But how fickle is fortune, especially in the times of great revolutions! How suddenly she sometimes changes her garments! Just as Mr. Slippey was about to extend his hand and take hold upon this felicity, there suddenly but noiselessly appeared before him, leaning against a pile of salt, the tall form of Mr. Elias Humphrey. This unexpected occurrence so surprised Mr. Slippey that he could not find words with which to make a single remark by way either of remonstrance or of interrogation. Mr. Humphrey seemed for a moment to expect some such remark. But Mr. Slippey was so slow in beginning that he began himself. In the same sad tone in which he had spoken in the afternoon, possibly even more sad, he reminded Mr. Slippey of some of the favors which he had conferred upon him, and mildly reproached him with ingratitude in refusing the loan of a single sack of salt at a time when of all others in his life he, Mr. Humphrey, most urgently needed it.

Mr. Slippey began to feel a little, a very little better, for at first it occurred to him that this must surely be Mr. Humphrey's ghost. As soon as he heard his well-known voice, although his language was certainly much improved, he became partially reassured. He was on the point of asking him to take a seat, and of telling him that he had been thinking about the matter in order to see if some arrangement could not be made. But while he was getting ready to say all this, his visitor with even an increased sadness of tone and exaltation of manner and expression, informed him that he knew what he was going to say, but that it was now too late.

"Williamson Slippey, don't you see where you are and where you are going?"

Mr. Slippey looked around and concluded that he was in his own store-room, before a warm fire, in his own arm-chair, by the side of his own table, on which was a mug with the remains of what was a most excellent whiskey-stew, and that he was not going anywhere just then. He would probably have denied about the stew, but there was the demijohn, which he had forgotten to hide; and then somehow Mr. Humphrey looked as if he would be hard to fool. So Mr. Slippey was making up his mind to answer this double question by putting another to Mr. Humphrey; and that was, how *he* came where *he* was? It was right here that Mr. Slippey thought he clearly had Mr. Humphrey. But he was so slow in making up this answer that Mr. Humphrey began upon him again.

"Williamson Slippey, you are the most altered man I ever saw. Five years ago you came to this place, a poor, little, insignificant fellow, and put up a little store. It was such a little thing that none but poor men like me traded with you. I helped you along in various ways. You have forgotten them now, and I have not come here especially to remind you of them. What I did for you I did because, poor as I was, I wanted to see you do well. I knew that there was not much in you any way; yet I knew you were poor, and I did think you were honest, and even somewhat kind-hearted."

In spite of Mr. Slippey's growing discomfort, he was touched by these remarks; for he had never before heard Mr. Humphrey (whom he considered an unlearned man) employ such expressive language. Mr. Slippey, at the allusion to his former virtues, felt his eyes to be growing a little moist. Mr. Humphrey continued:

"You used to seem to be satisfied with reasonable profits upon your merchandise, and to be willing to allow to other people fair prices for what they might have to exchange. Indeed, I have sometimes known you to give little things in the way of charity. And then, Slippey, you certainly were a sober man. You can't deny that, for you know that I have often heard you when you would be trying to make little bits of temperance speeches."

Mr. Slippey looked at the demijohn and then at the mug. As he could not deny, he thought, as the lawyers do sometimes in hard cases, that he would confess and avoid.

"Ca — case — case o' sickness, 'Lias. Ca — case — "

But Mr. Humphrey paid no attention to his plea.

"But now, since this unhappy war has come, you have gradually grown to be an entirely different man. You have speculated, and speculated, and speculated. The more money you have made the stingier you have become, even to your own family, and the more hard-hearted to the world. You have prophesied about the blockade not being raised, and about the continuance of the war, and the prospective rise in the price of salt, until you have not only become bereft of every sentiment of charity for a poor man, even one who has befriended you as I have, but this night, yes this very night, you are a traitor and an enemy to your country."

Mr. Slippey seemed not to have the remotest idea of what to say in answer to such talk as this. He felt that somehow he had lost his opportunity in the beginning, and that Mr. Humphrey had gotten the advantage of him so completely that now it seemed useless to try to recover it. He could only throw back his head, and with eyes and mouth gaze at, and, as it were, take in Mr. Humphrey. The latter, conscious of his advantage, pushed on.

"Yes, sir, I repeat it, you are a traitor to your country. You have been afraid, actually afraid, that the blockade would be raised, and that poor men like me would be able to get those things which if they do not get they must die. The cries of the sick and the dying, not only of those who are dying from pestilence and wounds, but from that more unhappy malady the longing for home; the anguish of old men and women and children for the absence and death of sons and husbands and fathers, and the miseries of all the poor for the want of corn and meat and clothes and shoes, — all these are nothing to you. You have speculated in many ways. But lately you have been confining your operations to salt: to salt, of all things the most needed and the hardest for poor people to get. You have bought up salt until you actually lie to your own wife both as to the quantity which you have and the places where you keep it. Not satisfied with what you have and the ruinous prices at which you sell it, you sometimes try to imagine that you are the sole proprietor of all the fossil-beds and brine-springs of Cheshire and Worcestershire."

Now Mr. Slippey thought that if there was anything that he would have been willing to swear to, it was that Elias Humphrey had never heard of Cheshire and Worcestershire, or of fossil-beds and brine-springs; and he was getting confirmed in a suspicion which he had that the latter had been in the store long before he had exhibited himself. Mr. Slippey therefore had some vague notion of saying to Mr. Humphrey that he did not consider such conduct exactly fair. But still he could not but feel that the advantage was yet on the side of Mr. Humphrey, and that the latter was using it with a skilfulness that was becoming very oppressive.

"Ah, yes," resumed Mr. Humphrey, now lifting his right arm, "you have dealt in salt until every thought of your mind and every impulse of your whole nature are of nothing but salt. Everything you look at and everything you think about are connected in your mind with salt. If you could you would turn your own wife and children into salt, believing that thus they would be of more value to you than as they are now. You are in a worse condition than the poor wife of the exiled Lot. She was changed into salt only for disobedience in turning to look back once more upon the graves of her fathers and the home of her youth. You have become a living, moving pillar of salt, because a disastrous war has made this necessary article of life precious as gold; and aside from the riches you make out of it, you love to be pointed at by the lean hands of the poor, and hear of them saying, '*There goes a man of* SALT.'"

Mr. Slippey began to perspire.

"Quotin' Scripter on me to boot!" he feebly muttered. Mr. Humphrey had now gotten so far above him, and he saw he had heretofore so far underrated him both as to the amount of his information and his powers of speech, that he became completely hacked. Mr. Humphrey continued his pursuit.

"Hard-hearted man, and proud! Hard-hearted as Abimelech, son of Jerub-baal, who murdered his seventy brethren, and having taken Shechem and slain its people, beat down the city and sowed its desolated streets with salt! And proud! Yea, this poor little salt merchant expects to be famous, even as David gat him a name when he returned from smiting of the Syrians in the Valley of Salt, being eighteen thousand men."

Mr. Slippey began to feel as if the roots of his hair would not be sufficient to keep it from rising from his head and leaving it perfectly bald.

"And then to think," Mr. Humphrey went on — "only to think how utterly mean and contemptible you have become! What an arrant coward! What an egregious liar! Before the war and before conscription you used to like to be considered a smart young fellow. But you have lately been growing older and older with a rapidity unprecedented in human life. You have gotten into the habit lately of speaking of yourself as an aged man, weary with cares and the weight of years. Ahead of conscription in the beginning, you intend to keep ahead of it to the end. As soon as it was hinted that if the war should continue another year the Governor would call out the militia up to fifty-five years of age, you went right to work talking about things that happened before you were born, and saying that younger men than you must fight the battles of the country. You mean to keep ahead of conscription and yet keep up the activity of a man of business. If it were necessary for your purposes, you would be as old as the Wandering Jew. And you have this advantage of the enrolling offi-cers: you come of such a low family, and your father was so mean and poor and ignorant that there was no family Bible in which to record the date of your birth, and there is not a respectable man living, at least in this neighborhood, who has ever concerned himself enough about you to know anything of your age. All this you know, and you glory in it. And yet you don't see where you are and where you are going."

Here Mr. Humphrey paused, and looked as if he intended to move himself in some direction. Mr. Slippey, hacked as he was, now thought surely he must say something.

"Ta — take — take a — take a seat, 'Lias, which — I should say — Mister, Mis-ter Humphrey. Ta — take a — seat — and let me — ex — explain."

Mr. Humphrey, instead of complying with this request, moved off a little to one side and stopped. Mr. Slippey, without moving his body, merely turned his head and looked at his visitor with a sort of cock-eyed expression. It was extremely inconvenient, and made him perspire more and more.

"Tha—thake a—theat—pleathe—won't you thake a—"

Mr. Humphrey, without heeding these words, came at him again in this wise:

"But you could not do all this without some compunctions. To repress these you have taken to intemperance—to whiskey-stew, forsooth! Day after day have you been tossed to and fro in the maddening vortex of speculation, never resting, never seeking rest. Only when the night has come, forsaking the couch of the wife of your bosom, forsaking the society of the children who have been born to you, and who, if properly nurtured and admonished, might have become swift and unerring arrows in the full quiver of a stout and virtuous old age, you have been coming to this miserable hole in order to steep your reason and your conscience in the fumes of a fiery fluid that is consuming the last substance of your vitality. The amount and the quality of the whiskey that you have consumed within the last six months are perfectly shocking to humanity. When the old-time whiskey gave out or got too high for your mean, stingy soul, you began on blackberry. That got too high, and you went to potato. Mean as that was, you went lower yet: to tomatoes and persimmon. Oh, how you have cheated the poor people in this neighborhood out of persimmon whiskey! A little pocketful of salt for a big bottleful of persimmon whiskey! And then, lower yet, China-berry! China-berry! Who but the men of this generation would ever have thought of making whiskey from China-berries?—China-berries which only cows and robins eat; thus taking away the principal article of food from the innocent Robin-Redbreast, the sweet songster of the grove."

These words about the robin affected Mr. Slippey to tears. He saw himself to be so much worse than he had believed that he began to despise himself. Yet he could but feel that some little injustice was done him in this last charge, having acted from, as he thought, no wanton disregard of the wants of that favorite bird.

"Tha—thake a—theat—Mith—Mith—Humph—and let me exth—exthpl—"

But Mr. Humphrey was deaf to his entreaties.

"And now, within the last week, you have descended to the very bottom of this last infamy, and taken to *Sorghum:* to SORGHUM! I repeat it," almost roared Mr. Humphrey, "of all vile potations, the vilest, Sorghum; the very most fatal device which war and the evil spirit have concocted together for the ruin of this unhappy country. There you sit even now with an exhausted mug of stew made of sorghum four days old; and to say nothing of your looks, which are wretched in the extreme, the very odors you and your mug and demijohn dispense are such that were the very vulture here, the vulture that loves to riot in corruption, and had he the opportunity of preying upon your dying carcass, he would consult the dignity of his bill, turn his head, plume his dusky wings, and fly away to distant shores."

Great drops of sweat now formed upon Mr. Slippey's face, and were coursing one another down his nose.

"And now," asked Mr. Humphrey with earnest compassion, "don't you see where you are and where you are going? No he don't. The miserable creature don't! Oh Williamson Slippey, don't you see that you are dying and going to *perdition?*"

The poor man had had no idea of being so near his earthly end. Notwithstanding his advance of all conscriptions, both past and prospective, he yet had felt within himself the supplies of a life of many years to come, and in his blindness had believed that sorghum-stews were furnishing strength far behind his age. But now these words fell upon his ears with the import of doom. His heart ceased to beat. His tongue could no longer articulate. Earthly objects were fading from his vision, and with unutterable horror he beheld the approach of the eternal burnings. Oh for a little more of life! Oh for the opportunity of repenting and of distributing his salt among the poor! Too late! On the fires came rolling and roaring. Feet foremost Mr. Slippey glided to meet them.

"Oh! Oh!! oн!! oн!!! oн!!!!" screamed the unhappy man, and gave it up.

At least so he believed.

But Mr. Slippey fortunately was mistaken. He was not quite dead, although the fire and the sorghum-stew had come near finishing him. He had fallen to sleep and to dreaming, and had subsided in his chair until his head was hanging over the arm next the fire. Its weight and that of his other upper parts had pushed one leg so far in that direction that his trowsers caught the blaze and his calf began to burn. The fire and the shriek awoke the sleeper, and it was half a minute before he could convince himself that he was not where Mr. Humphrey had said he was going. With many a slap and some kicks, having found out the state of things and extinguished the flames, he went with speed to the door, opened it, and thought that the cool night-air never had felt so fresh and so nice.

The next morning Mr. Slippey was observed to have on a new pair of trowsers and to limp slightly. On that day he sold out his whole stock except two sacks, which before night were in Elias Humphrey's smoke-house. In a very short time Mr. Slippey with his family started off in a southwesterly direction from Atlanta, and it was supposed succeeded in getting to Texas, whither he seemed to be bound.

1864

In the West, Grant's siege at Vicksburg had brought the city to a crisis. When the Daily Citizen *was reduced to a square foot of wallpaper and townspeople were forced to eat rats, the city surrendered, and the last two hundred miles of the Mississippi River came under Union control. While Grant eventually moved east to the railroad juncture at Chattanooga and his army's November charge up Missionary Ridge, the occupying forces that remained behind were left to police the open river, a virtual impossibility as cargo moved out of Memphis each day and smaller boats on the river then slipped to shore. "The lack of an adequate river patrol," Joseph Parks has observed, "left the military commander powerless to regulate trade except at the Memphis landings, and high prices offered for goods along the river proved too tempting for many a boat captain." The shortage of necessities such as boots and coffee, flour and salt was so acute and the illegal trade in smuggled goods so steady that as much as $20 million to $30 million worth of contraband supplies got passed along to waiting guerrillas and Confederate forces during the two years after Memphis fell in mid-1862. Even the dismal cold at the end of 1863 did not halt commerce or diminish the task in "A Night on the Mississippi" of a Union detail sent to investigate.*

◆○◆

Ross Guffin

"A NIGHT ON THE MISSISSIPPI"

(*Putnam's*, April 1870)

On the morning of the 31st day of December, 1863, it was reported to the commanding officers of Fort Pillow that there was a trading-boat on the Mississippi river above Osceola, largely supplying the Confederate soldiers and guerillas, then swarming in that region, with articles contraband of war.

It was a part of the duty of the garrison at Fort Pillow to guard against this illicit trade. Although all traffic along the Mississippi had been interdicted, except such as might be specially permitted by the agents of the Government, there were not wanting adventurers, who, for the sake of the large gains promised, took the risk of smuggling.

These daring fellows, having placed their goods in small boats or skiffs, would choose a dark night and quietly drop down the river, passing the guards and batteries at Cairo and Columbus; when they had a clear space for their operation of one hundred and thirty miles, from Columbus to Fort Pillow, unguarded, save by a few patrolling gunboats and occasional scouting parties. These eluded, when far enough down they would pull off into some slough, bayou, or small tributary to the Mississippi and there dispose of their effects at enormous prices.

Notwithstanding the vigilance of the forces left to guard the rear, as the armies of the West pushed their column further to the South, there were left behind numerous companies of partisan rangers, guerillas, and outlaws, and Confederate soldiers at home recruiting and gathering supplies. These were continually prowling about West Tennessee and Arkansas; and all these, besides citizens in sympathy with the rebellion, became the aiders, abettors, and patrons of the smugglers. Though these law-breakers were occasionally caught, and severely punished, the smuggling was continued with varied success until the close of the war.

The report, which came well accredited to Fort Pillow, placed the offenders in a slough, on the Arkansas side, at a point five miles above Osceola and twenty miles above Fort Pillow.

Lieutenant Edward Alexander, of the Fifty-Second Indiana Volunteers, commanding the provost-guard, was ordered to proceed at once, with a sufficient detachment from his command, to the designated point, and look after the reported transgressors.

Eight men were soon detailed and supplied with forty rounds of cartridges each, and rations for one day only, as they expected to return that evening.

The men fall in and stand, in four files, ready for the command. They have been selected for their work, and you will look long before you find an equal number finer in appearance, or more soldierly in bearing. They are all young, strong, and brave; and yet are ranked as veterans in the service. The Lieutenant, stepping in front, gives the command, and they move off, marching with steady, measured tramp to the river. Here they quickly embark in a yawl, which, with four well-manned oars, shoots rapidly up the river despite the strong current against it.

The day was warm and cloudy, with a slight mist, and a dense fog, rising from the river, rolled back over its banks, enveloping every thing in gloom. Such days are common to the great river at this season of the year, and in their dreary darkness there is a kind of painful stillness that weighs upon the spirit and fills the heart with dismal forebodings.

Nothing daunted by their sombre surroundings, the men pull stoutly. They shoot out from under the high bluffs of Fort Pillow; have passed the mouth of Cane Creek, and are well up with Flower Island, that looks down upon them drearily enough, its solitary home and dilapidated fence in front scarcely discernible in the bed of fog. On glides the boat, along the winding thread of the river, through the thick forests that line the banks on either side, and reach out as far as the eye can see. On the Tennessee shore the land is low, and the thrifty young timber, mostly cottonwood, stands so thick that the eye can penetrate but a short distance; while on the Arkansas side a bank, twenty feet high, rises perpendicularly from the water, and the rich soil above is overgrown with mammoth forest-trees that might have withstood the tempests of centuries, and now reach their arms far out and up toward the clouds that gather thick above them. The dark, towering trees, and the clouds hanging ominously high above their heads, seem to stand off as if each were defiant of the other. The wind moaning through the stripped and bare branches gives additional dreariness to the dull, dark day. The river is clear of islands, except an occasional sandbar that rises gradually out of its bosom and swells up to a height of several feet with considerable width, and then stretching away up the river, grows less and breaks off with a sudden jog, or again gradually disappears under the surface of the water.

The journey is half performed, and the yawl is passing a bar larger than its neighbors, which stretches away, a distance of a mile, to where a thick clump of trees covers its head. This is known to navigators of the river as "Bulletin Tow-Head." The men pass it coolly, little dreaming of the fate that awaits them there, on their return.

This passed, they come in sight of the village of Osceola, standing out in its little clearing on the western bank. A few scattering houses, mostly of logs, all look dingy and dirty, and it will hardly pass for the capital of Mississippi County, Arkansas, until you find the huge, misshapen loghouse a few rods from the river, and learn that it is the Court-House, and that twenty yards removed stands the jail, built of logs also, but neater, more substantial, and almost as large, as the Court-House.

It is related that, before the war, the denizens of the village and vicinity were wont to collect daily in these public buildings, and play cards and drink whiskey; the aristocratic class always occupying the jail, as the more comfortable.

Our party tarry here but a short time, and reëmbarking, push off, and pull on up the river. Another long stretch around a long bend, and the designated point is reached. The day was far spent before the Lieutenant had completed his search, and was ready to return. Captain E. D. Leizure, an experienced river-man, joined the Lieutenant's command on reëmbarking for the fort.

The men are tired, and the oars swing listlessly over the waters, while the swift current drives the boat rapidly down the river. The gloom of the morning had gradually deepened during the day, and the mist had changed into a steady rain. Osceola is reached and passed. The day is wearing away and growing more and more stormy. The river is very full, and the wind, now blowing a stiff gale, catches the yawl and hastens it forward over the waste of waters. The wind rises still higher, the air grows colder, the rain turns to snow and falls in great white flakes, obscuring the view of the helmsman. Night is coming on. The boat leaps forward with the waves; at this rate two hours will land it at the fort. But the yawl is becoming unmanageable; the wind and waves contend with the men for the mastery. Darkness now adds to the perplexity, as it settles deep and heavy around the struggling oarsmen. The party are still nine miles from the fort; they are wet, tired, and cold — are tossed and driven by the elements and hemmed in by the night.

What is to be done? It is proposed to abandon the yawl. What then? There is no human habitation for miles around. The party is in the midst of a vast wilderness of waters that extends far out over the marshes and lowlands of the Tennessee side, and away across westward to the dense forests of Arkansas, that give no show of hospitality, but, with dim outline, stand out against the sky, dark, wild, and cheerless.

The darkness thickens; the light, now faded out of the sky, lingers but faintly along the surface of the river. Peering through the gloom, the men trace the outline of a sandbar, near at hand, by its snowy cap, that gleams out a white streak along the middle of the mighty river. The wind, roaring from the thick growth of cottonwood on the Tennessee shore, forces the yawl rapidly toward the bar. The men strain every nerve to clear it, but in vain. The boat strikes the bar far down toward the point, and the waves carry it high upon the land.

There is no use in contending with the elements; the boat is abandoned, and the men set out to walk up the bar, hoping to find on the higher ground drift-wood to make a fire. Having gone nearly a quarter of a mile, they come upon the stump and roots of an old tree, half buried in the sand, and around which vegetation had grown up the summer before.

The grass and weeds are gathered, and the roots broken up, as well as the darkness will permit, and an effort is made to kindle a fire. But every thing is saturated with water and refuses to burn. Captain Leizure thinks of his carpet-sack, which contains his under-clothing. Immediately this is opened, and one after another the articles taken out, torn in shreds, and the burning match applied; and though some of these burn, they fail to ignite the materials gathered for the fire.

At length, when every means has been exhausted without avail, the men turn back to the boat, as the last hope. To remain on this bleak island over night, without fire, in the cold, which is already severe and rapidly growing more so, would be certain death.

The boat can only be made available by taking it up and carrying it across the bar, whence the wind and waves will take it to the Arkansas shore. It is quickly carried across the bar, and launched into the water on the other side, which is found too shallow to float it. The Lieutenant sends three men with Captain Leizure to drag the boat out into deep water, where all may embark; but just as the boat is well afloat, a powerful gust of wind strikes it, and shooting out from under the hands of the men, it rushes away into the darkness with the waves. Captain Leizure and one of the men have jumped in and are whirled away from the other two, who are left standing with the oars in their hands. The Captain and his companion resign themselves to their fate, being totally unable to return.

The men in the boat, whirled suddenly off, hear the shouts of their luckless comrades, until the voices are drowned in the noise of the storm; and then they see the flash and hear the report of a discharged musket; it was a signal-gun.

The boat sweeps madly on — where to touch, or when? It is at the mercy of the angry elements; it may be cast on another bar from which there can be no escape, or suddenly capsized, and the men may find a grave at the bottom of the restless river. But in another moment it strikes the shore. The waves dash over it. The water freezes as it falls. The soldier is frozen to his seat, and, benumbed with cold, he refuses to rise. His gun lies frozen into the ice formed on the water in the boat, and there it will remain untouched. The tried and faithful companion of years is now no longer wanted to defend a life too far gone to be held worth the preserving.

With great difficulty Captain Leizure succeeds in arousing his companion, and after long search and effort climbs up the steep bank with him, and into the woods. And now, if a fire can be kindled they are saved, otherwise they perish. The brave soldier who has faced the cannon, and braved the hardships of nearly three years' campaigning, sinks under the intense cold, and begs to be let alone to die. But the dauntless Captain works the harder to keep him up. A large log is found, and twigs and chunks of wood are heaped against it for a fire; but they have been wet through, and are now covered with ice. They have only two matches. Their clothes have been thoroughly drenched, and are even frozen stiff. Captain Leizure takes from his breast-pocket a large leathern pocketbook, and finds that the papers it contains are dry. They are bonds and notes of the value of many thousands of dollars — no matter how many, it is a question of life or death. The papers are ready for the match. It is struck, but it misses fire. The two lives now depend upon the one remaining match. It is struck, and, God be praised! it burns, the paper catches, then the twigs; the fire is made; the men are saved.

Leaving them by their growing fire, let us glance into the hotel at Fort Pillow. The commander of the garrison has given a supper, and the large dining-hall

is filled with happy people; brave officers, respectable citizens, and charming women.

It is the farewell of loyal hearts to the year that gave freedom to the slave — that brought the first real success to our arms — that gave us Vicksburg, Gettysburg, and Missionary Ridge — that had brought promise of the rebellion's overthrow.

The perils and escapes, the achievements and hopes, the rewards and promises of the closing and of the coming year are earnestly and eloquently discussed; and so the old year goes out, carrying with it the blessing of the loyal millions, and the new year steps in.

The party breaks up, and we walk out into the cold, dark night. The thermometer is now seven degrees below zero.

"Captain, have Lieutenant Alexander and his men reported?" asks the Post-Commander, Colonel Wolfe, as he draws my arm in his, and we walk away to our quarters.

"Not yet," is my reply.

"What can have become of them?" he rejoins. "I fear for their safety if they are out this dreadful night." And well you may, my brave Colonel; for even now, as we walk, where are they?

Left standing on the bar, the boat gone, with no hope, nor even possibility of its returning, the Lieutenant and his men determine to go back up to the higher ground and try once more for a fire. But in this they are doomed to a second failure.

Their matches all exhausted, and the cold winds howling about them, there is but one hope left: that by constant motion they may keep alive till morning comes and brings relief.

A beat is chosen, and there these veteran soldiers pace up and down the space of one hundred yards through the long, dreary hours of that awful night. The snow is already several inches deep and still falling. The constant tramping of the men wears it off the beat. And still they walk wearily on. At eleven o'clock the cold is intense; the snow has ceased to fall, and being caught up by the winds sweeping over the bar, is whirled into great drifts. Every thing is now freezing. Still back and forth, along the beaten path, plod the jaded men.

It is an hour later. One of the men, overcome with fatigue and cold, sinks down in his tracks, and falls to the ground, *dead*. His comrades go to him, take him up, chafe his limbs, breathe into his nostrils, and strive in every way to recall him to life; but it is in vain; the spirit that animated the fallen body has gone to Him who gave it.

The young Lieutenant, whose bravery had made him conspicuous on the battle-field, then turned to his men, and standing a moment in silence, thinking, doubtless, of the kind mother who dwelt far away to the North, and who might at that very moment be praying God's blessing on her dashing boy, addressed his last words to the men entrusted to his command, saying: "Boys, there is no use striving any longer; it is now only about midnight, and one of our number is already frozen to death. We cannot hold out till morning; there is no hope, we must all die."

Then, stepping aside, he drew the cape of his great-coat about his head and laid down. The snow blew over him, but he knew it not; he was asleep. Two others follow his example; their lives depart with the departure of the dying year. The new year comes, and with it the clouds break away, and the North Star shines out.

Guided by its light, the four remaining ones walk up the bar; but scarcely have they set out, when one poor fellow staggers and falls dead, only a few rods from his frozen comrades. The other three are tired, benumbed, disheartened, yet still they follow the star which guides them to life. It leads them over a mile of bleak desert, across a thick slough, and into a thick wood at the head of the island. This shelters them from the cutting wind until morning dawns; and peering out from the Arkansas shore, they descry a house, from which presently issues a man; it is Prior Lea, a well known Union man. They attract his attention, and, crossing to them in a skiff, he takes them to his house. And now, although they have already suffered untold agonies, their sufferings have only begun.

Once in the house, they sink insensible to the floor. The good host and hostess do all they can for the poor fellows, but it avails little. They are far gone, life hangs by a slender thread, which may snap at any moment.

The thermometer is now eight degrees below zero, and every thing without is freezing still. All about Fort Pillow there are signs of life. The smoke is curling in white columns over the low-made chimneys of the little huts called barracks; the guard has been relieved, and the men are coming in from the outposts, benumbed with cold, and in some cases with their fingers and ears frost-bitten; the soldiers dodge in and out of their quarters busied about the morning work; messengers and orderlies hurry rapidly over the snow-crested hills; and yonder, at post head-quarters, the color-sergeant commits the flag to the halliards and sends it to its place to the top of the tall staff, and there, high up in the clear sky, in the bright light of the new-born year,

"Flash its broad ribbons of lily and rose."

The men draw close around the fires, and talk of last night's cold. Frost flies in the air, and great cakes of ice are floating in the river.

Still there are no tidings of the Lieutenant and his men. About noon Captain Leizure and his companion, worn and stupefied, having made their way, from the fire where we last saw them, to a house nearly opposite the fort, cross the river in a skiff and report to the officers. The post-surgeon, Dr. J. W. Martin, is at once summoned, and a party got ready to search for the ill-fated ones who come not back. Captain Leizure, though almost exhausted from the previous night's exposure, volunteers to go as a guide.

In about two hours the steamer *Duke of Argyle* heaves in sight, beating her way slowly up against the strong current and running ice. The party board her, and she pushes on up the river. She comes in sight of the fatal bar just as the sun is setting in the red West. She is made fast on the Tennessee shore, and the boats are lowered as the twilight deepens into night. The thermometer is below zero; every thing around is freezing, except the mighty river, whose current sweeps on, bearing on its bosom the masses of ice that gather as they go. The deck-hands refuse to man the boats, until a file of soldiers, with loaded muskets, is brought up to enforce the officer's commands.

Landed upon the island, and aided by the light of a lantern, they soon discover the tracks of the unfortunate men who had landed there twenty-four hours before.

Hopes are entertained for their safety. We follow the trail, and presently come upon a cartridge-box, half buried in the snow and ice, the belt cut with a knife. Our hearts sink; the fate of one poor man is told. One life must have been despaired of, when, with hands too numb to unbuckle the belt, it was cut, and the cartridge-box fell from the body of a soldier in the enemy's country. With sad hearts we follow up the track. Now we see the well-paced beat, and piled at intervals along it we find the half-covered and frozen bodies of the lost Lieutenant and three of his men. A little further removed to the north, on the crust of ice, lies stretched upon his back another, who has met his last enemy; his face is pale and rigid, and his eyes, wide open, are seemingly fixed upon the stars that twinkle overhead and give back his bright, cold, comfortless look.

Well, we can do no good for these, and the others have shared the same fate, unless a kindlier fortune has taken them out of the cold ere this. To remain longer on this cold, barren spot would be to add to the number of the dead. So the search is abandoned for the night, and we turn for the steamer. But who will steer the boat? the helmsman who brought it over is so overcome by the cold that he cannot guide it back. Who will take his place? "I will," said Captain Leizure, and stepping aft, took the helm. The boat glides away. It is over a mile to the steamer, and it will take many a stroke to carry us to her. The oars are vigorously plied, and on goes our little boat, Captain Leizure holding her steady on her course.

The running ice must be avoided, and the current taken advantage of; but this is done, for a master-hand is at the helm.

The breath freezes as it escapes the nostrils; the stoutest must yield to the cold if we are out long; but every stroke of the oars brings us nearer the steamer. Here we are at last. The yawl strikes the bow of the steamer with a jar, and Captain Leizure falls at our feet, insensible. We take him up, lift him on to the deck, and carry him thence into the cabin. The surgeon administers restoratives, applies the proper remedies, and soon he is revived, and the life which had been so nobly given to others is brought back to its possessor.

The next day the search was renewed, and the three living men traced up to Mr. Lea's, where we have already seen them.

Physicians waited upon them; every care and attention that could be, was bestowed upon them; amputation, of both feet and hands, was found necessary, and performed on two of them, who, after undergoing inexpressible agonies for a short time, died; while the third, James Hendrixson, after a long and painful illness, recovered, and lived to serve his country yet longer.

The frozen corpses of the Lieutenant and the four men were taken to Fort Pillow, placed in coffins, and sent home. Such were the horrors of one night on the Mississippi.

*Vigilance was often the lot of the war's women as well, particularly those who vol-
unteered to nurse the wounded. There were many more such women, whom Jane
Schultz has called "soldiers of care," than have usually been acknowledged. Schultz
has counted some twenty thousand North and South, including the working-class
volunteers without Alcott's polish and the black laundresses and cooks whose contributions Izilda could so easily ignore. Many of these volunteers followed recruits
to camp and then to the makeshift hospitals erected near battlefields for emergency
care or the churches, hotels, and private homes that provided temporary facilities.
When general hospitals were outfitted in 1861, more quickly in the North than in the
South, female nurses were not at first thought respectable by hospital surgeons, a
prejudice that remained strong enough in Washington and Richmond to ally female
hospital workers more often with the patients whose care they advocated than with
the doctors whose orders they took. The outspoken "nuss" in "Mrs. Spriggins, the
Neutral," who watches the quinine while she tends the soldiers, is a reminder of those
ordinary women whose forgotten service is worth recalling and whose unruly voices
were increasingly worth catching in print.*

◦•

G. J. A. Coulson (Alcibiades Jones)

"MRS. SPRIGGINS, THE NEUTRAL"

(*Southern Magazine*, February 1871)

In daily travel between my country home and the city, I encounter various
specimens of the *genus homo,* and have learned to distinguish the denizens of
different localities with a good degree of accuracy. Certainly the natives of different latitudes are readily distinguished by a patient observer of the habits
of the animal; and the contrasts presented are the more sharply defined and
the more unmistakable in proportion to the distance separating their birth-
places. As I have opportunity I propose to give the reader of THE SOUTHERN
MAGAZINE such slight "pencil sketches" of those different specimens as may
convey entertainment or instruction, or both, and I begin by begging to introduce to their acquaintance an estimable lady who rejoices in the name of
Mrs. Spriggins.

It was in war-time, 1864, and in the depth of winter, that I saw her. The
snow was a foot deep. She mounted the train at a way-station, and hobbled
along the aisle of my car, carrying a brass-bound valise. She stood some five

"OUR HEROINES: UNITED STATES SANITARY COMMISSION"

feet eleven on her crutches (for she was lame), broad and muscular, aged about 60, and was a formidable looking personage. As she clattered along the aisle, the men on either side glanced at her over their newspapers or drew their legs away from the threatening valise, and then fell back upon their greedy mess of lying "latest intelligence" from the scene of strife. But nobody made way for her; nobody offered her a seat. There were seventy-one Yankee men in that car, and I honestly believe the woman would have stood on her crutches till the train reached the terminus, if the seventy-second man had been similarly unfortunate.

When I had her comfortably seated, her valise packed away behind the stove, her crutches poked under the seat, she turned her sharp gray eyes upon me as I stood by her, and commenced conversation.

"I'm werry much obleeged to you, I'm shore!" she began. "I s'pose you know me? My name is Spriggins, Missis Spriggins."

"No, madam," I answered, "I cannot say that I do. I am a comparative stranger here" —

"Ah, that 'counts for it. I'm purty well beknown hereabouts, and I thought you was so kind to me mebbe 'cause you know'd I had been kind to our boys." While I was considering what sort of reply to make, she went on: "Any noos this mornin'? I guess not. Them papers is mostly lies anyhow. I come from the front last Toosday."

"From the front?"

"Yes. I've been with our boys goin' on three year. I nusses them when they gits sick or wounded. I'm horspittle nuss. So them devilish Rebs has got to answer for breaking my leg as well as breaking up our Gov'ment."

"I never heard that they made war on women."

"Well, the cusses didn't exackly shoot me, but I slipped down on the ice at the horspittle. But there wouldn't have been no war if there wasn't Rebs, and if there hadn't been no war they wouldn't have had no use for nusses and horspittles. So *I* say they are to blame for my broken leg!"

There was no reply to reasoning so cogent as this, so I remained silent. Mrs. Spriggins didn't.

"You see, I've been in it from the fust. Me and my darter went to Vaginny a-nussin, with a rigiment from hereabouts. My darter she got married. He warn't much. He was a 'Piscopy man, a sorter chaplin. I'm a Methodist. Anyway he died, and my darter is a widdy. So am I.—Them cusses beats all! I had one last summer a-nussin. He was a pris'ner, and shot bad in the leg. But bless you, they never die! He got well, and his leg got well, and he's fightin' agin his country this very minnit, I guess, as bold as brass. That feller laid up in the horspittle a-gruntin' with his leg, and eatin' about a half-bushel of Injun bread a day, when he was well as I was. He sneaked out one night and got clear off. The horspittle warn't garded much. He used to sing 'Wish I was in Dixie,' and goodness knows *I* wished he was too! When he did go he stole four bottles of Keneen and my scissors. There was a little fight about a week afterwards, and our boys got whaled severe. One of 'em that got hurted was brought to my horspittle, and he says, 'Missis Spriggins, do you remember that Johnny Reb you nussed a month?' 'Yes,' says I. 'Well,' says he, 'I seed him to-day. He was a-turnin' our boys over that was killed, and a-cuttin' open their pockets with a pair of scissors. When he come to me, he says, 'Hello, Yank, aint you dead?' 'Not much,' says I. 'Got any tobacco?' says he. 'A small chunk,' says I. 'Which pocket?' says he. 'Right,' says I. So he jest kneeled down and cut my pocket open, as cool as a kowcumber, and took my tobacco. He had to run a minute afterwards, because the reserve was comin' up, and he hollered back to me— 'Say, Yank, tell Miss Spriggins her scissors is fust rate!' "

I had to laugh at this story, and after a little hesitation Mrs. Spriggins joined me, qualifying her mirth with the observation that "it was the biggest piece of impudence she had ever heard tell on."

"They *was* raal good scissors," she resumed with a sigh, "they was surgeons' scissors. One of the doctors lent 'em to me out of his case."

It did not appear polite to press the question of ownership too far, though I was curious to know whether the Johnny Reb had robbed her or the surgeon;

and if the latter, whether or not it was Uncle Samuel's loss or merely private property. The four ounces of quinine were undoubtedly "Gov'ment" stores, which was a comfortable reflection.

"Did you say he took some medicine also?" I inquired.

"Yes, he did—four bottles of K'neen! They was worth their weight in gold to them Rebs. We needed 'em too. A good lot of our boys was down with ager, which they cotched in the swamps. There was plenty of castor oil layin' about which he might have stole, and nobody would a-minded. But he went in for K'neen!"

By this time the train had reached the terminal station, and the seventy-one loyal citizens vacated the car with exemplary rapidity, crowding and crushing each other as if the car were a-fire or the enemy of mankind in hot pursuit of them. Our car was the last on the train, and was outside of the depot. With some difficulty I assisted Mrs. Spriggins to alight, and struggling through the deep snow we at last got on the sheltered platform. I had her valise, and asked her some questions about her destination.

"I'm goin' on the horse-car," she said; "it ort to be at the other eend of the depot. If you wouldn't mind hurryin' up a leetle, mebbe you could catch it, and make the driver wait till I git there. Tell him it's Missis Spriggins on crutches—he knows me, leastways he ort to."

I "hurried up" as requested, banging the valise against my legs with rude abrasion at every step. The horse-car was there, and vacant. By the time that I had tucked the "infernal machine" in the car, Mrs. Spriggins arrived, clambered in, and flopped into a seat.

"I'm shore I'm very much obleeged to you," she said, "you've been quite some kind to me. But I've always found gentlemen kind to me when they knowed that I was takin' care of our boys in the horspittles."

My shins were smarting and my temper was a trifle ruffled. There was nobody else within ear-shot, and it was not likely that I should see Mrs. Spriggins again, and I longed to speak disloyally. It was not a popular amusement in that locality, and the opportunities for safe explosions were infrequent.

"Madam!" I said, with severe dignity, "that consideration did not affect *me*. I am a Southerner, and a rebel in every pulsation of my heart. I have waited upon you because you are a woman, and because not one of the loyal citizens on the train paid you the slightest attention."

She caught my coat with a firm grip as I was moving away.

"Look heer, Mister, I don't b'leeve any of them Rebs can ever git to heaven at any price. But I nusses all sorts in the horspittle; and when I'm nussin a sick or wounded soger, pollyticks don't make no difference to me. Sometimes they are our boys, and sometimes Rebs, but in the horspittle I'm always *nootral!*"

The hard road to claiming a voice lay for many black men through enlistment, as Alcott's Robert Dane and the men of the 54th Massachusetts discovered. After emancipation was proclaimed in January 1863, thousands volunteered to serve in regiments of the United States Colored Troops, even under white officers who might be hoping for rapid advancement. While most regiments did not immediately see combat duty or the same monthly pay as white volunteers, they ran a considerably greater risk in the field when Jefferson Davis swore that they and their officers would not be exchanged: they would be reenslaved or executed if captured. By the spring of 1864, as deteriorating prisons filled, the upshot was increasing rage, especially along the Mississippi River, where hundreds of black soldiers were garrisoned at Fort Pillow. In April, when Lionel Booth had just arrived to take command from William Bradford, the fort was attacked by partisan rangers under Nathan Bedford Forrest, a man whose military audacity owed something to early want and what Richard Fuchs has called "a maelstrom of discontent." In "Buried Alive," that maelstrom descends to leave colored regiments and the Northern public reeling.

◆◇◆

"BURIED ALIVE"

(*Harper's Weekly*, 7 May 1864)

My name in Daniel Tyler, and my skin is dark, as my mother's was before me. I have heard that my father had a white face, but I think his heart and life were blacker than my mother's skin. I was born a slave, and remained a slave until last April, when I found deliverance and shelter under the flag that my master was fighting to dishonor.

I shall never forget the day when freedom came to me. I was working in the fields down in Alabama, my heart full of bitterness and unutterable longings. I had dreamed for two long years of escape from my bondage; the thought sung to me through the dark nights, and filled all the days with a weird sort of nervous expectation. But my dreams had proved nothing more than dreams; the opportunity I yearned for did not come. But that day, working in the fields, suddenly along the dusty road there flashed a long column of loyal cavalry, the old flag flying at its head. How my heart leaped at the sight; how, like a revelation, came the thought: "This, Daniel Tyler, is your opportunity!" Need I tell you how I acted upon that thought; how, in one second of time, I leaped out of slavery into freedom, and from a slave became a man?

Well, joining the flashing column, I rode with them for days, coming at last into Baton Rouge, and thence, having joined a regiment of my own people, came to Memphis. Thence four hundred of us came to Fort Pillow. But there are not four hundred of us to-day, for three hundred and odd were murdered in cold blood only a week ago by Forrest's rough-riders.

It was a day of horrors — that 12th of April. There were seven hundred of us in all in the fort — three hundred whites of the Thirteenth Tennessee Cavalry, and four hundred blacks, as I have said, all under command of brave Major Booth. The fort consisted simply of earth-works, on which we had mounted half a dozen guns. We knew that Forrest had been pillaging the country all about us, and imagined that perhaps he would pay us a visit; but the thought did not alarm us, though we knew, those of us who were black, that we had little to expect at the hands of the rebels. At last, about sunrise on the morning of the 12th, Forrest, with some 6,000 men, appeared and at once commenced an attack. We met the assault bravely, and for two hours the fight went on briskly. Then a flag of truce came in from Forrest, asking an unconditional surrender, but Major Bradford — Major Booth having been wounded — declined to surrender unless the enemy would treat those of us who were black as prisoners of war, which, of course, they refused to do, and the fight went on. The enemy, in the next few hours, made several desperate charges, but were each time repulsed. At last, about four o'clock in the afternoon, they sent in another flag. We ceased firing out of respect to the flag; but Forrest's men had no such notions of honor and good faith. The moment we stopped firing they swarmed all about the fort, and while the flag was yet withdrawing, made a desperate charge from all sides. Up to that time only about thirty of our men had been hurt. But in this charge the enemy got within the earth-works, and forthwith there ensued a scene which no pen can describe. Seeing that all resistance was useless, most of us threw down our arms, expecting, and many begging for, quarter. But it was in vain. Murder was in every rebel heart; flamed in every rebel eye. Indiscriminate massacre followed instantly upon our surrender. Some of us, seeking shelter, ran to the river and tried to conceal ourselves in the bushes, but for the most part in vain. The savages, pursuing, shot down the fugitives in their tracks. There was Manuel Nichols, as brave a soldier as ever carried a musket. He had been a free negro in Michigan, but volunteered a year ago to fight for the Union. He, with others, had sought a shelter under the bank of the river, but a cold-blooded monster found him, and putting a pistol close to his head, fired, failing however to kill the brave fellow. He was then hacked on the arm, and only a day after died, delirious, in the hospital. Then there was Robert Hall, another colored soldier, who was lying sick in the hospital when the massacre commenced. The devils gashed his head horribly with their sabres, and then cut off part of his right hand, which he had lifted in a mute appeal for mercy.

"THE MASSACRE AT FORT PILLOW"

Then there was Harrison, of the Thirteenth Tennessee, who was shot four times after surrender, and then robbed of all his effects. Before I was shot, running along the river bank, I counted fifty dead Union soldiers lying in their blood. One had crawled into a hollow log and was killed in it, another had got over the bank in the river, and on to a board that run out into the water. He laid on it on his face with his feet in the water, and when I saw him was already stark and stiff. Several had tried to hide in crevices made by the falling bank, and could not be seen without difficulty, but they were singled out and killed. One negro corporal, Jacob Wilson, who was down on the river bank, seeing that no quarter was shown, stepped into the water so that he lay partly under it. A rebel coming along asked him what was the matter; he said he was badly wounded, and the rebel, after taking from his pocket all the money he had, left him. It happened to be near by a flatboat tied to the bank. When all was quiet Wilson crawled into it, and got three more wounded comrades also into it, and cut loose. The boat floated out into the channel and was found ashore some miles below. There were, alas, few such fortunate escapes!

I was shot near the river just about dark. Running for my life, a burly rebel struck me with his carbine, putting out one eye, and then shot me in two places. I thought he would certainly leave me with that, but I was mistaken. With half a dozen others, I was at once picked up and carried to a ditch, into which we

286

were tossed like so many brutes, white and black together. Then they covered us with loose dirt, and left us to die. Oh, how dark and desolate it was! Under me were several dead, and right across my breast lay a white soldier, still alive! How he clutched and strained! How, hurt and weak as I was, with only one hand free, I struggled for air and life, feeling my strength waning every moment! It was a strange thing to lie there buried, and yet be able to think and pray. Maybe, friend, you have known what agony was, but you never had such pains of soul as I had down there in that living grave. I thought I could feel the worms gnawing at my flesh; I am sure I had a taste of what death is, with the added pain of knowing that I was not dead, and yet unable to live in that dark, dismal tomb. So I clutched and strained and struggled on, digging upward as I could with my one puny hand. At last—oh joy!—a faint streak of light looked in; my hand had carved an avenue to the world of life! But would I dare to lift my head? Might not some rebel, standing by, strike me down again on the moment? But I could not die *there* in that grave; I *must* escape. Slowly, painfully, I rolled the burden from my breast—*he* was dead by that time—and then carefully crept out from that living death. It was dark, and no one was near. A moment I stood up on my feet; then—

The next thing I remember I was in the hospital where I am now. They had found me just where I fell, and brought me to a place of safety, where, after a while, consciousness returned. I have been here a week now; and I think I shall get well.

I lie in the cot where poor Robert Hall lay when he was butchered by the rebels. They showed me, yesterday, a letter he had written the day before the massacre to his wife. He had learned to read and write at Memphis, after his enlistment, and used to send a message to his wife and children, who still remained there, every week or so. This was his letter which a surgeon had helped him put together:

"DEAR MAMMY"—it ran—"I am very sick here in the hospital, but am better than I was, and hope to get well soon. They have been very kind to me; and I find it very sweet to suffer for the dear flag that gives me shelter. You must not worry on my account. Tell Katy she must not forget to say her prayers and to study her lessons carefully now while she has an opportunity. And, mammy, take good care of the baby; I dreamed of her last night, and I think how sad it would be to die and never see her little face again. But then chaplain says it will all be right in heaven, and he knows better than we do. And, mammy, don't forget we are free now; teach both the darlings to be worthy of their estate."

That was poor Hall's letter—it had not been sent, and we have no heart to send it now. He will never see the baby's face here; but then God may let him see it up yonder!

I hope to recover and get away from here very soon; I want to be in my place again; for I have something to avenge now, and I can not bear to wait. Poor Hall's blood is crying to me from the ground; and I want to be able, sometime, to say to Manuel Nichols's wife, up there in Michigan, that *his* fall has had its compensation. And may God speed the day when this whole slaveholders' rebellion—what remains of it—shall be "Buried Alive!"

The zeal of the West and its regimental cost were more evident in the Eastern theater after Grant assumed command of all Union armies in March 1864 and joined the Army of the Potomac in the field. As General-in-Chief, Grant conceived a bold strategy for moving against Confederate armies on several fronts, but his field position while Meade commanded the Army of the Potomac was ambiguous, which was soon apparent in the dense tangle of Virginia's north woods. As Union soldiers commenced some sixty days of nearly continuous fighting that would carry them through the Wilderness, Spotsylvania, and Cold Harbor in May and June, they faced entrenched fire that was unrelenting and lethal. At Spotsylvania on May 12, both terrain and orders were confusing enough in a downpour that Winfield Scott Hancock's success against the Confederate line was sufficient only to claim bloody trenches for hours of inconclusive combat, what Earl Hess describes as "a hell of flying metal and desperate survival." Late that night, the continuing barrage brought down a large oak tree, a measure of the holocaust that a disheartened captain surveys in "A Night in the Wilderness." As he recalls the scene, the battle's opening engagements at places like Alsop's farm and its early expense when the distinguished John Sedgwick dies setting up artillery are only the first movements in a savage drama of shrinking ammunition and muddy death.

◆○◆

"A NIGHT IN THE WILDERNESS"

(*Galaxy*, May 1871)

Brown and I live together in a disconsolate, bachelor way, and in our common parlor, sitting-room, or "other room," as it is generally called, over our after-supper pipes, we discuss the incidents of our rather uneventful lives.

Brown, though, has had one great event in his life — his twenty or thirty days' service with the militia in 1863 — and he is determined that I shall not forget how much I missed in staying at home throughout the war.

I remember well the day he enlisted for the emergency; the grand heroic air with which he told me that the time had come for him to go; his elaborate preparations; his most affecting farewell to the few of us who could not or did not go; and his return, looking like a veteran of many years, torn, dirty, hungry, and tired, but with a proud consciousness of having served his country in the hour of her peril.

And during the eight years which have since elapsed he has been constantly reminded of those days.

A poor dinner down town reminds him of a poorer one in '63, and a good dinner recalls one which tasted better; while sun and rain, rest and fatigue, alike revive the memory of the great era of his life.

So the other evening, when I said it seemed too rainy to go out again, I was not surprised to hear that it was nothing to rain which he had gone through, nor unprepared for the story which followed.

The story had not progressed very far, however, when there was a knock at the door, and there entered Turner, who has a room on the floor above us, and who often stops in on his way up and down stairs.

Turner is a quiet little man, who generally plays the part of audience in our evening meetings, though occasionally breaking out in a loquaciousness which apparently surprises himself as much as his hearers.

He said "Good evening," and "Don't let me interrupt you," and took his seat by the fire.

"Oh! it's nothing," said Brown. "How do you flourish?"

"Brown has just started one of his favorite stories of hardship in the militia days," said I.

"Well, go on, Brown," replied Turner; "I'll be delighted to hear."

"That's not fair," rejoined Brown. "You fellows who really saw active service, and were in all manner of fights and marches, won't talk about them; and so we militia, don't you see, have to talk enough for both, if for nothing else, to prevent these stay-at-home chaps from forgetting that there was a war; but then it's not fair to ask us to keep at it when you're around. I never heard you tell an army story yet. I wish you would. Tell us about some battle or other."

And I added, "Yes, Turner! do make an exception in this case, and tell us about some battle, or about the bravest thing you ever did, or of anything that you remember and think about."

"I don't think," said Turner, "that one of ten thinks of battles in which he was engaged, or of brave actions—at least not of any that a moderately modest man can well speak of; but constantly to a man's mind comes unbidden the recollection of days and nights which were remarkable only for their supreme discomfort, when there was no special gallantry, and possibly no very hard work, but when he felt the peculiar sense of loneliness and horror such as only a soldier can feel.

"Such were some of the days and nights in the Wilderness and around Spottsylvania; and particularly I remember the night of the 12th of May, 1864, when our division made the first of its many movements to the left.

"I often think of that night. I was especially reminded of it this evening, as I walked up in the rain; and if you care to hear, I will try to give you some idea of it."

"THE CAMPAIGN IN VIRGINIA — 'ON TO RICHMOND!'"

Of course we urged him to go on; and, settling himself in his chair, Turner began:

"The whole army had had a hard week of it, and our brigade was in some respects worse off than most.

"From the 5th, when we arrived at Allsop's Orchard, just in time to save the preceding division from annihilation, there had been a continued excitement.

"We had been almost constantly under fire of one sort or another, and had on many of the days made at least two charges. Time after time we had advanced — sometimes to a real attack, sometimes for a feint; whichever it was, it made little difference; the fighting was equally stubborn, the losses equally great, the results equally unhappy.

"In these hopeless attacks we had lost many of the best men of the brigade. Here fell my one friend — the only man in the command whom I had known before the war — gallantly leading his men; and immediately after our heroic general was shot. To the hospital with the wounded general, and to the North with his dead body went the other aide, and I only remained; the others of our large staff had all been either wounded or captured in the Wilderness.

"Every one in the brigade had lost a comrade, while all had lost their commander; and it is not strange that we looked on the place as a slaughter-pen, or that on the afternoon of the 12th, after a more than usually sanguinary morning, we hailed with joy the order to withdraw from the works and to mass in rear of the lines — to rest, we thought.

"The regiments were not all disposed when the general of division rode by and called to our new brigadier to follow the division flag, 'and be quick about it.' So we moved off, leaving a New York regiment on the skirmish line, to be replaced by one from the brigade which had taken our place in the works, and to follow as best it could.

"We had been under arms since three o'clock in the morning, and the men were tired, wet, and hungry; but although many, I do not doubt, swore and growled inwardly, there was only apparent the greatest alacrity. I remember wondering if they all thought with me that any place must be better than that which we left.

"Getting in rear of the lines, we moved rapidly to the left, past the scene of General Sedgwick's death, through and over earthworks only recently abandoned; through a dense wood, where the trees were riddled with shot and the ground strewn with *débris*; down a steep ploughed hillside; through a bog, where we floundered saddle and waist deep; over a turbulent, swollen creek, and so on, down a country road, along a hill-crest covered with batteries of Parrott guns, and out to the front, over the battle-field of the morning, the enemy opening on our poor straggling column as it wound its way to the front over the dead and among the broken and scattered arms.

"A half-mile march brought us to a hollow basin where we were sheltered from the enemy's fire, and the column halting, the men flung themselves down in the mud fairly worn out.

"Here ensued a conference between several general officers and one of the colonels of our brigade, which I understood had reference to storming some positions with the troops of our brigade, which the generals seemed to look upon as *fresh*. An orderly, as he handed me some coffee, said in a despairing tone, 'They'd better put us in, and finish us up.' I told him to be quiet, but possibly thought as he did about it.

"The brigadier, calling me from my coffee, sent me back to bring up the regiment which we had left behind, as we might need all our force.

"As I rode back, I before long met any number of men of the regiment who by short cuts had nearly reached the brigade, and they all agreed in saying that the regiment was just behind them. But I was much less fortunate than its stragglers, and I had ridden almost back to the spot we had left in the morning, and had fairly given up when I got track of it, and after a little found it wandering off after a division of another corps. So it was well into the night, and the rain, which had held up since morning, had recommenced when I reported them to the brigadier.

"He pointed out two of his regiments, and said the others—I think we had seven in all at that time—had gone out to the enemy's works, which they were holding. The regiment which I had just brought up might rest for the present.

"Here an officer from the front arrived and reported the men out of ammunition. The brigadier said, 'Lieutenant, I've sent word to division headquarters again and again that my men would soon be out of ammunition, and I told the general when he was down here that he must help us, and I don't know what else I can do. However, Captain,' turning to me, 'you'd better go and see if you can't find some cartridges.'

"So taking a squad of men, and leaving my poor jaded mare to rest, I started on foot to hunt up an ammunition train. That of our division had not been seen for several days, and at division headquarters they did not know where it or any other was; and I could get so little information from either general or staff, that I was turning away when a voice under a blanket said, 'Captain! I saw a lot of wagons down by General Hancock's headquarters before dark.'

"In answer to my question of 'Where's that?' the owner of the voice pointed uncertainly into the darkness, and I as uncertainly started to follow his guidance. We tramped on through rain and mud, through hospitals and headquarters without number, found any number of ammunition wagons which had been emptied, and after making a pretty large circuit came across a sergeant who had some of calibre .577, but who had conscientious scruples against letting it go out of his own division.

"I partly persuaded him, and partly took possession of all I could find, and giving him a slip receipt we made our way back to headquarters. The two regiments which I had left there some time before had gone out to the works, and the —— New York was to follow as soon as the ammunition had been distributed. The men were all asleep, as it was the first chance many of them had had for nearly two days, and we had no little difficulty in arousing them. While the cartridges were being handed around, a forlorn emaciated man, bowed almost double with pain, came up to the regimental commander and begged to be excused from going out; he had had a double share of skirmish duty, he said, and had had diarrhoea for a week. He had hardly finished the recital of his woes when I heard the sing of a stray bullet past my ear, and the sick man with a hopeless shriek fell at our feet, dead. Excused.

"Presently the regiment started out, led by the lieutenant who had come in, with whom I went to learn the way, and to inspect the condition of affairs.

"We wound about through hollows and along a sunken road, where the men were protected from the straggling fire of the enemy, and guided by the glitter of the musketry we reached the 'angle.'

"General Hancock had in the morning driven the enemy from the crest which he occupied, and forced him back to an inner line of works. Part of this line our troops carried; but at 'the angle' they had not been able to go out, though they reached and held one side of the embankment. Our brigade had relieved one from the Sixth Corps, and the instructions were to keep up a constant fire during the night, to prevent the enemy attempting either to charge over the works, or to repossess them in force, and to hinder those who remained in the trenches getting themselves or the three or four caissons away.

"It was a gloomy enough place. Our men lay close against the soft mud of the embankment, and rose occasionally to fire over. It was very dark, and I could only distinguish the black mass of men and the line of the earthworks, with the outlines of the trees beyond. None of the enemy were visible, though an occasional blaze from their rifles showed that they were very close, and their balls, which flew past us generally over our heads, went scudding on over the fields to the troops resting in the rear. When two or three pieces were discharged at once, the glare lightened the place for a moment, and made apparent to the eye the discomforts which in the darkness were so apparent to the other senses.

"I looked up and down the line and tried to form some idea of the position, and to distinguish the several regiments in the dark mass. Discovering the Eighty-fourth New York, I crawled up among the men, and putting my head close to the top log of the parapet, I could see against the sky one or two of the hostile caissons, the others being lost in the darkness except when the blaze beyond lightened the background.

"While the lieutenant who had guided us out was putting the newly arrived troops into a vacant space, I found the colonel who had charge of the party. In a sudden blaze of light, I saw him standing behind the line with legs apart and firmly planted in the slippery soil, his hands resting on his sword-hilt in front of him, his head strained forward and his eyes peering into the darkness with an expression of intense eagerness and anxiety, as though determined to see how strong the enemy was, and what he contemplated. I have known that man, after a steady gaze, tell of approaching lines or see movements of the enemy which would not become apparent to others for some moments, though they had field-glasses and he none. I stepped up to his side and waited for him to notice me. He continued to look until it was all dark again, and then, putting his mouth close to my ear, he said in a loud whisper, 'Captain! are they *never* going to help us? We'll soon be entirely out of ammunition, and already some of the men are using what they can get from the dead. One regiment is firing rebel buck and ball with wads. That'll keep up a noise as long as it lasts; which won't be long, and then, if the rebels intend coming over as they say, we can't do anything. The men are perfectly worn out, and unless we keep them firing they'll go to sleep. They certainly ought to relieve us; but if they can't do that, for God's sake send us ammunition.'

" 'Send us ammunition,' echoed the other regimental commanders.

"I told them that we had brought every cartridge I could get; that the brigadier had again and again applied for reinforcements, or for ammunition; and that the general of division had replied that he knew all about it and that we must be patient.

"I wanted to stay with them, for though I knew I could really be of no use, there is a satisfaction in sharing misery which you cannot alleviate, and I felt how hopeless another appeal would be; but I consented to go back and to make one more effort for relief of some sort.

"I had carefully noted the three cedars and one pine tree by which the brigadier had made headquarters, and had, I thought, faithfully observed the direction as we came out, and so determined to abandon the sheltered but circuitous route by which we had reached the works, and to make a straight line to the rear. I struck back into the pitchy darkness, and had gone some distance before I began to suspect that I was not quite right. I repeatedly stopped to examine the ground, as I first descended a hill and then walked through a meadow; and as each time I waited to see the light at the works, it was behind me, I felt assured; but as I reached the top of the hillock from which I had expected to see headquarters, I concluded that I was astray. The sky was dark and heavy; the rain fell in fine cutting drops, which the fitful gusts of wind whirled into my face and fairly blinded me when I attempted to look where I thought the road should be. The wind moaned and sighed among the cedar and thorn bushes, which swayed to and fro with melancholy measure, as though in lamentation for the dead that lay under and around them, and bore to my ear many indistinct and indefinite sounds, which I first tried to define and then to locate. I could hear the tramping and whinnying of horses and mules, the rattling of chain harness, and the distant rumble of moving trains; but where they were, and whether ours or in the enemy's country, I could not tell. Several times I thought I heard troops moving, but the sound either died away or the dark mass I took for men proved, on approach, to be a group of bushes. I felt satisfied that I had gone far enough to bring me to my destination, but I could not imagine why I found no troops. There were several spots of faint light, as of distant camp fires, but I could not tell how far away they were or which might be at division headquarters. I could see occasional flashes of light in several directions, but I could hear no musketry. I stooped down and brought against the sky one after another the trees and lines of hills, and tried in vain to recall them; and finally taking the direction of the wind for a guide, I ran down the side of the hill and struck up a ravine.

"After going a little way a bullet flew past me from behind, and I felt reassured. I was in the midst of a marsh; and while at one step I mounted up on a hummock, at the next I was plunging knee-deep in mud and water. I stumbled over knapsacks and blankets which lay around, and tripped my feet in dead men's caps and straps. I sprang over a turbid pool to what seemed solid earth, and shuddered as I felt under me the yielding body of a man. As I plodded on I could distinguish the Confederate and Union dead lying, some with faces turned up and some curled in heaps upon the ground. Occasionally there seemed ahead of me to be moving forms, but as I came up to them they vanished away, or I found only a cedar bush which gritted its branches together in derision. Behind bushes or logs I found wounded men who were trying to keep themselves alive, and each of whom asked me whether it would not soon be day. Further on, and I caught again the red glare at the works, which leered at me through the darkness. I took a turn to the left and seemed to strike a path. Dark forms flitted by me, men going to the front or straggling to the rear; now and then I heard the singing of a musket ball, spending itself as it passed me and now and then the moan of a straggler who had been hit.

"I do not know how long I wandered thus. Several times I changed the direction of my walk and started out with fresh confidence, each time to find myself no more successful than before, and occasionally discovering that I was walking toward the front.

"Thus I was blindly wandering on, hopeless of discovering my way, when I was suddenly aroused by the command '*Halt*,' given in a hoarse foreign voice, by a dark object on the ground, which, as I approached, straightened out into the figure of a man. I should scarcely have been surprised had I learned that I was outside the skirmish line, as I used to have a peculiar luck that way, and was relieved when I learned that the sentry belonged to a provost guard, and had been posted there before dark to keep men from skulking to the rear. He was an outlandish foreigner, and I could get nothing from him regarding his regiment or division, or where the nearest troops were; he only knew that he had been there since before dark. I asked, 'Where's the next post of your guard?' and he pointed to an indistinct form some distance off, and toward this I walked, hoping to find an American, or at least an intelligent being, who could tell me something.

"But on reaching the figure I found, sitting on a bank, propped against a hedge, his musket lying across his knees, a soldier perfectly dead. I could find no mark of bullet and no stain of blood, but his flesh was cold and had the clammy dead feeling which I had learned so easily to recognize. He sat with his arms hanging down, his head thrown back, and the heavy rain was beating down on his calm young face.

"Was there to be no end to my wanderings in the dark? And were all men dumb and dead to me?

> Yet half I seemed to recognize some trick
> Of mischief happened to me. God knows where—
> In a bad dream perhaps. Here ended then
> Progress this way.

"I sat down and tried to collect my thoughts. The sounds which before I seemed to recognize were only now the sighs of the Valley of Death. The forms around me rose. The trees, the flitting shadows, the scattered arms, the silent dead sailed by in gloomy procession, and taunted me as they mournfully danced in time to the sighing branches. The sights, the sounds, the very earth itself seemed all unearthly now, and nothing real but my own aching head.

"Slowly the procession of dead things floated down, slowly the sad sounds became only the low sighings of the wind; and as the rain lulled I arose, and as I did so caught sight of a tree I recognized as having passed in the afternoon. Thankfully I put myself upon the road, and as I now knew where I was, the distance to headquarters seemed interminable. I started and ran along the slippery path, and as the first faint blue streaks of light began to brighten the horizon, I saw the patient horses standing, and found the brigadier.

"I was about to ask if he had heard from the front lately, and to offer some explanation of my absence; but he broke out with 'Hello, Captain! I thought you'd gone up! I've just managed to get some regiments to relieve ours. Smith's gone out with them, and when our men come in you see if you can get them together and mass them up as close as you can.' He gave a sigh of relief, which I heartily echoed, and curled himself down beside his tree.

"How I lost my way and where I wandered is quite as inexplicable to me now as then. I had often missed my way for a time in going about at night in the woods or over fields, but I never felt so strongly the sense of loneliness and horrid helplessness as I did when every direction seemed the wrong one, as I stood in the dark shivering with cold, with the uncommunicative dead around me. It is not a noble or heroic feeling, but it is one which all soldiers have at one time or another had; and as it is the least like home experiences, I have tried to tell you of it. The next morning's sight was more sickening, but it did not make the same lasting impression on me."

We sat all three looking into the gray ashes in the grate for some time, when Brown broke silence with, "And how about next morning?"

So Turner resumed: "After the regiments had all come in and had with a good deal of difficulty been got into shape, I came back and lay down in the mud. When I awoke the sun was several hours high and the rain of the night before was steaming out of the men and horses. I was anxious to see the scene of last night's skirmish, or whatever it was, and asked permission to ride out.

"All firing had ceased at daylight, and the sun showed very few live Confederates, but God knows there were plenty of dead ones. The enemy's works were very strong and had been made with much care — the inside built up with logs, over which the earth from the interior ditch was thrown. They had also been ditched in front, and it was this which enabled our men to come close up to them, where, standing in the ditch, they were as well protected as those on the other side. At every twenty or thirty feet there were heavy traverses which had been made to protect the guns. The ditch behind the work was literally filled with dead, and the rain which had settled in it was crimson red. In front the ground was strewn with our dead, and on the crest of the parapet lay the bravest, who had tried to go over. These bodies, lying directly in the line of both fires, were chopped and hacked by balls. There was one poor fellow the back of whose head and whose whole body was perforated like sponge, and flesh and clothing were hashed up together in a red and blue mass, but whose face, when we turned it up from the mud in which it was buried, looked as peaceful and quiet as if asleep.

"Behind, the dead had fallen thick; those first in the ditch had fallen, and on these others had kneeled to fire, to be likewise killed, and they lay twisted and intertwined. The space in rear was covered with those who had tried to escape, but who while crawling off on hands and knees had been shot, and had fallen on their faces. Behind every stump and stock were the corpses of some who had striven to cover themselves; and in one place behind a traverse a man had used a dead comrade as a shelter, but as he had risen to fire had been shot, and had become the rain shelter for a third who had fallen dead over the two.

"I walked about the place, and was just climbing over the works on my return when I saw in the ditch a young Confederate, who lay in blood-stained water, with the upper half of his body upon a dead man and with two others across his legs. His eyes were open, but glazed, though there seemed a slight animation in them, and they moved dreamily as I looked at him, while he made a slight movement with the arm which was disengaged. I could not see where he was hit, nor could I be sure that he was conscious. I told some men to come over to get him out, which they did with reluctance, as the enemy were keeping up a constant 'picking off' from the new line to which they had withdrawn during the night; but before they had extricated him an orderly came for me from the brigadier, saying our brigade was moving and that I was wanted at once; so I mounted and rode after the command."

Turner rose, and after poking among the gray coals he found a red spot, and with a paper relit his pipe, and saying "Good-night," left the room.

   We heard his step along the entry and listened to him going up stairs; and as we heard him close the door of his room behind him Brown said, "I believe, on the whole, I'm glad I didn't see a battle."

After Spotsylvania's inauguration into trench warfare, the futile bloodletting at Cold Harbor in June 1864 put an end to Grant's Wilderness campaign. But massive casualties did not put an end to glory elsewhere. In the Shenandoah Valley the following October, Philip Sheridan stole victory from the Confederates under Jubal Early by personally turning Union forces back from a humiliating rout. After the battle of Cedar Creek, Early's army fell apart and Confederate command subsided enough for Valley slaves to think about leaving their cabins for Union camps. They would not be welcomed, since armies could not feed them and soldiers could not imagine a place for anything but their unpaid labor. But slave families nevertheless followed Union troops in what Thavolia Glymph has called "collective escapes," whose nighttime urgency William Faulkner once described as "just walking fast in the dark with that panting, hurrying murmuring, going on." For the families finding their way in "The Freedman's Story," the arrival of Union soldiers brings opportunity and, late in the war, the undeniable summons of liberty's dark road.

◆◦◆

M. Schele De Vere

"THE FREEDMAN'S STORY"

(*Harper's Monthly*, October 1866)

[I have thought that a plain, unvarnished account of a servant's trials in his efforts to secure his freedom might not be uninteresting. It is given as nearly as possible in his own words. Oby is now with me, my dining-room servant. He has learned to read himself what I have written.

CHARLOTTESVILLE, VIRGINIA   M. S. DE V.]

My name is Oby; they say it is because my father was an Obeah man, when he lived down South in Florida and drove a stage. I have heard him say, to the contrary, that he belonged, at the time I was born, to a man by the name of Overton, and that that is my true name. So when I went down to town the other day, and the Provost-Marshal asked me if I could sign my own name, I boldly wrote down "Mr. Overton Paragon."

I was raised at this place by people who were ever so kind to me as long as I can remember them; but that was not very long, for they were poor white folks and could not keep me, or my mother, or my father either. So we were hired out to a very good master, who took good care of father especially, because he had hired him for more than twenty years, and I was living with them in his house, though I could not do much work, being rather weakly and, I am afraid, lazy too. One fine day master comes down stairs and says to father: "Uncle James, you have served me faithfully these ten years, and you know I only bought you because I did not want your master to set you in your old days to hard work. But I do not like to own you, and you are free. You can go whenever and wherever you choose. I can not give you your freedom in any other way, because the laws of the State do not permit me to do so, and we all have to obey the law; but you must understand that you can stay or go as you choose."

Father could not say much, for he was not handy with his tongue, but he told master that he did not want to leave him as long as he cared to keep him. But when master had gone up again, he comes in and tells mother, and Uncle Henry, who was there, tells him he had better go across the line and live at the North. Father had been there when master sent him all the way to Boston with a fine horse—his name was Topaz—and they tried very hard then to make father stay. But he did not like their ways; he said they were not genteel at all like our old family servants, and he came back and was mighty glad to be again in Old Virginia. So father staid, and mother staid, and I was taken up to the dining-room, and mistress taught me to wait, and to wash the china and the glass.

I was nearly grown—I may have been about nineteen or twenty years old—when the Yankees came right down upon us. We had been expecting them often before, and many is the time Uncle Henry came running in where mother was and cried out, "God be thanked, they are coming, they are coming!" And mother asked him, "Who are you talking about?" and he would say, "Our deliverers, the Yankees, whom God sends to make us all free!" But mother did not like his ways at all, and when he was gone she would take me and brother Henry by her little stool close to the fire and say: "Now, boys, don't you think you'll be so much better off when you are free. Folks have to work every where, free or slave, black or white; and it's much better for you to be with genteel folks, and go to church, and have nothing to do with poor niggers, than to be way off, where you have not any body who cares for you."

Mother was mighty good to us, and I know she meant it all for the best, but, to save my life, I could not help thinking of what Uncle Henry said, and what a fine thing it would be to be free, and to have twelve dollars a month and nothing to do. So I went over to Colonel Wood's Aleck and we talked it over behind the wood-pile, where nobody could hear us, and he told me how he knew a plenty more who would go away as soon as ever the Yankees came. He said they were fighting for us, and if we wanted to go we need not run away by night, like a poor three-hundred-dollar nigger, but we might ride off on a fine horse, in the middle of the day, and our masters could not say a word against it for fear of the Yankees. So I promised I would join him, and when we heard that General Sheridan was coming this way, with a hundred thousand men, we knew that the Confederates could not stand before him, and we agreed we would go off all together.

I remember it well; it was a dark night, but the stars were all out and the mud awfully deep, when all of a sudden Uncle Henry comes rushing in by the side gate, quite out of breath, and tells us that General Early has been beaten all to pieces, and that the Yankees are coming across the mountains. They did not know any thing of it in town, and I had heard master say at supper-table that we need not be afraid; the Yankees would again go up the Valley to Lexington and pass us by. But we knew better, and mother would have told mistress, whom she was mighty fond of, but Uncle Henry would not let her, and mother was terribly worried about it. He told us that we must all put on our Sunday clothes, and be very polite to the soldiers, because they were coming to make us all free, and we were just as good now as they. Father was very uneasy about us, for he did not believe half of what the others said, and shook his head and groaned as he sat before the fire and smoked his pipe; but he said nothing, only now and then he would look up, and when mother looked at him at the same time, he would shake his head and sigh, until it made me feel quite badly, and I did not know what to do.

At night, when the white folks had all gone to bed, we, Aleck and I, took an ash cake and a piece of middling, and we ran up the turnpike, miles and miles, until we came to the top of the long hill, where Doctor White's house stood before it was burned, and there we sat the livelong night, and watched the camp-fires against the dark mountain side, thinking what the Yankees were doing up there, and why they did not come to help us all. It was very hard to trot back again in the morning early, and to go to work splitting wood for the cook before breakfast, but Aleck and I thought if we could but once see the blue-coats coming down the hill, and their horses standing by the side of the lake, we would be perfectly happy.

And so it did come about one fine, clear morning. On Monday a man in gray had come racing up the turnpike, looking right and left under his broad-brimmed, slouched hat, and gone into town. Uncle Henry had met him as he came up, and shook his head and said: "Now, I should not wonder if that was a real Yankee." They all laughed at him, and asked him if he did not see the Confederate gray and the ragged hat the man wore. But he shook his head and said: "Now, I'll tell you, boys, it may be so, and it may not be so; but that man there did not ride like one of our folks, and he had his eyes too busy and his hand too near his revolver to be one of our soldiers." That morning early there came two, and three, and at last a whole number of these graycoats, and somebody said in a whisper, as we were standing at the stile close to the turnpike, "Those are the Jessie Scouts, you believe me!" But we looked at the old man who said so, and as nobody knew him we did not believe him. It was all the same true; it turned out afterward that they were Jessie Scouts, as they called them from General Fremont's wife; and there had been a dozen of them in town all day long, and nobody had known them. We knew how little our soldiers cared about spies and that sort of men, and so it was not very difficult to come in and find out every thing.

But on Tuesday, early in the morning, as soon as master had had his breakfast, we all slipped out and went down to the road, where we found a great many people standing about and talking of what the Yankees were going to do with the house, and the servants, and the town itself. Down by the lake, where the road from the house comes into the turnpike, and not far from the little lodge, stood a heap of gentlemen, who had come up from town to beg pardon of the General, and to ask him not to burn them all out. They were mightily scared, and Mr. Fowler, the tailor, who is a great goose, as I have heard it said often and often, looked white and shook in all his limbs. It could not be from the cold, for although the rain had stopped overnight, it was quite mild in the morning. Alongside of them, but a little apart, stood master and some of his friends; I don't know if they had come too to ask the Yankees to spare the house. Soon one man came flying down the hill, and then another, and then three or four together, galloping right by us without ever stopping, and just crying one after another, "They are coming! they are coming!" I slipped up close to where master stood, and I could hear them say that it was a mighty hard thing to stand there and not to know whether they would have a house over their head next night or not; and what would become of the ladies and of the little ones. One I heard say distinctly, "Oh, gentlemen, we'll all go up before night, sure enough!" William Gibbons, who preaches down in the big bath-house every Sunday, said the gentleman was very wicked, for if God would take us up we must all be ready at any time; and he, for one, was quite willing to go to heaven.

Every now and then somebody would cry out, "There they are!" and we all looked up to the top of the hill, behind which the road was hid, and when a man slowly rose over the brow and it turned out that he was on horseback, we thought sure enough there were the Yankees. So we stood hours and hours, and just when we thought they would not be coming that day, two men rode up the hill and down again slowly, then three more, then a dozen or more all in a body, with flags in their hands; and at last the whole turnpike was blue, and we knew for a certainty they were come. We just looked at one another, and I felt mighty queer; but Uncle Henry and all the others, who stood way down by the stile, looked exactly as if they were going to shout to the sky and to jump out of their skin. Aleck looked at me too, and winked, and shut his eyes, and shook all over, till I could not help myself, and I laughed, and they all laughed, and it set the others down at the stile a-laughing, and we held our sides and did not mind master and his friends looking at us as if they did not like it at all.

When the first officer came up to where Mr. Fowler stood, he rushed forward and came near falling between the horses' feet, and they all cried out together, I don't know what; but the tailor had the biggest mouth, and he talked loudest. So I suppose they heard him, and one of the officers said something about private property being spared, but public property must be given up.

Just then master walked up himself, like a real gentleman that he is, and although he was on foot and had not even a spur on his boot, he looked as good a man as the big officers on their fine horses. One of them told him he was not the General, but he would send up a guard as soon as they got into town. Then they moved on, and such a sight! They looked very different from our poor Confederate soldiers, with their sleek horses and bright swords, and there was not a ragged jacket or a bare foot among them all. They had, every one of them, a pile of good things strapped up behind and before their saddles, and a good many had a fine horse by their side with all sorts of packages and parcels strapped upon their back, ever so high, but nobody in the saddle. But I thought, what wouldn't I give if I could but ride one of those fine horses and be a soldier and as good as any white man! I looked at Aleck, and I saw he thought so too; and what is best about it, it did not last long, and it all came true, sure enough. We stood there and looked and looked until we were tired, for there was no end to the horses, and the big guns, and the wagons, and oh, they had every thing so nice and so whole, though they were bespattered from head to foot; I did not think soldiers could look so well. At last they were nearly all gone, and I and Aleck went back.

When we came to the other side of the lake we saw Miss Mary and some of the other young ladies standing by the window up stairs, and some of them were crying; but Miss Mary waved a little flag, such as our soldiers have, right in the face of the Yankees. But master looked up and gave her such a look! Miss Mary went away from the window, and when they sent for her to come down to dinner, she told Flora to tell master she had a bad headache and did not want any dinner. Soon after the bell rang, and when I went to the front-door there stood a big Yankee officer, with his sword by his side and the mud all over him, and he asked in a very soft voice if master was at home. I did not like much his talking of my master and he a Yankee, but I knew I must be polite to strangers, and I asked him to please walk in. He said he wanted to see master, would I request him to come to the front-door for a moment. I can't tell exactly what it was, but there was something in the officer's voice, and in the way he spoke to me, that made me feel a big man, and as if nobody ought to call me Oby any more. Master is mighty good to me, but he always talks to me as if I was a little baby and had not any sense at all. Now the officer spoke right sternly, though his voice was so soft, but somehow it did not hurt me in the least, and I felt all the better for it. I ran in and told master, who came out at once, not at all flurried but like a grand old gentleman, and he begged the officer very politely to walk in. But he would not come in, and merely told master that he was on General Sheridan's staff, and that he wished to know where he should place the guard. I wanted badly to hear what they were going to say to each other, but master sent me down stairs to tell Aunt Hannah to cook a big dinner for the soldiers. We had done that often enough when our poor Confederates came by, and there was not much left in the smoke-house; but when the folks in the kitchen heard it was for the Yankees they were going to cook they set to work with a will. Aunt Hannah said she would sit up all night to work for them blessed Yankees, and Flora laughed and cried out that she hoped there was a handsome captain coming to take her to Boston.

Now I did not like that at all, for Flora was a mighty sweet girl; she was not one of your mean black niggers, but quite light, and had the most beautiful hair I ever saw in my life, and a waist—why she could wear Miss Mary's dresses, who is not bigger than a grasshopper, and they were still too large for her. So I sat down angrily, and turned my back upon them, and whistled to myself. All of a sudden there comes a hand and shuts up my mouth, and a voice says to me: "Why, Oby, you are not at all gallant to-day!" Up I jump and make her a fine bow, and say, "Oh, Madam, I did not know you was here, I hope you are well." She did not say a word, but looked at Aunt Hannah and looked at me, and then she burst out a-laughing and cries: "Oh, Mr. Paragon, you must look sharper, or one of these days Miss Flora will bloom in another garden." They had spoilt her mightily, and told her that her name meant "Pretty Flower." The young ladies on whom she waited gave her quantities of nice things, and when she went down on Sunday to church she looked every bit as pretty as a lady, and prettier too. Colonel Wood's Aleck was very sweet on her, and he and I had had many a fight about it—who was to escort her to preaching, and who was to hand her into supper, when Aunt Betsy's daughter was married. She went more with Aleck than with me, and many is the cry I have had about it; but then she would look so sweetly at me, and say with such a soft voice: "Get along, you handsome nigger!" that I could not help myself, and all the money I ever got went to buy her ribbons and candy.

I went up to her and said: "Now, sweet angel, don't you be angry with me, and you shall have that big red shawl that hangs out at Mr. Abraham's store window"; and I put my arm around her and was just going to—when there came such a pull at the door-bell that I jumped up and thought the Yankees were breaking into the house.

I ran up the stairs as fast as I could, and as I was trying to unlock the door—we did not use to do it, and so the key would not turn very quickly—somebody rang and rang until I got frightened out of my wits. When I opened the door there stood Miss Polly, as red as a peony, her dress all in tatters, and her hair hanging about her as I had never seen a lady do in all my life, and rushes by me to master's study. Master had just come out to see what was the matter, and she ran nearly over him. Then she began telling him to come, for God's sake, to her house; how the Yankees had come there and broken every thing to pieces, and were misbehaving shamefully. I did not believe a word of it, for they had been very polite to us all and to master too; but he did not say a word, put on his hat, gave Miss Polly his arm, and walked right off with her. I followed him, for I thought he might want me, and I heard Miss Polly rattling away like a water-mill, telling him how the soldiers had come to the house, and first broken into the kitchen and eaten all the dinner that there was, and then came into the sitting-room and asked for whisky. Her brother, who had been shot in the Valley and was lying with a broken leg on a couch, had gotten very angry and called them names. The Yankees did not like that, and went to work smashing every thing in the house. So she ran over to our house to get help.

When we crossed the road—it was knee-deep in mud—we saw Miss Emma, with her three little children, sitting on the big oak stump right by the house, crying bitterly, and in the house all the windows and doors smashed, and such a row as I have not heard in my life. Master puts Miss Polly down by her sister's side, and tells her to sit quiet, and then he walks as boldly up to where the Yankees were as if he were General Sheridan himself. I was afraid to go after him, so I staid by the ladies, who, I thought, wanted somebody to protect them, and they were so full of the misfortune they told me every thing. All the silver was gone, and all the china was broken, and the pictures cut to pieces, and the books thrown out of the window; and as they were telling me the soldiers came out. Some had a pillow-case full of flour, another a tureen filled with meal, and still another had two big gold watches in his hand. At last one came out with a silver cup in his hand. When Miss Emma sees him she jumps up and catches hold of it, and says, "You sha'n't take away my poor baby's cup!" "But I will," says the soldier—a great big fellow with a sword by his side. "But you sha'n't!" cries Miss Emma again, and the big tears ran down her cheeks. And there they pulled, she on one side and the gentleman on the other side, and I thought she was going to fall down, when master comes out and very quietly puts his hand upon the soldier's arm, and says, "You will surely oblige the lady and let her have the cup." The Yankee looked quite bewildered, but he had let go, and Miss Emma ran back to her seat with her baby in her arm; and the baby held the cup with her dumpy little fingers, as if she knew what she held, and master looked pleased and said: "I am glad, Sir, you can act so handsomely." I thought the soldier had a great mind to tell him he did not want any of his praise; but I know most men were rather afraid of master, he looked so stiff and so stately; and he went slowly away. Then master called out in a clear, loud voice: "Mike O'Rourke! Mike O'Rourke!"

I was half frightened, when all of a sudden there stepped out from behind a big oak-tree a great red-haired Yankee, with a sword, and a carbine, and a pistol in his belt. "What do you want?" says he. Master answered, "Were you not placed here as guard, Sir, to protect this house?" "Well, I believe I was." "And when these marauders came, and the ladies begged you to protect them, you ran away and hid?" The soldier looked as if he did not like at all being talked to in that way, and perhaps he had not a very good conscience; so he said, in a sulky tone: "I could not stop all those fellows; they were too many for me!" Master said, very quietly: "You know very well that your orders are to do your duty, and to shoot down the first one who breaks the safeguard." The Yankee looked rather taken aback; but then he cried out very angrily, "I don't know what all this is to you, Sir, but I would have you know that it is very hard for a man whose house has been burned over his head, down in Pennsylvania, by these beggarly rebels, and whose old father and mother have been driven out by night and ruined for life, to stand here and protect people who, for all I know, may have been the very ones to do so to me." With that he turned on his heel and walked to the house. I don't know what master thought; but he looked rather puzzled, and went up to Miss Emma and began talking to them in a low voice.

Soon after the Yankees made a great uproar in the house, and then they came out, one by one, the red-haired man shoving them out with a laugh and a curse, until the house was clear again. I had been watching them, so that I did not hear what master said to the ladies, but just as the last one went down the hill I heard Miss Polly crying bitterly, and saying: "And would you believe it, Sir, one of these wretches told me I was the ugliest woman he had seen in the Confederacy; and as for Emma, she was too ugly to live?" I looked hard at master, to see what he would say to that, but I thought he was trying all he could not to laugh. Then he smiled and gave his arm to Miss Emma, and asked her when she had heard from her husband, and they all went back to the house.

The red-haired man came out and sat down on the bench in the veranda; and when he sees me standing there, he says, "Come here, man, and bring me some water; and, look here, bring me some whisky too, or I'll cut your head off!" I was certainly afraid he would do it, too, so I ran as fast as I could to Uncle Tony close by, who I knew had some apple brandy, and telling him that it was for a Yankee soldier he gave me some. I ran back to the Irish gentleman — for I knew him to be Irish, because we have so many of those folks around us, working on the canal — and brought him the whisky. I was running for the water too, but he called after me, and said he was not thirsty now, I need not go for water. So I sat down on the grass by his side, and looked up at him, and got hold of his sword, and made the little wheels on his spurs play as fast as they would go.

All of a sudden he looks at me and says: "Hallo, Cuffee, how would you like to have a fine horse and ride along with us all?" My heart jumped when I heard him make such an offer; but I did not know if he was in earnest, so I only laughed and laughed until he could not help himself and had to laugh too. But after a while he looked very sober, and said: "Nonsense, Cuffee, nonsense; don't laugh that way, but tell me soberly would not you like to go with me and become a soldier?" When I saw that he was really in earnest I jumped up and said, as loud as I could, "Yes, Sir, that I will, and I have long waited for the day, God be thanked it has come at last, and I shall be a free man!"

He told me then to follow him, and we sent over to Burr's Hill, where the General had his head-quarters, and the red-haired man's regiment had their camp. When we got there I found out that he belonged to the artillery, and the whole wood was filled with guns, and wagons, and horses, and all about the hill were fires lit, and the men were sitting around them eating their supper. I felt all of a sudden as hungry as a rattlesnake, for there they had coffee, and white sugar, and lemons, and all the good things we had not seen at our house for ever so long. We went past them all, until we came close to the house, and there I saw a great number of colored gentlemen standing around in a circle, and in the middle were some Yankee soldiers. Just as we came up I heard one of them say, "Here is another fine lot; what's the bid?" I felt as if I was turning to stone, when I found out that he held Bob, my second cousin, by his right ear, and pushed him forward in the bright light. I thought sure enough it was all the old story over again, and we were not free yet, but to be sold just as we were before. Somebody cried out, "I'll give a ham!" and another, "I bid a loaf of sugar!" Now I wondered more than ever, for Bob was a powerful fellow, and could plow better than any man on the plantation, and that was no price at all, even in Confederate money. But I soon found out that they were only offering something for the right to choose their servants, and that we were really free, only we could not choose our masters, but they chose us.

When I understood that right, I turned round and said, very politely, "Master, I wish you would not offer me to any body but keep me yourself. I would rather be your servant than any body's else." He seemed to be quite pleased at being called Master, and slapped me on the shoulder, and said, "Well, Cuffee, if you wish it, you may do so." I did not like to be called Cuffee, which is not respectable for a nigger who moves in good society; so I said, "Master, my name is Oby; and if it is the same to you, I would rather you should call me by my name." I don't think he heard me, for he said nothing for a while, and then he showed me his horse, a fine big bay, and told me to rub him down: "But mind you do it well," he said, "or you will be bucked." I did not know what he meant by that, for the boys had often called me a "Buck," and I had always taken it for a compliment. I soon found out however what it was, for Jack, the doctor's boy, who was up here too, and who had refused to cook supper for his new master, because he was so tired from doing all they had made him do ever since dinner-time, lay not far off, bound up in the most curious way I have ever seen, and was hollowing most awfully.

My bay did not give me much trouble, only he had an ugly way of kicking, when you touched him at a particular spot; and he was so quick at it that I got one or two kicks against my shins before I was aware of it. I disliked it mightily, for I did not know then that his kicking was to save my life when nothing else could help me. They did not offer me any supper that night, so I ran home and told Flora all about it, how the soldiers said I was free now, and how I was to have a fine horse and become a sure enough soldier, and have my fifteen dollars a month, all to myself.

She was not half as glad as I thought she would be, and asked me if I thought it was better to be the servant of a Yankee than to serve a gentleman like master. I did not like her saying so at all, for I could not tell her why I liked it better; and still, I knew it *was* better. I had thought I would ask her to come along with me and become my wife, when we got to the North. But somehow I had not the courage, she looked so wicked out of her eyes; and then Aunt Hannah stood by, and although she made-believe she was busy with her pots and plates I knew she had heard every word I said. But I could not help looking at Flora, and just to say, "Oh, Miss Flora!" and I thought she looked as sweet as a rose-bud, when she cast her eyes down and picked at the pretty belt I had given her the Sunday before, and seemed to think very hard.

Just then Aleck came up, and asked me when I was going away. That put me in mind, that last week master had called us all up into the hall and told us, if we wanted to go when the Yankees came, we must be sure not to sneak off like a parcel of runaway niggers, but to come up like men and tell him, and he would see to it that we had some clothes and something to help us on the way when we went. I thought it was my duty to go up stairs and tell him that I had made up my mind to leave. I pulled off my shoes and went up softly into the veranda, where I knew he would be sitting. And so he was, in his old arm-chair, with Maida right across his feet and Miss Lucy sitting by his side, reading to him out of the big old Bible he uses at prayers, when we come up in the morning and the evening. She read so low I could not hear where she was, but I made out that it was something about God being our rock and a very present help in trouble; and when I looked at master I saw the big tears were coming down his white cheeks slowly, one by one. I knew then he was thinking of young master, who lay dead and killed way off in Spottsylvania, and nobody knew where. When I saw that I could not go up to him to save my life, so I slipped down again, and did not know what to do.

Master had always been mighty good to me, and I had never wanted any thing on this earth but he had given it to me; and I knew as long as I staid with him, and he had any thing to live on, he would provide for me. But I wanted badly to be a free man, and I knew I could never earn fifteen dollars a month, as I could at the North; and perhaps they were going to give us each a farm, and we would not have to work any more. It was a bad night for me, and my head turned all around in a whirl; now I wanted to stay, and now I wanted to go. But when the red streaks came out over the mountain, and then the big sun rose right behind the old cherry-tree at the tobacco patch, I remembered what William had said, when he preached to us at Uncle James's funeral, about the rising of the Sun of Liberty, and our going to glory here upon earth, by the word of Mr. Lincoln, and I ran as fast as I could to Burr's Hill, and told them all that I had come to be free.

My new master showed me a beautiful horse that I was to ride, and when the light came through the trees and I could see every thing clear, I saw it was Master William's great big stallion. I did not like to get on him, because every body about here knew him, he had stood so often down in town, but I was told to take him down to water, and I did not like to be bucked like Bob. I went down to the spring, and I could not help thinking he was the handsomest horse I had ever laid eyes on, and it would be a great thing for me to ride alongside of all the gentlemen on such a fine horse. When I came back to the fire they showed me a quantity of bags and bales, all nicely fixed in white cotton sheets, which I had to strap on the horse; there was just enough room left between the pile in front and the pile behind to get into the saddle. They did not give me any breakfast either, but I did not mind that much, for soon the bugles sounded — it made me feel like a gentleman to be called by a bugle like all the others; and my new master, who was a corporal or a major, had some other gentlemen under him, and when the guns were all ranged in beautiful order, the Colonel came out and looked at us, and off we marched with the music at our head.

First came the Colonel and some officers, then came the music, with all sorts of instruments such as I had never seen before; after them came men who bore a number of flags, which I knew nothing of, and after them, before all the regiment, came we colored people, about fifty of us, all on fine horses, and the happiest boys ever you saw in your life. It was glorious. But when we got to the corner by the tobacco-house, where the gate has been out of order for many years and the lane is quite low and narrow, they all stopped and we could not go any farther. The mud was awful, and the horses could not pull the heavy guns and the wagons.

Just then who must come up but master. I felt mighty badly, but I could not run away, and I looked for my new master to stand by me and let them all know that I was free. When master's eye came slowly down the line and at last fell right upon me, I thought I was going to sink into the ground. It made me feel sick. When I looked up again he was making his way through the horses and the cannons right up to me, and did not mind the mud, and the way the soldiers all looked at him, and the horses that wanted to kick him. When he came up to where I sat on my horse, he just said, "Oh, Oby!" and before I knew what I was doing, I was out of the saddle and standing right before him, with my new cap in my hand. He said, in his quiet way, "Oby, you know you are not strong enough to sleep out in the open air; you have not even a blanket, and it is not three weeks since you were sick with pneumonia. Come home, my boy, and don't distress your father and your mother. You know it will kill them!"

I knew that what he said was but too true; but then again, when I looked at the fine horse I was on, and all the gentlemen around me, I felt quite undecided. Master said again, very quietly, "Come home, Oby!" and I followed him, I did not know why. But just as we were getting out of the crowd, on the side of the road, my new master came dashing up to where we were, and with a terrible oath told me to mount my horse and be ready to start. I was so frightened I did not know what to do. Master never said a word, but just looked at me as if he pitied me from the bottom of his heart, and I could not stand that; I did not think of father and mother at home, nor of Flora, nor of the nice times we had had together in the fields at night, but I just looked at master and went away with him. But the soldier was not satisfied yet; he came straight up to us, and swearing worse than ever, he said to master, "How dare you, Sir, force that man away? Do you not know that he is free, and has a right to go where he will?" Master changed color; I knew he was not accustomed to be spoken to in that way, and I wished I had never thought of enlisting as a soldier. But he said nothing at all, and although the soldiers all turned around, and my new master pulled out his carbine and cocked it, he made his way between the horses and the guns, I following him close by, until we came out on the other side of the column, and then he said very quietly, "Now, Oby, go home and tell your father not to distress himself about you any farther." I was just running up the road, when I heard somebody galloping up, and as I turned round I saw it was a great officer, with a sword in his hand, who rode up to master and asked him what was the matter. I could not hear his answer, but the officer said, "We do not force servants to go with us, and if your boy wants to stay, let him stay."

When I came home I found father and mother, Uncle Henry, and all of them in mother's room, and when they saw me they all cried out, "Oh, Oby, what have you been doing?" Well, it made me right angry to be treated thus like a baby, and I went out into the yard. There stood Flora, and what must she do but come up to me in the prettiest way of the world and drop me a little courtesy, and say in a little lisping way, "Oho, Mr. Paragon, you had not the courage to go with your friends? Don't you look like a little whipped boy? Shall I ask Miss Lucy for some candy for you?" It made me mad to hear her talk so, when she had all the time been telling me that I ought to stay, and not run away like the poor stupid field-hands.

I turned round without looking at her, and ran over to Uncle Bob, to ask him what I ought to do. He was not in, but Aunt Betsy was there, with the children about her, packing up all her things. I wondered what she was doing, but she would not give me any answer, and I was too mad to go home again; so I staid and waited for Uncle Bob to come home again. They had some nice middlings that day, and goody-bread with the sweetest cracklings I ever ate, and we all laughed, and talked, and I danced a jig for Aunt Betsy, and others came in until the house was full.

Late in the evening Uncle Bob came home, and such a sight he was! He had a double harness hanging over his shoulders, and a saddle on his head, and his hands full of bags and satchels, and a big gun under his arm. He looked very tired, and threw it all down; then he opened the door again and laughed, and when we went out there to see what it was, we found a nice carryall and two good, strong horses fastened to the fence. I knew the carriage well; it belonged to old Miss Mary Fitch, and the horses were Uncle Bob's master's. I did not like his goings on much, but he was an old man and I had no right to say any thing to him. When he had had his supper he lit his pipe and looked around him, and when he noticed me he opened his eyes wide, and said, "Why, Oby, I thought you had gone with the Yankees!" I felt mightily ashamed. I had to tell him all about it, and when I had done he called me out and whispered to me, "Now, look here, Oby, don't you make a fool of yourself, but come along with me to-night and be a man." He talked and talked, and before I knew exactly how it was, I had promised to go with him. He had a way about him that few could resist, and when he wanted you to do any thing he was sure to get you to do it.

It was a dark night, the moon was behind the clouds, and at times you could

"NEGROES ESCAPING OUT OF SLAVERY"

not see the hand before your eyes. Uncle Bob had hitched up and put Aunt Betsy and the four children inside the carryall; he sat on the box, and every corner behind and before was stuffed full with bags and parcels. I do not know why they took so much; but Aunt Betsy would take every thing; and there was her spinning-wheel, and her split-bottomed rocking-chair, and the cradle for the baby. Then there was Colonel Wood's Aleck, and Dr. White's Jimmy, and I. We walked pretty fast, and listened with all our might, for we thought we might meet some gentleman and he might stop us. But there was nobody about that night; every body was afraid of the Yankees, and kept very close. Besides, the roads were awful, and Uncle Bob's horses could hardly pull the carryall at a snail's pace. Every now and then they would stick fast in the mud, and then we had to take rails from the fence and put them under the wheels and help Uncle Bob. It was not half as pleasant as riding on a fine horse among a crowd of gentlemen, or even sitting at home in mother's room and having a nice supper. After a while Uncle Bob became angry, and the next time the horses stalled he pitched Aunt Betsy's wheel into the road; then went the chair, and the cradle, and a great many other things. Aunt Betsy did not dare say a word, but she groaned and groaned. It sounded awful in the dark night and in the black woods where we were. At last we could not get any further, and just then we saw a light through the trees, and when we whipped the horses on both sides to get nearer to it we found an army wagon in the middle of the road, with the mud over the hubs of the wheels, and one of the mules half-dead and half-buried in the mud. The drivers and some of the escort had made a roaring fire in the woods, and we joined them. I was so sleepy I fell down where we stopped, and did not know what happened any more.

I was just dreaming of my young master's calling me to saddle his pony when somebody touched me on the shoulder. I could not wake up at once. It always went hard with me to wake in the morning, and then I heard somebody call my name. It sounded very sweet to me somehow, though I did not know where it came from, and when I got my eyes open at last I thought I was dreaming still. For there was Flora standing by my side, looking up at the top of the tree, as if she did not know I was lying right before her. After a while she turned her eyes all around her, and when they came back to me she cried out, "Why, Oby, if that is not you! Where on earth do you come from?" Now that was a nice question to ask me; so I just jumped up and laughed heartily; and then she began laughing too, and before I knew what I was doing my arm was round her waist and I had kissed her twice. She pretended to be very angry, but I only laughed the more, and at last she told me how she had heard from Uncle Bob's son, who stays at master's mill, that I had gone along with him. Then she had made a little bundle of her nicest clothes and had followed us all the way, never saying a word, until she felt so cold in the morning she could not stay away any longer from the fire. When I asked her what she had come for, she said: "You would not have me let Aunt Betsy go away with all those babies and no one to take care of them? And then, might not somebody have come and frightened Mr. Paragon out of his wits and sent him home again crying?" At first I did not know how to take her, but there was something funny in her voice that I knew well enough from of old. So I jumped up, as quick as a squirrel, and before she knew what was coming I had my arms around her once more, and kissed her as hard as I could. We must have made some noise, for all of a sudden there was a crowd around us, and all cried out upon Flora and wanted to know how she got there and what she came for.

We were still talking and laughing in the jolliest way, as if there was no trouble in the world, and we were down at a corn-shucking, when bang went a shot, and another, and before we knew what was coming the wood was full of smoke that could not get out fast enough through the branches of the pine-trees. We all stood still, and my heart beat fast enough, not that I was much afraid of the shooting, but I thought it might be the gray-jackets, and if they should catch us and carry us back! I would not have minded the going back so much, for I knew they would not have punished us, but I could not have stood before master and seen him look at me again, as he did when he wanted me to come home with him from among the artillerymen. I did not stand long idly there, but I just took Flora's hand and told her to come along, and then I pitched Aunt Betsy and the little ones into the carryall, and all the bundles I could find. I was as in a dream, but it was not long before the horses were put in, and Uncle Bob was cracking his whip, and we were running after them as fast as we could.

When we were a little more quiet again we looked around, and then we found out that we had left our friends the Yankees, and were quite alone by ourselves. There were about five or six colored ladies with us, some of them had babies on one arm and a big pile of clothes and such things under the other; then there were one or two elderly men who looked scared and did not know, I believe, what they were doing, except that they must go on, on until they got to the North; and lastly, there were three or four little children who were just running along with the rest of them for the fun. After a while I began to feel hungry, and when I looked at Flora in the bright daylight I thought she looked hungry too; at all events she was very pale and drooping, and I saw she had no shoes on, and could hardly walk. I went to help her, but she tried to hold up, and said it did not matter. I saw, though, it would matter pretty soon, for we had not a mouthful of bread nor meal among us, and, except Uncle Bob, who was rich enough, there was no one among us who had any money. And here we were alone, left by our natural friends and protectors, and not likely to be received on any plantation.

It seemed that all of our party felt the same way, for no one said a word. Every now and then one of the children would begin to whine and be told to hush up. Then some girl would laugh right out and suddenly stop short, as if she was frightened at the sound of her own voice. Uncle Bob, who knew best, had his hands full to drive his tired horses and to pull the carryall, with its heavy load, through the awfully bad roads. I walked steadily on, Flora right behind me, Indian file, and what with the cold, drizzling rain, wetting us to the skin, and the loads of mud that stuck to our feet, and the heavy thoughts that weighed on our minds, we did not make a very merry couple. I thought, every now and then, what a glorious time I would have at the North. I knew I could make as good a shoe as any white man, and I thought of a nice little shop I might have in Cincinnati, where Peter Hite went when he was made free, and of Flora being my good wife, really married, and the beautiful things I was going to buy for her, so that she might look a real lady. But in the midst of my thoughts I stumbled against a big, old root, or Flora sighed behind me, and then coughed a little to put me on a false track, or asked me some question, to show that she was not sad at all, and my dreams were gone in a moment, and I saw all our troubles clear before me again.

We tramped on until late in the evening, when we met an old field-hand, with a bag of potatoes on his back, who told us we were still eight miles from the canal, and that he had seen no Yankees any where. We asked him to let us have his potatoes, but he said he did not want to have any thing to do with run-away niggers, and was going away to leave us, when Uncle Bob came up and asked him what he would take for them in greenbacks. When he heard us speak of greenbacks he became very polite at once, and sold them for ninepence to Uncle Bob, who made him promise to bring some fat middling and some corn-meal up to the old tobacco house, where we meant to spend the night. We all went in there, and it was a nice enough place for us to get dry in; there was some hay in a lean-to on one side, and I made a nice little bed for Flora; but we did not dare make a large fire for fear they might see it at the house and send the overseer down to turn us out. Uncle Bob got his middling, and Aunt Betsy cooked all they had for herself and her children, asking me and Flora to come up and help ourselves. I did not like much going there, when there were so many others who had nothing at all to eat, but Uncle Bob told me to make no hesitation — he always loved big words — and to partake of his victuals. I took Flora by the hand and pulled her along with me to the fire. Aunt Betsy looked at us, and I thought she was going to have a hearty laugh, but somehow there was none of us that night could laugh heartily, and we ate just to satisfy our hunger, but it did not taste good. Then we had a chew of tobacco, and Uncle Bob proposed we should sing a psalm about the mansions in the sky, and hal-lelujah, but we broke down pretty soon, and then we all lay down, one here, one there, as we were sitting. I was tired enough, but I could not sleep; the thoughts would come into my head. I could not drive father and mother out of my head, and every time I saw them in my mind they looked so sad it made me feel very badly. Then the children cried and moaned and asked for something to eat; and some of the old ones groaned too, and cried out: "O Lord, O Lord a-mercy!" — it was very hard to hear it all and not be able to help them in any way. So I was right glad when the mist broke in the morning and the sun rose, first red, like blood, and looking as if it were angry at us, and then clear and bright, like the dayspring from on high.

I ran down to the spring, where there was a plenty of water, to wash, and when I came back I saw Flora talking very anxiously to Aunt Betsy. They hushed up when I came near, but I could see well enough that Flora had been crying, and that somebody had given her an old pair of shoes that were twice as big as her feet. She did not have big splash-feet, like a field-hand nigger woman, but hers were nice enough for any white lady. I felt mighty sorry for her; she was not accustomed at all to rough work, and down at home she had hardly ever been sent out of the house. I knew she could not stand it long, and I was determined to make her go back. I did not mean to speak to her directly. I knew she would not listen to me if she once had made up her mind; but I thought she would mind what Aunt Betsy would say to her. I took the old lady aside, and told her all about my fears and troubles, and she promised at once to talk to Flora and to persuade her to go home again.

I went behind the big oak-tree, lest she should see me, and I noticed Aunt Betsy going up to her and talking to her very friendly and very soberly. But I must have been too curious, for no sooner had she ended than Flora comes straight up to where I stood and said: "And of all men, Oby, that you should want me to go back!" and with that she broke out into such sobs and sighs that I did not know what to do, and just had to beg her to stay and to go along with us. I told her I would stand by her as long as I was alive, and she could trust me now and forever. In the meantime they had all gotten ready to start, and as there was not much over from last night for breakfast, we were soon on the tramp again.

It was an awful time, though, we had; the road was worse than ever, for Sheridan's men had been right ahead of us, and they had trampled the mud knee-deep, and if the carryall once got into the ruts the army wagons had made, there was hardly any way to get it out again. We were soon left behind, for we had to pull the horses out when they stuck fast, and to mend the harness, that was all the time breaking, and take the rails from the fence and pry the carriage up to let the poor starved horses pull it out again.

At last we came to a sandy stretch in the pine woods, where it was a little better, and as we turned round a corner, there, right in the fence, lay Aunt Phoebe, and by her side two of her little babies, the one three years old and the other about nine months, and never a word did any one of them say. I went up to Aunt Phoebe and shook her, and asked her what was the matter. At first she would not answer at all; at last, when Flora came up and whispered into her ear, and begged her to speak to her, she said, very faintly, that she could not possibly go a step further, and that she had not a drop of milk left for her baby. Aunt Betsy came down too, and when she saw what was the matter, and turned the children round and found them look ashy pale, she called for Uncle Bob and fell to crying bitterly. He came up slowly, and looked at them all without saying a word. Then he pulled the mother and the children together into the fence-corner and put a quarter, a silver quarter, into the hands of Aunt Phoebe and left her there. We all followed him back to the carryall with our hearts ever so heavy, but what could we do? I asked Uncle Bob if he thought she would die? He did not look at me at all, but just said in his beard, "I don't know; maybe she will, maybe she won't; perhaps it's better for her to die than to live on as she has done."

After that we were sadder than ever before. Poor Flora lost her big shoes every other step, and most of the ladies had to throw away their bundles, and even then they could hardly get along. Whenever we met a colored man we asked him how far it still was to the canal, for we knew we would meet the Yankees there sure enough, and they would not let us starve, but give us all rations. It seemed as if we were never getting nearer to it, for every time we asked it was still some four or five miles, maybe six. We met some white gentlemen, too, on the road, but they just looked at us with stern faces and rode by. Once we came to a little bit of a house by the way-side, and saw an old lady sitting by the door, with a cat lapping up the milk in a gourd she held on her lap. I could not stand seeing that, so I walk up to her and make her a polite bow, and say, "Oh, Missis, I see you are a mighty good lady, won't you be so kind as to give me a little of that milk for a poor girl who is half dead over yonder?" The old lady looked at me and then at Flora, who was standing at the gate, staring with her big eyes at the gourd as if she had never seen milk in her life. After a while she said, "Well, I don't care; take it if you want it." I was just taking the gourd by the handle, being careful not to spill a drop, when a great big man in a gray uniform and a large revolver in his hand comes out of the passage, and swearing at me, as they did in the army, says, "Now, you rascal, you clear out here or I'll shoot you down like a dog!" I felt so mad I would have liked to run up to him and snatch the pistol out of his hand and shoot him myself; but I did not have the courage, that is the truth of it, and I knew also I must not get my friends into trouble before we got to the soldiers again. When I came back to where Flora stood I saw she had dropped down upon a big rock they used to get on horseback by, and when I spoke to her she said she could not get any further. That finished me, and I swore to God Almighty I would have something for her or take a man's life. But just then something came between me and her, and when I looked up there was the old lady with the gourd in her hand and a piece of corn-bread I had not seen before, and she said: "Never mind my son, boy; he is in bad humor because all our servants have left us in a body yesterday and taken our horses with them. Poor child, what is the matter with her?" And then she took Flora's hand in hers and rubbed it, and told her to sit up and eat and not to cry any more. I talked to her too, and after a while she did set up, and the way the milk and the bread went! It would have been a pleasure to me to see how she enjoyed it; but I was terribly hungry myself, and I counted every mouthful she took and every gulp that went down. When she had done, she stood up and looked much better, and then she thanked the old lady, as she had learned to do from Miss Lucy. The old lady had big tears in her eyes and looked mighty sad; she said something about God's Providence, which I did not understand, and about somebody's being ground between the upper and the nether millstone, which, I think, is somewhere in the Bible.

We had to walk fast enough to overtake the others, who had gotten far ahead of us, and it was late in the evening when we saw them all standing in a crowd together on a high place. The sun was just about setting, and the sky was golden, and as we looked at them we could see every ray of their clothes and every hair on their head. They all talked very loud, even Uncle Bob, who seemed to be very angry. We came up slowly, for we were terribly tired, and Flora could hardly drag one foot after the other. When we came up to where they stood, we saw we were on the side of the canal, and there on the tow-path sat Aunt Hannah, crying and screaming all together, and the others stood around her and looked as angry as could be. We pressed close up to Aunt Betsy, and I asked her in a whisper what was the matter. "Oh, Oby!" she said, "just think of it, Aunt Hannah was the first to see the canal, and she walks right up to where we now are and takes her poor little baby — it was not more than two months old — and before we knew what she was about she had thrown it into the water, and there it lies now. Oh, Oby, these are awful times! God have mercy upon us!"

I could not say a word. I had never seen or heard of such misery in my life. Flora went quietly down to where Aunt Hannah was rocking herself, weeping like a child, and then screaming out aloud, and sat down by her and tried to take her hands and to soothe her. But Aunt Hannah would not be soothed; she cried out: "Leave me alone, you! leave me alone! You don't know what it is to have a baby and to see it die on your breast. She is happier down there than she could ever have been in this world. I only wished I was there too. Can't you leave me alone? or give me something to eat? I have not eaten any thing since day before yesterday, not a mouthful. Oh, my baby, my baby! She was the sweetest child I ever had!" And with that she began screaming again, as if she were distracted. I could not stand it any longer; so I touched Flora and told her to come along, Uncle Bob was going and we must try to get something ourselves, or we would be starved too, or get mad like poor Aunt Hannah.

Flora got up and followed me, but she did not say a word. The tears were just running down her cheeks, and she did not mind it in the least. Uncle Bob was driving along on the tow-path, and we all followed in a long string, very slowly. At last we came to another turn, and there, right before us, lay a big mill, and behind it the town. On the mill-race stood a soldier in blue, and I could have shouted aloud, for now I knew our troubles would surely be at an end. I do not know what made me so bold, but I walked right up to the soldier and asked him if he did not know somebody that wanted a really good servant. He looked at me and then at Flora, who was standing behind me, and said: "You mean two good servants, don't you? I can't afford keeping a servant, but there is the sutler; I heard him inquire a little while ago for a handy fellow, who understood horses and knew how to make coffee and such things."

I hardly let him finish, for that was exactly what I was good for, and Flora made beautiful coffee. I just asked him where the sutler was, and when he showed me some way down the street a splendid team of four gray mules, standing before a large, fine house, and said that was the sutler's wagon, I took hold of Flora's hand and ran down as fast as I could. But when I came between the mules and the house I saw a whole crowd of servants standing around the door and crying out: "Take me, master, take me!" I thought it was all over, and I had lost my first and last chance, when Flora suddenly let go my hand and fell down like a log of wood, right between the wheels of the wagon. I tried to lift her up, but there was such a crowd, and the mules began to kick, and I thought she was going to die right away. Just then a man who had been inside the wagon popped his head out, and seeing Flora lying there, he asked: "Hallo, what is the matter, my man?" I told him as well as I could, and begged him for mercy's sake to help me, for Flora was sure enough dying. He laughed and stepped down leisurely over the swingle-trees, with a piece of hard tack in one hand and a bottle in the other. He poured some out of the bottle into his hand and rubbed her head with it, then he poured some down between her teeth, and when I could see next, she was sitting up with her head leaning against the wheel, opening her eyes as if she had been fast asleep, and munching a little bread in her mouth. I thanked the gentleman for having saved her life, but he only laughed the more. Then he asked me if I was not hungry too; and before I could say a word he pushed a whole pile of crackers into my hands. When Flora was all right again, he asked us what we were going to do with ourselves, and we told him as fast as we could, for we were both mighty grateful to him for his kindness. Then he told us that he was the sutler himself, and that if we promised to do well and be faithful servants to him he might find something to do for us both. He called to his clerk, who was in the house, and told him to see to it that we got a place to sleep in and some supper. When I looked a little around me I saw they had a beautiful flag flying from the top of the house, and that was the first night I slept under the Stars and Stripes, a free man.

Food was hardly easier to come by in northern Mississippi when Union troops evacuated Corinth in January 1864. They had occupied the important railroad juncture, where the Mobile and Ohio line crossed the Memphis and Charleston, ever since taking over Confederate headquarters following the battle of Shiloh and fighting to hold the town in October 1862. That was sufficient time to encourage two soldier newspapers, the Corinth War Eagle *and the* Corinth Chanticleer, *but the raids that had begun with systematic Union foraging in 1862 had been hard on Southern households. Their shortages were not eased when Forrest's cavalry reclaimed Corinth as a base during 1864, after Union troops had torn up tracks, burned down public buildings, and departed. "The little city," writes Margaret Greene Rogers, "witnessed more military activity and strategy than any other in the Confederate West." The inevitable skirmishing and incessant provisioning were difficult as well for Union and Confederate soldiers who fell sick in alarming numbers. But their continuing disruption in "Road-Side Story" beggars the area's homesteaders in ways that quinine and calomel could not cure. During the war's final winter, as Confederate engineers rebuilt the railroad that would help carry John Bell Hood to misguided assaults on Franklin and Nashville, a refugee woman and the family she has left shiver in one of the coldest winters on record while they wait, like so many others, to go home.*

◆◦◆

"ROAD-SIDE STORY"

(*Land We Love*, August 1866)

The reception-room where I awaited the cars was lonely, and I was glad to hear steps in the hall coming that way. Traveling arouses all the curiosity in my nature; I lose myself in vague wanderings about this or that person; not idle prying, I trust, but an expanding interest in the joys and sorrows of my fellow-creatures. The footsteps were those of a woman, and I straightway fell to wondering what manner of creature would appear. Fantasias in verse and song to the unseen flocked to my busy brain, to fly like frightened birds before the presence of the odd-looking little old woman, who stood in the entrance for a few seconds with that hesitating air of untraveled persons, and quickly found for herself and bundles the most unobtrusive spot in the room. A thin, sallow boy followed with an idiotic air and odd maneuvers. I am a polite man by nature as well as training, so I stirred the fire, and invited her nearer it, as I marked an occasional shiver under a threadbare shawl. "Thank you, sir; come,

Davy!" The tone was pleasant, the fire likewise, for her timid manner fled before its sparkle, and my companion proved rather agreeable than otherwise to look upon, with her restless eyes, under a white ruffled cap, surmounted by a well taken care of, but exceedingly worse for the wear bonnet, and a clean checked, homespun dress, just meeting the tops of a pair of stout shoes. Even the threadbare shawl had an air of doing its best, however little that might be. Several remarks passed relative to the belated trains, dreadful state of the roads, etc. Traveling seemed a new thing; and from the brisk manner in which its disadvantages were set forth for my edification, a fear arose that I was going to be bored. Now, if there is one kind of bore who possesses superior qualifications to another in this particular, it is the ungrammatical bore; the difference is as marked as between a well-polished gimlet and a rusty auger. The tidy old lady was very intelligent by nature, but several errors had struck my sensitive ear, and brought conviction that the weather and cars might be enlarged upon disagreeably; thereon I grew communicative myself, and after a roundabout dissertation on these already exhausted subjects, remarked that I was affected by an uncomfortable drowsiness, rose with a yawn, drew on my army overcoat, settled myself for the night, and advised her to do the same. The two left to themselves talked in a low tone; the boy was evidently her son, and I was touched by her tenderness in many simple ways. She made him take off his jacket, turn it round and round before the fire, took sewing materials from an emaciated pocket-book, darned a place here and there holding it up with an air of satisfaction. It was one of the gray jackets we were all wearing then, like the one I had on, only his was worn almost white with faded blue trimmings, while mine was so much better I could not resist holding up an arm by way of contrast, breathing a blessing on the mother who made it, and the sister who had so cheerfully given up her pretty opera-cloak for the facings of brother's new uniform; but the contrast was painful unless I had owned another jacket to give the boy, so I pulled my cape over the bright red cuff, and wished I had on my old one. Watching the faces before me, hearing her suppressed tones and his silly chuckle, I dozed away and could have slept had it not been for steps sounding again in the hall. The clerk of the house came in with such a flourish, confound him! that Morpheus fled amazed from my couch. I wanted to collar and choke him, not for waking me up solely — that was an aggravating circumstance, but not the exciting cause of my indignation. I remembered the shabby old lady found her way in alone, while a fashionable, handsomely-attired young lady was ushered in with all that parade and needless ceremony so annoying to real gentility. I argued, the one is rich, the other poor — sometimes I hate wealth, it narrows so many hearts and cracks so many brains! Resentment against the younger, in behalf of the elder lady, filled my breast. I hated the former before I looked at her; indeed I would not vouchsafe a glance from under my old slouched hat to one who had suddenly grown rich, and fancied herself in position by possession of a few dollars. I knew she was one of that class by the rustle of her sweeping dress. Bah! the fool! I muttered in my chivalric defense of the silent representative of poverty, who, I fancied, was already enduring heroically the arrogance of a "parvenu." A ripple of a laugh fell among my thoughts, a pleasant sound of itself, and for another reason—in the solemn earnestness of warfare men and women laughed seldom, it was chiefly little children who could laugh as in the olden time. Before I was quite aware of my intentions, I raised the brim of my hat to look at that face, while the shine of a laugh lay on it. A glance was enough to remove all preconceived ideas of the lovely woman before me. I called myself a fool as heartily as I had called her one. "Parvenu," indeed! How refined in style, how delicate in manner! Had the other been wife and heir at law to Croesus, she could not have found a more attentive listener. My aforesaid curiosity manifested itself in the most vehement manner—what if the train came before I divined whether that soul was as fair as the body! Were those eyes as honest as bright? Was that hair God's glorious crowning, or a "switch," held on with curious frettings of spikes and pins? Was it a dimple or shadow on that faultless chin? Were those roses on lip and cheek to the manor born, or parasites? At this juncture I wondered if she was married or single; strangely enough, the conversation grew suddenly interesting and important. I found myself wide awake at the next remark, which, singularly too, replied to my speculations. "Yes, ma'am; my husband," said the red lips proudly. It was a sweet word, sweetly spoken; I never thought so before, nevertheless it ruffled my composure; this may have risen from a commendable fear that she may not have been happily married; however, a resolution was offered and adopted to hate her husband, modified only by a providing clause that the man could give satisfactory evidence of his fitness to stand in that relation. This was a cool, sensible proceeding, and I gave myself due credit for disinterestedness in my devotion to the sex; at the same time acknowledging my capacity for hating or loving, men or women, suddenly and fervently, on the slightest provocation. That I was just to the lady's husband was evident to any observer. Why was she traveling alone? He was doubtless an idle, drunken skulker from the army; or why that wistful sadness that flitted now and then from those lustrous eyes? Possibly she might think well of the scapegrace, or might not; in either event it was furthermore resolved, that if he intruded himself in our midst, and offered the slightest indignity, stranger as I was it should be resented. I might restrain my rage until I whirled him out of her presence, but it was doubtful, very doubtful indeed! Don Quixote could not have been by half so crestfallen in his famous retreat from the windmills, as I after this desperate onslaught against the missing husband. I discovered myself a fool beyond a shadow of disputation when I heard her say: "We have all suffered, but my husband still lives, thank God!" It occurred to me at that moment more might be said than either lady would desire me to hear; and, with all my interest in others, I wish to know nothing of the penetralia of a human soul, which is not voluntarily given to my keeping.

I arose, and replenished the dying fire, for which I was repaid by looks of gratification from my companions; even the boy giggled in his sleep, and carried his hands to and from the fire to his mouth, as if the flames were food. Naturally, as it came to us all in those days, the war was our theme. Men and women could not sit silently together then, when all held hands in the game whose stake was life or death! The devotion of our women, especially, and their heroic sacrifices, I enlarged upon. "Still," I continued, "there are instances rare, I grant, where avarice has laid violent hands on the hearts of women as well as men." "There are dreadful necessities forced on us now," returned the young lady.

"Necessities? Would you call selling a draught of water to a thirsty man a necessity? Would you think water could be bartered and sold?" queried I.

"No, there's no excuse for that, none!" she added warmly. The old lady began to speak and checked herself, laying her wrinkled hand on Davy's restless fingers.

"It *has been done*, I bought it, and I grieve to say, a woman sold it," I repeated sorrowfully.

"What? Where?" ejaculated both voices simultaneously.

"Ten miles from Corinth, Miss., at a cabin-door." The old lady interrupted me with a deprecatory gesture and a flood of tears. "Pardon me, dear madam," said I eagerly.

"Forgive me, O forgive me!" she pleaded. "It was all along of poor Davy, all for poor, hungry Davy!"

The other lady joined me in entreaties that she would spare herself the recital of such unhappy memories, but she would speak, and this was the way she told her story.

"I must tell you why I sold the water, it does me good here," putting her hand to her throat. "I wanted to tell when the soldiers took it from my hand, but the words choked me and would never come. I was afraid they'd judge me hard and am glad to tell. It is not very long, sir, in words, but some days would stretch themselves out into years, just like I've seen the little saplings throw long shadows across my yard when the sun was sinking down. My old man was dead, I was a widow when my Davy here was a bit of a shaver, toddling around alone. I lived in a nice little home, not fine as yours, ma'am, but you know the old saying, 'A rich man's castle's no dearer than the poor man's cot.' He was handy with his hammer and plane, and we knocked about it inside and out, until when fine folks passed that way, they'd say, 'What a snug little cottage!' And little it was to be sure, but then it was mine, and it's the best of all good feelings to know a thing is a body's own; then again, after my husband died, it was all the dearer for the sake of him that built it. We three lived there then, Matty, Davy and me. Well, after a while Matty grew up and married, left me and her brother until when the war came, she come back to us, saying, 'I've come back home, mother, it's so dark over at my house when John is gone.' Poor thing! It never got light again, for John never set foot in the door any more! Two widows lived and worked together, bearing the same hard pain. We didn't have time to sit down and cry in idleness, for if there was no more soldier clothes to make for John, there was plenty more, who had no mother, sister, nor wife to work for 'em, and we hadn't the heart to stand by and see 'em go off, without helping them on. Most of my work was spinning and knitting, on account of failing eyes; but Matty's tears fell day after day over as many a pretty web of cloth as you ever laid your eyes on; they was none the uglier for that." Davy stirred in the large chair, but lay back again docile as an infant under her touch, and her oft-repeated whisper of "Hush, Davy dear!" I saw something was the matter with him, the great eyes across the hearth exchanged glances with mine and rested on him pityingly. "Well, we worked on, every body was working, rich and poor, and we wouldn't be outdone by nobody, if we did have heavy hearts; for that manner, every body's hung heavy, but it was all for duty, and you know there's no choice in that. My Matty was brave as any body. When John went off, he looked back and saw her smiling, and kissing her little brown hands at him; but when he was clear out of her sight, she fell down as still as the dead. Then she come home next day, light of tongue and hands and feet to hide the aching for my sake, like she hid it for his. Ah me! It's the first lesson and the last, and it comes easy to us all to hide the hardest achings from them we love, and laugh when they step on the hiding-place, to keep 'em from finding it.

"Old folks take no notice of how time slips off. When I wasn't thinking of Davy as nothing but a stripling he comes to me one day and tells me the 'Time was come for him to go.' 'Where,' says I, 'my son?' 'To fight for you and Matty.' My old heart fell, for he was my baby, but I just said, 'Davy, you are too young.' 'But, mother,' he kept on, 'who learnt me we was never too young to do right, when we knew the right way?' He didn't look then like he does now, poor Davy! And I was so proud of my boy, he was a mighty child for learning, and found so many better ways of saying things than I did, that he worked me up to thinking his way; but it was pitiful to see him go, he was so young and tender. When he walked out of the door in his proud way of stepping, with his musket on his shoulder, I got old all of a sudden, and it come to my mind how Abraham laid his Issac on the altar, and I prayed it might go well with me and my baby as it went with him and his; but with all the hoping and praying, I went weak and tottering the whole winter long. Then another aching come for Matty's sake. Her father died of a cough, and folks used to say she looked like him; but I never thought so, until she took to coughing the same hollow way. I tried to make her careful of it, but she loved to work; since John was dead and Davy gone, she loved it more and more. She used to say, 'Young hands is fitter for work than old ones, mother, and it makes trouble lay lighter for them that's gone, to work for them that's here.' Then again she'd say, 'Let me work, it feels like I was standing guard in his place.' I knew what she meant, and she'd work with all her might, like she stood at the head of a regiment, leading our boys to glory! We got along very well, thank God, until the cavalry got to dashing round. The stock, gardens, fields, barns, and houses suffered where they went, people got to leaving their homes, for homes wasn't homes any more and women wasn't safe to stay at 'em. There was a running to and fro like the prophet said would come, but, eh Lord! I couldn't make my mind to leave my home until I was called to the Father's mansion in the skies. The way they did would make me mighty mad, but I never said much until they killed my cows, then I give 'em a piece of my mind. 'Matty,' I'd say, 'that's what I call stealing.' 'Why, mother,' she'd say, 'it's capturing!' Sometimes when I couldn't laugh with her, she'd tell me, 'Never fret, mother dear, if Davy comes back they can't make us poor.' And then the tender-hearted thing would speak up for the raiders, saying, 'They must be hungry men, and may be they don't know it's widows they are taking from.' 'Hungry, indeed!' says I, 'do you reckon they'll eat that dress of yours, and my shawl, and the coffee-mill, and the saddle, and —' She'd put her hand over my mouth, and I'd quiet down and say, 'If they'd come and ask me, I'd give and welcome, according to the Scripture, and for Him that tells us to love our enemies.' 'But mother,' she'd keep on, 'we'll try to think kinder of 'em; there's men that's mad and blind rushing 'em on us, and it an't one half that knows what for.' Not that she hadn't as much pluck as me, for when she saw a wrong done, her cheeks would turn like sun-red peaches, and her eyes flash sparks like my old man's anvil, but she'd grown so serious and forgiving in her ways. She'd often say, 'Ah! mother, it an't for long any how. I'll go to father and John, and Davy will come back a man to take care of you.' I'd try to keep dark, but my fears was great, there used to be stains under her eyes for two or three hours every day, and then they'd fade out white as lint, leaving my heart aching and aching, worse and worse for the day that was sure to come. I thought she worked too much, and took to doing all I could in her place, she'd cry, and say, 'It hurts me worse than weaving to see you work, mother.' One day I went off to look up work, and get her physic from the hospital, when I come back she was lying on the trundle-bed, so tired she didn't even know the sun was shining through the window on her shut-up eyes. My Matty was likely, and likelier than ever when she was sleeping. I laid my bundle down and sat watching her while I rested, we was growing closer and closer to each other in them sad days. I begun to feel gentle and watchful over her as though she was a little one at my breast. I knew she was going fast, and I felt like every minute away from her was wasting time, she'd so soon be gone. I crept close and kissed her soft, thinking not to wake her; but she started up scared and laughed at her weak trembly ways, and her sleeping like a grand lady in the daytime, until she coughed so hard, I made out I was too serious to hear her pretty voice, and talked myself to keep her quiet, in my anxious way, about the times being so hard, and every thing getting from bad to worse over the country. I was fearing we'd have to leave the old place after all, or suffer for our bread. I was low-hearted in my ways, and she was hoping in hers, like her father was. She put her arm round me and talked on, while she smoothed my hair away under my cap with her little fingers, making me ashamed that an old woman like me, should be learning faith in God out of her own child's mouth, when it ought to have been me teaching and she learning. Long weeks went by in the same way of working and talking light for each other's sakes, when a day come that looked a little brighter than the rest, and we thanked God for the sun and the blue sky. Matty had got so she could not stand about much, and the old chair sat by the window every day, holding her in its ragged arms. She always had a pretty way of talking and she sat there with her eyes looking a long way off, as if she learnt all her sweet words from the sky. This time she said softly, 'Mother, I don't blame the boys for fighting for Dixie, it is such a beautiful land! I used to think it was prettier than heaven when John was here.' The sun was shining, and I thought when I followed her eyes out of the window, that if all the blood that was flowing was to flow in vain, the living would be slaves and only the dead men free! A shadow fell across the door and I knew it was Davy's. Matty sprang past me, and turned back. I stopped and looked, then we fell into each other's arms like two dead women! It was Davy, but not the Davy that went away, he was a boy, and this was an old man's face that laughed in ours, and threw his bony arms about, crying, 'I'm so hungry! so hungry!' We kissed each other, and then rose to kiss him, but he bit my face until I screamed and fell back shuddering with pain, and afraid to look that way again. Matty led him to the hearth; the old chair and the clock and my wheel seemed to stir his heart, for he wasn't so wild, and looked around laughing as if he knew it was home, but it was a foolish laughing that hurt our hearts, and we knew he never was to be right-minded any more. I needn't name the place where he had been, for

Davy can hear it in his sleep, and then there's no calming my poor daft boy, and when I see him in his worst ways, I think I lose myself and say too bitter things of them I'm trying hard to forgive. He's forever dreaming he's hungry, waking or sleeping, and never knows he's got enough. It's a hard thing for a mother to look on, and know it will never pass away! Matty and I couldn't smile any more, we'd look at each other with wet faces and still tongues, sometimes there wouldn't be a word spoke in that house all day long, but, 'I'm so hungry! so hungry!' We didn't look up often, it was so hard to see a skeleton sitting on the floor, laughing at the specks floating through his fingers to the light, or eating forever and ever, whether any thing lay before him or not; you think it's a sad sight now, but it was a sadder one then for I had nothing but bread some days to put in his hands. I was afraid he'd eat the flesh off mine or Matty's when we'd give it to him. I couldn't leave them by themselves to hunt for work, and it was only the little I had hid from the raiders that was left to live on. God knows how long it was, for we lost the count of weeks and months, and knew nothing but day and night until Davy's words seemed to eat our lives away! To pray and sleep was all the comfort we had, except loving each other more and more every day. One night I woke smelling fire, and Matty was coughing like she'd choke to death. O my God! I had a hard shaking ague with the hot flames leaping round me, and not a minute to save any thing but our lives, that was awful; but when I saw the black savages yelling outside, I'm an old woman and a strong one, but I fell against the wall with the horror on me! Matty led me and Davy out like children, the weak was strong in them days, and she knelt down with the flames flashing on her face and prayed to God to save us, and He did, for when they came near her, more than mortal strength was in her hands, and they shrunk off afraid she was so death-like and beautiful! We never asked black nor white for any thing; we was too proud, and we walked away, glad to leave the horrible sights and sounds and to get Davy where he wouldn't laugh so wild in our ears. The weather had turned bitter cold and though the sun had shone on the snow the day before, it lay sharp and white under our bare feet. I can shut my eyes now and see Matty leading the way in her white gown like a spirit. We walked awhile and rested awhile all night and the next day, and the next night we huddled together by a fallen tree and slept. Next morning we come to the cabin you told of, sir, and felt safe when we found it was close to our own soldiers. I got something to eat and work to pay for it from them, many a one helped me along by a kind word when he'd nothing else to give, but my poor girl never got over that night's sleep in the snow. Her eyes sunk deeper and deeper, the blood stole up from her heart and down from her cheeks, and one night I heard it gurgling through her lips, and rose up to see my darling die. I held her close to the fire, and tried to warm her cold

hands in my bosom. She smiled
and raised 'em up slow and tried
to smooth my hair down, in her
old way, but they fell round my
neck and I leaned my face down
to hers, it hung so heavy with
the aching. I couldn't wake
Davy, he'd a laughed, and I'd
never heard her whispering,
'Mother! Mother! There's no
more hunger nor thirst, nor
any more sorrow there!' It was
'mother! mother!' to the last, till
I felt Death unlock her slender

fingers from my neck and we fell back in the darkness. Davy woke me up in
the morning, laughing and running his bony hands over his dead sister's face.
I couldn't leave her there with him, I was afraid he'd bite her white cheeks, so
I buried her without a coffin, and dug the grave myself. If her sweet lips could
have spoke, I knew she'd say, 'Never mind, mother, it's only Matty's old dress
you are laying by, she's got a new one up in heaven!' Thinking of the things she
used to say, I took comfort from her silent face, laid the earth on it soft as any
kisses, and come away to live for Davy. I knew there was many a one willing
to help, but I couldn't go to find 'em, and there was no passing in and out of
Corinth until orders was given to leave. When the soldiers scattered from the
main body, hunting for water, they found me in my door, weak and sick of
starvation; there was a few handfulls of parched corn left, but I couldn't eat a
grain, fearing my boy'd go wild for the want of it, any more than I could beg
the men for their bread. To them that had the money I sold water, and give it
to the next that come for part of their rations. It was all I could do until we
eat enough to get strength to come away. The well give out in a short time and
then we staggered off and left Matty all alone by the road-side. It's there I'm
going now, for we found friends to help us along, and God has dealt kindly
with me and Davy, he an't so wild-like since he's got better to eat than bread.
A heap of the old settlers has gone back I hear, and if I can earn enough to
build a cabin by the side of Matty's grave, I'll stay there until we're called to
meet father and Matty and John."

I sat still in the dim light of morning, and saw a fair, smooth hand, and a
wrinkled hard one clasped together in sisterhood of grief and tenderness. The
boy gazed about vacantly, eating an imaginary meal with claw-like fingers,
and muttering in painful childishness, "I'm so hungry! so hungry!" These were

the only sounds, until we three bowed our heads and wept together. The trains came at last—the old lady was going westward, and as the cars moved slowly past under the shed, I saw another handkerchief beside mine wave a blessing. Something flew in my eyes just then, it may have been a cinder, for it passed away as I raised my hat in answer to a smile of recognition from the beautiful face that had been my "*vis-a-vis*" across the hearth in the wayside hotel. We all have our stories, she had hers, but you are tired, my friend.

Good night!

1865

"THE UNION ARMY ENTERING RICHMOND"

Loss and homeless wandering were less often the fate of Confederate families in urban areas, particularly those with large ports and steady contraband traffic. While some cities like New Orleans and Memphis had been occupied early enough to provoke more resistance than rags, others persevered despite the blockade and the approach of Union troops. That was especially true of Richmond, which became the Confederate capital shortly after the war began. Unlike other cities in the largely rural South, Richmond was a manufacturing center with flour mills, tobacco factories, and the Tredegar Iron Works, which could convert to producing the cannon and rails that the Confederacy would badly need. And yet the industrializing city remained Southern, as Emory Thomas has pointed out. "Men of industry and capital might dominate the city's marketplaces," Thomas has observed, "but planters and their wives still ruled Richmond's drawing rooms." While laboring families and refugees clamored for bread in the spring of 1863, and Corinth homesteaders worried about water, Richmond's ladies might still follow the fashions set abroad. At least in the better homes of "The Skeleton in the Closet," families apparently discovered their own way of improvising amid shortages.

◆○◆

Edward Everett Hale (J. Thomas Darragh)

"THE SKELETON IN THE CLOSET"

(*Galaxy*, June 1866)

I see that an old chum of mine is publishing bits of confidential Confederate History in *Harper's Magazine*. It would seem to be time, then, for the pivots to be disclosed, on which some of the wheelwork of the last six years has been moving. The science of history, as I understand it, depends on the timely disclosure of such pivots, which are apt to be kept out of view, while things are moving.

I was in the Civil Service at Richmond. Why I was there, or what I did, is nobody's affair. And I do not in this feuilleton propose to tell how it happened, that I was in New York in October, 1864, on confidential business. Enough that I was there, and that it was honest business. That business done, as far as it could be with the resources entrusted to me, I prepared to return home. And thereby hangs this tale, and, as it proved, the fate of the Confederacy.

For, of course, I wanted to take presents home to my family. Very little question was there what these presents should be—for I had no boys nor brothers.

The women of the Confederacy had one want, which overtopped all others. They could make coffee out of beans; pins they had from Columbus; straw hats they braided quite well with their own fair hands; snuff we could get better than you could in "the old concern." But we had no hoop-skirts — skeletons, we used to call them. No ingenuity had made them. No bounties had forced them. The Bat, the Greyhound, the Deer, the Flora, the J. C. Cobb, the Varuna, and the Fore-and-Aft all took in cargoes of them for us in England. But the Bat and the Deer and the Flora were seized by the blockaders, the J. C. Cobb sunk at sea, the Fore-and-Aft and the Greyhound were set fire to by their own crews, and the Varuna (our Varuna) was never heard of. Then the State of Arkansas offered sixteen townships of swamp land to the first manufacturer who would exhibit five gross of a home-manufactured article. But no one ever competed. The first attempts, indeed, were put to an end, when Schofield crossed the Blue Lick, and destroyed the dams on Yellow Branch. The consequence was, that people's crinoline collapsed faster than the Confederacy did, of which that brute of a Grierson said there was never anything of it but the outside.

Of course, then, I put in the bottom of my new large trunk in New York — not a "duplex elliptic," for none were then made — but a "Belmonte," of thirty springs, for my wife. I bought, for her more common wear, a good "Belle-Fontaine." For Sarah and Susy each, I got two "Dumb-Belles." For Aunt Eunice and Aunt Clara, maiden sisters of my wife's, who lived with us after Winchester fell the fourth time, I got the "Scotch Hare-bell," two of each. For my own mother I got one "Belle of the Prairies" and one "Invisible Combination Gossamer." I did not forget good old Mamma Chloe, and Mamma Jane. For them I got substantial cages, without names. With these, tied in the shapes of figure eights in the bottom of my trunk, as I said, I put in an assorted cargo of dry-goods above, and, favored by a pass, and Major Mulford's courtesy on the flag-of-truce boat, I arrived safely at Richmond before the Autumn closed.

I was received at home with rapture. But when, the next morning, I opened my stores, this became rapture doubly enraptured. Words cannot tell the silent delight with which old and young, black and white, surveyed these fairy-like structures, yet unbroken and unmended.

Perennial Summer reigned that Autumn day in that reunited family. It reigned the next day — and the next. It would have reigned till now if the Belmontes and the other things would last as long as the advertisements declare; and, what is more, the Confederacy would have reigned till now, President Davis and General Lee! but for that great misery, which all families understand, which culminated in our great misfortune.

I was up in the cedar closet one day, looking for an old parade cap of mine, which I thought, though it was my third best, might look better than my sec-

ond best, which I had worn ever since my best was lost at the Seven Pines. I say I was standing on the lower shelf of the cedar closet, when, as I stepped along in the darkness, my right foot caught in a bit of wire, my left did not give way in time, and I fell, with a small wooden hat-box in my hand, full on the floor. The corner of the hat-box struck me just below the second frontal sinus, and I fainted away.

When I came to myself I was in the blue chamber; I had vinegar on a brown paper on my forehead; the room was dark, and I found mother sitting by me, glad enough indeed to hear my voice, and to know that I knew her. It was some time before I fully understood what had happened. Then she brought me a cup of tea, and I, quite refreshed, said I must go to the office.

"Office, my child!" said she. "Your leg is broken above the ankle; you will not move these six weeks. Where do you suppose you are?"

Till then I had no notion that it was five minutes since I went into the closet. When she told me the time, five in the afternoon, I groaned in the lowest depths. For, in my breast pocket in that innocent coat, which I could now see lying on the window seat, were the duplicate dispatches to Mr. Mason, for which, late the night before, I had got the Secretary's signature. They were to go at ten that morning to Wilmington, by the Navy Department's special messenger. I had taken them to ensure care and certainty. I had worked on them till midnight, and they had not been signed till near one o'clock. Heavens and earth, and here it was five o'clock! The man must be half way to Wilmington by this time. I sent the doctor for Lafarge, my clerk. Lafarge did his prettiest in rushing to the telegraph. But no! A freshet on the Chowan River, or a raid by Foster, or something, or nothing, had smashed the telegraph wire for that night. And before that dispatch ever reached Wilmington the navy agent was in the offing in the Sea Maid.

"But perhaps the duplicate got through?" No, breathless reader, the duplicate did not get through. The duplicate was taken by Faucon, in the Ino. I saw it last week in Dr. Lieber's hands, in Washington. Well, all I know is, that if the duplicate had got through, the Confederate government would have had in March a chance at eighty-three thousand two hundred and eleven muskets, which, as it was, never left Belgium. So much for my treading into that blessed piece of wire on the shelf of the cedar closet, up stairs.

"What was the bit of wire?"

Well, it was not telegraph wire. If it had been, it would have broken when it was not wanted to. Don't you know what it was? Go up in your own cedar closet, and step about in the dark, and see what brings up round your ankles. Julia, poor child, cried her eyes out about it. When I got well enough to sit up, and as soon as I could talk and plan with her, she brought down seven of these old things, antiquated Belmontes and Simplex Elliptics, and horrors without a name, and she made a pile of them in the bed-room, and asked me in the most penitent way what she should do with them.

"You can't burn them," said she; "fire won't touch them. If you bury them in the garden, they come up at the second raking. If you give them to the servants, they say, 'thank-e, missus,' and throw them in the back passage. If you give them to the poor, they throw them into the street in front, and do not say 'thank-e.' Susy sent seventeen over to the sword factory, and the foreman swore at the boy, and told him he would flog him within an inch of his life if he brought any more of his sauce there; and, so — and so," sobbed the poor child, "I just rolled up these wretched things, and laid them in the cedar closet, hoping, you know, that some day the government would want something, and would advertise for them. You know what a good thing I made out of the bottle corks."

In fact, she had sold our bottle corks for four thousand two hundred and sixteen dollars of the first issue. We afterward bought two umbrellas and a corkscrew with the money.

Well, I did not scold Julia. It was certainly no fault of hers that I was walking on the lower shelf of her cedar closet. I told her to make a parcel of the things, and the first time we went to drive I hove the whole shapeless heap into the river, without saying mass for them.

But let no man think, or no woman, that this was the end of troubles. As I look back on that Winter, and on the Spring of 1865 (I do not mean the steel spring), it seems to me, only the beginning. I got out on crutches at last — I had the office transferred to my house so that Lafarge and Hepburn could work there nights, and communicate with me when I could not go out — but mornings I hobbled up to the Department, and sat with the Chief, and took his orders. Ah, me! shall I soon forget that crisp Winter morning, when we all had such hope at the office. One or two of the army fellows looked in at the window as they ran by, and we knew that they felt well; and though I would not ask Old Wick, as we had nicknamed the Chief, what was in the wind, I knew the time had come, and that the lion meant to break the net this time. I made an excuse to go home earlier than usual; rode down to the house in the Major's ambulance, I remember; and hopped in, to surprise Julia with the good news, only to find that the whole house was in that quiet uproar which shows that something bad has happened of a sudden.

"What is it, Chloe?" said I, as the old wench rushed by me with a bucket of water.

"Poor Mr. George, I 'fraid he's dead, sah!"

And there he really was—dear, handsome, bright George Schaff—the delight of all the nicest girls of Richmond; he lay there on Aunt Eunice's bed on the ground floor, where they had brought him in. He was not dead—and he did not die. He is making cotton in Texas now. But he looked mighty near it then. "The deep cut in his head" was the worst I then had ever seen, and the blow confused everything. When McGregor got round, he said it was not hopeless; but we were all turned out of the room, and with one thing and another he got the boy out of the swoon, and somehow it proved his head was not broken.

No, but poor George swears to this day it were better it had been, if it could only have been broken the right way and on the right field. For that evening we heard that everything had gone wrong in the surprise. There we had been waiting for one of those early fogs, and at last the fog had come. And Jubal Early had, that morning, pushed out every man he had, that could stand; and they lay hid for three mortal hours, within I don't know how near the picket line at Fort Powhatan, only waiting for the shot which John Streight's party were to fire at Wilson's wharf, as soon as somebody on our left centre advanced in force on the enemy's line above Turkey Island stretching across to Nansemond. I am not in the War Department, and I forget whether he was to advance *en barbette* or by *échelon* of infantry. But he was to advance somehow, and he knew how; and when he advanced, you see, that other man lower down was to rush in, and as soon as Early heard him he was to surprise Powhatan, you see; and then, if you have understood me, Grant and Butler and the whole rig of them would have been cut off from their supplies, would have had to fight a battle for which they were not prepared, with their right made into a new left, and their old left unexpectedly advanced at an oblique angle from their centre, and would not that have been the end of them?

Well, that never happened. And the reason it never happened was, that poor

337

George Schaff, with the last fatal order for this man whose name I forget (the same who was afterward killed the day before High Bridge), undertook to save time by cutting across behind my house, from Franklin to Green streets. You know how much time he saved—they waited all day for that order. George told me afterward that the last thing he remembered was kissing his hand to Julia, who sat at her bed-room window. He said he thought she might be the last woman he ever saw this side of heaven. Just after that, it must have been, his horse—that white Messenger colt old Williams bred—went over like a log, and poor George was pitched fifteen feet head-foremost against a stake there was in that lot. Julia saw the whole. She rushed out with all the women, and had just brought him in when I got home. And that was the reason that the great promised combination of December, 1864, never came off at all.

I walked out in the lot, after McGregor turned me out of the chamber, to see what they had done with the horse. There he lay, as dead as Old Messenger himself. His neck was broken. And do you think, I looked to see what had tripped him. I supposed it was one of the boys' bandy holes. It was no such thing. The poor wretch had tangled his hind legs in one of those infernal hoop-wires that Chloe had thrown out in the piece when I gave her her new ones. Though I did not know it then, those fatal scraps of rusty steel had broken the neck that day of Robert Lee's army.

That time I made a row about it. I felt too badly to go into a passion. But before the women went to bed—they were all in the sitting-room together—I talked to them like a father. I did not swear. I had got over that for awhile, in that six weeks on my back. But I did say the old wires were infernal things, and that the house and premises must be made rid of them. The aunts laughed—though I was so serious—and tipped a wink to the girls. The girls wanted to laugh, but were afraid to. And then it came out that the aunts had sold their old hoops, tied as tight as they could tie them, in a great mass of rags. They had made a fortune by the sale—I am sorry to say it was in other rags, but the rags they got were new instead of old—it was a real Aladdin bargain. The new rags had blue backs, and were numbered, some as high as fifty dollars. The rag man had been in a hurry, and had not known what made the things so heavy. I frowned at the swindle, but they said all was fair with a pedlar—and I own I was glad the things were well out of Richmond. But when I said I thought it was a mean trick, Lizzie and Sarah looked demure, and asked what in the world I would have them do with the old things. Did I expect them to walk down to the bridge themselves with great parcels to throw into the river, as I had done by Julia's? Of course it ended, as such things always do, by my taking the work on my own shoulders. I told them to tie up all they had in as small a parcel as they could, and bring them to me.

Accordingly, the next day, I found a handsome brown paper parcel, not so very large, considering, and strangely square, considering, which the minxes had put together and left on my office table. They had had a great frolic over it. They had not spared red tape nor red wax. Very official it looked, indeed, and on the left-hand corner, in Susie's boldest and most contorted hand, was written, "secret service." We had a great laugh over their success. And, indeed, I should have taken it with me the next time I went down to the Tredegar, but that I happened to dine one evening with young Norton of our gallant little navy, and a very curious thing he told us.

We were talking about the disappointment of the combined land attack. I did not tell what upset poor Schaff's horse; indeed I do not think those navy men knew the details of the disappointment. O'Brien had told me, in confidence, what I have written down probably for the first time now. But we were speaking, in a general way, of the disappointment. Norton finished his cigar rather thoughtfully, and then said: "Well, fellows, it is not worth while to put in the newspapers, but what do you suppose upset our grand naval attack, the day the Yankee gunboats skittled down the river so handsomely?"

"Why," said Allen, who is Norton's best-beloved friend, "they say that you ran away from them as fast as they did from you."

"Do they?" said Norton, grimly. "If you say that, I'll break your head for you. Seriously, men," continued he, "that was a most extraordinary thing. You know I was on the ram. But why she stopped when she stopped I knew as little as this wineglass does; and Callender himself knew no more than I. We had not been hit. We were all right as a trivet for all we knew, when, skree! she began blowing off steam, and we stopped dead, and began to drift down under those batteries. Callender had to telegraph to the little Mosquito, or whatever Walter called his boat, and the spunky little thing ran down and got us out of the scrape. Walter did it right well; if he had had a Monitor under him he could not have done better. Of course we all rushed to the engine-room. What in thunder were they at there? All they knew was they could get no water into her boiler.

"Now, fellows, this is the end of the story. As soon as the boilers cooled off they worked all night on those supply pumps. May I be hanged if they had not sucked in, somehow, a long string of yarn, and cloth, and, if you will believe me, the wire of some woman's crinoline. And that French folly of a sham Empress cut short that day the victory of the Confederate navy, and old Davis himself can't tell when we shall have such a chance again!"

Some of the men thought Norton lied. But I never was with him when he did not tell the truth. I did not mention, however, what I had thrown into the water the last time I had gone over to Manchester. And I changed my mind about Sarah's "secret-service" parcel. It remained on my table.

That was the last dinner our old club had at the Spotswood, I believe. The Spring came on, and the plot thickened. We did our work in the office as well as we could—I can speak for mine, and if other people—but no matter for that! The 3d of April came, and the fire, and the right wing of Grant's army. I remember I was glad then that I had moved the office down to the house, for we were out of the way there. Everybody had run away from the Department; and so, when the powers that be took possession, my little sub-bureau was unmolested for some days. I improved those days as well as I could—burning carefully what was to be burned, and hiding carefully what was to be hidden. One thing that happened then belongs to this story. As I was at work on the private bureau—it was really a bureau, as it happened, one I had made Aunt Eunice give up when I broke my leg—I came, to my horror, on a neat parcel of coast-survey maps of Georgia, Alabama and Florida. Now I was perfectly sure that on that fatal Sunday of the flight I had sent Lafarge for these, that the President might use them, if necessary, in his escape. When I found them, I hopped out and called for Julia, and asked her if she did not remember his coming for them. "Certainly," she said, "it was the first I knew of the danger. Lafarge came, asked for the key of the office, told me all was up, walked in, and in a moment was gone."

And here, on the file of April 3d, was Lafarge's line to me:

"I got the secret-service parcel myself, and have put it in the President's own hands. I marked it 'Gulf coast,' as you bade me."

What could Lafarge have given to the President? Not the soundings of Hatteras Bar. Not the working-drawings of the first Monitor. I had all these under my hand. Could it be—"Julia, what did we do with that stuff of Sarah's that she marked *secret service?*"

As I live, we had sent the girls' old hoops to the President in his flight.

And when the next day we read how Pritchard had arrested him, we thought if he had only had the right parcel, he would have found the way to Florida.

That is really the end of this memoir. But I should not have written it, but for something that happened just now, on the piazza. You must know, some of us wrecks are up here at the Berkeley baths. My uncle has a place near here. Here came to-day, John Sisson, whom I have not seen since Memminger ran and took the clerks with him. Here we had before, both the Richards brothers, the great paper men, you know, who started the Edgerly Works in Prince George's County, just after the war began. After dinner, Sisson and they met on the piazza. Queerly enough, they had never seen each other before, though they had used reams of Richards's paper in correspondence with each other, and the Treasury had used tons of it in the printing of bonds and bank-bills. Of course we all fell to talking of old times—old they seem now, though it is not a year

"THE FLIGHT OF THE CONFEDERATES"

ago. "Richards," said Sisson, at last, "what became of that last order of ours for water-lined, pure linen government-callendered paper of *sureté?* We never got it, and I never knew why."

"Did you think Kilpatrick got it?" said Richards, rather gruffly.

"None of your chaff, Richards. Just tell where the paper went, for in the top of that lot of paper, as it proved, the bottom dropped out of the Treasury tub. On that paper was to have been printed our new issue of ten percent., convertible, you know, and secured on that up-country cotton, which Kirby Smith had above the Big Raft. I had the printers ready for near a month waiting for that paper. The plates were ready — very handsome. I'll show you a proof when we go up stairs. Wholly new they were, made by some Frenchman we got, who had worked for the Bank of France. I was so anxious to have the thing well done, that I waited three weeks for that paper, and, by Jove, I waited just too long. We never got one of the bonds off, and that was why we had no money in March."

Richards threw his cigar away. I will not say he swore between his teeth, but he twirled his chair round, brought it down on all fours, put his elbows on his knees and his chin in both hands.

"Mr. Sisson," said he, "if the Confederacy had lived, I would have died before I ever told what became of that order of yours. But now I have no secrets,

I believe, and I care for nothing. I do not know now, how it happened. We knew it was an extra nice job. And we had it on an elegant little new French Fourdrinier, which cost us more than we shall ever pay. The pretty thing ran like oil the day before. That day, I thought all the devils were in it. The more power we put on the more the rollers screamed; and the less we put on, the more sulkily the jade stopped. I tried it myself every way; back current, I tried— forward current—high feed, low feed; I tried it on old stock, I tried it on new; and, Mr. Sisson, I would have made better paper in a coffee-mill! We drained off every drop of water. We washed the tubs free from size. Then my brother, there, worked all night with the machinists, taking down the frame and the rollers. You would not believe it, sir, but that little bit of wire—" and he took out of his pocket a piece of this hateful steel, which poor I knew so well by this time—"that little bit of wire had passed in from some hoop-skirt—past the pickers—past the screens—through all the troughs—up and down through what we call the lacerators, and had got itself wrought in, where, if you know a Fourdrinier machine, you may have noticed a brass ring riveted to the cross-bar, and there this cursed little knife—for you see it was a knife, by that time— had been butting to pieces the endless wire web every time the machine was started. You lost your bonds, Mr. Sisson, because some Yankee woman cheated one of my rag-men."

On that story I came up-stairs. Poor Aunt Eunice! She was the reason I got no salary on the 1st of April. I thought I would warn other women by writing down the story.

That fatal present of mine, in those harmless hour-glass parcels, was the ruin of the Confederate navy, army, ordnance and treasury: and it led to the capture of the poor President too.

But, Heaven be praised, no one shall say that my office did not do its duty!

The flight of Jefferson Davis is reminder enough that the war did not end with the fall of Richmond in early April or even with Lee's surrender to Grant at Appomattox Courthouse on April 9. Abraham Lincoln was assassinated less than a week later, and John Wilkes Booth was himself shot on April 26, the day Joseph Johnston surrendered his forces in North Carolina. Davis continued to urge prolonged fighting until he was captured in Georgia mid-May, just after Richard Taylor in Alabama surrendered all remaining Confederate forces east of the Mississippi. The Army of the Trans-Mississippi under Edmund Kirby Smith held off negotiating terms until the end of May in New Orleans, a surrender that was not signed until June. By that time, Union armies had already paraded down Pennsylvania Avenue singing "John Brown's Body." Soldiers there and elsewhere were eager to go home, and they chafed at the time left to serve on three-year enlistments. As "Sentenced and Shot" reveals, they took reassignment grudgingly, with what Jeffry Wert has called "a smoldering resentment." In Louisiana, where Sheridan was gathering an army to subdue unrest in Texas and George Armstrong Custer was posted to ready Western cavalry units for departure, the mirage of homecoming slipped away and the low rumble of defiance began to build.

◆○◆

Richard M. Sheppard

"SENTENCED AND SHOT"

(*Lakeside Monthly*, November 1870)

When the war closed, I was "in at the death"; — otherwise I should not have this story to tell.

Shreveport, 1865, made amends for Sumter, 1861.

A braggart could have fired the first gun — none but a hero the last; and while the first battle was lost by recruits, the last was won by veterans.

It was simply brave and generous to fall in the first charge, — but it was purely noble and heroic to die in the last. The first fresh rush of patriotic blood from the heart to the head could have easily carried the recruit up to the cannon's mouth; — but it was quite another thing that carried him through a four years' war, and flung him into the thickest of the last charge, to die as the enemy sounded the final retreat.

Life becomes very dear when you have fought your way from Bull Run to Petersburg — from Belmont to Mobile. To be shot by a rebel at Alexandria,

"THE SOLDIER'S DREAM"

Virginia, in 1861, is not at all like being shot by your friends at Alexandria, Louisiana, in 1865.

I returned from Shreveport to New Orleans after the surrender of Kirby Smith's army—all that was left of it—just in time to be ordered by Sheridan to report to Custer for duty with the second Cavalry Division of the Military Department of the Gulf. The orders were to rendezvous at Alexandria, Louisiana, and after due preparation, to march across the country into Texas, for the purpose of re-establishing the authority of the Government—to follow up victory with occupation.

Among the regiments ordered to report to the General there, was the ill-fated Second Cavalry. It had suffered somewhat from indifferent field officers, but more from that bad fortune which overtook so many Western regiments in the shape of garrison duty in small squads or squadrons, so scattered as to make each a sort of independent command, which in the end resulted in a loss of discipline and the ruin of those bonds of sympathy that bound most regiments firmly together. To lead such a regiment into a hotly-contested fight would be a blessing, and would effectually set at rest all such trouble; but their fighting had been altogether of the guerilla kind, and there was no regimental pride of character, simply because there had been no regimental deed of valor.

Two colonels had resigned—one to accept promotion, and the other to return home,—and a lieutenant-colonel had failed to succeed to their spread-

344

eagles; and the majority of the regiment would have rejoiced if, in his wrathful disappointment, he had thrown away his silver leaves and gone home too. But he never dreamed of it. Whether justly or unjustly, he was despised by his command; and only held his place by sheer force of will, backed by the authorities above him.

Such was the condition of the regiment when it reported for duty. Tired out with the long service, — weary with an uncomfortable journey by river from Memphis, — sweltering under a Gulf-coast sun, under orders to go farther and farther from home when the war was over and the one desire above all others was to be mustered out and released from a service that became irksome and baleful when a prospect of crushing the enemy no longer existed, — all these, added to the disaffection among the officers, rendered the situation truly deplorable. In fact, the men of the whole division were more or less discontented, and would have been troublesome under any commander and any circumstances that kept them in the service; but to be thoroughly organized and subjected to the discipline necessary to the maintenance of good order, and to be forced to treat with consideration the very people whose country they had acquired a chronic habit of devastating — and that, too, by a man whom they called a "yellow-haired circus-rider from the Shenandoah," — this seemed to them to be almost beyond the limit of human endurance.

The command had hardly pitched their tents and kindled their camp-fires before the spirit of reckless disregard of authority began to manifest itself. The men hated the Commanding General and staff "on principle," without regard to what they did. "No *Eastern* man can put on style over us!" "Bright buttons and spurs don't make a soldier!" "It's too late to teach us Army of the Potomac notions!" "The war is over, — why don't they send us home, instead of sending this upstart Major-General, with his first mustache, to lord it over us?" These are such speeches as one could hear at almost any hour of the day or evening, when wandering through the camp; and they were delivered with such emphasis and ill-suppressed bitterness that the effect was exceedingly ugly.

Immediately the men, singly and in squads, began to go on extemporaneous raids through the adjoining country, robbing and plundering indiscriminately in every direction. "They're all d——d rebs, let's *go for them!*" — and they did it with an evident relish. They seemed to have no idea that a conquered and subdued people could possibly have any rights that the conquerors were bound to respect. But such expeditions could not be permitted; indeed, the General was under orders to treat the people kindly and considerately, and he obeyed orders with the same punctiliousness with which he exacted obedience from his command. Therefore the most rigorous and explicit orders were issued against "jayhawking" of every kind, and the offenders were severely punished. But the

"BRIGADIER-GENERAL GEORGE A. CUSTER"

ordinary punishments were found to be utterly inadequate. The guard-house, police duty, extra duty, etc., had lost their terrors; and punishments had to be devised that would reach a class of men and offences unprovided for in the "Regulations."

The storm which had been brewing so many months in the ranks of the Second Cavalry, suddenly burst upon it. A paper, demanding the resignation of the Lieutenant-Colonel, had been largely signed by officers and men, and presented to him. This was the flint that struck out fire. In half an hour the officers whose names appeared on that fatal list were deprived of their swords, and the catastrophe was no longer to be avoided. Blood was in the eyes of the soldiers, and none in the cheeks of the officers; — vengeance was in the hearts of the men, and fear in the souls of the commanders. There was a quick roll of the drum — a few explosive orders — a sudden rush — a sort of dizzy whirl; the Lieutenant-Colonel narrowly escaped, — and, by a quick movement of the guard, a Sergeant and several men, whose names were on the paper, were arrested and lodged in the guard-house. A double force was posted to prevent the rescue of the prisoners — and the immediate danger was over.

After the storm, the calm. The anxiety of some men to get into trouble is only exceeded by their solicitude to get out of it. It happened so with these. The violence and headlong haste of the action was eclipsed only by that of the reaction. To the swordless officers musing in their separate tents, and the imprisoned soldiers discussing the affair behind their bars, there came, in due time, repentance and regret.

Through the clemency of the man whom they sought to destroy, there was at last afforded, on certain conditions, the opportunity to erase their names from the black muster-roll, and secure restoration to duty. Some quickly, others reluctantly, but finally all, availed themselves of the absolution — except one, the Sergeant, the leader, the prime mover and champion of the affair.

He scorned forgiveness; it implied an acknowledgment of guilt. He would stand by the deed; whatever the law called it, he held it just resistance to tyranny. He had sought no man's life. He had felt — "We cannot live together; therefore do thou go thy way, and I will mine"; — and he had simply said so. If that were a crime, he could not help it. No matter if a thousand men *were* cowards, *he* had not the blood of a poltroon in his veins. He should never promise — touch his hat, and, bowing low, beg to have his name blotted out of that list. His soul revolted at it. He would live and die by that solemn protest against the authority of a domineering coward and incompetent commander.

So the law took him and tried him before a General Court-Martial, found him *Guilty,* and sentenced him "to be shot to death." The General approved the finding and sentence of the court; and the day and hour of the execution were fixed in an order that was read, on a certain evening at dress-parade, to each regiment of the division. And with the words of that order, a cloud fell on the whole command.

The law was inexorable, and the court had no alternative. Being guilty, this was the punishment prescribed, without that saving clause which puts the offender at the mercy of the court — "Or such other punishment as the court may direct." But did he deserve death? Not a man in all the command believed it. The men knew it was the letter of the law that was slaying him; but how to invoke its spirit, and whether the spirit could save him if it would, sorely puzzled them. They were satisfied that he should be punished, but by something less severe and irrevocable than death.

With what crushing weight the thought came home to their hearts, that a good soldier, a true patriot, was to be shot for a technicality, at the end of a long war through which he had faithfully served! How they talked about that lonesome, weary wife, and her eager and expectant children, away at the North, watching with bated breath the opening of the mail that was so soon, if not to-day, to bring her the news of the final discharge of the Second Cavalry! Who could hold a pen to write this other news in its stead? Who could send home to her the picture of her own sweet face, with the curl of baby's hair on the glass, as he had worn it next his heart so many years, through all danger by flood and field, and write the words — "This, with his undying love, he bade me send to you — his last request"?

Did ever the reluctant days drag a man to such hopeless, bootless doom?

If only he had fallen on some fierce battle-field, madly striking for his country! If only he had been slain on the picket-line, piloting the grand old army to victory! If he could have died in the hospital, slowly wasted away by incurable wounds or disease, or been sacrificed in a Southern prison, enduring outrage and starvation with the fortitude born of honor and patriotism! If only in any way his blood might have been reckoned as a part of the price paid for liberty and free government!

But no — none of these. The very record of his devotion to his country's cause, and of his faithful years of untiring service, was to be blotted out. His memory was to be blackened forever, and his name to become a legacy of shame to his children; — and yet they knew he was conscious of no crime!

Was it possible to save him in any way? Could he be pardoned, or his sentence be commuted? Yes, but only one man could do it — the General. *Would* he do it? Only one man in all the command could ask it and hope to be heard — the Lieutenant-Colonel. Would *he* do it?

The days of respite passed rapidly, and the anxiety and sympathy for the doomed man constantly increased in a cumulative ratio. At last the indispensable man arrived at division headquarters with a "Petition for Pardon," and asked the staff to sign it. Every valid reason that could be found was urged, and he went away with all our names. He fared the same at the brigade headquarters; and by the time he reached the commanders of regiments, who all signed it, the report had rejoiced the hearts of every tent-squad in the whole division. They *knew* it would be granted, — the General could not avoid it; he wouldn't *dare* to shoot him in the face of that list of names. There was a threat of vengeance lurking in every expression of joy. "If —," "If —."

Armed with the petition, the Lieutenant-Colonel went to the General, and, gathering up all the eloquence of all the arguments, laid the case before him. He would "consider the matter"; — and the Colonel was dismissed.

A day passed by without an answer. Another, and still no reply. The third — some anxiety was manifested. The fourth — the solicitude increased. On the fifth day the old fear seized them. The sixth — not a word spoken; — to-morrow, "between the hours of ten and twelve o'clock — " they lay in squads, scattered through the camps, talking until late into the night, not caring to sleep; and the *reveille* seemed to break in upon their first nap.

The morning wore away in the midst of its usual duties.

Seven o'clock — Breakfast. There was the usual hum throughout the camps, the neighing of the horses, and the voices of the men calling back and forth as they straggled in, each to his own mess. Once more, as they drank their coffee and ate their hard-bread and bacon, grumblingly denouncing the shortcoming of the *commissariat,* they wondered if it were yet possible for the General to speak.

Eight o'clock — Sick-call. The orderlies reported their latest candidates, the surgeons prescribed, the hospital stewards provided for them; and the sick men, lying on their cots in anguish, turned to inquire of their new neighbors if the word had yet been spoken.

Nine o'clock — Guard-mounting. The first-sergeants hastily summoned their "details" and reported to the adjutants on the parade-grounds. The ceremony over, the corporals proceeded to post the "first relief"; and each man, as he resigned his charge and "fell in" at the rear, asked eagerly for the news.

Nine-and-a-half o'clock — the bugle sounded "Boots and Spurs."

There were no more questions. From the mere force of habit, the men obeyed the summons; and by ten o'clock the whole division was in motion. Silently, sullenly, the troops moved away from camp, down the main road; and, one brigade after another, regiment by regiment, were formed in hollow-square around a large vacant sugar-field adjoining the town. The General and staff passed through the line, moved forward to the centre of the square, and, being drawn up in line, awaited the appearance of the solemn *cortege.*

Slowly down the road from the guard-house it came, entered the square, and marched along the inward-facing lines of troops, entirely around the open space — the guard, the firing party with arms reversed, the wagon drawn by four large horses, with their sad-faced driver seated above; and in the wagon, with their arms pinioned behind them, each on his own coffin, facing the rear, rode two men, and took their last leave of their comrades.

This second man was a private from the Fourth Cavalry, and was tried and condemned by the same court as the Sergeant, for desertion — the third or fourth offence. He had been a vagabond and criminal before he became a soldier; and never having been a patriot, he was a deserter from the first, and was paying the just penalty of his crimes, without even the pity and commiseration of his own mess-mates.

The sunshine; the cloudless sky; the songs of birds; the graceful swaying of the long festoons of Spanish moss in the near woods; the shallow, murky river hastening away to the Gulf; the dreary old tumble-down village behind its dilapidated levee; the long-haired, swarthy, ill-clad remnants of the late Confederate army gathered at the street corners; the distrustful, impoverished citizens moving about disconsolately; the *débris* of two armies scattered in every direction; the outlying, devastated sugar-plantations covered with camps, and this one the scene of an imposing military execution; — these were the obvious details of a never-to-be-forgotten picture. Down into the hearts of five thousand men it sank — photographed by the indelible and impalpable chemicals of the mind, there to remain forever. They felt the wheels of that monstrous hearse tugging at all their heart-strings, as if they strove to chain them with their sympathies, and forever hold them back from the end of that sorrowful journey.

At last the procession reached the place of entering, filed out into the field, and halted a short distance in front of the General and staff. The men were assisted down from the wagon and seated upon their coffins at the foot of their graves. Eight men, with pallid faces, halted in line a few paces before them, and exchanged their carbines for those specially loaded for the occasion by the Provost Marshal, who had charge of all the arrangements. He had loaded seven of them with ball, but the eighth with a blank cartridge — leaving the men in merciful uncertainty, allowing each to think that perhaps his was the harmless shot.

There was no more delay. Everything was done quickly, and with the utmost precision. The Provost Marshal read his warrant for the execution, drew the fatal caps over the eyes of the prisoners, stepped back a little, and, in the midst of the most awful silence, commanded:

"*Attention! — Ready!*"

The clicking of those eight locks was horrible. The victims stirred a little, as it were involuntarily. The air seemed stifling. The calm, monotonous regularity of the commands was excruciating. The apparently heartless and business-like manner of the Marshal was maddening.

Instantly he slipped to the side of the Sergeant, and lightly pulling his sleeve, led him a few steps aside; then, before the action could be fully realized, commanded:

"*Aim! — Fire!*"

There was a crashing blast — a cloud of smoke — a dull, heavy "thud" as the soldier fell back dead on his coffin, and the Sergeant fell limp and motionless into the arms of the Marshal, who stooped down upon one knee to set him on the other, and, pulling off the black cap, nursed him back to life and consciousness.

There was a murmur of grateful applause along the whole line. The General had not been intimidated, and yet had granted the prayer of his men. He had punished the Sergeant severely, and yet been merciful to them both; he had spared the life of the one, though *sentenced*, and kept a knowledge of it from the other, though *shot*.

We didn't know then that the Second Cavalry went out to the execution with loaded carbines, and forty rounds in their cartridge-boxes; if we had, we might not have felt quite at ease — but it could have made no other difference.

For soldiers who were mustered out at last, returning home was not always what they had expected or what had been supposed by those they left behind. Like the country for which the war had been fought, the households and communities to which regiments returned were suddenly reckoning with what they had lost and with how much they could simply resume. Nowhere was that clearer than in Zoar, a society built on nonviolent principles outside Cleveland. Zoar had been founded in 1817 by German Separatists fleeing Lutheran condemnation in Wurtemberg. During the decades before the war, their experiment had prospered as a farming venture where property was held in common, where men and women could vote, and where the communal garden followed an elaborate design recalling the Biblical promise of the New Jerusalem. Open to trade and yet increasingly closed to new members, the society sought to remain what Edgar Nixon has called "a European culture in American soil." Yet a Republican hatred of slaveholders or "Sklavenhalter" was undeniable, even if threatening to the society's peace. After war was declared, some twenty young men defied Zoar's trustees and enlisted in the 107th Ohio Volunteer Infantry, despite the principles of their upbringing and the worldliness they would encounter. The jubilant families to which they return in "Wilhelmina" are similarly caught, like many insular towns of the nineteenth century, between the commitments of the past and a more wayward communal future. For Woolson's Zoarites and her visiting narrator, it is a precarious moment that an unexpected black daughter hopes to fill.

❖◦❖

Constance Fenimore Woolson

"WILHELMINA"

(*Atlantic Monthly,* January 1875)

"And so, Mina, you will not marry the baker?"

"No; I waits for Gustav."

"How long is it since you have seen him?"

"Three year; it was a three-year regi-mènt."

"Then he will soon be home?"

"I not know," answered the girl, with a wistful look in her dark eyes, as if asking information from the superior being who sat in the skiff, a being from the outside world where newspapers, the modern Tree of Knowledge, were not forbidden.

"Perhaps he will reënlist, and stay three years longer," I said.

"Ah, lady, — six year! It breaks the heart," answered Wilhelmina.

She was the gardener's daughter, a member of the community of German Separatists who live secluded in one of Ohio's rich valleys, separated by their own broad acres and orchard-covered hills from the busy world outside; down the valley flows the tranquil Tuscarawas on its way to the Muskingum, its slow tide rolling through the fertile bottom-lands between stone dykes, and utilized to the utmost extent of carefulness by the thrifty brothers, now working a saw-mill on the bank, now sending a tributary to the flour-mill across the canal, and now branching off in a sparkling race across the valley to turn wheels for two or three factories, watering the great grass-meadow on the way. We were floating on this river in a skiff named by myself Der Fliegende Holländer, much to the slow wonder of the Zoarites, who did not understand how a Dutchman could, nor why he should, fly. Wilhelmina sat before me, her oars idly trailing in the water. She showed a Nubian head above her white kerchief: large-lidded soft brown eyes, heavy braids of dark hair, a creamy skin with purple tints in the lips and brown shadows under the eyes, and a far-off dreamy expression which even the steady, monotonous toil of community life had not been able to efface. She wore the blue dress and white kerchief of the society, the quaint little calico bonnet lying beside her: she was a small maiden; her slender form swayed in the stiff, short-waisted gown, her feet slipped about in the broad shoes, and her hands, roughened and browned with garden-work, were yet narrow and graceful. From the first we felt sure she was grafted, and not a shoot from the community stalk. But we could learn nothing of her origin; the Zoarites are not communicative; they fill each day with twelve good hours of labor, and look neither forward not back. "She is a daughter," said the old gardener in answer to our questions. "Adopted?" I suggested; but he vouchsafed no answer. I liked the little daughter's dreamy face, but she was pale and undeveloped, like a Southern flower growing in Northern soil; the rosy-cheeked, flaxen-haired Rosines, Salomes, and Dorotys, with their broad shoulders and ponderous tread, thought this brown changeling ugly, and pitied her in their slow, good-natured way.

"It breaks the heart," said Wilhelmina again, softly, as if to herself.

I repented me of my thoughtlessness. "In any case he can come back for a few days," I hastened to say. "What regiment was it?"

"The One Hundred and Seventh, lady."

I had a Cleveland paper in my basket, and taking it out I glanced over the war-news column, carelessly, as one who does not expect to find what he seeks. But chance, for once, was with us, and gave this item: "The One Hundred and Seventh Regiment, O.V.I., is expected home next week. The men will be paid off at Camp Chase."

"Ah!" said Wilhelmina, catching her breath with a half sob under her tightly-drawn kerchief, "ah, mein Gustav!"

"Yes, you will soon see him," I answered, bending forward to take the rough little hand in mine; for I was a romantic wife, and my heart went out to all lovers. But the girl did not notice my words or my touch; silently she sat, absorbed in her own emotion, her eyes fixed on the hill-tops far away, as though she saw the regiment marching home through the blue June sky.

I took the oars and rowed up as far as the island, letting the skiff float back with the current. Other boats were out, filled with fresh-faced boys in their high-crowned hats, long-waisted, wide-flapped vests of calico, and funny little swallow-tailed coats with buttons up under the shoulder-blades; they appeared unaccountably long in front and short behind, these young Zoar brethren. On the vine-covered dyke were groups of mothers and grave little children, and up in the hill-orchards were moving figures, young and old; the whole village was abroad in the lovely afternoon, according to their Sunday custom, which gave the morning to chorals and a long sermon in the little church, and the afternoon to nature, even old Christian, the pastor, taking his imposing white fur hat and tasseled cane for a walk through the community fields, with the remark, "Thus is cheered the heart of man, and his countenance refreshed."

As the sun sank in the warm western sky, homeward came the villagers from the river, the orchards, and the meadows, men, women, and children, a hardy, simple-minded band, whose fathers, for religion's sake, had taken the long journey from Würtemberg across the ocean to this distant valley, and made it a garden of rest in the wilderness. We, too, landed, and walked up the apple-tree lane towards the hotel.

"The cows come," said Wilhelmina as we heard a distant tinkling; "I must go." But still she lingered. "Der regi-mènt, it come soon, you say?" she asked in a low voice, as though she wanted to hear the good news again and again.

"They will be paid off next week; they cannot be later than ten days from now."

"Ten day! Ah, mein Gustav," murmured the little maiden; she turned away and tied on her stiff bonnet, furtively wiping off a tear with her prim handkerchief folded in a square.

"Why, my child," I said, following her and stooping to look in her face, "what is this?"

"It is nothing; it is for glad, — for very glad," said Wilhelmina. Away she ran as the first solemn cow came into view, heading the long procession meandering slowly towards the stalls. They knew nothing of haste, these dignified community cows; from stall to pasture, from pasture to stall, in a plethora of comfort, this was their life. The silver-haired shepherd came last with his staff and scrip, and the nervous shepherd-dog ran hither and thither in the hope of finding some cow to bark at; but the comfortable cows moved on in orderly ranks, and he was obliged to dart off on a tangent every now and then, and bark at nothing, to relieve his feelings. Reaching the paved court-yard each cow walked into her own stall, and the milking began. All the girls took part in this work, sitting on little stools and singing together as the milk frothed up in the tin pails; the pails were emptied into tubs, and when the tubs were full the girls bore them on their heads to the dairy, where the milk was poured into a huge strainer, a constant procession of girls with tubs above and the old milk-mother ladling out as fast as she could below. With the bee-hives near by, it was a realization of the Scriptural phrase, "A land flowing with milk and honey."

The next morning, after breakfast, I strolled up the still street, leaving the Wirthshaus with its pointed roof behind me. On the right were some ancient cottages built of crossed timbers filled in with plaster; sun-dials hung on the walls, and each house had its piazza, where, when the work of the day was over, the families assembled, often singing folk-songs to the music of their home-made flutes and pipes. On the left stood the residence of the first pastor, the reverend man who had led these sheep to their refuge in the wilds of the New World. It was a wide-spreading brick mansion, with a broad-side of white-curtained windows, an inclosed glass porch, iron railings, and gilded eaves; a building so stately among the surrounding cottages that it had gained from outsiders the name of the King's Palace, although the good man whose grave remains unmarked in the quiet God's Acre, according to the Separatist custom, was a father to his people, not a king.

Beyond the palace began the community garden, a large square in the centre of the village filled with flowers and fruit, adorned with arbors and cedar-trees clipped in the form of birds, and enriched with an old-style greenhouse whose sliding glasses were viewed with admiration by the visitors of thirty years ago, who sent their choice plants thither from far and near to be tended through the long, cold lake-country winters. The garden, the cedars, and the greenhouse were all antiquated, but to me none the less charming. The spring that gushed up in one corner, the old-fashioned flowers in their box-bordered beds, lark-spur, lady slippers, bachelor's buttons, peonies, aromatic pinks, and all varieties of roses, the arbors with red honeysuckle overhead and tan bark under foot, were all delightful; and I knew, also, that I should find the garderner's daugh-ter at her never-ending task of weeding. This time it was the strawberry bed. "I have come to sit in your pleasant garden, Mina," I said, taking a seat on a shaded bench near the bending figure.

"So?" said Wilhelmina in long-drawn interrogation, glancing up shyly with a smile. She was a child of the sun, this little maiden, and while her blonde companions wore always their bonnets or broad-brimmed hats over their pre-cise caps, Wilhelmina, as now, constantly discarded these coverings and sat in the sun basking like a bird of the tropics. In truth, it did not redden her; she was one of those whose coloring comes not from without, but within.

"Do you like this work, Mina?"

"Oh — so. Good as any."

"Do you like work?"

"Folks must work." This was said gravely, as part of the community creed.

"Wouldn't you like to go with me to the city?"

"No; I's better here."

"But you can see the great world, Mina. You need not work, I will take care of you. You shall have pretty dresses; wouldn't you like that?" I asked, curious to discover the secret of the Separatist indifference to everything outside.

"Nein," answered the little maiden tranquilly; "nein, fräulein. Ich bin zufrieden."

Those three words were the key. "I am contented." So were they taught from childhood, and—I was about to say—they knew no better; but, after all, is there anything better to know?

We talked on, for Mina understood English, although many of her mates could chatter only in their Würtemberg dialect, whose provincialisms confused my carefully learned German; I was grounded in Goethe, well-read in Schiller, and struggling with Jean Paul, who, fortunately, is "der Einzige," the only; another such would destroy life. At length a bell sounded, and forthwith work was laid aside in the fields, the workshops, and the houses, while all partook of a light repast, one of the five meals with which the long summer day of toil is broken. Flagons of beer had the men afield, with bread and cheese; the women took bread and apple-butter. But Mina did not care for the thick slice which the thrifty house-mother had provided; she had not the steady, unfanciful appetite of the community which eats the same food day after day, as the cow eats its grass, desiring no change.

"And the gardener really wishes you to marry Jacob?" I said as she sat on the grass near me, enjoying the rest.

"Yes. Jacob is good,—always the same."

"And Gustav?"

"Ah, mein Gustav! Lady, *he* is young, tall,—so tall as tree; he run, he sing, his eyes like veilchen there, his hair like gold. If I see him not soon, lady, I die! The year so long,—*so* long they are. Three year without Gustav!" The brown eyes grew dim, and out came the square-folded handkerchief of colored calico for week-days.

"But it will not be long now, Mina."

"Yes; I hope."

"He writes to you, I suppose?"

"No. Gustav knows not to write, he not like school. But he speak through the other boys, Ernst the verliebte of Rosine, and Peter of Doroty."

"The Zoar soldiers were all young men?"

"Yes; all verliebte. Some are not; they have gone to the Next Country" (died).

"Killed in battle?"

"Yes; on the berge that looks,—what you call, I not know"—

"Lookout Mountain?"

357

"Yes."

"Were the boys volunteers?" I asked, remembering the community theory of non-resistance.

"Oh, yes; they volunteer, Gustav the first. *They* not drafted," said Wilhelmina, proudly. For these two words, so prominent during the war, had penetrated even into this quiet valley.

"But did the trustees approve?"

"Apperouve?"

"I mean, did they like it?"

"Ah! they like it not. They talk, they preach in church, they say 'No.' Zoar must give soldiers? So. Then they take money and pay for der substitute; but the boys, they must not go."

"But they went, in spite of the trustees?"

"Yes; Gustav first. They go in night, they walk in woods, over the hills to Brownville, where is der recruiter. The morning come, they gone!"

"They have been away three years, you say? They have seen the world in that time," I remarked half to myself, as I thought of the strange mind-opening and knowledge-gaining of those years to youths brought up in the strict seclusion of the community.

"Yes; Gustav have seen the wide world," answered Wilhelmina with pride.

"But will they be content to step back into the dull routine of Zoar life?" I thought; and a doubt came that made me scan more closely the face of the girl at my side. To me it was attractive because of its possibilities; I was always fancying some excitement that would bring the color to the cheeks and full lips, and light up the heavy-lidded eyes with soft brilliancy. But would this Gustav see these might-be beauties? And how far would the singularly ugly costume offend eyes grown accustomed to fanciful finery and gay colors?

"You fully expect to marry Gustav?" I asked.

"We are verlobt," answered Mina, not without a little air of dignity.

"Yes, I know. But that was long ago."

"Verlobt once, verlobt always," said the little maiden confidently.

"But why, then, does the gardener speak of Jacob, if you are engaged to this Gustav?"

"Oh, fader he like the old, and Jacob is old, thirty year! His wife is gone to the Next Country. Jacob is a brother, too; he write his name in the book. But Gustav he not do so; he is free."

"You mean that the baker has signed the articles, and is a member of the community?"

"Yes; but the baker is old, very old; thirty year! Gustav not twenty and three yet; he come home, then he sign."

"And have you signed these articles, Wilhelmina?"

"Yes; all the womens signs."

"What does the paper say?"

"Da ich Unterzeichneter,"—began the girl.

"I cannot understand that. Tell me in English."

"Well; you wants to join the Zoar Community of Separatists; you writes your name and says, 'Give me house, victual, and clothes for my work and I join; and I never fernerer Forderung an besagte Gesellschaft machen kann, oder will.'"

"Will never make further demand upon said society," I repeated, translating slowly.

"Yes; that is it."

"But who takes charge of all the money?"

"The trustees."

"Don't they give you any?"

"No; for what? It's no good," answered Wilhelmina.

I knew that all the necessaries of life were dealt out to the members of the community according to their need, and, as they never went outside of their valley, they could scarcely have spent money even if they had possessed it. But, nevertheless, it was startling in this nineteenth century to come upon a sincere belief in the worthlessness of the green-tinted paper we cherish so fondly. "Gustav will have learned its value," I thought, as Mina, having finished the strawberry bed, started away towards the dairy to assist in the butter-making.

I strolled on up the little hill, past the picturesque bakery, where through the open window I caught a glimpse of the "old, very old Jacob," a serious young man of thirty, drawing out his large loaves of bread from the brick oven with a long-handled rake. It was gingerbread day also, and a spicy odor met me at the window; so I put in my head and asked for a piece, receiving a card about a foot square, laid on fresh grape leaves.

"But I cannot eat all this," I said, breaking off a corner.

"Oh, dat's noding," answered Jacob, beginning to knead fresh dough in a long white trough, the village supply for the next day.

"I have been sitting with Wilhelmina," I remarked, as I leaned on the casement, impelled by a desire to see the effect of the name.

"So?" said Jacob, interrogatively.

"Yes; she is a sweet girl."

"So?" (doubtfully)

"Don't you think so, Jacob?"

"Ye-es. So-so. A leetle black," answered this impassive lover.

"But you wish to marry her?"

"Oh ye-es. She young and strong; her fader say she good to work. I have children five; I must have some one in the house."

"Oh, Jacob! Is that the way to talk?" I exclaimed.

"Warum nicht?" replied the baker, pausing in his kneading, and regarding me with wide-open, candid eyes.

"Why not, indeed?" I thought, as I turned away from the window. "He is at least honest, and no doubt in his way he would be a kind husband to little Mina. But what a way!"

I walked on up the street, passing the pleasant house where all the infirm old women of the community were lodged together, carefully tended by appointed nurses. The aged sisters were out on the piazza sunning themselves, like so many old cats. They were bent with hard, out-door labor, for they belonged to the early days when the wild forest covered the fields now so rich, and only a few log-cabins stood on the site of the tidy cottages and gardens of the present village. Some of them had taken the long journey on foot from Philadelphia westward, four hundred and fifty miles, in the depths of winter. Well might they rest from their labors and sit in the sunshine, poor old souls!

A few days later, my friendly newspaper mentioned the arrival of the German regiment at Camp Chase. "They will probably be paid off in a day or two," I thought, "and another day may bring them here." Eager to be the first to tell the good news to my little favorite, I hastened up to the garden, and found her engaged, as usual, in weeding.

"Mina," I said, "I have something to tell you. The regiment is at Camp Chase; you will see Gustav soon, perhaps this week."

And there, before my eyes, the transformation I had often fancied took place; the color rushed to the brown surface, the cheeks and lips glowed in vivid red, and the heavy eyes opened wide and shone like stars, with a brilliancy that astonished and even disturbed me. The statue had a soul at last; the beauty dormant had awakened. But for the fire of that soul would this expected Pygmalion suffice? Would the real prince fill his place in the long-cherished dreams of this beauty of the wood?

The girl had risen as I spoke, and now she stood erect, trembling with excitement, her hands clasped on her breast, breathing quickly and heavily as though an overweight of joy was pressing down her heart; her eyes were fixed upon my face, but she saw me not. Strange was her gaze, like the gaze of one walking in sleep. Her sloping shoulders seemed to expand and chafe against the stuff gown as though they would burst their bonds; the blood glowed in her face and throat, and her lips quivered, not as though tears were coming, but from the fullness of unuttered speech. Her emotion resembled the intensest fire of fever, and yet it seemed natural; like noon in the tropics when the gorgeous flowers flame in the white, shadowless heat. Thus stood Wilhelmina, looking up into the sky with eyes that challenged the sun.

"Come here, child," I said; "come here and sit by me. We will talk about it."

"But she neither saw nor heard me. I drew her down on the bench at my side; she yielded unconsciously; her slender form throbbed, and pulses were beating under my hands wherever I touched her. "Mina!" I said again. But she did not answer. Like an unfolding rose, she revealed her hidden, beautiful heart, as though a spirit had breathed upon the bud; silenced in the presence of this great love, I ceased speaking, and left her to herself. After a time single words fell from her lips, broken utterances of happiness. I was as nothing; she was absorbed in the One. "Gustav! mein Gustav!" It was like the bird's note, oft repeated, ever the same. So isolated, so intense was her joy that, as often happens, my mind took refuge in the opposite extreme of commonplace, and I found myself wondering whether she would be able to eat boiled beef and cabbage for dinner, or fill the soft-soap barrel for the laundry women, later in the day.

All the morning I sat under the trees with Wilhelmina, who had forgotten her life-long tasks as completely as though they had never existed. I hated to leave her to the leather-colored wife of the old gardener, and lingered until the sharp voice came out from the distant house-door, calling, "*Veel*-hel-miny," as the twelve o'clock bell summoned the community to dinner. But as Mina rose and swept back the heavy braids that had fallen from the little ivory stick which confined them, I saw that she was armed *cap-a-pie* in that full happiness from which all weapons glance off harmless.

All the rest of the day she was like a thing possessed. I followed her to the hill-pasture, whither she had gone to mind the cows, and found her coiled up on the grass in the blaze of the afternoon sun, like a little salamander. She was lost in day-dreams, and the decorous cows had a holiday for once in their sober lives, wandering beyond bounds at will, and even tasting the dissipations of the marsh, standing unheeded in the bog up to their sleek knees. Wilhelmina had not many words to give me; her English vocabulary was limited; she had never read a line of romance nor a verse of poetry. The nearest approach to either was the community hymn-book, containing the Separatist hymns, of which the following lines are a specimen: —

"Ruhe ist das beste Gut
Dasz man haben kann":

"Rest is the best good
That man can have," —

and which embody the religious doctrine of the Zoar Brethren, although they think, apparently, that the labor of twelve hours each day is necessary to its enjoyment. The "Ruhe," however, refers more especially to their quiet seclusion away from the turmoil of the wicked world outside.

The second morning after this it was evident that an unusual excitement was abroad in the phlegmatic village. All the daily duties were fulfilled as usual at the Wirthshaus: Pauline went up to the bakery with her board, and returned with her load of bread and bretzels balanced on her head; Jacobina served our coffee with her slow precision; and the broad-shouldered, young-faced Lydia patted and puffed up our mountain-high feather-beds with due care. The men went afield at the blast of the horn, the work-shops were full and the mills running. But, nevertheless, all was not the same; the air seemed full of mystery: there were whisperings when two met, furtive signals, and an inward excitement glowing in the faces of men, women, and children, hitherto placid as their own sheep. "They have heard the news," I said, after watching the tailor's Gretchen and the blacksmith's Barbara stop to exchange a whisper behind the wood-house. Later in the day we learned that several letters from the absent soldier-boys had been received that morning, announcing their arrival on the evening train. The news had flown from one end of the village to the other, and although the well-drilled hands were all at work, hearts were stirring with the greatest excitement of a life-time, since there was hardly a house where there was not one expected. Each large house often held a number of families, stowed away in little sets of chambers, with one dining-room in common.

Several times during the day we saw the three trustees conferring apart with anxious faces. The war had been a sore trouble to them, owing to their conscientious scruples against rendering military service. They had hoped to remain non-combatants. But the country was on fire with patriotism, and nothing less than a *bona fide* Separatist in United States uniform would quiet the surrounding towns, long jealous of the wealth of this foreign community, misunderstanding its tenets, and glowing with that zeal against "sympathizers" which kept star-spangled banners flying over every suspected house. "Hang out the flag!" was their cry, and they demanded that Zoar should hang out its soldiers, giving them to understand that if not voluntarily hung out, they would soon be involuntarily hung up! A draft was ordered, and then the young men of the society, who had long chafed against their bonds, broke loose, volunteered, and marched away, principles or no principles, trustees or no trustees. These bold hearts once gone, the village sank into quietude again. Their letters, however, were a source of anxiety, coming as they did from the vain outside world; and the old postmaster, autocrat though he was, hardly dared to suppress them. But he said, shaking his head, that they "had fallen upon troublous times," and handed each dangerous envelope out with a groan. But the soldiers were not skilled penmen; their letters, few and far between, at length stopped entirely. Time passed, and the very existence of the runaways had become a far-off problem to the wise men of the community, absorbed in their slow calculations and cautious agriculture, when now, suddenly, it forced itself upon them face to face, and they were required to solve it in the twinkling of an eye. The bold hearts were coming back, full of knowledge of the outside world; almost every house would hold one, and the bands of law and order would be broken. Before this prospect the trustees quailed. Twenty years before they would have forbidden the entrance of these unruly sons within their borders; but now they dared not, since even into Zoar had penetrated the knowledge that America was a free country. The younger generation were not as their fathers were; objections had been openly made to the cut of the Sunday coats, and the girls had spoken together of ribbons!

The shadows of twilight seemed very long in falling that night, but at last there was no further excuse for delaying the evening bell, and home came the laborers to their evening meal. There was no moon, a soft mist obscured the stars, and the night was darkened with the excess of richness which rose from the ripening valley-fields and fat bottom-lands along the river. The community store opposite the Wirthshaus was closed early in the evening, the houses of the trustees were dark, and indeed the village was almost unlighted, as if to hide its own excitement. The entire population was abroad in the night, and one by one the men and boys stole away down the station road, a lovely, winding track on the hill-side, following the river on its way down the valley to the little station on the grass-grown railroad, a branch from the main track. As ten o'clock came, the women and girls, grown bold with excitement, gathered in the open space in front of the Wirthshaus, where the lights from the windows illumined their faces. There I saw the broad-shouldered Lydia, Rosine, Doroty, and all the rest, in their Sunday clothes, flushed, laughing, and chattering; but no Wilhelmina.

"Where can she be?" I said.

If she was there, the larger girls concealed her with their buxom breadth; I looked for the slender little maiden in vain.

"Shu!" cried the girls, "de bugle!"

Far down the station road we heard the bugle and saw the glimmering of lights among the trees. On it came, a will-o'-the-wisp procession: first a detachment of village boys each with a lantern or torch, next the returned soldiers winding their bugles, for, German-like, they all had musical instruments, then an excited crowd of brothers and cousins loaded with knapsacks, guns, and military accoutrements of all kinds; each man had something, were it only a tin cup, and proudly they marched in the footsteps of their glorious relatives, bearing the spoils of war. The girls set up a shrill cry of welcome as the procession approached, but the ranks continued unbroken until the open space in front of the Wirthshaus was reached; then, at a signal, the soldiers gave three cheers, the villagers joining in with all their hearts and lungs, but wildly and out of time, like the scattering fire of an awkward squad. The sound had never been heard in Zoar before. The soldiers gave a final "Tiger-r-r!" and then broke ranks, mingling with the excited crowd, exchanging greetings and embraces. All talked at once; some wept, some laughed; and through it all, silently stood the three trustees on the dark porch in front of the store, looking down upon their wild flock, their sober faces visible in the glare of the torches and lanterns below. The entire population was present; even the babies were held up on the outskirts of the crowd, stolid and staring.

"Where can Wilhelmina be?" I said again.

"Here, under the window; I saw her long ago," replied one of the women.

Leaning against a piazza-pillar, close under my eyes, stood the little maiden, pale and still. I could not disguise from myself that she looked almost ugly among those florid, laughing girls, for her color was gone, and her eyes so fixed that they looked unnaturally large; her somewhat heavy Egyptian features stood out in the bright light, but her small form was lost among the group of broad, white-kerchiefed shoulders, adorned with breast-knots of gay flowers. And had Wilhelmina no flower? She, so fond of blossoms? I looked again; yes, a little white rose, drooping and pale as herself.

But where was Gustav? The soldiers came and went in the crowd, and all spoke to Mina; but where was the One? I caught the landlord's little son as he passed, and asked the question.

"Gustav? Dat's him," he answered, pointing out a tall, rollicking soldier who seemed to be embracing the whole population in his gleeful welcome. That very soldier had passed Mina a dozen times, flinging a gay greeting to her each time; but nothing more.

After half an hour of general rejoicing, the crowd dispersed, each household bearing off in triumph the hero that fell to its lot. Then the tiled domiciles, where usually all were asleep an hour after twilight, blazed forth with unaccustomed light from every little window, and within we could see the circles, with flagons of beer and various dainties manufactured in secret during the day, sitting and talking together in a manner which, for Zoar, was a wild revel, since it was nearly eleven o'clock! We were not the only outside spectators of this unwonted gayety; several times we met the three trustees stealing along in the shadow from house to house, like anxious spectres in broad-brimmed hats. No doubt they said to each other, "How, how will this end!"

The merry Gustav had gone off by Mina's side, which gave me some comfort; but when in our rounds we came to the gardener's house and gazed through the open door, the little maiden sat apart, and the soldier, in the centre of an admiring circle, was telling stories of the war.

I felt a foreboding of sorrow as I gazed out through the little window before climbing up into my high bed. Lights still twinkled in some of the houses, but a white mist was rising from the river, and the drowsy, long-drawn chant of the summer night invited me to dreamless sleep.

The next morning I could not resist questioning Jacobina, who also had her lover among the soldiers, if all was well.

"Oh yes. They stay—all but two. We's married next mont."

"And the two?"

"Karl and Gustav."

"And Wilhelmina!" I exclaimed.

"Oh, she let him go," answered Jacobina, bringing fresh coffee.

"Poor child! How does she bear it?"

"Oh, so. She cannot help. She say noding."

"But the trustees, will they allow these young men to leave the community?"

"They cannot help," said Jacobina. "Gustav and Karl write not in the book; they free to go. Wilhelmina marry Jacob; it's joost the same; all r-r-right," added Jacobina, who prided herself upon her English, caught from visitors at the Wirthshaus table.

"Ah! but it is not just the same," I thought as I went up to the garden to find my little maiden. She was not there; the leathery mother said she was out on the hills with the cows.

"So Gustav is going to leave the community," I said in German.

"Yes, better so. He is an idle, wild boy. Now, Veelhelminy can marry the baker, a good steady man."

"But Mina does not like him," I suggested.

"Das macht nichts," answered the leathery mother.

Wilhelmina was not in the pasture; I sought for her everywhere, and called her name. The poor child had hidden herself, and whether she heard me or not, she did not respond. All day she kept herself aloof; I almost feared she would never return; but in the late twilight a little figure slipped through the garden-gate and took refuge in the house before I could speak, for I was watching for the child, apparently the only one, though a stranger, to care for her sorrow.

"Can I not see her?" I said to the leathery mother, following to the door.

"Eh, no; she's foolish; she will not speak a word; she has gone off to bed," was the answer.

For three days I did not see Mina, so early did she flee away to the hills, and so late return. I followed her to the pasture once or twice, but she would not show herself, and I could not discover her hiding-place. The fourth day I learned that Gustav and Karl were to leave the village in the afternoon, probably forever. The other soldiers had signed the articles presented by the anxious trustees, and settled down into the old routine, going afield with the rest, although still heroes for the hour; they were all to be married in August. No doubt the hardships of their campaigns among the Tennessee mountains had taught them that the rich valley was a home not to be despised; nevertheless it was evident that the flowers of the flock were those who were about departing, and that in Gustav and Karl the community lost its brightest spirits. Evident to us; but, possibly, the community cared not for bright spirits.

I had made several attempts to speak to Gustav; this morning I at last succeeded. I found him polishing his bugle on the garden bench.

"Why are you going away, Gustav?" I asked. "Zoar is a pleasant little village."

"Too slow for me, miss."

"The life is easy, however; you will find the world a hard place."

"I don't mind work, ma'am, but I do like to be free. I feel all cramped up here, with these rules and bells; and, besides, I couldn't stand those trustees; they never let a fellow alone."

"And Wilhelmina? If you do go, I hope you will take her with you, or come for her when you have found work."

"Oh no, miss. All that was long ago. It's all over now."

"But you like her, Gustav?"

"Oh, so. She's a good little thing, but too quiet for me."

"But she likes you," I said desperately, for I saw no other way to loosen this Gordian knot.

"Oh no, miss. She got used to it, and has thought of it all these years; that's all. She'll forget about it, and marry the baker."

"But she does not like the baker."

"Why not? He's a good fellow enough. She'll like him in time. It's all the same. I declare it's too bad to see all these girls going on in the same old way, in their ugly gowns and big shoes! Why, ma'am, I couldn't take Mina outside, even if I wanted to; she's too old to learn new ways, and everybody would laugh at her. She couldn't get along a day. Besides," said the young soldier, coloring up to his eyes, "I don't mind telling you that — that there's some one else. Look here, ma'am"; and he put into my hand a card photograph representing a pretty girl, overdressed and adorned with curls and gilt jewelry. "That's Miss Martin," said Gustav with pride; "Miss Emmeline Martin, of Cincinnati. I'm going to marry Miss Martin."

As I held the pretty, flashy picture in my hand, all my castles fell to the ground. My plan for taking Mina home with me, acustoming her gradually to other clothes and ways, teaching her enough of the world to enable her to hold her place without pain, my hope that my husband might find a situation for Gustav in some of the iron-mills near Cleveland, in short, all the idyl I had woven, was destroyed. If it had not been for this red-cheeked Miss Martin in her gilt beads! "Why is it that men will be such fools?" I thought. Up sprung a memory of the curls and ponderous jet necklace I sported at a certain period of my existence, when John— I was silenced, gave Gustav his picture, and walked away without a word.

At noon the villagers, on their way back to work, paused at the Wirthshaus to say good-by; Karl and Gustav were there, and the old woolly horse had already gone to the station with their boxes. Among the others came Christine, Karl's former affianced, heart-whole and smiling, already betrothed to a new lover; but no Wilhelmina. Good wishes and farewells were exchanged, and at last the two soldiers started away, falling into the marching step, and watched with furtive satisfaction by the three trustees, who stood together in the shadow of the smithy, apparently deeply absorbed in a broken-down cask.

It was a lovely afternoon, and I, too, strolled down the station road embowered in shade. The two soldiers were not far in advance. I had passed the flour-mill on the outskirts of the village and was approaching the old quarry, when a sound startled me; out from the rocks in front rushed a little figure, and crying "Gustav, mein Gustav!" fell at the soldier's feet. It was Wilhelmina.

I ran forward and took her from the young men; she lay in my arms as if dead. The poor child was sadly changed; always slender and swaying, she now looked thin and shrunken, her skin had a strange, dark pallor, and her lips were drawn in as if from pain. I could see her eyes through the large-orbed thin lids, and the brown shadows beneath extended down into the cheeks.

"Was ist's?" said Gustav, looking bewildered. "Is she sick?"

I answered "Yes," but nothing more. I could see that he had no suspicion of the truth, believing as he did that the "good fellow" of a baker would do very well for this "good little thing" who was "too quiet" for him. The memory of Miss Martin sealed my lips. But if it had not been for that pretty, flashy picture, would I not have spoken!

"You must go; you will miss the train," I said, after a few minutes. "I will see to Mina."

But Gustav lingered. Perhaps he was really troubled to see the little sweetheart of his boyhood in such desolate plight; perhaps a touch of the old feeling came back; and perhaps, also, it was nothing of the kind, and, as usual, my romantic imagination was carrying me way. At any rate, whatever it was, he stooped over the fainting girl.

"She looks bad," he said, "very bad. I wish—but she'll get well and marry the baker. Good-by, Mina." And bending his tall form, he kissed her colorless cheek, and then hastened away to join the impatient Karl; a curve in the road soon hid them from view.

Wilhelmina had stirred at his touch; after a moment her large eyes opened slowly; she looked around as if dazed, but all at once memory came back, and she started up with the same cry, "Gustav, mein Gustav!" I drew her head down on my shoulder to stifle the sound; it was better the soldier should not hear it, and its anguish thrilled my own heart, also. She had not the strength to resist me, and in a few minutes I knew that the young men were out of hearing as they strode on towards the station, and out into the wide world.

The forest was solitary, we were beyond the village; all the afternoon I sat under the trees with the stricken girl. Again, as in her joy, her words were few; again, as in her joy, her whole being was involved. Her little rough hands were cold, a film had gathered over her eyes; she did not weep, but moaned to her-self, and all her senses seemed blunted. At night-fall I took her home, and the leathery mother received her with a frown; but the child was beyond caring, and crept away, dumbly, to her room.

Then next morning she was off to the hills again, nor could I find her for several days. Evidently, in spite of my sympathy, I was no more to her than I should have been to a wounded fawn. She was a mixture of the wild, shy crea-ture of the woods and the deep-loving woman of the tropics; in either case I could be but small comfort. When at last I did see her, she was apathetic and dull; her feelings, her senses, and her intelligence seemed to have gone within, as if preying upon her heart. She scarcely listened to my proposal to take her with me; for, in my pity, I had suggested it in spite of its difficulties.

"No," she said mechanically; "I's better here"; and fell into silence again.

A month later, a friend went down to spend a few days in the valley, and upon her return described to us the weddings of the whilom soldiers. "It was really a pretty sight," she said, "the quaint peasant dresses and the flowers. Afterwards, the band went round the village playing their odd tunes, and all had a holiday. There were two civilians married also; I mean two young men who had not been to the war. It seems that two of the soldiers turned their backs upon the community and their allotted brides, and marched away; but the Zoar maidens are not romantic, I fancy, for these two deserted ones were betrothed again and married, all in the short space of four weeks."

"Was not one Wilhelmina, the gardener's daughter, a short dark girl?" I asked.

"Yes."

"And she married Jacob the baker?"

"Yes."

The next year, weary of the cold lake-winds, we left the icy shore and went down to the valley to meet the coming spring, finding her already there, decked with vines and flowers. A new waitress brought us our coffee.

"How is Wilhelmina?" I asked.

"Eh — Wilhelmina? Oh, she not here now; she gone to the Next Country," answered the girl in a matter-of-fact way. "She die last October, and Jacob he haf anoder wife now."

In the late afternoon I asked a little girl to show me Wilhelmina's grave in the quiet God's Acre on the hill. Innovation was creeping in, even here; the later graves had mounds raised over them, and one had a little head-board with an inscription in ink.

Wilhelmina lay apart, and some one, probably the old gardener, who had loved the little maiden in his silent way, had planted a rose-bush at the head of the mound. I dismissed my guide and sat there alone in the sunset, thinking of many things, but chiefly of this: "Why should this great wealth of love have been allowed to waste itself? Why is it that the greatest power, unquestionably, of this mortal life should so often seem a useless gift?"

No answer came from the sunset clouds, and as twilight sank down in the earth I rose to go. "I fully believe," I said, as though repeating a creed, "that this poor, loving heart, whose earthly body lies under this mound, is happy now in its own loving way. It has not been changed, but the happiness it longed for has come. How, we know not; but the God who made Wilhelmina understands her. He has given unto her not rest, not peace, but an active, living joy."

I walked away through the wild meadow, under whose turf, unmarked by stone or mound, lay the first pioneers of the community, and out into the forest road, untraveled save when the dead passed over it to their last earthly home. The evening was still and breathless, and the shadows lay thick on the grass as I looked back. But I could still distinguish the little mound with the rose-bush at its head, and, not without tears, I said, "Farewell, poor Wilhelmina; farewell."

Aftermath

Homecoming at war's end was even more complicated for those who were no longer slaves. Their antebellum places in planters' residences or slave quarters were often untenable, especially when they were the scenes of black injury as well as white ruin. By 1865, the expectations that had bound plantation life in cabins and kitchens were gone. As Leslie Schwalm has pointed out, "Slaves had watched the appearance and substance of planter power weaken, as planters became increasingly unable to purchase or afford even the most basic necessities; as they became subject to the impressment of their crops and their slaves; and as voluntary and involuntary removal uprooted the local and familial ties that had held plantation communities in place for generations." During the itinerant years both before and beyond Appomattox, plantation houses were regularly occupied and abandoned, especially along the North Carolina coast, where Union troops captured cities like New Berne early in 1862. The result was that freedpeople relocated as much as planters reconstructed, but in both cases families carried memories of what they had lost and what they still hoped to regain. In other cabins and other kitchens, in the North and in the South, the war brought new households together, as "A True Story" reveals. Whether through occupation or relocation, they were households in which memories mattered so much that authority and deference could be redefined.

◆◦◆

Samuel Clemens (Mark Twain)

"A TRUE STORY, REPEATED WORD FOR WORD AS I HEARD IT"

(*Atlantic Monthly*, November 1874)

It was summer time, and twilight. We were sitting on the porch of the farmhouse, on the summit of the hill, and "Aunt Rachel" was sitting respectfully below our level, on the steps, — for she was our servant, and colored. She was of mighty frame and stature; she was sixty years old, but her eye was undimmed and her strength unabated. She was a cheerful, hearty soul, and it was no more trouble for her to laugh than it is for a bird to sing. She was under fire, now, as usual when the day was done. That is to say, she was being chaffed without mercy, and was enjoying it. She would let off peal after peal of laughter, and then sit with her face in her hands and shake with throes of enjoyment which she could no longer get breath enough to express. At such a moment as this a thought occurred to me, and I said: —

"Aunt Rachel, how is it that you've lived sixty years and never had any trouble?"

She stopped quaking. She paused, and there was a moment of silence. She turned her face over her shoulder toward me, and said, without even a smile in her voice: —

"Misto C——, is you in 'arnest?"

It surprised me a good deal; and it sobered my manner and my speech, too. I said: —

"Why, I thought — that is, I meant — why, you *can't* have had any trouble. I've never heard you sigh, and never seen your eye when there wasn't a laugh in it."

She faced fairly around, now, and was full of earnestness.

"Has I had any trouble? Misto C——, I's gwyne to tell you, den I leave it to you. I was bawn down 'mongst de slaves; I knows all 'bout slavery, 'case I ben one of 'em my own se'f. Well, sah, my ole man — dat's my husban' — he was lovin' an' kind to me, jist as kind as you is to yo' own wife. An' we had chil'en — seven chil'en — an' we loved dem chil'en jist de same as you loves yo' chil'en. Dey was black, but de Lord can't make no chil'en so black but what dey mother loves 'em an' wouldn't give 'em up, no, not for anything dat's in dis whole world.

"Well, sah, I was raised in old Fo'ginny, but my mother she was raised in Maryland; an' my *souls!* she was turrible when she'd git started! My *lan'!* but she'd make de fur fly! When she'd git into dem tantrums, she always had one word dat she said. She'd straighten herse'f up an' put her fists in her hips an' say, 'I want you to understan' dat I wa'n't bawn in de mash to be fool' by trash! I's one o' de ole Blue Hen's Chickens, *I* is!' 'Ca'se, you see, dat's what folks dat's bawn in Maryland calls deyselves, an' dey's proud of it. Well, dat was her word. I don't ever forgit it, beca'se she said it so much, an' beca'se she said it one day when my little Henry tore his wris' awful, an' most busted his head, right up at de top of his forehead, an' de niggers didn't fly aroun' fas' enough to 'tend to him. An' when dey talk' back at her, she up an' she says, 'Look-a-heah!' she says, 'I want you niggers to understan' dat I wa'n't bawn in de mash to be fool' by trash! I's one o' de ole Blue Hen's Chickens, *I* is!' an' den she clar' dat kitchen an' bandage' up de chile herse'f. So I says dat word, too, when I's riled.

"Well, bymeby my ole mistis say she's broke, an' she got to sell all de niggers on de place. An' when I heah dat dey gwyne to sell us all off at oction in Richmon', oh de good gracious! I know what dat mean!"

Aunt Rachel had gradually risen, while she warmed to her subject, and now she towered above us, black against the stars.

"Dey put chains on us an' put us on a stan' as high as dis po'ch, — twenty foot high, — an' all de people stood aroun', crowds an' crowds. Al' dey'd come up dah an' look at us all roun', an' squeeze our arm, an' make us git up an' walk, an' den say, 'Dis one too ole,' or 'Dis one lame,' or 'Dis one don't 'mount to much.' An' dey sole my ole man, an' took him away, an' dey begin to sell my chil'en an' take *dem* away, an' I begin to cry; an' de man say, 'Shet up yo' dam blubberin',' an' hit me on de mouf wid his han'. An' when de las' one was gone but my little Henry, I grab' *him* clost up to my breas' so, an' I ris up an' says, 'You shan't take him away,' I says; 'I'll kill de man dat tetches him!' I says. But my little Henry whisper an' say, 'I gwyne to run away, an' den I work an' buy yo' freedom.' Oh, bless de chile, he always so good! But dey got him — dey got him, de men did; but I took and tear de clo'es mos' off of 'em, an' beat 'em over de head wid my chain; an' *dey* give it to *me*, too, but I didn't mine dat.

"Well, dah was my ole man gone, an' all my chil'en, all my seven chil'en — an' six of 'em I hain't set eyes on ag'in to dis day, an' dat's twenty-two year ago las' Easter. De man dat bought me b'long' in Newbern, an' he took me dah. Well, bymeby de years roll on an' de waw come. My marster he was a Confedrit colonel, an' I was his family's cook. So when de Unions took dat town, dey all run away an' lef' me all by myse'f wid de other niggers in dat mons'us big house. So de big Union officers move in dah, an' dey ask me would I cook for *dem*. 'Lord bless you,' says I, 'dat's what I's *for*.'

"Dey wa'n't no small-fry officers, mine you, dey was de biggest dey *is*; an' de way dey made dem sojers mosey roun'! De Gen'l he tole me to boss dat kitchen; an' he say, 'If anybody come meddlin' wid you, you jist make 'em walk chalk; don't you be afeard,' he say; 'you's 'mong frens, now.'

"Well, I thinks to myse'f, if my little Henry ever got a chance to run away, he'd make to de Norf, o' course. So one day I comes in dah whah de big officers was, in de parlor, an' I drops a kurtchy, so, an' I up an' tole 'em 'bout my Henry, dey a-listenin' to my troubles jist de same as if I was white folks; an' I says, 'What I come for is beca'se if he got away and got up Norf whah you gemmen comes from, you might 'a' seen him, maybe, an' could tell me so as I could fine him ag'in; he was very little, an' he had a sk-yar on his lef' wris', an' at de top of his forehead.' Den dey look mournful, an' de Gen'l say, 'How long sense you los' him?' an' I say, 'Thirteen year.' Den de Gen'l say, 'He wouldn't be little no mo', now — he's a man!'

"I never thought o' dat befo'! He was only dat little feller to *me*, yit. I never thought 'bout him growin' up an' bein' big. But I see it den. None o' de gemmen had run acrost him, so dey couldn't do nothin' for me. But all dat time, do' *I* didn't know it, my Henry *was* run off to de Norf, years an' years, an' he was a barber, too, an' worked for hisse'f. An' bymeby, when de waw come, he ups an' he says, 'I's done barberin',' he says; 'I's gwyne to fine my ole mammy, less'n she's dead.' So he sole out an' went to whah dey was recruitin', an' hired hisse'f out to de colonel for his servant; an' den he went all froo de battles everywhah, huntin' for his ole mammy; yes indeedy, he'd hire to fust one officer an' den another, tell he'd ransacked de whole Souf; but you see *I* didn't know nuffin 'bout *dis*. How was *I* gwyne to know it?

"Well, one night we had a big sojer ball; de sojers dah at Newbern was always havin' balls an' carryin' on. Dey had 'em in my kitchen, heaps o' times, 'ca'se it was so big. Mine you, I was *down* on sich doin's; beca'se my place was wid de officers, an' it rasp' me to have dem common sojers cavortin' roun' my kitchen like dat. But I alway' stood aroun' an' kep' things straight, I did; an' sometimes dey'd git my dander up, an' den I'd make 'em clar dat kitchen, mine I *tell* you!

"Well, one night — it was a Friday night — dey comes a whole plattoon f'm a *nigger* ridgment dat was on guard at de house, — de house was head-quarters, you know, — an' den I was jist a-*bilin'*! Mad? I was jist a-*boomin*! I swelled aroun', an' swelled aroun'; I jist was a-itchin' for 'em to do somefin for to start me. *An'* dey was a-waltzin' an a-dancin'! *my!* but dey was havin' a time! an' I jist a-swellin' an' a-swellin' up! Pooty soon, 'long comes *sich* a spruce young nigger a-sailin' down de room wid a yaller wench roun' de wais'; an' roun' an' roun' an' roun' dey went, enough to make a body drunk to look at 'em; an' when dey got abreas' o' me, dey went to kin' o' balancin' aroun', fust on one

376

"THE ESCAPED SLAVE IN THE UNION ARMY"

leg an' den on t'other, an' smilin' at my big red turban, an' makin' fun, an'
I ups an' says, "*Git* along wid you! — rubbage!' De young man's face kin' o'
changed, all of a sudden, for 'bout a second, but den he went to smilin' ag'in,
same as he was befo'. Well, 'bout dis time, in comes some niggers dat played
music an' b'long' to de ban', an' dey *never* could git along widout puttin' on
airs. An' de very fust air dey put on dat night, I lit into 'em! Dey laughed, an'
dat made me wuss. De res' o' de niggers got to laughin', an' den my soul *alive*
but I was hot! My eye was jist a-blazin'! I jist straightened myself up, so, — jist
as I is now, plum to de ceilin', mos', — an' I digs my fists into my hips, an' I
says, 'Look-a-heah!' I says, 'I want you niggers to understan' dat I wa'n't bawn
in de mash to be fool' by trash! I's one o' de ole Blue Hen's Chickens, *I* is!' an'
den I see dat young man stan' a-starin' an' stiff, lookin' kin' o' up at de ceilin'
like he fo'got somefin, an' couldn't 'member it no mo'. Well, I jist march' on
dem niggers, — so, lookin' like a gen'l, — an' dey jist cave' away befo' me an'
out at de do'. An' as dis young man was a-goin' out, I heah him say to another
nigger, 'Jim,' he says, 'you go 'long an' tell de cap'n I be on han' 'bout eight

377

o'clock in de mawnin'; dey's somefin on my mine,' he says; 'I don't sleep no mo' dis night. You go 'long,' he says, 'an' leave me by my own se'f.'

"Dis was 'bout one o'clock in de mawnin'. Well, 'bout seven, I was up an' on han', gittin' de officers' breakfast. I was a-stoopin' down by de stove,—jist so, same as if yo' foot was de stove,—an' I'd opened de stove do wid my right han',—so, pushin' it back, jist as I pushes yo' foot,—an' I'd jist got de pan o' hot biscuits in my han' an' was 'bout to raise up, when I see a black face come aroun' under mine, an' de eyes a-lookin' up into mine, jist as I's a-lookin' up clost under yo' face now; an' I jist stopped *right dah,* an' never budged! jist gazed, an' gazed, so; an' de pan begin to tremble, an' all of a sudden I *knowed!* De pan drop' on de flo' an' I grab his lef' han' an' shove back his sleeve,—jist so, as I's doin' to you,—an' den I goes for his forehead an' push de hair back, so, an' 'Boy!' I says, 'if you an't my Henry, what is you doin' wid dis welt on yo' wris' an' dat sk-yar on yo' forehead? De Lord God ob heaven be praise', I got my own ag'in!'

"Oh, no, Misto C——, *I* hain't had no trouble. An' no *joy!*"

Between the sensational tales in the *Saturday Evening Gazette* that paid her board during the 1850s and her more familiar success with *Little Women* (1868–1869) and *Little Men* (1871), LOUISA MAY ALCOTT (1832–1888) published several other narratives of the war, including "A Hospital Christmas" (1864) in the *Commonwealth*, "The Hospital Lamp" (1864) in the *Daily Morning Drum-Beat*, and "The Blue and the Gray: A Hospital Sketch" (1868) in *Putnam's*. All touch on her wartime experience at Georgetown's Union Hotel Hospital, where she served as a nurse for six weeks in 1862–1863 before contracting typhoid fever. Her account of those weeks in *Hospital Sketches*, published serially mid-1863 in the *Commonwealth*, concludes with the Emancipation Proclamation on New Year's Day 1863. By November, when "The Brothers" first appeared, black regiments had been raised in states like Massachusetts, Michigan, Connecticut, Kansas, and Louisiana, and the Bureau of Colored Troops had been established. After the war, Alcott edited Boston's *Merry Museum* for children between 1867 and 1870, and serialized novels such as *Work* (1872–1873) in the *Christian Union* and *Silver Pitchers: A Temperance Tale* (1875) in the *Youth's Companion*, while she vigorously supported the movement for women's rights.

During the early 1860s, MARK TWAIN was still SAMUEL CLEMENS (1835–1910), a steamboat pilot on the Mississippi until the outbreak of war put an end to commercial river traffic. Returning to Missouri, he answered the call for militia volunteers by enlisting in the Marion Rangers, a home guard regiment organized in 1861 to protect the border state from a Union invasion. Though the Marion Rangers were disbanded in a few months, Twain lasted only two weeks, a sorry contribution he later lampooned in "The Private History of a Campaign that Failed" (1885) for the *Century's* celebrated series on *Battles and Leaders of the Civil War* (1884–1887). At the time, he was lucky to escape charges for desertion, especially after he departed for Nevada and stayed until the war ended. That was long enough to become a journalist for the Virginia City *Territorial Enterprise* and to appropriate the river name he would make famous. In 1874, when Twain's first and reportedly "true" story for the *Atlantic Monthly* was published, the Freedmen's Bureau was closing down, Northern support for hard-won civil and political rights was ebbing, and the ex-slaves who should have been legally safeguarded were left to rise on their own.

GEORGE JAMES ATKINSON COULSON (1819–1882) published regularly during the 1870s. Born in Baltimore, where he would co-edit the *Baltimore American* before the war, he lived thereafter in Maryland's Cecil County on the Delmarva peninsula and contributed often to the editorial pages of *The Cecil Democrat*. A man of business for years with A. T. Stewart and Company, he also wrote wrote "Cats" (1869) and "Toothache" (1870) for the *New Eclectic*, "Played Out" (1879) for *Lippincott's*, and "Suffrage" (1872) and "Aggressive Ruffianism" (1872) for the *Southern Magazine*, where his novel *The Odd Trump* was serialized beginning in 1874. That book was published a year later in New York, along with a series of five others in New York or Philadelphia shortly afterwards. His story of a "nootral" hospital nurse appeared during 1871 in postwar Maryland, when Baltimore was as much a crossroads for Southern refugees and Northern commerce as the border city had been during the years of the war.

JOHN OSCAR CULVER (1830–1912) volunteered near Milwaukee in August 1861 and served as a paymaster with the Department of the Missouri, headquartered in St. Louis, until he was mustered out a major in November 1865. He returned to Wauwatosa, Wisconsin, and published occasional stories, including "The Plaintiff Nonsuited" (1867) in the *Atlantic Monthly* and "The Founders of Globe City" (1868) in *Putnam's*. During the 1870s, he coedited the *Wisconsin State Journal* (the "Official State Paper") before moving on to California, mining operations, and further postal duties. By the 1880s, he was traveling widely across the West as a Post Office Inspector, a position that also allowed him to visit mines and to invest in the machines needed to make them work. Reconstruction had long since ended in those years, but in 1866, when his story of an itinerant paymaster appeared, guerrilla William Clarke Quantrill had just been replaced by outlaw Jesse James in Missouri, and Arkansas was troubled by the competing factions that would carry skulking violence into the 1870s.

REBECCA HARDING DAVIS (1831–1910) was raised in Wheeling, Virginia, an industrial center that became the first capital of the new state of West Virginia in 1863. By that time, Harding had published her celebrated "Life in the Iron Mills" (1861) in the *Atlantic Monthly*, been feted in Boston by editor James T. Fields, and married aspiring lawyer Lemuel Clarke Davis. Her stories of the Civil War as wrenching, costly, and morally charged circulated in the wartime *Atlantic Monthly* and later in *Lippincott's* and the *Galaxy*, where her novel about race and Reconstruction's retreat entitled *Waiting for the Verdict* was serialized in 1867. When "Ellen" came out in Boston two years earlier, the war had ended for almost everyone except the refugees without homes and the families that had been shaken by loss.

By 1862, when her letter to the editor appeared in *Harper's Weekly*, CHARITY GRIMES had been dead for a decade. At least Frances M. Whitcher (1814–1852) had passed away, after creating that rambunctious character, among others, to satirize the women of Elmira, New York. Whitcher's vernacular sketches of small-town narrowness and hypocrisy, which were published in Neal's *Saturday Gazette* and *Godey's Lady's Book* during the 1840s, so riled her husband's Episcopalian flock that he was forced to resign. After she died, her husband's second wife finished her novel and published it with later sketches in 1867; she may have been responsible for further poetic contributions from Charity Grimes to *Harper's Weekly* such as "Gineral Butler" (31 January 1863), "Lines tu Jeff Davis" (7 February 1863), and "Lay ov the Moddern Konservativs" (16 May 1863). Still, it was humorist Petroleum V. Nasby who produced a dramatic version of Whitcher's *Widow Bedott* in 1879, when Bedott was played by the cross-dressing Neil Burgess.

Ross Guffin (1836–1903) enlisted in the 52nd Indiana in October 1861, after studying at Antioch College, taking his degree from the University (now Butler), and then graduating from Harvard Law School in July. He was immediately elected first lieutenant of Company G and fought at Fort Donelson, Shiloh, and Corinth. In mid-1862, his infantry regiment was transferred to Memphis and then to garrison duty at Fort Pillow, where he was promoted to captain and served as provost marshal. Guffin took part later in General Sherman's Meridian campaign in Mississippi during 1864 and joined the staff of General A. J. Smith before resigning at the end of that year. In 1865, he began practicing law in Memphis, moved to Missouri in 1867, and settled in Kansas City the following year. An energetic Republican with moderate views, he continued to practice law and filled several political offices, including Assistant City Counsellor, U.S. Attorney for the Western District of Missouri, and Collector of Customs at Kansas City. When "A Night on the Mississippi" was published in 1870, Guffin was writing a good deal for newspapers and magazines since his political success was still in the offing. He would go on to oversee the allotment of Indian lands in Utah and to become the superintendent of the Sac, Fox, and Iowa peoples in the Oklahoma Territory, where he eventually died of wounds he received while garrisoned at Fort Pillow.

Edward Everett Hale (1822–1909) was not a Southerner in the Confederate Civil Service but a bonafide New Englander. His uncle was the celebrated Edward Everett who out-talked Lincoln at Gettysburg, while his great uncle was the Revolutionary War hero Nathan Hale, who regretted that he had only one life to give to his country. His father owned and edited one of Boston's foremost newspapers, the *Daily Advertiser,* and Hale himself married the niece of Henry Ward Beecher and Harriet Beecher Stowe. For over forty years, he was an ordained minister at Boston's Second Congregational Church, and he was then unanimously elected to serve as chaplain of the United States Senate from 1903 to the year of his death. Opposed to slavery and committed throughout his life to social reform, Hale was active in the Emigrant Aid Society, the U.S. Sanitary Commission, and the Freedmen's Bureau, before penning the "lend a hand" novels that would inspire a nationwide club movement during the 1880s. Although he founded and personally oversaw the more entertaining *Old and New* a decade earlier, helped edit the *Army and Navy Journal* during the war and the *Sunday School Gazette* as a young Worchester minister during the 1840s, he is probably best remembered for his story "The Man Without a Country" (1863), first published anonymously in the *Atlantic Monthly*. During a prolific career, he wrote volumes of history, sermons, autobiography, and travel accounts, many of which first appeared with close to a hundred lighter stories in magazines as diverse as *Sartain's* and the *Christian Union*, *Harper's Monthly* and *Our Young Folks*, the *Independent* and *McClure's*. "The Skeleton in the Closet," which was reprinted in 1868 to accompany "The Man Without a Country," was first published by Hale's brother-in-law Frederic Beecher Perkins in the *Galaxy* a year after the war ended. In 1866, the cascade of veteran memoirs that Hale's story tweaks was only just beginning. But his breezy affability while tracking Richmond's "skeletons" was scarcely shared in a city that stood in ruins.

CHAUNCEY HICKOX (1837–1905) was born in Ohio and married in Connecticut, where he enlisted during October 1862 in the 27th Connecticut Infantry; he mustered out with the regiment in July 1863 as a sergeant. He then joined the 8th Massachusetts Volunteer Militia Infantry and served as a second lieutenant for 100 days in 1864. At the time of the militia's third brief tour, depleted ranks were filled by companies from the western part of the state, where Hickox served briefly as a newspaperman with the Springfield *Daily* and *Weekly Republican*. Although he came to the regiment late, the 8th Massachusetts or "Minute Men" had answered Lincoln's first call for volunteers and arrived in Washington for three-month service amid the exuberant disorder of the war's first spring. After hostilities ended, Hickox returned to Washington as a clerk in the Pension Office, where he remained for the rest of his life. During those years, he wrote often for the magazines and contributed essays like "Shall Punishment Punish?" (1877) to the *Galaxy* and "The Presidency" (1881) to *Lippincott's*, along with a number of stories. When "Job and the Bug" appeared in 1871, Ulysses S. Grant had risen from general-in-chief to president, but his enviable stature at war's end had been dimmed by the scandals of his administration and the morass of Reconstruction, even in the nation's capital.

JOHN DANIEL IMBODEN (1823–1895) was born and reared in the Shenandoah Valley, where he was a superintendent of schools as well as a lawyer who served in Virginia's House of Delegates before the war began. When his state seceded, he organized the Staunton Artillery and later the 1st Partisan Rangers, a cavalry brigade he led on a memorable raid that destroyed railroad bridges and captured livestock during the spring of 1863. He was therefore well positioned to cover Lee's muddy retreat from Gettysburg, which he handled just as resourcefully in print when the *Century*'s series on *Battles and Leaders of the Civil War* (1884–1887) was expanded and published separately in 1887. His earlier account of the same events for the *Galaxy* varied intriguingly; when "Lee at Gettysburg" appeared in 1871, the revered general had died the year before, and the high esteem in which he was held was only beginning to take on the dimensions of Lost Cause myth.

A Georgia native and Maryland emigré, RICHARD MALCOLM JOHNSTON (1822–1898) was a sometime lawyer and sporadic teacher before he accepted a professorship of belles lettres and oratory at Franklin College (now the University of Georgia), where he was engaged when the war began. First in Georgia and then in Maryland after 1867, he opened private boarding schools and published the humorous tales of "Dukesborough" that he started writing in the 1850s. As a master of rural fiction, he later made his reputation with stories in *Harper's Monthly, Cosmopolitan,* and the *Century* during the 1880s and 1890s. He also published novels and travel accounts, historical essays and literary studies, as well as personal nonfiction like "Middle Georgia Rural Life" (1892) for the *Century* and "Dogs and Railroad Conductors" (1898) for *Lippincott's.* His story of Williamson Slippey's salt, published in 1870, suggests the entrepreneurial gumption that would make Atlanta the premier city of the New South.

When Virginia seceded, clerk WILLIAM HUMPHREYS KEMPER (1840–?) enrolled in the Alexandria Artillery as part of the 17th Virginia Infantry under his brother Delaware Kemper. He then transferred to the 18th Battalion, Virginia Heavy Artillery, in mid-1862 and was promoted to first lieutenant by the end of the year, after serving Colonel Stephen D. Lee with distinction as his adjutant at Sharpsburg. Kemper ran afoul of military regulations in August 1863, but his sentence was remitted and he was reassigned to General William Booth Taliaferro at Charleston, where he went on to serve as an adjutant of light artillery on James Island in 1864. He was ultimately paroled in May 1865 at Tallahassee as a member of General Sam Jones's staff. After the war, he hoped to become editor of the *Farmville Mercury,* especially after contributing such light-hearted pieces as "A Pinch of Snuff" (1873), "Plea for Shams" (1873), and "The 'Cabinet Mystery'" (1873) to the *Southern Magazine.* That position fell through, however, and he eventually departed for the west. In 1873, when his "little story" appeared, the Southern Historical Society had already been organized in New Orleans and moved to Richmond, and the *Southern Magazine* was about to become the society's official organ until the Southern Historical Society "Papers" were published independently starting in 1876.

Captain HENRY KING (1842–1915) was a newspaperman and an outspoken Republican from an early age. He enlisted as a private in the 50th Illinois and later served on the staffs of Generals McPherson, Dodge, and Sherman. After the war, he emigrated to Topeka and edited the *Kansas Magazine* (1872–1873), a short-lived literary phenomenon. In the 1880s, he moved to the St. Louis *Globe-Democrat,* which he edited for more than thirty years. By then he had already contributed numerous magazine stories and essays, such as "At Kawsmouth Station" (1879) in the *Atlantic Monthly* and "Over Sunday in New Sharon" (1880) in *Scribner's Monthly,* at a time when the border country of Kansas and Missouri was only slowly materializing in national magazines. In 1874, when "The Cabin at Pharaoh's Ford" appeared, much of the area was still the "far frontier" and beckoning, just as Reconstructive opportunities for freedmen in the South were disappearing and an exodus to Kansas was about to begin.

ELLEN DOUGLAS LARNED (1825–1912) was not the "Ellen Leonard" of Harper error but the celebrated local historian who would soon begin publishing in earnest. Born in the small town of Thompson, near Hartford, and named for the Sir Walter Scott heroine that her father favored, Larned would publish several meticulous histories, including a two-volume *History of Windham County* (1874–1880) and a *History of Woodstock* (1886) as well as occasional essays in the *Connecticut Quarterly.* She was a weather observer for sixty years, beginning more than a decade before the U.S. Weather Bureau was founded in 1870, the year she became the first female member of the Connecticut Historical Society. She later served as the society's vice-president from 1889 until her death. She was a charter member of the Elizabeth Porter Chapter of the Daughters of the American Revolution and a lively supporter of the Woman's Christian Temperance Union. Her early misattributed story of the New York draft riots was striking enough for the Harpers to reprint as *Three Days' Reign of Terror, or the July Riots of 1863, in New York* later in 1867. By that time, some years after the "terror" Larned described, the Democratic working class had helped frustrate both the wartime draft in New York City and the Republican prerogatives that would shape reconstructive policies elsewhere, while Tammany Hall had edged the city's Union League Club out of political ascendancy and into the pages of the *Nation,* founded in 1865 and edited by E. L. Godkin and Wendell Phillips Garrison.

A contract surgeon in Philadelphia during the war, SILAS WEIR MITCHELL (1829–1914) served initially at the hospital in the old armory building and then at the Hospital for Nervous Diseases at Turner's Lane. He was among the first to study battlefield shock and the treatment of pain, particularly in his coauthored *Gunshot Wounds and Other Injuries of Nerves* (1864). Although George Dedlow was fictitious, the hundreds of soldiers Mitchell examined were not, nor were the thousands of pages of notes he kept or the tens of thousands of morphine injections whose administration he pioneered as the country's foremost neurologist. In the hospital wards and the subsequent literary work for which he was increasingly known, particularly after his novel *In War Time* was serialized by the *Atlantic Monthly* during 1884, Mitchell was convinced that mind and body interacted powerfully. For men of the growing middle class, he would later prescribe a vigorous outdoor life as the avenue to good health, while for women he would come to favor the rest cure and the protracted seclusion that would drive Charlotte Perkins Gilman to near insanity, as "The Yellow Wallpaper" (1892) in the *New England Magazine* revealed.

Nephew of Catherine Beecher, Henry Ward Beecher, and Harriet Beecher Stowe, FREDERIC BEECHER PERKINS (1828–1899) taught school, was admitted to the bar in Hartford, and served as librarian of the Connecticut Historical Society while he published Barnard's *American Journal of Education* in the years before the war. During the 1860s and 1870s, he edited a host of magazines, such as the *Galaxy,* the *Independent,* the *Saturday Magazine,* and the *Library Journal,* while contributing regularly to these and others with pieces like "Spiritism" (1866) for the *Nation,* "An Imaginary Conversation" (1869) for *Putnam's,* and "Devil-Puzzlers" (1871) for *Old and New.* He left his first family, including the daughter who would become Charlotte Perkins Gilman, in 1860 and left the East for the San Francisco Public Library in 1880. A man of wit, literary craft, and capacious knowledge, he was at ease in the electric world of New York magazines and attuned to the city's head-long commercial rush in 1863, when his story of Wall Street's speculative boom appeared.

NORA PERRY (1831–1896) began writing as a child and began publishing fiction and poetry before she was twenty. Her best-known poems in the 1850s were "Tying Her Bonnet under Her Chin" (1859) in the *National Era* and "After the Ball" (1859) in the *Atlantic Monthly.* At about the same time, Perry became Boston correspondent for the *Providence Journal* as well as the *Chicago Tribune;* she then published stories like "Clotilde and the Contraband" (1862) and "Margaret Freyer's Heart" (1863) in *Harper's Monthly.* Thereafter, she favored stories for girls in such magazines as the *Galaxy,* the *Atlantic Monthly,* and *Scribner's.* In 1867, when her story of New Orleans resistance and domestic espionage appeared, the city had just survived an alarming race riot, the Southern states had been partitioned into occupied military districts, and Louisiana's Knights of the White Camelia were beginning to coalesce.

Born in Sweden and educated in Germany, MAXIMILIAN SCHELE DE VERE (1820–1898) emigrated in 1843 to Boston, where he studied Greek at Harvard. The next year he accepted a professorship in modern languages at the University of Virginia, an appointment he would hold for fifty-one years. He was prodigious during that time with his scholarly contributions in comparative philology, the development of the English language, and the emergence of idiomatic American speech, especially *Americanisms: The English of the New World* (1871). In addition, his numerous magazine essays ranged widely to include such topics as "Early German Philosophers" (1859) for the *Christian Review,* "Prince Eugene" (1864) for the *Southern Literary Messenger,* "Foxes and Fox-Hunting" (1868) for *Hours at Home,* "Wonders of the Deep" (1869) for *Putnam's,* and "Low Life in Nature" (1871) for *Scribner's.* In 1866, when his story of a fugitive slave household was published, the Freedmen's Bureau had been created the previous year and ex-slaves were negotiating labor contracts in Virginia, while lynchings were on the rise and black families were fighting for the schools, businesses, and churches they had built.

RICHARD M. SHEPPARD (1832–1900) enlisted as a private with Philadelphia's elite in the 6th Pennsylvania Cavalry or "Rush's Lancers" during 1861. After a year on provost duty in defense of Washington, the regiment served in almost every major campaign that the Army of the Potomac undertook, and Sheppard rose through the noncommissioned ranks to become a second lieutenant in early 1863 and regimental quartermaster by the end of that year. In the spring of 1865, the Rush Lancers were made part of the 2nd Provisional Cavalry before being mustered out in August, but Captain Sheppard was detached to serve with General Sheridan before Sheppard, too, left the army at year's end to return to Philadelphia for good. His single story, appearing in 1870 when Custer had been posted to Kansas and the Western Indian campaigns, chronicles actual events in Louisiana as the war wound down and the Second Wisconsin Cavalry was growing restless.

Republican RICHMOND WOLCOTT (1840–1908) graduated from Illinois College in 1859, when the school under Edward Beecher was publicly committed to the abolition of slavery. In August 1861, Wolcott enlisted as a private in the 10th Illinois Infantry and served as a regimental hospital steward. He resigned a captain in September 1864 and returned to the study of law; after the war ended, he married, moved to Springfield, and opened his law practice. During the years of the war, the 10th Illinois fought along the Mississippi River at New Madrid and Island No. 10, as well as in and around Mississippi, Alabama, and Tennessee before being reassigned to General Sherman's campaign in Georgia and the Carolinas. When Wolcott's story of unflinching Western service appeared in September 1862, after his earlier "Taken Prisoner" had been published by the *Continental Monthly* in March, General Grant's army had moved from a costly victory at Shiloh to capturing Corinth and seizing the Memphis and Charleston Railroad, the Confederacy's single through line from the Atlantic to the Mississippi.

CONSTANCE FENIMORE WOOLSON (1840–1894) was the grandniece of James Fenimore Cooper, though, unlike him, she knew the West about which she wrote firsthand. Her family moved from New Hampshire to Ohio shortly after her birth; with her father, she visited the Separatist Society of Zoar when she was growing up and wrote of "The Happy Valley" (1870) for *Harper's Monthly,* the first magazine piece she published. Her illustrated fiction, poetry, and travel essays soon appeared in such magazines as *Appletons' Journal, Putnam's,* and the *Century.* Her lake country sketches were later augmented by contributions from the South after she relocated to St. Augustine in 1873 and then from Europe after she moved abroad in 1880. During the Civil War, when she was still in Cleveland, she sold autographs as part of the "post office" she ran in one of the city's sanitary fairs, which were organized to raise funds for the U.S. Sanitary Commission. By 1875, when her story of Zoar enlistments mistakenly put the 107th Ohio Volunteer Infantry at Lookout Mountain instead of Gettysburg, Woolson had already gone south, the "Sanitary" was on its way to becoming the American Red Cross under Clara Barton, and Zoar was in decline, its intricate garden summoning fewer and fewer society members to communal allegiance.

ILLUSTRATION SOURCES

Frontispiece: "The House-Tops in Charleston during the Bombardment of Sumter," *Harper's Weekly*, 4 May 1861, 273.

PRELUDE

"Negroes Leaving Their Home," *Harper's Weekly*, 9 April 1864, 237.

1861

"The Spirits Abroad — The Spirit of Disunion," *Harper's Weekly*, 28 July 1860, 472.

"The Stampede from Bull Run," *Illustrated London News*, Supplement, 17 August 1861, 167.

"Scenes of Camp and Army Life," *Harper's Weekly*, 6 July 1861, 422.

1862

"The Great Uprising of the North," *Harper's Weekly*, 12 April 1862, 248–49.

"The Gold Panic in Wall Street," *Harper's Weekly*, 21 March 1863, 188.

"The Starving People of New Orleans," *Harper's Weekly*, 14 June 1862, 380.

"Federal Picket on the Potomac," *Illustrated London News*, 7 December 1861, 567.

"The Rebel Army Crossing the Fords of the Potomac," *Harper's Weekly*, 27 September 1862, 613.

"A Sharp-Shooter on Picket Duty," *Harper's Weekly*, 15 November 1862, 724.

"Lincoln's Last Warning," *Harper's Weekly*, 11 October 1862, 656.

"General Stuart (Confederate) with His Cavalry," *Illustrated London News*, 4 October 1862, 368.

1863

"Rendezvous of Mosby's Men in the Pass of the Blue Ridge," *Illustrated London News*, 21 January 1865, 56.

"The Battle of Gettysburg — Longstreet's Attack," *Harper's Weekly*, 8 August 1863, 504–5.

"The Harvest of Death—Gettysburg, July 4, 1863," *Harper's Weekly*, 22 July
1865, 452.

"The Riots at New York," *Harper's Weekly*, 1 August 1863, 484.

"A Negro Regiment in Action," *Harper's Weekly*, 14 March 1863, 168–69.

"The Battle of Antietam—Carrying Off the Wounded," *Harper's Weekly*,
11 October 1862, 649.

"Pay-Day in the Army of the Potomac," *Harper's Weekly*, 28 February 1863,
136–37.

"The Union Prisoners at Richmond, Virginia," *Harper's Weekly*, 18 January
1862, 45.

"The Prisons at Richmond—Union Troops Prisoners at Belle Isle," *Harper's
Weekly*, 5 December 1863, 781.

"Destruction of a Rebel Salt Factory," *Harper's Weekly*, 15 November 1862, 732.

1864

"New Year's Day," *Harper's Weekly*, 2 January 1864, 8–9.

"Our Heroines: United States Sanitary Commission," *Harper's Weekly*, 9 April
1864, 229.

"The Massacre at Fort Pillow," *Harper's Weekly*, 30 April 1864, 284.

"The Campaign in Virginia—'On to Richmond!' " *Harper's Weekly*, 18 June
1864, 392–93.

"Negroes Escaping Out of Slavery," *Harper's Weekly*, 7 May 1864, 292.

"Arrival of Union Refugees at Kingston, Georgia," *Harper's Weekly*,
10 December 1864, 785.

1865

"The Union Army Entering Richmond," *Harper's Weekly*, 22 April 1865, 248–49.

"Paris Fashions for March, 1865," *Harper's Weekly*, 25 March 1865, 189.

"The Flight of the Confederates," *Illustrated London News*, 22 July 1865, 64.

"The Soldier's Dream," *Harper's Weekly*, 7 November 1863, 709.

"Brigadier-General George A. Custer," *Harper's Weekly*, 19 March 1864, 177.

"Return of Veteran Volunteers on Furlough," *Harper's Weekly*, 23 January 1864,
56–57.

AFTERMATH

"A Slave Auction at the South," *Harper's Weekly*, 13 July 1861, 442.

"The Escaped Slave in the Union Army," *Harper's Weekly*, 2 July 1864, 428.

CIVIL WAR GLOSSARY

adjutant A regimental officer chosen by the colonel to pass along orders, monitor operations, and complete paperwork as his chief of staff.

ambulance A two- or four-wheeled hospital vehicle issued to Union regiments in varying numbers and routinely appropriated for non-medical uses, even after a trained ambulance corps was organized in the Army of the Potomac midwar and a more informal "infirmary corps" began serving Confederate medical needs in 1862.

ambuscade A sudden attack or ambush by men in hiding.

annual Less a magazine than a gift book that was prepared each year for the Christmas season as a miscellany with mezzotints, which were often colored by hand and designed for women in ever increasing numbers during the 1840s.

Aqueduct Bridge A structure of heavy gneiss piers built to carry laden canal boats across the Potomac between Georgetown and Rosslyn, Virginia, where Key Bridge would later stretch. Completed in 1843, the canal bridge was drained during the war and replaced by a roadway to transport troops, while the elaborate aqueduct link to Great Falls upriver provided millions of gallons of water daily to Washington and the city's struggling hospitals.

ash-cake A flat cake made of corn and baked in a frying pan, on a hot stone, or in the ashes of an open fire.

ball with wads Essentially a blank, as there was no powder to propel the ball, no matter how much the wads increased its accuracy.

bandy A game also known as goff that was played with a long curved bat called a bandy and a hard leather ball stuffed with feathers, which was hit into a series of small holes in as little time and with as few strokes as possible.

battalion An infantry unit of five hundred to eight hundred men at full strength, what was once a regiment in the Regular Army and took its name as the unit formerly thought the best size for going into battle. During the Civil War, an infantry battalion was roughly half as large as a regiment and was generally commanded by a major or a lieutenant colonel.

battery An artillery unit of men and cannon that, along waterways, dated back to the "first system" of national defense authorized in 1794 or the "second system" built into the nineteenth century. These early fortifications were earth or wood and could include two stories, parapet guns, and furnaces for heating cannonballs, arrangements that made such structures considerably more elaborate than the mobile units of inland battlefields.

Bedouin A gypsy or an Arab nomad in the desert and thus any wanderer in the United States thought likely to steal; often poor and often Irish.

biting a cartridge The fastest way to rip open the paper containers of muzzle-loading powder that left black circles around hurried mouths.

bivouac A temporary encampment, after battle or on a march, that was often more orderly in the open fields Federal soldiers favored than in the woods where Confederates found shelter. Both armies knew that bivouacking near the field of recent combat meant collecting better equipment for the battles to come.

block house A modest building generally made from logs and perforated with loopholes for muskets or small cannon so that bridges or tracks or occupied territory could be guarded.

Blue Hen's Chickens Residents of the state of Delaware as far back as the Revolutionary War, when a Delaware officer and breeder named Caldwell declared that true gamecocks had to be born of blue hens. The name stuck to his company, which fought stoutly as the blue hen's chickens in Carolina. Although the border between Maryland and Delaware and so rights to the term were long contested,

blue hen's chickens also came to apply more broadly to any state's feisty, hot-tempered fighters, especially women.

blue-jacket A Union soldier wearing the dark blue "blouse" that the regular army favored as far back as the Revolutionary War. After the colorful but dangerous confusion of early regimental uniforms in 1861, Northern military authorities imposed standard issue, along with the graduated sizes that would persist in American men's clothing.

blue ruin Cheap liquor with a kick, generally corn whiskey or gin.

bombazine A lustreless blend of wool and silk that was used as far back as the sixteenth century for mourning clothes and has since been used for umbrellas.

Boots and Spurs Variant of "Boots and Saddles," a bugle call to pack up and leave camp.

border-rider A horseman along the English-Scottish border during the many lawless years before the clans were finally suppressed in 1745; Sir Walter Scott, among many others, later spread the ballads that told of their bloody vengeance as cattle thieving quietly continued. Supporters of the Catholic Stuarts were most likely to pledge candles as offerings measured by a piece of string to the length of a saint's relic or effigy or, in this case, the heavy two-handed swords called "whingers" that clansmen carried.

brickbat Hefty chunks of brick that could be hurled in place of stones.

brigade Roughly four regiments of infantry or cavalry that were commanded by a brigadier general and became the smallest viable tactical unit. Brigades served from the same state for the duration, even as the war depleted both their numbers and their state's control.

buckhorn A homemade knife that was often part of a soldier's private arsenal. In the war's early months, soldier knives could run to foot-long blades with curved or serrated edges and the rough deer-horn handles that were used, along the frontier, to mark the deal in card games so that players would "pass the buck."

bucking The common army practice of punishing misconduct by tying a soldier's wrists around his folded knees and passing a stick over his arms and under his legs for a good long while.

bushwhacking A guerrilla attack made by those hiding in thickets, often the deserters, fugitives, and raiders who terrorized public roads and civilian homes before returning with their plunder to the bush.

butternuts Southern sympathizers living in the North and the Western states of Iowa, Illinois, and Indiana, where they sometimes attacked squads of Union soldiers. First in the West and then across the blockaded South, Confederate troops were also known as butternuts, from the oily fruit of butternut trees used to dye homespun uniforms brown.

caisson A wooden carriage for field artillery and ammunition, as well as the spare wheel that could save any standardized vehicle or punish any offending artilleryman lashed to it for a spell.

calibre .577 Ammunition for muzzle-loading British Enfield rifles and close enough for .58-caliber American Springfield rifles to be used interchangeably with minimal clogging, which helped simplify Union ammunition supply and rearm scavenging Confederates.

Camp Chase Early in the war, a training camp for Western regiments near Columbus, Ohio, where Confederate officers taken prisoner were later transported as Union victories mounted in the West.

canister Artillery projectile consisting of many small metal balls or any available scrap metal packed with sawdust into a thin cylinder that was shot, sometimes two or three together, from smoothbore cannon and was effective up to five or six hundred yards.

carbine A short rifle that was used fatefully by John Brown in prewar Kansas and at Harper's Ferry. During the war, the carbine was generally a cavalry weapon that by 1865 was usually breechloading, repeating, and deadly.

carpetbag Customarily a wool traveling bag used by those who carried little luggage, like the men who were later said to descend on the postwar South in the hope of lining their pockets quickly.

cartridge-box A black leather container that usually held forty rounds for Union infantry. Confederate soldiers increasingly abandoned such boxes as too heavy when cartridges could be carried in pockets and knapsacks.

Chain Bridge The first bridge across the Potomac, built in 1797 and once literally suspended from chains. By 1861, this upriver connection between Maryland's Little Falls and the Leesburg Pike in Virginia was essential to Washington's plan of defense and had been rebuilt on rough stone piers that remain to this day.

chevron A sleeve badge of rank for noncommissioned officers (two stripes for corporals, three for sergeants) with embroidered emblems such as a small diamond or star further signifying different branches of service.

chloroform An anesthetic introduced by the British and used more widely for amputations than ether. Although shortages drove some surgeons to whiskey and stoic reserve, particularly in the South, Confederate hospitals even late in the war could usually count on captured supplies.

coffin plate The small piece of metal on a coffin's lid that carries the name of the deceased.

company Roughly a hundred men organized regionally from prewar militias, military schools, and early volunteers that retained close local ties and elected the company's captain and lieutenant, at least until promotion by merit and then service by subscription tightened army control.

contraband Any forbidden property that was shipped, traded, or confiscated during wartime. Union soldiers often found their packages from home inspected at headquarters for the contraband liquors they were not supposed to receive, and Confederate officers during the war's last months quietly allowed the contraband cotton trade that secured the drugs and food, especially bacon, their troops sorely needed. The term was also extended to the slaves of treasonous masters with no right to their return, a designation that began early in the war and was soon used by Northern newspapers to mean fugitive slaves who reached Union lines.

corn-husking Usually an evening occasion at harvest time, when plantation slaves were gathered in competing teams to remove corn husks, and planters made sure that the whiskey jug passed, singing began, and an all-night dinner and slave ball ensued.

corn pones Corn cakes cooked by slaves while their antebellum masters ate wheat biscuits. Deriving their name from the Indian *apohn* or bread, the cakes were often served with broth or grease and were carried in Confederate haversacks throughout the war.

corps Originally Napoleon's preferred unit for organizing armies of fifty thousand or more, a unit that was imported into Union and Confederate armies slowly so that corps commanders could be selected after battlefield experience proved their capacity to lead three to four divisions. Separated into several corps, an army could advance and forage over a wider front.

Cuffee A pervasive reference to a slave, which might come from the Ashanti name Kofi, from the African word for a male child born on Friday, or from the English slang *cove* or fellow.

division Three or four brigades commanded by a major-general and favored early by Confederate tacticians, until they likewise turned by 1862 to the larger corps. Divisions usually included artillery batteries, up to two cavalry regiments, and army cattle, which were often moved by division.

double-quicking A longer stride of up to 180 steps per minute that made advancing armies more mobile. On the battlefield, the greater speed once reserved for a bayonet charge made infantry attacks less vulnerable to the greater range and accuracy of defending rifles and yet more likely to lose their orderly pace in a mob rush.

dress-parade A camp review sounded by bugle call just before 6:00 P.M., when uniforms were inspected, shortcomings were reprimanded, and general orders were read concerning charges and courts-martial.

earthworks Fortifications made quickly from dirt and wood, which protected entrenched troops and their lines of communications even better when loopholes and head logs frustrated enemy sharpshooters.

echelon Ranked arrangement of infantry battalions that assured their steady progress in battle.

Election (or 'lecshun) cake A thick pancake first made during the eighteenth century in Hartford, Connecticut, where such cakes were sold by the baker's dozen during March town meetings to encourage voting the straight ticket.

en barbette An arrangement of mounted cannons that fired high and over a parapet rather than straight and through its opening.

ether An anesthetic whose use was promoted in Boston (beginning with tooth extractions in the 1840s) but did not spread quickly. During the 1850s, chloroform was favored in Philadelphia and more southerly states that resisted Boston practices, even though ether was less toxic and less dangerous to the lungs and the heart despite its combustibility.

euchre A card game for two or more players that was popular across the country, even among Southern ladies, who played a four-handed game as partners aiming for five points. Soldiers commonly gambled as they played, however, which is why the roads to battlefields were often littered with the playing cards they did not want relatives to find in their personal effects.

Examiner (Richmond) A powerful daily advocate of the Confederacy and yet a tart critic of Jefferson Davis's administration. Founded by the outspoken John M. Daniel in 1847, the newspaper was traded across picket lines and sold in Richmond prisons for 25 cents an issue or $1 a week, before folding as Union troops advanced on the city in 1865.

F.F.V.s (or First Families of Virginia) Old colonial families descended mainly from English merchants and sea captains of the seventeenth century, later remembered as aristocratic cavaliers when nineteenth-century New Englanders began celebrating their Puritan roots and Revolutionary fathers. With political tensions and class distinctions on the rise, Northerners used the abbreviation to deride the home-grown "chivalry" that began with families like the Byrds and Fitzhughs, the Pages and Fairfaxes, the Randolphs and Lees, who had made Virginia prominent.

fine-cut A wad of tobacco cut into thin strips for chewing.

flash novel A racy book about the artful dodging of thieves, gamblers, and harlots, particularly when dressed in outrageous imitation of upper-class finery. Tending toward cheap engravings and gaudy bindings, titles like J. D. Vose's *Seven Nights in Gotham* (1852) picked up the riotous slang that also characterized New York newspapers of the 1840s, like the *Sporting Whip* and the *Weekly Rake.*

flatiron A metal iron that could become red-hot on the stove or in front of the fire, which meant that it had to be picked up with a padded holder, cleaned repeatedly to remove soot and starch, and used

with care on large stretches of fabric (such as petticoats, shirts, and nightgowns) to prevent scorching.

fusillade Any outburst of firearms, from massed infantry rifles to mortar shelling.

Gilderoy A red-haired Scots lad or gillie (hence, "gillie roy") named Patrick MacGregor, a notorious highwayman whose "kite" or body was hanged in 1636 higher than those of his fellows.

goody-bread and cracklings A rich corn bread mixed with roasted pork rinds and generally made by slaves.

grape Artillery cluster charge consisting of iron balls, plates, and rings wrapped in canvas around a central bolt; when fired, the bolt broke to release a very effective shot up to several hundred yards.

graybacks Confederate soldiers in the short jackets of cadet gray worn early in the war, as they had been for decades at West Point. Union soldiers were quick to transfer the nickname to their inevitable lice.

greenbacks A common term for the paper money issued in the North after the Legal Tender Act of 1862. Named for the green ink used on their reverse side to stymie counterfeiters, greenbacks became a reliable national currency without the disastrous inflation produced by Confederate bluebacks, later called shucks as they grew more worthless.

guidon A swallow-tailed pennant used to identify a cavalry company or troop, generally of fringed damask about three feet wide and posted around pitched tents or on the line of march.

gunboats Small Union craft that were flat on the bottom, wide in the beam, and protected by an iron "turtle shell." Developed first on the Mississippi River, which they subsequently patrolled, gunboats were clunky enough in appearance to lend their name to the regulation shoes that Union soldiers wore.

hardtack A hard flour-and-water cracker roughly three inches square with small holes and often lots of maggots or weevils. A daily Union ration of nine to ten "worm castles" could be carried in a haversack and later cracked with a gun butt, crumbled into coffee, or fried in pork grease to make "skillygalee."

haversack A regulation bag of painted cloth roughly a foot square, big enough to carry ammunition, camp equipment, rations, and personal effects. Issued to Union troops and later captured by Confederate soldiers, haversacks outlasted the morocco cases, patent-leather satchels, and even bundled knapsacks that marching regiments soon threw away.

Herald (New York) The cheap and sensational newspaper founded in 1835 by James Gordon Bennett, whose Democratic politics and Southern sympathies meant its pages were long opposed to Lincoln and emancipation despite the paper's support for the war effort. With as many as thirty or forty special correspondents filing reports plus attention to business news, the *Herald* could claim a circulation of more than one hundred thousand in the United States and abroad, with particular influence in the South and Britain.

hominy A corn porridge named for an Indian word meaning "corn without skin" and later called grits when made from small-grained kernels that were soaked, boiled, and whitened, especially in the South.

India rubber Vulcanized rubber that was invented by Charles Goodyear in 1843 and first used by the army during the war with Mexico. Early in the Civil War, some regiments carried India rubber canteens, until they proved less resistant to heat than gourds. Waterproof blankets, which could also be worn as ponchos or laced together as shelters, enjoyed growing popularity, although performance reports were mixed.

"Injun" (or Indian) bread A bread or hoecake made in the South of Indian corn often mixed with eggs and wheat, rice, or rye meal.

jayhawking Marauding attacks to terrorize and plunder, particularly in Kansas and particularly to exterminate proslavery Missourians even before the war began.

Jessie scout A Union spy dressed in a Confederate uniform and named for Jessie Benton Fremont (wife of Union general and first Republican presidential candidate John Fremont), who suggested the ploy.

jobbing Undertaking work for a settled price, either as local labor or as large-scale wholesaling that delivered imported shipments to retailing merchants.

linseed poultice A concoction made to curb inflammation, reduce fever, ease weariness, or soothe pain, especially when the poultice was warmed.

Long Bridge A mile-long Potomac causeway and the main thorough-fare connecting Fourteenth Street with the Alexandria Road south. Later to become the Fourteenth Street Bridge, the wooden struc-ture was completed in 1809, rebuilt toll-free in the 1830s, and opened to railroad cars by 1861, when Federal regiments and their supplies began crossing the river into war.

long taw A marble game in which the taw, or shooter, is rolled along a lane at the marbles to be hit and taken.

Lucifers Wooden shafts about three inches long, one-sixth of an inch wide, and one-twentieth of an inch thick, whose London name around 1830 came from the Latin for "light-bringer."

magnetic patient One who sought to heal debility through the co-hesive charge of magnetic forces, especially after Friedrich Anton Mesmer at the end of the eighteenth century began passing a magnetic wand over sufferers in his perfumed consulting room.

malaria A disease commonly called ague or the shakes and widespread in the armies mobilized across the swampy land of the South, where poisonous vapors were blamed in-stead of the mosquitoes that soldiers called gallinippers.

mash Ground grain, often corn, that was boiled with water as a warm feed for horses and cattle or as a fermenting pulp on its way to becoming whiskey.

middling The poorer bacon or fatback that was cut from hogs butchered between the hams and the shoul-ders, generally as the meat ration of slaves.

Minié ball A conical lead bullet with a hollow base that was standard issue on both sides and that tore through rifled barrels and soft bodies to leave ugly wounds.

Mississippi sawyer A slave laborer who worked in the sawmills of Mis-sissippi's extensive pine forests, often from early light to sunset. In humid weather when tempera-tures ran high, moving raw lumber, firing boilers, and manning carriage blocks was backbreaking work, as was handling six- or seven-foot saws before postwar machinery eased their demands.

morphia An opiate that was infre-quently used by antebellum physi-cians.

mortar Short, squat rifled cannon that was effective at lobbing shells over enemy earthworks during a long-range attack or siege.

Murder Bay A growing slum between B Street and Pennsylvania Ave-nue, where smelly outhouses, the fetid Washington Canal, and the local fish market made swampy land squalid even before thousands of escaped slaves built wartime shanties and regiments of Federal troops camped near the prostitutes that General Joseph Hooker would try to curb.

musket Initially the smoothbore muzzle-loaders of the Mexican War and the Revolution, which were later rifled to increase accuracy, acceleration, and penetrating power. On the march, this main infantry weapon could also serve as a clothes line for soldiers fording streams and a bayonet post for bivouacking regiments putting up tents.

natural A simpleton who was thought to deserve kindness and protection by the 1840s, after Wordsworth's widely read poem "The Idiot Boy" (1802) portrayed such an innocent as uncorrupted and thus closer to pristine nature.

neuralgia Shooting pain along a nerve or, more generally, any painful debility and thus a handy term if diagnosis was vague or the mind seemed to be mysteriously at work.

Obeah (or Obi) A Caribbean religion born in Africa, like those who followed it in ever smaller numbers into the nineteenth century. Its secret magic for hire was available within slave communities for those seeking to heal or to harm.

parole d'honneur Literally "word of honor," which captured soldiers gave early in the war before prisons were set up. Initially, it was enough to swear not to aid the enemy or to bear arms until exchanged.

Parrott gun A cast-iron cannon that was rifled for greater accuracy and banded in wrought iron at the breech for greater reliability. The gun was cast by Robert P. Parrott in varying sizes that were occasionally unsound, especially as they grew larger; but they were always inexpensive and thus were among the weapons produced by the West Point Foundry in such numbers that it was said the national eagle should be replaced by the parrot.

percussion cap A small powder-filled metal cover that was inserted in a rifle's breech to ignite its charge when the hammer fell. Replacing earlier flints, percussion caps ensured better wet weather performance and an improved rate of fire.

phrenologist One versed in the twenty-seven to thirty-five mental faculties, such as memory and calculation, that could be specifically located in the cranium and measured on the head.

picket Guard along an army's periphery, where solitary soldiers watched for the reconnoitering enemy or, occasionally, became friendly enough across the fifty to one hundred yards separating army lines to exchange coffee and tobacco as well as newspapers and thus intelligence reports.

point in tierce The third of six fencing positions and one of the few positions from which saber attacks were customarily executed.

Port Tobacco A small town in southern Maryland where Confederate spies often crossed the Potomac into Virginia, and where John Wilkes

Booth later hid in the swamps after assassinating President Lincoln.

President's levee A decorous afternoon or evening gathering at the White House, where the President and the First Lady traditionally received visitors of all classes on an equal footing.

provost guard Military police, generally a company or two under the command of the provost-marshal.

provost-marshal The army's chief law-enforcer in the field, with jurisdiction over soldiers, prisoners, and anyone coming into camp.

quadrille An orderly dance of couples in the square formations popular at midcentury, before more unrestrained dances like the waltz swept in.

quinine The Civil War's popular "dose" for whatever ailed, from bowel troubles and toothaches to rheumatism and fevers. When quinine grew harder to come by in the blockaded South, malaria was treated with a mixture of whiskey and tonics made from tree bark, and even Northern surgeons used substitutes such as wild cherry syrup, blue pills, cod liver oil, or various combinations with whiskey.

ramrod A metal rod used to ram a bullet down a rifle barrel after a load of black powder, then removed unless an addled soldier forgot.

rebel buck A reference to the "buck and ball" combination of buckshot and round ball, a load suitable for the aging .69-caliber smoothbores that many Confederate soldiers brought into the war. Their muskets were inaccurate beyond fifty yards, but the load was so effective at close range that the 11th Kansas called their regimental newspaper the *Buck and Ball* when its single issue appeared in Arkansas during December 1862.

redoubt A field fortification, often a small temporary parapet that enabled defensive fire.

regiment Initially ten to twelve companies or just over a thousand volunteers drawn from the same state, until losses through battle, disease, and desertion soon reduced their number. New recruits and then conscripts usually formed new regiments of infantry, cavalry, or artillery, a practice that left older regiments and their colonels short on bodies if long on pride.

Regulations A revised edition of the manual on military discipline that General Winfield Scott assembled for the regular standing army in 1820, largely as a translation of French procedures under Napoleon. Updated for a burgeoning and mainly volunteer army in 1861, General George McClellan's *Regulations for the Army of the United States* was echoed in 1862 by a similar effort to organize citizen-soldiers in the Confederate states.

round shot Hollow globes of thin metal filled with lead or iron balls that showered long-range targets with deadly hail.

St. Vitus's dance A brain disease that produces convulsive movements, erratic speech, and growing madness.

sabre A traditional cavalry blade that grew shorter, lighter, and less effective during the course of the war, when ineptitude and reduced numbers as well as handier carbines generally transformed cavalry charges with greater consequence if less glamour.

schooner A swift two- or three-masted sailing vessel that was named for its capacity to "scoon" or skim the surface of Massachusetts waters, where the ship was first launched into American commerce in the early eighteenth century.

Scotch cap A small, visorless headdress made of wool with a tuft on top, which could be folded up and carried in a convenient pouch.

Scribbler's Scrap-Book A slighting and generic reference to gift books and literary miscellanies like *The Ladies' Scrap-Book*, which was published in Hartford during 1854. Such parlor literature reflected the popular pastime of compiling scrapbooks, a domestic pursuit shared by men, women, and young children.

Seven-Up A version of the English card game All Fours, which was brought to the colonies by English settlers and remained a favorite pastime through the nineteenth century until poker usurped its popularity. Two or three could play, or four in pairs, and they played in this variant until somebody scored seven points.

Sharp's rifles Generally breech-loading single-shot rifles made in the North by Christian Sharp and valued for their accuracy and rate of fire, which outstripped Confederate smoothbores and rifled muskets. Nearly ten thousand Model 1859 rifles were issued to Union infantry and almost eighty thousand shorter carbines were supplied for Union cavalry use.

sharpshooter A crack shot who could pick off a single enemy soldier at up to a mile and sometimes more, particularly with the telescopic sights, breech-loading rifles, and specialized ammunition that snipers were among the first to receive.

shebang A makeshift home assembled in the open air by Union soldiers, each of whom carried half a shelter tent that could be joined to form the "whole shebang" housing at least two. Confederate soldiers contrived more homemade structures for three or four out of whatever was on hand.

silver leaves The embroidered insignia of lieutenant colonels, which was sewn in the middle of the shoulder straps worn by officers.

six-pounder rifle A five-foot rifled cannon whose name carried the memory of the smoothbore's solid iron shot weighing six pounds. With new lightweight projectiles, the "pounder" came to refer less to projectile weight than to bore diameter, and with new cannons of larger sizes the six-pounder generally declined.

skiff A small boat with a flat bottom and a sharp nose that was cheap to build and, on rivers, as widely used in the nineteenth century as outboards are today.

skilpot A common pond turtle or terrapin with a small, striped, yellow head, apt to sun on a convenient log.

skirmish The irregular engagement of a small company of men, advancing cautiously behind trees and out of the brush to harass the enemy, either in clandestine attacks or in anticipation of more significant action to come.

slouched hat A soft felt hat with a wide brim favored by camp followers, Confederate soldiers, and even Union generals like Custer and Sheridan, who set aside a government-issue kepi for the greater comfort and protection of a civilian slouch.

sorghum A tasty cane syrup produced mainly in the West and then in the wartime South, where sugar supplies were diminished by the Union blockade and sugar plantations in Louisiana were occupied early on by Northern troops.

specie The coins or hard currency that guaranteed the value of treasury notes, although the South suspended redemption until war's end and thereby ensured runaway inflation.

spread-eagles The silver-embroidered insignia of full colonels, as well as the patriotic bombast that Civil War colonels often uttered as political appointees.

stag dance Camp dance without women, although soldiers sometimes borrowed bonnets and hoopskirts and often drank freely to enliven the cotillions and waltzes, polkas and jigs got up with banjo and fiddles.

straps Shoulder markings worn by Union officers in place of epaulettes and sometimes removed in the field to leave the smaller rank insignia that the enemy could not so readily discern.

sutler A civilian merchant in camp or nearby, whose premises might be a shack or a tent where off-duty soldiers gathered and whose prices for cookies and condensed milk, tobacco and stationery, playing cards and sutler's pies (among other foodstuffs and merchandise) were generally steep. Although most Northern regiments were assigned a sutler by army regulation, Southern troops with less money were increasingly lucky to find a roadside cart that sold pies and cakes.

traverse A barricade often constructed of earth to protect an artillery battery against attack from the sides.

Tribune (New York) The leading antislavery newspaper founded in 1841 by Horace Greeley and read daily by more than two hundred thousand, including Lincoln. In July 1863, New York mobs set fire to the newspaper's building out of fury at Greeley's Republican fervor and support for the Union draft.

trussel A rectangular wooden framework for a military bridge or railroad track, which was engineered by combining vertical and diagonal support timbers (often precut) to intercept the semicircular arches that helped distribute heavy loads.

very old Tommy Likely a reference to the soldier's or workman's daily food allowance, especially of the soft bread (instead of biscuit or hardtack) that could easily grow stale.

vidette Mounted guard that communicated enemy movements by signal and thus also the name of a soldier newspaper, printed in 1862 by John Morgan's men as they moved with the Confederate general from Tennessee to Kentucky and back again.

Washington cake Traditionally the holiday confection made at Mount Vernon from raisins and currants, candied fruit and lemon juice, brandy and sherry, and the whites of forty eggs beaten with a bundle of twigs.

Washington Canal A waterway meant to secure Washington's commercial prosperity by linking the Potomac River and the Eastern Branch (later the Anacostia River) and thus bringing canal traffic within sight of the Capitol. Begun in 1810 after financing delays that would recur, the Washington Canal was opened in 1815 and connected in 1833 to the Chesapeake and Ohio Canal and its

promise of national commerce; but tides and debris confounded maintenance, city politics and Congressional inattention stymied progress, and contractors by the 1850s were so open-handed and unreliable that the canal had become a virtual sewer, whose stinking trench along Constitution Avenue (then B Street) would be filled in permanently once hearings began in the 1870s.

Whitworth projectile An iron hexagonal shot for the largely Confederate cannon designed by Sir Joseph Whitworth, whose unusual rifling gave his "bolts" remarkable distance, impressive accuracy, and an unnerving sound.

yawl A long, light boat usually propelled by four or six oars.

Zouaves Often, antebellum militia companies from such states as New York, Pennsylvania, and Illinois, where they copied the baggy red trousers, tight blue jackets, and tasseled fezes of French North African troops. More sprightly than combat-ready in the war's early months, the New York Fire Zouaves nonetheless suffered the Union's first casualty in action when Colonel Elmer Ellsworth attempted to take down a Confederate flag at Alexandria's Marshall House.

BIBLIOGRAPHIC ESSAY

Both the headnotes and the glossary entries in this collection are indebted to sources that deserve acknowledgment and that may themselves interest students of the war. Where particular stories are intriguing, it may also help to know whose research provides a likely place to begin further study, especially as the voluminous scholarship on the Civil War, ambient culture, and wartime literature continues to grow. What follows is an effort to "walk chalk," as Twain's Aunt Rachel might say, from the war's prelude to its aftermath.

For the antebellum clash at homesteads like "The Cabin at Pharaoh's Ford" and the vicious attacks that would ensue as the crisis in Kansas became grim, see Don E. Fehrenbacher, "Kansas, Republicanism, and the Crisis of the Union," in *Sectional Crisis and Southern Constitutionalism* (Baton Rouge: Lousiana State University Press, 1995), 45–65; Gary L. Cheatham, " 'Desperate Characters': The Development and Impact of the Confederate Guerrillas in Kansas," *Kansas History* 14 (1991): 144–61; and Michael Fellman, *Inside War: The Guerrilla Conflict in Missouri During the American Civil War* (New York: Oxford University Press, 1989), especially 3–22. The most reliable account of the underground railroad remains Larry Gara, *The Liberty Line: The Legend of the Underground Railroad* (Lexington: University of Kentucky Press, 1961), which is usefully supplemented by James R. Shortridge, *Peopling the Plains: Who Settled Where in Frontier Kansas* (Lawrence: University Press of Kansas, 1995), 15–45; and Richard B. Sheridan, "From Slavery in Missouri to Freedom in Kansas: The Influx of Black Fugitives and Contrabands into Kansas, 1854–1865," *Kansas History* 12 (1989): 28–47. Estimates of fugitive migration via the midwestern "train," now hard to verify, are cited in Stephen B. Oates, *To Purge This Land with Blood: A Biography of John Brown* (New York: Harper and Row, 1970), 259; pertinent correspondence is reprinted in Wilbur H. Siebert, *The Underground Railroad from Slavery to Freedom* (1898; rpt. New York: Russell and Russell, 1967), 347–50. For the widespread convergence of antislavery imperatives and domestic ideology, see Karen Sanchez-Eppler, *Touching Liberty: Abolition, Feminism, and the Politics of the Body* (Berkeley: University of California Press, 1993), 14–49; Carolyn L. Karcher, "Rape, Murder, and Revenge in 'Slavery's Pleasant Homes': Lydia Maria Child's Antislavery Fiction and the Limits of Genre," in Shirley Samuels, ed., *The Culture of Sentiment: Race, Gender, and Sentimentality in Nineteenth-Century America* (New York: Oxford University Press, 1992), 58–72; and Gillian Brown, *Domestic Individualism: Imagining Self in Nineteenth-Century America* (Berkeley: University of California Press, 1990), 13–38.

Margaret Leech provides a lively description of the disarray that pervades "Job and the Bug" in *Reveille in Washington, 1860–1865* (1941; rpt. New York: Carroll and Graf, 1991), 1–86. Also illuminating are Constance McLaughlin Green, *Washington: Village and Capital, 1800–1878* (Princeton, NJ: Princeton University Press, 1962), 1: 230–43; Benjamin Franklin Cooling, *Symbol, Sword, and Shield: Defending Washington During the Civil War* (Shippensburg, PA: White Mane, 1991), 1–42; Donald Beekman Myer, *Bridges and the City of Washington* (Washington, DC: U.S. Commission of Fine Arts, 1974); Cornelius W. Heine, "The Washington City Canal," *Records of the Columbia Historical Society* 53–56 (1953–56): 1–27; and, on nearby unrest, Robert I. Cottom Jr. and Mary Ellen Hayward, *Maryland in the Civil War: A House Divided* (Baltimore: Maryland Historical Society and Johns Hopkins University Press, 1994); and Harold R. Manakee Jr., *Maryland in the Civil War* (Baltimore: Maryland Historical Society, 1961). Several other volumes have been particularly useful, here and throughout this collection, in recalling what magazine readers once knew: Dorothy Denneen Volo and James M. Volo, *Daily Life in Civil War America* (Westport, CT: Greenwood Press, 1998); Benjamin W. Bacon, *Sinews of War: How Technology, Industry, and Transportation Won the Civil War* (Novato, CA: Presidio Press, 1997); Paddy Griffith, *Battle Tactics of the Civil War* (New Haven: Yale University Press, 1989); Herman Hattaway and Archer Jones, *How the North Won: A Military History of the Civil War* (Urbana: University of Illinois Press, 1983); H. L. Scott, *Military Dictionary* (1861; rpt. Westport, CT: Greenwood Press, 1968); Phillis Cunningham and Catherine Lucas, *Costumes for Births, Marriages, and Deaths* (London: A. and C. Black, 1972); John H. Young, *Our Deportment: or, The Manners, Conduct, and Dress of the Most Refined Society* (Chicago: Union Publishing, 1882); and *The Manners That Win, Compiled from the Latest Authorities* (Minneapolis: Buckeye, 1880). For the euphoria of the war's early months, see Maury Klein, *Days of Defiance: Sumter, Secession, and the Coming of the Civil War* (New York: Knopf, 1997); and Mark Wahlgren Summers, " 'Freedom and Law Must Die Ere They Sever': The North and the Coming of the Civil War," in Gabor S. Boritt, ed., *Why the Civil War Came* (New York: Oxford University Press, 1996), 177–200.

For the heady days of "A True and Simple Tale of '61," when Fort Sumter fell and Confederate patriotism abounded, see Gary W. Gallagher, *The Confederate War* (Cambridge, MA: Harvard University Press, 1997), 63–111; Larry M. Logue, *To Appomattox and Beyond: The Civil War Soldier in War and Peace* (Chicago: Ivan R. Dee, 1996), 18–30; George C. Rable, *The Confederate Republic: A Revolution against Politics* (Chapel Hill: University of North Carolina Press, 1994), 20–38; and Drew Gilpin Faust, *The Creation of Confederate Nationalism: Ideology and*

Identity in the Civil War South (Baton Rouge: Louisiana State University Press, 1988), 22–40. The vigorous response of Southern women may be examined in Drew Gilpin Faust, Thavolia Glymph, and George C. Rable, "A Woman's War: Southern Women in the Civil War," in Edward D. C. Campbell Jr. and Kym S. Rice, eds., *A Woman's War: Southern Women, Civil War, and the Confederate Legacy* (Richmond, VA: Museum of the Confederacy; Charlottesville: University Press of Virginia, 1996), 1–27; and Anne Firor Scott, *The Southern Lady: From Pedestal to Politics, 1830–1930* (Charlottesville: University Press of Virginia, 1995), 80–102. For the larger effort to organize a Confederate medical service and for the subsequent treatment of Southern soldiers, see Frank R. Freemon, *Gangrene and Glory: Medical Care During the American Civil War* (Madison, NJ: Fairleigh Dickinson University Press, 1998), 28–34, 77–83, 124–33, 147–59, 214–20; *"Every Kind of . . . Wound and Disease": Hospital Life within the Confederate Medical Department* (Richmond, VA: Museum of the Confederacy, 1997); Glenna R. Schroeder-Lein, *Confederate Hospitals on the Move: Samuel H. Stout and the Army of Tennessee* (Columbia: University of South Carolina Press, 1994); Horace H. Cunningham, *Field Medical Services at the Battles of Manassas* (Athens: University of Georgia Press, 1968), especially 23–41; and Bell I. Wiley, *The Life of Johnny Reb: The Common Soldier of the Confederacy* (Indianapolis: Bobbs-Merrill, 1943), 244–69. Shelby Foote's description of the Manassas "panorama" appears in *The Civil War: A Narrative*, 1: *Fort Sumter to Perryville* (New York: Vintage–Random House, 1986), 78; Drew Gilpin Faust's assessment of the "foundations of personal identity" is elaborated in *Mothers of Invention: Women of the Slaveholding South in the American Civil War* (Chapel Hill: University of North Carolina Press, 1996), 3.

The rush to enlist that unsettles "Ellen" and the subsequent camp life of Union troops are remembered in John D. Billings, *Hardtack and Coffee, or, The Unwritten Story of Army Life* (1887; rpt. Lincoln: University of Nebraska Press, 1993), 34–89; Daniel E. Sutherland, *The Expansion of Everyday Life, 1860–1876* (New York: Harper and Row, 1989), 1–26; and Bell I. Wiley, *The Life of Billy Yank: The Common Soldier of the Union* (Indianapolis: Bobbs-Merrill, 1952), 17–65. Reid Mitchell describes the army's "substitute families" in *The Vacant Chair: The Northern Soldier Leaves Home* (New York: Oxford University Press, 1993), 158. For the manner in which regiments were supplied during the war, see David Michael Delo, *Peddlers and Post Traders: The Army Sutler on the Frontier* (Salt Lake City: University of Utah Press, 1992), 101–38; and Erna Risch, *Quartermaster Support of the Army: A History of the Corps, 1775–1939* (Washington, DC: Center of Military History, U.S. Army, 1989), 333–452. For the nineteenth-century place of "naturals" like Ellen, see James W. Trent Jr., *Inventing the Feeble Mind: A History of Mental Retardation in the United States* (Berkeley: University of California Press, 1994), 7–39. For related studies of wartime children rather than the childlike, see Emmy E. Werner, *Reluctant Witnesses: Children's Voices from the Civil War* (Boulder, CO: Westview

Press, 1998); and James Marten, *The Children's Civil War* (Chapel Hill: University of North Carolina Press, 1998).

For accounts of the first battle with staggering casualties, a toll that "Hopeful Tackett—His Mark" reckons with obliquely, see Larry J. Daniel, *Shiloh: The Battle That Changed the Civil War* (New York: Simon and Schuster, 1997); Joseph Allan Frank and George A. Reaves, *"Seeing the Elephant": Raw Recruits at the Battle of Shiloh* (Westport, CT: Greenwood Press, 1989); and James M. McPherson, *Battle Cry of Freedom: The Civil War Era* (New York: Oxford University Press, 1988), 392–414, one of many discussions that make McPherson's single-volume history of the war essential reading. Also useful in evaluating the early and consequential war in the West is Benjamin Franklin Cooling, *Fort Donelson's Legacy: War and Society in Kentucky and Tennessee, 1862–1863* (Knoxville: University of Tennessee Press, 1997), especially 26–57. To discover who enlisted in the North and what Union soldiers apparently fought for, particularly after Shiloh, see James M. McPherson, *For Cause and Comrades: Why Men Fought in the Civil War* (New York: Oxford University Press, 1997), especially 163–78; Logue, *To Appomattox and Beyond*, 3–17; Reid Mitchell, *Civil War Soldiers* (New York: Viking, 1988), especially 56–89; Gerald F. Linderman, *Embattled Courage: The Experience of Combat in the American Civil War* (New York: Free Press, 1987), especially 61–79; Maris A. Vinovskis, "Have Social Historians Lost the Civil War? Some Preliminary Demographic Speculations," in Maris A. Vinovskis, ed., *Toward a Social History of the American Civil War: Exploratory Essays* (New York: Cambridge University Press, 1990), 1–30; and, for another perspective on the "Star-Spangle' Banger," Scot M. Guenter, *The American Flag, 1777–1924: Cultural Shifts from Creation to Codification* (Rutherford, NJ: Fairleigh Dickinson University Press, 1990), 66–87. Melville's line from "Shiloh" is cited and "guns in the West" are discussed in Stanton Garner, *The Civil War World of Herman Melville* (Lawrence: University Press of Kansas, 1993), 137–46. Timothy Sweet examines the poem as part of Melville's *Battle-Pieces* and a damaged pastoral tradition in *Traces of War: Poetry, Photography, and the Crisis of the Union* (Baltimore: Johns Hopkins University Press, 1990), 165–200.

The spirited commerce at the mouth of the Mississippi that makes New Yorkers drool in "Thomas Elliott's Speculations" is described by Stephen R. Wise, whose brisk observation about New Orleans as an international entrepôt may be found in *Lifeline of the Confederacy: Blockade Running During the Civil War* (Columbia: University of South Carolina Press, 1988), 21. For other blockade alternatives, see James W. Daddysman, *The Matamoros Trade: Confederate Commerce, Diplomacy, and Intrigue* (Newark: University of Delaware Press, 1984); Stanley Lebergott, "Through the Blockade: The Profitability and Extent of Cotton Smuggling, 1861–1865," *Journal of Economic History* 41 (1981): 867–88; and, for a discussion of the covert trade in cotton, Paul W. Gates, *Agriculture and the Civil War* (New York: Knopf, 1965), 105–8, 125–26. The Confederacy's loss of a key port is chronicled in Chester G. Hearn, *The Capture of New Orleans, 1862* (Baton Rouge: Louisiana State University Press, 1995). New York's wartime economic role is examined in Edwin G. Burrows and Mike Wallace, *Gotham: A History of New York City to 1898* (New York: Oxford University Press, 1999), 864–82; Charles R. Geisst, *Wall Street: A History* (New York: Oxford University Press, 1997), 35–63; and Ernest A. McKay, *The Civil War and New York City* (Syracuse: Syracuse University Press, 1990), 94–103. When a slip of paper in Perkins's story can throw everything "higher than Gilderoy flew his kite," it is worth noting that nineteenth-century colloquialisms are glossed in a number of key sources: Charles Earle Funk, *A Hog on Ice and Other Curious Expressions* (New York: Harper and Row, 1948); John S. Farmer and W. E. Henley, *Slang and Its Analogues, Past and Present* (London: By subscription, 1890–1904); John S. Farmer, *Americanisms — Old and New: A Dictionary of Words, Phrases, and Colloquialisms* (London: Privately printed by Thomas Poulter, 1889); M. Schele De Vere, *Americanisms; The English of the New World* (New York: Scribner, 1872); and, up to the PS, Frederic G. Cassidy, ed., *Dictionary of American Regional English* (Cambridge, MA: Belknap–Harvard University Press, 1985–).

The protracted occupation of New Orleans and the corrosive effect that "Mrs. F.'s Waiting Maid" reveals are examined in Faust, *Mothers of Invention*, especially "To Relieve My Bottled Wrath," 196–219; Stephen V. Ash, *When the Yankees Came: Conflict and Chaos in the Occupied South, 1861–1865* (Chapel Hill: University of North Carolina Press, 1995), 76–107; Gerald M. Capers, *Occupied City: New Orleans under the Federals, 1862–1865* (Lexington: University of Kentucky Press, 1965); and, more generally, George C. Rable, *Civil Wars: Women and the Crisis of Southern Nationalism* (Urbana: University of Illinois Press, 1991), especially "Duty, Honor, and Frustration: The Dilemmas of Female Patriotism," 136–53. Mary P. Ryan theorizes the increasingly haphazard line between public and private for those in New Orleans and well beyond in *Women in Public: Between Banners and Ballots, 1825–1880* (Baltimore: Johns Hopkins University Press, 1990), 130–71. The unique position of the city's several Creole populations is considered in Joseph G. Tregle Jr., "Creoles and Americans," in Arnold R. Hirsch and Joseph Logsdon, eds., *Creole New Orleans: Race and Americanization* (Baton Rouge: Louisiana State University Press, 1992), 131–85. For the perpetual difficulty of defining the term creole, see Berndt Ostendorf, "Creolization and Creoles: The Concepts and Their History," in John Lowe, ed., *Pelican Eyes: Louisiana Culture and the Nation* (Jackson: University Press of Mississippi, submitted). Unusual in its polyglot settlement, New Orleans nonetheless proved instructive in its covert activities; for the wider role of the war's female spies, South and North, see Elizabeth Young, *Disarming the Nation: Women's Writing and the American Civil War* (Chicago: University of Chicago Press, 1999), 149–94; and Lyde Cullen Sizer, "Acting Her Part: Narratives of Union Women Spies," in Catherine Clinton and Nina Silber, eds., *Divided Houses: Gender and the Civil War* (New York: Oxford University Press, 1992), 114–33. Sharon Kennedy-

Nolle's shrewd observation may be found in her "Introduction to the 1998 Edition," *Belle Boyd in Camp and Prison* (Baton Rouge: Louisiana State University Press, 1998), 17.

The more supernatural disturbances of "Believe in Ghosts!" are considered further and well beyond the years of the Civil War in Daniel Cottom, *Abyss of Reason: Cultural Movements, Revelations, and Betrayals* (New York: Oxford University Press, 1991), especially "The Experience of Personation," 50–77. See, too, Barbara M. Weisberg, "They Spoke with the Dead," *American Heritage* 50 (September 1999): 84–92; Stephen Prothero, "From Spiritualism to Theosophy: 'Uplifting' a Democratic Tradition," *Religion and American Culture* 3 (1993): 197–216; Ruth Brandon, *The Spiritualists: The Passion for the Occult in the Nineteenth and Twentieth Centuries* (London: Weidenfeld and Nicolson, 1983), especially "Knock, Knock, Who's There?", 1–41; Ernest Isaacs, "The Fox Sisters and American Spiritualism," in Howard Kerr and Charles L. Crow, eds., *The Occult in America: New Historical Perspectives* (Urbana: University of Illinois Press, 1983), 79–110; and R. Laurence Moore, *In Search of White Crows: Spiritualism, Parapsychology, and American Culture* (New York: Oxford University Press, 1977), especially "Nineteenth-Century Spiritualism: The Foundation of Its Appeal," 3–39. For greater skepticism about the paranormal and useful discussions of mental states, including "brain fever," see German E. Berrios, "Delirium and Cognate States: Clinical Section" and Stephen Jacyna, "Delirium and Cognate States: Social Section," in German E. Berrios and Roy Porter, eds., *A History of Clinical Psychiatry: The Origin and History of Psychiatric Disorders* (New York: New York University Press, 1995), 3–22, 23–33. For the differing experiences of standing picket, see James I. Robertson Jr., *Soldiers Blue and Gray* (Columbia: University of South Carolina Press, 1988), 58–59, 139–44; and David Kaser, *Books and Libraries in Camp and Battle: The Civil War Experience* (Westport, CT: Greenwood Press, 1984), 83–87.

The place of scouts in military operations like the nip and tuck described in "The Sergeant's Little Story" is evaluated by Edwin C. Fishel in *The Secret War for the Union: The Untold Story of Military Intelligence in the Civil War* (Boston: Houghton Mifflin, 1996), 1–7, 569–71; Fishel's comments are usefully augmented by William A. Tidwell, *April '65: Confederate Covert Action in the American Civil War* (Kent, OH: Kent State University Press, 1995), 30–56; and Charles E. Taylor, "The Signal and Secret Service of the Confederate States," *Confederate Veteran* 40 (1932): 302–5, 338–41. For the origins of India rubber and slang uses of buckhorn knives, see Bill Bryson, *Made in America* (London: Secker and Warburg, 1994), 107–8, 320; for their Civil War use, see Risch, *Quartermaster Support of the Army,* 358–59, on India rubber; and Wiley, *The Life of Johnny Reb,* 295, on Confederate knives. Wartime card games and the sergeant's other pastimes are discussed in Volo and Volo, *Daily Life in Civil War America,* 145–47; Billings, *Hardtack and Coffee,* 61–72; Wiley, *The Life of Billy Yank,* 247–74; and Wiley, *The Life of Johnny Reb,*

36–58. See Schele De Vere, *Americanisms*, 327, for the German roots and "universal popularity" of euchre.

The most comprehensive study of the battle that "On the Antietam" portrays is still Stephen W. Sears, *Landscape Turned Red: The Battle of Antietam* (New York: Ticknor and Fields, 1983), where the lingering memory of the silence once the battle ceased is noted (335). For the further experience of combatants, see John Michael Priest, *Antietam: The Soldiers' Battle* (New York: Oxford University Press, 1994); more evaluative assessments may be found in Gary W. Gallagher, ed., *Antietam: Essays on the 1862 Maryland Campaign* (Kent, OH: Kent State University Press, 1989). Because the engagement occurred roughly sixty miles from Washington, where Mathew Brady's operatives were ready to haul the equipment and supplies they needed to the field, the battle of Antietam has left a particularly rich photographic record. See William A. Frassanito, *Antietam: The Photographic Legacy of America's Bloodiest Day* (New York: Scribner, 1978), especially 37–54; Alexander Gardner, *Gardner's Photographic Sketch Book of the Civil War* (1866; rpt. New York: Dover, 1959), plates 19–23, with Gardner's own text; and Oliver Wendell Holmes, "My Hunt after 'the Captain,' " *Atlantic Monthly* 10 (December 1862): 738–64. For the competing and surprisingly picturesque view that special artists brought to illustrated magazines, see Frank H. Schell, "As an Artist Saw Antietam," *Civil War Times Illustrated* 8 (June 1969): 14–22; William P. Campbell, *The Civil War: A Centennial Exhibition of Eyewitness Drawings* (Washington, DC: National Gallery of Art, 1961); Edwin Forbes, *Thirty Years After: An Artist's Story of the Great War* (New York: Fords, Howard, and Hulbert, 1890), 257–58; and Theodore R. Davis, "How a Battle Is Sketched," *St. Nicholas* 16 (July 1889): 661–68.

The immediate consequences of emancipation that "A Letter from the Country" helps trace are discussed by Phillip Shaw Paludan in *"A People's Contest": The Union and Civil War, 1861–1865* (Lawrence: University Press of Kansas, 1996), where his observation about the stakes for white Americans appears (198). See, too, David W. Blight and Brooks D. Simpson, eds., *Union and Emancipation: Essays on Politics and Race in the Civil War Era* (Kent, OH: Kent State University Press, 1997); Mark Grimsley, *The Hard Hand of War: Union Military Policy toward Southern Civilians, 1861–1865* (New York: Cambridge University Press, 1995), 120–41; James M. McPherson, " 'The War Will Never End Until We End Slavery,' " in *What They Fought For, 1861–1865* (Baton Rouge: Louisiana State University Press, 1994), 47–69; Frank McGlynn and Seymour Drescher, eds., *The Meaning of Freedom: Economics, Politics, and Culture after Slavery* (Pittsburgh: University of Pittsburgh Press, 1992); and David W. Blight, "No Desperate Hero: Manhood and Freedom in a Union Soldier's Experience," in Clinton and Silber, *Divided Houses*, 55–75. John Hope Franklin pays particular attention to Lincoln's document and the "hundred days" between announcement and signature in *The Emancipation Proclamation*

(Wheeling, IL: Harlan Davidson, 1995), 47–78. Those interested will find a recipe for Washington cake in *The American Heritage Cookbook and Illustrated History of American Eating and Drinking* (New York: American Heritage; Simon and Schuster, 1964), 602; a recipe for 'Lecshun or Election cake may be found in Imogene Wolcott, ed., *The Yankee Cook Book* (New York: Coward-McCann, 1939), 252–53.

The three branches of military service that "T. J.'s Cavalry Charge" describes are examined in Robertson, *Soldiers Blue and Gray*, where the decisive role of the infantry is acknowledged (19). For an account of the "fun and fury on the field" that draws all three branches together, see Carlton McCarthy, *Detailed Minutiae of Soldier Life in the Army of Northern Virginia, 1861–1865* (1882; rpt. Lincoln: University of Nebraska Press, 1993), 94–115. More particular attention may be found in Thomas S. Dickey and Peter C. George, *Field Artillery Projectiles of the American Civil War* (Atlanta, GA: Arsenal Press, 1980); Stephen Z. Starr, "Cold Steel: The Saber and the Union Cavalry," in John T. Hubbell, ed., *Battles Lost and Won: Essays from "Civil War History"* (Westport, CT: Greenwood Press, 1975), 107–24; "Infantry Equipments," *Army and Navy Journal* 1 (28 November 1863): 213; and, for an overview of related scholarship, Joseph T. Glatthaar, "Battlefield Tactics," in James M. McPherson and William J. Cooper Jr., eds., *Writing the Civil War: The Quest to Understand* (Columbia: University of South Carolina Press, 1998), 60–80. Billings pegs less vigorous soldiers like McSnorter in *Hardtack and Coffee* when he describes "Jonahs and Beats," 90–107.

The unsuspected bravery that "Colonel Charley's Wife" reveals has prompted considerable research in recent years. For revised estimates of cross-dressed military service, see Elizabeth D. Leonard, *All the Daring of the Soldier: Women of the Civil War Armies* (New York: Norton, 1999), 165, 310–311 n. 2; and DeAnne Blanton, "Women Soldiers of the Civil War," *Prologue* 25 (spring 1993): 27. In the growing field of additional scholarship, see Young, *Disarming the Nation*, 149–94; Lauren Cook Burgess, introduction to *An Uncommon Soldier: The Civil War Letters of Sarah Rosetta Wakeman, alias Private Lyons Wakeman, 153rd Regiment, New York State Volunteers, 1862–1864* (New York: Oxford University Press, 1996), 1–13; Thomas P. Lowry, *The Story the Soldiers Wouldn't Tell: Sex in the Civil War* (Mechanicsburg, PA: Stackpole Books, 1994), 118–22; and Janet E. Kaufman, " 'Under the Petticoat Flag': Women Soldiers in the Confederate Army," *Southern Studies* 23 (1984): 363–75. For a sense of the partisan fervor in "Mosby's Confederacy," see Jeffry D. Wert, *Mosby's Rangers* (New York: Simon and Schuster, 1990), 114–27.

The first three days in July 1863 and the war's pivotal battle in Pennsylvania continue to receive exceptional attention, particularly the headlong charge by George E. Pickett that both "The Fourteenth at Gettysburg" and "Lee at Gettysburg" describe. Of recent note are Jeffry D. Wert, *Gettysburg: Day Three* (New York: Simon and Schuster: 2001); Michael Fellman, *The Making of Robert E. Lee*

(New York: Random House, 2000), 141–64; Peter S. Carmichael, "'Every Map of the Field Cries Out about It': The Failure of Confederate Artillery at Pickett's Charge," and Gary M. Kross, "'I Do Not Believe That Pickett's Division Would Have Reached Our Line': Henry J. Hunt and the Union Artillery on July 3, 1863," in Gary W. Gallagher, ed., *Three Days at Gettysburg: Essays on Confederate and Union Leadership* (Kent, OH: Kent State University Press, 1999), 270–83, 284–305; John Michael Priest, *Into the Fight: Pickett's Charge at Gettysburg* (Shippensburg, PA: White Mane, 1998); Gabor S. Boritt, ed., *The Gettysburg Nobody Knows* (New York: Oxford University Press, 1997); Emory M. Thomas, *Robert E. Lee, A Biography* (New York: Norton, 1995), 287–303; Kathy Georg Harrison and John W. Busey, *Nothing but Glory: Pickett's Division at Gettysburg* (Gettysburg, PA: Thomas Publications, 1993). The kaleidoscopic aftermath of Lee's defeat has also been examined with care; see Gary W. Gallagher, "Lee's Army Has Not Lost Any of Its Prestige: The Impact of Gettysburg on the Army of Northern Virginia and the Confederate Home Front," and A. Wilson Greene, "From Gettysburg to Falling Waters: Meade's Pursuit of Lee," in Gary W. Gallagher, ed., *The Third Day at Gettysburg and Beyond* (Chapel Hill: University of North Carolina Press, 1994), 1–30, 161–201; Gregory A. Coco, *A Strange and Blighted Land: Gettysburg, The Aftermath of a Battle* (Gettysburg, PA: Thomas Publications, 1998); Garry Wills, *Lincoln at Gettysburg: The Words That Remade America* (New York: Simon and Schuster, 1992); and John W. Busey, *These Honored Dead: The Union Casualties at Gettysburg* (Hightstown, NJ: Longstreet House, 1996). Like Antietam, Gettysburg was immediately photographed with disquieting results, as William A. Frassanito has twice demonstrated; see *Early Photography at Gettysburg* (Gettysburg, PA: Thomas Publications, 1995), and *Gettysburg: A Journey in Time* (New York: Scribner, 1975). Just as comprehensive in scope is Carol Reardon, *Pickett's Charge in History and Memory* (Chapel Hill: University of North Carolina Press, 1997), where the stirring sight from Cemetery Hill is described (19). What Billings had to say about army wagons may be found in *Hardtack and Coffee*, 350–76, including his engaging description (352).

The most nuanced study of the sudden upheaval in "Three Days of Terror" is Iver Bernstein, *The New York City Draft Riots: Their Significance for American Society and Politics in the Age of the Civil War* (New York: Oxford University Press, 1990), where the tenor and spread of the protest is first acknowledged (5) and then examined from the perspective of the rioters (17–42) as well as the tonier classes (43–72). For further coverage, see James W. Geary, *We Need Men: The Union Draft in the Civil War* (DeKalb: Northern Illinois University Press, 1991), especially 103–115; and Adrian Cook, *The Armies of the Streets: The New York City Draft Riots of 1863* (Lexington: University Press of Kentucky, 1974); as well as the briefer discussion of civil disorder and its municipal aftermath in Burrows and Wallace, *Gotham*, 887–99; and McKay, *The Civil War and New York City*, 195–215. Peter Levine offers a more statistical approach to Union conscription in "Draft Evasion in the North during the Civil War, 1863–1865," *Journal of American History* 67 (March 1981): 816–34. For the activities of women as urban violence grew, see Mary P. Ryan, *Civic Wars: Democracy and Public Life in the American City during the Nineteenth Century* (Berkeley: University of California Press, 1997), 135–80.

The storied assault on Fort Wagner and the cresting fortunes of "our boys" that "The Brothers" celebrates are examined in Martin H. Blatt, Thomas J. Brown, and Donald Yacovone, eds., *Hope and Glory: Essays on the Legacy of the Fifty-Fourth Massachusetts Regiment* (Boston: Massachusetts Historical Society; Amherst: University of Massachusetts Press, 2001); James M. McPherson, "The *Glory* Story," in *Drawn With the Sword: Reflections on the American Civil War* (New York: Oxford University Press, 1996), 99–109; Luis F. Emilio, *A Brave Black Regiment: The History of the Fifty-Fourth Regiment of Massachusetts Volunteer Infantry, 1863–1865* (1891; rpt. New York: DaCapo Press, 1995); Jim Cullen, " 'I's a Man Now': Gender and African American Men," in Clinton and Silber, *Divided Houses*, 76–91; and J. M. W. Appleton, "That Night at Fort Wagner. By One Who Was There," *Putnam's* (July 1869): 9–16. For the recuperative role of women like Nurse Dane and their fitful challenge to gendered norms, see Freemon, *Gangrene and Glory*, 35–40, 84–91; Elizabeth D. Leonard, *Yankee Women: Gender Battles in the Civil War* (New York: Norton, 1994), 3–49; Jane E. Schultz, "The Inhospitable Hospital: Gender and Professionalism in Civil War Medicine," *Signs* 17 (1992): 363–92; Kristie Ross, "Arranging a Doll's House: Refined Women as Union Nurses," in Clinton and Silber, *Divided Houses*, 97–113; Glenna Matthews, *The Rise of Public Woman: Woman's Power and Woman's Place in the United States, 1630–1970* (New York: Oxford University Press, 1992), 120–46; and Lori D. Ginzberg, *Women and the Work of Benevolence: Morality, Politics, and Class in the Nineteenth-Century United States* (New Haven: Yale University Press, 1990), 133–73. Alcott's own observation may be found in *Hospital Sketches* (1869; rpt. Boston: Applewood Books, 1986), 74. The increasing literary attention her volume has received may be sampled in Young, *Disarming the Nation*, 69–108; Mary Cappello, " 'Looking about Me with All My Eyes': Censored Viewing, Carnival, and Louisa May Alcott's *Hospital Sketches*," *Arizona Quarterly* 50 (autumn 1994): 59–88; and Jane E. Schultz, "Embattled Care: Narrative Authority in Louisa May Alcott's *Hospital Sketches*," *Legacy* 9 (1992): 104–18.

For the prevailing views of wartime trauma and the treatment of pain that Silas Weir Mitchell and "The Case of George Dedlow" helped revolutionize, see Freemon, *Gangrene and Glory*, 46–50, 192–96; Chris Alam and H. Mersky, "What's in a Name? The Cycle of Change in the Meaning of Neuralgia," *History of Psychiatry* 5 (1994): 429–74; Martin S. Pernick, *A Calculus of Suffering: Pain, Professionalism, and Anesthesia in Nineteenth-Century America* (New York: Columbia University Press, 1985), especially 93–124; and Silas Weir Mitchell, George R. Morehouse, and William W. Keen, *Gunshot Wounds and Other Injuries of the Nerves* (Philadelphia: Lippincott, 1864). For the less scientific practices that eased trauma as well, see Bret E. Carroll, *Spiritualism in Antebellum America* (Bloomington: Indiana University Press, 1997), 120–51; and Ann Braude, *Radical Spirits: Spiritualism and Women's Rights in Nineteenth-Century America* (Boston: Beacon Press, 1989). Lisa A. Long's revealing observation about the dimensions of psychic loss appears in her paper, " 'When the sensation Lenses become destroyed': S. Weir Mitchell's Civil War Medicine," MLA Convention, 1995; a similar attention to physical trauma and Mitchell's narrative audacity may be found in Laura Otis, *Membranes: Metaphors of Invasion in Nineteenth-Century Literature, Science, and Politics* (Baltimore: Johns Hopkins University Press, 1999), 37–63; Stephen Meuse, "Phantoms, Lost Limbs, and the Limits of the Body-Self," in Michael O'Donovan-Anderson, ed., *The Incorporated Self: Interdisciplinary Perspectives on Embodiment* (Lanham, MD: Rowman and Littlefield, 1996), 47–64; Lisa Herschbach, " 'True Clinical Fictions': Medical and Literary Narratives from the Civil War Hospital," *Culture, Medicine, and Psychiatry* 19 (June 1995): 183–205; and Debra Journet, "Phantom Limbs and 'Body-Ego': S. Weir Mitchell's 'George Dedlow,' " *Mosaic* 23 (winter 1990): 87–99.

For the guerrilla malevolence that threatens Union operations in "Robbed of Half a Million," see Michael Fellman, "Inside Wars: The Cultural Crisis of Warfare and the Values of Ordinary People," in Daniel E. Sutherland, ed., *Guerrillas, Unionists, and Violence on the Confederate Home Front* (Fayetteville: University of Arkansas Press, 1999), 187–88. Of particular interest in the same volume is Robert R. Mackey, "Bushwhackers, Provosts, and Tories: The Guerrilla War in Arkansas," 171–85. The vicious, irregular fighting on lonely stretches of Western roads and the war's less familiar developments in Arkansas and Missouri are discussed in Daniel E. Sutherland, "Guerrillas: The Real War in Arkansas," in Anne J. Bailey and Daniel E. Sutherland, eds., *Civil War Arkansas: Beyond Battles and Leaders* (Fayetteville: University of Arkansas Press, 2000), 133–53; Thomas A. DeBlack, "1863: 'We Must Stand or Fall Alone,' " in Mark K. Christ, ed., *Rugged and Sublime: The Civil War in Arkansas* (Fayetteville: University of Arkansas Press, 1994), 59–103; Carl H. Moneyhon, *The Impact of the Civil War and Reconstruction on Arkansas: Persistence in the Midst of Ruin* (Baton Rouge: Louisiana State University Press, 1994), 124–41; Leo E. Huff, "Guerrillas, Jayhawkers, and Bushwhackers in Northern Arkansas During the Civil War," *Arkansas Historical Quarterly* 24 (1965): 127–48; Michael Fellman, "Women and Guerrilla Warfare," in Clinton and Silber, *Divided Houses*, 147–65; and Fellman, *Inside War*, especially 81–131. For soldier pay and its perennially welcome arrival, see Billings, *Hardtack and Coffee*, 97–98; Robertson, *Soldiers Blue and Gray*, 78–79; Wiley, *The Life of Billy Yank*, 48–49; and Wiley, *The Life of Johnny Reb*, 136–37.

For the physical ailments that sap the Union soldiers of "In the 'Libey,' " see Frank L. Byrne, "Prison Pens of Suffering," in William C. Davis, ed., *The Image of*

War, 1861–1865, 4: Fighting for Time (Garden City, NY: Doubleday, 1983), 402–3, as well as Byrne's entries on "Prisoners of War" and "Prisons" in Richard N. Current, ed., *Encyclopedia of the Confederacy* (New York: Simon and Schuster, 1993), 3: 1256–64, 1265–69. The warden of the Libby, among other prisons, is profiled in Arch Fredric Blakey, *General John H. Winder, C.S.A.* (Gainesville: University of Florida Press, 1990), 153–201; on captivity more broadly, see Robertson, *Soldiers Blue and Gray*, 190–213; William B. Hesseltine, ed., *Civil War Prisons* (Kent, OH: Kent State University Press, 1962), especially 60–79; and William B. Hesseltine, *Civil War Prisons: A Study in War Psychology* (1930; rpt. New York: Ungar, 1964), especially 114–32. David Kaser considers what Libby prisoners were able to read, when they could subscribe to Richmond's several newspapers and hope for a Testament or a tract like "What Did the Angel Wipe It Out With?" from the United States Christian Commission under flag of truce; see *Books and Libraries in Camp and Battle*, 62–65. For the curious fate of the Richmond warehouse when it was moved to Chicago years later, see Bruce Klee, "They Paid to Enter Libby Prison," *Civil War Times Illustrated* 37 (February 1999): 32–38; and William B. Meyer, "The Selling of Libby Prison," *American Heritage* 45 (November 1994): 114–18.

Atlanta's Civil War boom, which helps explain why a necessity could be hoarded with such great expectations in "Mr. Williamson Slippey and His Salt," is described by Mary A. DeCredico in *Patriotism for Profit: Georgia's Urban Entrepreneurs and the Confederate War Effort* (Chapel Hill: University of North Carolina Press, 1990), 130. For the growing scarcity of salt, among other Southern shortages as the war continued, see James L. Roark, "Behind the Lines: Confederate Economy and Society," in McPherson and Cooper, *Writing the Civil War*, 201–27; William Blair, *Virginia's Private War: Feeding Body and Soul in the Confederacy, 1861–1865* (New York: Oxford University Press, 1998), 33–54; John Solomon Otto, *Southern Agriculture During the Civil War Era, 1860–1880* (Westport, CT: Greenwood Press, 1994), 19–45; John E. Stealey III, *The Antebellum Kanawha Salt Business and Western Markets* (Lexington: University Press of Kentucky, 1993), 191–97; Gates, *Agriculture and the Civil War*, 73–108; and Ella Lonn, *Salt as a Factor in the Confederacy* (1933; rpt. University: University of Alabama Press, 1965), especially 35–53. Both Southern speculation and the anger it provoked are discussed in James M. Russell, *Atlanta, 1847–1890: City Building in the Old South and the New* (Baton Rouge: Louisiana State University Press, 1988), 92–100; and Randall C. Jimerson, *The Private Civil War: Popular Thought during the Sectional Conflict* (Baton Rouge: Louisiana State University Press, 1988), 214–19. For the increasing production of sorghum, which Mr. Slippey takes to using in his stews, see Gates, *Agriculture and the Civil War*, 145–49; and Schele De Vere, who notes in *Americanisms* that the substitute was far from vile: "*Sorghum* became not only itself a favorite with soldiers and all classes of society, but soon acquired a general meaning, denoting anything specially pleasant or desirable" (287).

The lucrative profiteering that "A Night on the Mississippi" reveals is evaluated in Joseph H. Parks, "A Confederate Trade Center under Federal Occupation: Memphis, 1862 to 1865," *Journal of Southern History* 7 (1941): 297–98. Peggy Robbins has assessed the value of Memphis smuggling in "Union Soldiers and Confederate Civilians Mingled Together . . . When the Yankees Held Memphis," *Civil War Times Illustrated* 16 (January 1978): 31. The complications of extended Union rule in the city are detailed in John F. Marszalek, *Sherman's Other War: The General and the Civil War Press* (Kent, OH: Kent State University Press, 1999), 108–30; Jeffrey N. Lash, " 'The Federal Tyrant at Memphis': General Stephen A. Hurlbut and the Union Occupation of West Tennessee, 1862–1864," *Tennessee Historical Quarterly* 48 (1989): 15–28; Thomas H. Baker, "Refugee Newspaper: The Memphis *Daily Appeal*, 1862–1865," *Journal of Southern History* 29 (1963): 326–44; and Gerald M. Capers, *The Biography of a River Town. Memphis: Its Heroic Age* (Chapel Hill: University of North Carolina Press, 1939), 135–61. The unusual perspective of A. E. Frankland, a Confederate Jew, appears in Maxwell Whiteman, ed., "Kronikals of the Times: Memphis, 1862," *American Jewish Archives* 9 (1957): 83–125. For a broader discussion of an occupied people's tactics of resistance, smuggling among them, see Ash, *When the Yankees Came*, 38–75.

Jane E. Schultz discusses the considerable tasks of volunteer nurses like "Mrs. Spriggins, the Neutral" in " 'Are We Not All Soldiers?': Northern Women in the Civil War Hospital Service," *Prospects* 20 (1995): 38–56, where her title's allusion to Mary Ann Bickerdyke and her own subsequent term appear (51). For the ample service of the war's women, which reached beyond nursing to sanitary fairs, soldiers' aid societies, and factory jobs, see Judith Ann Giesberg, *Civil War Sisterhood: The U.S. Sanitary Commission and Women's Politics in Transition* (Boston: Northeastern University Press, 2000), especially 85–112; Jeanie Attie, *Patriotic Toil: Northern Women and the American Civil War* (Ithaca, NY: Cornell University Press, 1998), especially 248–67; Stephen B. Oates, *A Woman of Valor: Clara Barton and the Civil War* (New York: Free Press, 1994); Massey, *Women in the Civil War*, 3–24; Leonard, *Yankee Women*, 50–103; J. Matthew Gallman, "Voluntarism in Wartime: Philadelphia's Great Central Fair," in Vinovskis, *Toward a Social History of the American Civil War*, 93–116; and Mary Denis Maher, *To Bind Up the Nation's Wounds: Catholic Sister Nurses in the U.S. Civil War* (New York: Greenwood Press, 1989).

Richard L. Fuchs examines several perspectives on events at Fort Pillow and the controversy that "Buried Alive" helps amplify in *An Unerring Fire: The Massacre at Fort Pillow* (Rutherford, NJ: Fairleigh Dickinson University Press, 1994), where his charged assessment of Forrest appears (29). For somewhat different evaluations, see Kenneth Bancroft Moore, "Fort Pillow, Forrest, and the United States Colored Troops in 1864," *Tennessee Historical Quarterly* 54 (1995): 112–23; and Jack Hurst, *Nathan Bedford Forrest: A Biography* (New York: Knopf, 1993), 164–81, where a more textured portrait of Forrest emerges without minimizing Fort Pillow's butchery. The larger issue of black military service is considered in Ira Berlin, Joseph P. Reidy, and Leslie S. Rowland, eds., *Freedom's Soldiers: The Black Military Experience in the Civil War* (New York: Cambridge University Press, 1998), 1–50; Howard C. Westwood, *Black Troops, White Commanders, and Freedmen during the Civil War* (Carbondale: Southern Illinois University Press, 1992); Joseph T. Glatthaar, *Forged in Battle: The Civil War Alliance of Black Soldiers and White Officers* (New York: Free Press, 1990); and Dudley Taylor Cornish, *The Sable Arm: Black Troops in the Union Army, 1861–1865* (1966; rpt. Lawrence: University Press of Kansas, 1987). For the observations of black soldiers who wrote home, like Robert Hall, see Berlin et al., *Freedom's Soldiers*, 83–175; and Edwin S. Redkey, ed., *A Grand Army of Black Men: Letters from African-American Soldiers in the Union Army, 1861–1865* (New York: Cambridge University Press, 1992). For a sense of how much their service actually changed perceptions of their race, see David W. Blight, *Race and Reunion: The Civil War in American Memory* (Cambridge, MA: Belknap–Harvard University Press, 2001), especially 338–80; Kirk Savage, *Standing Soldiers, Kneeling Slaves: Race, War, and Monument in Nineteenth-Century America* (Princeton, NJ: Princeton University Press, 1997), 162–208; Sidney Kaplan, "The Black Soldier of the Civil War in Literature and Art," in Allan D. Austin, ed., *American Studies in Black and White: Selected Essays, 1949–1989* (Amherst: University of Massachusetts Press, 1991), 101–23; and Jimerson, *The Private Civil War*, 86–123.

Earl J. Hess describes the horrific fighting that "A Night in the Wilderness" spills into a postwar boarding house in *The Union Soldier in Battle: Enduring the Ordeal of Combat* (Lawrence: University Press of Kansas, 1997), 69; his remarks may be usefully augmented by Gerald F. Linderman's discussion of "disillusionment" during the Wilderness campaign in *Embattled Courage: The Experience of Combat in the American Civil War* (New York: Free Press, 1987), 240–65. William D. Matter provides a striking tribute to the courage of Spotsylvania's beleaguered soldiers in *If It Takes All Summer: The Battle of Spotsylvania* (Chapel Hill: University of North Carolina Press, 1988), while he focuses on issues of authority in "The Federal High Command at Spotsylvania," in Gary W. Gallagher, ed., *The Spotsylvania Campaign* (Chapel Hill: University of North Carolina Press, 1998), 29–60. For coverage of the nearly uninterrupted engagements over two costly months, see Noah Andre Trudeau, *Bloody Roads South: The Wilderness to Cold Harbor, May–June 1864* (Boston: Little, Brown, 1989); for the greater detail that Brown's boarding house friends could not stomach, see Gordon C. Rhea's three volumes to date: *The Battle of the Wilderness, May 5–6, 1864* (Baton Rouge: Louisiana State University Press, 1994); *The Battles for Spotsylvania Court House and the Road to Yellow Tavern, May 7–12, 1864* (Baton Rouge: Louisiana State University Press, 1997); and *To the North Anna River: Grant and Lee, May 13–25, 1864* (Baton Rouge: Louisiana State University Press, 2000).

Thavolia Glymph speaks for the escaping slaves of "The Freedman's Story" in " 'This Species of Property': Female Slave Contrabands in the Civil War," in Campbell and Rice, *A Woman's War*, 61; William Faulkner describes what white Southerners overheard in "Raid," part of his story cycle entitled *The Unvanquished* (1938; rpt. New York: Vintage Books–Random House, 1966), 94. Among historians, there is a growing sense that slaves were not "freed" docilely but often ready to claim their liberty. See Ira Berlin, Thavolia Glymph, Steven F. Miller, Joseph P. Reidy, Leslie S. Rowland, and Julie Saville, eds., *Freedom: A Documentary History of Emancipation, 1861–1867* (New York: Cambridge University Press, 1982–); Clarence L. Mohr, *On the Threshold of Freedom: Masters and Slaves in Civil War Georgia* (Athens: University of Georgia Press, 1986), especially 70–75; Barbara Jeanne Fields, *Slavery and Freedom on the Middle Ground: Maryland During the Nineteenth Century* (New Haven: Yale University Press, 1985), and Vincent Harding, *There Is a River: The Black Struggle for Freedom in America* (New York: Harcourt Brace Jovanovich, 1981), 219–97. For groundbreaking studies of the slave life that Oby Paragon leaves behind, see Eugene D. Genovese, *Roll, Jordan, Roll: The World the Slaves Made* (New York: Vintage, 1974); John W. Blassingame, *The Slave Community: Plantation Life in the Antebellum South* (New York: Oxford University Press, 1979), especially 105–48; and, for what slave quarters looked like, John Michael Vlach, "Not Mansions . . . But Good Enough: Slave Quarters as Bi-Cultural Expression," in Ted Ownby, ed., *Black and White Cultural Interaction in the Antebellum South* (Jackson: University Press of Mississippi, 1993), 89–114, as well as Brenda Stevenson's reply, 115–23. Thoughtfully diverging views appear in James M. McPherson, "Who Freed the Slave?", in *Drawn with the Sword*, 192–207; George M. Fredrickson, *The Black Image in the White Mind: The Debate on Afro-American Character and Destiny, 1817–1914* (Middletown, CT: Wesleyan University Press, 1971), especially 165–97; and Louis S. Gerteis, *From Contraband to Freedman: Federal Policy toward Southern Blacks, 1861–1865* (Westport, CT: Greenwood Press, 1973), 11–32.

Margaret Greene Rogers provides a compact history of the war that touched northeastern Mississippi where "Road-Side Story" is set in *Civil War Corinth, 1861–1865* (Corinth, MS: Rankin Printery, 1989), with particular attention to its strategic significance (41). For a lucid assessment of what the Confederacy forfeited when Union troops captured the city, see Peter Cozzens, *The Darkest Days of the War: The Battles of Iuka and Corinth* (Chapel Hill: University of North Carolina Press, 1997). For John Bell Hood's Tennessee disaster in 1864, when Corinth served his army as supply depot, see Winston Groom, *Shrouds of Glory: From Atlanta to Nashville— The Last Great Campaign of the Civil War* (New York: Atlantic Monthly Press, 1995); Wiley Sword, *Embrace an Angry Wind: The Confederacy's Last Hurrah: Spring Hill, Franklin, and Nashville* (New York: HarperCollins, 1992); and Foote, *The Civil War: A Narrative*, 3: 654–710. The cramped lives of the South's devastated families are examined in Mary Elizabeth Massey, *Refugee Life in the Confederacy* (1964;

rpt. Baton Rouge: Louisiana State University Press, 2001); Massey, *Women in the Civil War*, 291–316; Laura F. Edwards, *Scarlett Doesn't Live Here Anymore: Southern Women in the Civil War Era* (Urbana: University of Illinois Press, 2000); Joan E. Cashin, "Into the Trackless Wilderness: The Refugee Experience in the Civil War," in Campbell and Rice, *A Woman's War*, 29–53; Faust, *Mothers of Invention*, 30–52; Rable, *Civil Wars*, 181–92; and Paul D. Escott, " 'The Cry of the Sufferers': The Problem of Welfare in the Confederacy," *Civil War History* 23 (1977): 228–40.

The disposition of Richmond on the verge of volunteer regiments, civil servants, refugees, wounded soldiers, and Union prisoners, as well as the beguiling hoops of "The Skeleton in the Closet," is described by Emory M. Thomas in *The Confederate Nation, 1861–1865* (New York: Harper and Row, 1979), 98–104, where the continuing appeal of the city's drawing rooms is noted (102). For fuller portraits of the Confederacy's capital city, see Greg D. Kimball, *American City, Southern Place: A Cultural History of Antebellum Richmond* (Athens: University of Georgia Press, 2000), 217–52; Ernest B. Furgurson, *Ashes of Glory: Richmond at War* (New York: Knopf, 1996); Sallie Brock Putnam, *Richmond During the War: Four Years of Personal Observation*, ed. Virginia Scharff (1867; rpt. Lincoln: University of Nebraska Press, 1996); Mary Boykin Chesnut, *Mary Chesnut's Civil War*, ed. C. Vann Woodward (New Haven: Yale University Press, 1981); Emory M. Thomas, *The Confederate State of Richmond: A Biography of the Capital* (Austin: University of Texas Press, 1971); and John Moncure Daniel, *The "Richmond Examiner" During the War* (1868: rpt. New York: Arno, 1970). The war's final months are best documented by Mark Grimsley and Brooks D. Simpson, eds. *The Collapse of the Confederacy* (Lincoln: University of Nebraska Press, 2001); Nina Silber, *The Romance of Reunion: Northerners and the South, 1865–1900* (Chapel Hill: University of North Carolina Press, 1993), 13–38; Rable, *Civil Wars*, 202–20; Jimerson, *The Private Civil War*, 238–51; and Gaines M. Foster, *Ghosts of the Confederacy: Defeat, the Lost Cause, and the Emergence of the New South, 1865 to 1913* (New York: Oxford University Press, 1987), 11–35. For a brief history of hoops, as well as other women's clothing during the Civil War, see Lauren Taylor, "A Common Thread," *Civil War Times Illustrated* 24 (May 1985): 32–41.

The restlessness of the Union's lingering regiments in "Sentenced and Shot" and the sequence of events once Custer arrived in Alexandria, Louisiana, are reported by Jeffry D. Wert in *Custer: The Controversial Life of George Armstrong Custer* (New York: Simon and Schuster, 1996), 232–36, where his gauge of Western defiance appears (232). An account by Custer's wife, Elizabeth, has also been reprinted as *Custer in Texas: An Interrupted Narrative; Including Narratives of the First Iowa Cavalry, the Seventh Indiana Cavalry, the Fifth Illinois Cavalry, the Second Wisconsin Cavalry, and the Military Mutiny in Custer's Command While in Louisiana* (New York: Sol Lewis, 1975), which John M. Carroll has compiled, edited, and written. For more temperate ways of disciplining citizen-soldiers, see Billings, *Hardtack*

420

and Coffee, 143–63; Robertson, *Soldiers Blue and Gray*, 122–44; Wiley, *The Life of Billy Yank*, 192–223; and Wiley, *The Life of Johnny Reb*, 217–43.

The more sequestered society of Zoar, where veterans return in "Wilhelmina," is examined most intelligently by Edgar Burkhardt Nixon, whose great-grandfather was the society's gardener for more than fifty years. See "The Society of Separatists of Zoar" (Ph.D. thesis, Ohio State University, 1933), where the German community's initial vision is described (1). For further discussion, see Kathleen M. Fernandez, "The Separatist Society of Zoar," *Communities: Journal of Cooperation* 68 (winter 1985): 27–31; Jack Killey, "The Eccentric Experiment: A Friendly, Vital People," *Western Reserve Magazine* 8 (May–June 1981): 55–59; Emilius Oviatt Randall, "The Separatist Society of Zoar," *Ohio Archaeological and Historical Quarterly* 8 (1900): 1–105; George B. Landis, "The Society of Separatists of Zoar, Ohio," *American Historical Association*, Annual Report for 1898 (1899): 163–220; Robert Shackleton, "In Quaint Old Zoar," *Godey's* 133 (November 1896): 513–17; and Catherine R. Dobbs, *Freedom's Will: The Society of the Separatists of Zoar—An Historical Adventure of Religious Communism in Early Ohio* (New York: William-Frederick Press, 1947), although Dobbs's research is not always trustworthy and the volume must be read with a cautious eye. Zoar was one of many collective settlements in nineteenth-century America, whose history in and out of Ohio may be traced in Yaacov Oved, *Two Hundred Years of American Communes* (New Brunswick, NJ: Transaction Books, 1988), especially 447–65; Alice Felt Tyler, *Freedom's Ferment: Phases of American Social History to 1860* (Minneapolis: University of Minnesota Press, 1944), especially 128–30; Charles Nordhoff, *The Communistic Societies of the United States* (1875; rpt. New York: Schocken Books, 1965), especially 99–113; and William Alfred Hinds, *American Communities: Brief Sketches of Economy, Zoar, Bethel, Aurora, Amana, Icaria, The Shakers, Oneida, Wallingford, and the Brotherhood of the New Life* (Oneida, NY: Office of the American Socialist, 1878), 23–38. A history of the German regiment in which Zoar volunteers served has recently been reprinted; see Jacob Smith, *Camps and Campaigns of the 107th Regiment Ohio Volunteer Infantry, From August, 1862, to July, 1865* (1910; rpt. Navarre, OH: Indian River Graphics, 2000). For literary commentary on Woolson's story, together with "The Happy Valley" (1870) in *Harper's Monthly* and "Solomon" (1873) in the *Atlantic Monthly*, see Sandra Parker, ed., *Home Material: Ohio's Nineteenth-Century Regional Women's Fiction* (Bowling Green, KY: Bowling Green State University Popular Press, 1998), 175–79; Sharon L. Dean, *Constance Fenimore Woolson: Homeward Bound* (Knoxville: University of Tennessee Press, 1995), 106–7; Carolyn VanBergen, "Constance Fenimore Woolson and the Next Country," *Western Reserve Studies* 3 (1988): 86–92; and John Dwight Kern, *Constance Fenimore Woolson: Literary Pioneer* (Philadelphia: University of Pennsylvania Press, 1934), 31–34.

The upheavals in black family life that "A True Story" traces, both during and after the Civil War, are evaluated in Ella Forbes, *African American Women During the Civil War* (New York: Garland, 1998), especially 9–35; Deborah Gray White, "Female Slaves in the Plantation South," in Edward D. C. Campbell Jr. and Kym S. Rice, eds., *Before Freedom Came: African-American Life in the Antebellum South* (Richmond, VA: Museum of the Confederacy; Charlottesville: University Press of Virginia, 1991), 100–21; Ira Berlin, Francine C. Cary, Steven F. Miller, and Leslie S. Rowland, "Family and Freedom: Black Families in the American Civil War," *History Today* 37 (January 1987): 8–15; and Jacqueline Jones, *Labor of Love, Labor of Sorrow: Black Women, Work, and the Family from Slavery to the Present* (New York: Basic Books, 1985), especially 44–78. Leslie A. Schwalm's observation about weakening plantation ties may be found in *A Hard Fight for We: Women's Transition from Slavery to Freedom in South Carolina* (Urbana: University of Illinois Press, 1997), 114–15. For the later fate of the black cook, whose role as mammy has proved extraordinarily long-lived despite Aunt Rachel's rebuke, see Doris Witt, *Black Hunger: Food and the Politics of U.S. Identity* (New York: Oxford University Press, 1999), 21–53; Mary Titus, " 'The Dining Room Door Swings Both Ways': Food, Race, and Domestic Space in the Nineteenth-Century South," in Anne Goodwyn Jones and Susan V. Donaldson, eds., *Haunted Bodies: Gender and Southern Texts* (Charlottesville: University Press of Virginia, 1997), 243–56; Maurice M. Manring, "Aunt Jemima Explained: The Old South, the Absent Mistress, and the Slave in a Box," *Southern Cultures* 2 (1995): 19–44; Diane Roberts, *The Myth of Aunt Jemima: Representations of Race and Region* (New York: Routledge, 1994), especially 1–22; and Cheryl Thurber, "The Development of the Mammy Image and Mythology," in Virginia Bernhard et al., eds., *Southern Women: Histories and Identities* (Columbia: University of Missouri Press, 1992), 87–108.

INDEX

Page numbers for illustrations are in italics.

Kathleen Diffley is Associate Professor of English at the University of Iowa

and author of *Where My Heart Is Turning Ever: Civil War Stories and*

Constitutional Reform, 1861–1876.

MAY   7 2003